Ruth Walker was born in Cincinnati, Ohio. After she married George St. Clair Walker, who was in the Air Force, they lived in fourteen different states, including Hawaii, and travelled extensively in the Far East. Their only child, Sharon, was born in the Philippines. Ruth Walker's first novel was published in 1964 and she has written several others since, including the bestselling titles *Air Force Wives* and *The Club*.

GW00630971

Also by Ruth Walker

Air Force Wives
The Club

Rings

Ruth Walker

HEADLINE

First published in Great Britain in 1990
by Judy Piatkus (Publishers) Ltd

First published in paperback in 1991
by HEADLINE BOOK PUBLISHING PLC

10 9 8 7 6 5 4 3 2

ISBN 0 7472 3587 2

Printed and bound in Great Britain by
Collins Manufacturing, Glasgow

HEADLINE BOOK PUBLISHING PLC
Headline House
79 Great Titchfield Street
London W1P 7FN

To Lola Ruth Walker-Marcia,
who watched the clowns with me

BOOK ONE

Mara's Story

PROLOGUE

SHE WAS OLD, VERY FRAGILE, AND HER LIMP HAD BECOME more pronounced as she approached her eighty-second birthday. Even so, she carried herself with the same arrogance as when she had dazzled a whole generation with her beauty, her supple body, her extraordinary talent.

Her hair, once a vibrant red, had lost its fire and was now ash-gray, but the old pride was still there, and she held herself very straight, ignoring the encroachment of age, and scornfully refused the help of the limo driver who'd been sent to pick her up at the Showman's Rest Home in Sarasota, where she'd been living for the past seven years.

She had fought many battles during her long life; some she had won, others lost, but she'd never given in to self-pity, never backed away from a fight. She was proud of that, proud that she had lived her life without once crying foul. So she wasn't going to give in now, certainly not to anything as trivial as the infirmities of old age, especially with half the other inmates—her word for them—of the rest home gawking at her from the spacious front veranda.

The driver, a young black man, wasn't offended by her haughty glare. He grinned cheerfully, tipped his cap, and went ahead to open the rear door for her. He helped her in, then whistled his way around the long, gray limo and slid into the driver's seat.

"Great day for an outing, ma'am," he said over his shoulder, and she relented enough to smile and nod before she leaned back and closed her eyes to discourage any further conversation. As they pulled away from the curb, she reflected that it was unlikely that she'd miss anything even if she did fall asleep. After all, she knew every inch of the highway from Sarasota to Orlando, their destination.

Not that she intended to do any napping. She had too much
to think about, to sort out. She also had a decision to make,
something she'd been postponing for three decades. And a decision she wished she could postpone even longer, if the truth
be known.

Truth . . . What a strange word *truth* was. As if it were a
constant, something that could be spelled out in precise terms.
There was no such thing as perfect truth, only truth as seen
through different eyes. Would telling her granddaughter the truth
about herself, should she decide that way, hurt and wound Michelle?

Would the truth, at this late date, rob her granddaughter, the
person she loved the most, of a golden fantasy Michelle had
harbored all her life? There was an even more personal fear,
too—that Michelle would lose all respect for her. Should she
risk such a loss in order to set the record straight?

The decision must be made today for the simple reason that
it might be her last chance. That old mossback, Dr. Robbins,
had just the same as told her so yesterday when he'd forbidden
her to go on this outing. "Your stamina is too low," he'd said.
"Perhaps by spring you'll be able to get out again."

But there had been that pity, the pity she couldn't abide, in
his eyes, and she'd known that he didn't believe she'd still be
alive come spring.

Well, she had no intention of letting her worn-out old heart
quit on her, not yet. Michelle needed her, needed her advice,
her good counsel. A little more time wasn't too much to ask.
Another couple of years—well, she wasn't going to think about
that, not now. She'd never stewed over things that couldn't be
helped.

As for Dr. Robbins, doctors had been wrong about her before.
She just might outlive the old fool yet.

She stifled a laugh, imagining his reaction when he found out
she'd lied to Loretta, her companion-cum-jailer, and convinced
that silly twit that he'd given permission for this excursion today.
When he chastised her about it—and he would!—she was going
to look him straight in the eye and tell him that he was a dod-
dering old fool who should have retired twenty years ago. . . .

Her expression was so ferocious that the driver, glancing at
her in the mirror, asked quickly, "You okay, lady?"

"Keep your eyes on the road, young man," she said, and had
the satisfaction of seeing him straightened in his seat, his eyes
studiously avoiding the mirror.

She permitted herself a thin smile. No, the fire hadn't gone out of this old bag of bones, not yet. Her displeasure could still make grown men quail—and wasn't that some kind of epitaph for an old lady who was past eighty?

Oh, Jaime, she thought, her smile fading. *You wouldn't've liked old age. It's dreary and lonely, and all you have is memories to keep you warm. . . .*

What had someone—funny, she couldn't remember who— once called memories? The solace of the old? God knew she had more than her share, some good, some bad. She'd been up, higher than most people, had been down just as low, and now, with time sifting the ashes of her life, she wasn't sure if she could trust her own memory. Had she enhanced the high points with her imagination, while conveniently forgetting how wretched the worst had been? Maybe old age did that to you, evened out the highs and the lows of your life.

One memory she was sure of. She could still see Jaime's image as clearly now as when they'd been lovers—his ardent face, his smile, the strong, lithe body that had brought her so much ecstasy, so much pleasure—and so much pain.

Strange. He seemed so close today, almost as if he were sitting beside her on the backseat of this fancy limousine Michelle had sent for her. If she reached out, she might touch him—no, the driver was watching her in the mirror again, his face concerned. It was enough to know that Jaime was near, watching out over her. There had been times when his face had grown so dim that she'd had to refresh her memory with his picture, the one he'd given her after they'd become lovers.

"So you won't forget me," he'd said, his smile a little strange.

"As if I ever could," she'd said, and then he'd kissed her and they'd made love that whole long, lovely afternoon.

How long ago that was, and yet he did seem so near today. Was that because she would soon be seeing their granddaughter, who in many ways was like him, who had his smile, his—what did they call it these days? Charisma?

And my get-up-and-go, she thought, smiling again. *So like both of us. Impulsive and quick-tempered like me. Tenacious and sweet-natured like Jaime. And passionate like both of us . . .*

And they had been passionate. That part had never changed, the consuming passion they'd felt for each other. Even now, so many years later, she could still remember so clearly the deli-

cious thrill of being in Jaimie's arms, of having him make love
to her. . . .

The limo, braking to a sudden stop, brought her back to the
present. She opened her eyes, hoping they had arrived at their
destination, but it was only a slowdown, commonplace on this
busy highway that linked Sarasota with Orlando.

"Sunday drivers," the driver said, his glance apologetic.
"Don't worry. I'll get you there on time."

"I'm sure you will," she said, the words a little tart because
she resented the interruption of her reverie.

She closed her eyes again; her thoughts drifted. Did she regret
any of it, the mistakes she'd made, the people she'd hurt? Oh,
yes. There were so many things to regret. But not Jaime. No,
she had never regretted giving her heart into his keeping. The
aching loneliness of life since his death was worth it. To have
lived her life without him would be far worse.

Other things she did regret. In her blind ambition, she'd tram-
pled over others, used them. She'd been arrogant and vain and
unthinking. Still was sometimes, if it came to that. And she'd
paid the price for her mistakes, paid in pain.

But then, pain was part of living. So was love—for the lucky
ones. God, she had loved that man—and he had loved her. Nothing, not anything that had happened later, could change that.

What was it Jocko, her old friend, had once said, the first
person she'd known to use that phrase? No pain, no gain? And
she'd had more than her share of pain, starting at the very beginning, at her birth. But then, hadn't she had more than her
share of gain, of happiness and moments of great joy, too?

Her head slipped forward. She dozed. . . .

CHAPTER 1

MARA WAS SEVEN YEARS OLD THE FIRST TIME SHE RAN AWAY from her *vitsas*. Although her family had adopted the name Smith, their Romany name was Kaldaresha, and they were English gypsies, dark-skinned, stocky people, who had immigrated to the new land when Mara was two. She was small for her age, green-eyed and fair-skinned, but even so, she wouldn't have stood out among the other children so much if it hadn't been for her flaming red hair.

The hair was the bane of her life. Not only did it set her apart, but it was a constant reminder to her tribe that she was the daughter of a *gadjo*, that her mother, at the age of sixteen, had run off with a British sailor.

Four months later, when he deserted her and went back to sea, Pearsa returned, pregnant with Mara, to be taken back into the family only because of her skill as a fortune-teller. Even so, she probably would have gone before the tribal elders and been declared *maramay*, which would have meant she was unclean and therefore no longer existed in the eyes of her people, if her father hadn't been *baro*, head of the Kaldaresha tribe.

Pearsa's *vitsas*, the extended group of families that bore the Kaldaresha name, never forgot that she had been defiled by a *gadjo*. No Romany would marry her now; it was even risky to sleep with her. It was well-known that any child she bore could be deaf and dumb, that any man she slept with might lose his manhood.

By the time Mara was four, she already knew that she was an outcast, ignored by the adults, the butt of merciless teasing from other children. Born with more than her share of pride, it was doubly hard on Mara because she often defied her elders, not showing the proper shame for her *gadjo* blood.

7

Pearsa, who saw the ex-lover who had deserted her in Mara's red hair, her pale skin and green eyes, never defended her. Once, when Mara was hurting from a bruised face and a cut lip because several of her cousins had ganged up on her, she'd made the mistake of going to her mother in tears, looking for comfort. The whipping her mother had given her brought home yet another time that not only were tears a waste of time, but she was on her own and it was up to her to fight her own battles.

What cut the deepest was the knowledge that if Pearsa once stood up for her, it would be different. After all, Pearsa, who spoke the *gadjo* language, was not only a skillful fortune-teller, but the tribe's best *boojo* woman, whose time-honored swindles earned much-needed money for her family.

When Mara was seven, she attacked an older cousin who had called her unclean once too often. Although he was twice her size, she managed to bloody his nose before two of her aunts separated them. Yaddo, Mara's grandfather, beat her with a belt until his arms were tired, but it wasn't the raw welts on her back that broke her heart. It was her mother, who not only didn't interfere but who watched the whipping in stony silence.

Mara had endured the beating without crying, too proud to show weakness in front of her cousins, but her mother's rejection was almost too much to bear. She'd always known that Pearsa was indifferent to her; she hadn't known until now the depth of her mother's dislike.

Ignoring the gleeful taunts of her cousins, she went to the creek that ran through their campground. She stripped off her bloody clothes and waded out into the creek, splashing cold water over her back until the bleeding stopped, then returned for her clothes and washed them out in the creek. After she'd wrung them as dry as she could, she put them back on and returned to the campground.

The sodden cloth clung to her thin body as she threaded her way through the raggle-taggle collection of wagons and carts, the drab, round-topped tents and other makeshift shelters, toward the small tent she shared with her mother. It was only after she had crawled inside and was hidden from prying eyes that she allowed a single sob to escape her lips. She shivered convulsively, an added reason for despair. Roms, she'd been told so often, were immune to the cold; the fact that she wasn't only pointed out her *gadjo* blood.

She stripped again, draped her wet clothes over an old crate to dry, and wrapped herself in the worn blanket that kept her warm at night. As she lay on her felt sleeping mat, her thoughts were dark, far more painful than the stinging welts on her back.

Finally she cried, but not for long. Crying was a weakness—and she wasn't going to let any of them know, especially her mother, how much they'd hurt her, not just physically but inside, where it didn't heal. What's more, it was time to give up the dream that someday Pearsa would change and become the loving mother she wanted so desperately. She was alone; she had to live with that, accept it.

She wiped her eyes, got up from her sleeping mat, and went to the canvas bag that held her meager wardrobe. She selected a long-sleeved blouse and a voluminous skirt, an old one of her mother's that had been cut down to fit her, and dressed quickly. Pulling the blanket around her, she lay back down, and was drowsing when her mother came into the tent.

There was a flare of light against Mara's closed eyelids, and the smell of sulfur and coal oil in her nostrils as Pearsa lit a lantern and set it on top of the fruit crate that served them as a table. Mara watched her mother as she began to undress, and despite her resolution not to expect any comfort from Pearsa, she felt a wave of longing that this time it would be different.

Even then, she wouldn't have run away if her mother had shown the slightest concern, if only to turn and look at her. But Pearsa didn't even glance in her direction. She was humming as she brushed the tangles from her long black hair and braided it for bed.

Mara wanted to howl out her pain and grief. She wanted to pound her fists on her mother's oblivious back. Most of all she wanted her mother to love her. Her eyes glistening with tears she'd vowed never to shed again, she watched while Pearsa snuffed out the flame in the lantern.

Like the other women of their tribe, who ran to stockiness, Pearsa had picked up weight as she grew older, and the warped legs of her cot groaned as she settled under her blanket. When Mara heard the deep, regular breathing of sleep, she rose from her mat and felt her way to the ironstone crock where their bread was stored. There was a soft clinking sound as she lifted the lid. She froze, listening. When the cadence of her mother's breathing didn't change, she wrapped the hunk of bread into a head kerchief and tied the ends into a knot.

Just before she left the tent, she paused to listen to the familiar sound of her mother's breathing. It was part of her life, something she fell asleep with every night. Would Pearsa care that she was gone—or would she be relieved, glad to see the last of her? Knowing the answer, she resolutely turned away and went out the door.

The campground was silent as she slipped out into the moonlit night. She heard a snuffling sound, but it was only a dog, who examined her with an inquisitive nose, then drifted away again. *Even the dogs hate me,* she thought, and the loneliness welled up again. As silent as a ghost, she stole through the tents and wagons, keeping to the shadows.

By necessity, her plans were vague because she had no idea where she was. The tribe had rented the meadow where they were camped from an elderly farmer, a widower. She'd heard the women laughing at him because he believed that one of them would give her favors in lieu of rent. Of course, this would never happen, but the farmer didn't know that, nor would he tell anyone how he'd been duped when they vanished, as they always did, in the night.

Mara didn't question this. It was the way, the ancient way, and it was all she knew.

Her whole world began and ended with the tribe. She had little curiosity about what lay beyond their campsites. She only knew that for the past few weeks they had traveled over land as flat as a board, through golden wheat fields that rippled like waves in the wind, that the farm people who came to their camp—the men to trade or buy horses, the women to have their fortunes told or to buy a trinket—were sturdy people who showed their suspicion with every look.

So it didn't matter in which direction she set out, only that she get away as far as possible by morning.

She walked all night, stopping only occasionally for a few minutes rest. Despite her growing weariness, her fear of being caught kept her trudging along a dirt road, hiding in a wheat field the rare times when a farm truck or automobile rattled past.

When dawn came, she moved off across a field. It was autumn, and the wheat reached far above her head, shutting her into a fragrant, golden world. Once, when she came to a creek, she stopped to drink deeply of the cool, clear water, and to eat. But she only broke off a small piece of the bread, knowing it might be a long time before she could steal some food. Eventually she hoped to find a refuge with people gullible enough to take her in. But not for a while. She was still too close to the campground.

She wasn't worried about finding a place to stay. That she

didn't look like the rest of her tribe was something they were glad to take advantage of, because she could pass as a *gadjo* child. With her eyes wide with innocence, her fair skin and red hair so different from the *gadjo*'s idea of a swarthy gypsy child, she would engage the farmer woman's attention while her cousins slipped into the house through another entrance to pick up anything of value that they could carry away. So she was confident that she could convince some farm couple that she was a *gadjo* child who had been deserted by her parents. With luck, they would take her in.

When the ache in her legs, the blisters on her feet, and the stinging welts on her back made a rest necessary, she stopped again. She ate some of the bread, then pulled handfuls of wheat and made herself a nest. She curled up on the wheat and soon was asleep.

When she awoke, it was getting dark. The sky, which had been so blue all day, had clouded over, hiding the moon, and she moved carefully now, fearful not only of the dark, which, as everybody knew, held such horrors as the Maro, demons of the night who ate human flesh, but also other dangers, such as dogs and boys on the prowl.

The sky seemed to open up as she was hurrying down a road she'd stumbled upon. In seconds she was drenched to the skin. Her long, cumbersome skirt flapped against her bare ankles, and water dripped from her hair. Although she was wearing her cotton head scarf, she regretted now that she hadn't taken her mother's warm wool shawl.

She passed a building, dark and anonymous in the rain, then two more, and realized that she was coming into a town. When she heard men's voices up ahead, she turned aside, looking for a place to hide. The voices came closer; she edged backward until her back touched something wet and cold that gave slightly under the pressure of her hand. When she realized it was a tent, she flung herself down on the wet ground and wriggled under the canvas siding.

It was pitch-black inside, but it was also dry and, without the wind, much warmer. She stifled a startled cry when there was a flare of light, a lantern. Two men had come into the tent; they stood by the entrance, talking quietly. She looked around, frantic for a place to hide, and when she saw a platform, covered with canvas, she slid under the skirting and huddled there. Had the men seen her? Were they coming even now to drag her out into the light?

But no one came, and after a while the light went out and the voices faded. Still, she didn't move. Like a rabbit that finds itself surrounded by hounds, she froze for another few minutes. When nothing happened, she slumped down on the spongy material that carpeted the ground under the platform. It smelled like wood, and she decided it must be coarse sawdust.

She wrung out her clothes as best she could, then ate a few bites of soggy bread, saving the remainder for later. She was very thirsty, and she wished that she'd let some of the rain run into her mouth. Since there was nothing she could do about that now, she dug out a small nest in the sawdust and curled her aching body into a ball to keep warm, her head cushioned on her arms.

Although every inch of her body ached, a deeper pain was even more hurtful as she was assaulted by fear, by despair. Would there ever be a time when she was not alone, not despised for something that wasn't her fault? Even if she was taken in by the *gadjos*, wouldn't it be much the same? Somehow she had to find a place where she would be accepted, a place where she belonged. . . .

Her thoughts scattered; she fell asleep.

A dim, gray light awakened her. It was still raining—hard. When she heard voices, she huddled down in her small nest, fighting fear. The rain, drumming on the canvas tent, finally slackened, and she was able to make out a few words, but they made no sense to her. She knew someone had told a joke when there was prolonged laughter. The noise intensified, accompanied with slapping sounds, shouts. Someone began whistling, and the tune was so cheerful that involuntarily she smiled.

Unable to resist her curiosity, she crept toward a place in the canvas skirting where two pieces overlapped. Carefully she parted them and peered out.

The tent was much larger than she'd expected; the floor was covered with the same barklike wood shavings she'd been sleeping on. The people, both men and women, were oddly dressed in tight-fitting clothes that reminded her of the long johns she'd seen hanging on *gadjo* clotheslines. Her eyes widened as she watched them do such things as tumbling on canvas mats, turning flip-flops, one after another. A man and a woman, both wearing black, tight-fitting jersey pants, were walking on ropes stretched tightly between two poles. One man, to her amazement, was balancing three chairs, two on his hands, one on his chin.

Understanding finally came to her. These people were like Marco, a Hungarian Rom who had married into their tribe. He had been accepted because he was an acrobat who earned money for the tribe by entertaining the *gadjo* who came to their camp to trade. So these people must be entertainers—were they also Hungarian Roms like Marco? She had heard stories about the degenerate Hungarian tribes, who mingled freely with the *gadjo*, sometimes even marrying them—or had she fallen in with a Spanish tribe, which was even worse?

She studied them doubtfully. No, these people weren't Roms. Some of them were blue-eyed and fair-skinned. One, a man with bulging muscles, had hair the color of ripe wheat. So they were *gadjos*—was this one of the *gadjo* shows that played at the fairs?

A small, bone-thin man, who was standing alone, watching the others, glanced in her direction, and she ducked back, her heart throbbing with fear. Although there was no shout of discovery and no one came to rout her out of her hiding place, she didn't dare return to the flap.

After a while she ate her remaining chunk of bread, wishing there were more. Her throat was so dry, it was hard to swallow. Her stomach rumbled again, and she explored the scarf she'd used to carry the bread, hoping to find a crumb or two, but it was all gone. Shivering with cold, she piled the sawdust up around her and fell back to sleep.

A clatter awakened her. She crept to the flap opening and peeked out. A group of men, wearing work clothes, were busily setting up wooden benches in the tent. As they worked, they talked back and forth in the *gadjo* language, joking and laughing and calling out what she realized were good-natured insults. They, too, were *gadjos*—she didn't know whether to be relieved or not.

When the men had finished putting up the benches, they went away. Before she could relax again, several men, carrying odd-shaped objects, came into the tent and climbed up on the structure above her. A burst of music vibrated through the wooden platform: she realized she was hiding under a bandstand.

People began to fill the seats, some of them occupying the wooden chairs in the center section, others the blue-painted benches on each side. Another group, mostly children and half-grown men, settled down in the sawdust in front of the benches.

Mara stared hungrily at the small brown bags of popcorn and peanuts, the candy bars, and most of all, the bottles of orange pop they were buying from a vendor in a red-striped jacket. For a bottle of that pop, she was almost willing to trade her one treasure, a tiny silver necklace she wore around her neck, except that it was the only gift her mother had ever given her. Pearsa had stolen it from a farmhouse, and because it had been too small for her own neck, she had tossed it into Mara's lap. Mara had hidden it away, afraid her mother would take it back. Not for food or a bottle of that orange pop would she part with it, even now.

The musicians had been tuning their instruments, and now a blast of brassy music made her start. Mara watched as a flap in the rear of the tent parted and a group of men, dressed in gaudy costumes, their faces painted white and red and black, came tumbling in, followed by a gray animal so huge and grotesque-looking that she cringed back, afraid.

A doll of a woman, her red costume glittering in the light of the kerosene lanterns that lined the ring in the center of the tent, rode atop the lumbering beast. Mara forgot her fear as she watched the woman wave, bestowing gracious smiles upon the audience. It seemed to Mara that the woman was looking directly at her, and a warmth filled her, making her smile, and suddenly her hunger and thirst, even her aching body, didn't matter. All that mattered was the act unfolding before her eyes, the dazzling color of the costumes, the breathtaking action, the magic.

Like a docile dog, the huge beast performed one trick after another, standing on his back feet, balancing on a huge barrel, ending with a lumbering dance. And all the time the tiny woman atop the beast smiled graciously, looking like a queen in her glittering costume. It was all Mara could do, when the act was finished, not to scream her approval like the rest of the crowd.

The thin man she'd seen before, now splendidly dressed in red and gold, announced the next act in ringing tones, and she watched, hardly breathing, as several men did a tumbling act that took her breath away.

As one act followed another, a hunger that wasn't for food stirred in Mara. How grand it all was, how happy these people in their dazzling clothes—and how different from her own drab life. She shivered under the force of her envy. To be one of them, to live among them—what joy! But of course, it was impossible. Why would they take in a Rom child who had no useful skills?

Despite her fascination with the acts, she couldn't ignore her growing thirst, her aching back. She had slumped down to relieve the pressure on her knees, when the thin man announced a new act.

"And now, the artiste you've all been waiting for, the lovely, the talented, the incomparable—Miss Dolly Lee!"

His words were greeted with such wild applause and cheers that Mara returned to the opening again. As she stared at the woman standing alone in the center of the ring, she forgot her thirst, forgot her blistered feet and aching back. The newcomer, to Mara's bedazzled eyes, was incredibly beautiful with her long, blond hair and red, red lips, her eyes outlined in black. She was dressed in white, from her feathered headdress to her tight-fitting slippers, a silver-white that sparkled in the light of the electric lanterns. Her smile, as she waved to the crowd, was dazzling.

The thin man finished his introduction. The woman began to climb up a taut rope, and the audience grew quiet, as if they were holding their breath. Looking like a white butterfly Mara had once caught, then freed because it was so beautiful, the woman climbed higher and higher, stopping now and then to swing outward, one hand and one foot anchored in a twist of the rope, smiling down at the audience.

When she reached the top, she flung herself forward, catching a small wooden swing. As she twirled with breathtaking speed above the crowd, her body seemed as limber as if she'd been born without bones.

It was magic.

Mara, desperate not to miss a thing, recklessly pushed the canvas open wider so she could stare into the upper reaches of the tent. When the woman flung herself upward and backward, she cried out in fear. A split second later, the woman caught the swing with her heels, and this time Mara's cry was relief.

But her own cry brought her back to reality, and she ducked back, pulling the canvas together, afraid that someone had heard her. Although she didn't dare look out again, she knew when the woman finished her act because the audience burst into applause, and cries of "Bravo!" filled the air.

Mara crouched in the sawdust, her mind in a whirl. She could almost feel the warmth, the waves of approval, surging from the audience, enveloping the woman. How she yearned to be in her place, to be loved, admired, applauded, to shine like a star. For that she would do anything, give anything.

She lost herself in a dream. It was she, grown to a woman— beautiful, graceful, dressed in white—who soared above the stands. Below, the crowd watched, full of admiration, of love, while above, where no one could reach her, hurt her, she performed, full of grace as she twisted and twirled on the magical swing. . . .

Caught up in her private dream, she didn't notice when the audience filed out, when the band stopped playing and departed. The canvas suddenly parted, and a hand reached in and caught her by the nape of the neck, taking her by surprise.

She fought like a wild animal, but it was an uneven battle; eventually her arms were pinned to her side. "What we got here? A swamp rat?" a deep voice said.

Although she only understood a word or two, she read the man's amusement, and some of her panic dissolved. She was caught, but it wasn't hopeless. She knew the tricks that usually worked with *gadjos*. All her instincts in full bay, she began to cry, wailing out her distress. The man, she noted through her fingers, looked embarrassed.

"Hey, kid, I ain't gonna hurt you. I'm going to find your folks. They must be looking all over for you."

Mara cried harder, and he added hurriedly, "Look, if you don't stop crying, I'll hafta turn you over to the sheriff. You don't want that, do you?"

Mara caught the dreaded word "sheriff" and stopped crying.

"There, that's better. Now you tell me where we can find your folks, and maybe I'll forget you snuck in here without paying."

"Why you tormenting that child, Arnie? She's scared to death," a woman's voice said.

Mara peeked between her fingers again. Her breath escaped in a loud gasp. In all her life, she'd never seen such a big woman. Was she a demon, a ghoul, or just a very fat *gadjo*?

"I'm trying to find out her name," the man said. "How about it, kid? I'm Arnie Malichi, and I own this circus. This here is Miss Tanya, the fattest woman in the world. How about telling us *your* name?"

Mara looked down at her bare feet; she didn't answer.

"I don't think she understands English," the woman said. "Or maybe she'd deef." She looked Mara over carefully. "Sure a raggle-taggle youngun. If it wasn't for that red hair, I'd say she was one of them gypsies."

The man grunted. "Well, whoever she is, she spells trouble. If we turn her loose and something happens to her, we'll get the blame. Best we turn her over to the law—"

Mara made an involuntary sound of protest, and the man gave

her a hard stare. "She can hear, all right. And I don't have time to mess around with her," he said.

"Don't you bully that child," the woman scolded, and Mara's cunning began to stir. Despite the woman's alarming size, she wasn't dangerous—and she had weaknesses that any Rom child could take advantage of.

Mara stared at Miss Tanya with beseeching eyes. "I got wet in rain. I hide where warm. Fall asleep. People come, show start, I scared. Don't have no—" The word eluded her.

"You didn't have no ticket," the woman supplied for her.

"Just what we need, another deadbeat," the man said, but he was smiling now. "Okay kid, what's your name, and how can we find your ma and pa?"

"Rosa—" she said, using her *gadjo* name. "Rosa Smith. I live over there." She made a vague gesture. Her stomach rumbled and she had a sudden idea. "Very hungry. You got food?"

The man slapped his forehead. "Talk about nerve! Not only is she a deadbeat, but now she wants a free meal!"

"Oh, feed her," the woman said. "The kid's hungry."

"Okay, but you can do the honors. You got enough food in your truck to feed an army."

"Up your kazoo," the woman said, making a gesture Mara understood too well. She looked at the woman with renewed interest. Miss Tanya didn't act like any *gadjo* women she'd ever seen before.

"Come along, Rosa," the woman said, and lumbered off toward the exit.

A few minutes later, Mara was sitting at a table inside a box-like hut that had been built on the flatbed of a truck, stuffing her mouth with food. She demolished two sandwiches, made from a highly spiced meat she didn't recognize, and a large hunk of yellow cheese, followed by a slice of chocolate cake. She licked the icing off her fingers, eyeing the remainder of the cake, and when the woman went over to the door to look out, her step shaking the whole structure, Mara moved swiftly to stuff a piece of the cake and a hunk of cheese into her kerchief. When the woman came back, Mara was finishing off a mug of tepid milk, her eyes wide and innocent.

"Nature calls. I have to go to the donicker," Miss Tanya said. "You stay here until I get back."

Mara nodded as if she meant to obey. Much as she wanted to stay with this woman, who she knew would feed her well, she knew it wasn't going to happen. These people were like the Roms, always under suspicion for their roaming ways. The last thing they'd do was take in a strange child. Better to find some elderly farm couple who were gullible enough to swallow her story about a mother who'd deserted her—but oh, how she ached to live with these people, to learn how to soar above the crowd on a swing, admired by everyone. No one would care that she was half-Rom, half-*gadjo*, only that she made them gasp with fear.

Pausing only long enough to stuff the remainder of the cheese into her kerchief, she slipped out the door and down three sturdy steps to the ground. She wasn't even tempted to appropriate a silver brooch that was lying on the table. It would be too dangerous, and besides, the fat woman seemed more like a Rom than a *gadjo*.

She had almost reached the edge of the campground when she ran headlong into Arnie Malichi. He put his hand on her shoulder, holding her there. "Okay, Rosa. This man is the county sheriff. He'll see you get back home."

The man standing behind him was stout, barrel-chested; his hair was cropped very short and he was frowning. "Jesus, Malichi, why you wasting my time with a gypsy kid?"

"Gypsy? With that red hair?"

"They come in all colors, a bunch of damned mongrels, you ask me. Hell, they even breed with their own kin," the man said, spitting on the ground.

Mara forgot prudence, the necessity of never angering a *gadjo*, especially a lawman. Her teeth bared, she flew at the sheriff. Before she could rake his face with her fingernails, he flung her off and she landed in a heap on the wet ground.

"Okay, you wolf cub, that's it," the sheriff growled. "Your tribe's over on Muskie Road, staying at old John Prindle's place. One of these days he's gonna end up with a shiv in his back, letting that trash camp out in his creek bottom, but that's his problem. I'm turning you over to your folks, and I hope they beat the begeezers out of you."

He jerked her to her feet, and pushed her ahead of him. She looked back and caught a last glimpse of Miss Tanya, standing in the door of her wooden hut. She couldn't see the expression on the fat woman's face because the lamplight was behind her, but she was sure Miss Tanya was sorry to see her go.

Her punishment, from her mother, was the worst beating of her life, but she never regretted running away. As the blows rained upon her head, her neck, her back, they didn't seem to matter. She was lost in a dream that she was back in the circus

tent, watching a woman flying through the air, the center of all
eyes, the object of love, of admiration. The woman had red hair
instead of blond, because this time the woman was her.

The bruises and welts from her beatings soon healed, but now
she had a dream that would never tarnish, not even when, in
time, it became more realistic.

CHAPTER 2

IT WAS MARA'S FIFTEENTH BIRTHDAY. SHE LAY ON HER COT
in the hot, fetid darkness of the aging bus she'd been sharing
with her great-aunt, Sophia, since her mother's death, brooding
over her grievances.

The bus was a rusted-out Ford that had once hauled Allentown, Pennsylvania, children back and forth to school before
the Great War. It still bore the words *Allentown School District*,
painted in fading blue letters, on its sides, although no one in
the Kaldaresha tribe could read them.

The back half of the bus was used to store tribal supplies—
sacks of flour, sugar, cans of gasoline. To convert the rest to
living quarters, the seats had been removed and it had been fitted
with two canvas folding cots, a rickety table, a couple of oak
stools, and a battered oak icebox that held utensils and metal
dishes. All the windows had been boarded over to provide privacy, effectively shutting out any outside air that might have
cooled off the bus.

Not that there was any breeze outside. Cincinnati, Ohio, in
midsummer, especially the river bottoms in the basin of the city,
was like a furnace, even late at night.

Around Mara, the darkness reeked of unwashed female bodies, of coal oil from the rusty lantern that provided the only light
when the door was shut. Her own cot, with its worn blanket and
greasy pillow, was Mara's place of refuge. A couple of nails,

pounded into the side of the bus near her cot, held most of her clothing. The rest of her possessions were stored in the small sea chest that she'd inherited from her mother, dead from lung fever for three years now.

Her greatest treasure was the small wooden box that held Pearsa's tarot cards. Not that Pearsa had given them to her willingly; death had done that.

She kept the box hidden under her pillow, not only as a talisman against spells and other evil things, but because she had a superstitious fear of anyone else handling them. Everybody knew that the magic in the tarot cards was easily contaminated by unclean hands.

Mara ignored her surroundings, including the heat and the fusty odors the old bus never lost, not even after a rare cleaning and airing. At the moment, she had other things to think about, such as her dream, the one that she'd harbored so long and which had never seemed so impossible as it did today.

Now that she was fifteen, no longer a child, she realized the obstacles that stood in the way of her becoming a circus performer, but that hadn't ended the dream. One day, by some method she was still uncertain about, she would soar beneath the canvas roof of a grand circus tent, and then the applause, the admiration, would be for her. She would be very rich, and no one would ever order her around again.

Her cousins had mocked her when she'd coaxed the scar-faced Marco into teaching her a few acrobatic tricks, when she persisted in doing the exercises he told her would give her upper body the strength an aerialist needed to perform even the simplest tricks. They'd made even more fun of her efforts to learn to speak the awkward language of the *gadjo* by talking to the outsiders who visited their campsites.

Her grandfather had been quick to use her talent when dealing with the *gadjo* in their own language was important. But it was her skill as a fortune-teller, learned from her mother, that had led to her engagement to Lazlo.

Mara made a face, thinking of the trap she'd fallen into. No matter how much Lazlo lusted for her, he never would have made a marriage offer if she didn't possess a skill that would bring money into his tribe. Her mistake was letting anyone know how good she was with the tarot cards. After all, she never got to keep the money she made except when she managed to slip a few stray coins in her skirt pocket.

Many things had changed in the past eight years. For one

thing, she was fifteen, a woman now, and while her status in the family hadn't improved, the beatings had stopped—and so had most of the insults. Her temper, always so quick to flare, had proven to be something even her cousins respected. No one was eager to risk her sharp tongue or her sharp fingernails these days.

But even her reputation for a fiery temper hadn't helped once Lazlo had seen her at the funeral rites held every year in Cincinnati to honor those in the far-flung branches of the Kaldaresha family who had died during the year. He was the head of the Razamona family, related to the Kaldareshas by marriage, and he reeked of the Turkish tobacco he smoked incessantly. Even that wouldn't have been so bad if he ever bathed. He was also more than four times Mara's age. Not that any of this mattered to her grandfather. Yaddo smelled a large dowry, and he would have sold her to the devil for that.

Mara rolled over on her back and stared up at the water-stained ceiling of the old bus, thinking of the quarrel that had erupted when she'd told her grandfather what she would do to Lazlo if the toad tried to take her to bed. It involved a sharp knife and the part of his body he was reputed to be so proud of.

"He's fat and ugly and he smells like a goat," she said. "In fact, I'd rather sleep with a goat."

Her grandfather exploded into one of the rages he was famous for. He called her names that blistered her ears and then he marched her to the bus and pushed her inside.

"You'll stay here until your aunt comes to dress you for the meeting with the Razamona family tomorrow. And if the bargaining goes well, you'll marry Lazlo tomorrow afternoon, and there'll be no sulking, no tantrums." She started to speak, and he made a threatening gesture. "Not another word. Would you shame your family by disobeying your grandfather?"

Behind her grandfather's bulky figure, she saw her cousin's avid face and knew that Anna was hoping she would go too far and be beaten. Anna had always been the ringleader of the group who tormented her—maybe, Mara thought scornfully, because she herself was squat and heavy-featured, and although she was already nineteen, no man had ever made an offer for her.

As for her aunt, Anna's mother—Carmano wasn't even pretending that she didn't enjoy seeing Mara in disgrace again.

"This is a good match for you," her grandfather went on, his tone milder now. "Lazlo is very rich. He owns a Packard and a fine caravan. You'll live like a queen."

"He's ugly. He's over sixty and he smells like a goat—"

The slap sent her reeling backward. Even in her pain, she noted that her grandfather had been careful to strike her on the side of the head, where the bruise wouldn't show. She lay on the bus floor where she'd fallen, staring at him so contemptuously that his swarthy face turned dark red.

"You'll get more of the same if you give me any more trouble. You should be grateful a rich man like Lazlo is willing to marry a half-breed."

"And one without a *sumadjii*, too," her cousin said spitefully.

At Mara's involuntary wince, Anna eyed her with satisfaction. It was a source of shame to a Rom woman if, on her wedding day, she didn't wear the neckpiece of strung coins that would someday pass down to her from her mother. Mara's mother, who had returned to her *kumpania* with only the clothes on her back, had left no *sumadjii* for her daughter.

"Your aunt has been talking to Lazlo's mother about the dowry," her grandfather said. "The old lady drives a hard bargain, but they have almost come to an understanding." He rubbed his hands together briskly. "Your aunt is providing your gown so you won't disgrace us. And you'll do your part or—"

"And I say I won't. You can beat me all you like and I still won't do it. If I just sit with my eyes closed and don't scream and fight when Lazlo and his friends come for me, than he will be offended and demand his dowry back. You'd never live down the disgrace."

It wasn't an idle threat. The marriage would be official when Lazlo's oldest male kin and her grandfather shared the *pliashka* and then embraced. But later, when she was "kidnapped" by her groom and his friends, the honor of her family would be measured by her resistance. But should she not resist, should she sit there passively when Lazlo and his friends came to drag her away to his caravan, it would shame her *kumpania*, and everybody would suspect that she was not as pure as represented. Such things had started blood feuds. The least that would happen was that the Razamonas would demand the return of her dowry.

"You think you can defy me?" her grandfather growled. "But what if I scar that face you're so vain about so no other man will ever offer for you?"

"You wouldn't do that," she said with more confidence than she felt. Driven too far, it was very possible Yaddo would lose his temper and cut her. There was another danger, too. There were drugs that put a person into a stupor, without a will of their own. What if she was given a drug?

"You ungrateful little witch!" It was her aunt, who until now had held her tongue. She oozed spite as she wagged her finger at Yaddo. "It's the *gadjo* blood in her. What was it I said when Pearsa came back, her belly swollen with that *gadjo*'s bastard? 'Turn her out,' I said. 'She's bad luck,' I said. But no, you wouldn't listen. Just because she was always your favorite, you took her back, but haven't we had bad luck ever since? Did you ever see such a run of bad luck as we've had since we came to this wretched country?"

Mara scrambled to her feet. "Any bad luck *you've* had, you made yourself," she said hotly. "And Mama paid her way—and so have I. And never a word of thanks, old woman!"

"It was her duty. No thanks was due her—and besides, she was unclean. She was lucky Yaddo took her in," Anna said.

The world around Mara turned red. She was upon her cousin in a moment, snatching at her hair, scratching her face. They rolled on the floor, knocking over the table and breaking an ironstone bowl before Yaddo managed to separate them. His face twisted with anger, he shook Mara until she was dizzy, but when her cousin tried to attack her again, he warned her off.

"She's no good to us if her face is marked up," he growled. "Lazlo demands she be perfect, not even a mole."

"She'll get hers when his mother is in charge," Carmano told her daughter, her black eyes brimming with malice. "The old lady will see that this one is kept busy, waiting on her. The first time Mara opens her mouth, she'll find herself stretched out on the floor. I just wish I could be there to see it."

Mara's grandfather ordered the two women to get back to their cooking. Before he left, he warned Mara what would happen to her if she tried to leave the bus. Although she told herself that she wasn't afraid of his anger, she was still here, listening to the sounds of activity outside.

There would be dancing later, after the oldest man from each *kumpania* had sung the old songs. And tomorrow there would be feasting, because her grandfather would pauperize himself rather than come up short on the wedding meal.

The tables would be groaning with crusty brown chicken, with beef and pork cooked with aniseed, all roasted slowly over hot coals. There would be goose, too, its skin crackling crisp, bowls of yogurt with cucumbers and tomatoes, and *booklet*, the pancakes stuffed with meat she loved so much. And beans—

green ones in sour cream, white beans in a vinegar sauce, and
chick-peas cooked with fat pork. There'd be olives, ripe and
salty, and best of all, pastries dripping with honey.

Mara's mouth watered, just thinking about that food. They
would all stuff themselves, and Lazlo, the pig, would eat more
than anyone else. An image floated through her mind, of Lazlo's
porcine eyes, his lustful stares, his sly pinches, and she knew
that even her grandfather's rage was preferable to such a fate.

It wasn't that she was averse to love. It was right and natural
for a woman to sleep with a man. But he should be someone
she found attractive, someone she would be content to spend
her life with. What a difference if it were Yolo, Lazlo's youngest
son, she was marrying—Yolo with his dark eyes, his strong body,
his passionate glances.

Just thinking about Yolo made her body grow hot and heavy
and damp. Since she'd first seen Yolo, three days ago at the
beginning of the funeral ceremonies, she had thought of little
else. And she was sure he felt the same way about her. He
couldn't seem to keep his eyes off her, and once, when no one
else was around, he'd whispered that he was mad about her. The
sweat had broken out on his forehead, and she'd felt a warmth
in her belly when she saw the telltale hardening inside his trousers.

Oh, yes, he wanted her. She knew that much about men. Ever
since she was eleven and her body had started to ripen, she'd
been the target of men's hot glances. Even her uncles found
reasons to touch her, stroke her arm—when no one was looking.
So she knew the power she had over them. What's more, she
liked it, liked knowing that just brushing her skirts against a
man could arouse him. And she wanted to be with one, become
a woman, but it was the son she wanted, not the father.

She knew all about that part of love, what men and women
did in the dark together. The old women talked about it, made
sly jokes about the size, the shape, of men's penises, about their
staying power, how a man could please a woman—and a woman
please a man.

A sound outside interrupted her thoughts. A moment later,
the door opened and Sophia came in. Sophia, her great-aunt,
was a widow who'd lost her standing in the family because she
had no children. Although they weren't close, she seldom
scolded Mara, although she was quick to give advice. Sometimes, when it was her turn to fill the plates with food, she saw

that Mara got more than her share. Once, she'd even given Mara an embroidered blouse that still had a lot of wear in it.

In no mood for talk, Mara pretended to be asleep. She watched under her eyelashes as a match flared. From the trouble Sophia was having lighting the lantern, she'd had too much wine. When she almost lost her balance, she muttered a curse under her breath and began to undress.

Mara knew that she'd come to sleep off the wine. Most of the encampment would be in bed early, resting up for the wedding tomorrow. Which meant she could move around with relative freedom—but how would that help? Yes, she could escape, but to what? To live among the *gadjo*? No Rom tribe would take her in, not only because she would surely be declared *maramay*, but for fear of her grandfather's anger. She had no money except for the handful of coins hidden away in her sea chest. Her only clothes were the castoffs of others, not fit for looking for work among the *gadjo*, even as a scrubwoman.

Yes, she could speak their language, but everybody knew how dangerous *gadjo* men were to an unprotected Rom woman. Times were very hard for *gadjo* men right now, with so many veterans of the war in the Old Country looking for work. And when times were hard, it was the Roms who suffered. It had always been that way. Gypsies were easy prey because they couldn't call upon the police for help. In fact, it was often the police who brutalized Rom women.

Mara brooded over the stupidity of the *gadjo*, who thought Gypsy girls were promiscuous. Didn't they know that an unmarried girl's virginity was guarded as carefully as the *sumadjii* she would someday inherit from her mother? Only when the tribe was in danger of starving did the women sell themselves, and then only married women or widows or those who had already lost their virginity.

Not that they hesitated to flaunt their charms to get a *gadjo* to open his wallet. She herself was an expert at the sidelong glance that promised so much. How else could she soften up a *gadjo* and make him susceptible to her *boojo* scheme?

It would be suicide to run away without the protection of a man. Ugly stories about *gadjo* men who forced themselves upon Rom women came to her mind. But what if she wasn't alone? What if Yolo was with her? She would be safe with him. She'd seen how he threw his knife in the competitions, how strong his body was. He could find work, maybe on a horse farm or at a racetrack. They could pass as Spanish or Rumanian and melt into the *gadjo* world. As for her dream—well, she wouldn't have to give it up. Yolo was good with horses. Maybe he could get a job in a traveling show where she could learn how to perform on the swing. It wasn't impossible. Her spirits lifted as it came to her that this might be the chance she'd been waiting for since she was seven. . . .

The door opened and her aunt came into the bus. She dropped a plate of food on the cot beside Mara. "Here, girl, I brought you something to eat. If it was up to me, you'd go hungry tonight. But your grandfather said bring it, and I always obey, as a woman should."

Mara's silence seemed to annoy her, because Carmano made an impatient sound. "Well, eat, eat, or I'll take it away again."

Silently Mara picked up a boiled egg. She examined it carefully, and when she saw the shell hadn't been broken, she peeled and ate it. Surely an egg was safe. But the spicy pork or the stuffed pancakes could be drugged. And then she would fall asleep, not to awaken until dawn, when it would be too late.

So she twisted her face and groaned, holding her stomach. "I think I'll wait awhile before I eat the rest. I've got a stomach-ache," she said.

"It's the meanness in you coming out," her aunt retorted. But she left the food behind when she flounced out of the bus. Mara waited a minute to make sure she was gone before she slid off the cot and went to shake her great-aunt's shoulder.

"What—what?" Sophia said groggily.

"Are you hungry?" Mara asked.

Sophia opened her eyes. "What is it, Mara?" she grumbled. "Can't you let me get some rest? You know I'll be up early, getting the chickens ready for roasting."

Mara presented the plate of food. "Here—Carmano brought me some food. I'm not hungry—too excited, I guess. No use it going to waste."

"So you've decided to be sensible, have you?" Sophia pushed herself upward and took the plate. "Your grandfather has only the best in mind for you. You'll have a rich husband, and who knows? His mother is very old. She can't last forever. Once she's gone, things will be better."

She took a bite of the pork, went on talking around a mouthful of food. "It won't be so bad—how long can the old fool perform like a man? A few months and you'll have some peace. Later, when you're a rich widow with your own truck and caravan, you can find yourself a young man to warm your bed. Just pick one who's an orphan and you won't have to take orders from another mother-in-law.''

She finished off the food, smacking her lips. ''Very good—maybe a bit too much marjoram in the pork.'' She blinked sleepily, looking like a plump owl, and Mara took the empty plate out of her hand. ''Sleepy—better get some sleep,'' Sophia muttered. By the time Mara had set the empty plate back on the table, her great-aunt was already snoring.

Mara felt a little guilty—but not too much. Sophia was the only one of her aunts who was good to her, but she wouldn't be blamed for her escape once they realized what had happened. . . .

Outside the bus, the sounds of revelry had faded, and Mara knew it wouldn't be long before everybody had returned to their own cots and mats and hammocks for the night. Moving swiftly, she got together her things. There wasn't much—a couple of skirts, several blouses, undergarments, the one good shawl that had been her mother's.

When she'd wrapped everything in the shawl and tucked the bundle under her cot, she blew out the lantern and settled back on her cot to wait. Since she was still fully dressed under her blanket, she was glad that the bus was beginning to cool off. Her caution was justified when her aunt returned, carrying a shielded lantern, and bent over her. Mara forced herself to breathe heavily, as if she were drugged, and Carmano grunted with satisfaction.

''Now who's so smart, you little coyote?'' she said.

After Carmano left the bus, Mara threw back the blanket, but she didn't get up immediately. She lay there awhile, the enormity of what she was planning overwhelming her. After Yolo and she left, they would be branded *maramay*, untouchables. They would no longer exist in the eyes of their families—or any other Rom. Not such a sacrifice for her, who had always been an outcast, but what about Yolo? He was his father's favorite son, born when Lazlo was already in his early fifties, and someday he would inherit a good share of his father's possessions. And what if she'd misread those yearning glances, those burning looks, the words he'd whispered after he'd kissed her?

Heat invaded her body as she remembered that kiss. She had been in the barn at the edge of the fairgrounds, where her grandfather kept his trade horses. Yolo had followed her inside, and that's when he'd kissed her, his lips so hot, they seemed to scorch her mouth. In the soft darkness of the barn, her heart had swelled as if it might burst, and her breath came so fast that she was sure he would think she was sick. But then, Yolo was breathing hard, too. And that wasn't the only thing about him that was hard. As he shoved against her, she felt the outline of his male organ, pushing, pushing, pushing into her abdomen.

A weakness came over her, as if she'd drunk too much wine; there was a hot, aching sensation between her thighs. He squeezed her breasts, then probed under her skirt until she thought she'd faint. He whispered he was hot for her, that they had to be together, no matter what, and she would have flung herself on him and let him take her, there and then, only they'd heard someone coming. Yolo had muttered a curse and then slipped out the back, leaving her still burning.

So wasn't she foolish to be having doubts now? Once she'd given herself to Yolo, he would do anything she wanted. She had listened to other women, found out what men liked, how to keep a man happy. She'd see that it was always good for him, so he'd never tire of her. . . .

She stiffened as she heard voices just outside the boarded-up window near her cot. Since they weren't bothering to lower their voices, she recognized Tondo, her oldest uncle, and Lazlo.

"You're a lucky man, Lazlo," her uncle said. He was a heavy man, thick-chested and short; she had always been wary of him because of the way he stared at her, his eyes hot, when no one was looking. "A tender bit like that to warm your bones at night is enough to make a man young again." And then he added slyly, "Or send a man to an early grave."

There was a coarse laugh. "Nothing like a fresh young pullet to keep a man young," Lazlo said.

"Well, you can thank the family for keeping her pure," Tondo said. "The young bucks started sniffing around her skirts when she was eleven."

"Which is your way of telling me that old hag, Carmano, will try to hold me up for a bigger dowry tomorrow." Lazlo's voice was sour. "Don't forget—Mara's half-*gadjo*. If I wasn't such a tolerant man, I'd never think of marrying your sister's bastard."

"Ah, well, we've never been sure it wasn't a Rom that fathered the girl. Red hair isn't unknown to our people. And maybe there's a little *gadjo* blood in your family, too. Seems to me I've heard a few rumors about—wasn't it your grandmother, something about her and an English tinker she took up with?"

"Nothing to it," Lazlo said hastily. "We Razamonas have

always been careful with our women. If it wasn't for the girl's skill with tarot cards, I wouldn't consider her for a moment.''

"You mean your mouth doesn't get wet when you look at those beauties under her blouse?'' Tondo's voice was insinuating. "Are you sure an old man like you can keep up with a young bride? Maybe you should buy her for your son. I just saw him in the horse barn, sleeping off the wine he's been guzzling all evening. Maybe a young bride would keep him from drinking so much.''

"When the time's ripe, something will be arranged for the boy. A good clean girl who can bear him sons. A man my age, who already has sons, can take a few chances, but a young man has to be careful. Of course, I wouldn't be unhappy if Mara produced another son for me. She looks healthy enough, if a bit thin for my tastes.''

"Your tastes! You'd bed a cow in heat if you got the chance. How many cuckoo eggs have you left in other men's nests?''

"Never mind that. If I find out that girl's been tampered with, your family will answer for it before the council—''

Still wrangling, they passed out of Mara's hearing. She was shaking with anger, but the conversation served to erase any lingering doubts she had. Never, after the things Lazlo had said about her, would she marry him! And if they somehow forced her into marriage, she would slit his throat while he slept.

She settled down to wait until the camp was quiet. How convenient that Yolo was in the barn, sleeping off the wine he'd drunk today. Had it been the thought of his own father taking her to bed that made him drink too much? All the better! He'd be that much more eager to run off with her. She'd make him so happy that he'd never regret turning his back on his family. And oh, how wonderful to love and be loved, to not be alone anymore. . . .

Mara awoke with a start. Despite her intentions, she'd fallen asleep. Luckily no light came in through the cracks around the windows, so it was still night. Except for a dog barking and an occasional slap of tires on the street that bordered the fairgrounds, there was no sound outside. She slid off the cot, her senses alert. Sophia moved in her sleep and muttered something, but she didn't awaken. Mara eased the bundle out from under her cot and felt her way through the bus and out the door.

There was no moon, but a row of street fixtures at the edge of the fairgrounds gave off a dim light. For a few minutes she listened to the distant sounds of the city before she headed for

the barn. The dilapidated building that Yaddo had appropriated
to shelter his trade horses was located at the far side of the
encampment. She knew she was getting close when she heard a
horse whinnying. Would Yolo still be there—or had he returned
to his truck?

She had heard that his grandmother had given him a fine
truck, only three years old, for his eighteenth birthday. The old
woman doted on him, it was said, and not just because he acted
as her chauffeur and drove her back and forth to the various
Chicago storefront *ofisas* where she told fortunes. Surely, since
the truck was his, he would use it for their getaway. She would
like living in such a fine vehicle. Not only did it have a canvas
cover, but it was said he slept on a real feather mattress, another
present from his grandmother.

She saw the barn up ahead, looming gray and silent in the
murky light. The door was standing open, and she left her
bundle outside when she went inside, just in case she had to
make a hasty retreat. The pungent odor of horseflesh made
her nostrils flare. Enough light came through a broken window to reveal the stalls and the gray mounds of the horses
stabled there.

She crept forward, and when she turned in to the first empty
stall, her foot touched something soft. "Yolo?" she whispered.

"Who is it?" Yolo's voice asked.

"It's me, Mara," she said.

The man sat up, groaning. "Mara? What are you doing here?"

"You said you wanted us to be together. Everybody was
asleep, so—here I am."

He understood then. She heard his breath rattle in his throat
and then he was reaching for her, pulling her down beside him
on a mound of sweet-smelling hay. As though he could see in
the dark, his hands found her breasts. He pushed her backward
and covered her with his body, his lips, hot and wet, pressing
against her mouth.

Mara felt as if she were swelling all over—her lips and breasts
and the tender flesh between her thighs. Yolo released her so he
could pull up her skirt, and her heart leapt in anticipation of
what was to come.

He slid his hand between her thighs, and now he was breathing so hard that she was afraid the whole *vitsas* would hear him.
He slid away from her long enough to pull off her blouse, then
her skirt and her cotton undergarments, exposing her flesh to

the night air. He tore off his own clothes and flung himself down beside her again.

As his tongue made love to her mouth, to her breasts, she clawed at him frantically, wanting him to hurry, wanting to be initiated into the mysteries that she'd only heard about until now. He whispered words in her ear, words that inflamed her further. The odor of wine colored his breath, but she didn't care. All that mattered was the aching and burning that sent her squirming against him, making inarticulate sounds in her throat.

He fondled the soft mound between her thighs, slid his fingers inside to explore the hot moistness there, and then he was forcing her hands down upon his own body.

"Make me feel good," he moaned.

He groaned as she stroked his flesh, so velvety soft and yet so rigidly hard. When he pushed her thighs apart roughly and told her he wanted to see her, she lay back against the hay. There was the scratch of a match against wood, and the odor of sulfur, and she quivered with excitement as he stared down at her naked body, spread out before him like some exotic feast. In the flickering light of the match, his eyes had a glazed, feverish look, and his face was very red, as if he were holding his breath. He wet his lips with his tongue, and she saw that he was holding his swollen member in his left hand.

The match flickered out and he fell between her thighs, taking her by surprise. She gave a keening cry as pain arched through her. Yolo cursed and clapped his hand over her mouth, still moving frantically against her, and suddenly the pain was replaced by new sensations, wild and exciting. As he thrust, thrust again, a glaze shimmered at the edge of her eyesight, and the world was reduced to one thing—this ache, this need, this glorious pleasure.

She writhed against him, frantically trying to get closer. "Let me do it—oh, you're killing me," he whispered hoarsely.

But she didn't want him to do it. She wanted to be in control, to have him fill her completely, to move this way or that to satisfy the special needs of her womanhood. Frantic that he would finish first and rob her of her satisfaction, she seized him by his buttocks and thrust herself upward, opening herself fully to him. When the relief she craved came, it convulsed her body with a pleasure so intense that she went into a frenzy, scratching and clawing at his shoulders.

A moment later, Yolo gave a cry, and the gushing of his seed

filled her. Slowly, slowly, she came down to earth again. So that
was what love between a man and a woman was all about. It
had been everything she'd expected, and yet she felt—empty,
sad. Was it because she had just lost her only treasure, the thing
that made her valuable to the family? Or was it something else,
the suspicion that something important, she knew not what, had
been missing?

A feeling of urgency replaced the sadness.

"I brought my clothes," she whispered. "I won't have to go
back to the bus. If we leave now, we can be in Columbus by
morning. Oh, Yolo, I promise I'll make you happy! You won't
ever be sorry that you left the family!"

Yolo didn't answer. He lay across her, very still, but it was
only when he began to snore that she realized he was asleep.
She struggled out from under him and shook him fiercely, but
he only muttered, "Go away."

Bewildered, she crouched beside him. How was it possible
that he could fall asleep so quickly? Had he passed out from the
wine? No, that couldn't be. Drunken men couldn't perform with
a woman—or so she'd heard.

For the next few minutes she tried desperately to awaken
Yolo, but it was useless. He lay on his back, and no amount
of whispering or shaking or tickling could arouse him. In the
end, she knew she had no choice but to leave him there and
return to the bus. Already the sky was turning gray, and in a
little while the women would begin to stir, starting the fires
and tending to their children, getting an early start for the
wedding.

If she waited any longer, someone was sure to see her with
her hair wet with sweat, her mouth swollen with kisses, her body
reeking with the odor of love.

As she pulled her clothes back on, she fought against bitter
disappointment. Everything had gone wrong—what should she
do now? She had given up her one treasure, her virginity, and
for what? It was already late—even if Yolo awakened soon and
came for her, would they have time to escape?

Carrying her bundle, she crept through the silent camp,
back to the bus, without seeing anyone. Quickly she undressed again, cleaned herself as best she could by splashing
her body from the bucket of water they kept under the table.
Although she was sick with disappointment, she hadn't given
up all hope. In the morning, when her aunt came to dress
her, she would pretend to be ill. God knew that part would

be easy. She felt nauseous, and there was a throbbing pain behind her eyes.

She would use her illness as an excuse not to eat any breakfast, no matter how they coaxed. That way she couldn't be drugged. When Lazlo and his friends came to kidnap her, she would just stare at him listlessly, not putting up the fight expected of her. He would be furious, of course, and surely he would demand his money back. Everybody would be angry at her and she would be in disgrace—but when hadn't she been in disgrace because of her *gadjo* blood?

She huddled under her blanket, her face to the wall, the bundle of clothing hidden under her cot, and in her weariness, she dozed off into a troubled sleep. Her first indication of trouble was when the bus door was flung open so hard, it banged against the wall. As she sat up, the blanket clutched around her, it seemed to her that the bus was filled with people, that they were all talking at once—and all staring at her as if she'd suddenly grown an extra head.

Before she could sort them out, her aunt pulled her off the cot. "Bitch! Filthy bitch!" she shouted.

"Who is he?" her grandfather roared. Before she could answer, Yaddo hauled her up by one hand and was dragging her through the bus, not giving her a chance to grab her blanket. When they reached the door, he flung her on the ground, then stood over her. His face was engorged with blood, and his lips were so blue that she wondered if he was having a fit. Aware of the people crowding around, she pulled up her knees to hide her breasts. Under the weight of those silent, judging stares, she felt raw and exposed, as if her skin had become transparent.

Her grandfather raised his fist, as if to crash it into her face, but her great-aunt stopped him.

"You don't know if it was Mara," Sophia said. "Anna could have made a mistake."

"It was Mara," Anna said shrilly. Her eyes held a malicious triumph. "I went outside to relieve myself, and that's when I saw her sneaking through camp. I followed her to the barn and I heard them inside, moaning and groaning and rolling around in the hay. Then she came out and went back to the bus."

"There wasn't any moon last night—how can you be sure it was Mara?" Yaddo said. "If you're lying—"

"There's one way to find out if she's been with a man." It was Lazlo's mother. She was a large, elderly woman with coarse features and iron-gray hair. Although it was just past dawn, she was already fully dressed in a long black skirt and blouse, her hair pulled back so tightly that her face looked like a peeled onion.

Mara's aunt nodded, her face grim. "I'll need help—she's as strong as a wildcat."

Before Mara realized fully what she meant, several of the women had grabbed her and were dragging her back into the bus. She fought them with all her strength, but in the end there were too many of them, and they spread-eagled her across the table, held her down while Carmano and Lazlo's mother examined her.

It was a nightmare, a humiliation so crushing that she wanted to die. When the two women found unmistakable evidence of her guilt, a wail rose from Carmano's throat.

"Unclean! Unclean!" she cried. She slapped Mara across the face, would have done more if the other women hadn't pulled her away, not from any kindness toward Mara, but because punishment must come from her grandfather. Screaming insults, her aunt rushed outside to tell Yaddo that his granddaughter had disgraced him, just as her mother had done before her. Mara tried to sit up with some idea of covering herself, but the other women, their faces like rock, held her there until her grandfather came.

He yanked her by the hair and dragged her outside, flinging her into the dust.

"You are unclean. I cast you off," he roared. "I curse you for the shame you've brought your family today."

"Who is the man?" Lazlo demanded, pushing forward. "You can do whatever you want with her, but I demand the right to punish the man."

Mara covered her face with her hands, waiting for Yolo to step out of the crowd and confess his guilt. When no one spoke, she sought out his face in the circle around her. His eyes were sick, his face ashen, but he didn't speak, and it was then she knew that she'd been a fool, that she had mistaken a boy's lust for a man's love.

She didn't betray him. Even when her grandfather began to beat her with his belt, demanding she tell him the name of the man who'd befouled her, she remained silent.

After a while, the world around her dwindled down to grayness, and the only reality was the rise and fall of Yaddo's belt. Her last thought before she lost consciousness was that if she

survived the beating, she would never again, not as long as she
lived, trust another man.

CHAPTER 3

*T*HE DIRT ROAD *HORACE PERKINS* PLODDED ALONG WAS NAR-
row, very dusty. The morning sky had already taken on the
first white haze of noon heat, but it was still cool under the
sycamore trees that met overhead. It was mid-July, and Horace
should have been feeling good, because he thrived on hot
weather, but the truth was that he was thoroughly disgruntled
with his life.

The year of 1920 had been a bad year for Horace B. Perkins,
owner of Doc Perkins's Traveling Medicine Show, the purveyor
of the famous Redman's Elixir. From the time they'd left Nash-
ville, where they wintered every year, there had been a series
of mechanical breakdowns among the show's five vehicles—an
ancient Hudson touring car and four over-the-hill trucks, one of
which pulled the wooden caravan that Berty, Horace's woman,
was so proud of.

Their bad luck had started just after they'd left their home
quarters, a storefront in an overcrowded neighborhood in Nash-
ville. Their supply truck had thrown a rod, and then the cage
car that housed Big Benny, a Russian bear of uncertain age and
even more uncertain disposition, had broken down, costing them
several days' delay while some yokel garage owner sent away to
Lexington for parts. To top that off, Big Benny had rolled over
and died one night, probably from old age, leaving them without
an animal attraction.

The weather, which had started out as miserable, had wors-
ened, washing out several stops—stops where Horace had hoped
to recoup their finances. Since the medicine show was exploring
new territories this year, their route was an unfamiliar one. Such

things as which officials could be bribed to look the other way when it came to water connection permits and peddler's licenses had made every stop precarious.

Having to seek new territories was a sore spot with him. The year before, he'd been unwise enough to take on a new driver, who had systematically plied his real trade of pickpocket at the various stops along the route that had long been profitable and relatively safe from harassment. The driver's vocation made the show unwelcome in Ohio towns like Careytown and Highland and Leesburg, where various lawmen and irate citizens were waiting for him, arrest warrants in hand, should he be foolish enough to return to central Ohio.

In other words, he was in one helluva pickle.

It didn't help that Berty, his woman, had warned him that the driver had a sly look about him. Lord knew, he'd always tried to keep the show clean. After all, the elixir really did do some of the things he claimed for it, and with prohibition a certainty, the high alcohol content was bound to make it even more attractive to his steady customers in Ohio. So he'd blown it again, and now he was having a hard time feeding his crew.

The latest disaster to befall the show was the sudden departure of his only decent entertainer, the buxom, sexually generous Bonny Banks. She had run off with their mechanic/driver, who ate like a horse but who had managed to keep the vehicles running with a minimum of breakdowns and wasn't too unconvincing as the hero in their melodrama.

So now he only had three acts—a magic lantern show about to fall apart, Redman the Indian, who did war chants, and Berty, who belted out the latest songs.

Berty's voice hadn't improved with age, and sometimes she didn't even hit the middle notes when she was singing "When My Baby Smiles at Me," or "Who Ate Napoleons with Josephine when Bonaparte Was Away?"

Of course, he could still project a pretty good image of a medical man when he went into his spiel about having been forced to take his miracle "cure" directly to the people because the medical profession had prevented him from marketing his elixir through regular channels.

He never really claimed to be a doctor, but he billed himself as Doc Perkins, and through the years had come to think of himself as a bona fide physician. For years he and Berty had earned a good living on the road, but folks were getting more sophisticated, what with radio and movies wising them up, and the old spiel wasn't working so good. At their last spot, there'd been less than twenty-five people—and only seven had bought the elixir.

Which was why the free entertainment was even more important that it used to be. Once a magic lantern show, a war dance from a red Indian, and a saucy dance by a nubile girl, posing either as an Indian or Egyptian maiden, had been enough to draw them in. Now they demanded more before they'd stay around long enough to hear his spiel, extolling the miracles of the magic elixir.

The elixir, oddly enough, was really quite effective for such things as minor upsets of the stomach and constipation. It also tasted so awful that it had worked many a cure on that basis alone. With its high alcohol content—Horace made sure his testing gauge always showed at least 22 percent—it was especially popular with farm wives in the teetotaler Bible Belt. He'd built up quite a market for it in central Ohio and western Pennsylvania before he'd made the mistake of hiring on that pickpocket bastard.

Now Bonny Banks, who hadn't had much of a voice but who had been plump and pretty, the perfect heroine for the melodramas, was gone. To top it off, Redman, who brewed the elixir, insisted he needed new herbs for another batch. Hence this side trip into the Kentucky foothills, a delay they could ill afford.

Horace was a large, fleshy man with dark brown eyes his wife called soulful when she was in a good mood, cow's eyes when she was not, a flowing mustache that was turning iron-gray, and a sizable paunch that he carried with the aplomb of a banker. Although it was assumed by most people he met that he drank, because of the broken veins in his rather bulbous nose, the truth was that a beer or a glass of wine to be sociable was his only indulgence. His vices lay in a different direction—in the turn of a card, the rattle of a pair of dice.

Horace strolled on, using his cane to neatly separate queen's lace and tiger lily blossoms from their stems, taking a certain satisfaction in bashing the innocent wildflowers. It occurred to him that he'd never worried about money when he'd been Horace Perkins, a talker on the Coleson Bros. Circus midway. That was before he'd run off with Berty. That she just happened to be married to one of the circus's owners was the reason that he'd been blacklisted by every respectable circus in the country.

He'd been working as a candy butch in a run-down mudshow when he'd met Redman in a Memphis bar. The Indian had of-

fered him a swig of the concoction he'd sworn was a tribal rec-
ipe, guaranteed to cure just about anything that ailed man or
beast. Horace, who had developed an irksome rash, had taken
a chance and swigged down a jigger of the vile-tasting stuff.
When it cured his hives, he was sure he had a gold mine. Not
only could he go into business for himself, but it meant he
wouldn't have to take any more shit off men who'd been in
diapers when he was first starting out as a midway talker.

The next morning, he hunted up the Indian, who was sleeping
off his drunk, and they'd come to an understanding. Redman—
he had no other name—would supply the medicine. In addition,
he would dress up in fringed leather and beads and whip up
some war chants. He, Horace, would do the rest, and make
Redman one helluva rich Indian.

Getting Berty to let loose of their nest egg, which she was
hoarding for their old age, was the next step. He made a few
promises, such as giving up gambling, and eventually she forked
over enough to buy a couple of beat-up trucks and the other
equipment, including their caravan, which he'd bought dirt cheap
from a down-and-out Gypsy, and they'd set out on their first
circuit.

They'd been at it ever since. They hadn't gotten rich, but until
lately, they'd made enough to keep afloat and live a pretty good
life, one they both enjoyed.

For a while Horace entertained himself, as he often did, with
a scheme to find out the formula for the elixir, a secret Redman
guarded carefully. When this palled, he wondered how it was
that Berty had stuck by him all those years. Of course, she'd
never gone hungry, but how much longer could they keep going?

"It's your own fault," she'd said just this morning when he'd
complained about the rotten take from their stop in Compton.
"You got bad judgment about people. Like taking on that tart
Bonny. Didn't I warn you? Didn't I tell you she was trouble?
And now look what's happened."

He'd known she was right, which was why he'd lost his temper. He regretted calling her a fat cow. Okay, she was thirty
pounds heavier than when they'd run off together, but no way
was she a cow. Cows were placid and easygoing, and Berty had
more spit than a dozen other women.

So as soon as he figured out the best way to get back in her
good graces, he would return to camp and make his peace. It
wasn't any fun when she wouldn't talk to him—or worse still,
when she wouldn't listen to him talk.

He settled himself on a fallen log beside the road and took a cigar out of his waistcoat pocket. He trimmed the end with his pocketknife, then primed it with saliva. There was an acrid smell as he struck a wooden match against the sole of his shoe and lit the cigar.

Lately he'd been hoarding his supply of Havanas, making them last, and he inhaled the fragrant smoke blissfully. In the act of tapping off the ash against the log, he froze, listening. That noise—it sounded like a baby mewling. But what would a baby be doing out here on this dirt road, miles from any house?

The sound came again, leaving him in a quandary. Although he had the innate caution of the perpetual outsider, he was also a very curious man. So he carefully cut off the end of his cigar with his pocketknife and put the remainder back in his waistcoat pocket before he rose and looked around.

The whimpering sound had come from behind a stand of scrub pine. He pushed through the scrubs and found himself standing at the edge of a ditch, which was bordered by shoulder-high hawthorn bushes. At first he didn't see anything out of normal, and then, as he was turning away, he caught a flash of pink through a break in the bushes.

A body, he thought. *My God, it's a naked body.*

The suspicion chilled him. The last thing he wanted was to be anywhere near the proximity of a possible crime. But still— what if someone was hurt down there in that ditch and he could help?

In the end, he pushed aside the bushes to get a better look, and discovered he'd been right. It was a body, a woman, and she was stark naked. She was lying on her back, her legs twisted to one side, and her body bore the kind of bruises and welts that could only come from a beating.

Her hair, which covered her face, was a fiery red, and she possessed one of the finest female bodies he'd ever seen—and Horace had been, in his day, quite a connoisseur of the naked female form.

His first thought was that she was dead. Then she moved her head, and Horace felt a strange kind of shame. It seemed obvious to him that she'd been raped, a crime committed by a man. And he was a man. Not that he'd ever in his life forced himself upon a woman. But still—he *was* a man.

His hesitation was short. The girl made the same mewling sound he'd heard before, and he eased himself down the side of the ditch, holding on to the shrubs for support. Halfway down, he lost his footing and slid the rest of the way, ending up in an ignoble heap at the bottom of the ditch. He picked himself up, dusted off the worst of the sand, before he warily approached the girl.

His first act was to shrug out of his seersucker jacket and put it over her to cover her nudity. She gave a cry of surprise and Horace hurried into speech.

"There now, girl, you'll be just fine. I'm going to leave for a few minutes to go fetch Berty—that's my woman. She'll take care of you."

The girl lay very still for a moment. When she pushed the hair away from her face, he saw that her eyes were a brilliant green, shot with tiny black lines, like a cat Berty had once had.

Before he could speak again, the girl moved backward in a crablike movement. He'd thought she would be grateful for his offer of help, but she bared her teeth, her eyes spitting fire, and he retreated a few wary steps.

She said something in a language he didn't recognize, but it was obvious she was cursing him. When he tried to interrupt and reiterate his good intentions, she snatched up a small rock and threw it at him.

The rock hit him on the side of his neck, and he gave a yelp of pain. "That wasn't nice," he said, feeling aggrieved. "I didn't have anything to do with—with what happened to you. I was just out taking a walk when I heard a noise—look, here's my card. I'm a perfectly respectable businessman."

She looked at the card he offered, then at him, and it was obvious she thought he was crazy. Horace felt a sudden urge to laugh. If Berty saw him handing a business card to a naked woman in the middle of nowhere, she'd never let him live it down.

Unexpectedly the girl reached out and snatched the card from his hand. She turned it over, examined both sides, then let it fall to the ground. Her unblinking stare made him fidget with embarrassment. "What's your name, miss?" he asked.

She didn't answer. She huddled under his jacket, watching him, but when he told her again that he was going to get his wife, she surprised him by nodding.

A few minutes later, after he had labored up the side of the ditch and was standing at the top, he looked back. She was still watching him, and if she was feeling any gratitude, it didn't show on her face. He was wondering if she'd still be there when he got back with Berty when his foot struck an object, hidden in the grass. He bent, picked up a small wooden box. Aware of the importance of time, he thrust it into a trouser pocket and hurried toward the road.

It took him a while to explain the situation to Berty. She interrupted him several times to tell him how stupid he was. "Naked women!" she said in disgust. "You're even crazier than I thought. What on earth's wrong with you? You know what the hicks around here would do if you got mixed up in a rape. They'd string you up before you ever went to trial! It'll take us about ten minutes to pack up and get out of here—and another hour to reach the county line."

He almost gave in to Berty's fears, but then the image of the girl, alone and defenseless, tugged at his conscience. The least they could do was to take the girl some clothes, he told Berty firmly.

Still grumbling loudly, Berty dug into an old trunk for an assortment of well-worn clothing. Horace watched her warily, having second thoughts again. She was usually right about people, which was why he felt so uneasy as he led the way toward the ditch where he'd found the girl.

A little to his surprise, she was still there, huddled under his seersucker jacket. As soon as she spotted him, she jumped to her feet, clutching the jacket in front of her, ready for flight. Then she saw Berty, coming along behind, and her relief was apparent. The bruises and welts were even more extensive than he'd thought. They covered her legs and thighs, and what he thought was mud on her face was great purple bruises.

Berty sucked in a startled breath, then made a *tish*ing sound with her tongue. As Horace helped her down the side of the ditch, he knew it would be all right now. For all her scathing remarks about him being a softheaded fool, she had her own soft spots—and abused women were one of them.

"This is Berty," Horace said. "She's going to help you."

The girl stared at Berty, at the clothes draped over Berty's arm.

"I brung you some clothes," Berty said. She made a gesture to Horace to turn his back, and he was careful not to smile, because she knew that he'd already seen everything the girl had. A few minutes later, when Berty told him it was all right to turn around, the girl was fully clothed. Not only did Berty's old cotton dress cover her adequately, it swathed her small body from neck to feet.

Berty shook her head. "I'll have to take those things up,"

she muttered, and Horace knew he'd been right, that she would take the girl under her wing.

"And you can stop smirking," she added testily. "I'm a Christian, ain't I? I got a heart."

"You got the biggest one I ever saw," he said fervently, and earned a wintry smile.

"I ain't forgot what you called me," she said. "And don't think your sweet-talking is gonna get you back in my bed for a while."

She turned to the girl. "What's your name, honey?" The girl didn't answer, and she looked impatient. "You understand me all right. And you got a tongue in your head. So what's your name?"

Again the girl surprised Horace. "Rosa," she said. "Rosa Smith."

"Smith is it? From that accent, I would've guessed you'd have some foreign kind of name. Your ma a foreigner?"

"Spanish," Rosa said, so quickly that Horace was sure she was lying.

"I figgered that was a Spanish accent," Berty said, nodding.

The girl didn't answer. When she swayed, then sat down heavily on the ground, he took a concerned step toward her. Berty reached her first, making the tutting sound again. She patted the girl's thin shoulder and told her that everything would be all right, not to worry.

Between the two of them, they got the girl on her feet and up the side of the ditch. She leaned heavily on Berty as they started down the road. Once in the caravan, they got her settled in a rush-bottomed chair. Berty bustled around, warming some barley soup on their two-burner kerosene stove. Horace wasn't surprised that after the first cautious bite, the girl dug into the soup hungrily. One of Berty's many assets was her cooking ability.

When she'd finished off the soup and a large hunk of Berty's bread, the girl stared around the small caravan, her eyes appraising the wood paneled walls, the ruffled curtains, the copper pots that hung above the stove, the circus poster on the wall.

Horace studied her in turn. Hair that could truly be called flame-colored, uncut and shaggy, but glossy and thick . . . skin, as pale and poreless as ivory . . . green eyes, wary but not afraid . . . hands rough, as if she did hard work, but nails neatly filed, all except two that were broken to the quick.

Funny how hard it was to judge someone when you didn't have their clothes to go by. A person's shoes, for instance, told you a lot—and why was she staring at that old circus poster as if she couldn't quite believe her eyes? Was it possible that she was with a circus?

"You got folks that'll be worried about you, Rosa?" he asked.

A look he couldn't interpret crossed her face. Anger or sorrow or grief—it could be anything. But one thing he was sure of— she was hurting bad, and it wasn't just physically.

When she shook her head, Berty asked, "You an orphan?" The girl looked uncertain, and Berty added, "You know—are your ma and pa dead?"

Rosa nodded, and Berty's face softened.

"You cook good," Rosa said unexpectedly.

Berty looked pleased. "So you've found your tongue. Well, that's a help. What we don't need around here is another person who lets on he don't understand good, decent English."

"Now, Berty, you know Redman just don't like to talk to females. He can speak up when it's necessary."

She snorted. "To you, maybe, but he ain't never said one word to me. Pretends he don't even hear me."

"Well, he's an Indian. Maybe they don't talk to their womenfolk."

She gave him a baleful look and began clearing away the soup bowl and spoon. "You want to rest now, you're welcome to curl up on the mat over there," she told Rosa. "We'll be moving on shortly. You're welcome to come along with us as far as Beattyville—that's our next stop."

The girl frowned. "Stop?"

Horace beamed at her; he stood and made a deep bow. "Horace P. Perkins—at your service. Purveyor of the famous Redman's Elixir, guaranteed to cure chilblains, constipation, and stomachaches, remove warts, both large and small, and has even been known to heal hangnails—"

He went on with his patter, noting that she was listening intently.

When he ran out of steam, she said, "Medicine show. I hear about them."

She yawned suddenly, her eyes watering. Without another word, she slid off the chair, then curled up on the mat Berty had pointed out and was soon asleep.

Berty refilled Horace's coffee mug. "What you think happened to her?"

"Some kind of family fight, I'd say."

"You talking about a husband? Why, she's just a youngster."

"Could be some of her own relatives. Maybe she did something they didn't like and they turned her out. She doesn't act like she's got a home to go back to. Those foreign families have their own ways. I don't figure it for a—you know, her being molested. No signs of that I could see."

"And you were looking pretty hard, too."

"Now, Berty—I got eyes, don't I?" He paused a moment, thinking. "How old you think she is?"

Berty shrugged. "Thirteen—maybe fourteen. Those Latin girls develop real young."

"What are we going to do with her?"

"Put some salve on them cuts, feed her a few meals till she gets back her strength, then turn her over to the law. We sure can't take on any more mouths to feed, not the way things are with us," she said.

He knew she was right, but he felt a small regret. The girl had gotten under his skin, the way she hadn't cried and carried on, even though she was hurting. She had grit—and he did admire women with grit.

"Well, we don't have to make any decision right now. Let's see what happens by the time we get to Beattyville."

It was later, as Berty was busy securing her dishes and other breakables in preparation for their coming trip along winding hill roads, that Horace remembered the wooden box he'd found by the side of the road. He took it out of his pocket, opened it, and when he saw the tattered deck of cards inside, a lot of things came clear.

Knowing his wife's prejudices, he waited until Berty went outside to take down some wash before he stuffed the box in a drawer where his underwear was stored. He'd dispose of those telltale fortune-telling cards later—when Berty wasn't around. Because it wouldn't do to let her see them. She would never let him live it down if she found out he'd brought a Gypsy waif into her spanking clean caravan.

CHAPTER 4

*A*LTHOUGH *MARA'S EXPERIENCE WITH THE GADJO HAD BEEN* limited to tarot card readings, plus her part in various *boojo* schemes, she had become shrewd at sizing them up. So she'd known within minutes that she didn't have anything physical to fear from either the tall, gray-haired man or the woman.

Her first impression was that they must be rich. The man wore a fancy watch on a heavy gold chain stretched across his waistcoat, and there were several gold rings on the woman's fat fingers.

Their caravan had given her a real shock. Although they weren't Roms, they lived in a Rom caravan, like those she'd seen when her family's path crossed other Rom tribes. Occasionally someone brought one over from the old country, and they were a source of great pride. Had these people stolen it? Surely no Rom would ever sell such a treasure.

It was very clean, too, which made her uneasy. The wooden walls were heavily waxed, the copper pots that hung from a wall rack were as shiny as mirrors, and there was no dust on the polished wood floor. The windows, which were made of real glass instead of isinglass, sparkled as if they'd just been washed. Why would a woman waste her time and energy cleaning and polishing when the dust blew back in the next day?

And the wash she'd seen strung outside on a rope—why would two people need so much underwear, so many shirts and dresses and petticoats? It didn't make sense—but then, *gadjos* didn't make sense to her, never had. So easy to fool and yet so dangerous. She mustn't let down her guard, not for a minute, even though these *gadjos* had been so kind.

On the other hand, she didn't have much choice. She had to

stay here until she could fend for herself. Where could she go, looking like this, her face all bruised and swollen?

For a moment her grief, the feeling of deep loss, threatened to overwhelm her, but she stifled the sob that rose in her throat. It wouldn't do to show weakness in front of these strangers. From their conversation when they thought she was asleep, they had no suspicions that she was a Rom. The man would be easy to fool, but maybe not the woman. Those sharp eyes didn't miss much. And yet—Berty had brought her clothes, had fed her, let her sleep in her caravan. Maybe it would be safe to relax her guard—but just a little.

The couple was still talking when she fell asleep. When she awoke, the caravan was filled with cooking odors. She sat up, sniffing hungrily. It might not be easy to lull the woman's suspicions, but as long as she stayed here, she had no doubts that she would eat well.

"How you feeling, girl?" the woman asked, and Mara saw that Horace was gone, that Berty was watching her.

"My back—is very sore."

"And no wonder. Well, I'll put some salve on it and it will heal fast. Take off your dress and sit there at the table."

Her touch was light as she applied the sweet-smelling salve. Although there was an initial sting, the salve soon did its work, and by the time Mara slipped her dress back on, she already felt better. She yawned widely, her eyes drifting toward the built-in bed that filled one wall. Horace, who had come back into the caravan, started to say something, but the woman spoke first.

"We're fixin' to move out in a couple of hours—if that red Indian doesn't hold us up. When we get to Beattyville, you keep out of sight and you can stay with us until we get to Lexington. You can find work there, I expect."

Mara hid her relief. Although she had no idea how far it was to Lexington, at least they weren't going to throw her out immediately. "You sell—" Mara paused, the word eluding her.

"Redman's Elixir." Horace laid his finger alongside his nose and winked. "Its real attraction is its alcohol. The smart ones know what's what, which is why they buy it. Cheaper than whiskey any day."

Mara smiled at him. This kind of thinking she understood. He might be a *gadjo*, but he thought like a Rom.

At her smile, the man's eyes flickered; for a moment he looked disconcerted. "Berty here, she's our star attraction," he said quickly. "Sings like an angel."

"More like a crow these days," Berty said, "but they're still getting a bargain 'cause the show is free."

A thought struck Mara. "I dance good," she said.

Horace's eyebrows rose. "Now, do you, little lady? Some of those Spanish dances?"

Mara hesitated. Could the dances she knew pass for Spanish? "Yes, Spanish," she said firmly.

Horace glanced at the woman as if looking for guidance. When she said nothing, he turned back to Mara. "Maybe you could help us out. We're kinda short on talent right now."

"With them bruises?" Berty said sharply. "The locals would have us up for child beating."

"I didn't mean right away. It wouldn't hurt to see what she can do. No harm in that, is there?"

The woman's mouth tightened. "Do what you want."

She went to a tiny zinc-lined sink and began washing dishes, her back to them. "Where's that Indian, Horace?" she said over her shoulder. "If he don't get back soon, we won't have time to eat and reach Beattyville by nightfall."

"Oh, he'll be along as soon as he gathers his plants." Horace looked at Mara. "We'll be eating in another hour. Why don't you curl up over there on the bed, Rosa, and get yourself some rest?"

The woman turned and gave Horace a hard look. "I'll be needing the bed for my afternoon nap," she said shortly. "Rosa can sleep in one of the trucks. Lots of room in the cab for a little one like her."

"Why, you don't never take a—" His wife's hostile stare stopped Horace, and he rubbed his chin, looking embarrassed. Mara watched the flush on his face with interest. He didn't like it that his wife wouldn't let her sleep in their bed. She wasn't offended. After all, what did he expect? In the same circumstances, she'd feel the same way about a *gadjo* sleeping on her cot.

Berty went outside to throw out the dishwater, and Horace gave Mara a sheepish grin. "Berty's got a big heart, Rosa. Just don't get her riled up."

Mara didn't bother to answer, realizing that he was just making conversation. She was staring at the circus poster again, trying to decide if it could be the same woman she'd seen long ago, the substance of her dreams ever since.

"That's Sadie Lucke," Horace told her. "She isn't as well-known as some, but there's never been another aerialist like her."

"She is real woman?"

"Oh, she was real, all right."

"She dead?"

"For several years now. The things that lady could do on a swing. Defied the laws of gravity, she did."

He gave her absorbed face a closer look. "You got circus fever?" he asked. At her blank look, he added, "You like circuses?"

"I only saw one," she said.

"Well, that's all it takes." There was a faraway look in his eyes. "I was with it for almost twenty years. It was a great life."

"What you do? Tame wild animals?"

Berty came in the door and caught the question. "Him? He's scared shitless of animals. Last time he worked a circus, he was a talker on the midway. Turned tips for the girlie show."

The couple exchanged glances. Horace looked away first. "Anything you want to know about circus life, just ask," he said expansively. He took the watch from his waistcoat pocket and looked at it. "Right now, you best get some rest. You can sack down in the Hudson. Soon as the Indian gets back with his herbs, we'll eat our supper and then we'll be moving out."

Mara took the blanket Berty handed her and went outside, hitching up her too-long skirt with one hand so she wouldn't trip. She paused to look around, trying to decide which of the four vehicles she should crawl into. A young boy, probably in his late teens, came out of the bushes. He stared at her but didn't speak. Neither did she. Although she had no idea what a Hudson looked like, she wasn't going to ask him to point it out, and reveal her ignorance. Behind her, Berty and Horace were talking—arguing, if raised voices meant anything—but she didn't bother to listen.

Her first impression, that they was rich, had faded. The woman had complained about not having enough money to buy supplies if they didn't do well at the next stop. If she helped them to earn money by dancing, they should be willing to feed her and give her some money. She was a good dancer. Not as good as some of her cousins, but better than Anna—that cow.

And these people wouldn't know the difference. Only another Rom would realize that she'd never really mastered the subtleties of the dance.

Unexpectedly a soul-searing grief welled up inside her, a grief that cut so deep that she gasped out loud. She would never see her people again. Even if, by some chance, their paths crossed, they wouldn't acknowledge her existence. She was dead—none of them, not her cousins or her grandfather, not Yolo, who had betrayed her, nor Sophia, who had been kind to her, would speak to her, look at her. It was time to face the truth, that she was alone now, completely on her own.

Since she was no longer a Rom, she would be a *gadjo*. She would live like them, think like them, be one of them. The *kumpania* had turned their backs on her? Well, she spit on them. From now on, for better or worse, she was a *gadjo*.

CHAPTER 5

M ARA'S INTRODUCTION TO REDMAN CAME AN HOUR LATER. She had dozed fitfully, curled up in the cab of one of the trucks, finally drifting off to sleep only to have a large brown hand shake her awake.

"What you do in my truck?" the man demanded. "I don't let no woman in my truck."

To Mara, used to the short, stocky men of her tribe, he seemed very tall and very alien with his blue-black hair, his black eyes, and deeply lined, copper-brown skin. Although he was obviously middle-aged, his hair showed no gray, and his face could have been carved from a block of dark walnut.

She slid out of the truck, afraid that he'd haul her out bodily if she didn't. She also found her voice. "Horace say I sleep in this truck."

He glared at her so menacingly that she took a step backward. But only one. It was her pride that prevented her from turning tail and running.

"This my truck. Gotta papers for it. He don't say who sleep in my truck." But he stopped moving toward her. "Who you?"

"I'm Mar—Rosa," she said.

"What kind name that? Mar-Rosa?"

"Rosa. My name is Rosa."

His grunt indicated disbelief. "You go away now," he said.

Since there was nothing else she could do, Mara retreated, well aware how foolish she must look with Berty's too-long skirt flapping around her ankles. For the next hour, she took refuge in the shade of a huge water oak. The sun had already dropped below the top of the hills when Berty called her. "Rosa—come help with supper. You can start by setting up the planks for the table."

A few minutes later, Mara surveyed the food she'd carried to the plank table—bowls of mashed potatoes and white beans, a large hunk of ham, rice and roasted corn and two loaves of bread—and decided there was enough food for an army instead of the five people who gathered for the meal. Used to grabbing whatever she could from her *kumpania*'s communal table, she had to force herself not to bolt down the food on her plate.

As she ate, using an unfamiliar fork instead of a spoon, she looked the people over. There was the Indian, of course, who ate steadily, ignoring everybody else. Another was the half-grown boy she'd seen earlier; he kept his eyes on his plate, shoveling in the food as fast as he could chew and swallow it. The other man, who was several years older, had long, untidy hair, crescents of grease under his fingernails, and needed a shave. He eyed her so boldly that she avoided looking at him.

Only Horace made any attempt at conversation. As genially as if he were entertaining in a fine home, he spoke about the weather, the state of something he called the economy, about someone called Warren Harding, who he seemed to think would give away the country to the bankers.

Berty sat a bowl of cooked greens down in front of him with a thump, saying, "What you should be worrying about is the Klan. Getting stronger all the time here in the South. Don't ever know when you'll step on their toes." Her eyes held malice as she glanced at the Indian. "They don't take to people with dark skin. Maybe we should keep the Indian out of sight until we reach Cincinnati."

Redman ignored her and went on eating.

"Now, now, Berty," Horace said.

Berty poured coffee into heavy white mugs and passed them around. She didn't eat with the others, but there was nothing servile about her as she waited on the men. In so many ways she reminded Mara of the Rom women, and yet—no Rom would contradict and argue with her man the way Berty did. She wondered, as she dug into her own food, if she'd ever understand these *gadjos* and their strange ways.

It was later, while Berty was washing dishes, dunking them in lukewarm water and scrubbing them with a bar of brown soap that smelled like lye, that she told Mara she'd better get to bed early because they would be moving on before dawn the next day.

"That red Indian held us up or we'd already be in Beattyville," she added sourly.

"When you want me dance for you?" Mara asked.

"That's up to Horace," Berty said.

And Mara had to be content with that.

The next day, after a harrowing early morning trip along the hairpin curves of a mountain road, they made their first stop. Although the odor of bear was overwhelming in the front seat of the cage truck, which was packed with planks and canvas, Mara had been so exhausted that she'd slept through the night without waking once. Where the others slept, she had no idea.

The teenager—his name was Tommy—drove the truck. He still hadn't addressed his first word to her, which suited her just fine.

Beattyville was nestled in the bend of a narrow river, surrounded by a forest of evergreens. That they were the objects of both curiosity and suspicion as the men set up a large tent on a vacant lot near the center of town, Mara was immediately aware. She didn't realize that others had noted the hostility until she heard Berty say, "This town's been burned."

"But not by us," Horace said.

Mara watched with interest as they made their preparations. On a sawhorse table, the Indian laid out a row of beaded moccasins, an assortment of tomahawks, and feathered headbands. The other men put together benches made of planks and set up a rickety-looking stage inside the tent. Berty arranged, under a net covering, a display of popcorn balls, rich with molasses, white squares of candy she called divinity fudge, and long sticks of licorice. She put Mara to work blowing up balloons.

"Get the kids here and their parents will come, too, to keep them out of mischief." Berty gave Mara a sharp look. "You stay out of sight tonight. Don't want these folks getting wrong ideas."

That evening, banished to the darkened caravan, Mara watched from the window. Because of the balmy evening, the front of the tent had been rolled up to let in any stray breezes. Most of the plank benches were full; the people, the men and boys wearing bib overalls and work shoes, the women and girls in cotton dresses, stared silently as the men set up signs on each side of the rickety stage.

The program started with a greeting by Horace. Wearing a black coat, gray striped trousers, a wide red tie, and a high hat that was shabby but carefully brushed, he reminded Mara of a *gadjo* preacher, the leader of a mob who had once raided their campsite, looking for a lost child.

Silver-tongued and confident, at least outwardly, he spun an earnest tale about the afflictions that had tormented him before he was lucky enough to stumble upon the magic elixir, a blending of curative herbs known only to a few Indian medicine men.

Redman, his gaunt face smeared with paint, did a war chant, pounding out the rhythm on a drum. Mara snickered as he danced in a circle, whooping so loud that she wondered if he was going to leave them all deaf. Then Berty sang in a husky voice that sometimes lost the melody. She was wearing rouge and lipstick now, and her robust figure looked as if it had been poured into her red satin gown. To Mara's surprise, she was accompanied by the pimply-faced youth, who played a fiddle reasonably well.

Horace returned, again exhorting the benefits of the elixir. His face glistened with sweat, and his words were so convincing that she wondered why Berty hadn't used the elixir on her own welts and abrasions. She was still sitting in the dark when Horace and Berty came back to the caravan. Horace lit a lantern, and she knew from his glum face that they hadn't done as well as they'd hoped.

"Well, we didn't get well, but at least we have traveling money now." Horace shook his head. "I just couldn't turn the tip tonight. Maybe I'm losing my touch. Some of them up and left before I did my final spiel."

"Can't blame them. Just that wild Indian and me to entertain them," Berty said. "They get better stuff at home on the radio. Maybe we should try to fix the magic lantern and use it again."

"Nonsense. You were in good voice tonight," he said.

Mara eyed the coins Horace turned out on the table. "Why you not let me dance?" she asked.

Horace glanced at Berty. "We could give her a try tomorrow night when we get to Vincent," he said. "We aren't going to have ten sales if we don't do something. You think you can cover those bruises?''

Berty looked Mara over. ''Well, there's a pot of greasepaint in the trunk. I don't think it's dried up yet. I can cut down one of my old costumes. Too tight for me anyway.'' Her voice sharpened as she asked Mara, ''You ain't fooling about the dancing, are you? These rurals—they can turn ugly when they think they're being cheated.''

Mara tapped her chest. ''Good dancer,'' she said, pumping confidence into her voice.

Their next stop wasn't really a town. It was a general store, set at the crossroads of two highways, and flanked by three houses. To Mara's surprise, there was a crowd of more than fifty people waiting on the benches when the show began.

Mara was pleased with her costume, although it was more confining than she was used to, with its high-necked white blouse and ankle-long skirt. Still, the skirt was bright red, and Berty had pressed out the wrinkles with a flatiron. From the same trunk that the costume had come from, she produced a red scarf to make a sash for Mara's narrow waist.

Standing in the rear of the tent, Mara gave an experimental kick and was delighted with the show of lace-trimmed petticoats. Berty had insisted that she wear dark lisle stockings to hide her bruises, but she wished she could dance barefooted, the way the Rom women did.

To her surprise, when she was introduced, Horace pointed out the bruises on her throat and arms. ''This little lady is living proof of the power of Redman's Magic Elixir,'' he intoned. ''She was in a bad accident just a few days ago—and look how her bruises faded when she used the elixir as an ointment. And in a minute you'll see how it banished the stiffness in her limbs, caused by the fall.''

Horace's speech filled Mara with dismay. For the first time, she felt nervous about dancing in front of all these strangers. Surely, as gullible as she knew the *gadjos* to be, they wouldn't believe his claims. The tribe bought a common brand of horse liniment, put it in their own bottles, and sold it as a Rom remedy. She was pretty sure that the base of the elixir was the same patent medicine, spiced up with alcohol and herbs to disguise its characteristic odor.

But no one challenged Horace, and she gave her skirts a final flip and ran out into the middle of the plank stage.

* * *

Berty disapproved wholeheartedly of Horace pointing out Rosa's bruises, especially since she'd spent so much time trying to hide them. In fact, she disapproved of the girl—period. There was something too secretive about her, the way she pretended not to understand any questions she didn't want to answer. Not that she'd pestered the girl with questions—and neither had Horace. He was all too willing to accept everybody at face value. Which was why they were so often broke.

Well, she intended to keep a close eye on that little baggage. Someone had given her a beating, and there had to be a reason for that. It wasn't rape. There would have been unmistakable signs—bruises on the inside of her thighs and breasts. No, the girl had been whipped by someone who had avoided hitting her breasts and genital area. Had she been caught stealing from her own family? Or something worse? And just what was she, anyway? She didn't know a word of Spanish. Twice Berty had slipped a couple of Spanish words into their conversation, but Rosa had only looked at her blankly, obviously not understanding.

Berty shook her head, watching Rosa as she ran out into the center of the small stage. She had to admit that the crowd was showing more interest than they had when she sang—or that wild Indian did his chants. Well, she had no false pride. She knew that she was over the hill as a singer. And there was no denying the crowd was intrigued by Rosa. Funny how different she looked up there on the stage. Ordinarily she was as expressionless as the Indian, but now her face positively glowed. Yes, she liked the spotlight, all right.

She could dance, too, which was a surprise. Although there was nothing structured about her dancing, it was exuberant, graceful, and if you could believe the stares of the men, provocative. Even Tommy, his pimply face flushed, was gaping at her like a kid looking at a candy bar as he sawed away at his fiddle, playing his version of a tango.

As Rosa pranced, kicking her heels high in the air, as she flung back her head and snapped her fingers, then grabbed her skirts in both hands and shook them so vigorously that she showed a tantalizing glimpse of lisle hose and white thighs, Berty knew that she was winning over her audience in a way that she herself had never done, even when she was in her prime. Briefly she felt a flash of envy, of pique, but she shrugged it off. After all, they all would benefit if the audience was disarmed by Rosa's talent.

As he stood beside her at the edge of the stage, Horace's beaming face showed no such doubts. He rubbed his hands together in a frenzy of satisfaction, and Berty knew that he was right, that the girl could only swell their bankroll.

"So what you think?" Horace asked. "Should we give her a job?"

It was a rhetorical question, but she answered it anyway. "We don't know a thing about her. We could find ourselves murdered in our bed some morning."

"Nonsense. She's harmless as a baby. And not much older either."

"Well, you'll do what you want, like always. Don't know why you bother to ask my advice. But don't forget I warned you."

Mara reveled in the applause of the audience. It was her first taste of this kind of approval, and she discovered she wanted more, was eager to perform again. She also basked in Horace's lavish praise after the show. But Berty's "You did fine—but watch the way you kick up your skirt" was so grudging that she knew it was time to win the woman's goodwill.

Horace might think he ran the medicine show, but it was Berty who really did. Besides, food and sleeping space and every stitch she wore came from Berty. There was something else, too. Since she would be passing as a *gadjo* from now on, she needed to learn how to act like one, think like one. And it never was too soon to start, using Berty as her model.

She ran over the various stories she had used in the past to ingratiate herself with *gadjo* women, but none of them seemed to fit. No, there was only one way to win Berty over, and that was by doing more than her share of chores—and not complaining about it.

Early the next morning, she arrived at the caravan with an offer to help with breakfast preparations. Later, she did the dishes and then hauled water from the creek behind the general store without being told so she could help Berty scrub out the caravan, something she had no patience with. What did all that scrubbing do except wear out things, anyway? But she did like being clean, and when Berty suggested she take a towel and a bar of the brown soap down to the creek to wash her hair, she didn't argue.

When she returned, everybody had almost finished packing up to leave. Her wet hair swinging around her shoulders, she hastened to help Berty tie down the cupboard doors and lash the chairs into place.

"You're going to be a lot of help, Rosa," Berty said approvingly. "Let's see what we can do about finding you a change of clothes."

That night, they spent in a state camping grounds, and after the dishes had been cleared off, Horace and the other men, including the Indian, used a park table to play cards. After Mara had finished the dishes, she served mugs of coffee to the men, then settled down on the grass nearby to watch.

The cards reminded her of her own lost tarot cards. What had happened to them? No one in the tribe would dare try to use them, of course, because they would consider them unclean, along with their owner. Had they burned them—as they must have burned her clothes and other possessions?

Her thoughts were so hurtful that she turned her attention to Horace. Although the evening air was cool, his face glistened with sweat. "Horace—he got fever?" she asked Berty, who had joined her on the grass.

"He's got fever, all right. Gambler's fever. He'll gamble the coins off my eyelids when I'm in my coffin, I suspect. And that reminds me, I found some cards in Horace's drawer when I was putting away his underwear. He says he picked them up near that ditch where he found you. You know anything about them?"

Mara's heart leaped. "Cards?"

"Yeah. Funny-looking ones. They're in a wooden box."

"They are mine," Mara said carefully. "When those men rob me—" she gave Berty a sidelong glance "—they take everything. I guess they drop box."

"Well, if they're yours, you'll be wanting them."

Berty heaved herself to her feet and went into the caravan. When she came back, she was carrying the small wooden box.

Mara had a hard time concealing her elation. As long as she had the cards, she could always earn money by telling fortunes. At least she wouldn't have to beg on the streets if these people kicked her out.

She realized Berty was watching her, obviously waiting for some kind of explanation. "Friend give me cards," she said.

"Queer-looking, you ask me."

Mara tucked the box into her pocket. "I go to bed now. Where I sleep tonight?"

Berty pulled at her lower lip with her thumb and forefinger, a gesture Mara had already learned meant she was trying to make up her mind about something. "You can sleep in the cab of our truck tonight," she said finally. "There's a lot more space behind the front seat than in the other trucks. We can fit a couple blankets in here, give you something comfortable to sleep on."

Mara knew what a concession this was, but she only nodded, knowing more wouldn't be welcome.

The next morning, while she was helping Berty make popcorn balls, she offered to tell her fortune.

"My friend—she show me how," she added.

"I don't believe in that heathen stuff, but it might be interesting," Berty said. "Soon as we finish here, you can show me how you do it."

After they were finished with the popcorn balls, Mara got out the box and tipped the cards out on the table. Something fell on the floor, and when she bent to pick it up, her breath caught sharply. It was the silver necklace her mother had given her long ago—but how had it gotten in the box? She always kept it in the sea chest. Someone had put it in there—was it her grandfather? No, he would never do such a thing. So it must have been Sophia, who knew how much she treasured the necklace—and why.

Unexpectedly her eyes stung with tears, and her mouth writhed, out of control. Afraid that Berty would see her pain, she let a few cards slip to the floor, using that as an excuse to avert her face while she picked them up. When she was back to normal, she handed Berty the cards and told her to shuffle them while asking a question or making a wish, then cut them three times.

She laid the cards out in the form of a cross. Although she felt no compulsion to reveal what they really said, she was curious what lay in Berty's future.

She couldn't help a smile when she saw the Fool, playing his flute so merrily, his eyes on the sky, ignorant of the abyss that opened before his feet. If ever a man fit that card, it was Horace. But when she laid the next card, the Chariot, in reverse, beside the Fool, the smile slipped off her face.

"Well?" Berty prompted. "What do you see?"

Mara turned the next card over. It was the Ten of Diamonds. "I see money. Much money," she said.

"Going in which direction—out or in?" Berty's voice was dry. "And what else do you see, Rosa? It's something you don't like."

"Cards show good luck, not bad," Mara said quickly, vexed with herself. "Many people buy elixir. Show make money. Way off in future—maybe not be so good health. Cards say take care of self, not go out in cold wind."

Berty's eyes were skeptical, but she didn't press her any further, for which Mara was grateful. When she'd seen the card, her mother's saying for the Chariot in reverse had come to mind. "Out of the strong comes forth sweetness. From the weak, the bitterness of misery." And the Chariot card was resting next to the card that represented Horace, who for all his bombast was a weak man.

Mara finished laying out the spread. She tapped the final card—the court card, Judgment. "This is future. Tomorrow, next day, day after, everything good. Much money. Maybe then comes time not so good. But in end, things come out all right."

Berty looked thoughtful. "You're good," she said. "You give one bad thing to make the good things seem true. Too bad we can't use your talent to make money."

"Why I not tell fortunes? I willing."

" 'Cause this is the Bible Belt, girl. We'd be run out of town."

Her words didn't make any sense to Mara. Roms told fortunes everywhere—here in Kentucky, in Ohio, wherever they roamed. She started to ask Berty what a Bible Belt was, but she caught herself. This was the kind of ignorance that could give her away to someone as sharp as Berty. She stored the words away in the back of her mind. Tomorrow, when she got the chance, she'd ask Horace to explain them to her.

She put the cards away in the wooden box, along with the silver necklace.

CHAPTER 6

MARA LAY HIDDEN BEHIND A GROWTH OF WILD OATS AT the edge of a small Alabama roadside park. The weeds were lush with mid-March growth, and she was careful to keep her head down, her cotton skirt tucked under her so that it wouldn't blow up and betray her presence to Berty's sharp eyes. Under Berty's supervision, she'd spent the whole morning doing the wash, hanging it up to dry, and cleaning the caravan, and she was in no mood for further chores.

Pensively she reviewed the past nine months. In most ways she'd been well treated, but in others she was no better off than when she'd been with her own family. It wasn't that she was lazy. It was just that Berty's standards of cleanliness were impossibly high. Scrubbing floors that weren't dirty, scouring pots and pans after every meal until they shone like mirrors, turning out bedding to air so often, just wasn't necessary.

Even so, if it weren't for other things, she could put up with this. After all, she'd learned so much about being a *gadjo* from Horace and Berty, could even talk like them—most of the time. But she didn't like having to go to Horace for every cent she needed. Just yesterday, when that peddler had come by their campsite, she'd yearned for those shiny gold earrings with the red stones and had almost convinced Horace to buy them for her when Berty came out of the caravan and ran off the peddler. If she drew wages, she could get what she wanted. But even buying a bottle of cream soda was impossible without some money of her own.

Oh, Horace always had an excuse for not paying her wages like he did the others. "Things are tight. Our expenses eat up the profits" was his usual excuse. She'd heard that so many times, she could scream. It wasn't even true. She'd made it her

59

business to watch at the window when Horace and Berty were counting the evening take, and there was a lot more money than they told the others.

Besides, it was her dancing that kept the customers around long enough for Horace to sell them the elixir. So why didn't they pay her? It was so unfair! Berty kept her so busy that the only reason she'd managed to get away today was because an old friend of Horace's had come by, diverting Berty's attention.

She had been hanging the wash up to dry when the stranger had come up. "I'm looking for Horace Perkins," he'd said, taking off his panama hat and wiping the sweat off his forehead. He was wearing a seersucker suit like the rich farmers in the area wore, but his shoes and tie had a city look. "I saw his poster at the barbershop in town and figured he'd be camping out here."

Mara pointed to the caravan. "He's over there."

"Thank you, miss," he said, but he didn't move away immediately. "You wouldn't happen to be old Horace's kid, would you?"

"No—I work for him and Berty," Mara said.

"Well, you're a very pretty lady," he told her, smiling widely. "You ever been with it?"

"With it?"

"The circus. You're pretty enough to be a performer."

Mara's interest soared; for a moment she found it hard to breathe. "You are with a circus?"

"Advance man for Bradford Circus, at your service."

"What does that mean? Advance man?

"Why, that I have the most important job in the circus," he said, lifting his eyebrows as if surprised at the question.

"He's also the biggest con artist in the business," Horace said from behind them. "How's it going, Charlie?"

Hardly able to contain her impatience, Mara watched as the two men slapped each other's shoulders, laughing and calling each other names that sounded like insults to her.

"But what the advance man *do* in the circus?" she finally asked.

"Well, I go on ahead of the circus, make sure the lot we've rented is ready, put advertisements in the local newspapers, and set up interviews with radio stations and papers if I can. I give out free ducats where they'll do the most good and hire local kids to paper the town with posters." He winked at Horace. "Like I said, I'm the most important man with the circus."

Horace laughed, and then they were reminiscing about old times. When they both agreed how easy a target circus people were for crooked officials and hostile lawmen, Mara nodded to herself. Just like Roms—it was strange how much like Roms these traveling show people sometimes were.

Noting Mara's interest, Charlie said expansively, "Hey, kid, I got a present for you. I was taking it home for my kid, but he's got a hundred of them." He winked at Horace again. "If you was a little older—or younger—I might ask for a kiss in payment. But as it is—" He reached in the satchel draped over his arm and took out a piece of tightly rolled paper.

Mara accepted it gingerly, wondering if it was some kind of *gadjo* joke. But when she unrolled the paper, her breath caught in her throat. It was a poster—a circus poster. Brilliantly colored, it showed a group of men doing handsprings and tumbling over each other. She looked at the bright lettering, wishing she could read what it said.

After a long study, she rolled it up carefully and tucked it under her arm. When the two men headed for the caravan, she tagged along, forgetting the wet laundry. She sensed a reservation in Berty's greeting to the stranger. Not that she wasn't polite. She poured the men mugs of coffee, then went on with lunch preparations, not joining in on the conversation.

For once, Mara was glad that Berty pounced on her to peel vegetables for soup. During the past months she had become adept at understanding the *gadjo* language, so she could follow the men's conversation even though they used words strange to her like *bally* and *dookie wagon*. In fact, she was so absorbed in their conversation that she stopped peeling until Berty told her brusquely to get back to work.

The man noticed her sullen look and asked, "You didn't tell me what you do, miss," he said.

Horace answered for her. "Rosa here's just about the dancingest gal I've ever seen. Whirls around like one of those Indian dervishes."

"Time you finished hanging up the wash, Rosa," Berty said abruptly, and there was nothing to do but leave. She was just hanging up the last sheet when the man left the caravan.

When she thanked him for the poster, he nodded, then said, "If you can dance as good as old Horace says, you should be working for the circus, little lady." He glanced toward the caravan, then hurriedly tucked a card in her hand. "Here, keep this. Our winter quarters are near Orlando—that's down in Florida. You ever decide you want to change jobs, you go see Mr. Sam and give him this card and tell him Charlie Schoor sent you.''

Mara stared down at the card in her hand. What was written there was a mystery to her, but she wasn't about to admit that to this stranger. She tucked the card into her pocket.

"This circus—they have dancers?''

"Indeed they do. But they come and go. Mr. Sam is getting the show together right now for the season; he can always use a good dancer, and the pay isn't bad. How much they paying you here?''

"My meals and a place to sleep. I have to ask Horace for money if I want to buy anything. Sometimes he don't give me any.''

"Well, Horace is a good man, but he does like to gamble,'' Charlie said.

He tipped his hat and went strolling off toward his touring car. Mara stared after him, turning his words over in her mind. Was Horace gambling those nights he snuck off alone? Was that why he didn't pay her wages?

She finished hanging the sheet and then she slipped away and hid herself in the grass because she had a lot of thinking to do.

It wasn't that she needed time to make up her mind about leaving. She had known for a long time that if she ever wanted to realize her dream, she had to go where she could learn how to be an aerialist. So it had been inevitable, the moment Charlie Schoor had given her the card, that she would leave. But there were plans to be made. She would need money. It would be useless to demand it from Berty, nor would she get any from Horace. But there was another way—and it wouldn't really be stealing. So why did she feel so guilty? Why did she keep thinking that Berty and Horace needed her, that she would miss them?

Early next morning, while everybody in camp was still asleep, she stole into the caravan where Berty and Horace were sleeping. She opened the drawer where she'd seen Berty put their earnings and slipped several bills off the cache she found there. Since it was dark, she didn't know how much it was, but she hoped it was enough to pay her bus fare to Florida. If not, she'd just have to hitchhike. She had already packed her clothes, what she intended to take with her, in a small canvas satchel she'd found in the supply truck. There wasn't much, just blouses and skirts and a couple of cotton dresses Berty had cut down for

her—and the poster Charlie Schoor had given her. But, she reflected, it was a lot more than she'd arrived with.

Also, it was *gadjo* clothing. No one would suspect these days
that she was a Rom—or so she hoped. She'd lost a lot of her
accent during the past few months, and it wasn't by accident.
She'd always had a gift for mimicking—and Berty and Horace
had been her models. Eventually no one, not even another Rom,
would be able to tell she wasn't a *gadjo*.

She was walking along the access road that led to the state
highway when she heard footsteps coming up fast behind her.
She whirled and saw it was Horace. He was wearing his old
seersucker robe, and his hair was rumpled, his face very pale
in the moonlight.

"So you're leaving us, Rosa," he said, his voice heavy.

"I very tired, being on the road all the time," she lied. "I
want to get job and—and settle down."

"So why are you sneaking out in the middle of the night?"

She swallowed hard. "Because I don't like say good-byes,"
she improvised, and then discovered it was true.

"Why don't you come back to the caravan and talk to Berty?
If something's bothering you, maybe we can work it out."

"Nothing bothering me," Mara said quickly. "I just need
make change. You always say we should look out for number
one 'cause no one else will."

Horace blinked; there was a dry, rasping sound as he ran his
hands over his jaw. "I do say that a lot, don't I? Well, you'll
need some money to tide you over until you find a job. Wait
here and I'll fetch you some."

Aware of the bills in her pocket, Mara started to tell him she
didn't need his money, but then he added, "We'll just call it a
loan," and she was silent.

Horace, she had often noted, saw things the way he wanted
to and was never confused by the truth. It obviously hadn't occurred to him that she'd worked—and worked very hard—for
board only the past few months.

A few minutes later, when Horace returned, he wasn't alone.
He caught her outraged stare and smiled sheepishly. "Thought
you'd like to say good-bye to Berty, too," he mumbled.

"What's this about you leaving, Rosa?" Berty demanded.
She was wearing a voluminous muslin nightgown and felt slippers; she looked angry and out of sorts. "After all we've done
for you, I expected a little gratitude."

Mara started to remind Berty that she'd earned the food they'd given her, but it suddenly came to her that Berty's cross words came from hurt, not anger. "You been good to me," she said instead. "I very grateful. But I work for you long time for just board."

"If you'd come to me and said you were leaving, like any decent person would, I would've told you that I've been holding back your pay so you wouldn't spend it on gewgaws."

She put several bills in Mara's hand. "I took out the money you already helped yourself to," she said, her voice dry. "I figure five percent of the profits after expenses, minus your board and them clothes I gave you, is fair."

Mara stared at the bills in her hand. It was money she'd earned, every penny of it, so why did she feel so guilty? Dammit, this was *gadjo* logic—was she beginning to think like them?

"Thank you for what you done for me," she said, but somehow the words seemed inadequate. Suddenly she knew what would make it right. She reached in the pocket of her skirt and took out the small wooden box that held her tarot cards. Her hand trembled a little as she got out the silver necklace. She pressed it into Berty's plump hand. "I want you to keep this. You can wear like bracelet," she said.

She let Berty, then Horace, hug her, kiss her cheek, but she refused again to wait until morning, saying she planned to catch a milk truck into Atlanta. She promised to take care of herself and watch how she spent her money, not to take up with some masher.

But as she trudged down the road, heading for the highway, where she hoped to hitch a ride to the Greyhound bus station in Atlanta, she found herself wishing she'd done things a little differently, maybe even stayed on until they found someone else to take her place.

As for the necklace—she didn't regret her impulsive gesture. It was time, finally, to put the past, the hurt and humiliation and anger, behind her and get on with the rest of her life.

CHAPTER 7

M ARA ARRIVED AT BRADFORD CIRCUS'S WINTER QUARTERS in the early afternoon of a bright March day. To save money, she had hitchhiked most of the way from Tallahassee. She was weary to the bone; the cotton dress she was wearing was dusty and wrinkled, and she had spent half of the money Berty had given her on bus fare and food, but that didn't matter. She was finally here, where she wanted to be, at the circus's winter quarters, eager and ready to take the next step toward realizing her dream. Which was why she was smiling so broadly as she thanked the strawberry farmer and his wife who had picked her up in Orlando.

They had asked her numerous questions, obviously assuming it their right since they'd shared their rusty farm truck with her, and she had been forced to make up a story to explain why she, a girl alone, was hitchhiking. Not that hitchhiking was all that unusual. More and more, people were traveling with the aid of their thumb, most of them war veterans looking for work, but a surprising number women and even whole families.

"And so your mama is gone now and you're trying to locate your pa?" the weather-beaten farmer had said.

"Yes, sir. Last I heard, he was with Bradford Circus. He's an advance man," she said, using the Rom trick of adding a seemingly idle detail to give a lie believability.

"Well, well. I hope you find him. A young girl like you shouldn't be alone in the world."

And what if I told you I was a Gypsy? she had thought, remembering the insults that had been flung at her and her family so often by *gadjos. You wouldn't let me near your truck for fear I'd steal your wheels or give you lice. . . .*

The truck rattled off, and she looked around, trying to get her bearings. The Florida sun beat down upon her bare head, but she was too excited to notice it. The odors, carried by the wind, made her nostrils quiver—the musky, sweet-sour scent of the elephants tethered nearby in a grove of cottonwood trees; the wild, civet odor of what could only be big cats; the familiar smell of a stable; the briny tang of damp sawdust, spread over a muddy spot in the road. For a moment she was seven years old again, caught up in the magic of her first circus. . . .

The sound of a hammer brought her back to the present. Several men, wearing rough work clothes, were repairing the roof of a weather-beaten barn nearby. When one of them stopped to wipe the sweat from his face, she caught his eyes.

"Where is man named Mr. Sam?" she called.

The man silently pointed to a sign, nailed to a post in front of her, then returned to his work. Since she couldn't read the words written on the sign, she went on, past a long row of tents, most of them so old that their original color had faded to a nondescript gray. She soon found herself in an area of oddly assorted vehicles, trucks and buses with boarded-up windows, and even an ancient touring car that must have been built before she was born.

Some of the trucks had canvas tents set up on their flatbeds; others were attached to the wooden and metal caravans that the *gadjos* called trailers. She saw a woman, standing beside a small tent, but she disappeared inside before Mara could ask directions.

Farther on, she came to three wheelless railroad cars, set up on cement blocks, that formed three sides of a square. One had a barred window at one end, and was painted red, while another was a blinding silver in the sun. The third had been painted blue; it sported an awning that shaded one side.

A few minutes later she had stopped to set down the satchel and rub circulation back into her numb hand when she saw a man approaching. As he drew closer, she realized that he was older than she'd first thought, probably in his thirties. His hair was black, his skin olive, and his high-bridged nose came straight down from his forehead. After one incurious look in her direction, he would have walked past if she hadn't spoken.

"Please—can you tell me where I find Mr. Sam?" she asked.

His coal-black eyes examined her, taking in her wrinkled dress, her dusty shoes, the battered satchel at her feet; although there was only indifference on his face, suddenly she wished she hadn't stopped him.

"What do you want with Mr. Sam?" he asked.

"I need job."

"What kind of job?"

She hesitated, tempted to ask what business was it of his. "Anything he need," she said finally.

"Don't you have any special skills?"

"Skills?"

"Flier. Rigger. Laborer," he said, his lips twisting. "If it's anything less reputable, I think you should know that this is a Sunday school show."

She wanted to ask him what a Sunday school show was, but instead she said, "I am dancer."

"In that case, Mr. Sam might talk to you. He put out a call ad for hooch show girls in *The Clipper* last week." He pointed back the way she'd come. "You must've passed the Blue Wagon. Didn't you see the sign?"

"I not see sign."

For some reason, this made him smile. Not that she liked him any better for it. An uneasiness that bordered on fear sent a shudder through her. "I'm going that way. You can follow me," he added, surprising her.

"Thank you. I ask man where I find Mr. Sam, but he not answer me."

"Circus people don't like strangers," he said. "How long you been hoofing?"

"Hoofing?"

"Dancing."

"Most my life. I do it for money first time last year."

"You don't look old enough to be out of school," he said, but there was no real interest in his voice, and she wasn't surprised when he started on again. She followed him, having to hurry to keep up with his long stride. Although he wasn't tall, he gave the illusion of height, something to do with the way he walked. As if he owned the world, she decided, and the uneasiness stirred again.

The man stopped to light a cigarette, and she set down her satchel, glad for a chance to catch her breath. "You from around here?" the man asked.

"I am not from these parts," she said.

He gave her a strange look. " 'I'm not from these parts, I was born somewhere else. The wheel of fortune turning, turning, brought me here.' "

Mara felt a small shock. His words were from an old Rom

song. Had he realized what she was? "That very pretty," she said, widening her eyes. "You make it up?"

"It's a song. A Romany song."

"Romany?"

"Gypsy." He flipped his cigarette down, stepped on it, and she snatched up her satchel. They went on, eventually coming to the three railroad cars she'd passed earlier. He pointed to the blue one in the middle.

"You'll find Mr. Sam there, in the Blue Wagon." He gave her a long, brooding look. "Let me give you some free advice. State your business and then shut up. Mr. Sam doesn't take to gabby women."

He was gone before she could thank him. She stared after him, wondering why, when the day was so warm, she felt so chilled. *Someone's walking on my grave,* she thought, borrowing one of Berty's sayings.

She climbed up on the platform at the end of the car and knocked on the frame of a screen door.

A man's voice barked, "Yeah? What is it?"

Although his words weren't an invitation to come in, she opened the screen door and went inside. It was comfortably cool, with an electric fan lazily turning in the ceiling. There was a large typewriter on one of two desks, a table, which held an electric burner, a coffeepot, and a tray of sweet rolls; several wooden cabinets, a wall of shelves stuffed with books and piles of paper.

"When you've finished gawking, maybe you'll tell me what the hell you want," an irritated voice said, and she turned her attention to the man seated behind a large rolltop desk.

He was small, wiry-built, with bony wrists and a long, deeply grooved face. His hair, which showed streaks of gray, was carefully combed to cover a small bald spot on the top of his head. In his seersucker suit and white shirt and tie, he reminded her of the Cincinnati undertaker her *kumpania* dealt with every year.

"I would like job," she said with as much dignity as she could muster. "I am hooch dancer."

She would have said more, making up some lies about her experience, but she remembered the dark-haired man's advice in time. She was acutely aware of her dusty clothes, her disheveled hair as he looked her over, and she wished now that she'd stopped at a gas station and washed up before hitching that last ride.

"Well, you look healthy enough. A bit too skinny. The town-ers like the hooch dancers to carry a little flesh. You any good?"

"I am very good," she said firmly.

"Well, adequate will do. It's the flesh they come to see."

He got up and poured himself a mug of coffee. Her mouth watered as she looked at the plate of sweet rolls.

"You hungry?" Mr. Sam asked, and she realized he'd caught her glance.

"Yes, sir," she said.

"Help yourself."

She started to thank him, but he had already returned to the papers on his desk. She poured coffee into a mug, added a generous amount of cream and three teaspoons of sugar, and took the largest roll on the plate. She devoured it quickly, stand-ing up because he hadn't offered her a chair. Since the man was busy with his papers, she took another roll and slipped it into her pocket.

He looked up when she sat her empty mug down. "Go talk to Ruby. You'll find her in the wardrobe building. Tell her I said to give you a tryout. You'll have to satisfy her, you understand. I don't interfere with her operation."

Mara thanked him, but he had already turned back to his desk.

Mr. Sam didn't go back to work immediately after the red-headed left the Blue Wagon. By the time she had reached the door, he'd already decided that he'd made a mistake. It was his experience that girls that pretty seldom wore such tacky clothes. Which could mean trouble up ahead. Good-looking women who could take care of themselves were one thing. The kind like this redhead, who was obviously underage and still wet behind the ears, spelled trouble, and that he didn't need.

So it had been stupid to send her to Ruby just because he'd felt sorry for her. Okay, the way she'd gobbled down that roll and then snitched another one had gotten to him. Which was crazy. Lots of people went hungry these days what with the recession, the strikes, inflation. God knew he couldn't feed them all. He had his own people to take care of, and with all the aggravations the government piled on businessmen these days, it was hard enough to keep his head above water without taking on new trouble.

He often wondered what the old man would have said about such things as Prohibition and women voting. He and his old man had fought like a couple of starved dogs hankering for the same bone, but he'd learned everything he knew about running a circus from his father.

And now he had his own son. Would there still be a circus for Michael to run someday? Maybe, maybe not. It wasn't like the old days, when the circus was king and just about the only entertainment available for ordinary people.

And he was wasting time, stewing about things he couldn't change when he had a stack of manifests to check over. The show was starting out in late April this year, a little later than usual, their first stop a five-day run in Atlanta. If the season of '21 was a good one, they would make their nut and have funds for new equipment and new canvas all the way around next year. Maybe there would even be enough to buy that five-kilowatt electric light plant he had his eye on. Until then the show would have to make do with the old carbide and mantle lights. He finished his coffee and returned to work.

Mara found the wardrobe building, but not until she'd wandered around for almost half an hour, finally asking another workman for directions. This one, luckily, was willing to point out a small whitewashed building, which sat alone a few hundred yards away.

Ruby, she discovered, was a large, middle-aged woman with arms as muscular as a man's, and a pair of very hard eyes. As she looked Mara over, it was obvious she wasn't impressed.

"How old are you?" she demanded.

"Eighteen," Mara said, stretching it by two years.

The woman gave a snort. "Fifteen, sixteen at the most," she said flatly. "Well, Mr. Sam says to give you a tryout, and that's what I'll do. But get one thing straight. I do my own hiring."

She didn't wait for an answer. She motioned for Mara to follow and went striding off, not looking back, finally stopping in front of a large tent, one of several clustered together. A group of people were already there, including two women. They were wearing black tights, and were practicing a tumbling act on dirty gray mats. No one paid any attention to the newcomers.

"Okay, let's see you do the hooch," Ruby said.

Mara hesitated. What was the hooch? Was her audition over before it began? "I not sure what is the hooch," she said finally.

Ruby's face lengthened. "Why does it always happen to me?" she asked the air above Mara's head. She did a quick turn, rolling both her broad hips and her eyes. "That's the hooch. Maybe you call it something else."

Mara decided it looked simple enough. Her confidence flooded back as she made the same maneuver several times, exaggerating the swing of her hips.

"Okay, let's see what else you can do."

A few minutes later, after Mara had demonstrated her dancing skills, Ruby told her she was probably making a mistake but she had the job. Mara was careful to hide her glee as she listened while Ruby ran through a list of rules concerning such things as being on time, keeping herself clean, and mending her own costumes.

"And no johns," Ruby said. "What you do when the season's over is your own business. But on the road, my girls are squeaky clean and they don't make la-la with towners or circus guys, whether for free or for pay. As far as you're concerned, it's Sunday school every day. There's a curfew, an hour after the evening show, which gives you time to hit the privilege tent for a snack before you go to bed. And I expect you to be in your bunk, lights off, by curfew. You break the rules and you're out on your ass. No exceptions. No second chances. I don't have time to baby-sit a bunch of silly tarts. You understand?"

"I understand, but I am not tart," Mara said, drawing herself up to her full five-foot height.

"Don't be so damned thin-skinned. Come along now. I'll introduce you to the other girls. You all bunk together, so you'll see a lot of them the next few months. I like things nice and peaceful. No fighting, no backbiting, and no trouble."

A few minutes later, when Mara met the other women of the dance troupe, she doubted they were as squeaky clean as Ruby believed. Most of them looked a little shopworn to her. Only one, a slightly built, dark-haired girl, seemed friendly.

"You can take the bunk above mine," she said. "I hope you don't snore."

She giggled when Mara shook her head. "Don't worry about the dance routines. A six year old with three legs could learn them. And I hope you can sew. We've got a wardrobe lady, but we hafta do our own mending 'cause she's usually busy taking care of the artistes."

"Artistes?"

"You know—the performers."

"Ain't we performers?"

"Us? Listen, honey, even the roughies outrank the hooch show girls. It's a real scruffy job. On the other hand, it's better than slinging beer to a bunch of ass pinchers. I was working in this roadhouse near Albany when I met Sammy Jack—he plays brass in the Big Top band, see? He fixed me up with this job, and I been here ever since. In the winters, I work for a forty-nine camp in Tampa.''

She caught Mara's bewilderment and shook her head. ''Say, you're a real First of May guy, aren't you? And before you ask, that's a greenhorn. First thing you gotta do is learn how to talk circus. A forty-nine camp is—well, sort of a dance hall. You know—the girls dance with the customers and get a cut of their bar tab. Hard on the feet. Which is why I sign up for the circuit every spring.''

She grinned at Mara. ''So what's *your* story?''

Mara hesitated, decided that the truth was safe. ''I was dancer in medicine show. A friend of show owners, name of Charlie, come by. He is advance man for this circus. He say use his name if I want job here.''

''That's gotta be Charlie Schoor,'' the girl said. ''For God sake—don't get mixed up with that phony. For one thing, he's not the advance man. He heads one of the poster hanger crews. Who'd trust him to check out sites or negotiate contracts?'' The girl paused to give her a speculative look. ''Say, what's your name? Old Ironpants didn't say.''

Mara started to tell her *Rosa*, then changed her mind. Most Roms had two names, one they used among themselves and one for everybody else. But she was a *gadjo* now. She didn't need two names.

''Mara,'' she said.

''Pretty name. Irish, ain't it? What's the rest of it?''

''Just Mara,'' Mara said, unwilling to use either her Rom name or Smith, the one they used with outsiders. To her surprise, the girl didn't press her further.

''I'm Sally,'' she said, smiling at Mara. ''Sally Garmish.''

The rest of the afternoon, Mara practiced the dance routine under Sally's tutelage. As the other dancer had said, it wasn't all that difficult. The routine consisted of a few turns and high kicks, a strutting, leg-kicking step that Sally called a cakewalk, all accompanied by strenuous wriggling of the hips. Since she was expected to know it by the coming Sunday, when the locals would be treated to a free preview of the coming season's show, Mara kept on practicing on her own after Sally left the workout barn to go to supper.

Later, she bought an overcooked sausage on a stale roll and

a bottle of orange soda at a small booth set up to service the local people who came to watch the performers practice, and took it back to the ramshackle building Sally called the dorm. Perched on the upper bunk she'd been assigned, with her legs dangling over the side, she ate the sandwich and drank the orange soda, saving the roll she'd snitched from Mr. Sam's office for breakfast, then undressed down to her underwear and slid under the rough, khaki-colored blanket. She was bone-tired and still a little hungry, but she was content. The hooch dancers might be at the bottom of the pecking order, as Sally said, but she had a job with the circus. Tomorrow she'd start looking around for someone to teach her how to fly.

The next morning, she was awakened by women's voices. Since everybody was talking at once and no one was paying any attention to her, she slid down from her bunk and dressed quickly, not wanting anyone to see her shabby underwear. Not, she tried to convince herself, that she really cared what they thought. After all, she wasn't any too impressed with them either. From their talk, they were interested in two things only—men and having a good time.

She was glad that it was Sally who took her around the grounds, introducing her to the people they met. Most of them were polite, a few friendly, but she sensed a wariness that she recognized as suspicion toward the outsider. She also recognized something else. As Sally had warned, the girls of the dance troupe were at the bottom of the heap.

From the speculative looks of the men Sally introduced her to, she knew she'd been right about the women. As for Sally, she admitted freely that she sometimes accepted "dates" with men.

"Sammy Jack—he's my friend in the band—looks out for me so I don't get roughed up."

"I thought we couldn't go out with men."

"What Ruby don't know won't hurt her—or Mr. Sam," Sally said smugly. "A lot of the girls do it." She gave Mara a sidelong glance. "Sammy Jack's okay. He keeps half the money, but he stays around close in case—well, you never know. Some crazy guys out there."

Mara shuddered. No matter how tough things got, she could never sell her body—and besides, breaking the rules and maybe getting fired was the last thing she wanted to do. That afternoon, when Sammy Jack, who played the saxophone in the circus band, came around to see her with a "proposition," she told him politely that she didn't need a pimp.

"Hey, watch your mouth," he told her, frowning.

"I just say I got no need for pimp," she said, unimpressed by his yellow leather shoes, the big ring on his little finger—or his threatening glare.

"Yeah, well, you be careful. You could get in big trouble, insulting people like that."

He stalked off, leaving her standing in front of the ring tent where she'd been practicing. Mara wasn't sorry that she'd let him know where she stood, but maybe she shouldn't't've called him a pimp. Berty had explained what it meant to her once, but it must not be a word you used in public. Mara gave an exasperated sigh. So many things that were new to her. She just wished she could hurry up and learn them.

"It isn't any of my business," a man's deep voice said behind her, "but that fellow is bad news."

Mara looked around, then down. A very small man, a miniature man really, was looking up at her. He was leaning on a brass-topped cane, and the smile that creased his face was surprisingly attractive.

"Lord Jocko," he said, bowing. "Your humble servant—well, maybe not so humble, but still your servant."

She studied him with fascinated eyes. He really did look like the English lord her mother had once described. In his gray suit that fit his small body like a glove, an immaculate shirt with a stiff collar, and a wide, silk tie, he looked out of place in the Florida sun. His accent was strange, too—not the soft drawl of the workmen, the quick, sharp speech of the easterners in the show, or the flat midwestern monotone.

"My name is Mara," she said.

"So I've been told." He looked her over, taking his time. "Rom?" he asked.

Mara felt a jolt of surprise: she suddenly found it hard to breathe. "Why you say that?"

"Your accent. From one of the English tribes, I'd say. I'm quite a student of accents, having a rather broad one of my own. And don't worry. It's still your secret. I know a lot of secrets I don't tell."

Mara was silent, not sure if she trusted him. Somehow he'd guessed she was a Rom—but she didn't believe it was her accent that had given her away. More likely, it was a lucky guess—and she'd fallen right into his trap. In the future, she'd have to be more careful. These circus people had a way of catching you off guard. . . .

"It's almost time for dinner. So how about joining me in the cookhouse?"

"Hooch dancers can eat with artistes?" she asked doubtfully.

"By invitation. Where have you been eating, by the way? You weren't with the troupe last night or this morning at breakfast."

"I bought soda and sandwich at food stand."

He groaned and rolled his eyes. "Ptomaine heaven," he said. "That slop is strictly for the local gawkers who come to watch the artistes rehearse."

He gestured toward a large, three-pronged tent. "The cookhouse flag is up—let's see what's on the menu today, shall we?"

As they walked toward the tent, Mara adjusted her step to Lord Jocko's shorter ones. She was bemused to learn that he had been with Bradford Circus for almost ten years, and she wondered why he made such a point of telling her that he didn't work in something he called the "ten-in-one" but as a clown. He seemed a little annoyed when she told him that she'd never heard of Lord Jocko's famous firehouse act.

When they reached the cook tent, he pulled two cardboard tickets from his pocket and handed them to the elderly man at the door.

"One for the lord and one for the little lady," he said grandly.

The man grinned, showing toothless gums. "You're a real card, Lord Jocko," he said.

Mara waited until they were seated at a long, narrow table before she asked, "You are English lord?"

"Of course. Just like you're Spanish—or Arabian or whatever you call yourself. And I just happen to have a bond certificate I'd like to sell you."

Mara didn't ask him what he meant. Too many of the things these people said went over her head. If they ever realized this, they'd know how ignorant she was and take advantage of her. She realized he was staring at her again. What had she said—or not said—this time?

"Just out of the crib. A baby crib, that is," he said, sighing. "Well, that won't last long. You'll either wise up fast or—" He hunched his shoulders in a shrug. "And what a pity if you wise up too fast. I just might take you under my protection and see that doesn't happen."

"I take care of myself," Mara said stiffly.

A waiter, a middle-aged black man, came up for their order.

He treated the midget with such respect that Mara commented on it after he'd left.

"We anomalies—to use the polite word—are treated well because the ten-in-one show brings in the money. Actually, we're something of an embarrassment, which is why the anomalies eat half an hour before Cookie raises the flag. Since I happen to be Clown Alley's star act, I'm considered an artiste, so I usually eat with my compadres over there."

He pointed to a nearby table where several men sat. Although they came in all ages, shapes, and sizes, they had one thing in common—they were a noisy group, exchanging insults and engaging in rough horseplay.

"You, my friend, are neither an artiste nor management, which is why you ordinarily wouldn't be sitting in the short end of the cookhouse. I tell you this to save you embarrassment. The dance troupe girls sit at their own table in the long side of the tent. I hope I haven't hurt your feelings?"

"No. I want to fit in," she said earnestly, and then wondered why he laughed.

"Didn't Ruby tell you that meals are part of your pay?" he asked. "She should have given you a supply of meal tickets when she hired you—like the ones I gave old Jake at the door."

"She call them ducats. I not know they were for getting meals," Mara said, ashamed of her ignorance.

Jocko shook his head. "You'll have to pick up the circus lingo or you're in big trouble." He helped himself to a pickle from a relish dish, took a bite. "So—what brought you to the circus? Do you want to be an artiste, a star? Do you see yourself in the center ring, riding a rosinback horse—or maybe doing a tumbling act? Do you want wealth, fame, the fawning attention of an adoring audience?"

He finished off the pickle and wiped his hands on a napkin. "Do you have a chance in hell of making it? Not likely," he went on. "Doing the hooch is strictly dead-end, going nowhere. Or maybe that's all you want, a bunk at night, food, and enough money to buy a few trinkets?"

Because of his accent, it took a few seconds for his words to sink in. Mara was prepared to give him an evasive answer, only to hear herself saying, "I want to work on swing. I want to be good performer—and very famous."

Jocko frowned at her. "Oh, you do, do you? Well, you're not alone. It's the will-o'-wisp of fame that draws people to the circus, the dreamers and the misfits and the anomalies like me. This is never-never land, an illusion—''

"But I have to learn *how* to be performer," she interrupted. "I need teacher."

"Most fliers learn from their parents—which puts you at a disadvantage. You're pretty old to be starting out on the trapeze or the rings. Do you have a head for heights?"

"High places not bother me," she said quickly, although this possibility had never occurred to her before.

"That's a plus. Getting someone to teach you how to fly— that's a problem. Most of the aerialists are married men."

"What this got to do with—"

"You're much too pretty, little one. Their wives aren't going to stand still for their men getting cozy with someone who looks like you. The only unmarried flier—actually he's an aerialist since he does a solo—is Leo Mueller, but he's not a man that you could influence, even with that Mary Pickford smile."

"Who is this Leo Mueller?" she said.

"He's just coming in the door, my single-minded friend."

Mara looked around and recognized the man who had directed her to Mr. Sam's wagon. "So that is his name," she said.

Jocko's eyes sharpened. "You've already met Leo?"

"He take me to Blue Wagon, where I find Mr. Sam when I first come here."

"Well, don't count on him taking you on as a student. He only has one use for women. He came here from Barnum & Bailey, and he's a loner. I have to admit he's got star quality— half the circuses in the country have tried to recruit him. Although he does a solo these days, he's one of the best catchers in the business."

"What is catcher?"

He rolled his eyes. "You *are* a babe in the woods. The catcher is the one who catches the fliers. He calls all the turns, and if his timing is off—" He ran his finger across his starched collar.

"But I want to do solo act."

"Already you're picky, and you don't even know circus lingo."

"I can learn. I am very smart," Mara said.

He laughed so hard that tears came into his eyes. When she frowned at him, he sputtered something about being sorry, but she'd taken him by surprise.

"Maybe it's best you don't go around telling people how smart you are," he added. "Let them find out the hard way."

He launched into an anecdote about his early days as a clown, and ordinarily she would have drunk in every word, but her attention was on Leo Mueller. He must have sensed her interest, because he turned his head slowly and gave her a long, expressionless look. Again, a shiver rippled through her. No wonder he was a loner. He reminded her of a copperhead snake—sleek and beautiful and very dangerous. What woman would want to nestle up to *him* in the dark?

"Does he—this Leo—have a woman?" she asked, breaking in on the midget's rambling story.

"A long string of them. In bed, out of bed, good-bye, lady. He's bad news, just like that bum Sammy Jack, only worse. No one messes with him. Even Mr. Sam treats him with kid gloves. The rumors are that he cut up a fellow just before he came here—some say in Canada, some in upper New York. Fight over a woman. Not that he gives a damn about women."

He grinned and thumped his chest with his knuckles. "Now me, I love women—and they love me."

Mara smiled automatically, but her eyes were still on Leo Mueller. No special woman—and the ones he did have didn't last long. Did that make it harder—or easier?

As she watched, Leo pushed back his chair, got up, and left the cookhouse. As far as she could tell, he hadn't spoken to one person during his stay, even though the cookhouse was almost full now.

While she listened to Jocko with half an ear, she tried to plan her strategy. If she could believe the midget, Leo Mueller had no trouble finding plenty of willing women to warm his bed, so it was unlikely that would be his price. He would want money, and she had—well, not a lot, but some money was left from what Berty had given her, and she'd be earning more when the circus went on the road.

As soon as she got the chance to talk to him alone, she would ask what he'd charge to give her lessons and then she'd bargain with him. She was good at that. Her aunts had often used her to drive a good bargain with the *gudjo* who bought their leather handiwork at the county fairs. She wouldn't pay him, of course, until she'd had her lessons, but she wouldn't try to cheat him. That would be too dangerous.

She set about pumping Jocko about Leo Mueller, so casually that she was sure he didn't realize what she was up to.

"He's a perfectionist, which is why he works solo, I suspect," Jocko said. "He doesn't let anyone see a new trick until he's perfected it, not even Mr. Sam."

He looked at Mara, and there was worry in his deep-set eyes now. "He's the show's biggest drawing card. He could have fangs and horns and Mr. Sam would still cater to him. Everybody in the circus, from the lowest swamper to Mr. Sam, is dependent on the star acts, the ones who bring in the customers. Do you understand what I'm saying, Mara?"

"No. What you mean?" she asked.

"You're thinking about asking him to give you lessons, aren't you?"

Mara didn't deny it. "He can say no if he want to. Why he get mad if I ask?"

Jocko sighed. "I see you've made up your mind. But be careful. This man is a real Bengal, and he doesn't have any conscience. He also gets offended very easily." He smiled at her suddenly. "I say this as a friend—we are friends, aren't we?"

Mara looked at him with troubled eyes. Suddenly it was important to be honest with this little man who had gone out of his way to be kind and helpful. "I never have friend before," she confessed. "I not sure how to act."

The smile slipped off Jocko's face. He studied her for a long time as if weighing her words. "Then I'll teach you how," he said. "I very much want to be your friend, Mara."

CHAPTER 8

THE NEXT AFTERNOON, MARA WAS SITTING ON THE SMALL wooden footlocker that was allotted to each dancer for her belongings. She was mending a rip in the costume she'd been issued by May Mayberry, the wardrobe mistress, when Sally came in and flung herself down on her bunk.

She was still wearing her practice clothes; her face looked

drawn and pale, and there were dark circles under her eyes. "I'm really bushed," she said. "These late nights are getting to me."

Mara didn't know what to say, so she said nothing.

"Sammy Jack was asking about you," Sally went on. "Look, Mara, the guy's okay. He's real careful about—well, you don't have to worry about some ape getting rough. And the money's good. You could make five, maybe ten bucks, a night. You can't get by on what they pay you here, you know. Mr. Sam holds back part of your money until the end of the season. He says it's so we have a stake for the winter, but hell, he ain't our daddy."

When Mara was still silent, she sighed. "Okay, I tried. If you change your mind, let me know."

"I not change my mind," Mara said.

Sally shifted her position. "So where did you disappear to this afternoon?" she asked.

"I went to workout tent to practice."

"Well, don't wear yourself out. Wait until the First of May and we start the circuit. Sometimes it's four or five one-dayers in a row. We'll be lucky to get three hours sleep a night."

"The first of May? That is whole month away," Mara said, remembering that there had been extra horseplay in the cookhouse that morning because it was the first of April, what the *gadjos* called April Fool's Day. "I hear circuit start last week in April."

"Actually, it's the last day in April. First of May is an expression that means—well, the day we start. It can be in March or April." Sally grinned slyly. "That's what you are, a First of May guy. You will be until you've put in a year on the road."

Mara frowned at her. "Will people be friendly then?"

Sally shrugged. "It takes time. People come and go so fast that most of the old-timers don't bother with you until you've been around awhile. And the families will never be friendly, not with a hoofer. They think they're special because they're artistes. Hell, the papas watch their daughters like hawks and marry them off to guys they can use in their act."

"Like the Roms," Mara said without thinking.

"Roms?"

"Some people I hear about once," Mara said, annoyed with her slip.

"Yeah. Well, you should get around more. There's a lot to learn about this life."

Mara considered her words. "Maybe I watch artistes practice. I heard Leo Mueller has got new trick."

"Oh, hey! Stay away from Leo. He always practices alone, and he don't want no audience."

"Where he practice?" Mara said, careful to sound indifferent.

"In the ring barn real early in the mornings." She frowned at Mara. "You ain't interested in him, are you? He and Danielle—she's the French flier who joined the Duncan Brothers last year—has got a hot thing going. She's turned up with bruises a few times, but she can dish it out, too. Those scratches on his neck don't come from no cat."

"He got a woman?"

"He always has a woman. But if you've got any ideas along those lines, forget it. He goes for artistes. Too good for the likes of us. Besides, he ain't someone you wanta mess around with."

She went off to wheedle a bucket of hot water from the cookhouse, and Mara brooded over her words—and her warning about Leo—while she finished her mending. The costume, when she tried it on, showed an amazing amount of bare skin. She was trying to ease the tiny skirt that matched the skimpy tunic down over her thighs when Sally returned, hauling a bucket of hot water.

"Say, you really fill out that top. You're going to put some noses out of joint when the girls—"

She broke off when two of the women came in. They looked Mara over, but neither said anything, and Mara, who still felt uneasy in the presence of *gadjo* women, slipped between two stacks of bunks to change back into her practice clothes.

That afternoon, at the free Sunday matinee that was held as a goodwill gesture to the locals each year, she appeared with the dance troupe for the first time. Ruby briefed her in advance.

"What the customers want to see is lots of bare skin. We gotta keep the costumes decent, 'cause this is Bible Country, but when you dance show a lot of leg and wiggle your ass. Look like you're having one helluva good time. Kick up your heels and let them get a good look at your treasures, but no touchy-feely. There's always a bunch of do-gooders hanging around the hooch show, itching to spoil the fun, so be careful. We don't need that kinda trouble."

The performance held two surprises for Mara, starting with the behavior of the audience, almost totally male. They ranged in age from teenagers to whiskery old men, and although they stared holes in the dancers, there were no suggestive remarks, no cursing. In fact, they seemed content to just look. The second surprise was that she found herself enjoying the dancing. Or maybe, she thought, it was being before an audience she enjoyed.

After the first dance routine, the talker, a fat, jolly-looking man named Bert, introduced the girls, one by one, mostly with fanciful stories.

"And this little lady is fresh out of France," he said when he got to Mara. "Some of you veterans may have caught her act at the Café De Paree. She's the prettiest little thing to come out of France in years. Anyone who agrees yell, 'Yeah!' "

There was a deafening roar of "yeahs," and Mara felt herself flushing. Later, when they began the next routine, she found that the last vestige of nervousness was gone. Although there had been no demand for excellence in Ruby's speech, she put extra verve in her dancing and was gratified by the applause when Bert motioned for her to take an extra bow.

"You really throw yourself into it, don't you?" Sally whispered. "Well, that'll change when we get on the road and we're grinding out six shows a day."

That night, after the lights were out, Mara lay awake, making plans. They would be starting on the circuit in a month, and once on the road, there would be little spare time. So this might be her last chance to persuade Leo to train her. Which meant she needed to be up early, dressed and out of the dorm before the others got up.

The next morning, it was still dark when she climbed down from the top bunk and pulled on the tights and man's work shirt she'd scrounged from the wardrobe mistress for her practicing sessions. She was tempted to wear her one decent outfit, a skirt and a blouse, but she decided against it. It was important to make Leo believe that she'd come to the ring barn to get in some early morning practice. And why would she be wearing a skirt and blouse to rehearse in?

This early in the morning, before the cookhouse flag was up, she felt very conspicuous as she hurried toward the ring barn. Like the other buildings in the circus's winter quarters, it was old but in good repair. Even before she reached the door, she heard the whine of moving rigging and knew that Leo was already there, practicing.

She slipped inside, careful not to make a sound. The air was warmer here; it reeked of the ever-present Florida mold, of musty canvas mats, of human sweat and liniment and less definable things. She eased down to a squatting position in the shadows, glad for the chance to get her nerves under control before she confronted Leo.

In the cold light of dawn that came in through long, narrow windows set high in the walls, he swung from a ring at the top of the barn. Weightless as a shadow, he executed turns and twists that made her breath catch in her throat for their daring—and beauty. How could a man who looked like that be cruel and dangerous, the way people said he was? Could the circus be wrong about Leo Mueller?

After a series of one-handed swings that seemed to defy gravity, Leo hooked his leg around a rope to rest. His face glistened with sweat, and it was obvious he'd been working out for quite a while. In his black, skin-tight practice clothes, he was as lean and supple as a cat, and unbidden, a shudder rippled through Mara. "Bad news," Jocko had called him. Was that what he would be to her?

"You, there. What the hell you doing here?" he called, and she realized he'd seen her in the shadows.

She tilted her head to stare up at him and tried out a smile. "I am here to practice. That not allowed?"

He studied her, his eyes enigmatic, before he slid down the rope and stalked toward her.

"Don't you know the ring barn is off limits while I'm practicing?" he demanded.

"I very sorry. Nobody tell me," she said, and then launched into the speech she'd rehearsed. "I hear you got trouble lately, but I not know people watching you practice make you nervous. I go now."

She turned to leave, but he grabbed her upper arm, stopping her. "What do you mean—I got trouble lately?"

"I hear you lose your—" She broke off, biting her lower lip. His hand tightened on her arm. "Who told you that?"

"The girls—they talk after lights out. I not know who say it."

This time the silence was so long that she wet her lips nervously, finally risking a look at him.

He was smiling, but it wasn't a pleasant smile. "What did you really come here for?" he said softly, and she knew that somehow, by some gesture or wrong word, she had given herself away.

"I want you give me lessons, how to fly," she said, knowing it was time for honesty.

"And just how did you intend to pay for them? My services come very high," he said, his voice a purr.

"I have money," she said, trying to pump sincerity into her voice.

"You little liar. From the looks of you when you came here, you didn't have two dimes to rub together." He bent closer, his hot breath brushing her cheek. Somehow she managed not to flinch. "So just how do you plan to pay me? With a roll in the hay? What makes you think I'd be interested? I can get all the classy women I want. I'm not in the market for a dime-a-throw tart."

His assumption that she was offering her body didn't anger her, but his insult, that she was a dime-a-throw tart, did. Her temper flared, out of control; without thinking, she slapped him across the face. Her hand was well callused from hard labor, and the slap rocked his head back.

Lightning fast, he was upon her. He shook her like a terrier with a rat. Afraid for her life, she fought him, scratching and biting with all her might. But the more she struggled, the tighter his fingers bit into her flesh and the harder he shook her. Knowing there was little satisfaction in hurting someone who can't feel pain, she finally went limp and let her head loll backward as if she had fainted.

Leo swore viciously, but he stopped shaking her. "Okay, you can drop the act," he snarled. "You're not out."

She remained limp, hoping he wouldn't just drop her. She expected him to check her breathing or take her pulse, so she was totally unprepared when he pinched her hard—in the breast. Somehow she managed not to cry out, although the pain was excruciating, and again, Leo cursed.

She moaned, then let her eyelids flutter open. When she met his cold stare, she knew that she hadn't fooled him, not for a moment. She blinked hard, fighting tears, sure that her too-quick temper had ruined any chance she had of enlisting his aid.

"So maybe you aren't a dime-a-throw tart," he said, and there was a flicker of amusement in his black eyes now. "And I just might take you on after all. I'll make you a deal. I teach you to well, not fly. That takes too long and we don't have the time. But I'll teach you enough so you can audition for the aerial ballet three weeks from now. And then you pay me off any way I choose."

Mara fought a rising excitement. She knew what the aerial ballet was—eight girls who performed complicated tricks in unison on ropes extended from the ceiling of the big top. But Leo's last statement—that was unclear. "What that mean? Any way you choose?" she asked finally.

He smiled, a cold, narrow-eyed smile. The mark of the slap showed plainly on his cheek, but she couldn't make herself feel sorry, even though it could have cost her this chance. "That's where the gamble comes in. Maybe I'll ask for every cent you earn for the next year—or just for a kiss. Or I could want more than a kiss. Are you a gambler? Or are you all talk? It's up to you."

She stared at him, her thoughts whirling. What did he want? Surely not her body. The woman she'd seen him with in the cookhouse was a beauty. She was also an artiste, like Leo, which would make a difference to a man with his pride. So was this some game he was playing with her? And did it really matter? This might well be her only chance to be trained by a top performer. Did she dare refuse?

"Don't take too long making up your mind, because I just might change mine again," Leo said.

Mara wasn't fooled. He wouldn't change his mind. He enjoyed keeping her dangling and off balance. The thing was, if his price was her body, could she keep her part of the bargain? The very thought of being intimate with him repulsed her. On the other hand—she wasn't a virgin. She knew what to expect. Surely it wouldn't be all that bad. And maybe he only wanted money. . . .

"Okay," she said. "But if you want—if it ain't money you want, I do it only once."

He gave her a contemptuous smile. "If that's my price, once is all I want."

He bent to pick up his jacket. "Meet me here tomorrow morning—at six o'clock sharp. Not a minute later or a minute earlier. I don't want you inside the barn while I practice. You understand?"

Mara nodded, unable to speak. It was happening. It wouldn't be easy, but then—when had anything ever been easy for her? But after she'd learned all she could from Leo Mueller and she'd paid his price, whatever it was, she would be one step closer to her dream.

CHAPTER 9

M R. SAM HAD MORE THINGS ON HIS MIND THAN THE PER-
sonal problems of his employees, so he groaned when he
saw Ruby rapidly approaching the Blue Wagon. Dammit—that
woman did get under his skin. He'd always been leery of tall,
full-breasted women. His mother had been almost six foot tall
and strong as a man, and his memory of the hidings she'd given
him for real and imaginary crimes until he was old enough to
put an end to it still made his shoulders sting.

The screen door rattled as Ruby came into the railroad car.
He regarded her warily. "What's up, Ruby? And make it short.
I'm busy as hell."

"This is important, Sammy," she said. She was the only
person who dared use that name for him, but he'd never been
able to call her on it. "It's that new girl, the redhead."

"So? If she isn't working out, can her."

"I can't complain about her work. The marks really go for
her when we do the Sunday previews. You should hear them
whistle. Some of them come every Sunday, just to gawk at her.
One even sent her candy like she was a goddamned star."

"So what's your complaint?" Mr. Sam said, losing his patience.

"She's been sneaking out real early in the mornings, going to
the ring barn. You know what that means. She's got something
going with Mueller. And that's the problem. If I kick her out
and Leo gets sore—well, he could take a powder."

Mr. Sam regarded her gloomily. She was right. Mueller was
touchy, unpredictable, but his name on a poster meant overflow
crowds. He also attracted automatic publicity to the circus wherever they went. More lies had been printed about him than about
the Siamese twins, Chang and Eng. If the flier had screwed all

86

the women he was rumored to have screwed, he would have to
be triplets. But that kind of notoriety brought the women into
the big top in droves, just to see the devil perform.

As for the girl, she was nothing, unimportant, even if the
marks did like her. The truth was, he didn't approve of the hooch
operation. He kept it in the show only because it drew the men,
who came to see a flash of white thigh, a provocative smile, and
then stayed on to play the midway games and stuff their mouths
with hot dogs and popcorn. Besides, Ruby kept the girls in
line—most of the time.

But if Mueller was interested in the redhead, it could mean
trouble. This was something to handle with kid gloves—or
maybe not to handle at all. After all, Mueller's women never
lasted long. Once he lost interest in the redhead, he'd fire her.

"I don't know what your problem is," he said, feigning anger. "You couldn't be worrying about her morals."

Ruby gave that remark the contempt it deserved. "She's already causing trouble in the troupe. I ain't saying it's her fault.
She keeps herself clean, and minds her own business, but she
gets too much attention from the marks—and the circus guys.
The other girls don't like it. One of these nights, they're going
to gang up on her. When they find out she's fucking Mueller—
well, it's gonna be one big mess."

Mr. Sam winced. For all that he was third-generation circus,
he had a streak of prudery and he disapproved of women cursing. But he had to admit that Ruby was right again. Trouble at
this point—at *any* point— he didn't need.

"Okay, I'll check into it," he said. Pointedly he turned back
to the stack of railroad schedules on his desk, hoping that maybe,
for once, he'd get the last word with Ruby.

But Ruby, being Ruby, didn't allow him this triumph. "You
be sure and do that, Sammy," she said, and stomped off.

The next morning Mr. Sam got up half an hour earlier than
usual, having set his alarm clock for five-thirty. His own personal winter quarters, a small bungalow located in a corner of
the winter quarters property, was surprisingly comfortable, certainly more so than the tents, converted vans and buses, old
pullman cars, and shacks in various stages of disrepair that
housed the others. True, his official address during the winter
months was the three-story mansion he'd built for his wife south
of Orlando, but this time of the year, after "call" ads had been
placed in theatrical publications, summoning the artistes and

other key employees back to work, he moved into the cottage so he could be there for the inevitable emergencies that arose.

His wife, a former equestrienne, was no longer interested in the circus. She preferred to stay at home and devote her considerable energy to "good works." His son, Michael, who was seven, was off at school in the East, learning—at his mother's insistence—how to be a gentleman.

Despite their differences, Mr. Sam was, in the main, faithful to Belle, more by default than anything else. Sometimes, it was true, he had a discreet dalliance with someone who took his fancy, but it was always short-term—and it was never anyone on his payroll. Most of the time he was celibate—and often lonely.

In a few years, when Michael finished school, if all went as Mr. Sam planned, his son would take some of the burden of running the circus off his shoulders. Meanwhile, the circus took up all his energy and time, even during the winter months. It hadn't been easy, building the run-down show he'd inherited from his father into what it was now one of the few prosperous circuses in the country that was still family-owned. Or, in circus jargon, upgrading Bradford Circus from a high-grass to a low-grass operation.

Mr. Sam often thought a circus was like one of the exotic orchids his wife cultivated in her fancy greenhouse. For all its flash, it was surprisingly tough, and yet it needed constant pruning and cultivating and fertilizing to flourish.

The war years had been hell. He'd had to scrounge acts and personnel, especially the strong younger men who did the hard labor, wherever he could get them. Things were better now, what with some of the old acts and other help returning, but it was still a headache, putting together a first-class show.

The best acts, of course, gravitated to the big shows like Barnum & Bailey, attracted by the top wages, the amenities offered star acts, and by the publicity—how the artistes did love publicity! Which left a limited number of top acts to be divided up among the smaller circuses.

Since he'd been lucky enough to sign on Leo Mueller, who had some kind of grudge against Barnum & Bailey, it was up to him to keep the man happy.

If that juicy little dancer had caught Leo's fancy, then something could be arranged, an accommodation made. Why not take her out of the hooch troupe, where she was causing a problem, and give her a token job elsewhere—say, as stage assistant to that new magician he'd just hired? She had the looks for it, and how much talent did it take to twitch her ass and hand props to a magician?

Having solved the problem to his satisfaction, Mr. Sam should have been able to put the whole business out of his mind, but it rankled his pride that he'd been put in the position of pimping for Leo Mueller. If the arrogant bastard wasn't such a drawing card, he'd dump him in a minute. Maybe, before he did anything, he should find out just what the hell was going on between those two. . . .

Which was why the next morning, when he should've still been in bed, he headed for the ring barn.

The sky toward the east was streaked with pink when Mara slipped out of the dorm. Although she usually was indifferent to her surroundings, which had changed so often during her life, she had a special affection for Florida. Despite the bugs, of which there were plenty, there was something special about the sunlight, which had a golden quality, and about the freshness of the breezes, which, even this far from Tampa Bay to the west, held a tinge of salt.

The trumpeting of an elephant made her smile. The bull who serviced the females during the winter was in *musth*, she'd heard, and she wondered if this strange condition, during which the bull sometimes became violent, had anything to do with the mating instinct. If so, he had her sympathy. Although it annoyed her, she sometimes was tempted to accept one of the propositions she got. Not that she ever intended to fall in love again. She didn't have to get knocked in the head more than once to learn her lesson.

As she hurried toward the ring barn, she kept a wary eye out for anyone else who might be up and about. There were no guards, not in winter quarters, but the cooks would soon be heading for the cookhouse to start coffee, cook up huge batches of oatmeal and cream of wheat, roll out dozens of biscuits. In a few days, all but the temporary laborers, who would be hired as needed along the route, would have arrived, and final preparations for the summer season would begin.

The elephant gave another hooting cry, and she felt regret that she hadn't yet visited the menagerie. Well, there would be time for that once she was in the ballet. She would also get to see the show from beginning to end instead of catching bits and pieces of it in rehearsal. Someday, sooner or later, *she* would be part of the show in the Big Top, the center of all eyes. She didn't doubt this. No matter what it cost, she would be an artiste. But

she wanted it to happen now, not off in the future sometime. . . .

She was near enough now to the ring barn to hear the snap of
the trapeze, the swish of the ropes Leo was working out on. She
had learned to wait outside until the sounds stopped, and even
after she went into the tent, to stay in the shadows until Leo
turned his attention to her. At the best of times, he was sharp-
tongued and impatient with her shortcomings. He demanded so
much and never paid her a compliment, no matter how well she
did, and yet—wasn't this what she wanted? To learn everything
she could from a really good teacher?

Jealousy stirred as she thought of the aerial ballet women,
who had been practicing for almost a week now. She'd learned
most of their names as, one by one, they had reported in, most
of them coming from winter jobs at supper clubs around the
country.

There was Pearl, the blonde from Missouri, who held the
pivotal position in the act, and Marcella, who was dark-haired
and very pretty. Then there was Clinker, a thin, pale-skinned
girl who looked as if a strong wind would blow her away. All
of them were different, some not as pretty as others, but they
had something she wanted desperately—a place in the aerial
ballet troupe.

Mara clenched her hands into fists as she waited for Leo to
finish rehearsing. The audition for the two open slots, one week
away now, was a challenge she wished were behind her. What
if she didn't measure up? What if, after she'd done her routine,
Mr. Sam told her, "Sorry. You're not ready—who's next?"

No, she wouldn't die if that happened. But it would hurt. God,
how it would hurt!

The ballet women were considered artistes, although much
further down the ladder than other performers. Sally had told
her once that they were highly competitive with each other. Most
aspired to better jobs—a place in a featured aerial act, a replacement for a female flier who was having a baby, or even to team
up permanently with a male aerialist who needed a female partner.

Only a few ever made it out of the chorus, but the possibility
was there, a stepping stone to the top. When her chance came,
she would be ready for it. But first—yes, first she had to win
that spot. . . .

It had been a surprise, a painful one, that she hadn't taken to
it naturally, as she'd confidently expected. Every trick she learned

was agonizingly hard. By now, she should be working on a routine, and yet Leo kept her endlessly practicing the same moves, telling her she wasn't ready yet to put them together into a routine.

And the thing was—he was right. She knew it in her heart. She would make it—but it would be harder than she expected. Much harder.

Unconsciously she sighed, and Leo, who had the hearing of a cat, stopped practicing and directed a hard look into the shadows where she was squatting.

"You might as well come out," he growled. "You've already broken my concentration."

She stepped forward, into the early morning light that streamed in through the overhead windows. "I'm a little early," she said, although she knew she wasn't.

"Well, let's get on with it. You need every bit of practice you can get. You been doing those muscle-building exercises I gave you?"

"Two hundred a day," she said.

"Double them. You've got a lot of catching up to do. You should have started on the trap by the time you were six, seven at the most. You'll never be a top act, but you may become adequate. Luckily, that's enough to get you on the ballet in this two-bit circus."

"This is very good circus," she protested. "Everybody say that."

"And you're a dunce. Let's see what you can do with a few flip-flops—to start."

During the next hour, Mara put everything else out of her mind. As she sweated and strained, trying to keep every movement graceful, her timing perfect, her muscles felt as if they were on fire. She was doing a flange turn, a maneuver that involved flipping her body upward, rolling it over in a complete turn, which she found particularly painful because it put such a strain on her upper body, when she slid out of a roll-over too soon. Pain shot through her shoulder and upper arm muscles, but she suppressed a moan and grimly corrected her position. This time, she did it perfectly.

"That's enough for today," Leo said, slapping his thigh with the towel he used to dry off after a workout.

"How did I do?" she couldn't resist asking.

"You were rotten," he said, his voice flat. "You're going to have to practice more. Come here tonight at seven. I've reserved the tent for a couple of hours to practice my two-and-a-half. When I'm finished, I'll work with you for a while. Run along now. I want to take down my rigging.''

Lithely he climbed up the rope toward the top of the barn. She watched him enviously. Would she ever be half as graceful? Sometimes she doubted it—no, she wasn't going to think like that. She *was* going to make it. She had to. Because what else did she have?

She was leaving the barn when she almost bumped into Mr. Sam. He had a strange look on his face, as if he wanted to laugh. ''How long has this been going on?'' he growled.

''What you mean, Mr. Sam?''

He made an impatient gesture. ''How long has Leo been training you—and why? You been putting out to him?''

She flushed, but she didn't look away. ''It is business deal.''

''And I'm going to heaven when I die. Well, it's none of my business as long as it doesn't interfere with the show. But if there's any trouble, out you go. You hear me, girl?''

''I not cause trouble,'' she said.

But of course, trouble was already brewing.

The next morning, Leo began putting together a routine for her. Although she'd practiced all the moves before, now she did them in a series, and it was grueling, painful, nerve-racking. It didn't help that Leo, a hard taskmaster, was impossible to please. The slightest deviation and his wrath came down upon her fast. It was obvious to Mara that he'd never heard of praise.

''You look like a cow with St. Vitus's dance,'' he yelled at her when she made a clumsy move during a flange. ''You're beating the fucking air like you're chopping wood. When you do the flanges, put a little flash in it. You want to show how hard they are, so try to look like you're in pain—''

''I *am* in pain,'' Mara muttered—under her breath.

''—and when you're finished, give them a big smile because you've just done a very hard trick. If you're lucky, they won't catch on that a six-year-old child could do better.''

Forgetting her resolution to hold on to her temper, Mara glared down at him. ''It is hard trick, not easy.''

''For someone without talent, maybe. If you want that slot, I advise you to talk May Mayberry into lending you a flashy costume for the audition. It might give you an edge—but I doubt it.''

She wanted to call him a few names, but instead she returned to the flange, doggedly putting everything she had into it. This time, when she lifted her body and rolled it upward, over her arm, she did it perfectly.

Even so, she expected another of his insults, but he said, "That's better. Not the best I've ever seen, but better."

He stared up at her, his black-eyed gaze moving over the sweat-stained tights that clung to her hips and thighs. She was sure she knew what he was thinking. If she got the job, he would collect his fee—and his price might be her.

But—she gave a tiny shrug that was pure Rom—anything could happen before then. Even if Leo did want his payment in bed, well, it would only be once. She would live through it, just as she had lived through other unpleasant things.

When she dragged her exhausted body outside, Jocko was waiting for her. He should have looked out of place in his English-tailored tweed suit and a bowler hat, but somehow he didn't.

"So the rumors are true. You do have something going with Leo Mueller. I thought you had more sense."

"He gives me lessons so I can try out for aerial ballet," she said.

"That bastard doesn't do favors for nothing. So how are you paying him, Mara?"

Mara breathed in slowly, let the breath out, determined not to lose her temper. "I got money," she said.

She expected a disbelieving stare, but instead he said, "How about breakfast? I could use some friendly company."

"You got plenty friends." Despite herself, there was a touch of resentment in her voice.

"Here, here. Is that self-pity I hear? Poor little waif. All alone in the world, are we? And only got one friend to her name, too."

She stiffened at his mocking tone. "I not alone in the world."

"And just where are your relatives?"

"Circus people mind own business," she said crossly.

"Most of them do. But I'm a very curious fellow."

"You very curious fellow, all right."

"Say, you made a joke. How about that."

"Why you surprised? I can make jokes."

"A sense of humor is honed by leisure. How much leisure have you had in your life?"

Mara shrugged; she gave him a sad smile. "I lie about relatives. I grow up in orphan place."

"Good try. You can embroider on that when you're a star and the press comes around, looking for a good story."

She forgot her pique and smiled at him. "You think I be star?"

He studied her thoughtfully. "It's possible. I caught the hooch show last Sunday. You stood out like a peacock among a covey of peahens. Star quality is the name for it. I've got it. That bastard Leo has it. You have it. But you need a lot of talent, too. Just what is Leo teaching you?"

Jocko listened silently as Mara described the routine Leo had set up for her. He nodded when she was finished. "It's obvious he's put some thought into it. He's smart not to push you too far, too fast. Reasonably simple tricks, but flashy ones. The flange can be spectacular. There's an Alsatian woman over at B&B who's making a name for herself with the flange turn. Call it what you want—magnetism, charm, showmanship—but she has it. And you have it, too, my young friend. Yes, I think you could be a star. But you have a lot to learn first—and only part of it is skill. To begin with, you need to do something about the way you talk. Good, clear English—that's the way to go."

Mara turned his words over in her mind. "You teach me right way to talk—yes?" she asked.

"I could. But do I want to? That's the question you should be asking."

"I not understand. Ain't we friends?"

Jocko laughed. "I'm teasing. Of course, I'll do what I can—starting tonight, over supper. As for your routine—I think you should concentrate on your flanges. That will make up for a lot of other deficiencies."

"I hate flanges. They very painful. Look what rope did." She showed him the lacerations on her left wrist.

"That's part of the price you have to pay for fame. How do you think I feel, dressed like a buffoon, taking pratfalls? But those pratfalls pay off. The flanges will pay off for you. However, you should have some medication on those welts. I'll take you to the menagerie to see Doc McCall. He'll fix you up."

Mara wasn't insulted at his offer to take her to the circus's veterinarian. She had heard of Doc McCall, and knew that everybody went to him for minor ailments and injuries. Town doctors were reluctant to treat circus people. For one thing, they didn't want them sitting in their waiting room with other patients. There was also the matter of payment. How could a doc-

tor send a bill collector after someone who might be several
hundred miles away the next day?

But Doc McCall came cheap—and besides, in the opinion of
the circus, a good vet could teach those fancy towner doctors a
few tricks. . . .

They found the veterinarian, an elderly man with a shock of
white hair, in the cat barn, lecturing one of the beast boys. A
sloe-eyed lioness watched them sleepily from a nearby cage.

"No wonder she's got a stomach upset," Doc McCall scolded.
"Cats are susceptible to every infection in the book. When I say
those cages should be kept clean, I'm talking about a thorough
scrubbing with plenty of soapy water, followed by a good rinse.
You oughta be able to eat off the floor of that cage when you get
done. I'll let it ride this time 'cause you're new at the job, but
you slip again and I'm going to have your ass."

The beast boy, who looked as if he'd just been attacked by a
tiger, scurried off, and the veterinarian turned his attention to
Mara's wrist. He got out alcohol, bandages, and a jar of salve.
The salve was familiar. It was the same one the Roms used on
their horses.

After he'd cleaned and sterilized the lacerations, he applied a
thick coating of salve to her wrist and bandaged it lightly. "Use
the salve twice a day until it's used up," he told her. "It'll
toughen the skin. And watch for infection. Any puffiness or
redness and I want you to come back to see me. Lots of molds
and fungus in this climate. It never gets cold enough here to kill
them off."

Mara nodded, her attention on a huge male tiger, who was
prowling up and down in the nearest cage, stopping frequently
to shake his massive head and stare at them with tawny-gold
eyes. When he gave a moaning grumble, Mara pushed her hand
between the bars, ignoring Doc McCall's sharp warning.

"He not bite me," she said confidently.

The tiger sniffed her fingers, made a coughing sound, then
rubbed his nose against her hand.

"Got a way with animals, have you?" Jocko drawled.
"Maybe you're aiming for the wrong career. You'd be a sensation cracking a whip and strutting around in a holding cage."

Mara didn't like the amusement in his eyes, or his jocular
tone. She withdrew her hand, thanked the old vet, and asked
what she owed.

"It's on the house," he said. "I enjoy treating a human patient
once in a while, especially a pretty one like you."

Once outside, Jocko told her, ''You've made a new conquest. Now you have two friends—but I'd watch that one. He likes the ladies.''

''Men all alike,'' she said crossly.

Jocko raised one eyebrow. ''You including me in that statement?''

Mara smiled at him. ''No, not you. You different.''

To her chagrin, Jocko doubled up, laughing. ''That's the best laugh I've had in a long time,'' he wheezed, wiping his eyes with an immaculate handkerchief.

''Why you laugh at me?'' she said angrily. ''I not like it.''

''Oh, neither do I. But it earns me a damned good living. In fact, if I didn't spend my money as fast as I make it, I'd be a rich man by now.''

''I didn't mean—''

''I know you didn't. And that's what's so rich. You really don't see me as a freak, do you? And in gratitude, I think I'll take you under my wing and teach you some things you'll never learn from Leo Mueller.''

''What things?''

''Showmanship. How to sell yourself to an audience. How to grab more than your share of the attention, even if there's two other acts performing in the arena.''

''Like that woman who does the flanges?''

''Exactly. Little Lillian Leitzel. She never misses a chance to promote herself. I hear she's jealous as hell of anyone who steals the limelight from her, but when she gets her own way—then she's so gracious that everybody loves her. So use your brain. When you get to the top, play the star with outsiders, but not with your own people.''

''But everybody hate Leo—and he is star act.''

''That's different. Leo's a very dangerous man. Do you want everybody to be afraid of you?''

''I want people to like me. But I not let people walk on me.''

''I don't think you'll ever have that particular problem,'' Jocko said, his voice dry.

They had reached the cookhouse: the odor of frying bacon made Mara's mouth water. ''I am hungry,'' she said.

''So you are. Hungry for everything life can give you. Just remember—it's hard going up the rope, but coming down only takes a few seconds.''

* * *

A week later, along with four other women, Mara auditioned for the aerial ballet. She had spent hours practicing on her own, as well as the time she spent with Leo. While she knew that she had improved immensely, she couldn't help the doubts that tormented her as she hurried toward the ring barn.

The ring barn was crowded, not only with the auditioning women, but with spectators, including Jocko, who gave Mara a jaunty wave, and, to her surprise, Leo, who stared at her with his cold black eyes. Had he come to see her win—or fail? Well, she meant to win that slot, no matter what price he demanded. Consciously she straightened her shoulder and gave him a confident smile.

The first two women who tried out, Mara dismissed immediately. Although their routines were adequate enough, they went through them with a lack of style that she was sure would never impress Mr. Sam or Oly Johnson, the ballet boss.

The fourth girl, a slender blonde with a sunny smile, was different. Looking as if she was enjoying herself, she performed her routine with the kind of energy that Mara envied. She was also head and shoulders above Mara in the complexity of her routine.

Mara wasn't surprised when Mr. Sam and Oly Johnson talked to the girl briefly, then told her to go see May Mayberry to be fitted for a costume.

Mara consoled herself with the knowledge that there was still another vacancy in the chorus, but some of her confidence ebbed as she watched the fourth woman rapidly execute a complicated series of turns and moves on the ropes, including several that Mara knew she herself was incapable of. The only thing that gave her hope was that after the girl had slid back down the rope to the tanbark, Mr. Sam told her to stand by, they'd get back to her.

And then it was Mara's turn. She threw off the shawl she was wearing over her costume, and put everything she had in the smile she directed at Mr. Sam and Oly Johnson. She had practiced that smile in the only place where privacy was possible, the women's washhouse, in front of a cracked mirror someone had tacked up. She knew the smile was effective. She'd tried it out on Jocko and he'd pretended to faint.

And now as she stood smiling at Mr. Sam and Oly Johnson, she was sure from their expressions that her practice was paying off. The costume she wore, although well worn and patched in a number of places, was emerald-green, setting off her coloring, and she was glad she'd taken Leo's advice to borrow it from the wardrobe department. Oddly enough, she really felt the pleasure she was trying to project.

She stood there for a moment longer, and then she nodded to the huge man, one of the workmen, who was holding the rope taut. She began to climb, not scrambling up quickly like the other aerialists had, but taking her time, flirting with the audience with her smile, her graceful little gestures, following the advice that Jocko had given her.

When she reached the halfway mark, she paused to give the rope an exuberant little swing, as if she was having the time of her life. There were gasps from below as she dropped a few inches, only to catch herself up short with her leg. When she gave her audience a sly little smile, they laughed, knowing they'd been taken in. Like her slow ascent, Leo hadn't taught her this maneuver, and she wondered what he was thinking, watching in the audience.

Then she had reached the trap and was doing a slow series of turns and swings, making sure her slender body showed to best advantage. Since music wasn't used during auditions, she was surprised when someone started whistling a rollicking little tune. It was a peculiar two-toned whistle that sounded like an instrument, and it kept perfect time with her saucy little swings.

She had pinned back her hair with two wooden combs, and now, surreptitiously, she loosened them so that on her next whirl they fell, as if by accident, to the tanbark below. Her hair, released from restraint, tumbled down, almost to her waist, and as she did a twisting maneuver on the trap, it floated around her, enveloping her in a flame-colored veil.

When she had finished her trapeze routine, she switched to the swiveled rope that hung from the top of the barn and did her first flange. But not as one of the other aerialists had—with seeming effortlessness, making it seem easy. No, she did her best to make the audience see how painful it was, how the rope bit into her wrist, how her shoulder ached as she flung her body upward, rolling over her arm several times. And then, when she stopped, she let them see something else—her satisfaction that she had done seven flange turns . . . and done them well.

Both Leo and Jocko had warned her not to expect applause, but as she flung out her arms in a final bow, there was a ripple of applause, and one shrill whistle that made her smile.

Using only her hands, she descended the rope, and took another bow.

Surreptitiously she studied the expression on Mr. Sam's face,

wishing she could read his mind. Both he and Oly must know
that her routine was relatively simple, but what else did they
think as they consulted each other quietly? Mr. Sam glanced
down at the clipboard he was holding. "What's your last name,
girl? It only says Mara here."

"Just Mara, Mr. Sam."

"Okay, just Mara, you get a week's trial. You could stand
some more experience, but the web doesn't take all that much
skill. You've got showmanship. Maybe it's enough. Report in to
Cal Armor tomorrow morning."

Mara was floating on air as she left the tent. Her face felt very
hot, as if she had a fever, and she was having a hard time breathing normally. She had stopped to catch her breath, to savor not
only her exhilaration but relief, when Leo caught up with her.

"Feeling pretty proud of yourself, are you?" he said. "Who
taught you that drop trick?"

"No one. I do it myself," she said.

"Clever. You're a very clever girl. But are you also an honest
one? I hope so, because I always collect my debts one way or
another."

"I not—I don't have job yet," she said. "Mr. Sam say one
week's trial."

"But that wasn't our bargain. The bargain was that I *train* you
for the audition. I don't remember anything being said about
you getting the job."

Mara fought to keep her anger from showing. He was right—
and she had fallen so easily into his trap. "Okay. How much
you want?"

His black eyes glittered. "Not how much. It's *what* I want—
and I want you. Tonight at eight—at my digs."

She met the triumph in his eyes, and she wanted to turn and
run away, but she forced herself to smile. "I will be there," she
said with dignity. "But then we are even."

She strolled off, resisting the impulse to run. She thought she
heard his laugh behind her, but she didn't look back.

CHAPTER 10

*O*NE OF THE ADVANTAGES OF BEING IN WINTER QUARTERS, Mara had been told, was that the usual two buckets of water allotted daily to each performer while on the road was increased to as much as the person was willing to carry from the spigots outside the cookhouse. It was pride, not vanity, that made her carry enough buckets of water to the women's washhouse, a small, tin-bottomed shack near the dorm, to scrub not only herself but her hair, using a bar of sweet-smelling soap she'd bought at the canteen Mr. Sam maintained for the convenience of his employees.

Afterward, she sat in the sun outside the dorm, drying her hair, thinking about the ordeal ahead of her when she went to Leo's "digs."

Ever since she'd refused Sally's second request to "set her up" with Sammy Jack, Sally had been cool to her. Today she evidently decided to try again, because she sauntered over to ask, "Sure you won't change you mind and let Sammy Jack line up some dates for you?"

Mara shook her head and went on tossing her long hair with her hand.

"Say, you were great this morning at the audition," Sally said. "Those flanges were really impressive."

Mara, not sure what impressive meant, cautiously said, "Thank you."

"Leo's been training you, huh? You two are kinda close these days, aren't you?"

"It is business deal," Mara said quickly.

"Yeah? Well, be careful. He's got a mean streak a mile long." Sally sighed. "He *is* a handsome devil, isn't he? You ever catch his act?"

"I see him rehearse."

"Well, you can watch him from the back door at dress rehearsal—if Mr. Sam doesn't catch you. Did anyone tell you there's going to be a parade in Atlanta? Mr. Sam is thinking about stopping them next year. Too hard to find good routes what with so many automobiles on the streets these days. We're in the spec, too, of course."

"Spec?"

"The spectacular. You know, the walk-around at the beginning of the show in the big top. The artistes hate them. They don't like having to change costumes so often. But I think they're fun. We rode on the elephants last year. Thank God, it's horses this year. A lot easier on the keister."

Mara felt a sudden lift to her spirits. *Spectacular* . . . Even the word was exciting. Jocko had talked about the spectaculars, one of the things about American circuses, like having three rings instead of one, that he considered superior to the European. She'd asked what European meant, not realizing that he was talking about the old country, and he'd shaken his head and muttered something about Roms living on a separate planet.

She realized Sally was still talking, this time about a feud that had erupted in Clown Alley between Lord Jocko and one of the other clowns. She listened politely, but she was glad when Sally wandered off again.

When the cookhouse flag went up, she went to supper with the other women, even though she had lost her appetite. She concentrated on her meal, paying little attention to the other girls, her mind on her coming encounter with Leo. How would it be, having him make love to her? Would he take his time, drag it out, or would it be over with quickly, the way she hoped? She had heard that Leo's women often turned up with bruises. Well, she wouldn't let that happen to her. He could take her to bed—that was the price she'd agreed to pay—but never again would she let anyone hurt her. . . .

The cookhouse was crowded now, very noisy. Jocko was sitting at the clowns' table, and when she caught his eye, he gave her a jaunty salute, which she returned with what she knew must be a weak smile. One of the girls caught the exchange. She giggled and asked, "Are his crown jewels really as big as they say?"—a remark Mara pretended not to hear.

There was a brief break in the noise. Mara looked up to see Leo stalk through the door. He headed for an empty table in the short end of the cookhouse, and she knew that no one would

join him, not even another artiste. She returned to her food—
and her own thoughts—and was taken by surprise when a hard
hand fell upon her shoulder. She looked up into Leo's opaque
eyes.

"Join me," he said.

She wanted to refuse, wanted to say she had finished eating
and was ready to leave, but instinct warned her it wouldn't be
wise. Without looking at the other girls, she rose and followed
Leo back to his table.

He didn't speak to her while he ordered his meal. Like the
other artistes and management, he was served by a waiter, although lesser souls lined up at the steam tables and grill and
carried their plates back to their table. There were other touches,
too—bowls of relish and pickles, chipped ice in the water pitcher,
baskets of hard rolls and bread.

"What do you want to eat?" Leo said.

Mara shook her head. "I eat already."

"Bring the lady a piece of pie and a cup of coffee," Leo told
the waiter.

Both of them were silent as they waited for their order. Leo
seemed to be lost in his own thoughts, and if he noticed the
attention they were getting, it obviously didn't bother him. Mara
wondered why he'd made such a point of seeking out her company. Surely he must know the gossip it would cause. It might
be okay for him to take a girl from the dance troupe to bed, but
not to eat with her in the cookhouse.

Ruby, who was sitting at a table with the wardrobe women,
was glaring at her. She wouldn't say anything to Leo, but Mara
knew she'd get a lecture from Ruby later. Had Leo done it for
just that reason?

Mara felt a burning sensation at the back of her neck, a sure
sign that she was battling her temper.

"Don't forget—eight o'clock at my digs," Leo said suddenly.

"What about curfew?" she asked.

"Don't worry about that. You'll be bunking with the ballet
from now on."

Mara forgot her resentment. "You mean—"

"You got the job."

"But Mr. Sam say I am on trial for—"

"He changed his mind. The slot is yours. And don't get too
cocky. You'll still be on trial from ticket to ticket."

Mara knew what that meant. Everybody was nervous on payday. A yellow ticket in your pay envelope meant you were out

of the show and expected to be off the lot by sundown. But that didn't matter. The slot was hers. She would keep it.

"If you think that old butch Ruby is a slave driver, wait until you work for Cal Armor," Leo said.

"I work hard, not mind. Someday I do solo, like you."

"You're a fool," Leo told her. "You'll be lucky to stay in the ballet. Maybe someday some second-rate troupe from a mudshow will take you on to do the front swings for their act, but you're never going to do a solo."

The waiter brought Mara's pie and coffee. She sat with her eyes downcast, pushing the dessert around with her fork, not even pretending to eat, as Leo gave her directions to his place, which he described as a junked pullman car that had been converted into living quarters. He sounded almost pleasant now, but Mara's anger wasn't defused.

In a few hours it will all be over, she thought. *And then I'll never have to speak to this coyote again.*

Mara lay on her bunk, still fully clothed, wondering if it was eight o'clock yet. It was almost totally dark outside—and she didn't dare be late. She slid off the bunk and asked Sally, who was playing cards with three other girls on an upturned fruit crate, what time it was. Sally pointed at the alarm clock on the shelf beside her own bunk and went on playing cards.

Since Mara couldn't tell time, that wasn't much help, but she thanked Sally and then got her purse out from under her pillow and went outside. From the buzz of conversation that erupted as soon as she closed the door, she knew they were tearing her apart right now. Well, the devil take them. They all broke curfew. And what would those cats say if she told them that she'd only been with one man, and then only once? They would laugh their silly heads off and make remarks she didn't understand half the time. Not that she didn't know when someone was making fun of her. Probably everybody in the circus knew about her patched drawers by now.

Leo's pullman car sat in a cottonwood grove, well apart from the conglomeration of tents and converted buses and old railroad cars that housed the rest of the circus people. Mara had little trouble finding it, but when she was standing outside, looking up at the iron platform at the end, she was reluctant to climb the metal steps.

The door opened and Leo came out on the platform to stare

down at her. "You're late," he said, then turned and went back inside without waiting for an answer.

Mara took her time following him. When she came through the door, she blinked in surprise. The wooden floor of the pullman was highly waxed, covered with richly colored carpets that glowed like jewels in the light of a glass-shaded lamp. An ornate cabinet sat against one wall, and the sofa and chairs, covered in dark red velvet, had graceful lines, unlike anything she'd ever seen before.

"Like it?" Leo asked softly. "Wait until you see the bedroom."

She turned to face him, and for the first time noticed he was wearing a dark red garment that looked like a short robe over his trousers. He must have caught her curiosity because he said, "It's a smoking jacket. What do you want to drink?"

She started to tell him that she wasn't thirsty, then changed her mind. "Orange soda," she said.

"I don't stock exotic drinks like that for my ladies, I'm afraid. I do have some wine. Imported Bordeaux."

He picked up a heavy glass bottle, poured a couple of inches of red liquid into a glass, and put it in her hand. Mara sipped it gingerly. The wine her family drank at weddings and other celebrations was bitter and left a metallic taste in the mouth. This wine went down so smoothly that she quickly emptied the glass.

"More?" Leo asked, and at her nod, filled her glass again.

"Sit down," he said, pointing toward one of the sofas.

Mara perched on the edge of the sofa cushion, holding the glass carefully so she wouldn't spill any wine. Casting around for something to say since it was obvious Leo wasn't going to speak, she said, "Your things very nice."

"What's this? Social chitchat?"

Mara's embarrassment dissolved in a rush of anger. "You say come tonight to pay debt. That is only reason why I am here."

Leo set his glass on a table. "Then we're wasting time, aren't we? So let's get down to business."

With deliberate slowness, he untied his belt and let the smoking jacket slip to the floor. He was nude above the waist; his chest was smooth and hairless, revealing the taut muscles of an athlete.

"Take off your clothes," he said. "Or maybe you'd like me to do it for you?"

Defiantly she stared into his eyes. What she saw there sickened her, but she was determined not to give him the satisfaction of showing her disgust. She unbuttoned the tiny pearl buttons down the front of her blouse, hoping he wouldn't notice the slight trembling of her hands. The blouse had been one of Berty's, cut down to fit her, and for a fleeting moment she wondered what Berty would think if she saw her now.

She slid off her blouse, then unfastened the belt of her skirt. It slipped to the rug, joining Leo's smoking jacket. Careful not to look at the man watching her, she took off her muslin petticoat, her cotton drawers, and when she was naked, she sat down again so she could take off her shoes and hose.

But Leo knelt before her. "I'll do that," he said.

He unbuttoned both her shoes before he drew them off. His hands were very hot against her skin as he rolled down her hose and slipped them over her feet. His eyes fixed on her face, as if gauging her reaction, he held her feet in his hands.

"Your feet are cold," he said softly. "I'll warm them up for you."

His hands, as he stroked her arch, her instep, were surprisingly gentle. Did this mean that he would be easy with her? If so, it might not be so bad after all, especially if it was over quickly.

She stiffened as he bent his head and pressed his lips against the arch of her foot. In a series of tiny kisses, his lips moved over her instep to her toes. When she realized that he was touching them with his tongue, a hot flush spread over her body.

Leo raised his head, his eyes roaming over her naked body. "What do you know. A natural redhead," he said.

He rained kisses on her foot and then up her leg, over her calf and knee, the inside of her thighs. She felt very hot, but this time it wasn't embarrassment. It was something else, something that shamed her. How was it possible to feel lust for this man she despised so much?

She moaned, sickened by the sexual hunger that swept her body, and tried to pull away, forgetting all her resolutions not to resist and get it over with as quickly as possible. But Leo held her there effortlessly while his hot mouth enveloped her nipples as if he meant to devour them. Her struggles stopped as the voluptuous needs of her body soared, became overwhelming.

He kissed her mouth finally, but it was not like Yolo's kisses. Yolo's kisses had bruised her lips; he hadn't insinuated his tongue into her mouth, probing it deeply, taking possession in an erotic imitation of the act of love. Her skin felt incredibly sensitive, and the heat spread from her loins to her breasts, to the rest of

her body, making her tremble. When his hand slid downward
to the soft mound between her thighs, she opened up to him,
mutely inviting him to explore further.

"Are you a virgin?" he murmured against her ear, and when
she shook her head, he added, "Good."

His fingers probed the soft moistness between her thighs,
finding with unerring skill the secret place that, in her ignorance, she hadn't realized men knew about. Yolo's lovemaking
had been fierce and ardent, but it had been that of a boy. This,
what Leo was doing to her now, was how a man made love.
With finesse and certainty, with the sure knowledge of experience. And she didn't want him to stop. God, she did love what
he was doing to her, the burning sensation in her tissues that
was almost pain, the frantic hunger, the pulsating waves of pure
pleasure.

Suddenly afraid that he would stop and deprive her of the
release she needed so badly, she pushed up against him, letting
him know her need, and he laughed, the sound jarring and intrusive.

Then he was bending to her, touching her intimately with his
lips, probing with his tongue, and she was sure she would die
from sheer pleasure. Sensation, wild and pulsating, rippled
through her, and she moved convulsively against the pressure
of his lips. When she was sure that she couldn't stand the frus-
trating torment a moment longer, he moved over her, covering
her, filling her, and now the pleasure was intensified as he rose
and fell above her, his eyes closed, his mouth set in a rictus grin,
his face wet with sweat.

Even in the midst of her pleasure, she felt a small surprise
that he was revealing his own need to her. But the thought slipped
away as the sensation he was arousing blossomed into mindless
and endless rapture. . . .

She was coming back down to earth again when she felt a
gush of warmth inside her. Leo collapsed upon her, his breathing rasping in her ear. Slowly, slowly, her mind cleared, and
bewilderment replaced the pleasure. How was it possible that
this man, whom she detested, had made her respond so easily?
Had it been the wine? Or was it some flaw in her own character?
Was she the tart others had accused her of being?

Suddenly she found Leo's strident breathing, the musky male
odor of his hot body, still joined to hers in the ultimate intimacy,
offensive. Desperate to get away, she squirmed out from under
him and stood up. When she met his eyes, she knew he recog-

nized her belated revulsion and was amused—or was it anger that made his smile so threatening?

"Well, you *are* a tiger, aren't you?" He touched the scratches on his neck. Had she put them there? She couldn't remember. Only that for a few minutes she had been a different person, wild and wanton and out of control.

She began to dress. Leo didn't try to stop her. He watched in silence as she hurried into her clothes, then dropped into a chair while she slid her hose, still rolled around her garters, over her legs.

She was putting on her shoes when he rose and came toward her. In the soft glow of the lamplight, his naked body glistened with sweat, and she looked away, knowing her own skin still showed the same telltale signs of lust.

"All that work for nothing," he said softly. "You're going to have to take them off again, you know. I'm not finished with you yet."

"I go now." In her agitation, she jumped to her feet. "I say you take me once, and you say that enough."

"So I've changed my mind." His voice grated against her nerves, and she realized too late that she'd pricked his pride when she'd left him so abruptly. "Why don't you finish your wine? That might stop you from doing anything rash like trying to leave before I'm done with you."

Mara's anger, always so close to the surface, soared out of control. She swept the glass of wine off the table with her arm. "You go to hell," she said, and started for the door.

Leo was upon her before she'd taken more than two steps. He flung her on the sofa and then fell on top of her, knocking the breath from her body. Before she could scream, he clamped his mouth over hers, silencing her. She struggled desperately, but he held her easily while he plundered her mouth.

The first time he'd been gentle with her, but now she knew that he meant to hurt her, to humiliate her. She clawed at his face, and he slapped her, so hard that she went limp. She knew that he was tearing off her clothes again, but she was too stunned to move, not even when he thrust her legs apart and fell between them.

This time when he took her, he forced an entrance, ruthlessly plunging into her again and again. Tears gathered under her eyelids and ran down her cheeks, and the world around her seemed to retreat, grow dim. She fought against the weakness, not wanting to be completely in his mercy. Through a red mist, she saw something—no, someone—looming behind Leo, and then there was a hollow sound, like a dropped melon bursting open, and Leo collapsed upon her, his head lolling on her breast.

She blinked hard, finally clearing her sight. Jocko, wearing one of the sardonic smiles that said the whole world was crazy, everybody but him, was standing over Leo. His walking cane, the one with the silver handle, was still in his hand.

"I seem to have come too late," he said, looking down at Leo's naked body. "My timing was off, old dear. One of my failings, I'm afraid."

She gaped up at him, trying to make sense out of his words. Shuddering, she wriggled out from under Leo's flaccid body. "Is he dead?" she said.

Jocko put two fingers against the pulse in Leo's neck. "Just knocked out. But he's going to have one hell of a headache when he comes to. Get your clothes and come with me. He won't be out long."

Mara grabbed up her clothes and stumbled after Jocko as he headed out the door. Although there was only a sliver of a moon, he seemed to have eyes that could see in the dark as he led her along a narrow path, finally reaching a small wooden trailer.

"My own private Clown Alley," Jocko said. "Go inside and get dressed. I'll wait out here."

Mara clutched her clothes in front of her, wondering why she felt more aware of her nakedness now than she had with Leo. "My blouse is torn—and I've lost some buttons, too."

"I'll take care of that—only, put something around that delectable body before I die of frustration."

Mara went inside the cottage. Still feeling disoriented, she draped herself in a quilt she found on a chair. Her legs felt weak, and she sat down quickly, fighting the desire to cry. She won that battle, but her body was shaking so badly that she had trouble breathing. She was still sitting there, huddled in the quilt, when Jocko joined her.

"I say—your clothes are a bit of a mess, aren't they?" he said, picking her blouse and skirt up off the floor. "Well, let's see what I can do."

Although he sounded unruffled, Mara was aware of their danger. She already knew that Leo was a vengeful man. What would he do to Jocko if he realized who had struck him from behind?

"If you're worrying about Leo, don't fret," Jocko said. "I doubt he knows who hit him. Even if he suspects, he'll keep it quiet rather than have anybody find out a midget did him in. It's that stiff-necked Rom pride—all of you seem to have it.''

Mara stared at him, trying to make sense of his words. ''Leo a Rom? That cannot be.''

''I'm sure he is. Under *maramay*, I'd guess.''

Mara shuddered violently. If Leo was a Rom, then she had lain with a man who was *maramay*, and now she was unclean, too. . . .

The absurdity of her thoughts struck her, and she felt a hysterical laugh building in her throat. Because, of course, she was already unclean, unclean and dead in the eyes of other Roms for over a year. . . .

''You are right,'' she said, remembering the Rom song Leo had quoted to her the first time they'd met. *The Wheel of Fortune turning, turning, turning*—why hadn't she guessed the truth then? ''Why I not see that, Jocko?''

Jocko cocked his head to one side. ''Oh, he's very clever about hiding what he is. He even got an education somewhere—and got rid of the accent. I'd guess that it happened when he was pretty young, and he's lived among—what do you call us? *Gadjos*?—most of his life. Maybe being ostracized by his own kind is what made him such a coldhearted bastard.''

''He knows about me,'' she said with certainty. ''He guess I am Rom first time he seen me. That is why he hates me.''

''Hates you? Well, maybe that's part of it. But he's also got a lust for you. Lust and hatred are a bad combination.''

She stared at him, knowing she owed him the truth. ''He did not rape me first time. I went to pay him for lessons. It was only to be one time. After it was over, I try to leave and he want to do it again. This time, he hurt me. I not know why he so mad.''

''Maybe you let him know how you hated every minute of the first time.''

Mara met the question in his eyes. ''I not hate it,'' she said simply.

Jocko's face darkened. He looked away. ''It's over now. Let's see what we can do about mending your clothes.''

He produced a sewing kit and a small box of assorted buttons. He refused her help, saying he was clever with a needle. Sitting cross-legged on a padded stool, he diligently applied the needle to her torn blouse.

Mara examined the trailer, bemused by the scaled-down furniture, including a child-sized bed, shaped like a sleigh. ''Like dollhouse,'' she murmured.

Jocko looked at her over his reading spectacles. "Don't let my size fool you. I'm not a doll. I'm a fully developed male—which is something you'll have to take on faith."

"I hear rumors," she said slyly.

"So you can still make jokes. That's good. Better see what you can do about your hair—there's a mirror and a hairbrush over there on the washstand."

Mara was dismayed when she looked in the mirror. Her face was pale, her hair a tangled mess, her eyes dull with shock. Using Jocko's brush, she put her hair back in order.

"That bruise on your jaw is already turning black," Jocko commented. He slid off the stool and went to get a jar of flesh-colored greasepaint from a drawer and handed it to her. "Better cover it up—you can take the jar with you. How come you're so fair, anyway? Most of the English Roms are swarthy and dark-haired."

"My father was *gadjo* sailor," she said. "My mother ran off with him. When he desert her, she went back to *kumpania*."

"Which made her something of a pariah, I suspect. I'm surprised they took her in."

"She very good fortune-teller. The family treat her like dirt," she said, the old grievance welling up and thickening her voice. "When she die of lung fever, they dig hole in potato field and bury her there. They say she don't belong in cemetery in Cincinnati where rest of the family is buried."

"Is that why you left?"

"They put me out. Yaddo—that's my grandfather—he very mad when I say I not marry old man he choose for me. So he beat me, say I am *maramay*, and dump me in a ditch naked and with no money."

Jocko whistled softly. "What happened to you then?"

"A man find me. He and his woman have medicine show. I dance in show. Then man come to see Horace, and he tell me Mr. Sam is hiring dancers for his circus. So I take bus to Tallahassee and then I hitchhike to winter quarters."

"You ran out of money before you got here? You know you won't get paid for three weeks after the show moves out, don't you? It keeps people from bolting when they find out how rugged circus life is."

"I got money. I get by okay."

"And so you shall, because you're tough. And tough people get by. Just don't make the same mistakes twice."

"I won't," she said shortly.

Jocko held out the blouse he'd been mending. "This should pass muster with your dorm mates," he said. "While you get dressed, I'll make us a cup of tea." He slid off the stool. "This business will all blow over. But if that bastard bothers you again, you come to me. I'll take care of him."

And because he looked like a cocky little boy, whistling in the dark, Mara had to smile. But she couldn't help thinking that he was wrong, that it wouldn't blow over all that easily.

CHAPTER 11

As MARA LAY IN THE DARKNESS OF THE DORM, UNABLE TO sleep, she wished she could take a sponge bath to wash away not only the physical evidence but her dark memories of the rape. She found herself straining her ears, questioning sounds that ordinarily she would have ignored. Was that creaking noise someone walking across the dorm toward her—or just an old board, springing back into place? And that rasping sound—a branch of one of the cottonwood trees, rubbing against the eaves of the dorm? Or someone easing open the door?

She knew her fear was irrational. Leo would never come here and seek her out among seven other girls. It was Jocko, alone in his trailer, who was so vulnerable. Despite his assurance that he was in no danger, that Leo couldn't know who had rescued her, it would be so easy for Leo to cripple the midget with his fists—or maim him with a knife.

She had looked into Leo's eyes and seen the darkness there. He was a dangerous man—hadn't she been told that so many times? Maybe he would bide his time, but eventually he would get his revenge—or was it possible that she was thinking like a Rom? Maybe Leo would be satisfied with the damage, the pain and humiliation, he'd already caused her. After all, he had completed the rape before Jocko struck him. Maybe that would be enough for him.

The next morning, as she sat with the other dancers trying to force down a few bites of food, she looked up just as Leo entered the cookhouse. Danielle Dubois, the French equestrienne, a small, dark-haired woman with large, lustrous eyes, was with him. If he knew Mara was there, he gave no sign as he led the way to his usual table. While his companion chatted away, carrying on a one-sided conversation, he sat silently, drinking coffee.

Since he didn't glance toward the table where Jocko was eating with the other clowns, or at Mara, sitting with the dance troupe, she allowed herself to relax a little. It seemed Jocko was right. The incident, humiliating and painful as it had been, was over. So why did she still feel so uneasy?

Luckily her new job gave her little time for worry. The ballet routine, which Leo had described as elementary, was difficult for her to learn, and her hours of practice left her little time for worry. To her surprise, the other seven women of the ballet chorus were friendlier than the dance troupe had been. Was that because they saw that she was no threat?

One of them, the slightly built strawberry blonde named Clinker, went out of her way to help Mara with the more difficult maneuvers of the routine, which consisted of a choreography of turns and whirls halfway up a rope, followed by synchronized maneuvers on a giant rope web.

Mara was warmed by this offer of help from a stranger, and she accepted with gratitude. She also practiced on her own whenever she could find a vacant rigging in the workout tent or ring barn. Most of the featured aerialists used their own equipment, but the rigging for the ballet chorus was provided by the circus. Only after she got a grudging "You're doing better, Mara" from Cal Armor, the ballet master, did she feel a little more optimistic about her chances of staying in the chorus.

The stipulation from the circus while still in winter quarters was for food tickets and housing only, so Mara was careful to never miss a meal. When the other women went into Orlando for an occasional treat of smoked mullet at one of its fish houses, she stayed behind, even though she was included in the invitations. Not only was she hoarding her remaining money, but she had little to say to these self-assured *gadjo* women, with their bobbed hair and their pretty summer dresses. Secretly she envied them their flesh-colored silk stockings and crepe de Chine chemises, although she had her suspicions, from their conversation, where most of these luxuries came from. Since she'd sold her own body to Leo for a few lessons on the trapeze, she didn't even have the solace of feeling superior.

It was Jocko who provided her with amusement these hectic days. His teasing, his wry comments and jokes, and most of all his compliments during their speech and showmanship lessons, made her smile. They never spoke of Leo—to her relief. Her sexual response to a man she hated was something she wanted to forget—and she often regretted that she'd told Jocko the truth.

Sometimes she ate with Jocko, but most of the time she ate with the ballet troupe, which was something of an ordeal. She'd never been good with other women, starting with her own female cousins. While they talked about film stars and the latest fashions, which they followed so avidly, about songs she'd never heard, and motion pictures she'd never seen, and most of all about men, she seldom spoke, for fear of showing her ignorance.

With more free time, she gravitated to the menagerie, where the garrulous old vet, Doc McCall, was always willing to answer her questions about the animals. She also came in for a share of his lectures, mostly about never forgetting that the beasts, no matter how friendly they might seem, were still wild animals, and as such, dangerous.

Although she didn't argue with him, it was hard to believe that the docile elephants would harm anyone except by accident. One young female named Connie became her special pet, and she brought sugar lumps and rolls from the cookhouse to feed to the greedy elephant. Sometimes, when no one else was about, she rubbed the bristly skin above Connie's small, intelligent eyes and whispered endearments into her fan-shaped ear. She could swear that the great gray animal understood Romany.

It was from Doc McCall that she learned more about the pecking order of the circus.

At the top, he told her expansively, was Mr. Sam, followed by the management staff, then the superintendents of the major departments such as traffic, advertising, tickets, wardrobe, concessions, the train master, and the all-important equestrian director, who was in charge of the big top.

"The towners call him the ringmaster, but his correct title is equestrian director," he said. "They also call the roughies roustabouts, and the talkers on the midway, barkers."

Then there were the "bosses" or foremen, who supervised

the canvas men, the menagerie, on an equal footing with others like Oly Johnson, in charge of both the ballet and the prop men, who assembled and disassembled the holding cage for the lion trainer and the props used in the clown skits.

Some jobs didn't fit into any of these categories, such as the mail agent, the bandmaster, Cookie, who ruled his fifteen-man crew with an iron hand, and Doc McCall himself, who obviously considered himself a cut above most of the other circus people.

The artistes, the aristocracy of the circus performers, had their own pecking order, starting with the equestrians and followed by the aerialists, the animal trainer, the high-wire walkers, the mat acrobats, and the animal acts. Not to Mara's surprise, the aerial ballet women ranked just above the dance troupe, which was at the bottom of the list.

Circus status extended even among the "roughies," the laborers and other working men. When Doc McCall explained that those who had skills—mechanics, electricians, rigging men—ate at a separate table from the common laborers, Mara thought of her own upper movement since she'd moved from the dance troupe to the aerial ballet.

For one thing, the converted railroad baggage car that housed the ballet women in winter quarters was located much closer to the cookhouse, washhouse, and the women's donicker than the dance troupe's dorm, and Mara realized now that this wasn't by accident. Even the assignment of the surplus army bunks the women slept in was affected. As the newest woman in the chorus, she'd been given the bunk closest to the door, where the drafts were chillier on windy nights.

The ten-in-one freaks—like Jocko, Doc McCall called them anomalies—were not considered artistes, but because they brought so much money into the circus, they were treated with respect and accepted by other circus folk, he told Mara.

Maybe so, she thought, *but they still eat half an hour before everybody else.*

"Mr. Sam won't use geeks or anyone too deformed," Doc McCall went on. "He's got a streak of the preacher in him. He's close with the buck, but he doesn't bend his values for the sake of the almighty dollar."

Mara already knew that the clowns held their own position of importance.

"To outsiders," Jocko had once explained, "it might seem an easy profession, just a lot of men in outrageous costumes and painted faces cavorting around the arena, but actually a clown has to be a skillful acrobat and have perfect timing. Without the diversion of the clowns, there would be long waits between acts when special props and riggings have to be put up."

He'd given her the grin that always held a touch of self-mockery. "Of course, there are clowns and then there are clowns. The ones, like me, who can come up with new skits every season are called producing clowns or sometimes Augustes. If I wasn't such a modest fellow, I'd point out that among clowns, I'm the crème de la crème."

It was curiosity that made Mara linger near the performers' entrance, which she'd learned to call the back door, after the ballet had done its first stint during the dress rehearsal of the season's show. The lion trainer's act was always first for the evening show, followed by the ballet chorus and two other acts, and then the clowns made their grand entrance into the arena, where they did twelve minutes of skits, most of them elaborately staged.

Careful to stay out of Mr. Sam's range of view, she waited for Jocko to appear. When he did, she had to put her hands over her mouth to stifle a laugh. He strutted into the arena importantly, wearing full evening dress, including a top hat, an idiot's smile painted in red on his otherwise all-white face.

Seemingly unaware of the derisive hoots of the other clowns, he bowed and waved to the audience, reminding Mara of the court card, the Fool, in her tarot deck. After first pantomiming to the stands what they intended to do, the other clowns began to stalk him. The audience, locals and invited guests alike, shouted shrill warnings, but Jocko cupped his ear with his hand as if he couldn't quite make out what they were saying.

And then, with perfect timing, things began to fall apart. First, he lost his hat when a large clown in an orange wig stole up behind him and zipped it off his head. He looked for it in vain, even though half the audience were screaming to him that the big clown had it. In rapid succession, he lost his tie, his jacket, his belt, never catching on that the other clowns were stripping him, garment by garment, of his dignity.

As the tormenting intensified, so did his bewilderment. His expression was so sorrowful that Mara found herself closer to tears than laughter. When he finally lost his trousers, leaving him standing there in bright polka-dotted shorts, amusement won out and she found herself laughing uproariously.

It seemed, she reflected, that something Jocko had once said to her, that to be truly effective, comedy must have a tinge of cruelty, was true.

"It's the old better-thee-than-me attitude," he'd said. "The crowd doesn't identify with the victim, you know. It's the bully they root for. This is their revenge for all the times they've been the victim themselves."

As she watched Jocko take one pratfall after another, each accompanied with screams of laughter from the stands, she wondered if maybe she could find a way to use something like this in her own act. If she ever hoped to be a full-fledged aerialist, she had to do something to set herself apart from the other girls.

In the center ring, the big clown picked Jocko up by the scruff of his neck and dropped him in a barrel of water. He held the midget under much too long, and she discovered that she'd stopped smiling, that her eyes were wet. She wiped the tears away, knowing how Jocko would jeer if he saw them. And then he'd tell her not to take it so seriously, that it was all an act that paid better than a bank president earned. So in the end, who got the last laugh?

Then, finally, the First of May arrived. It wasn't really May 1, of course. It was April 30, a Thursday, when the first half of the circus train pulled out of Orlando, heading for Atlanta.

Mara fought uneasiness as she stood on the platform of the sleeping car where she and the ballet women would bunk during the circuit. It was her first ride on a train, and while she wouldn't have admitted it to anyone, the puffing engine with dark gray smoke pouring from its stack was intimidating.

She had other worries, too. Her few performances so far had been in front of a tolerant audience, most of whom attended the rehearsals on Annie Oakleys, the free passes handed out to local politicians, journalists, and newspaper columnists as goodwill gestures. But what if she didn't perform well in front of a paying audience? She would find a yellow ticket in her pay envelope, would be stranded wherever she was fired because the circus didn't pay return fare to Florida until after the thirteenth week of the circuit.

She doubted if anyone would bother to say they were sorry. She had already noticed that circus people were as superstitious as Roms. Afraid her bad luck might rub off on them, the other ballet women would probably stay away while she was packing up her things. She'd seen it happen to one of the dance troupe women, who had lost her job after she'd started a fight with May Mayberry. And unlike herself, that girl had had friends.

If she was fired, no one would give a damn. Oh, Jocko might think of her occasionally, but why would he miss someone who had caused him so much trouble? Doc McCall would probably miss having an audience, and it was possible Clinker would say good-bye and wish her luck, but in the end, she would leave the same way she'd come—alone and friendless.

It was a sober Mara who went to bed that night, the clacking of the rails in her ears. As a new member of the troupe, she rated an upper bunk above the noisy wheels, but she didn't mind. In fact, there was something soothing about the sound, and she went to sleep with the click, click, click of the rails making words in her mind.

Gotta make good . . . gotta make good . . . Gonna make good . . .

The circus's first stop was Atlanta, a five-day engagement in conjunction with a seed growers' convention. The city was considered a "circus town," which meant the circus could expect large overflow crowds for their evening performances if not for their matinees. Mr. Sam, the rumor went, had pulled some kind of coup, locking up the conference hall lot right under the noses of the Lasky Circus, their biggest rival. It was only fair, one of the girls said, since Joe Lasky, Lasky Circus's owner, had pulled a dirty deal last year that had locked *them* out of Atlanta.

By the time the second section of the train, which carried the artistes, pulled off the main line onto the spur track near the conference center, Mara noted that the frenzied activity of setting up the circus was already well under way. Following the lead of the other women, she headed for the cookhouse, which was always the first tent to be raised. Like the other women, she ate heartily, even though she was too excited to be hungry, knowing it would be her last meal that day. She'd already learned that it was unwise to eat a full meal just before a performance.

A sleeping tent, tightly packed with folding cots and three dressing tables, had been set up for the troupe, which they shared with several other female performers, who did a tumbling act. After she'd eaten, Mara found a vacant corner in the tent and washed as best she could in the bucket of cold water allotted to her, then went to the wardrobe tent to put on her costume for the parade, which would take place in downtown Atlanta that afternoon.

Although the other women groused about the parade, Mara enjoyed it. She felt like a princess in her gauzy gown, shot through with silver and gold threads, and decorated with span-

gles. Even though she was one of eight women riding in an
ornately decorated carriage that was pulled by a team of six
white horses, she was sure some of the cheers from the spectators were meant for her, and instinctively she waved and bowed,
her smile dazzling.

When they returned to the fairgrounds, one of the other ballet
women, a blond girl named Hannah, remarked, "You really
fancy yourself, don't you, Mara? You'd think you was a star, the
way you were carrying on."

Mara eyed her coldly. "The circus pays us to make people
want to come to circus. I was just doing my job."

There was the sound of clapping behind her. She turned to
see a group of men, Mr. Sam among them, standing near the
carriage. Although she still hadn't straightened out their names,
she knew the men, who wore sober business suits, held mana-
gerial positions. Most of them were smiling, but which one had
clapped? It hadn't been Mr. Sam. He looked even more sour
than usual.

Just before the matinee performance, the second of the two
buckets of water allotted each performer arrived, brought by the
water boys, and like the other women, she gave herself a quick
sponge bath, no longer self-conscious about exposing her nude
body to the glances of the other women.

After she'd put on her costume, the same one she'd worn in
the parade, she edged forward to examine herself in the mirror
that served all the women in the dressing tent.

Clinker, generous as ever, told her she looked like a real
Arabian dancing girl with those green eyes and red hair. "You're
gonna knock them dead," she added, her tone admiring.

"Especially if she burns the ropes," said Hannah, who had
been watching.

At Mara's puzzled look, Clinker explained, "That's what they
call it when someone loses their grip on the rope and falls. And
don't worry. If it happens to anybody, it'll be someone who
thinks she's so smart that she gets careless."

Hannah gave her a hard look, and began putting nail polish
on her spectacularly long nails. Clinker grinned at Mara and
whispered, "She thinks she's hot stuff because she danced in a
Broadway show once."

"Broadway show?"

"Yeah—say, you really are a First of May guy. Is this your
first job?"

"I dance for medicine show for year," Mara said.

"Well, circus life is a lot different than a medicine show. Look, if you've got any problems, just come to me. I didn't realize—I guess I misunderstood a lot of things. You know how it is around the circus. Too many flapping tongues."

She made a face, as if her own words embarrassed her. "Relax, kid. Even the old-timers are nervous the first show of the season, because they know something's bound to go wrong. The first show always runs long no matter how many rehearsals Konrad calls. It's not his fault. He's one of the best equestrian directors in the business."

She paused to blot her lipstick. "So just take it easy, concentrate on what you're doing—and if the worst happens, like your tights fall off, just keep smiling."

As Mara walked with Clinker toward the backyard, the space behind the big top where the spectacular parade was assembling, she felt a sudden surge of confidence that, to her surprise, was strong enough to banish her doubts and fear. *It's starting,* she thought exultantly. *It's finally starting for me.*

The Arabian Nights was the theme of the Bradford Circus's 1921 season. The women from the aerial ballet, dressed in dancing girl costumes and riding the same broad-backed white percherons that had pulled their carriage during the parade in town, were accompanied by a bevy of clowns as they moved into the arena for the spec.

The clowns were dressed as court jesters, and the tiny bells sewn to their foolscaps tinkled merrily as they capered and gestured, emitting a chorus of whoops, chuckles, shrieks, and guffaws, smacking and being smacked with double-bladed paddles.

Jocko, in a black-and-white checkered costume, was the butt of a large share of the violence, but he got his own back in sly ways that brought shrieks of laughter from the audience.

Mara wasn't nervous, as she knew some of the other women were, to be perched on top the elaborately decorated percherons. She'd been raised with horses, and she rode with confidence, playing up to the audience, enjoying the attention and the music from the bandstand, which Clinker had identified as "The Sheik of Araby."

When the spec was over, the ballet troupe waited in the backyard for the music that would be their cue to start their act. They had been assigned the left ring, facing the lower-priced "blue" seats, while the center ring featured the equestrienne Danielle Dubois, and the right ring a Chinese tumbling act. Later, they would precede Leo Mueller's solo act with their web routine, and then they would be finished until the finale, when they did a final walk-around with the whole ensemble. If time was running short, and Konrad, the equestrian director, called for a shorter show, their second appearance would be the first act cut.

''Which shows how we rate,'' Clinker had commented to Mara earlier.

Their cue, several bars of ''Dardenella,'' came. They ran out into the arena, holding hands and smiling at the audience, who roared their appreciation at the sight of so many nubile bodies. Mara breathed in the odor of tanbark, of sawdust, of the popcorn and parched peanuts the vendors were selling in the stands, and her skin tingled as if she were charged with electricity.

She had dreamt about this moment since she was seven and had been caught up in the magic of her first circus. She wasn't a star yet, but she had no doubts, as she climbed the rope she'd been assigned, that it would happen eventually. She was willing to wait—but not too long. For now, this was enough. She was where she wanted to be, doing what she wanted to do, and the past didn't matter, because everything that had happened, even the worst of it, had had a part in getting her here.

Aware that she wasn't as experienced or as talented as the other women, she threw herself into the ballet routine, trying to overcome her shortcomings with sheer energy. As she swung gracefully from the rope, twisting and turning, moving in unison with the other women, smiling as if she were having the best time of her life, she became aware that she was getting more than her fair share of attention, that the applause that erupted so generously was for her more often than not, and she felt an exhilaration that was so seductive, so overwhelming, that when the twelve minutes allotted to their act was over, she was reluctant to leave the arena.

She took her bow with the rest of the chorus, then, flushed and excited, she ran toward the back door, falling a little behind the other girls. As a final wave of applause washed over her, she turned and made a saucy little bow, throwing the audience a kiss.

None of the other girls saw her, for which she was grateful. Already she regretted her impulsive gesture, especially when Oly drew her aside, saying he wanted a word with her.

''That thing you did at the end—it got a big hand,'' he said. ''I'm adding it to the act. Milk it for all it's worth.''

Mara returned to the other women, feeling a little numb. "What was that all about?" Clinker asked.

"Oly wants me to do some extra rehearsing," she said prudently.

"Really? I thought you were swell. How did you feel out there, Mara? Butterflies in your stomach?"

"I felt very good," Mara said.

"Yes, I could see you did. To me, it's just a way to earning a living. When my Johnny signed up with Mr. Sam, I got on with the ballet so I could be with him."

"You are married?"

One of the other girls snickered, and Clinker gave her a hard look. "Johnny and I are going to get married as soon as we save some more money."

"Do I know him?"

"You might have noticed him during rehearsals. He's a flier—with the Klinski troupe."

"You must be proud of him," Mara said, noting the flush on Clinker's cheeks.

"Yeah. Next year he'll rate bunks in the married car and then we can be together during the circuit. I'll still keep my job, of course. Mr. Sam don't allow any deadwood in his show. If you fill a berth, you gotta work."

"Your boyfriend—he teach you how to do tricks?"

Clinker looked amused. "My family's old circus, four generations of fliers. I was working on the traps by the time I was six. Johnny was an acrobat, part of a risley act, but he wanted to be a flier. When my oldest brother hurt his leg, Papa trained Johnny to fill in. That's when I met him." She sighed deeply. "Everything went up in smoke when my folks found out we were—you know, seeing each other on the sly. My pa's always been real strict with me and my sisters. He fired Johnny on the spot, and that's when I ran off with him."

Mara mulled over her words. "I broke off with my family, too," she said finally.

"Over a guy?"

Mara hesitated, then nodded.

"So what happened to him?"

"He change his mind."

"Tough—well, there's lots of guys around. You'll find another one."

"I don't want man. I want to do my job—and get very good at it."

"Well, you *could* use a little more work on your spins. If you want, I'll help you practice. I cut my teeth on the ropes."

Clinker was as good as her word. During the remaining days in Atlanta, she supervised Mara's morning workouts so well that Mara earned one of Oly's rare compliments after the Sunday matinee. Not that his praise was effusive.

"Not bad, Mara," he said. "Keep it up and someday maybe you'll be as good as Clinker."

It was a month later, when the circus reached Chicago, that Mara began to feel restless. It wasn't that the performances had lost their magic, only that she was greedy for more. When she stood at the back door and watched the fliers, she felt almost sick with envy. She wanted to be up there alone, to hear the crowd roar for her—and yet, the possibility that this would ever happen seemed even more remote than before she'd joined the ballet troupe.

Grimly determined to be ready should an opportunity present itself, she decided to change her appearance. Since she had finally drawn some pay, she went to a five-and-dime store near the fairgrounds and spent some of her money on cosmetics.

Clinker thought it was a lark, helping her. She showed Mara how to darken her eyelashes with mascara, how to outline her eyes with pencil, how to use lemon and egg white rinses to put gold highlights in her hair.

Although most of the other women, including Clinker, were wearing the new mannish bobs, with their hair cropped short on the sides, Mara resisted, just as she had resisted something called the Irene Castle bob. Her red hair, she knew, was one of the things that set her apart from the other ballet girls, and it was important to her that she not look like everybody else.

During a matinee performance, a few locks of hair slipped out of the silver net that matched her costume and swung around her shoulders. She got so much applause that she did it deliberately at the next performance, letting the net slip enough to release most of her hair. The cheers and yells for her to let her hair down the rest of the way were so loud and spirited that it aroused the ire of the equestrian act in the center ring.

Mara's first inkling of trouble was when Oly called her aside before the evening performance that evening. He wasn't alone. Konrad, the formidable equestrian director, was with him—and he looked Mara over with a scowl that told her she was in trouble. According to circus gossip, Konrad had a long history of being temperamental and hard to deal with. Like Mr. Sam, he seldom smiled, and even the top acts were careful not to offend him, because it was well known that he could be vindictive.

"What's this I hear about you causing trouble?" was Oly's greeting. He was a large man with a booming voice, and she was sure everybody in the backyard was listening.

"I not know what you mean—"

Konrad interrupted. "What's that accent, girl?"

Mara hesitated. What if he spoke Spanish—or Greek? "Hungarian," she said.

"Well, my Hungarian friend, it seems the customers in the star seats were so busy watching your hair fall down last night that they didn't pay much attention to our featured act in the center ring. I'd call that trouble, wouldn't you?"

"It was accident—"

"Come now. You knew exactly what you were doing." He rubbed his chin and gave Oly a sidelong glance. "I have to admit the sight of all that red hair tumbling down was easy on the eyes. Which is why Mr. Sam is going to give you a chance to do something special. How does that strike you?"

It took a moment for Mara to find her voice. "Swell," she croaked, borrowing one of Clinker's pet words.

"Okay, so work out a short routine—say, three or four minutes—and we'll see what Mr. Sam has to say about it. Maybe we'll give you a spot at the end of the ballet. No promises, you understand. And keep this under your hat."

Mara returned to the dressing tent in a daze. The other women were too busy talking to notice when she dropped onto her cot, feeling a little weak. A chance to do a solo spot—was this one of the jokes the old-timers played on First of May guys? No—Oly wasn't the type for practical jokes. And neither was Konrad. So it must be genuine, and if she hoped to get that spot, she had to come up with something special. But what? How could she possibly work up a three-minute routine good enough to win her a solo when the tricks she knew were all so ordinary?

She was late dressing, and the other women had already left for the privilege tent, where snacks were sold after the cookhouse was closed for the night. Mara was usually ravenous after the evening performance, but tonight, since she had some thinking to do, she headed for the women's sleeper

car instead. She had almost reached the path that led to the
railroad tracks when she spotted Jocko's diminutive figure up
ahead.

Wanting his advice, she called to him to wait up, and hurried
toward him. It wasn't until she was close that she realized something was wrong, that he was having trouble keeping his balance.

"Ho, ho, ho," he said, swaying a little. "If it isn't our little
Romany—and all alone tonight. I thought you ballet girls only
moved en masse."

"I want to ask your advice," she said, ignoring his greeting.
In a few words, she told him about Konrad's offer, ending with
an appeal for help.

Jocko was silent for a while, thinking. "Do you remember
me telling you about Lillian Leitzel, the Alsatian aerialist who
does the flanges?"

Mara knew where he was heading and shook her head. "I
hate the flanges. They hurt."

"Maybe—but it might be the only way you can get that solo
slot. All it takes is a lot of practice—and some guts. Sure they
hurt, but all we artists suffer for our art." He pushed back his
hat, revealing a large swelling on his forehead.

At her look of dismay, he smiled crookedly. "Not to worry.
My head is the harder part of me. But I'd still like to lay a paddle
alongside that Charlie's head. He bashed me with a piece of
board, did it deliberately."

"Which one is Charlie?"

"That's a generic term. A Charlie is a guy who wears blackface and does a tramp act. This one wears an orange wig and a
big ego."

"I know one you mean. Are you okay? You look funny."

"My stock-in-trade," he said, grinning.

"Maybe you should see Doc McCall."

"All I need is a patch of brown paper and vinegar on me
bruises and maybe a wee kiss from me nanny to make the pain
go away."

Mara stared at him, frowning. Usually Jocko's voice was deep,
but also slightly nasal. Now it was pitched higher and she didn't
recognize his accent.

Jocko giggled; he seemed to be having a hard time focusing
his eyes. "Just a wee joke. We Irish do like to twit the toffs, you
understand."

"I thought you were English," she said crossly.

"Oh, I'm English, all right, but I identify with the Irish. Salt of the earth, the Irish. Cock of the walk, the Irish."

"Maybe you have concussion. I better walk you home," she said, making up her mind.

"Oh, yes. Do that. Take the little man by the hand and lead him to his beddybye. And if you're in the mood to be kind, join him under the covers and really comfort him."

He burst into tears.

Mara didn't know what to say, so she said nothing. As if he were a small boy, she took Jocko's hand and led him down the road toward the railroad siding where the circus train was parked. To her relief, because she didn't want to see Jocko shamed, no one else was on the road. Tomorrow was their first still day since they'd left Florida. Most of the circus people, knowing they could sleep later in the morning, would be celebrating, either in the privilege tent or in one of the bars near the fairgrounds.

As a star, Jocko rated an end compartment in Clown Alley, where the clowns were quartered. When they reached the pullman car, he leaned against the platform railing while he fumbled in his vest pocket, finally producing a key. Since he couldn't seem to find the keyhole, she took it away from him and unlocked the door.

The compartment sprang to life when she pressed the light switch just inside the door. Although small, it seemed like a palace compared to the cramped quarters she shared with the ballet troupe. Jocko had once told her that privacy was the rarest of commodities in a circus, and therefore the most precious. Although she didn't entirely agree, having had so little privacy in her own life, she looked around curiously, wondering how it felt to have so much room to one's self.

Jocko sank onto the lower bunk, already made up for the night, and closed his eyes. "Ah," he said. "These old bones just can't take the bumps like they used to."

"You ain't old."

"Aren't old, not ain't—remember we talked about that last week? And believe me, I am old—for a midget." He opened his red-rimmed eyes to stare at her. "We don't live long, you know."

"I don't believe that."

" 'Struth. Course, we do live longer than the giants. Those poor laddies' hearts just wear out, you know. Me, I'm all heart." He thumped his chest, then winced and coughed.

Mara took a concerned step toward him. "How bad are you hurt, Jocko?"

"Fatally. Would you cry if I died young?" he said hopefully.

"I would not cry," she lied. "I would feel sad, very sad, but I would not cry."

"You carry it all inside, do you? Maybe that's best. Never show the bastards you're hurting. It gives them too much pleasure."

"What can I do for you?"

"Ah, my love, give me your sweet hand. Hold on tight until I fall asleep, and in the morning, I'll be me old self again."

He hiccuped, negating the pathos in his voice, and she had to stifle a laugh. "I could use another wee drop of the demon rum. One of my fellow clowns gave me a few slugs out of compassion, but it's wearing off and I could use more." He waved toward a shelf above a tiny sink. "You'll find the rum over there."

She found the bottle and a glass, poured it half-full of rum, and handed it to Jocko. Jocko sipped it slowly, humming to himself. Mara curled up at the foot of the bunk, watching him with sleepy eyes. A group of men, laughing and exchanging good-natured banter, passed the window. Somewhere in the distance, she heard a train whistle, then the clatter of wheels on the main line.

Jocko began to sing, waving his glass in time with the music. "What is name of that song?" she asked curiously.

" 'Tis a lullaby, lass."

"Did your mother sing it to you?"

"No, not me mum. It was Aggie of the red hair and green eyes who taught me this lullaby. She was my nanny until I was fourteen, and she was as Irish as Patty's old sow, and I loved her and her green eyes and her clever hands and her soft, soft bosom. When I was very good, she let me brush her hair. She felt sorry for this poor weak laddie who was never going to grow up. They believed that then, you know. It gave them solace, all of them so ashamed of this changeling who'd befouled their aristocratic nest."

He paused to finish off the rum in his glass, to wipe his mouth. "The doctors told them I'd never live to be a man. So they tolerated me. Detested me, you understand, but since I wouldn't be around long, they did tolerate me. Only, I fooled them. Fourteen and I was still there. Sixteen and seventeen—would I never get around to dying? Then I was eighteen and here was this perfectly healthy tiny man, a bloody embarrassment to the whole family. While I was growing up, they kept me out of sight, locked away in a wing of the ole manse. I never even saw the village until I was eighteen. They didn't know what else to do with me, so they sent me away to school, and that's how I escaped. I got an education, and then I joined the circus and I've never been back.''

"And Aggie?"

"She returned to Ireland when they finally decided I didn't need a nanny anymore. But I won't forget you, sweet Aggie." He began to hum again.

"Is that how they talk in Ireland?"

"Sure and 'tis the gift of the Irish. Their voices roll off the tongue like honey, all sweetness and smooth as silk. Just like Aggie. She missed her family, you see, all those brothers and sisters. Sometimes, because I still fit on her lap, she forgot that I wasn't really a little boy anymore, and then she would hold me and stroke me and even more. Ah, to be almost a man and be allowed to suckle Aggie's soft breast! It was heaven, heaven indeed. Sometimes, when I couldn't sleep and was a bother, she did something very naughty with those clever hands of hers so she could get some peace and quiet. They used to do that, you know, some of the nannies. It kept the little boys in line— under their thumb, so to speak.''

Tears formed in the corners of his closed eyelids and ran down his cheeks. "I get so lonely. I thought I'd find friends among the other little people when I joined the circus, but it didn't happen. They've got small minds to match their small bodies, and they're all so vain, regular little popinjays, always quarreling and preening themselves. That's why I prefer the clowns.''

He began to cry again. Not knowing what to say to comfort him, Mara took his hand. He climbed into her lap and snuggled up close, and when he buried his face in the valley between her breasts, she didn't push him away, because there was something so natural about sitting there, holding his childlike body in her lap.

"Ah, sweet Aggie," he murmured, and his mouth moved in a suckling movement against her nipple. She knew she should stop him, but she sat on, letting him nuzzle her breast, because his need was so great, his loneliness even worse than hers. He fell asleep, and she settled him on his pillow and covered him with a quilt.

"Sleep well, little man," she said before she left the compartment, careful to set the lock before she closed the door.

CHAPTER 12

*T*O MARA'S RELIEF, WHEN SHE RAN INTO JOCKO IN THE backyard two days later, he was his usual irascible self. He thanked her for seeing him to his compartment, made a wry joke about not being able to hold his rum, and then confessed that the end of the evening was a blur to him, that he'd been hung over royally the next morning.

Mara was only too happy that he didn't remember, especially when he added that he'd had a dream so delicious that he wondered if he shouldn't switch from bootleg whiskey to smuggled rum. When he changed the subject and asked if she had decided what to do for her solo act, she lied and told him she was still working on it.

The truth was, she hadn't even started putting it together yet. The circus was playing a series of one-night stands, covering several river towns in southeastern Ohio. Since the show started packing up even before the final performance ended and didn't set up the workout tent on one-night stands, she hadn't had a chance to do any practicing. Like the other girls, she fell into her bunk at night, totally exhausted.

Oly approached her at the end of the week. "You ready to show your stuff to Mr. Sam?" he asked. "He's clearing time Sunday morning to look at some new routines. The Chung troupe has made some changes in their pyramid trick, and Jocko and some of the clowns have put together a new gag. I think I can fit you in—provided you're ready."

Mara nodded, sensing a warning in his words. He was telling her that this might be her only chance for a solo spot. If only she could come up with something really special, she would find a way to practice, even if she had to bribe one of the riggers to erect rigging for her in the big top early in the morning, doing it on the sly. But first she had to come up with something different, spectacular—but what? What could she, a beginner who had barely made the ballet troupe, do that would earn her a solo slot?

She took the problem to bed with her that night, and as she drifted toward sleep, something Jocko had said about concentrating on the flange turns came to her. Was that the answer? A routine based on a large number of them would be difficult because they demanded unusual upper body strength, vastly concentrated energy—and showmanship to put them across. They were also painful and dangerous. But did she have a choice? It was either this or she would lose the chance she'd been given. What was that odd expression Jocko used? No pain, no gain? Well, the gains would be worth any amount of pain—provided she could bring it off.

The next morning, when they were alone in the women's dressing tent, she told Clinker about the audition, that she planned to feature the flange move in her routine. She was warmed by Clinker's enthusiasm and instant offer to help. "Flange moves are tricky, but if anyone can do them, you can," she said. "You'll need a lot of practice, but the ring tent will be up during the Indianapolis and Terre Haute runs. And I've got something else that might help."

She went to the small metal locker at the foot of her cot, dug through it, finally producing a midnight-blue costume, shot through with glitter threads.

"Here. This is a costume I wore when I did my act with the family. I don't have any use for it, so you might as well wear it. It needs a good airing, but it's in perfect shape."

Mara held it up against her body, admiring the flash of brilliant blue sequins sewn into the neckline. A sudden doubt dampened her excitement. "It is okay to wear costume to audition?"

"You can always plead ignorance 'cause you're still a First of May guy," Clinker said, grinning.

"It is very beautiful." Mara wanted to throw her arms around Clinker and hug her, but she was too shy—or maybe too wary. "You are good friend, Clinker," she said instead. "Someday I find way to pay you back for this."

"I'll remember that when you're a big star. I may need a job or something. I can't work the webs for the rest of my life."

Mara looked at her doubtfully. Was she making a joke? It occurred to her that Clinker looked tired—and sad. In fact, she hadn't been her usual cheerful self for several days.

"Something is wrong, Clinker?" she asked.

"Oh, everything's peachy-keen. Johnny's been mooning around over one of the Klinski girls, the blond one with the twitchy tail." She gave a mirthless laugh. "Well, what the hell. That's how I got him."

Mara looked into her friend's wounded eyes. Clinker was hurting. But what could she say to help? She wasn't good at dealing with other people's problems. She wasn't all that good dealing with her own.

"He's dog meat," she said, her voice flat. Since this was the worst insult she could think of, one a Rom would kill over, she was surprised when Clinker laughed.

"You come up with the strangest things sometimes," Clinker said, shaking her head.

There was a rush of voices as the door at the end of the sleeper flew open and three of the ballet troupe came in. They had been to the privilege car, and it was obvious that someone had filled their hose flasks for them, because they were giggling like schoolgirls. Mara, watching her friend, noticed how strained Clinker's smile was, how dispirited she looked, for all that she added her usual wisecracks to the spirited conversation.

Was it ever safe to trust a man? She had met Clinker's Johnny, and she hadn't liked the bold way he looked at her. Sometimes she wondered if men hadn't been put on earth just to torment women. An image of Leo, his eyes like black marbles, made her wince. He seemed always to be underfoot lately. When she went to the cookhouse, more often than not he turned up at the same time. Although he never looked directly at her, she was all too aware of his dark presence.

Once, when she'd been waiting in the backyard with the other women for their cue, she had looked up to find him standing in the shadows, watching her, his expression so menacing that the hairs on the back of her neck had stirred.

Clinker touched her shoulder, reminding her that it was time to get dressed, and she put Leo out of her mind. She had other, more important things to worry about—such as putting together a routine for the solo spot audition.

* * *

Five days later, the first day of a five-day run in Indianapolis, she strolled into the ring tent where the audition was to be held, her head high, her smile radiating a confidence she didn't feel inside. To her relief, only Mr. Sam, Oly Johnson, and those acts that had new material to add to their routines were there. Although performing for an audience was the breath of life to her, today was different. For the program she planned, she needed all her concentration, and other circus people, the most critical of audiences, would be distracting.

She watched with only half her attention as the Chung troupe, a family group of acrobats, demonstrated a novelty twist to the standard pyramid trick, followed by Jocko, looking as dapper as always, even in exercise clothes, who did a routine with several other clowns that made Mara laugh and forget her nervousness for a little while.

And then, finally, Oly Johnson was calling her name and it was her turn.

Her smile deliberately provocative, she let the cape she'd borrowed from Clinker, which covered her from shoulder to feet, slowly slide to the ground, revealing her skimpy costume. She stepped out of the puddle of velvet, shaking herself slightly as if she were a cat.

Moving slowly, still smiling, she approached the rope. Her climb was a small masterpiece, something she had practiced at length the past few days. Rather than climbing the rope the conventional way, she slid upward, feet first, curling her body around the rope, progressing a couple of feet at a time.

That she had everybody's attention, she knew when the man who held the rope, a giant of a man named Lobo, who she'd heard was a mute, watched her progress openmouthed.

She reached the Roman rings and began to swing in a series of twisters, a flashy move that involved rotating her body between the rings. It was not particularly difficult, but she made it seem so by the rapidity of her swings.

As she plunged forward, catching herself with her feet, then swinging outward, her arms outstretched, a move Clinker had taught her, she directed her smile at Mr. Sam, knowing that he was the one who made the final decision. Since she hadn't had the time to perfect anything unusually difficult, she tried to make up for it by milking everything she could from each move, each gesture, knowing that the only chance she had was to sell herself, her own personality.

When the first minutes of her routine were over, she swung

over to a rope that had been fitted out with a swivel. She hooked her arm around it and made a graceful bow, then began to do flanges as rapidly as she was capable of, even though she preferred to do them much slower.

One . . . two . . . three . . .

An ache started up in her shoulder, then radiated down her arm, but she didn't slow down. Though her wrist seemed to be on fire, she kept going, swinging her body upward, over her shoulder as fast as she could, then dropping down again, only to start over again, the swivel above her creaking as if urging her on.

Her left wrist had gone numb now, for which she was grateful, and still there had been no sound from below.

Nine . . . ten . . . eleven . . .

She had planned to do fifteen, but desperation drove her on. Down below, a baritone voice, Jocko's voice, rang out, "Sixteen . . . seventeen . . . eighteen . . ."

A surge of energy, unexpected but welcome, gave her the strength to go on. She reached twenty, knew it was time to stop, but she gritted her teeth, summoned up one last bit of energy, and did one more, then flung her free arm out in an exuberant gesture that said, "Hey, look at me!" Below, someone applauded, and while she knew it must be Jocko, she felt a renewed confidence.

She slid down the rope, pausing halfway down to do a complete swing, her right arm and leg flung out in a joyous gesture, her left foot and arm twisted in the rope as an anchor. When she reached the bottom, the big rope man was smiling, bobbing his head like the Kewpie doll she'd bought at one of the midway concession stands with her first pay.

Aware of her audience, she smiled at him, then stood on her toes and gave him a kiss on his leathery cheek. His face turned fiery red, and as she walked toward Mr. Sam and Oly, she wondered if they thought this was a planned part of her act.

"Not bad," Oly said, which was his highest praise.

She smiled her appreciation, but it wasn't Oly who mattered. Mr. Sam was watching her with eyes that showed no warmth, and she braced herself for rejection.

"So why was your routine ten minutes long?" he demanded.

"I can cut flanges down—"

"How many flanges can you do?"

Mara hesitated, not knowing what to say. "How many you want, Mr. Sam?"

Mr. Sam glanced at Oly. "Sassy britches, isn't she? Well, let's give her a try, Oly. Get May and her women to whip her up a costume. White, I think, to show off that hair." He turned his attention back to Mara. "You think you can do twenty-five flanges, girl?"

Again, Mara hesitated. Her whole body ached; the tremor in her legs made it difficult to stand erect, and her wrist felt as if it had been scorched by fire, even though she had followed Clinker's advice and had soaked it in salt water several times a day to toughen the skin. She'd barely been able to do twenty-one flanges today. How could she manage four more?

On the other hand, how could she not?

She took a deep breath. "Duck soup, Mr. Sam," she said—which was another of Clinker's expressions.

"Okay, we'll give you one shot at it. You've got ten days to get it together. The Klinski troupe gave me notice, so there'll be a vacant time slot when we reach St. Louis on June twentieth. Twelve minutes, left ring, following the ballet routine. You'll be playing to the blue seats, and they're a tough audience, so don't get your hopes up too high."

Before she could thank him, he turned on his heel and walked away. Oly shook his head. "You sure you wanna do this? Twenty-five flanges twice a day will be murder." He gave her a thin smile. "Of course, if you bleed a little, you'll have them in your pocket. They love to see the red stuff flowing down a female arm."

Mara frowned at him. "That is joke?"

"Yeah, a joke. Forget I said it. Wrap some tape around that wrist, you hear? You don't want any infections."

After he had left, Mara stared after him. He had sounded—well, almost fatherly. A sudden surge of excitement drove the thought away. She had done it! She had a twelve-minute solo spot! Of course, she had to do fifty flanges a day to keep it, but that was a small price to pay. What was a little pain next to doing a solo?

Oly caught up with Mr. Sam outside the ring tent. "Whatta you think?" he asked.

"About what?"

"About the redhead's routine."

"That it was just that—routine. Luckily, Leo's women don't last long, so we play along, keep him happy, and hope it peters out soon."

Oly shook his head. "I think you're letting your prejudices cloud your judgment, Sam. I was watching that big guy, Lobo, while the girl was performing. He's held rope for every little twit that's come along the past twelve years, but you would've thought he'd just been given an Annie Oakley to heaven when she kissed him. She's going to be a drawing card. Mark my word."

"Maybe. But I don't like being put in the position of pimping for that bastard Leo. Let him do his own courting."

"Something funny about that business. Mueller practically forces you to give the girl a solo spot, and yet he never goes near her. What the hell's going on, anyway?"

"Who knows? Who cares? Maybe they get together late at night. All I know is he put on the pressure and I had to cave in or lose our top artiste. But as soon as he dumps her, she's off the lot."

"Well, it's your show," Oly said. "But I'll tell you something—I think she's going to make you eat your words."

Mr. Sam gave him a wolfish smile. "Maybe. But she's also going to have a mighty sore wrist the next time she crawls in bed with that bastard. Double those twenty-five flanges every day and you've got one sore little bimbo. In fact, I got my doubts she can do them."

Oly shrugged. "You could be wrong. We'll find out when we reach St. Louis, won't we?"

CHAPTER 13

MARA LAY IN HER UPPER BERTH, PRETENDING TO BE TAKING a nap, listening to the other women talking. It was a free day, between Fort Wayne and Indianapolis, and they were taking advantage of it to go into town.

They had invited her to join them, but she'd given the excuse that she didn't feel well. They were all wearing their best outfits, the pumps and flesh-colored hose, the barrel-shaped skirts and big-brimmed hats she coveted, and she was very much aware how she'd stand out among them in her shabby, outdated clothes.

But that wasn't the only reason she'd turned down the invitation. Today, at two o'clock, she was going to sign a contract with Mr. Sam.

Despite her excitement, she hadn't told the other women about the contract, not even Clinker. If she said too much, she would sound vain. Too little and she would seem secretive. It was a problem, all right. Maybe she'd ask Jocko's advice today when they had lunch together—which was the third reason why she couldn't go shopping with the other women.

Jocko had caught up with her yesterday as she was leaving the women's dressing tent.

"So you pulled it off," was his greeting.

She pretended ignorance. "Pulled it off? What does that mean?"

"Don't try that innocent act on me," he said. "You're signing a contract with Mr. Sam tomorrow at two."

His smug smile was irritating. "How do you know that?" she said stiffly.

"Oh, I have my sources. How about a celebration—say, lunch in town?"

She shook her head. "I got nothing nice to wear," she said.

His eyes twinkled at her. "My, my. You *are* changing. You sound just like a normal woman."

She glared at him. "What does *that* mean?"

"Never mind that. I can loan you—"

"I got money. I don't want to spend it."

"If you want to be a star, then dress like one. Call it an investment—like buying your own rigging eventually." He studied her thoughtfully. "Why don't I take you shopping before we have lunch? I'll borrow Mr. Sam's touring car and arrange for a driver. I'd learn to drive, only it could be a little sticky, reaching the brake pedal with twelve-inch legs."

Mara smiled at his joke. "Okay—but I don't want to spend much money."

"I promise you'll get bargains you won't believe," he said. "I'll pick you up at ten. That'll give us plenty of time to shop, have lunch, and get you back here in time to sign the contract."

As soon as Clinker and the other women left on their shopping trip, Mara climbed down from her berth and went to get a bucket of water. Although it was supposed to be delivered to the women each day, more often than not the ballet women had to fetch their own from the water car. The water sloshed on her skirt as she carried the bucket to the zinc-lined cubicle that served the sleeping car as a bathhouse. The water was very cold, but she hardly noticed as she washed and rinsed her hair, took a sponge bath, then poured the water into the drain in the floor.

She put on the cotton coverall she used as a robe, and with her hair wrapped in a strip of linen toweling, she left the sleeper and found a private spot over the rim of a hill, out of sight of the train.

Sitting in the sun, she tossed her hair with her hand to dry it, her thoughts on the coming meeting with Mr. Sam. He had offered it out of the blue, even before he saw her first solo performance, slated for the circus's final matinee in St. Louis. She had been floating on air ever since. A sudden flicker of fear struck her. When, in all her life, had things ever gone smoothly for her? Maybe it was wrong, dangerous, to feel so happy before she had signed the contract.

Almost as if her own thoughts had conjured up the devil, a hard hand grabbed a hunk of her hair and jerked her head backward. Above her, she saw Leo's inverted face. His eyes had a feverish look, and his skin was flushed. He smiled at her, and her flesh crawled with revulsion. Fear, primitive and instinctive, paralyzed her even before he slid his free hand around her throat, squeezed hard.

"See how easy it would be to break your neck," he purred. "Just one little twist and it would all be over for you. Then it would be Jocko's turn. If I stepped on that little maggot, I could squash him like a bug." He gave her hair another painful jerk. "For now, this is just a warning. In my own good time, I'll collect what's due me. And don't feel too cocky because you've got a solo. I could get you fired as easily as I got you that contract."

A moment later, she was alone.

Mara sat there frozen, trying to make sense out of Leo's threats. Collect what was due to him? But he'd already done that, already had her two times. Get her fired as easily as he'd gotten her the contract? But that wasn't true! She'd *earned* that solo spot. So why had he lied? And why had he waited so long to confront her? Did he want to make sure she had something to lose before he threatened her? It was all so crazy. . . . Was *that* the answer? Was Leo Mueller crazy, like most of the circus people believed?

A shudder, then another, ran through her. She realized she was cold to the bone, even though the sun was so hot. Suddenly the privacy she'd sought a few minutes earlier was terrifying. She grabbed up her towel and scrambled down the cindery side of the hill to the railroad spur. By the time she had reached the sleeper, she was shaking as if she had caught a chill.

But her own cowardly reaction shamed her. Leo had routed her so easily—and she's always prided herself on her own courage. Even when she'd had nothing else, she had always had that. Wanting to dispel the fear, she tried to whip up her anger. How dare Leo put his hands on her, threaten her, tell those lies! And why hadn't he done more? He hadn't tried to rape her, hadn't even kissed or fondled her. So what was he up to, anyway?

An hour later, Jocko came to pick her up in Mr. Sam's touring car. The driver was the big mute who had held Mara's rope during her audition. He smiled broadly, showing a set of very large teeth, when she spoke to him. He held the door open for her, then took his place behind the wheel and busied himself with the gear.

Jocko listened, looking very thoughtful, while she told him about Leo's threats, but to her surprise, he brushed them aside. "Don't fret about Leo, Mara. Just put it out of your mind, relax, and enjoy this outing. As for Leo getting you the contract—I doubt that very much. You were great at your audition—you even surprised me."

On the drive into Indianapolis, Jocko talked nonstop, telling Mara about his early days in the circus and his struggle to gain a reputation as a producing clown.

"Why didn't you get job with Barnum & Bailey?" she asked. "I hear all circus artistes want to work there."

"B&B is loaded with clowns. I'd just be one of the pack—or an anomaly, putting in a dozen shows a day in the ten-in-one. Here I'm a star. Consider this if you're ever tempted to try for the Big One. Better to be a big frog in a little pond. Which doesn't mean you have to sign your bloody life away today. Look, why don't I check out that contract for you? Mr. Sam's as honest as they come, but he's also a businessman. His standard contracts are pretty one-sided. They protect the circus, but don't do much for the performer."

Mara, silenced by a sudden thought, didn't answer him. That contract—how was she going to sign it when she didn't know how to write? She couldn't just make an X—it would be too humiliating, and besides, it would show a weakness other people could take advantage of.

"What is it, Mara?" Jocko asked. "Something bothering you?"

She glanced at the driver. Even though Lobo seemed to be absorbed in his driving, she lowered her voice. "I don't know how to read or write," she confessed.

Jocko whistled softly. "Now, why didn't I think of that? How would a Rom kid learn to read and write? Look, you only have to manage the four letters in *Mara*. I can teach you how before two o'clock."

"What about a last name?"

"Your name is Mara—period."

Mara smiled with relief. "Thank you, Jocko. You're very good friend—like Clinker. Someday I pay you both back."

"I'll settle for a kiss. As for poor Clinker, I suspect you'll get your chance pretty soon."

Knowing his penchant for gossip, Mara was tempted to change the subject. But she found herself asking, "What you mean?"

"It's that cretin she's so crazy about. He's leaving the show. The Klinski troupe has signed up with the Lasky Brothers Circus. Mr. Sam is furious. This is the fifth act Joe Lasky has lured away in two years."

"You sure of this?"

"I'm sure. That bloody Johnny is marrying one of the Klinski girls. Best thing that could happen to Clinker, but I don't think she'll see it that way."

Mara sighed. "She will be so hurt. Why men treat women like that? I am never going to let a man make me unhappy."

"Don't bet on it. When you fall for some fellow, you'll be just like the rest of us—ruled by your glands. I just hope he deserves you, but I doubt he will."

She was trying to decide if this was a compliment when the car pulled to the curb in front of an elegant-looking shop. The driver helped Mara out of the car as if she were made of spun sugar, but he left Jocko to struggle out of the backseat on his own.

"Wait here, Lobo," Jocko told the big mute imperiously.

Like he's been ordering people around all his life, Mara thought. And maybe he had. After the evening she'd put him to bed, she had asked Clinker what a nanny was, and had been told they were nursemaids, hired to look after rich people's kids.

The store was cool after the June heat outside. To Mara's surprise, there was no racks of clothing in sight, only deep sofas and chairs, muted lighting, a mirrored wall. A tall, thin saleswoman hurried toward them, her smile ingratiating. From the way she greeted Jocko, calling him Lord Denison, it was obvious she knew him—and valued his patronage.

"My friend is shopping for a day dress, something simple but with a flair," Jocko told her. "She'll need accessories—lingerie, hose, a scarf, pumps, that sort of thing—too."

Mara glared at him, aghast. "I don't have money for all that!" she protested.

"Not to worry. The prices here are quite reasonable." He looked at the saleswoman, his eyebrows twitching. "I'll have Mrs. Edwards put your purchases on my own account. We can settle up later, Mara."

"Oh, of course, Lord Denison," the woman said quickly. "Any friend of yours—"

"And we're in a bit of a rush," Jocko interrupted. After she'd hurried away, Jocko grinned up at Mara. "As you can see, I've dealt here before. The lady thinks I'm a real English lord. And loaded to the gills. Even if I had four arms, I'd get top treatment."

Mara mulled this over for a few seconds. "I don't want to cheat nobody. I don't do that no more—anymore—not since I left the *kumpania*," she said.

"Ah, Mara, you are a treasure. There's no cheating involved here. I'll pay the tab, and when you get the money, you can pay me back."

"And what if I cannot pay you? What if Leo tells Mr. Sam to fire me?"

"Believe me, that's not going to happen." He smiled, looking like a small, mischievous imp. "Besides, I have the utmost faith in your drive to succeed."

The woman returned, carrying an armload of dresses. Half an hour later, Mara was the proud possessor of not one, but two new dresses—she who had never before owned even one new garment. At Jocko's insistence, she also chose two pretty blouses and a skirt in the new shorter length, a selection of underwear—which Mrs. Edwards informed her the fashion magazines were beginning to call "undies"—plus a pair of low-cut pumps that made her ankles and legs look very slender.

Mara regarded her old clumsy shoes, hand-me-downs from Berty, with disdain, tempted to toss them out. Prudently she had the woman wrap them up, along with her other old clothes, including her patched underwear, to take away with her.

Wearing a pale green muslin shift with a lowered waistline that the saleswoman assured her was the latest style, and the prized new pumps, she accompanied Jocko to the restaurant he'd chosen. Although she was proud of her new dress, especially when the price was so low, she would have preferred a bright red one with a draped skirt that had caught her eye. Jocko had talked her out of it, but she still had a few wistful thoughts about it.

"Only the best for us," he said airily when she commented on the elegance of the restaurant—and the flattering attention of the dandy who ushered them to their seat. Again, Jocko was fawned upon, and since she'd seen him slip a bill into the man's hand, she wondered if it was this rather than his fake title that got him so much respect.

His diminutive size evoked sidelong glances and whispers from other patrons; like Jocko, she ignored the stares.

"I've arranged for someone to join us for coffee," Jocko said after he'd ordered for them. "I think you'll find him interesting."

Although Mara didn't recognize anything she was served, the food was so good that she stuffed herself, glad that Jocko seemed disinclined to talk. She leaned back finally with a sigh of satisfaction. "That was good," she said. "What is escargot?"

"Believe me, you don't want to know. This is one of the few restaurants in the vast wasteland of culture west of New York that serves it. Do you want dessert?"

Mara regarded the dessert cart with greedy eyes, finally choosing chocolate cake with chocolate icing. Jocko refused dessert, settling for coffee instead. When Mara had finished her cake, he produced a pad of paper and a pencil, placed them in front of her.

"Time for your lesson. It's easy—just watch what I do and copy it."

But it didn't seem easy to Mara. Although she could dip her hand into a *gadjo*'s rear pocket at a county fair and extract a fat wallet and never get caught, she found it incredibly hard to manipulate the pencil, which seemed to have a will of its own. It angered her that it took so many tries before she finally produced a decent copy of the four letters Jocko had written out for her.

"Now, here's where it gets a little tricky," Jocko said. "When you sign your name, Mr. Sam's going to ask you for the rest of it, and that's when you tell him you only have one name. What did you call yourself when you applied for a job with the circus?''

"Just plain Mara. I don't know what is written on my pay envelopes, but I think it has these four letters."

"Good. Just tell Mr. Sam that's all there is. If he persists, get a little testy."

"Why don't I make up last name? I have time to learn to write it—"

"Mara is enough. When you get very famous, it will be a plus. Nothing like a little mystery to enhance a reputation."

"You sure that will happen?"

"Aren't you? If you aren't, you've already lost the battle."

"I am sure," she said, wishing she felt as confident as she sounded.

"So let's hear no more doubts."

He looked up as a tall, thin man came into the dining room. "And that's my guest, Woody Stern," he said, pocketing the pencil and pad. "For the next few minutes, I want you to do a lot of smiling and no more talking than necessary. Take your cue from me."

Mara eyed the man curiously. *Old,* she thought; then, as he came closer, she decided it was his rimless glasses and unfashionably long hair that made him seem old. He looked so out of place in the fancy restaurant that she was surprised that the man Jocko called the maître d' was personally escorting him to their table.

At Jocko's invitation, the man sat down across from Mara. His eyes, very sharp behind the glasses, surveyed her. "I see you've brought a friend along for your interview, Jocko."

"You have that wrong, Woody," Jocko drawled. "It's my friend you're here to interview."

The man looked disappointed. "I'm sure she's a very nice person, but you're the celebrity."

"You'll have to trust me on this. Every time we play St. Louis, I give you a good story well in advance and a handle to hang it on. That hasn't changed. I promised you something special and you'll have it."

"What's the angle?"

"Cinderella—with one big difference."

"Such as?"

"This Cinderella started out as a princess—a Romany princess. The daughter of a king."

"Come off it. Gypsies don't have kings."

"A rose by any other name—" Jocko shrugged. "The point is that people believe they do."

"Okay. People believe they do. So her father was tribal leader or something. So let's call him a king and her a princess. Who's going to believe that?"

"Look at her. Doesn't she look like a princess?"

The man studied Mara closely. "You really a Rom, kid?"

Mara had been listening in bewilderment and growing anger. Jocko had promised to keep her secret, yet here he was telling this man that she was a Rom.

Jocko gave her a bland smile. "Say something in Romany for Woody, Mara," he said.

She glared at him and spat out a curse—in Romany.

"See? Romany."

"That could be Sanskrit for all I know. But what the hell. It's a good story—provided she has enough talent to make it worthwhile. What does she do, anyway? Get blown out of a cannon?"

Mara had had enough of being treated as if she weren't there. "I'm an aerialist," she said indignantly.

"Temper, temper," the man said, but he was smiling now. "She's got spunk, Jocko."

"Wrong word. Make that fiery-tempered," Jocko advised.

"That red hair—is it natural?"

Mara bristled again. "It is."

"I believe it. It matches the temper—and that white, white skin."

"Alabaster skin. Emerald-green eyes. Flame-colored hair—do I have to teach you your profession?" Jocko said.

"Got it," Woody said, obviously amused. "Is she good on the trap?"

Again Mara answered. "I am very good. I can do—uh, thirty flanges."

He whistled softly. "That's almost as good as Lillian Leitzel. It takes a lot of strength to do that many flanges. Is this on the level, Jocko?"

"Of course. Would the little lady lie? But she only does that many on very special occasions," Jocko added hastily. "She's a superb showman. When she's in the arena, no one watches the other performers. Put that in your article."

"You mean you haven't already written it for me?"

"You're the journalist."

"And you're a pushy little devil. This is almost as good as that yarn about you being English royalty. I looked it up once, you know. There *is* a titled family named Denison in Surrey, but they've never had a dwarf in the family."

"Midget. I'm a midget, not a dwarf. And you're missing the point. The circus is synonymous with magic, legends, fairy tales. People want to believe in midgets with titles, and Gypsy princesses."

"Well, why not? As long as it's good press, why not?"

"Then you'll write an article about Mara?"

"Maybe. What's her last name, by the way?"

"Just Mara. She does have a family name, but she can't use it—"

"Most Roms come with fifteen different names. They change them at the county line," Woody said.

"—because she has her pride. Her family disowned her because she wanted to join a circus. She swore then that she'd never use her family name—or any name except Mara. That's why I said it was a Cinderella story with a twist. She arrived in winter quarters without a dime to her name, but she was so talented that Mr. Sam hired her immediately. Now she's on the verge of stardom. It's an incredible story of talent and pure guts winning out over all the odds."

"Incredible is right. If she's so talented, how come I haven't read anything about her in *Billboard*? She's not on any of the posters I've seen around town or in the advertising Mr. Sam placed in our paper."

"Because Mr. Sam didn't have her under contract. Some technicality because of her age. Now she's eighteen, and she's going to sign with him this afternoon."

Woody regarded him thoughtfully. "You promise I won't be making a fool out of myself if I print all this as fact?"

Jocko placed his hand on his heart, looking very earnest. "I swear it's essentially the truth—with an interesting twist or two."

"It's those twists I'm afraid of. Okay, I'll play along with you, but I have a price. You know I'm a circus fan, a member of the Circus Fans of America, don't you? So in return for this favor"—he gave Jocko a sly look—"I get to play clown at an evening performance."

"It's a deal. I'll square it with Konrad, our equestrian director. How good are you on a horse? You want to be a Joey?"

"Just a plain hobo will do." Woody's voice was dry. "Don't do me any special favors."

"I'll tell the boys to go easy on you. Of course, you're taking a chance. They're a perverse lot."

"Don't I know it," the man groaned, but he was looking very pleased with himself, Mara decided.

For the next few minutes, he queried Mara. She reaffirmed Jocko's version of her story, and Woody Stern seemed satisfied—or if he wasn't, he kept his doubts to himself.

After he'd taken himself off, saying he had a deadline to meet, she surveyed Jocko with mixed emotions. His lies had been as convincing as any Rom *boojo* woman. But he wasn't a Rom. He was *gadjo*—how had he learned to lie so convincingly?

"You think he believe all those lies?" she asked.

"Not for a moment. But he'll print the article about you— and he'll make it sound believable. You have to have a gimmick, something different, in this game. You could be the greatest aerialist in the world, but without flash, something that sets you apart, you'll never become a star. That's the reason for the costumes, the animals, the drum rolls when the acrobats do a special trick or the clowns take a pratfall. It's all part of the game. Magic. Illusion. They want to be fooled, to be bedazzled. Everything in the circus must be larger than life. They lead such drab lives out on the prairies or in the industrial towns or on the gray streets of the big cities. They come to the circus looking for an escape from reality, and we give it to them. If the circus ever gets too sophisticated, too sleek and polished, it will lose the magic. But meanwhile it still works. That's why you're headed for the top. You have the touch. Not an especially great talent, but something extra that makes them believe in the magic for a little while."

His words stirred Mara. Of course—didn't she feel that magic every time the music started and the first clown appeared in the arena? Hadn't she felt it the day she'd seen her first circus? And that magic had never failed her even through the worst miseries of her childhood.

Suddenly, as if it had just happened, she found herself telling Jocko about a seven-year-old runaway who, hidden under a big top bandstand, had seen something so magical that it had changed her life.

"Man who owned circus was name Arnie. Fat lady was Miss Tanya—and woman on trapeze, I think it was Glory or something like that."

"Could've been Arnie Malichi's show. If so, the aerialist was Gloria Gibson—she worked for Arnie for years. Small-time mudshow, but clean," Jocko said.

"Is Gloria still with mudshow?"

"Lord, no. She must be in her late forties now."

"You know where she is?"

Jocko took out his wallet and dropped several bills on the silver tray at his elbow. "Would you believe that she fell in love with a visiting prince, got married, and is now living in a castle in Spain?"

"No. Why you lie like that?" she said crossly.

"I'm hurt by your mistrust. It's the truth, so help me."

"I think you got Rom blood in you," she grumbled.

"Not unless one of my female ancestors was fooling around with a raggle-taggle Gypsy-o. I'm the product of nine generations of English nobility. And no one in the circus is going to believe you're a Gypsy princess any more than they believe I'm an English lord. Which is what makes it so delicious. The exposé, that you aren't really a Gypsy, that some journalist is going to write about you once you're a star will give you priceless publicity. Later on, you'll issue a statement, saying that whole business was made up by a press man, that you're really from a noble Italian family. That should rate almost as much attention as the Fatty Arbuckle scandal."

"Who she?" she asked, and was nonplussed when he laughed uproariously. He wiped his eyes finally and told her, "Sorry. I apologize. Just don't change too much. Where would I get my laugh for the day? And it's time we head back to the lot. I think Mr. Sam is in for quite a surprise."

Not sure what kind of surprise he meant—and too irritated to ask—Mara didn't answer. One thing was becoming increasingly clear to her. There was a lot more to this business of being a *gadjo* than she'd suspected. Sometimes it seemed to her that they spoke a different language from the one she'd learned so painfully. Their words didn't seem to mean the same thing twice. Maybe these people thought differently. The rules seemed to change, according to whom she was with. How was she ever going to understand them?

"Since you never seem to know what the time is, I got you a little present," Jocko said, his voice so offhand that she was caught by surprise when he laid a velvet box on the table in front of her. She opened it carefully, half expecting something to

jump out at her. When she saw the tiny gold watch brooch, she
gave a cry of delight.

"But I can't tell time," she wailed.

"So I'll teach you. Who would have thought, when I was
studying my Latin verbs, that I would someday be teaching a
young Gypsy to tell time. How old are you, Mara? And I want
the truth this time."

"Seventeen—well, I will be seventeen."

"Sixteen . . . I thought as much. If anyone asks, be a little
coy, but intimate you're over eighteen."

"What is *intimate*?"

"Hint. You can do that, can't you?"

Her temper stirred. "You are very good friend, do lots of
good things for me, but I don't like it when you laugh at me."

"I apologize again. That's one of my worse traits. Put the
bastards down before they put me down. I promise not to do it
again to you. Pax?"

"Pax," she said, although she had no idea what the word
meant.

"Then we're friends again." He took his own watch out of
his vest pocket and looked at it. "It's time to go. And when we
go out the door, don't look back. It's a superstition with me to
never look back. It's bad for the liver."

Since this was one of his remarks that was meaningless to her,
Mara pinned the watch to her dress, admiring the way the tiny
stones that surrounded it flashed in the soft light of the restaurant. Those couldn't be real diamonds, of course, but that didn't
matter. It was the most beautiful thing she'd ever owned.

"I am going to keep watch forever," she told Jocko.

"It won't be the last gift you receive from a man," Jocko
said, and his voice held sadness.

Mara bent forward to kiss his cheek. "But it will always be
the one I like best."

Mara told Clinker about the contract three days later when
they were dressing for the matinee show. Although she lowered
her voice so the other girls wouldn't hear, she wondered why
she bothered. After all, they would all know when they reached
St. Louis and she did her first solo—but somehow it seemed
important to tell Clinker first.

Clinker hugged her excitedly. "I guessed it," she declared.
"I saw you and Jocko going into the Silver Wagon on our free
day, and I just knew Mr. Sam was giving you a contract for a

solo spot! I waited for you to say something, was going to just come out and ask you about it this morning, but then I heard that business about Leo Mueller and it went right out of my mind."

"Leo Mueller? What has happen to Leo?" Mara said sharply.

"You haven't heard? It's all over the circus. I hear Mr. Sam about had a fit. Leo is the circus's biggest drawing card—"

"What is happen to Leo?" Mara demanded.

"Why, he was picked up by the police while he was eating lunch at some restaurant in town yesterday. Someone phoned in an anonymous tip and they found hashish sewed into his jacket lining. I hear it took three of them to get handcuffs on him, and now the charge is assaulting an officer. He swears someone framed him. Nobody believes that, of course, except Danielle Dubois. Sure, no one likes him, but who would frame him?"

Jocko would, Mara thought. Jocko, who had a way with a needle and who thought like a Rom. Was that why he'd been so unconcerned when she'd told him about Leo's threats?

She shook her head, repudiating the suspicion. Why would Jocko do such a dangerous thing? No, it had nothing to do with Jocko—or with her. What's more, she intended to put it out of her mind. . . .

She began applying her makeup. As she looked in the mirror, she realized she was smiling. That's when it came to her that for the first time since Leo had raped her, she was free of fear.

CHAPTER 14

*D*URING THE NEXT TEN DAYS, AS THE CIRCUS PLAYED AN Kentucky county fair, then crossed the Ohio for a five-day run at another fair in Indiana, Mara concentrated upon improving her act. Clinker, unlike the other ballet girls, who obviously resented Mara's chance at a solo, was genuinely delighted. Generous as ever, she helped with the finer points of timing and presentation, showing her tricks that came from her own extensive experience. When Mara asked why she'd never tried for her own solo, she smiled a little wanly and said that she and Johnny planned to do a double after they were married. Jocko, true to his word, supervised what he called the showmanship factor, teaching her how to make the grand gesture (his words), how to play to the crowd. She didn't resent his constant corrections of her grammar, even though he was often a little sharp. After all, she needed every weapon she could get if she hoped to become a star.

Just before her debut in St. Louis, he brought her a wide copper bracelet and told her to wear it on her left wrist during her performance.

"Let the audience think the bracelets cover scars from doing the flanges. The trick is to make them believe that you suffer agonies for your art, just to give them entertainment."

"It *is* painful," she retorted.

"Pratfalls are painful, too. So is a fork-jump onto the back of a rosinback. Have you ever noticed how often the high-wirers miss their big plays the first time? Then they grit their teeth, climb back on the wire, and this time, they do it right. That's showmanship. How can the audience know how hard a trick is if it looks too easy? I get knocked about every walk-around. Pathos. This poor little clown getting the stuffing knocked out of him by those big bullies. But I always pick myself up and start back in again. That's showmanship. If you can convince the crowd that the flanges are painful and you're suffering, yet you can still come up with a brave smile, they won't notice that the other aerialists can outperform you by a country mile, old dear."

Mara was thoughtful after she left Jocko. She didn't need him to tell her that she didn't have the skills of the other featured artistes. But maybe she could give the audience something just as important.

The next morning, before the flag was up, she went to the cookhouse. When she asked Cookie, a round, jolly man who fit the traditional nickname of circus cooks, for a sliver of raw liver, he didn't seem surprised, and she wondered if, after years with the circus, anything could surprise him.

She put the piece of waxed paper he gave her in her pocket, and later, after she'd changed into the new white satin costume the wardrobe woman had made up for her, she made sure that everybody was busy with their own preparations before she unwrapped the tiny piece of liver and carefully slid it under the copper bracelet on her left wrist.

"Hey, you really look divine," Clinker said, her eyes admiring. "Old May really did a good job on that costume."

Mara ageed. When she'd first tried it on, she had been stunned by her resemblance to the woman who had inspired her dream of someday becoming an aerialist. For a moment, her eyes had smarted so much that she'd had to turn away from the wardrobe mistress, afraid her tears might be misunderstood.

"Thank you for your help, Clinker," she said now. The words came out a little stiff; she'd had so few occasions in her life to express gratitude. "If I can ever do anything for you, just ask."

"I've got everything I want," Clinker said, her voice lilting. "Johnny is meeting me after the evening performance. He's got something to tell me. He says it's real important." She hugged Mara suddenly, her thin face flushed and almost pretty. "I think he's bought me a ring. God, I'm happy, Mara."

Mara regarded her doubtfully. Did Johnny plan to take Clinker with him when he moved to the Lasky Circus with the Klinski troupe? Clinker hadn't mentioned that move—maybe Jocko was wrong about Johnny marrying into the Klinskis. Well, it wasn't any of her business, and yet—she hoped Clinker would get her ring tonight.

As they waited at the back door, ready to take their places in the spec line-up, she watched the audience over the heads of the clowns. Although it wasn't a straw crowd, with an overflow crowd sitting on the straw in front of the blue seats, all the stands, even the more expensive star seats in the middle, were full, unusual for an overcast afternoon that promised rain.

Above the blare of the band, she heard the deep-throated sound of the noisy crowd, a surprising number of them men, and it seemed to her there was too much milling around. Once there was a disturbance in the blue seats, and several of Mr. Sam's "pretty boys," the men who kept order in the Big Top, rushed to stop a fight that had broken out.

The applause, as the ballet women rode around the track on their white Percherons, usually a cue for sustained whistles and catcalls, was scattered, and some of Mara's high excitement faded.

Jocko, wearing his jester outfit, did a cartwheel in front of the ballet troupe and then made a low bow and doffed his peaked hat to her. Was he wishing her luck or trying to warn her that the crowd was restless today?

One thing in her favor—with the audience so unruly, Mr. Sam wouldn't have much time to watch the individual performances. In fact, no one of importance would be watching, not during a matinee.

But she was wrong about that. As she waited at the back door for the musical cue that would send her running out into the arena, one of the clowns came up.

"Knock 'em dead, princess," he said.

The voice was familiar. She looked closer and recognized Woody Stern, the newspaper journalist who had interviewed her earlier. He was done up in blackface with huge white dominoes outlining his eyes, the standard makeup for "guest clowns" to distinguish them easily from the regular clowns. This was supposed to assure that they got special treatment and didn't get knocked around.

Not that the clowns always followed this rule, Jocko had told Mara. On one notorious occasion, fed up with a rash of guest clowns who complicated their already complicated gags, they roughed up the governor of Indiana so badly that he ended up with a black eye. The legend went that he told everybody afterward he'd had the time of his life.

Mara nodded to Woody, noting that his real smile was almost as broad as the one painted on his face. Questions filled her mind. What if she failed tonight? What kind of article would he write about her then?

Her debut spot followed the clowns' second feature appearance, near the end of the show. Her cue—a few bars of "Stars and Stripes Forever"—came, and she ran out into the arena, was introduced briefly by Konrad, along with a risley group, a family of five brothers, and in the center ring, Danielle Dubois, the equestrienne.

After she'd climbed the rope the big mute held, and started her routine, she was aware that she wasn't doing her best. Once, when she paused at the end of a flashy series of twists to bow and smile brightly, she caught a glimpse of Mr. Sam, standing in the performers' entrance. From the sour expression on his face, he wasn't pleased, probably because the applause for all three acts was almost nonexistent.

Afraid of being ignobly returned to the ballet after one solo performance, Mara threw herself into the rest of her routine, projecting all the energy she could summon.

In the center ring, Danielle Dubois was taking her prize Arabian, Abdul, through its paces, and Mara was aware that most of the attention, even from the blue seats, was on the equestrienne. She tried to pump excitement into her smile, using the tricks Jock had taught her, but it was no use. She felt a choking panic; nothing she was doing seemed to attract the wandering attention of the audience.

Then Konrad's booming voice was announcing her flanges, explaining how difficult they were. It was a rare concession, giving a side ring act this special attention, and Mara felt a renewed surge of confidence. Her reception had been lukewarm, she told herself, but that was before they'd seen her perform the flanges.

Perched on a ring, she flung her arms out wide, smiling broadly, then swung over to the rope. She looped it around her wrist and then she was turning, twisting, throwing her body upward, arching her back, extending her legs and free arm, letting momentum straighten her body again. It was showy, exciting, but there was no gasp of appreciation from the audience, no counting of the flange moves. They watched, but in silence, obviously not impressed. Desperately, she increased her pace even though her shoulder was already aching so badly she was sure it was disjointed.

Then, from below, one lonely male voice called out, "Nine . . . ten . . . eleven. . . ."

Another voice, also male, took it up. "—twelve . . . thirteen . . . fourteen. . . ."

And then there were a dozen voices, and a rush of energy galvanized Mara. She increased her pace once more, and as she slipped into a roll, she brushed her hand against the brooch that held back her hair, and it fell to the tanbark below. When her hair billowed out around her, she heard a collective gasp from the crowd and knew she was finally getting their attention.

The crowd took up the chant, "—seventeen . . . eighteen . . . nineteen. . . ." and confidence flooded her. She went all out, not caring that later, she would regret it, glorying in being the center of attention. On her twenty-fifth turn, where she had planned to stop, she winced, as if she felt a rush of pain, and pressed hard against the bracelet on her left wrist, crushing the bit of liver hidden there.

"—twenty-three . . . twenty-four . . . twenty-five," the audience chanted.

She felt a trickle of blood from the crushed sliver of liver running down her arm, but still she went on, doing one more turn, even though she knew her twelve minutes were up.

Her smile a little trembly, she waved and blew kisses to the audience, and when she descended, stopping halfway down the rope to take a bow and do a saucy little turn, the crowd roared their approval of this brave little lady who had ignored her pain and the blood running down her arm to give them a good show. Exhilarated and excited, she dashed toward the back door, almost knocking Mr. Sam down.

"Watch your time. You ran over twelve minutes," he said, but his voice was less gruff than usual. "And get some salve from Doc McCall for that wrist."

Before she returned to the dressing tent to change her clothes, she discarded the sliver of liver in a trash bin. Not every time, she thought, but on the big shows, the really special ones . . .

Jocko was waiting for her when she came out of the tent. "Tricky, aren't you? Well, don't get caught. That sort of thing can backfire on you."

"How did you—what you talking about?" she said.

"Cookie is an old friend of mine, so it won't get around, but—be careful, you understand?"

"Okay," she said, relaxing.

"How about joining me for a snack? I've arranged for a cab, and I know a place down by the river that serves the best grilled bass in Missouri."

Woody Stern's article came out in the *St. Louis Herald* the next afternoon. Clinker brought a copy to Mara, who pretended she'd already seen it, because she was ashamed to admit that she couldn't read a word of it. From Clinker's excited comments, she knew the review was good, but it wasn't until she met Jocko in the backyard before the evening performance that she learned how good it really was.

He pulled the newspaper clipping out of the pocket of his tuxedo costume, and read it to her as they waited for the spec to begin.

" 'Yesterday at the State Fair, during a matinee performance of the Bradford Circus, a star was born,' " he read. " 'Her name is Mara, and she's a real live princess, the daughter of a man known as the King of the Gypsies. Princess Mara is only five foot tall, weighs in at a hundred pounds, but she's all woman, with flame-colored hair and a figure as perfect as any movie star's. She charmed an unruly crowd, had them eating out of her hand. . . .''

It went on in the same vein, and to Mara, listening to Jocko's baritone voice, it was so unreal that when he'd finished, she asked skeptically, ''Does it really say that?''

''It really does. This is the kind of publicity that's going to make you a star before you reach your twenty-first birthday, maybe even sooner.''

She beamed at him, but her smile faded quickly. ''None of ballet girls say anything about my solo. All Mr. Sam say was watch my time. I think I did okay, but—''

''Okay?'' Jocko shook his head in disbelief. ''What you did was rescue the show with that stunt of yours. You noticed how restless the crowd was, didn't you? There's been a lot of union trouble in this area lately, hard feelings between various union and management factions. As usual, the trouble spilled over onto the circus. Some of those bozos out there came here spoiling for a fight. They figure the circus is safe ground for a brawl.''

He paused to give her a grin. ''Luckily, your performance helped defuse the situation. You're going to get a lot of attention, because Woody tells me his article has been picked up by a couple of other newspapers in the area. What we have to do now is keep the momentum going. And that's Jim Boris's job. He's the show's publicity boss, but he usually needs a good kick in the ass before he moves. You leave it to me. I'll give him a kick he won't forget.''

He swaggered off to take his place in the spec line-up, and she reflected that she might not have many friends, but the ones she had were good ones. But the thought made her uncomfortable. When was the last time she'd gone out of her way to do something for Jocko or Clinker?

Clinker, for instance. Her eyes had been red-rimmed this morning at breakfast—and she hadn't been wearing an engagement ring. How had the meeting with Johnny gone last night? Had he finally told her he was leaving the show?

She took Clinker aside after the matinee. ''Are you okay?'' she asked.

''Oh, sure. I got my head bashed in last night, but aside from that, I'm just fine,'' Clinker said.

''Johnny hit you?'' Mara said indignantly.

''He didn't lay a hand on me,'' Clinker said. ''Can you believe this? After he told me he was marrying that Klinski slut, he wanted to screw me. Papa was right. He really is a louse.''

"You want me to put a curse on him?" Mara offered. "I can fix it so his thing won't work the next time he tries to screw that girl."

She didn't mean it for a joke. Although she'd never put a curse on anyone, because it was very dangerous and could rebound, she knew how to do it, so her offer was sincere. She was surprised when Clinker started to giggle, even more surprised when Clinker stopped giggling, told her she was the best friend she'd ever had, and burst into tears.

Mara hesitated, not sure what to do, and then, a little gingerly, she put her arms around Clinker and let her cry it out.

During the next two weeks, as the circus moved along its hectic circuit—four days in Topeka, a special one-day stop at Fort Riley, a five-day run in Wichita—Mara worked hard to improve her act. Not only for the audience, but for herself, her own pride. And also, although she didn't like to admit it, for the approval of the other artistes on the show.

She was getting more than her share of attention from audiences, but she knew she hadn't yet won over the other performers. They knew, none better, that she was faking some of it, making easy tricks seem difficult—not that they didn't use the same tactics. But she wanted to be what Jocko called an artiste's artiste, to earn their respect.

Most of all she wanted fame, and to her gratification, that part was already happening. She never knew what Jocko said to Jim Boris or whether he really did kick the publicity man's ass, but suddenly she was being interviewed by both newspaper and magazine journalists in the Silver Wagon, the pullman car that Mr. Sam used as his quarters on the road and also for meetings. She had been mentioned in the circus column in *Billboard* as a rising young star, even appeared on WLW, a Cincinnati radio station.

The reviews and interviews were invariably favorable. She was praised for her talent, her beauty, her showmanship. Some of them quoted freely from Woody's article, accepting her as a Rom "princess."

Not so oddly, no one in the circus believed the story was true. In fact, Clinker congratulated her on coming up with a new publicity stunt.

"Maybe you should dye your hair black," she said seriously. "Gypsies are really dark, you know."

Only one thing intruded upon her euphoria. She still hadn't

been given the center ring position for her performances—or her own private cubicle in the women artistes' dressing tent. Not that she really rated either. Only star performers who had proved their lasting power were allotted the center ring or had private dressing rooms.

Since her salary had increased so much, thanks to Jocko's intervention at contract time, she also was accumulating more money than she had ever dreamed was possible. Only after Jocko pointed out how vulnerable she was to theft, since she kept her money in the chest that contained her tarot cards, did she briefly consider opening a bank account. But she distrusted the banks so much that she finally made a deal with Mr. Sam to hold most of her money for her. It wasn't that she totally trusted him either, despite his reputation for honesty, but he was better than some banker off in Chicago or New York. Besides, since she couldn't write a check, how could she withdraw any money if she needed it?

Just before the season ended, an article came out in a circus fan magazine, comparing her favorably to Lillian Leitzel. Then Peter Standish, the mayor of Columbus, Ohio, saw her act and invited her to have lunch with him at his club. The officers of the club, which was all male, created a fuss about admitting a woman into their dining room, and suddenly the whole brouhaha was in the news section of the papers, not just in the entertainment columns.

"It's one of those breaks you can't plan," Jocko crowed, beaming like a proud father. "Play it for all it's worth. Wear that midnight-blue dress, the one with the tunic, you bought last week. But don't put on one of those abominable body shapers. The fashion editors might not praise you, but you'll turn the head of every man there—and believe me, every member who can make it will be in that dining room tomorrow to see what the shouting is all about."

He studied her through narrowed eyes. "As soon as you get to the club, make some excuse to take off your hat to show that gorgeous mane of hair. And be mysterious, silent, like Pola Negri."

"Who's that," she said suspiciously.

"She's a movie star, a vamp," he said. "And don't ask me what a vamp is, because I'm not sure it's something I can explain."

Mara dressed for the luncheon with Clinker's help. More and more she depended upon her friend's advice when it came to such things as clothes and makeup. Clinker buttoned up her dress, then arranged her hair in an elaborate twist that gave her added height.

"You really do look like a princess," Clinker said when she was finished.

Mara smiled at the compliment, but she couldn't help remembering Jocko's final instructions.

"Keep your mouth shut. Your grammar is still shaky as hell, although you speak better than most circus people now. The way you absorb other people's accents, you'll probably come back today with a midwestern twang and a whole new vocabulary. If something comes up that requires reading, like the menu, pretend to be nearsighted. Say you left your reading glasses on the train."

Mara seldom questioned his judgment about such matters. Too many times, Jocko had proved to be the wisest of advisers. Despite the vast differences in their background, they understood each other. Was this because both of them were outsiders, misfits?

By now, she had come to realize that Jocko had already achieved most of the things she hungered for. He was always being recruited by other shows, including the Lasky Circus, Mr. Sam's top rival. That he never used these offers as a source of subtle blackmail endeared him to everybody, even those who had experienced his razor-sharp tongue.

Despite their friendship, Mara was surprised that Jocko continued to share his fame with her. She knew there was a healthy ego behind his self-mockery. Whatever the reason, during the next two months, as they followed the circuit from Columbus to Dayton to Youngstown, from Youngstown to Cleveland to a hectic, rain-swept run in Peoria, he included her in any interview requests he received. The contrast between them, one so tiny and garrulous, the other so feminine and quiet, but both claiming to come from nobility, was more than newsworthy; it was a natural. The interviewers played it for all it was worth.

After a national magazine did a feature article on Mara, proclaiming her to be one of the brightest stars in the circus heaven, Mr. Sam called her into the Silver Wagon and not only offered her a raise, but the center ring, replacing Danielle Dubois, who was leaving the show.

Mara went back to her quarters on the train in a thoughtful mood. She was delighted about the raise, more so about the center ring spot, but there was something else she wanted, something that would assure her a place among the star acts, even those with larger circuses. From the moment her act started, she wanted to be alone in the arena, the center of all eyes, from the cheapest blue seat to the star seats in the center. And for that, she needed to be an undisputed star.

It took her two years to achieve her goal. During the 1922 and 1923 seasons, she never wavered from her objective. Putting first things first, she spent several hours a day practicing, sharpening her skills, slowly transforming her act into the kind that other performers respected.

She also set about doing everything she could to forge a solid reputation for reliability. Knowing that for some reason she couldn't pin down, Mr. Sam was still skeptical about her, she never missed a performance, not even when she got sick during one of the flu epidemics that periodically swept the circus. She had to work with a fever and a bad cough, but she was there every performance.

She was never late, was always willing to take part in the parade when one was scheduled, as well as in the spec, something most of the star acts scorned. She accepted lunch invitations from local and state politicians, gave interviews to reporters from even the smallest magazines and least important newspapers, anything to gain publicity, not only for herself but for the circus. Several times she even acted as a glorified front man to get special concessions from local authorities, thus easing Mr. Sam's job.

When she gave interviews, she took a cue from Jocko and always presented a different handle on which the journalist could hang his article, thus becoming a favorite with newspaper writers all along the circuit. She learned to dress in a flamboyant way that not only satisfied her own personal taste but was flattering to her vivid coloring and petite figure.

Since the flat-chested and angular styles currently popular were not becoming, she refused to wear them, even though Mr. Sam, in recognition of her publicity value, provided her with a clothes allowance now. But the fad for harem pantaloons and berets and bold, unconventional colors, as well as African jewelry made of bone and wood and mock jade, she adopted wholeheartedly.

Mr. Sam's attitude gradually changed—albeit grudgingly. But the day finally came, at the end of the 1922 season, when he invited her to sit in on the annual planning session with management and a few top performers. When her contract was renewed that winter, she asked for and got what she wanted, her own private cubicle in the dressing tent and a roomy compartment on the train. What's more, from now on when she performed, she would be alone in the center ring.

With Oscar Tanqueray, the bandmaster, she worked out a music program, in the main, following his advice but with some ideas of her own. After Konrad announced her act, there would be dead silence until she reached the center of the ring. A drum roll would accompany her up the rope, and only when she reached the top would the music start.

Whatever he might have thought privately, Oscar agreed with her demands. Maybe he thought it wasn't worth arguing about.

At the end of the 1923 season, Mr. Sam allotted Mara a larger compartment on the train, plus his permission for her to decorate it any way she chose—within reason. Mara offered Clinker a job, the pay to come out of her own salary. She needed someone to dress her hair, to keep her costumes and clothes in order, to answer the fan letters that were increasing dramatically, and to handle the bank account she planned to open so she could pay her bills by check, she told Clinker.

"And to be my friend," she added, and was embarrassed when Clinker's eyes filled with tears.

As if a wind had caught Mara up and was whirling her into the future, the pace of her life quickened. She was deluged with so many ardent suitors, bearing flowers and candy and invitations, that Mr. Sam insisted on assigning her a bodyguard.

Mara made her choice carefully, finally settling on Lobo, the big mute who held her rope when she was performing. Besides being a near-giant, he was undeniably ugly, with his blunt features, broad nose, and protruding forehead, and with her growing flair for publicity, she decided to use him in her act. Dressed in black, with flowing robes and a turban, he carried her out into the center of the arena. Perched on his shoulder, with the aplomb of the princess she was supposed to be, she smiled at the audience as if to say, "Doesn't everybody have a giant to carry them around?"

While she climbed the rope, he held it tight, and he looked so fierce that not even the bravest admirer dared approach Mara uninvited.

Her white costumes, too, became her trademark. "Never wear anything but white into the arena," Jocko advised. "The perpetual virgin," he added, which made her laugh.

By now, she had met her first movie star, who had soulful

eyes and a thick Mexican accent although he was supposedly from Brazil. Ramon was a circus buff, and he told her he had fallen in love with her the first time he'd seen her whirling so bravely overhead, ignoring the blood running down her arm. He wined and dined her and even proposed, and she suspected that he was vastly relieved when she turned him down.

"He's prettier than me," she told Clinker, who couldn't understand why Mara would refuse such a catch.

Clinker, who was a movie buff, had pictures of an even more famous Latin actor, Rudolph Valentino, on the wall over her berth, and she never missed a chance to see his latest movies. Privately, Valentino, with his liquid eyes and sleek black hair, reminded Mara a little too much of Yolo, but after she saw *Robin Hood*, she got a crush on Douglas Fairbanks and dreamed of a lithe, muscular man, dressed in green, chasing her through a dark forest.

When she admitted this to Jocko, he rolled his eyes. "I keep forgetting you're still only twenty," he said, making her bristle. Although Jocko was undeniably her friend, there were times when he became moody, sarcastic, even toward her. For one thing, he had taken a dislike to Lobo, calling him the Missing Link, which meant nothing to Mara, and the Geek, which did.

One of Mara's swains, a wealthy young lawyer, became so enamored with her that he followed her from town to town, showering her with gifts. She finally took pity on him and allowed him to seduce her, an experience she enjoyed as much as he did since he was a very good lover. But when he became possessive, she broke the affair off. Since the reason she gave him was that she couldn't keep her mind on her act when she was thinking of him, he took it like a good sport.

It was about this time that it dawned on her that she could do pretty much what she wanted concerning men as long as she was discreet. After that, she sometimes took a lover, satisfying her own strong sensual needs, but she never slept with anyone connected with the circus.

The movie actor, who was enjoying his misery, eventually confided his woes to a famous gossip columnist. Maybe Ramon thought it would make Mara take him more seriously. It didn't do that, but after the columnist broke the story, there were few readers of the gossip column who didn't know who Princess Mara was. Which may have been why, out of the blue, Mr. Sam gave Mara another raise, and her own private dressing tent.

And then, just when she thought she had everything she wanted, she met Jaime St. Clair.

CHAPTER 15

WHEN JAIME ST. CLAIR WAS NOT TOO MANY YEARS OUT OF diapers, he found out what it meant to be the only son of an enormously rich and totally ruthless father.

Ordinarily he wouldn't have been left alone, even inside the high walls of his father's estate in Westchester County, much less outside its iron gates. This day, the servants had been careless because both of Jaime's parents had gone into Boston for the day.

Instead of keeping an eye on the St. Clair heir as ordered, they indulged in a rare opportunity to raid the estate's wine cellar of some less distinguished wines, unlikely to be missed, and have a celebration. During their inattention, five-year-old Jaime wandered out through the gates, which had carelessly been left ajar, and down the road toward the highway.

When he was finally found, late that afternoon, he was playing touch football with a gang of older kids in a school yard a mile away. The kids—and Jaime—got quite a scare when the county sheriff, three of his deputies, and Jaime's father descended upon them.

Diabolically, Earl St. Claire didn't even scold Jaime, but all the servants, some of whom had worked for the St. Clair family for years, were fired. Jaime had been more than fond of several of them, from whom he'd gotten most of the affection in his young life, and their dismissal was far worse punishment than a dozen whippings would have been.

He never forgot the lessons he'd learned that day. It didn't curb his natural high spirits, but never again did he involve anyone else in his rebellions and pranks.

He also learned not to be so trusting. To a person, the servants had sworn that he hadn't left their sight that day except when he went to the bathroom, that he'd deliberately given them the slip by climbing out the bathroom window.

During his Choate and Harvard years, Jaime was one of the most popular men in school. Along with an extremely wealthy father from a New England Brahmin family, and unusual intelligence, he'd been endowed—some said unfairly—with all the physical attributes considered attractive by his generation—thick, curly hair, the color of ripe wheat, eyes so blue they were devastating to women, plus classical features, which included a well-shaped nose, a cleft chin, and teeth as even and white as expensive orthodontics could provide.

Add a tall, rangy body that was a natural on the dance floor and the tennis courts, a sunny smile that gave him an open-faced, approachable look, and it wasn't any wonder that his fraternity brothers called him "Killer."

It wasn't that he deliberately set out to bed so many women. It was just that he wasn't averse to taking advantage of what was offered so freely. After all, he liked girls, liked their soft voices and silky bodies, liked being with them, making love to them. It was inevitable that he would gain the reputation for being a hot lover. He looked the part and he acted the part. The truth was that while he'd slept with many girls, he had never been in love, didn't believe in love, was sure he was immune to it.

What's more, he was happy with things the way they were. After all, he had the best of all worlds, even if his mother was an alcoholic and his father a coldhearted snob.

Jaime seldom thought about the future. It had all been laid out for him the day he was born. After he got his law degree from Harvard, which had been his father's school, and passed the Massachusetts bar exam, he would go to work in his father's Boston law firm. Eventually he would marry some pretty, pleasant girl from a good family, give his father a couple of grandkids, preferably boys, and if his marriage was as dry and sterile as his parents' was, well, that's how the ball bounced and the cookie crumbled.

It was inevitable that he would arouse envy. Few men can have so much, all stemming from having been born into the right family and inheriting the right genes, and not gain an enemy or two along the way.

Jaime's nemesis was Martin Remington, the son of a superior court judge. They had known each other all of their lives, their families having adjoining estates, but they'd never been friends, even though they were approximately the same age, Martin being a year older. In fact, Martin was the closest thing to an enemy Jaime had. When he'd joined Martin's club at Harvard, which had been his father's choice for him, he'd expected trouble.

He wasn't disappointed.

During initiation, Martin saw that Jaime was given the full treatment, including a paddling that raised a few welts on his bare backside, and a disgusting mixture of epsom salts and croton oil that made him violently ill. He expected Jaime to blubber like a baby, but instead he took the whole thing in stride. He even joked about it, which won over everybody but Martin.

After Martin graduated, he remained at Harvard to take postgrad work, and he never missed a chance to bait Jaime or play upon his weaknesses. Not beyond a certain point, of course, and always with a cool approach, one that said, "Hey, I was just having fun, sport!"

One of Jaime's weaknesses was that he couldn't resist a dare. Not that he was foolish about it. But given reasonable odds, he just had to meet the challenge. His most notorious escapade involved a late-night climb up the hallowed ivy of one of Harvard's hallowed old halls and the appearance on the roof the next morning of a grossly vulgar display of two wax models, one male and one female. He won his bet and just managed not to get kicked out of school.

All in all, Jaime was enjoying his senior year. He would graduate with honors in June, which was one reason he was celebrating with friends at their favorite off-campus speakeasy. He was feeling pretty mellow, because his grades had actually evoked a rare compliment from his father. A rather pallid one, true, but still—a compliment.

"Good show" had been his father's exact words. "See that you don't muck up before graduation."

Which, Jaime reflected as he chugalugged a home-brew beer, was high praise from that stiff-necked, coldblooded bastard.

"I hear you made the dean's list again," Martin said. He had joined their table earlier, and his voice held more malice than usual. Jaime, who had just finished ordering his fifth homebrew, just grinned at him.

"Eat your fucking heart out," he said.

Everybody laughed. "Yeah, Martin," one of his friends said. "You look a little green in this light."

Martin flushed. "Well, we can't all be grinds," he said. Someone made a meow sound and they all laughed again because everybody knew that Jaime did less studying than anyone else in his class.

"How are you going to celebrate?" Martin said, ignoring the laughs. "You planning on bedding one of your Radcliffe fillies?"

Jaime's good humor frayed a little around the edges. He dated a lot of girls, and if they were willing, he joined them in bed, but he never talked about it, before or afterward. Never.

"Maybe I'll go hunting somewhere else this time," he said lightly.

"Where? You got a movie star in mind—or someone more exotic?" Martin jerked his thumb toward a four-color circus poster, hanging behind the bar. "How about that fancy piece of tail, the one who calls herself Princess Mara? I hear some spick actor tried to commit suicide when she turned him down. It was in all the gossip columns—"

"So that's what you're reading these days," Jaime said lazily. "No wonder your grades are rotten these days."

"And you're changing the subject," Martin said, his eyes glittering. "How about it? You think you can add this circus woman to your stable?"

"Why would he want to?" Ozzie Herman, who had been Jaime's roommate in his freshman year, asked. He gave Martin a hard look. "She's not his type."

"That shouldn't bother Killer here. How about it, Jaime? I've got a hundred says you can't even get the lady to come to the spring dance next week."

Jaime caught the malice in Martin's eyes, guessed its source. What was there about Martin that women didn't like? He wasn't bad-looking, and he could put on a good front—did they sense his utter contempt for their sex? Whatever the reason, he had a bad reputation among women of his own class. In fact, the ones he dated were townies, easy prey for Ivy League boys. . . .

"Don't be so sure," Ozzie, always loyal, said. "Jaime can get any girl he wants."

"Yeah, Jaime. Show the doubter how it's done." It was Tommy Leader, who had often been the bunt of Martin's sharp tongue. "All you can snag is a townie, Martin. Wasn't that one of the waitresses from Steve's Place I saw in your car last week? How much does she charge?"

Martin ignored him. "How about it, Jaime? Is it a bet? My hundred says you can't get the lady to come to the dance."

And Jaime, who had just downed his fifth beer, found himself nodding.

That night, he stayed up late, thinking about the challenge. He finally came to the conclusion that he needed all the information he could get on Princess Mara. From the poster, she was a knockout. It seemed obvious that if men tried to commit suicide over her, she also was a tease—and probably a publicity hound. But what else was she?

Luckily, he knew just where to go for information. One of his Choate classmates had gone into the family newspaper business after graduation from Princeton. Even though it was late, he picked up the phone, gave the operator his friend's number in Boston.

"It's good to hear from you, you old son of a bitch," his friend said, brushing off Jaime's apologies for ringing him so late. There was a two-year difference in their ages, Todd (Toddle to his friends) being the older, but their friendship was the deep-rooted kind that always picked up easily from where it had left off.

"How about doing me a favor?" Jaime said.

"Such as?"

"I made a bet with Martin Remington—"

Toddle's groan cut in. "You never learn, do you? How did he sucker you in this time?"

"You want to hear this or not?"

"I want to hear it."

"He bet I couldn't get a certain lady to come to the spring dance with me. I bet I could."

"What's the problem? You've got the magic touch with females, boy."

"It's not that easy. I've never met her."

"So who is it?"

"It's a circus performer named Mara something-or-other."

Toddle whistled. "Not Mara something-or-other. Princess Mara. She's supposed to be some kind of Gypsy princess, which no doubt is something a press agent dreamt up. But her talent is genuine enough."

"How come you know so much about her?"

"Hell, I've had circus fever ever since I saw my first parade, boy. I haven't missed the Big One in Madison Square Garden for five years. The smell of peanuts roasting is addictive. You should try it sometime."

"Not interested." Jaime didn't point out that the circus business seemed pretty tawdry to him. "I think I'd better know something about the lady before I make my move."

"How do you plan to go about it?"

"Find out her weaknesses. Use them to get acquainted and then ask her to the dance."

"You were right the first time. I don't think it's going to be that easy. She's got a reputation for being unapproachable. Which adds to her mystique, of course. Also, she's closely guarded, I understand. There's this big guy, a deaf-mute, who carries her out into the arena in her act. He's also her bodyguard. He's roughed up a few lovesick fellows."

"What else can you tell me about her?"

"Off the top of my head, that's about it. Look, why don't I dig around in the morgue at work and see what I can come up with? How much time do you have?"

"According to the poster I saw, her circus is playing Boston, starting a week from today. The dance is the day following the end of their five-day Boston run. Which might scuttle the whole thing. They could be playing Chicago that Friday for all I know."

"Well, I'd love to see you rub old Martin's nose in shit, so I'll get right on it. And remember—you owe me a beer for this."

"If I can pull this thing off, I'll owe you a whole keg, friend."

Two days later, a large brown envelope was delivered to Jaime's quarters. He sat down to read the contents. Fifteen minutes later, he laid the material aside, feeling glum.

It was surprising how contradictory the information about the circus woman was in the articles, news releases, and press notices Toddle had come up with.

Which of the "facts" about you are true, Mara-without-a-last-name? he mused, and discovered he was intrigued on a level that had nothing to do with his bet. *Are you really a genuine Gypsy princess, disowned by your family because you refused to marry the man your father chose for you? Are you a natural redhead—or are you a gorgeous fake who was born with brown hair in some mid-European country? Either your act is incredibly difficult—or it's all a matter of illusion and tricks. So just who the hell are you, anyway?*

He picked up Toddle's note and read it again. It reminded him of the keg of beer, then added the information that Princess Mara's circus would be playing Medford for three days before its Boston run, that the Friday of the spring dance was a "still" day for the circus, which meant the lady just might be available for the evening.

The next day, Jaime cut classes and drove into Medford to catch the matinee performance of the Bradford Circus.

At the fairgrounds, located in a large field adjacent to the city line, Jaime bought a box seat ticket for the matinee performance, then wandered along the midway, looking it over. To his inexperienced eyes, the circus seemed very prosperous. The rides and various signs were freshly painted, the canvas tents clean and obviously new; the personnel looked very respectable in their red-and-white striped shirts and caps. The food—hot dogs and hamburgers and sausages on a bun—at the concession stands looked fresh and well prepared. So it wasn't a—what did they call those sleazy carnivals? Mudshows?

When the Big Top opened, he was one of the first to file into the tent. Like the rest of the circus, signs of prosperity were everywhere. The wooden chairs in the boxes were padded, in first-rate condition, the red-and-white canvas of the tent looked new, and the colored sawdust that covered the ground was obviously freshly laid. Since it was a matinee, he had expected the audience to be predominately children and their mothers. To his surprise, there was a large proportion of adults, both couples and single men.

When the show started with a parade around the arena, he wasn't particularly impressed. The profusion of animals, of cavorting clowns and scantily clad girls, the bombastic music, seemed overdone to a man with reasonably simple tastes. Then the performance began with three surprisingly good acts, each one in a separate ring—Chinese acrobats, a ballet troupe of pretty girls executing turns on a rope web, and an equestrian display of what the bass-voiced master of ceremonies called high school horses—and his interest picked up.

This was followed by what seemed to Jaime to be a small army of clowns. He found himself laughing at a tiny midget, dressed in morning clothes. The clown's aplomb, as he careened dizzily from one mishap to another, completely oblivious that he was the butt of the other clowns' jokes, was both ridiculous and pathetic. He realized the man's genius when he discovered himself screaming out a warning when the little man, blithely unaware that he was being stalked by a tall clown with a maniacal look on his face, stepped off into nothingness at the end of a tilted board, only to land unhurt in the arms of a fat clown. The midget planted a kiss on the clown's cheek and then sauntered off, swinging his cane and tipping his top hat to the audience.

There were several other acts, including a chorus line of elephants that made the kids scream with delight. Then, finally, the band struck a dramatic chord and the drums gave a slow roll. The lights dimmed to near darkness and the music faded to dead silence. The crowd quietened expectantly, and even the vendors stopped hawking their wares in the stands.

A single spotlight moved over the audience, catching a face here and there, then moving on. It rose, up to the peak of the tent, as if to demonstrate the height of the big top, then slowly descended, finally focusing on a spot directly in front of the performers' entrance.

A tiny woman stood there. Even though she was motionless, every inch of her body radiated grace and confidence. A white feather cape covered her from shoulders to feet.

But it wasn't her spectacular costume that made Jaime's breath stop for a long moment. Her hair, gathered loosely at the nape of her neck by two silver combs, really *was* the color of flames, and her lips were full, sweetly curved, painted bright red. Her eyes glistened in the circles of light, and her skin had a luminous look that Jaime was convinced was natural, not makeup.

Although he was too far away to make out the color of her eyes, he already knew they were green. "Emerald-green," one of the press releases had called them. He had thought at the time how trite this was, a redhead with green eyes, but now he knew that nothing about this woman was trite.

There was an eruption of applause, and the woman's face came alive. She smiled, a joyous, all-out smile, and suddenly the tent was touched with magic. With one part of his mind, Jaime noted that the spotlight had turned pink, hence the aura, but another part, much more gullible, was convinced it was her smile that was magical.

The snare drums began a slow roll, and when it had ended, the ring announcer's voice boomed out into the arena.

"Ladies and gentleman, I give you—Princess Mara!"

The woman raised her arms in a sweeping gesture, then brought them down to her sides as she gave a deep, slow curtsy, as if paying homage to the audience. There was movement behind her, and a man, a giant of a man, dressed all in black, including a turban, stepped forward. He knelt in front of Mara, and she swung herself upward, using his thick thigh as a step to perch on his shoulder. *A human throne*, Jaime thought, suddenly amused by his own impressionability.

The band broke into a sprightly march, and the spotlight followed the giant and his passenger as he stalked forward, coming to a stop in the middle of the center ring. The giant relieved Mara of her cape, revealing her costume, a tight silver-and-white jacket and a filmy skirt, worn over white tights. Kneeling at her feet, the giant removed her bejeweled mules. Again using his thigh and then his shoulder as steps, the aerialist grabbed a white rope that dropped from the highest reaches of the Big Top to the arena below.

As the band played another march, she ascended the rope by a series of curious maneuvers, turning her body over her arm in such a way that she rolled a few feet upward along the rope with each turn. She took her time, stopping twice to hook her foot in the rope and leaning far out, head down, to blow kisses to the audience.

It was a masterful maneuver because it made the crowd part of the act, and they entered into the fun, waving back and returning her kisses, cheering her on. Jaime suspected the danger was far less than it looked, but it didn't matter. He found himself cheering her on, too.

Then she reached the rings at the top. Without any delay, as if she sensed it was time to earn her applause, she began an intricate routine of twists and turns and swings, her body control disciplined and graceful. And all the time, her smile, her every move and gesture, telegraphed her joy and pleasure at being there. Was it real, Jaime wondered, or was it all a very clever act?

As the band played "The Dance of the Hours" from *La Gioconda*, she finished the routine in a flurry of quick turns and breathtaking maneuvers, her insouciance total.

The applause swelled as she bowed once, then quickly descended to the floor. She took her bows, her expression a little bemused, as if she hadn't expected such a volume of applause. She blinked hard, gave a tremulous smile, and then she turned her face toward the master of ceremonies on his stand at the side of the arena, and held up two fingers on one hand, five on the other, then turned, to be swept up again to the top of the tent by the swiveled rope.

"Ladies and gentlemen," the announcer said, his voice hushed. "Princess Mara is deeply touched by your applause. Usually at matinees she does twenty of her specialty, the difficult—and very dangerous—move called the flange turn by circus people. Today, in appreciation of a special audience, she will attempt twenty-five flanges. It is my great pleasure to give you— Princess Mara!''

The drums rolled again, and the aerialist swung her small body up to the level of her shoulders, paused briefly, as if screwing up courage or saying a prayer, and then, using her shoulder as an axis, rolled her body over itself and dangled from one arm. At first, there was silence in the audience, as if the spectators were holding their breath, and then someone— suspiciously close to the performers' entrance, Jaime noted— shouted out a loud ''One!''

From then on, each roll of the drums was accompanied by the audience, chanting out numbers. When Jaime found himself joining in, he had to laugh again. What would his friends, who thought he was so sophisticated, say if they saw him now, rooting right along with the audience? That he was a gullible fool— or that the lady swinging from the rope in what probably was a routine trick was one very clever performer?

Halfway through the performance she must have loosened the combs that pinned back her hair, because suddenly they tumbled to the tanbark below and her red hair cascaded down, forming a halo around her head and hiding her face from the audience, who roared their approval. Jaime had been watching for this, alerted by articles he'd read, but he had to give her credit because he hadn't seen her touch the combs.

And then the last roll was finished—she had done not twenty-five but twenty-six—and she was taking her bows. Her face was very pale, and when she gently touched the copper bracelet on her wrist, she winced, which could have been genuine pain or could have been part of her act. Whatever the truth, Jaime found himself applauding, calling ''Bravo!'' every bit as loudly as the heavyset man in the next box, who actually had tears in his eyes.

Magic—the little lady was pure magic, he thought, watching as she milked the applause, her eyes bright with what he would have sworn were tears. How did she do it, he wondered, performance after performance? If she went all out during a matinee—what did she do for an evening performance? Thirty-five roll-overs?

Then she was descending the rope to the accompaniment of a fast-paced number from the bandstand. The giant, who had been holding the rope taut during the whole performance, his eyes never leaving her, plucked her from the rope before her feet could touch the ground and swept the feather robe around her. Perched on his shoulder, she left the arena, and Jaime discovered that he hadn't been breathing properly for the past ten minutes. He suspected it was the same with the rest of the audience.

The performance went on, but he saw very little of it. He was deep in thought—or was he deep in something else? Like lust? It couldn't be anything else. He was too experienced to fall in love at first sight with a circus performer, for Christ's sake! So call it what it really was. He had come here to win a bet, but all he cared about now was getting to know—in the biblical sense—Princess Mara, queen of the aerialists.

And wasn't *that* something to write home about?

After the final performance, a lion tamer act, followed by another walk-around by the clowns, Jaime sat for a while, waiting for the audience to file out of the tent. That they were more than satisfied with the performance was obvious from their reluctance to leave. That the show, discounting Mara's performance, was well above average, he was sure, although he knew nothing about circuses. But it was Mara who had excited them, buoyed them up and put sparkle in their collective eyes.

So yes, she was magic, just as the articles had said. But what else was she? Did she have her weaknesses? Did she have a soft heart? Could she be reached by appealing to her sympathy? Or how about greed and vanity? Was that the way to reach her—by flattery and gifts?

The woman interviewer of one article had described the stage-door Johnnys who hung around, trying to court her. So all he had to do was to think of a way to stand out in the crowd. . . .

CHAPTER 16

AFTER JAIME LEFT THE CIRCUS LOT, HE ARRANGED FOR ONE perfect white rose to be sent to Mara's dressing tent every hour for the rest of the day. He charged it to his father, since his own finances, from a trust fund his grandmother had left him plus his parental allowance, were at low ebb, and instructed the florist to put only one name, Jaime, on the card.

Most of the girls he knew would have laughed at the single rose ploy, which was something of a cliché, but he was pretty sure that despite the circus woman's fame, she was relatively unsophisticated.

The florist entered into his scheme with enthusiasm. "I saw Princess Mara in Philadelphia last year," he confided. "She's a beauty, all right. Good luck, sir."

That evening, Jaime rented a whole box of seats, then sat in the center of the box. Dressed in impeccable evening clothes, borrowed from his father's closet, with a tiny white rosebud in his buttonhole, he was the center of all eyes.

He applauded only once, this at the end of Mara's act.

When the show was over—and yes, she did do thirty-five flange turns—he got directions to Mara's dressing tent from a soft drink vendor for a healthy tip, and made his way there, sure he would have no trouble being admitted.

A thin-faced woman answered his knock and stared at him with unfriendly eyes. The giant, to his relief, was nowhere in sight.

"Yes?"

"My name is Jaime—Jaime St. Clair. I'd like to speak to Mara," he said.

"*Princess* Mara," she snapped.

"Princess Mara," he said agreeably. "I've been sending her flowers—"

She jerked her thumb over her shoulder. "Which ones?"

Jaime stared at the flowers that filled the tent. There were pink roses, yellow roses, coral roses, as well as a dozen other varieties, enough to stock a florist shop. He didn't see any white roses, although he was sure they must be there somewhere.

"Look, I know she's a very busy person, but I really do have a reason to see her—"

"Just go quietly and I won't have her bodyguard throw you off the lot."

She dropped the canvas door flap in his face.

Jaime gave a philosophical shrug. It looked as if he'd have to come up with something else if he hoped to get past the dragon lady.

He returned home in a pensive mood—home being a very large town house in Boston that he privately thought of as St. Clair Cathedral. To his surprise, since it was used only occasionally by his parents, who preferred their Westchester estate, his father was there, having a cognac in the room he sometimes used as a home office.

Earl St. Clair was that rare thing, a man, extraordinarily handsome in his youth, who had retained his looks all through the aging process. Not that he was all that old, Jaime reflected. It was just that, in his own mind, his father represented authority gone amuck. Right now he was eyeing Jaime's evening clothes with what could only be described as suspicion.

"This is a surprise. What are you doing in town?"

"Oh, I thought I'd take a break and see a show, sir."

"I hope you aren't neglecting your studies. I'm expecting honors from you, boy," his father said. "And if those are my clothes, see that you have them cleaned before you put them back in my closet."

He poured himself another cognac. He didn't offer Jaime one.

Jaime muttered something about studying for an exam and went upstairs. Strange, he reflected, that while he didn't have any problem getting along with other people, he'd never been able to win his father's approval. He couldn't remember his father ever touching him, although surely he must have when he was a child. As for his mother—she was a wispy, vague figure on the perimeter of his life, who spent an inordinate amount of time in bed with a variety of illnesses. If she had any opinions different from his father's, she'd never expressed them to Jaime.

Was it any wonder that he went out of his way to charm other people?

This last thought was surprisingly painful. Since he never deliberately courted pain, Jaime turned his thoughts back to the problem at hand. Getting that date with Princess Mara was going to be more difficult than he'd thought, but he wasn't giving up. It wasn't just the wager now; the lady intrigued him. The truth was, he wanted to get to know her for himself, find out just what made her tick. Did her voice match that lovely body, those classic features, that gorgeous mane of hair? Was she soft and feminine, the way she looked, or was she tough, reflecting circus life? Whatever the answers, he was eager to find out.

The next day, at the matinee performance, he rented the same box as before. Dressed in morning clothes that he usually wore to usher at the weddings of his friends' sisters, he was sitting in the box when the spec began. He had arranged for a flower to be sent each hour during the afternoon, only this time the flowers were small white orchids. The lady might overlook roses, but surely orchids would stand out above the crowd—or at least arouse her curiosity about the sender.

To make his point, he was holding a florist's box, containing a spectacular white orchid, which had cost him—or rather his father—more than enough to get him disinherited. Orchids, especially outsize ones, were considered vulgar by the girls he dated, but he was betting that a circus performer would be impressed, especially after catching a glimpse of her dressing tent, which looked like an interior decorator's nightmare.

When the show was over, after another spectacular performance by Mara—no, *Princess* Mara—he returned to the town house and put his mind to the next phase of his scheme. The idea was to get past Mara's bodyguard and the female dragon—and he was confident that he had a handle on that. After a long nap, he talked the caretaker's wife into broiling him a steak for an early dinner, and then dressed in his father's evening clothes again.

Carrying the florist's box, he returned to the circus lot. The first man he tried to bribe was a rough-looking roustabout in a dirty cap. After he cussed Jaime out, he warned him to get off the lot before he got himself beat to a pulp.

The second man he approached wasn't so fastidious. "You'd best stay away from her sleeper, 'cause there's guards what patrol the train," the man said, blinking nervously. "But there's a fire exit in the rear of her dressing tent. It snaps shut inside, so you'll have to figure out how to get the flap open.''

After Jaime paid him the money he'd promised, the man told him. ''If you get caught, you're on your own. I never seen you, understand? And listen, cap, you better keep an eye out for Lobo. He's got fists like meat hooks, and he don't let nobody near the princess.''

This warning didn't deter Jaime, but it made him careful later when he was running his pocketknife under the flap in the canvas. The snaps gave with a small popping sound, and a few moments later, having removed it entirely, he was easing his long legs through the opening.

To his relief, the tent was empty. He looked around with interest since he'd only had that one glimpse the day before. He couldn't help smiling as he took in the profusion of gaudy rugs, an ornate dressing table, covered with an assortment of bottles and jars and cosmetics, a small brass camp bed, piled high with bright cushions. *Grand Rapids out of the Arabian Nights,* he thought. Or was he being snobbish? Maybe this was the height of good taste for a Gypsy—if she really was one.

Prepared for a longish wait, Jaime settled himself on the camp bed. He was just getting out a cigarette when he heard a noise outside the tent. Quickly he ducked behind a screen and peered out through a crack between two sections. Which was lucky, because it was the thin-faced woman, carrying an armful of clothes, who entered. Humming under her breath, she began hanging up the garments in a portable clothes press.

Jaime eased down to a squatting position since the screen wasn't tall enough to hide his head. When he heard a voice outside, he put his eye to the crack again.

The voice was husky, low-pitched; he didn't recognize the accent, although he was sure it wasn't Spanish or French which he spoke with reasonable fluency. A moment later, Mara came into the tent, still talking over her shoulder.

''Go get yourself some chow at the cook tent,'' she was saying. ''Clinker's here—she can keep an eye out for visitors.''

She spotted the costume the other woman was hanging up. ''How does it look, Clinker?''

''They did a good job on that ripped seam, but you'd better try it on. You don't want any nasty surprises when you're doing your act,'' the woman said.

Mara began taking off her clothes, and Jaime, too fascinated to look away, discovered his mouth was dry. He had known that her figure was spectacular; he hadn't known that her breasts were snowy mounds accentuated by pale pink nipples, that her pubic hair was the same shade as the mane that graced her head, that there was an enchanting dimple above each of her buttocks. Although he wasn't unfamiliar with the naked female form, he discovered he was embarrassed. He was also fully and painfully aroused.

Mara slipped into the costume, then stood in front of a full-length mirror, twisting around to view herself from behind. Even such a mundane movement was full of grace. Feminine grace, he amended, and had to suppress a groan of pure frustration.

After a consultation with the woman she called Clinker, she seemed satisfied and seated herself at a dressing table. The two of them talked amicably as the woman arranged Mara's hair, brushing it until it shone, then pinning it back from her face with two silver combs.

The woman gathered up an armful of garments, said she'd take them to someone named May and then fetch some tea and fruit from the cookhouse. To Jaime's relief, she left the tent.

Mara was outlining her eyes with a thin black pencil when Jaime stepped out from behind the screen. For a split second she froze, the pencil dropping from her hand, and then she was off the stool and moving as fast as a cat toward the door. She was halfway there before he got out the first word.

"Please—don't be afraid. I just want to give you this in person."

He held out the orchid. She hesitated, her eyes wary as they took in his evening clothes, the florist box in his hand, his coaxing smile. He knew then that she wouldn't scream. He waited for her next move.

Mara's first impression of Jaime St. Clair was shock. She'd been to a lot of movies, having developed a taste for them, and her first thought was that Jaime St. Clair had stepped right out of one of those drawing room comedies that Jocko was addicted to and which she never understood, even when he explained them to her.

He's beautiful, she thought.

The man's smile broadened, and she had a crazy notion that he meant to lean over and kiss her—and that she wanted him to, very much.

The fear that he might guess what she was thinking brought her back to reality. Without a word, she started for the door again. But he moved quickly to take the top off the box. It was a white orchid, the largest one she'd ever seen.

"How did you get in here?" she demanded, then didn't give him time to answer. "No, I don't want to know. Just get out before I start screaming for help."

But he didn't move. "Look, I know this is very unorthodox, but I couldn't think of any other way to meet you. I'm Jaime St. Clair, and I'm really quite harmless. I've seen every one of your performances the past three days, and there's something I want to ask you. Will you listen?"

Mara was rarely indecisive, but she was now. Part of her sensed danger, but the rest of her wanted very much to hear him out.

"Have your say and then get out," she said finally. "The spec starts in a few minutes."

"I know. I was listening. But I wasn't watching. Do you believe me?"

Mara didn't. Not for a moment. If she'd been hiding behind that screen while this man, with his hair the shade of a fall wheat field and his eyes incredibly blue, stripped off his clothes, she would have watched every move he made. As for being offended—she didn't mind that he'd seen her nude. After all, she looked her best without clothes.

"What do you want to ask me?"

"My school club has a special Sweethearts' Dance every May. I'd be honored if you'd be my guest."

She stared at him in confusion. School? Surely he was older than that. "Aren't you pretty old to still be in school?"

Now it was his turn to look confused. "I'll be graduating in June. I'm twenty-two."

"And you're still in school? Were you sick or something?"

He was silent for a moment. "I see the problem," he said finally. "I'm talking about college. Harvard, to be specific."

"Oh . . . this dance. Why me? There must be lots of girls at your college you could ask."

A flicker of something—was it amusement?—showed in his eyes, but his voice was matter-of-fact as he said, "Harvard is a men's college."

"Well, anyway, you must have a lot of girlfriends. Why ask me?"

"Because you're the most beautiful woman I've ever seen."

"Why are you lying? You are, you know."

"Why do you say that?"

"I'm a Rom—a Gypsy. I can read faces."

"So what if I tell you the truth?"

She shrugged with studied indifference.

He stared at her fixedly. "I fell in love with you at the matinee performance three days ago. That's why I want to take you to the Sweethearts' Dance."

Mara felt let down, disappointed. She wasn't sure what she had expected—but not another lie. "Get out," she said, pointing at the door. "My bodyguard's right outside. One yell and he'll mess up your pretty face."

"Your bodyguard's eating his dinner at the cookhouse," he said softly. "But I'll leave, of course."

He put the florist box in her hand. "Will you do me one small favor? Will you wear my orchid during your act tonight? It would mean a lot to me."

She shook her head, but she didn't give him back the orchid.

"And here's my card," he went on. "If, for any reason, including curiosity, you should change your mind, call me. The dance is Friday. I understand that's an open date for the circus."

Mara refused the card, but he laid it on the edge of her dressing table anyway, then took her hand and bent his head to kiss her palm. Then he was gone, leaving behind the faint scent of after-shave—and the musky odor of a clean and healthy male body.

Mara wore the orchid, pinned to her waist, at the evening performance. Jaime St. Clair was sitting in one of the star boxes, munching on popcorn, looking totally at ease in his evening clothes. As she stood near the back door, waiting for the lights to dim, she was aware that he was staring directly at her. He rose, gave a deep bow, then sat back down, and a giggle escaped her throat. He looked so ridiculous—was he a little crazy?

"I see the monkey suit guy is back again," Oly Johnson, who was standing nearby, said. "A real ding-dong-daddy. Did he give you that orchid you're wearing, Mara?"

Mara pretended not to hear. Her cue came and she ran out into the spotlight, outwardly cool and inwardly surprisingly nervous. All through her act, she was aware of Jaime St. Clair, and didn't know whether to be sorry or glad when she looked back as Lobo was carrying her off the arena floor to find that his seat was empty.

He was at the matinee performance the next day, and again at the evening performance that night. By now, the whole circus

was buzzing about him, calling him her "monkey suit beau."
The fact that a white orchid arrived before each performance
fueled the gossip.

Mara told herself that he was a pest, a menace, not to be
taken seriously. But when he still turned up the next day, she
dug out the card he'd left her, had Clinker read off the numbers,
and then went to the Silver Wagon to use Mr. Sam's phone.

When Jaime answered, she told him loftily that she'd changed
her mind. Since she had nothing better to do on her free day,
she would go to his dance with him.

CHAPTER 17

CLINKER WAS VIOLENTLY—AND VOCALLY—OPPOSED TO
Mara's date with "Joe College." Not only didn't she like
college boys in general, calling them rich snobs, but she ob-
jected to this one in particular because he was too handsome.

"He's out to make a fool of you," she declared.

Although Mara had a few doubts herself, she found herself
defending Jaime St. Clair. "He was very nice," she said, her
tone short. "And anyway, *Jocko* comes from rich people, and
he's the most gentlemanly man I know."

A peculiar look crossed Clinker's face. "Oh, Jocko has his
quirks, too," she murmured.

"You shouldn't listen to gossip. Jocko is my friend. I don't
want to hear any talk about him."

Clinker shrugged. "He's a bloody snob. If he was normal-
size, he wouldn't even speak to you."

"And I say you're wrong," Mara retorted. "As for Jaime St.
Clair, there's no use trying to change my mind. I told him I'd
go with him, and that's the end of it. So why don't you help me
decide what to wear? I've never been to a dance. Do they dress

real fancy? There's that dress I bought last week. I haven't had a chance to wear it yet.''

Clinker muttered something about ''damned stubborn fool'' under her breath, but she dropped the subject of Jaime St. Clair. Mara wasn't angry. Clinker could be moody, much too bossy at times and she was jealous of Jocko, Doc McCall, and even poor Lobo, but she was loyal, protective, and also good company. Sometimes, when Clinker was down in the dumps, Mara tried to restore her good humor by telling her jokes. Since she never could remember the punch line, they weren't all that funny, but Clinker always laughed as if they were.

The black moods came whenever her friend heard news about Johnny. He had married the Klinski girl and was now well entrenched in the act—and he hadn't made any attempt to repay money that he'd borrowed from Clinker when they were still together.

Friday afternoon, Mara dressed carefully for the dance, and when she was finished, she was pleased with the results. Clinker had outdone herself, arranging her hair into an elaborate style she'd copied from *Vogue*, the magazine she was slavishly addicted to. The new gown, which reached just below Mara's knees, was emerald-green satin, cut to fall in a straight line to her hips, but it was the matching jacket, decorated with pearls and large splashes of tiny jet-black and crystal beads, that made Mara confident that she would look as stylish as anyone else at the party.

It wasn't until Jaime came to pick her up that she had her first doubt. When she opened the door flaps of her dressing tent, his eyes widened perceptibly, then narrowed, which could be a sign of approval—or shock. Mara, who had learned to read *gadjo* expressions at an early age, suspected it was the latter. He wasn't pleased; for some reason, he was embarrassed. But she assumed a haughty air, and told herself that she didn't care. What did a man, especially one still in school, for God's sake, know about women's fashions?

He'd parked his car in the visitor's lot. Mara had ridden in both ancient farm trucks and fancy touring sedans, including limos, but never in a sport roadster before. She was delighted by the tiny yellow car with its brass fittings and its rakish lines. She said as much to Jaime.

''It's a Stutz,'' he said carelessly. ''Too small for anything except knocking about in. When I go into my dad's firm, I'll have to buy something more dignified.''

''What kind of firm?''

"Law. I'm going to be a lawyer—if I pass the bar."

"What does that mean, pass the bar?" she said, and then listened while he talked about the difficulties of passing the Massachusetts bar exam.

"You must be awful smart," she said.

"Not really. But I'm a quick study," he said, smiling.

She nodded her understanding. "That's what Jocko says about me—that I'm a quick study. He could be a lawyer if he wanted. He studied law at Oxford—that's in England."

"I know. Who's Jocko?"

"Why—Lord Jocko, the midget clown. Surely you've heard of him. He's very famous."

"He's a clown and he studied law at Oxford and is an honest to goodness lord?"

Mara caught the skepticism in his voice and bristled immediately. "He did study law at Oxford. As for being a lord, that's his business."

"I stand reproved," he said, and started talking about the dance, which was a tradition with his club. When she asked what kind of club it was, he told her it was a Final club, on a par with one he called Porcellian.

"Like the Showman's League in Florida?" she asked.

"A little different, but yes, pretty much the same."

Again, there was that tone in his voice, as if he wanted to laugh, and she retreated into a dignified silence.

Half an hour later, they pulled up in front of a large stone building. She had expected it to be large, since a dance was being held there, but this was enormous. She studied the broad pillars in front and the ivy that covered most of the stone walls. Was this some kind of joke? Surely this must be Jaime's college.

Jaime slid out of the car, then came around to help her out. The sounds of music drifted toward them as they circled the building, finally stopping at the edge of a large courtyard. Glass-topped tables and white-painted iron chairs were arranged around a wooden platform where couples were dancing. To the rear of the platform, on a raised stage, a five-piece band was playing a lively tune. The only light came from strings of tiny bulbs that outlined the branches of the trees that surrounded the courtyard.

"Fairy lights," she said in awe, and earned Jaime's laugh.

It was when the dance ended and discreetly concealed flood lights in the shrubbery came on that she got her first good look at the other girls. There was a sameness about them, despite their varied coloring and heights. Most of them were very slim and if they all weren't pretty, they obviously thought they were. Few wore any makeup except bright red lipstick; and to a woman, their hair was shingled, and their pastel gowns were simple, featuring straight lines that emphasized their boyish figures. Except for a few strands of pearls or silver bracelets, worn on their upper arms, there was little jewelry.

When Mara realized how out of place she must look in her glittering jacket and rhinestone shoe clips, it took all her pride not to turn and run. It wasn't just her gown that was wrong; everything else about her was. With her fussy hairdo, her abundance of makeup, she looked ridiculous, like Jocko in the formal evening garb he wore in his act.

"Let's dance," Jaime said in her ear. He looked a little pale, and from the way he was pretending not to notice the stares, the whispers, she was sure she knew why.

Again pride came to her rescue. "I have to go to the donicker," she said with dignity.

He looked blank for a moment. "The donicker—oh, I see. Through that door and down the hall. You'll see the sign. I'll wait for you here," he said.

Her chin high, Mara headed for the door. At the end of a short hall, she saw a sign, tacked to a door. Hoping it said, "Ladies," she pushed it open and went inside. A dressing table and mirror, several white porcelain basins, and a row of stalls with wooden doors greeted her. She ducked in the last stall, glad the room was empty. The odor of pine disinfectant made her nose tickle as she dropped down on the seat.

She was still sitting there, trying to decide what to do, when the door opened and a group of chattering women came in.

"Imagine his nerve," one annoyed voice said, "bringing a cheap-looking creature like that to the dance."

"Didn't you know? He has a bet on with Martin Remington," a third voice said. "You know Jaime. He just can't pass up a dare. Now Martin is going to have to pay up, and I for one am going to laugh myself sick."

"So that's it. Martin is a real germ, the way he's always staring at—" She must have made a gesture because the other girls laughed.

"Well, I still say Jaime should've had more sense," the first girl said, her voice sulky. "It'll serve him right, having to dance with that tart all evening."

"Oh, I think he'll have plenty of company. Men like flashy

women, even your perfect Randy. You have to admit she's really striking-looking. I hear she's a Gypsy.''

''She's vulgar and cheap. That ghastly red hair and all those jet beads and rhinestones. Ugh. What I mean is—what if she has some kind of disease or something?''

The girls went on talking, but Mara put her hands over her ears, afraid that if she heard any more, she would storm out of the stall and scratch their eyes out.

Only when they finally left did she come out of the stall. She looked in the mirror, and something Jocko had said to her when she'd modeled the gown for him came back to her.

''A bit much, ole dear,'' he'd drawled.

Another time, he'd told her she needed a keeper when she went shopping. She'd thought he was talking about money, but of course, he hadn't meant that at all. Well, he was right. Maybe she did need a keeper when she went shopping. But that didn't help tonight. Eventually she would have to face those snobs out there, and she wasn't about to let any of them, including Jaime, guess how much it hurt to find out she'd been used.

What exactly was the bet? That he get her to come to the dance? Or was there more? Was he also supposed to get her in bed with him?

Her nostrils flared under a new rush of fury. She was going to get even. Oh, yes, she was going to pay him back. But first— she had to turn the tables on those cats who had called her a whore and a tart. . . .

She locked the door against interruptions, then returned to stare at her reflection in the mirror with dispassionate eyes. She could remove most of her makeup, take off her rhinestone necklace, but what about her dress? And her hair? Was its color really ghastly?

She took off the jacket and studied the dress beneath. Meant to be covered by the jacket, it wasn't too different from the dresses the other women were wearing, except for the color. The cut was simple, the neckline demure, and without the jacket, the color didn't seem so gaudy. As for her shoes—the crystal clips were removable. Without them, they looked like simple opera pumps.

But first things first.

It took her only a few minutes to scrub off her makeup, re-place it with a brushing of powder, a discreet application of mascara. She brushed out the elaborate hairdo Clinker had spent so much time on, then arranged her hair in a simple style that emphasized her high cheekbones and her full mouth. Since the lipstick in her purse was very red, she left it off, glad that her lips were naturally pink. True, some of the women had been wearing bright lipstick, but then, they didn't have her vivid coloring. Ghastly red hair indeed.

As she stood back and examined the result of her transformation, she began to smile. She looked—classy. No, make that striking-looking. The way a princess should. Maybe she wasn't really a princess, but her grandfather had been *baro* of the *kumpania*. That was something like a king, wasn't it?

"Just wait, Joe College," she said aloud. "You're going to be sorry."

She tucked the jacket, shoe clips, and jewelry into a cupboard under the basins, then soared out into the hall with her chin elevated. A few seconds later, her appearance on the terraced garden caused a very satisfying sensation. Jaime's mouth fell open. In fact, he looked as if someone had just kicked him in the stomach. Since it was another part of his anatomy she wanted to vent her rage on, she wasn't appeased.

She gave Jaime her most dazzling smile. "You were a real gent, not to say anything about the way I was dressed," she said sweetly.

"You'd look beautiful in anything," he said fervently, and she had to restrain herself from kicking him where it would hurt the most.

Two men came up, and Jaime introduced them to Mara. She smiled demurely, and let her toe tap in time with the music. With this broad hint, both men immediately asked for a dance.

Jaime took her arm. "First dance goes to the lucky escort," he said, and whirled her out onto the floor.

He was a skillful dancer, and Mara picked up the steps quickly, even though they were unfamiliar to her. When the dance ended a few minutes later, Jaime's friends took over, cutting in on each other every few minutes. When she finally declared that she had to rest, she was immediately surrounded by men, all wanting to bring her a cup of punch, to pay her compliments.

Wisely, she said little. It wasn't necessary. These men, she had already discovered, were little different from circus men. Although they asked her a few perfunctory questions about circus life, what they really wanted to do was impress her, to talk about themselves. A smile was all the reward expected in return.

Earlier, she'd seen Jaime dancing with a dark-haired girl she was convinced was one of the three who had insulted her in the powder room. He looked a little bored, and she waved and gave him a tiny smile, then returned her attention to her partner, a tall, sharp-featured man who was trying to find out if she really was a Gypsy princess. Since he'd told her his name was Randy, she put extra warmth into her smile.

A few minutes later, Jaime appeared at her elbow and whisked her away. "Time for you to catch your breath. You do know you're the most popular girl here, don't you?"

"Because I'm new," she said, shrugging.

"Because you're enchanting," he said, and she wanted to throw up. "What happened to your—uh, jacket?"

She looked him in the eye. "When I heard some girls talking about the over-dressed little tart you brought to the dance, I decided it was time to make some changes," she said evenly.

A flush reddened Jaime's cheekbones. "Look, it isn't that your clothes aren't—uh, in fashion—"

"They just aren't classy enough for your classy friends. I figured that out right away, no thanks to you."

"I was afraid of offending you, Mara."

"So you let those—those bitches do it for you."

"I was wrong. Am I forgiven?"

He sounded so sincere that she almost did. Until she remembered the bet. He still hadn't confessed to that. If he did—maybe she would forget about revenge.

But by the time he drove her back to the circus lot, he still hadn't mentioned it. Why had *she* been chosen as the object of the bet? she wondered. Was it because she was a circus performer? Did that make her so unacceptable to people of Jaime's class that the idea of him dating her was suitable for a bet? Her movie star and dozens of politicians and bank presidents and even one college president had seemed very proud to escort her to fancy restaurants.

On the other hand, they never brought their wives along, nor had she ever been invited to any of their homes.

They were walking across the circus parking lot, heading for the railroad spur where the train was parked, when Mara saw Lobo, standing in the shadows, watching them. She smiled to herself. Lobo was already sulking because she'd gone off the lot without him. By now, he'd be in the right mood for what she planned.

Jaime took her hand when they reached her stateroom. "May I come in for a bit?" he said, his voice husky.

Mara smiled at him. "Just for a few minutes."

Usually Clinker would be waiting up to hear all about her evening, but tonight she had taken advantage of the still day to go into Boston with some of her friends. She had left a lamp burning, and it cast a pinkish glow over the stateroom. As Mara looked around with newly educated eyes, she wondered what the women at the dance would say about the bright throw rugs, the piles of satin cushions, the collection of Kewpie dolls, sitting on a shelf. That the stateroom she was so proud of was cheap and vulgar, like its occupant?

The anger inside her simmered higher, but she managed a smile. "I'm really tired, so maybe you'd better go. But thank you for a very interesting evening. Oh, by the way—I'm glad you won your bet, Mr. St. Clair."

She watched with satisfaction as a flush spread over his face. *Not good enough, Joe College. You're going to feel more than embarrassment before this night is over—*

Her scream caught him by surprise. He said, "What the hell—" even as her second scream rent the air. When she ran her hands through her hair, disarranging it, he gaped at her, his eyes startled.

A moment later, Lobo came barreling through the door flap. He was upon Jaime with the speed that was always so surprising in a man his size. When he hit Jaime for the first time, Mara felt a rush of satisfaction, but when he didn't stop, when he hit him again, Mara was suddenly afraid. After all, she didn't want Jaime badly hurt—just shook up enough to teach him a lesson.

"That's enough, Lobo," she commanded sharply.

But Lobo didn't hear her—or pretended not to. He struck Jaime again, this time squarely on his nose, knocking him to the floor. Blood spurted, and Mara grabbed Lobo's thick arm before he could raise it again. "Stop it, Lobo," she said. "That's enough. He didn't hurt me."

For a moment, she thought Lobo was going to ignore her. But he lowered his arm, and gave her a brooding look.

"Wait outside," she said. "As soon as I get him patched up, you can take him back to his car."

Lobo lifted his arm, his hand clenched in a fist, but this time it was just a warning gesture to Jaime. He went out, carrying his shoulders high, and she knew he would sulk for days.

Silently she got a washcloth, dampened it. When she wiped the blood off Jaime's face, she saw that it came from a relatively small cut on his cheek, probably from Lobo's ring. She put a plaster on the cut, and all the time she administered to him, Jaime was silent. There were no recriminations, nothing. Both his eyes were swollen, as was his nose, and she knew he'd be sporting two black eyes the next day. Although she deeply regretted what she'd done, she wasn't about to admit it.

"And let that be a lesson to you," she said tartly when she was finished. "The next time you try to make a fool out of someone, just remember this."

The last thing she expected was his smile. "I *did* deserve it, didn't I? I was sorry the moment you said you'd come with me. I didn't think—which is one of my problems."

"So now we're even," she said.

"No, not even. You didn't deserve what I did to you, but I did deserve to have the stuffing knocked out of me. I want to make it up to you. Will you have dinner with me after the evening performance tomorrow night? I'll drive to Hartford—that *is* your next stop, isn't it?"

Mara stared at him in astonishment. Have dinner with him after what he'd done—and what *she'd* done? He must be crazy.

"Get out!" She pointed to the door. "And don't come back."

He didn't argue with her. Wincing a little, he limped toward the door. Just before he left the tent, he turned and said, "If you change your mind—you have my number."

She didn't bother to answer, and after he was gone, she closed and locked the door. As she got ready for bed, she brooded over the evening, and finally decided that it hadn't been a total waste. She'd learned some important lessons tonight. A star should look like a star, as Jocko was always saying, but there were better ways than just piling on more glitter.

She would learn those ways, learn more about fashion, about how to dress. No, she didn't want to look like those washed-out college cows in their pastel dresses, but she could be striking-looking—she did like that word!—and still not be overdressed or flashy. Jocko said she was a quick study. Well, she'd prove it.

So she owed Jaime St. Clair that—and she'd also learned another lesson, something she should have remembered after Yolo had betrayed her so cruelly. No matter how charming and sweet-talking a man could be, you just couldn't trust them, the handsome ones least of all.

The next day in Hartford, where the circus was playing a two-day engagement, a single white rose was delivered to

Maria's dressing tent. She couldn't read the card inside, but she was sure it was an apology.

She was tempted to toss the card away, along with the rose, but for some reason she didn't try to understand, she didn't. She put the card away in the bottom of her jewelry chest, and at the evening performance, she wore the white rose pinned to her costume.

CHAPTER 18

CLINKER WAS PASTING CLIPPINGS INTO A SCRAPBOOK. AS SHE applied her scissors to a copy of *Billboard*, which had a whole column on the Bradford Circus, with Mara's name prominently featured, she stopped to read the article again, even though she'd already read it aloud to Mara.

Although she knew that what some of Mara's rivals said about her was true, that she was hot-tempered and too quick to hog all the publicity, that she took advantage of her growing fame to milk the circus for all it was worth, she also knew that Mara had proved to be her friend a dozen times, starting back when Johnny had jilted her for that flat-faced Klinski bitch. And it was Mara who had given her a job when she needed it.

Had Mara caught on that she was having trouble working the ropes? She's been so careful to hide it, had gone to a towner doctor about the stiffness in her left arm and leg instead of consulting Doc McCall. Nothing serious, the doctor had told her, something to do with a fall she must have taken. Stay away from strenuous exercise; the stiffness probably would grow a bit worse, but nothing to worry about. After that, she'd been even more careful than ever, but Oly Johnson, who never missed anything, had caught on. He'd told her confidentially that when the season was over, maybe she should "retire."

Retire to what, she'd wanted to scream at him? Slinging hash in some crummy diner somewhere? Living with towners, when all she knew was circus life? Of course, Mr. Sam would have found her something to do, like taking tickets in a sideshow or working in the caramel popcorn stand. As a laborer, she would have moved out of the ballet sleeper into the cattle car with the rest of the female laborers, and taken her meals in the long end of the cook tent, been relegated to the bottom of the heap.

But Mara had saved her from that. No one had guessed the truth. They all thought it had been her own choice, giving up the ballet to be Mara's secretary—and good right hand—because she was tired of it, and she got the same respect these days that Mr. Sam's office staff did.

Of course, she earned her pay. Earned more than her pay, because the truth was, Mara could be pretty close with her money. *Still*, Clinker thought with satisfaction, *I've never shirked my duties, never will.* She protected Mara from unwanted visitors, saw that she got her rest, was her dresser, secretary, and errand girl, and she never gossiped about her even though she knew most of Mara's secrets.

For instance, she knew that Mara could barely write her own name, which was why she made a point of reading aloud anything in the trade papers or magazines that she thought Mara should hear. She also knew that Mara sometimes resorted to a trick in order to gain sympathy during her act. Who else could Mara trust to procure those bits of liver before important performances?

She was proud that she was Mara's best friend. There was Jocko, of course, but sometimes he talked too much, especially when he was drinking. She'd heard whispers that he used hashish these days, too. Everybody in the circus knew that he lived with pain from a back injury and made allowances for him. What a pity that he was in love with Mara. He went through agonies every time she had dinner with another man. . . .

That was another secret she knew—about Mara's lovers. Oh, there weren't many, and they never lasted very long. As soon as one began making a pest out of himself, getting jealous and tiresome, that's when she got rid of him.

Clinker sighed, thinking of her own love life—or rather, her lack of one. Since Johnny had let her down so badly, she'd avoided men. Not that she hadn't had her chances. But she'd lost interest in that sort of thing. Getting mixed up with a man only brought a woman misery.

Besides, she was too busy taking care of Mara. Like her music. Mara was totally ignorant about music. She didn't know one song from another, not even the old standards. It was as if she'd never heard a radio or seen a movie before she joined the circus. Which was why Clinker had taken a hand in choosing music for her act. She picked up recordings that seemed right, played them for Mara on the Victrola she'd bought, and when Mara took a shine to a song, then Clinker relayed the choice to Oscar Tanqueray.

Not that Oscar liked it. Once, he'd called Mara a nervy bitch, which had gotten back to her. The fireworks had really exploded then. Mara, her eyes shooting sparks, had dressed him up one side and down the other. When he went to Mr. Sam and threatened to quit, something he did at least once a month, Mr. Sam told him that he could apologize to Mara or leave. Oscar had apologized, an apology Mara had graciously accepted, and that had been that. One thing about Mara. She didn't hold grudges.

And then there were the things Clinker chose not to tell Mara. Like that piece in the paper she'd read recently about a street brawl in New Jersey. The story had only been a few lines long, wouldn't have rated that much if the victim hadn't been the son of a prominent local politician, but it had caught her eye because the attacker's name was Leo Mueller. Which had raised a few chills.

Manslaughter, they called it, and now this man, who either was or was not the Leo Mueller she knew, was a fugitive, having escaped from the station after being booked. Well, even if it was Leo, there was little chance he'd show up where people knew him—and where he'd been so unpopular. Which was why she hadn't read that particular news item to Mara. Why worry her? After all, Leo Mueller wasn't that unusual a name. . . .

Something else was bothering her these days. That college guy, the one who looked like a movie star—she'd spotted him twice in the past week. The first time, she hadn't been sure, having only seen him when he was all dolled up in evening clothes. This fellow, who'd been helping to put up canvas, was rough-looking, wearing work pants, a cap that covered his hair, and a ratty old sweater.

Then she'd seen him again, scrubbing down the elephants, and this time he wasn't wearing a cap, and she would swear it was the St. Clair fellow. Even in work clothes, you couldn't mistake that thick blond hair or that handsome face.

Which must mean he hadn't learned his lesson and was still chasing Mara. She wasn't surprised. All the men wanted Mara.

Didn't he realize that he didn't have a chance? Mara had told her the whole story. Well, maybe not all of it. But something had happened that night in Boston that had fired up Mara's temper, and she'd sicced Lobo on him. Served the rich boy right. That kind always thought circus women were easy.

Maybe she should put a bug in Lobo's ear. The big mute had taken care of him once. Maybe this time he should mess up that pretty face permanently. Well, she'd think about it.

Clinker finished pasting the last article, this one from an Indianapolis newspaper, in the scrapbook and put it away. Later, while Mara was taking her afternoon rest, she would read the latest entries to her. Mara was like a kid about that scrapbook. Even though she couldn't read it, she liked to browse through the book, looking at her own pictures. Something bad had happened to her before she came to the circus, something that made her crave attention more than most. Well, whatever it was, it was her own business. As far as she, Clinker, was concerned, this was one secret Mara could keep. . . .

Jaime, who was not given to doing anything that was inconvenient or uncomfortable, had gotten a job with Bradford Circus through pure funk. The night he'd left the fairgrounds in Boston, sporting two black eyes, a bloody nose, and more bruises than he could count, he had vowed to put the seduction of Mara out of his mind as a lost cause. But his mind—nor his body—hadn't cooperated, not at all.

He'd never wanted a woman as badly as he wanted Mara, so much so that he didn't want any other. Which was more than a little humiliating. After all, he wasn't some callow kid with his glands in an uproar from puberty. He was sexually mature, an experienced lover who enjoyed women, enjoyed sex, but wasn't overwhelmed by it. What's more, he was good at it. Never too quick to rush to climax, he tried always to leave his partner satisfied—he prided himself on that. Yet right now, he wanted to break into Mara's stateroom, take her quickly, furiously, without finesse, no matter what the consequences.

Which was insanity. What the *hell* was wrong with him? A belated adolescence? He didn't get crushes on women, never had, never would. Or so he'd thought. But now he seemed obsessed with Mara. Her image, that vivid little face, that lush mouth that promised paradise, that marvelous hair he wanted to bury his face in, those long, slender legs and cone-shaped breasts—God, they seemed to be etched under his eyelids, getting between him and his friends, his social life, other women. . . .

He had moped around his digs, turning down invitations, not answering the phone or the doorbell, until finally, just before graduation, Ozzie had crashed his apartment and asked what the devil was wrong with him. Jaime had confided in him, his best friend, expecting sympathy, only to watch Ozzie laugh himself sick.

After he finished mopping the tears out of his eyes, Ozzie's advice was, "You want this little circus queen, go after her. You've got the whole summer—so do something about it, you jerk." He stopped to grin at Jaime's sour expression. "Hey, why don't you join the circus? That way you've got a legitimate reason for being on the lot."

Jaime told him he was crazy, but the idea, once planted, wouldn't go away. He thought of a dozen reasons why it wouldn't work, but in the end, since he couldn't concentrate on anything else, he'd finally decided to take Ozzie's advice. In the fall he'd be taking more law classes, but he had the whole summer free. Maybe, if he saw Mara again, his obsession would go away.

Ozzie—as always, delighted to be involved in an intrigue—had pointed out that he couldn't get a job as a roustabout dressed like a college kid. So after graduation was out of the way in June, Jaime went to a Salvation Army store, bought a supply of work pants and shirts, socks and underwear, all a little the worse for someone else's wear.

When he put them on, he didn't need the glint in Ozzie's eye to know that there were few traces of Jaime St. Clair, man about campus, in this rough-looking man with a two-day-old beard, a watch cap, and work pants and shirt. Only his shoes, handmade in Italy, looked out of place. Since he wasn't about to give up foot comfort, not even for an obsession, he rubbed dirt on the shoes to take off the shine.

He'd been confident that he would be hired. Times were good, at least everybody *he* knew said they were, so why not? But he hadn't counted on the glut of unskilled laborers in the St. Petersburg area, where the circus was playing, out there looking for any kind of job.

As he waited outside a large, ornately carved circus wagon that looked like a relic from the Barnum days, he studied his competition. A few were big, burly fellows, but the majority was a scrawny bunch. In fact, some could have come straight out of Florida State Penitentiary, and for sure, they all looked as if they were used to very hard times.

So much for the glamour of the open road, he thought.

From the hard stares he was collecting, it was obvious that they had his number and recognized him as an outsider. Maybe he should have rubbed some of that dirt on his neck, he mused, as well as his shoes.

The middle-aged man who interviewed him was hard-eyed, impatient. When he asked for Jaime's work record, Jaime named two circuses he'd gotten from his prep school friend, the circus buff.

"They won't check up on you," Toddle had said. "But you can give yourself away in other ways. Keep your mouth shut and don't volunteer anything."

When the man asked what experience he'd had, he reeled off several jobs—laborer, elephant boy, canvas and bench man. Having been coached by Toddle, he was prepared to elaborate, but the man only nodded.

"Well, you look like a strong, clean-cut lad. I'll give you a try. You aren't a boozer, are you?"

Jaime started to say he was a teetotaler, changed his mind. "I take a drink now and then. Nothing I can't handle," he said.

"What you do on your own time is your business, but if you don't show up the morning after you get your pay, don't bother to come back. And this is a Sunday school outfit. No grifting, no brawling, no rough stuff. Any trouble and out you go." He looked Jaime over, frowning. "You from Boston?"

"South Boston," Jaime said, prudently naming the run-down working-class part of town.

"Thought so from that accent. In a bit of trouble back home, are you? Well, everybody minds their own business here. Just keep your nose clean."

Jaime's first day on the job was spent helping the work gang set up the game booths. His next was washing down the elephants, because the menagerie crew was shorthanded. He admired the big, gray beasts and thought he could get very fond of one, a gentle lady named Connie.

"You like the bulls?" the elephant boss asked when he caught Jaime slipping the elephant an apple he'd swiped from the cookhouse.

"Bulls? Isn't her name Connie?"

"They're all bulls here whether they're male or female."

The elephant boss, whose name was Cappy, went on talking

about elephant lore, and Jaime's genuine interest must have won his approval because he added, ''You're a good worker, cap. Maybe I'll ask Ralph to assign you here on a regular basis. You think you could go for that?''

''You bet.''

''Course, you weigh too much to be an elephant boy, but you can help out with the feed, cleaning up, like that.'' He gave Jaime a toothless smile. ''Hope you got a strong back—and a strong stomach. You wouldn't believe how much shit one of them bulls can drop in a day.''

Jaime had a picture of his father's face if he should ever learn that the son of Earl St. Clair, Boston's most conservative corporate lawyer, was shoveling elephant droppings for a living. He must have smiled, because Cappy slapped him on the back and told him he liked a guy with a sense of humor and they were going to get along just fine.

It was a lucky encounter because, he soon learned, Cappy was a dyed-in-the-wool gossip. Nothing went on that he didn't know—sometimes, Jaime suspected, even before it happened. During the next couple of days, it was easy to turn the conversation to Mara. He professed an admiration for her skill, and Cappy agreed, then went on to relay the story of her quick rise to fame. It was from Cappy that he found out about Leo Mueller.

''He really had a fix on Mara. That guy scared me—and I don't scare easy. Good performer, best I ever seen on the trap, but that black pride and hot temper of his was a bad combination. When he got caught with hash on him, he messed up a cop, and they tossed him in the slammer. Nobody here did any crying.''

''What do you mean, 'he had a fix on Mara'?''

''Why, he was crazy about that little gal. Stared at her like he could swaller her whole. Watched every one of her performances, too, and that ain't somethun happens often with the artistes.''

''She wasn't interested in this—uh, Leo?''

''Naw. Couldn't stand the guy.''

He went on to expound on Mara, her talent and spirit. When Cappy called her a natural, Jaime found himself nodding. She was that—in knowing how to play a crowd. And in his own way, so was he a natural—with women.

Was that why he was here, busting his butt shoveling elephant shit, because he'd run into a woman who thought he was a—what had she called him? A coyote?

Just what was he trying to prove, anyway?

By the end of the first week on the job, Jaime had learned more than he cared to about being a working stiff in a circus. He had expected to see Mara often. The reality was that he saw her only from a distance, and then only twice. Since he was hard at work during the matinee and evening performances, he couldn't even watch the show.

Two weeks after he'd joined the circus in St. Petersburg, he still hadn't met Mara face-to-face, much less had the chance to talk to her.

Mara had been fighting a headache for almost three days. It wasn't something new to her. She'd had them all her life. Sometimes they wracked her body for days, then disappeared for as long as a year. Usually they came when she was under some kind of pressure, but this one was a mystery. After all, her career was going well. She was fast becoming the best-known female artiste in the business, rivaling even Lillian Leitzel.

Mr. Sam, after a lot of grousing, had agreed to put one of the circus motor cars at her disposal, had even offered to arrange for her to take driving lessons from one of the show's mechanics. When she realized she'd have to pass a written test to get a license, she declined, which wasn't a hardship, because Lobo was only too glad to take her anywhere she wanted.

As for her personal life, she was getting along well with everybody, even Mr. Sam, who had actually been pleasant lately. Not that she was fooled. Her contract would run out at the end of the season, and he was afraid she would elope—as the circus people called it when anyone decamped for a rival circus.

Well, she had no intention of moving to another circus. But she did want her own private pullman, a parlor car like Lillian Leitzel had. For one thing, Clinker and Lobo could have private rooms on the pullman instead of having to sleep in dorm cars. What's more, she wanted to decorate the car's salon any way she liked. Ever since Clinker had read her that article about Lillian Leitzel's private car, which the reporter had called a "Turkish delight," she'd had her heart set on outdoing her biggest rival. As she pointed out to Mr. Sam—she needed an elegant setting for the times when, at his request, she helped him entertain his business associates and important bankers and politicians.

"Of course, I'll need my own cook," she added, and grinned to herself when he groaned. This was the demand she would give up after a lot of haggling—another old Rom bargaining trick.

Although Mr. Sam hadn't agreed yet, she was sure she'd get her pullman car next season. So everything was going well. Of course, she was a little worried about Jocko. Sometimes she smelled liquor on his breath, and he always seemed to have some woman in tow when she saw him around the lot. That he squandered a lot of money on women was well-known. Also, he had become more demanding, wanting a larger compartment, wanting the circus to pay for his clothes and his props, even though this went contrary to custom.

But they were still good friends. Sometimes they had dinner together and then they talked for hours, just like old times.

So what was the matter with her? She had been sleeping poorly, and when she did fall asleep, why did she invariably dream of that coyote Jaime St. Clair? The dreams were—well, embarrassing. In them, she and Jaime made love, and when she awoke, she would be covered with sweat, and then she couldn't go back to sleep. Maybe, when she had time, she should consult a doctor, a real one. Well, she'd think about it. . . .

It was late June, and the circus was ten weeks into the 1925 circuit, when Mara saw Jaime St. Clair. He was busy painting one of the rides, his back turned, but she recognized him right away. Her first reaction was ambiguous. The man had caused her all kinds of trouble—so why was she smiling? In the end, it was self-anger that made her stalk over to him and demand, "What are *you* doing here?"

He turned and looked at her. "I'm painting over the nasty words some moron wrote on the loop-de-loop cab," he said.

"You know what I mean. Why are you wearing those work clothes, pretending to be a roughie?"

"I *am* a roughie. I thought it would be a lark, working for a circus." He gave her a lopsided grin. "Of course, I didn't much enjoy the First of May treatment. I spent one whole day looking for a left-handed donicker."

Despite herself, she wanted to laugh. "It took you a whole day to figure out they were ragging you?"

"Yeah. But then, I'm not overloaded in the brain department."

"It serves you right. I hope the roughies really gave you a hard time."

"They did. They talked to me into drinking something they

call dynamite rum, which must have equal parts cayenne pepper
and croton oil in it, because it burned a hole straight through. I
spent the night sitting in said donnicker.''

This time she did laugh. ''You still haven't explained what
you're doing here.''

''I think that's obvious. Look, that was a rotten trick I pulled
on you, and I'm really sorry. I deserved that beating your bodyguard gave me. But doesn't that even things up? Can't we start
from scratch? Have dinner with me tonight. There're some great
steak houses here in Indianapolis. I can rent a car—''

''Just what makes you think I'd go out with a roughie?'' she
said, tossing her head.

''Then how about going out with Jaime St. Clair, who thinks
you look like a half-opened rose.''

''The flowers,'' she said. ''You've been sending me white
roses, haven't you?''

''You found me out,'' he said, grinning.

''Those roses cost more than you make in a month on this
job. They call what you're doing slumming, don't they?''

''They call it courting. It was the only way I could think of
to be near you. The funny thing is, I'm enjoying it—well, some
of it, like working for Cappy. I like the bulls. I think I'm in love
with a certain lady called Connie.''

Mara was startled into another smile. ''She's real special.
One of the first friends I made after I joined the circus.''

''So we do agree on one thing. Why don't we find out what
else we have in common. How about that dinner?''

But he'd spoken too quickly, too glibly, and she shook her
head.

''It'll be a cold day in hell before I go out with you, Mr. Joe
College.''

She turned on her heel, so quickly that she almost fell over a
coil of rope. She marched away, not looking back, so she had
no idea how he took her quick retreat.

The next day, the white roses didn't come. Had he given up
so easily? She was surprised at her own disappointment. After
all, it had meant nothing, his sending her those expensive flowers, since he was obviously rich. So wasn't it stupid for her to
feel neglected?

Sometimes she just didn't understand herself. . . .

The circus had a five-day run in Ft. Wayne, which the whole
circus welcomed after a series of one-night stands. Now the

women could catch up on their laundry, get their hair done, or
do some shopping at the local stores, and since there were no
breakdowns at night, everybody, including the tent men, could
socialize, down a few bottles of bootleg beer, knowing they
could get a full night's sleep afterward.

With a couple of nights of undisturbed sleep, Mara should
have felt refreshed, but instead she was depressed, bone-tired
as she returned to her dressing tent after the evening show. For
one thing, the crowd had been restless, even though they'd qui-
eted down during her performance. As she was leaving the backyard, one of the prop men told her that there'd been trouble on
the midway, some towner claiming that he'd been shortchanged
at the whirligig ride. Of course, this happened often. Circuses
and other traveling shows were always vulnerable to this kind of
accusation, which sometimes was justified.

"Bad apples creep in," Mr. Sam had told her once. "But we
toss them out as soon as we find them."

Mara shivered suddenly. All day she'd felt—well, uneasy, as
if something were going to happen. Something unpleasant. Her
eyes sought out the drawer where she kept her tarot cards. If she
hadn't given up that Rom stuff, she would lay out her cards.
Funny—she had started to throw them away a dozen times in
the past three years, but something always stopped her.

As for her uneasiness—it must be the trouble on the midway
that had triggered it off. No wonder she was nervous tonight.

She stripped to her chemise, hung her costume up on its padded hanger, but just as she bent to take off her slippers, she
heard a sound behind. She straightened, whirled around.

Leo Mueller was standing right behind her. He was smiling.
Too stunned to scream, she stared at him. How could Leo Mueller be here when he was in prison, a thousand miles away? Then,
as he took a step closer, panic blossomed inside her like a poi-
sonous flower. She started to run, hoping to reach the door, but
he was too fast. He seized her by the left wrist, held it so tightly
that even with the protection of her copper bracelet, pain shot
up her arm.

"Don't yell or I'll hurt you—bad," he said. He spoke softly,
making his threat far more convincing than if he had raised his
voice.

"If you hurt me, you'll go back to jail," she said, forcing
herself to sound calm.

"I'm never going back to jail." For a moment, his black eyes
blazed with anger. "There was trouble on the lot—who they

going to blame if they find you raped and strangled? Towners, that's who. You think you're so important Mr. Sam would risk having the train chained to the rails by kicking up a fuss? Who gives a damn about a circus slut?''

He jerked her closer, and when she realized he meant to kiss her, she kicked out, landing a solid one on his shin. He cursed viciously and pushed her face against his chest to stifle her screams. He smelled of sweat and tobacco and something else that made her skin curdle.

He smells of death, she thought.

Was this how her life was going to end? Being raped and killed by Leo Mueller?

But she had too much to live for. Her mind churned, fastened on a plan. She stopped struggling and collapsed against him. She began to cry. For a moment he froze, and then he pushed her away so he could look at her.

"What the hell's wrong with you?" he asked, so peevishly that, even in her fear, she wanted to laugh.

"You shouldn't say those things to me. It isn't *my* fault you went to jail," she said, snuffling.

He was quiet for a moment. "You set me up with the tin plates. I never use dope. That hash was planted on me.''

"Not by me. I was sore at you, but I wouldn't do that to you, to anyone. It must have been someone else.''

"Okay, I made a few enemies on the show," Leo said, and because he spoke so rationally, she breathed a little easier. "Maybe it wasn't you. We could have been good together, Mara. That first time you liked it. And then you made me crazy, the way you put on your clothes, the way you looked at me, like I was dirt. But maybe it isn't too late. You know you want me—''

She couldn't help it. A shudder of disgust ran through her body. Leo saw it, interpreted it correctly. His mouth twisted and a black anger blazed in his eyes. He was upon her again, crushing her face against his chest so she couldn't scream, couldn't breathe—

I'm going to die, she thought starkly.

Jaime knew it was a stupid move, going anywhere near Mara's dressing tent. But the fights that had broken out on the midway earlier troubled him, especially when he saw Lobo, the light of the battle in his eyes, in the middle of it, a struggling towner in each huge hand. Mara was probably surrounded by people right now, including the dragon lady, but he had to make sure that she wasn't alone and unprotected before he went off to his berth on the train.

Mara's dressing tent was the last one in a row set up for the convenience of those artistes who rated their own private tents. As he passed Clown Alley, the large tent where the clowns congregated, he heard men's voices, laughing and telling jokes. They sounded so normal that he told himself again that he was crackers, asking for trouble like this.

He passed several more dressing tents, noting that there were no lights showing around their door flaps. The performers, the evening show over, had already gone to the privilege tent or into town for a snack, because they could sleep later in the morning. They would do little drinking, if any. Dangerous tricks didn't mix well with hangovers. It was the working men who would be boozing it up at the local speakeasies. Liquor was their solace, their reward for what he was finding out was exceedingly hard work.

He reached the last tent in the row and stopped. A crack of light showed at the door flap and he knew someone was there. He heard voices—and one was a man's. So Mara was entertaining some lucky guy tonight. Did she have a lover? A siege of jealousy tightened his jaw. There had been no rumors about a lover—but why was he surprised? She was a beautiful, desirable woman—and, he would swear, a very sensual one. . . . The voices stopped, and feeling like a Peeping Tom, he started to turn away, but a sound stopped him. What had that been? A sigh? A cough? No, there it was again—as if someone was choking. . . .

He didn't stop to think. The same reflexes that made him so formidable on the tennis courts sent him racing for the door flaps. He burst through, not bothering to open it first, and the sight of Mara, half-naked and locked in the arms of a dark-haired man, paralyzed him briefly. Then he realized she was struggling, her face full of panic, and the blood rushed to his head, almost blinding him. A second later, he was jerking Mara out of the man's arms.

He hit the man a solid right on his chin, and taken by surprise, the man fell backward. He lay there on the floor, blood pouring from his mouth, and from the crazy way his jaw was moving, Jaime was sure it was broken.

"Try to get up, you bastard, and I'll kill you," he said, meaning every word of it.

But the fight had gone out of the man. He moaned, holding his jaw, and Jaime decided it was safe to look at Mara. To his surprise, she was just standing there, looking very calm.

"What are *you* doing here?" were her first words, the same ones she'd said earlier.

Jaime was too surprised to answer. As he stared at her, he realized that what he had taken for composure was shock. He took a step toward her, opened his arms. She didn't walk into them, but her face crumbled and she began to cry.

There was the sound of running feet outside, and Lobo rushed into the tent. He took one look at Mara, and his face screwed up into an ominous frown. He moved toward Jaime, but Mara stepped between them.

"Stop, Lobo," she said sharply. "It was Leo who tried to—" But she couldn't get the word out.

Lobo looked down and saw Leo on the floor. This time it was Jaime who stepped in front of him.

"His jaw is broken—and from all the blood, I think he bit his tongue when I hit him. Why don't you get him out of here? Let the police take over now."

Lobo reached down and jerked Leo to his feet. At Leo's groan, a savage grin split his ugly face. Pushing his captive in front of him, he left the tent.

"You think that guy is safe with Lobo?" Jaime asked Mara.

She didn't answer. She was busy wiping her eyes. "I was scared," she said, as if she needed to explain the tears. She hiccuped suddenly.

"Go wash your face and you'll feel better."

To his surprise, she disappeared behind the screen. He heard the clink of china, then the sound of water splashing into a bowl. A few minutes later, she was back, and now she was wearing a robe. This time, he was sure her calmness was genuine.

"Where's your maid, the dragon lady?" he asked.

"If you mean Clinker, she's already on the train. She's been sneezing all day, so I told her I'd get Lobo to walk me back to the train—and she isn't my maid. She's my secretary. She's also my best friend. Everybody on the show knows that."

"I want to be your friend, too, Mara," Jaime said softly.

She gave him a scornful look. "And what else do you want?"

Jaime hesitated, then decided to be honest. "I want to be your lover," he said.

She didn't laugh, but there was a sudden glint in her eyes as if she wanted to. "Well, you're honest enough. You wouldn't believe the men who want to be my friend—until they get me alone.''

''You're very beautiful, but you're more than that. You're a very special person.''

''You don't know anything about me.''

''I know you're the most exciting woman I've ever met. I know I'm in love with you.''

She started to say something. Later, he wondered just what she would have said if they hadn't been interrupted. This time it was Mr. Sam, the owner of the circus, and from the look on his face, he was not only worried, but madder than hell.

''You okay, Mara?'' he asked immediately.

''I'm okay,'' she said.

''Some of the boys are holding Leo. They roughed him up a little before I made them stop. Since he didn't hurt you, I'll tell them to dump him outside of town. Otherwise, I don't know if I could stop them from finishing off the job Lobo started.''

''I got a good scare, is all. Tell them to let him go.''

''Wait a minute—you mean you aren't going to turn him over to the police?'' Jaime said.

''And have Mara held here for weeks as a witness? You must be crazy—say, who the devil are you, anyway?''

''Jaime St. Clair. I work for—''

''I remember you now. You work for Cappy. What are you doing here?''

''I was passing the tent when I heard Mara—Princess Mara scream. I rushed in and found her struggling with that man. I hit him and—well, he stopped.''

Mr. Sam frowned at Mara. ''Where was Lobo?''

''He was helping your boys clear out the rowdies on the midway.''

''His job is to guard you.'' He looked at Jaime. ''And it's about time you took off for your berth, fellow.''

You're welcome, Jaime thought resentfully. He nodded at Mara, and started out. She waited until he had reached the door before she said, ''Thank you.''

He went back to the sleeper he shared with twenty-five other roughies. Stripped to his civvies, he crawled into his berth, but he couldn't sleep. Mara had thanked him—and she'd sounded as if she meant it. Did that mean that he'd finally gotten through to her?

Bingo, he thought. He was smiling as he drifted off to sleep.

CHAPTER 19

MR. SAM HAD A FAVORITE FANTASY, THAT HE WAS A LARGE, black, very sinister-looking octopus, with dozens of tentacles extending into every corner of the circus, not excluding the more intimate facets of his employees' lives. After all, a domestic quarrel—say, between the Battling Boques, the show's star equestrian couple—could mushroom into something serious enough to affect the whole circus.

And there had been more than one altercation lately, which, while not domestic, still could have been disastrous to the circus. That business of Leo Mueller's attempted assault on Mara, his top drawing card, for instance. He still shuddered when he thought of what the loss of their star act could have meant to season-to-season revenue.

And he would have hated it on a purely personal level, too. He'd always admired people who had spit, even if it was at his expense. Tempestuous and temperamental she might be, but Mara was a showman, through and through, and she never shorted her audience, not even at the most ill-attended matinee.

With most artists these days, how much they gave was in direct proportion to the size and enthusiasm of the audience. Many a time Mara had saved the show by whipping the audience into a frenzy and sending them home well satisfied that they'd gotten their money's worth.

She was also avaricious, prickly-tempered when she didn't get her own way, and out for herself. But then—so was he. Yeah, so was he.

It was no wonder that his nights lately were anything but restful. There were too many things on his mind—and he was a born worrier. He worried about the sudden decrease in revenues in the Big Top show—someone, probably one of the ducat sell-

202

ers, was knocking down, and he meant to find out just who it was.

Then there was inflation. The customers would only pay so much for a circus ticket, and yet the price of food, gasoline, and engine parts had gone sky high, not to mention the latest gouging from the railroads, who had upped their rates for yet another time.

The world was going to hell, but no one was paying any attention. Everybody was on a roller coaster ride, following fads, and spending money and generally acting crazy. He didn't understand what was happening, but he didn't like what he saw.

So he had a lot to stew about this morning as he walked from the cookhouse to the Silver Wagon, not the least of his worries being what that old fool Joe Lasky was up to. Once, before the war, it had been Bradford and Lasky Circus. But that was before the quarrel that had split the circus in two, almost throwing both into bankruptcy.

The trouble had started with the co-owners courting the same woman. Mr. Sam had won the lady's hand, something for which Joe Lasky had never forgiven him. He had stormed off, taking half the circus with him, to start his own show. Even though Lasky had married another woman within a year and now had two boys, the rivalry continued as if it had a separate life of its own.

As far as Mr. Sam was concerned, it should have died a long time ago. He certainly had no stomach for it. But there was no way he could overlook these latest tricks Joe Lasky had pulled. When the Lasky Circus had deliberately booked approximately the same route for the 1924 season, it had cut both their takes considerably. As for stealing acts, it just wasn't done.

Well, not openly.

God—just when he got a new act built up to where it had a following, old man Lasky wooed it away. The Constantini family was the latest of six acts who had defected to Joe Lasky in the past several years. Even though it was only late June, the big top show was two acts too short—and it was almost impossible to book a decent replacement once the season had opened.

Thank God for Mara. The customers didn't seem to notice how thin the program was spread when she was on the bill. And she never missed a performance. Even when she was under the weather with a cold or had the flu that time, she went on.

Without her—well, he would really be in the soup.

Of course, he'd have to be crazy to admit this to her. Give any artiste the idea he or she was indispensable, and they started demanding special privileges, like better train accommodations and even cuts of the profits.

His old man had had his failings, like a love of the sauce, but he'd known how to handle artistes. "They're like children, Sammy," he'd expounded once. "A little flattery is okay, but not too much. And watch the pay. They only squander it anyway. Whoever heard of an artiste who didn't die broke? So dole out the concessions one at a time."

When the old man died and Mr. Sam inherited his half of Bradford and Lasky Circus, he'd followed that advice. Of course, he didn't have Big Boy's glad hand or that wide good-humored smile, which covered a lot of sins. Mr. Sam was well aware that he was short on charm—and tact.

Which was why he sometimes lost a good act. In fact, it was beginning to look as if he might lose the biggest star the show had ever had if he didn't do something drastic, another reason he hadn't been sleeping well lately.

Mara was getting ready to elope to another show. He was sure of it. She'd been too sweet to him lately. She'd even stopped making demands. What else could that mean except that she had accepted another offer and now her conscience was hurting her?

Was it Joe Lasky, up to his usual tricks? Or was it the big one himself, John Ringling? All that publicity Mara had gotten lately—yeah, it could be she had her sights set on the Big One. Of course, they did have Lillian Leitzel, and Mara was never willing to share publicity. Well, *something* was going on. Maybe it was time to loosen the purse strings a little and give her a bigger cut.

He reached the Silver Wagon, unlocked the door, and went inside. It was stuffy with July heat, and he opened all the windows to let in the early morning breeze. He liked this time alone before the office crew reported in and the day's problems started—and start they would.

His twenty-four-hour man, who was one of the best "fixers" in the business, was having trouble with the local sheriff, who was sitting on the water permit, and who wanted—hell, who knew what he wanted? He'd find out soon enough. That was the one sure thing about a circus, that the local authorities would turn up sooner or later, usually with their hand out.

Maybe it was because there always seemed to be so much money around a show. Nickels and dimes and quarters changing hands right and left. It never seemed to occur to outsiders to wonder how big the nut was. The expenses of running a show with over six hundred employees were enormous. Just feeding that crew cost more than feeding the convicts of most state prisons.

Mr. Sam crossed to his battered old desk and sat down, but he didn't get to work immediately. He leaned back in his chair, his eyes closed, planning out the day. Doc McCall was complaining not only about the food the cats were getting but about the travel cages again, claiming they were unsanitary. He'd have to do something about that, maybe invest in some new ones.

And then the feud between Jocko and that charlie, Bubbles, was heating up again. Usually he let the clowns work out their own problems, but Jocko was too valuable to be out of the show with injuries. Well, he'd talk to Bubbles and tell him to lay off the rough stuff. If that didn't work, he'd can the damned bully. Maybe he should have done that a long time ago.

After all, Jocko was a producing clown, the best in the business. Most of the gags in the program were his—and he came up with new ones every year. What's more, he shared them with the other Joeys, including Bubbles. . . .

Someone coughed behind him. When Mr. Sam saw the portly man standing in the doorway, he plastered a broad smile on his face and surged to his feet.

"Come in, Sheriff Bentley," he said, summoning up his most hearty tone. "Just about to make some coffee. How about joining me?"

"I didn't come here for no coffee," the man said. "What's all this about banning local concessions?"

"Now, Sheriff, you know our policy. We like to cooperate with the local charities and such, but last time we was here, your people weren't too particular about who they hired to run their booths. Bradford Circus is strictly legit, you know."

"So you say. Well, maybe I'll just hang on to that water permit. For sanitary reasons. Seems to me there was a lot of garbage laying around the fairgrounds after you folks checked out last year," Sheriff Bentley blustered.

Mr. Sam fought back a desire to curse. "Let's not be hasty— tell me what exactly it is that you want. Maybe we can come to some agreement."

Although obviously not mollified, the sheriff took the chair Mr. Sam offered. "It's my wife, Elizabeth. She and her lady friends are trying to raise money for their garden club—"

Mr. Sam almost groaned out loud. If he let in one, then every

charity and club in the county would be on his back. And if he
didn't, then he could kiss that water permit good-bye.

"Mr. Sam—you in there?"

Even if he hadn't recognized Mara's voice, he would have
known who it was. The sheriff, already on his feet, had a dazed
look in his porky eyes. Like someone just kicked him in the
balls, Mr. Sam thought sourly.

"Come on in, Mara," he said, so heartily that she gave him
a surprised look. Her eyes took in the sheriff's flushed face, and
a mischievous smile played around her mouth.

"Why, I didn't know you had company." She gave the sheriff
her most dazzling smile. "Why don't you introduce me to the
gentleman, Mr. Sam?"

To Mr. Sam, who knew how quickly she could turn off that
charm, the next few minutes were nerve-racking. Even so, by
the time the sheriff left, he was finding it hard to hide his amusement. The man,- completely bedazzled by Mara, not only produced the water permit, but he forgot all about his wife's garden
club. In fact, when Mara asked him and his wife to be her guest
and sit in the owner's box at the evening performance, he practically slobbered.

After he'd seen the sheriff out, Mr. Sam turned back to Mara,
wondering what this was going to cost him. "So what are you
doing here so early in the morning?" he asked. "You usually
sleep in after a long haul."

"It's about my contract," Mara said. "I thought it was time
we had a private talk."

"What's this?" Mr. Sam said, instantly wary. "You aren't
satisfied with drawing the highest pay in the show? Who's been
talking to you? I hear old Lasky himself was out there last week
in Memphis, sitting in the blues. He was wearing false whiskers
and eyeglasses, but Oly Johnson spotted him. Did he make you
an offer?"

"I don't know what you're talking about." She gave him a
hurt look, and Mr. Sam's suspicions soared. As did his anger.

"Don't forget we got a contract—and it's got several months
yet to go."

"Why, Mr. Sam, you've got it all wrong! I came here to tell
you that I'm going to stop pestering you about that parlor car. It
isn't worth all the fuss. Which is what I told this agent I was
talking to—"

"What agent?" he interrupted.

"His name is Joseph Conti. Says he's from New York." Her

green eyes were wide and innocent. Too wide. Too innocent. Surely she knew that Joe Conti was the biggest circus talent agent in New York. Or did she? It was always so hard to tell with Mara. . . .

"He told me that according to my contract—I didn't see any harm in just letting him take a peek at it—I can accept winter bookings if I want."

"I have the final say-so about winter bookings!"

"Well, yes, that's true. But as I told Mr. Conti when he asked me to sign up with him, I'm so sure you won't give me any trouble about winter bookings—and other things—at contract time this year that I really don't need an agent."

She smiled at him, murmured something about meeting Jocko for breakfast, and was gone, leaving him sore enough to bite nails—and also totally alarmed.

It wasn't just that business about taking winter bookings. He could live with that. But she'd been much too reasonable, even sweet. And that wasn't like her, not at all. Which probably meant she'd already made up her mind to leave the show at the end of the season.

Well, it went against the grain, giving her a parlor car, but he couldn't afford to lose his star act. Sure, he had some great acts, but they didn't create publicity for the circus like Mara did. What could a journalist write about the Chungs, a family of fourteen acrobats, none of whom spoke English? Or about a lion trainer who hated reporters and refused to talk to them?

But Mara positively glowed during interviews, charming the hell out of even the most hard-nosed reporter. And she always came up with something different, something they could hang a story on.

So she had him over a barrel. She could go to the Big One or Lasky any time she wanted. And that meant he had to deal with her on her own terms.

That afternoon, after the matinee performance, Mr. Sam went to Mara's compartment, taking along a bottle of domestic champagne and a box of chocolates, like, he thought in disgust, a goddamned suitor. He offered to tear up her old contract on the spot, to sign a new one that would increase her salary ten percent, permit her to take winter season jobs—within reason. He would assign a parlor car to her, decorated and furnished in any manner she chose—within reason. What's more, the circus would pay Clinker's salary from now on, as well as Lobo's.

In return, she would appear at all circus promotion events, give interviews, and entertain dignitaries in her dressing tent and private car.

"And do it graciously," he added, already regretting the concessions he'd made.

"Why, of course! You know I love people," she said, looking surprised.

"Anything else you want?" he said, sarcastically.

"Yes." He was completely nonplussed when she leaned forward and kissed his cheek. "There," she said. "That wasn't so hard, was it?"

Mr. Sam didn't answer; he was afraid he might start swearing.

Jaime was lying on his bunk, trying to get some rest. He had spent the day cleaning out cages, hauling water, shoveling sawdust and less pleasant things, and every muscle in his body ached. Something else ached, too. His pride. A dozen times he'd made the decision to give it up, to return home, where he could sleep in a decent bed, take all the hot showers he wanted, change his clothes every hour if he liked. The only reason he was still here was the fact that he wasn't a quitter—at least not yet.

The worse thing was boredom. It wasn't so much the labor, although it was hard and grueling, but the people he had to put up with. The conversation was almost totally circus gossip or tales of the "good old days," when circuses had really been circuses—whatever that meant. The rest of the world, politics and art and literature, might not have existed, although he'd had a couple of good political arguments with the old vet, Doc McCall.

And there were other things. He was sick of snores and hacking coughs and strange odors in the hot confines of the working men's sleeping car at night. Sick of early risings and late nights, of breaking down the show at white-hot speed and then, after a miserable night in an airless sleeper, of putting the canvas up again. He was tired of taking crap from men who couldn't even write their own names, tired of being the butt of jokes because he was a First of May guy, of being dirty and sweaty and bored.

He'd always thought of himself as being democratic, as opposed to his father, who was the world's greatest reactionary. But he was learning that there were limits. If he had to hear one more scatological joke, he was going to barf. If that made him a snob, so be it. . . .

He drifted off to sleep, and the next morning, after what he had to admit was a decent and more than generous breakfast, he was assigned to the elephant stalls again by Ralph "Pops" Kobochef, the work crew boss. Four hours later, he was still cleaning out elephant stalls, and since it was hotter than hell, he was not happy about it.

True, it was better than some of the jobs he'd been handed since he'd joined the circus—such as cleaning the clown's dressing tent after a four-day run. Clown Alley seemed an appropriate name for it since he'd hauled a ton of garbage out of there. He winced, remembering the bobby trap someone had rigged, a tin can under pressure that had exploded in his face when he picked it up, covering him with talcum powder. Maybe he'd laugh about it someday when he was telling his grandkids about his circus days, but at the time, he'd had to grit his teeth to keep from lighting into those jokers. . . .

On the other hand—well, it *had* been funny. He must have looked like a marshmallow, white from head to toe.

He was grinning when he turned, a load of elephant droppings in his shovel, and almost tripped over Jocko, who was standing directly behind him.

"I want to talk to you," the midget said in a deep voice Jaime found incongruous with his size.

"Talk away," Jaime said. He deposited the droppings into a wheelbarrow, then leaned the shovel against the stall. He wiped the sweat off his face with his forearm, smiling down at the little clown.

Jocko didn't smile back. "Stay away from Mara," he said. "You spell trouble, and she doesn't need any more of that."

"You've got it all wrong. I wouldn't hurt her for the world."

"You really believe that, don't you? That only proves how stupid you are."

His words were a little slurred, and Jaime gave him a closer look. Had the little guy been drinking? Was it Dutch courage that made him so belligerent?

"Look, I only want to be her friend—like you," he said.

"Don't patronize me, you bastard. I'm a better man than you'll ever be."

"I don't doubt that." Jaime kept his voice even. "But you're wrong about me. I want what's best for her—"

"Then get the hell out of her life. You're a self-indulgent, rich jerk who gets everything he wants. Mara doesn't understand your type. She's naive and trusting and—"

"Mara? You're talking about the same girl who just talked
Mr. Sam out of a parlor car to herself?"

For the first time, Jocko's face softened. "That was a bit of
all right, wasn't it? But I'm not talking about finances. She thinks
she knows all about men, but she doesn't. She's never run up
against anyone like you before. And I don't want her hurt."

"I don't want to hurt her," Jaime said softly.

"Then get out of her life—"

"That's an Oxford accent," Jaime said. "So what are you
doing, playing clown in a circus?"

"When I could be standing on a stool behind a podium, trying
to get the students to stop giggling long enough to teach them
philosophy? Or do you see me in a law court, trying a case while
the jury snickers behind my back?"

"Maybe you should have taken a chance," Jaime said, and
then wished he could have recalled the words when Jocko gave
him a black look and stalked away.

A bottle fly buzzed around Jaime's face, and he brushed it
away absently. He wanted to refute Jocko's accusations, but he
couldn't. Because the man was right. He'd never thought beyond
his own gratification. He couldn't even offer Mara a long-term
relationship. The only reason he'd been able to tolerate the circus was because he knew that he could walk away at any time.

But to stay on for an extended time, even for the remainder
of the season—hell, that wasn't possible. For one thing, he would
be doing postgrad work in September. As for marriage, that was
totally out of the question. There were a dozen reasons why it
was impossible, starting with how his father would react. Also,
he would hate being Mr. Princess Mara—which was what would
happen if he stayed on as a drone.

And he couldn't take Mara back to Boston. She would be
miserable there. The circus was her life, her only life. So the
little guy was right. It was time he left. And yet—it was going
to be hard, walking away, just when he could see small signs
that she was beginning to weaken, that she was as aware of him
these days as he was of her. . . .

That evening, after the evening performance, he was waiting
for Mara in the backyard when she came out of the big top.
Lobo, the big mute guy who acted as her bodyguard, was close
behind her. He spotted Jaime and gave him a ferocious scowl.

"Can I talk to you, Mara—alone?" Jaime asked.

To his surprise, she didn't argue. "Mr. St. Clair can see me
to my dressing tent," she told Lobo. "I'll be okay."

Lobo's craggy face lengthened, but he turned and walked away, the set of his bulky shoulders radiating disapproval. Jaime wondered absently if the big mute was in love with Mara—like half the men in the circus.

When they reached her dressing tent, Mara dismissed Clinker, saying she had some business to discuss with "Mr. St. Clair." Whatever the older woman thought, she didn't argue, but she gave Jaime a look that could have scalded a pig as she went out, closing the flaps behind her.

"So what's on your mind?" Mara said.

Not for the first time, Jaime wondered at her accent. Sometimes her speech had a southern flavor, and other times, it reflected Jocko's Oxford accent. Was she an unconscious mimic or was it something she cultivated deliberately? And if things had worked out differently, and he had been around her long enough, would she have begun speaking with a Boston accent?

"Well, what is it? I don't have all night to waste on you," she said, her voice haughty.

"I came to say good-bye," he said. "I have to return to Boston. Personal business."

"Well, I'm sure I don't want to keep you here any longer when you must have packing to do. Good night—and good-bye, Mr. St. Clair."

Her voice was very cool, but there was something in her eyes that made him say, "I made a mistake, taking a job in the circus just to be near you. Which is something one of your friends just pointed out to me."

Before he could turn away, she attacked him. At first, he was too astonished to defend himself from her surprisingly hard fists as she flailed away at him. She landed a couple of painful blows on his chin before he put his hands up to protect his face.

"You conceited bastard," she raged. "As if I care what you do. I knew you were playacting all along. What was it? Another bet with your friends? How dare you act like I'm the one chasing *you*! Now get out of here before I yell for Lobo!"

She hit him again, this time on the ear, but he didn't move. When she burst into tears, he just stood there, not knowing what to do. After a while he put his arms around her, half expecting her to attack him again, but she collapsed against him, making little shuddering sounds.

Something primitive and self-serving took over. Jaime pushed her hair away from her face and kissed her wet lips. It was his last conscious thought for a long time. As if every bone, sinew, and muscle in his body had been waiting for this moment, he was lost in a sensual daze.

The kiss deepened, became more than a touching of lips and a meeting of tongues. He'd kissed so many girls before that he knew every nuance of the technique, but all that went out the window now. The kiss, lacking any form of gentleness now, was a ruthless demand for total surrender. Only when she gasped with pain did he release her.

Without a word, she began to undress—and so did he. Their eyes fixed greedily on each other's bodies, they removed their clothing until both of them stood naked, revealed to each other. He had time for one abstract thought, that his need for her was so urgent, it was going to be hard to hold back until she was ready, and then he picked her up in his arms and carried across the tent, seeking out her brass daybed like a spawning salmon returning to its birthplace.

He laid her on the bed, but he didn't join her, not immediately. Instead, he bent over her, exploring her with his eyes, his fingertips. He ran his forefinger along the curve of her full lips, down to her throat, between her breasts and over the soft mound of her belly, finally burying it in the downy triangle below. She writhed against it, making small, incoherent sounds, her eyes glazed and unfocused.

After a while he stretched out beside her, kissing her, finally rolling on top of her, and she opened herself to him immediately, pressing urgent hands against his buttocks as he buried himself in the soft, hot sheath of her body.

He had expected that making love to Mara would be special, if only because of his long wait, but it was more than that. It was total, a complete blocking out of everything except pure sensation. Even the small self-conscious part of himself that was always aware of appearance, of performance, was stilled as the rush to climax started.

Beneath him, Mara rocked and gasped and made small mewling sounds, and he was aware, as if they were joined in more than their bodies, of her frenzied need. Then everything seemed to implode and nothing else mattered except his own satisfaction.

When he came back to earth again, everything had changed. He had changed. Whatever it cost him, cost her, he knew that he wasn't going to walk away.

As if she'd read his mind—or maybe his *gadjo* face?—Mara laughed softly. "What was it you said about going back to Boston?'' she purred against his ear, and he laughed and pulled her over on top of him and began kissing her again.

The second time was slower, less frenzied. There was time to explore the depths of their hunger for each other. He realized finally what the Bible meant when it spoke of a man knowing a woman. Because there was so much to learn about this woman— how soft and resilient and giving that tough little body felt under his touch, how moist the delicate tissues between her thighs became when he kissed her there, how eagerly, generously, she returned his caresses. Most of all, he learned that the first time hadn't been a fluke, that the world could explode around him without notice when he was in the final throes of ecstasy.

"So what are we going to do about this?" Mara said when their breathing had returned to normal, reminding him that for all her sexuality, she was a very practical woman.

He didn't hesitate. He didn't even blink. "I think we'd better get married," he said, burying his face in the softness of her breasts.

CHAPTER 20

IN THE TWO YEARS SINCE HER MARRIAGE TO JAIME—AND THE year since their daughter's birth—Mara had encountered numerous questions about her marriage and had become adept at evading them. Today's interviewer was a woman, a journalist who had contracted to write an article about Mara for *Liberty Magazine*, and she was unusually insistent. She was tall, handsome, elegantly thin. Her eyebrows had been sacrificed to fashion, replaced by two penciled-in lines, and her dress, one of the new flounced styles that stopped just above the knee, was very stylish, unusually so for a working woman, Mara decided.

As she answered the journalist's questions, she pretended not to notice how the woman's eyes darted around the salon, taking in the stylish "moderne" furniture, the porcelain figurine of a winged woman who looked remarkably like Mara herself, and the expensive black lacquer accent pieces.

She wasn't surprised when the woman commented, "Your furnishings are delightful, but somehow I expected antiques. I understand your husband's family home is like a museum."

"Which is why he enjoys a change," Mara said sweetly— and, she realized immediately, indiscreetly.

"Then he really does come from the Boston St. Clairs?"

"He is from Boston," Mara said shortly.

"And his father is Earl St. Clair, the attorney?"

"His father's name is Earl, yes."

Clinker, who was always in evidence during interviews, leaned forward to replenish the tea in the journalist's cup. "Would you like more lemon, Miss Short?" she asked in her most genteel tones.

Distracted by the question, the woman asked for sugar, and when she returned to the interview, Jaime's ancestry was dropped—to Mara's relief. She always tried to shield Jaime from publicity, knowing his innate need for privacy. Unfortunately this wasn't always possible, and she suspected that at least some of his recent moodiness was caused by a particularly gushy magazine article that described him as "Princess Mara's golden-haired, aristocratic husband."

And yet, what could she do about it? As Jim Boris, the circus publicist, had pointed out, their marriage had all the ingredients of a fairy story. Rich man's son falls in love with famous circus aerialist, herself a princess, is estranged from his family when they marry. A year later, a beautiful child, a daughter named Victoria, is born to them. A fairy tale. The fact that Jaime was outrageously good-looking didn't hurt the legend.

"—possible to photograph your husband and you together? At your convenience, of course," Miss Short was saying.

"I'm afraid that isn't possible," Clinker said, again answering for Mara. "Mr. St. Clair is a very private person. He prefers to stay out of the limelight. You can understand that, considering his background. And if you don't mind, Princess Mara has a matinee in just an hour, and she must start getting ready. . . ."

Still talking, she stood, leaving the woman little choice but to stand, too.

"Well, I did want—how about a picture of your daughter? I hear she is a delightful baby."

"Oh, Vicky is delightful, but you must understand that for

security reasons, we prefer not to have her exposed to publicity. However, I'd be glad to set up an appointment for you to photograph Princess Mara's pullman car. Most outsiders are intrigued by how comfortably our artistes live on the road.''

As Clinker ushered the journalist out, Mara smiled to herself. Her friend had become an expert at handling visitors, even sharpeyed reporters. But her smile was short-lived, and unconsciously she sighed. For the past week, she'd felt depressed, a state rare to her since her marriage.

Or was it all that rare? Lately she'd been aware of an uneasiness, the source of which she couldn't put her finger on. Was it one of her premonitions? No, that was stupid. She'd put all that Rom nonsense behind her. These days she had everything a woman could possibly want, didn't she? A handsome, attentive husband, a healthy, beautiful daughter, a career that exceeded all her childhood dreams. She was very wealthy—no, not wealthy. Jaime had told her once that the rich called themselves rich. So she was rich, or so Clinker, who handled her financial records for her, was always telling her.

Her name was that rare thing for a circus performer—a household name even to people who had never been near a circus. Articles had been published about her in half the newspapers and magazines in the country, and there had been two books, purporting to be fiction but obviously based on what was common knowledge about her life. In both novels there was this fiery-haired heroine, a beautiful aerialist who performs astonishing feats on a trapeze, and who was, in one novel, a Gypsy princess; in the other, a Hungarian countess by birth.

Both novels included a romantic incident that had estranged her from her noble family. That much of the legend seemed to be set in stone—that she'd been disowned by her family because she'd fallen in love with an unsuitable man. And both novels ended, after numerous adventures and misadventures, with her marriage to a wealthy blue blood.

Then there were the articles, some of them bordering on the ridiculous because they were so far off the mark. It was almost universally accepted by now, after so many "exposés," that she was not a Gypsy. What she really was, no one had yet pinned down.

And never will, Mara thought complacently. Because there was no record of her birth anywhere in the world. She had no idea herself where she'd been born, although she knew it had been in England. To her family, she didn't exist, had never existed. Even if some reporter, more enterprising than the others, tracked down her *kumpania*, her relatives would stare at him with their veiled Rom eyes and deny her existence.

Which was why she'd never told Jaime the truth, why she'd let him go on thinking she was from Hungary, an orphan without any family. With his own ancestry, which could be traced back to something called "Hastings," how could she possibly tell him that she came from a race he considered inferior?

Just after Vicky's birth, he'd laughed one day while reading an article about her and said he was glad that ridiculous story about her being a Gypsy was dying out. He wouldn't want their daughter growing up thinking she had mongrel blood in her veins.

Before she realized what he thought of Gypsies, she would have told him the truth in time, but not after he'd shown his contempt for her race. Not that she hadn't wanted to point out a few truths, that her people were far more pure-blooded than his own mixed ancestry—English and Welsh and Scots. But she couldn't take a chance. Oh, he wouldn't stop loving her. He was too fair for that. But what if she saw contempt in his eyes? What if he changed, ever so slightly?

There were other secrets, too, she kept from Jaime.

He had no idea she was illiterate. Without Clinker to protect her secret, he would have guessed long ago. As it was, he thought it was vanity that prevented her from getting reading glasses and sometimes made it necessary for him to read something aloud to her. She knew she should tell him the truth, and yet—with his fine Harvard education, wouldn't he be ashamed of a wife who could barely write her first name?

She should have learned to read by now, of course. The thing was—if she took lessons at this late date, it was sure to leak out. There were few secrets around a circus. The word would get back to Jaime, and it would surely anger him, not only that she'd lied, but that all those stories about her noble birth, which he halfway believed, were pure fiction.

Several times she had thought of asking Jocko to teach her how to read, but then how could it possibly remain a secret? And besides, Jocko was so often difficult these days. There were rumors that he'd been in a couple of bar brawls, brought on by his own sarcastic tongue. He hadn't been hurt, just knocked around, but one of these days he would insult the wrong person when none of his drinking buddies were around to protect him. What was bothering him, anyway? He so seldom came around anymore. Only the baby seemed to draw him. Vicky's mother, he virtually ignored. . . .

Mara's face softened, thinking of the baby. Right now Vicky was sleeping in the nursery at the other end of the car. Her nanny, an import from England, was devoted to her—and no wonder. Vicky was a dream child, with her father's ice-blue eyes and fair skin. Although she had her mother's red hair, it was darker, more auburn than true red. In fact, she looked like the princess Jaime called her. "Princess Sunshine" was his favorite name for her. All she lacked was a crown.

"Why the grin, love?" It was Jocko, smiling at her from the open door. "Don't tell me. You've just talked Mr. Sam out of my percentage of the profits."

Although Mara smiled back, she felt a small hurt. True, she hadn't had much time for Jocko since her marriage, but that didn't mean her feelings for him had changed. Lately his remarks to her were often barbed by the same sarcasm he showed others, and sometimes he went too far and she had to hold tightly to her temper.

Not that she ever quarreled with him. How could she when she owed him so much? He'd been her friend when she needed one so badly—and he'd kept all her secrets, too, which was astonishing in a man who loved his gossip so much.

So she pretended not to catch the edge in his voice and said, "I was thinking of Vicky. She's just learning to sit up now, and she won't let anyone help her. Takes after me, I think."

Jocko's face softened. "The circus princess—everybody's favorite child."

"Yours, too, I expect," she said lightly.

"Well, blame it on my frustrated paternal instincts."

"Oh, one of these days you'll meet the right woman and start your own family," she teased.

"I've already met the right woman. But she doesn't have any time for me since she married her prince."

Mara decided it was time to change the subject. "So what's new from the circus rumor mills?"

Jocko settled himself on the low hassock Mara kept just for him. "I detect one of your husband's phrases here. A couple of years ago, you wouldn't have known what that meant."

"As a matter of fact, I think it's one of your phrases," she retorted.

"Touché. You know, you do that so well. You soak up everything you hear like a sponge, then make it your own. Even so,

I'm amazed he's never guessed your—uh, problem. Don't you think it's time you told him? After all, it's such a small secret. Half the circus is illiterate.''

"I will. When the right time comes."

"Don't you trust the guy to understand?''

She flushed. "Of course I trust him. I love him—and he loves me."

"Which isn't quite the same thing as trust, is it?''

"I don't know what you mean—no, don't answer that. I think we should change the subject."

He studied her for a long moment. She sensed something fermenting behind that stare, and she braced herself to hear something she didn't want to hear. But to her surprise, he nodded agreeably.

"Okay—let's see. The latest gossip . . . Have you heard about Konrad Barker's summer wife? They had this fight—dishes thrown, a lot of yelling—and after he stormed off, she got his supply of bootleg hooch and poured it out on the ground. When he came back and realized the mud he was wading through was his whiskey, it was instant divorce. But not before she broke every dish in his van.''

They were still laughing when Jaime arrived. He looked very tired, and his greeting nod to Jocko was perfunctory. Without speaking, he poured himself a drink from the bottle of scotch he kept behind the books in one of the black lacquer cabinets. Only after he'd finished it off did he bend his head to kiss Mara's cheek.

"So how is the menagerie business these days?" Jocko asked.

For a while they talked about a problem Jaime, who was menagerie boss, was having with a young rhino who wasn't adjusting to train travel. Although both men were polite, Mara was relieved when Clinker returned.

She gave the two men a disapproving look. "It's time you got ready for the spec," she told Mara.

Mara nodded, but it occurred to her that Clinker was getting a little too high-handed these days. Or, as Jaime would say, she was exceeding her authority. He resented Clinker's proprietary ways, but then, he didn't understand how much she relied on her friend.

Mara wondered, as she had so often lately, if he was happy with his job. When Mr. Sam had made Jaime menagerie manager at the beginning of this, the 1927 season, he'd had no problem taking over. Everybody in the show liked him these days—with three exceptions. And wasn't it ironic that it was her three best friends, Clinker, Jocko, and Lobo, who were the exceptions?

Jaime made the excuse there was something he'd forgotten to tell Cappy Hines, the elephant boss, to escape from the parlor car. Usually it was a haven he returned to each day after work, but not when it held Jocko, who made little attempt to hide his hostility.

More and more, he was bored with circus gossip, at which the midget and Clinker, Mara's assistant-cum-nursemaid, were so adept. After all, the circus was a splinter society, out of step with what was going on in the rest of the world. It was as isolated from reality as life inside a prison, with a preponderance of its inmates outcasts and misfits.

Which made him wonder why it held such a fascination for people from other walks of life—judges, politicians, movie stars, even a president or two. Was it because it seemed, to outsiders, such an irresponsible way of living? A happy-go-lucky world afloat in the middle of the grim reality of the real world?

Not true, at least where he was concerned. There was a grim sameness about life in the circus despite the constant change of scenery. It was a rigidly structured and pragmatic world without mental stimulation. And yet it was Mara's world, the only one she knew—or wanted. To her, leaving it would be unthinkable, something he could never ask of her. As for him—to be with Mara, the first person in the world whom he loved without reservation, he would put up with just about anything, even the restrictions of circus life.

His job, as menagerie manager, didn't help. Oh, Mr. Sam had fired the old manager for inefficiency, and there really had been an opening, but there were other men, much more qualified, like Cappy Hines, whom he could have promoted. It would be different if he'd been offered a job in management. After all, he was better-educated than anyone else in the show except, ironically enough, Jocko. So what the hell was he doing, ordering beast boys around, when he was capable of something much more challenging?

It didn't help that his father had pointed this very thing out to him in his latest letter. After the old man had disinherited him, he hadn't expected to ever hear from him again. Even so, out of a sense of duty, he'd sent his parents notification of Vicky's birth. The first letter from his father had been a surprise, especially since it held a conciliatory note, saying he'd decided to test the water and see if the two of them couldn't at least be civilized about "this business."

In this and later letters, Earl St. Clair had never made the mistake of attacking Mara directly. If he had, Jaime would have stopped writing—and the old man knew it. Getting those letters was strangely pleasant. Maybe because, for the first time in his life, his father was treating him like a man.

Not that he had encouraged the old man's hope that he would "regain his senses" and come back to Boston. He couldn't ask Mara to go with him, and since he couldn't live without Mara, that was that. God, he did love that woman! She was such a strange mixture of wisdom and ignorance, pragmatism and intuition. Sometimes she seemed able to read his mind. In fact, he had almost made the mistake of asking if this was because of her Gypsy blood.

He hadn't known about that until he'd found the fortune-telling cards, hidden away in the bottom of her jewelry chest. He'd been looking for a misplaced cuff link when he'd opened the chest. The tarot cards, so worn that it was hard to make them out, told it all.

And this, just after he'd made that stupid remark about being glad the rumor of her Gypsy birth was dying because he wouldn't want Vicky to believe she had Gypsy blood—no, damn it, he'd used the words *mongrel blood*—in her veins.

It was too late to do anything to negate that stupid, snobbish remark. She would never believe that he'd just been smarting off, that he didn't really give a damn what her ancestry was. After all, his own background was more than a little suspect, no matter how his relatives touted their blue blood. A great-grandmother with a rather shady past . . . an uncle, three generations back, who had made a fortune as a profiteer during the Civil War, ferrying contraband back and forth across the Ohio . . . a cousin who had done something unsavory in the stock market that had been quickly hushed up after he'd resigned his seat and gone into exile in Brazil.

But if he produced these relatives as evidence that his blood wasn't all that blue, she would read it as pity—or condescendence. And she would be outraged. So he'd said nothing. How could he explain that it made him love her more that she wasn't the royalty so many people assumed she was?

Well, no matter. He was coping, hanging on, and in the main, happy. But it was about time he did something about his own career. He'd been drifting, but that was all going to end—today.

He quickened his pace, heading toward the Silver Wagon van, which was both Mr. Sam's quarters on the road and the circus staff's meeting place. He caught Mr. Sam just as he was leaving for the evening performance.

"Do you mind if I walk along with you, sir?" Jaime said. No matter what his private opinion of the circus owner might be—obstinate, bullheaded, a miser—he was always polite to him.

"What's on your mind, Jaime?"

"There'll be an opening when Jim Boris retires at the end of the season. I could do his job."

"I'm not so sure. Twenty years he's handled promotions and publicity for the show, including much of the legal work, and he's done a good job. You think you can fill the shoes of a man like that?"

"Not at first. But I'm a fast learner."

Mr. Sam eyed him balefully. "I've had a few bad experiences with fast learners."

Jaime felt his temper stir. "Make up your mind before the end of the season. I'm not going to spend another year in the menagerie. Cappy should have been given that job in the first place."

"So now you're telling me how to run my business? You wouldn't have some idea that being married to Mara gives you special privileges, would you?"

"No, sir. I do not. But I think I'm ready for the publicist job. Don't you?"

For a moment, he thought Mr. Sam would explode into one of his famous tirades, but instead his pale eyes grew a twinkle. "Been thinking about you for old Jim's job. I wondered when you'd get up the gumption to ask for it. You can sit in with him starting tomorrow. When he retires, the job's yours—provided you can handle it by then."

Jaime didn't know what to say. Hadn't it been too easy? Was this more of the same old Mr. Princess Mara thing? If so, did it matter? All he wanted was the chance to prove himself. . . .

After he left Mr. Sam in the backyard, he took his time walking back toward the train siding. Although he seldom missed Mara's evening performance, which enchanted him as much now as it had the first time, there were things he wanted to thrash out before he told her the news. *And we'll live happily ever after,* he thought with only a tinge of irony.

He was passing the artistes' dressing tents now. From Clown Alley, the largest of the tents, he heard raucous laughter, a voice loudly singing an off-key ditty. He had never understood the relationship between the clowns. They played outrageous and sometimes dangerous practical jokes on one another, carried on furious feuds, and yet they stuck together in a way that excluded outsiders. But then, as Jocko had once pointed out to him, what would a circus be without its clowns?

He was thinking of his latest encounter with the irascible clown when he sensed a movement behind him. Instinctively he whirled and flung up his hand. The man who stepped out of the shadows was dark-haired, lean and familiar.

"Pay-up time," Leo Mueller said softly.

Jaime saw the knife in his hand. As it flew through the air toward him, he fancied he felt the cold wind of its passage preceding it. The knife sliced into him, plunging between his ribs. Darkness fell, blotting out Leo's thin smile; there was only time for one thought—regret that he would never get the chance to tell Mara one more time that he loved her before he died. . . .

Mara did her performance in a mechanical way, for once the magic that usually took place between her and an audience failing her. She was glad that, because of an unusually late start, Konrad Barker had given the musical signal for a "quick" show, which meant each performer was expected to cut four minutes out of his act.

Ordinarily Mara paid no attention to quick calls. She put in her full twelve minutes, no matter what the weather or other emergencies. But tonight she cut her flanges to twenty-five and only took a couple of bows after she'd descended the rope. Even so, the applause was generous, and usually she would have milked it for a while, but tonight she nodded at Lobo to carry her out of the arena even before the applause began to die.

Lobo waited patiently outside her dressing tent while she changed into slacks and a sweater. From the big top, she heard the blast of trumpets as the clowns tumbled their way through the final walk-around. The crowd had seemed subdued tonight—or maybe she'd imagined it because of her own mood. Something was eating at her—was she upset because Jaime hadn't been there to watch her performance?

At the door of the parlor car, she said good night to Lobo and told him to get some rest. But he shook his head and refused to leave. When she lost patience and reminded him brusquely that Jaime would look after her now, he gave her a brooding look and shambled off into the darkness.

She went inside, only to find the salon empty. Where was Jaime? Always, even when there was some emergency in the menagerie and he missed a performance, he was here when she returned, waiting to share a late snack with her. They would dissect the night's show, the audience, her performance, and his problems at the menagerie, and later they would go to bed and make love, because that part of their marriage had never lost its magic.

So where the hell was he? Had Jocko, when he assured her so earnestly today that Jaime never paid any attention to the women who flirted with him, really been trying to warn her?

A flash of jealousy galvanized her, and she picked up a chair and flung it across the room. *Damn him,* she thought, not meaning Jaime, but Jocko, for planting suspicion in her mind.

Well, it wasn't going to work. When Jaime got home, she wouldn't ask where he'd been and why he hadn't come to see her performance. She would be so loving, so affectionate, that he'd think he was in heaven. She wasn't worried about other women. She knew his needs so well, and she was all the woman he could handle, because she gave him what no other woman could. Of course, that didn't mean that if she ever found out he'd even *looked* at another woman, she wouldn't scratch the bitch's eyes out. . . .

She changed into a white satin robe, brushed out her hair, and then, because she was hungry, nibbled a pickle from the covered tray of snacks that Clinker had left out for them.

She thought she heard Vicky cry out in the nursery, but when she listened, there was no repeat of the sound. She didn't check on her, because the nanny slept in the same compartment and would consider it an affront if she did.

How strange that she should let a nurse tell her whether or not she could go into the nursery and pick up her own child. It wasn't a matter of spoiling her. Vicky was sunny-natured, well-behaved, unaware that she was not only the darling of her father and mother but the sweetheart of the whole circus—including Mr. Sam.

Restlessly she wandered around the salon, remembering how Jaime had protested when she'd given away her old furniture after they'd moved into the new pullman car. He'd told her he loved the old pleasure parlor look, but she hadn't been fooled. He had been secretly relieved when she brought in a professional decorator from New York. Personally she didn't like the moderne style, found it sterile and cold. But Jaime liked it, and that was all that mattered, to make him feel at home in her world.

Which was why she'd gone to Mr. Sam last week and demanded that he give Jaime a job that would keep that clever mind of his busy. So why wasn't he here tonight, waiting to tell her that Mr. Sam had offered him Jim Boris's job—and that he'd accepted?

She heard voices and the crunch of footsteps on the cinders alongside the car. Jaime—and he had brought company. Would he wait to tell her the news about his new job until after the company had left?

But when she went to open the door, a welcoming smile on her lips, it was Mr. Sam who stood on the platform. His face was so gray, her breath caught in her throat. She looked beyond him, saw Clinker, and she knew that they had come to tell her something terrible, something monstrous.

Instinctively she tried to ward it off. "No," she said hoarsely, and put up both hands to keep them out. But they came in anyway, moving heavily as if fighting a strong wind.

"I'm so sorry," Mr. Sam said, pity clouding his eyes. "It's Jaime. He's dead—Leo Mueller killed him. It happened near Clown Alley. Two of the tent men saw the attack. There was a fight—the bastard's dead, too. Killed by his own knife."

It was too much to absorb so quickly, too much terrible pain and grief, all at once. "Leo?" She turned the word over in her mind. "But Leo's in prison."

Clinker stepped forward. Her eyes, always prominent, seemed to bulge out of her head as if they were bloated with unshed tears. "He was out on parole from a manslaughter charge. A friend of mine saw him in New York last month. He—he asked about you—"

"And you didn't tell me?"

Clinker plucked at the collar of her shirtwaist dress as if it wore too tight. "Mr. Sam knew. Jaime did, too. It was his decision not to tell you. He arranged for Lobo to watch the car whenever he wasn't here. It never occurred to any of us that Jaime was the one that Leo—"

She began crying. Mara didn't move. She was waiting, in the way that a condemned person waits for the hangman's drop. Mr. Sam touched her arm.

"He didn't suffer long, if at all. It must have happened instantly."

He stopped, and she saw that tears were running down his face, filling in the deep creases beside his mouth.

Everything got very strange then. The bright colors in the room faded to a uniform gray and the light from the lamp grew dim. She started to tell him to stop Clinker from screaming like that because she'd awaken the baby, only to realize that the screams were coming from her own throat.

CHAPTER 21

NO MATTER HOW UNPLEASANT OR DANGEROUS OR PAINFUL the days of her life had been, time had always been Mara's friend, tumbling her past the bad parts, carrying her on to new adventures, new triumphs, and sometimes, new disasters. But she'd always accepted this as natural, the wheel of fortune turning, turning. She rode the wave with confidence, sure that time was on her side, that up ahead were all the things she yearned for—fame, fortune, the love of a good man, happiness.

And this was how it had been until now. In her ignorance she hadn't known that time could be an enemy, that every minute, every second, could be a slow poison that distorted everything around her, twisting her mind with agonizing questions.

Was it my fault?

Could I have stopped it?

Why did it happen to Jaime, not to me?

Why didn't I sense that Jaime was in danger and stop it from happening?

But of course, she *had* sensed it, but she'd misinterpreted and ignored the warning. . . .

During the first few days, shock protected her—minimally. Grayness surrounded her. Unrelieved with gay colors that might have taunted her, reminding her of how much she had lost, the grayness blurred the cutting edge of her grief. Even her own image in the lavatory mirror seemed gray, her hair dull, her eyes listless, her mouth, so naturally rosy, a thin, pale line of despair. She didn't care. For the first time in her adult life, Mara didn't care how she looked.

People came and went—Mr. Sam, Jocko, Clinker, Doc McCall, the artistes, Cookie and his crew, the workmen. They spoke to her, said the things that were supposed to be comforting and which sounded so hollow to her ears. Time heals all, one said, and for a brief moment, until apathy took over again, Mara felt a flare of hot rage.

Later she would realize that Clinker protected her from the worst of it, but in the days that followed Jaime's death, she was only aware of bewilderment. How could he be dead? Jaime, always so much more alive than other men, lying in a St. Clair family's cemetery plot in cold Boston? No, it couldn't be true. This was a nightmare, something dreamt during a long, cold night in the dead of winter.

During these days of grayness, she left everything to Clinker, who took over the chores of everyday living, who made the arrangements to ship Jaime's body back to Boston. She hadn't refused his father's request, because what difference did it make if Jaime lay in a lonely grave in South Carolina, where he'd died, or in his family's plot in Boston?

He was dead. Nothing would bring him back. Not all the prayers she'd never learned how to say, not all the tears that she couldn't shed. Better that he be buried where his mother could lay flowers on his grave. She couldn't give him that, and his family could.

It was when she finally had to acknowledge this reality that the real pain began. Over and over she relived the day of Jaime's death, wondering if she could have stopped it from happening if she'd done this, done that. She thought of Jaime every waking moment, and when she finally fell asleep nights, she dreamt about him. Not nightmares, which might have been easier to bear, but dreams in which he laughed with her, kissed her, made love to her, and told her secrets about his boyhood that she couldn't remember later, after she awoke.

She grew to dread sleep, because waking up was so painful, and she often sat up into the early hours, listening to the silence or, if the train was making a haul to the next date, to the clatter of the wheels that had once sung her to sleep so merrily and which now only reminded her of what she'd lost.

There was no solace in their child, although this was the platitude most often voiced, that at least she had Jaime's child to keep his memory alive. To Mara, the baby, with Jaime's eyes, Jaime's sunny smile, was a constant reminder of what she'd lost. She found herself avoiding Vicky as much as possible, sending her off with her nanny more often than not.

Around her, an affront to her grief, life went on.

The circus moved from South Carolina to Virginia, then crossed the Ohio River to play a series of one-night stands in southern Ohio, advancing along the circuit just as if she weren't slowly withering away inside. The sounds that came to her ears— the merry tinkle of the carousel, the hoarse cries of the midway talkers, the hoot of the steam calliope wagon—were pure torment, because they reminded her that just a few hundred yards away, people were have fun, getting on with their lives, just as if Jaime had never existed, never loved her, never fathered their child.

Two weeks after Jaime's death, Mr. Sam came to see her. He told her that the circus needed her, that she should start thinking about getting back to work.

"We all grieve with you," he said. "But the circus has to go on. You're our biggest drawing card—the profits are already falling off because we can't use your name in the advance advertising. We have that four-day run in Cincinnati next week, and we need a straw crowd or we're just not going to make our nut. Do you think you can be back to work by then?"

Mara stared at him with unseeing eyes. When she didn't answer, he gave her hand a pat, told her gruffly to think about it, and left.

Jocko came every day. She didn't look forward to his visits, but neither did she discourage them. Nothing he said, his wry jokes, his bits of news, his awkward attempts to comfort her, mattered. It was all grist for the mills of despair.

Jocko was sitting on the hassock he favored, regaling her with the latest scandal among the aerial ballet girls, when there was a knock on the door. Since Clinker was off somewhere, Mara decided to ignore it, hoping whoever it was would go away. She was resentful when Jocko rose and bounced over to fling the door open.

The man who entered was tall and lean, a stranger. Despite his gray hair, he was still a very handsome man. His resemblance to Jaime was so marked that Mara gasped and half rose to her feet. For a long moment they stared at each other before he turned his attention to the salon, viewing it, judging it, and then dismissing it in one sweeping glance.

"Who are you, sir?" Jocko demanded.

"Earl St. Clair. I want to speak to my daughter-in-law."

Jocko turned to Mara. "You want to talk to him?" he asked, his tone bellicose.

Mara hesitated, then nodded listlessly. What difference did it make now?

Jocko glared at Jaime's father, but he stepped aside. "You want me to stay here, Mara?" he asked, and when she nodded, he waved Earl St. Clair to a chair, then returned to his hassock. His short arms crossed at his chest, he concentrated his attention on the intruder.

Mr. St. Clair ignored him. As his cold eyes, a paler blue than Jaime's, looked Mara over, she was suddenly aware of her own appearance—no makeup, her hair hanging limp, her hostess gown wrinkled and carelessly buttoned.

"I've come to talk to you about your daughter," he said. "I'm sure you'll agree that the circus is no life for a child. This constant moving about, the sordid surroundings, the lack of roots, isn't good for her, especially since she only has one parent now. Since she *is* a St. Clair, the last of our branch of the family, we—her grandmother and myself—would like to offer her a home. We'll provide for all her needs, send her to a good school, and give her all the advantages. In return, I'm willing to settle an equitable amount on you to provide for your future. Jaime, as I'm sure you must know by now, had no money of his own, only the small trust account from his grandmother that terminated with his death. If you let the child live with us, she will be my heir."

As the meaning of his words sank into Mara's numb brain, a small current of anger stirred, struggled to get past her apathy, then died. What did it matter? Maybe it would be better for Vicky if she went to live with her grandparents. After all, this was no life for a child, not when she could have a fine home, the best education money could buy, and eventually inherit the St. Clair estate, which should have gone to Jaime. Because Vicky *was* his child, too, a St. Clair with all that meant. . . .

"Get out of here, you bastard!" The words made her start violently, and she looked at Jocko in amazement. His tiny hands doubled up into fists, his face an ominous red, he advanced upon

Earl St. Clair, looking like a small fighting cock. He was wearing the deer-hunting outfit he sometimes affected, and he should have looked ludicrous. Instead he looked dangerous, a person to take very seriously.

"Keep out of this, you freak," Earl St. Clair said, his lips barely moving.

It was the word "freak" that aroused Mara from her apathy. Suddenly all the pain and grief of the past few days exploded inside her and she was on her feet, pointing an imperious finger at the open door.

"Out! I want you out of here immediately," she stormed.

Jaime's father looked at her with cold eyes. "You'll regret this," he said. "Your daughter won't thank you when she's old enough to realize what you're throwing away. What can you give her that compares to what I'm offering? How much longer do you have before your career is over? Ten—maybe fifteen years? It only takes one slip and you'll never again—what is it you do? Swing from a rope? You'll end up in a dust heap somewhere— and you'll drag your daughter down with you. Consider all this before you say *no*."

There was enough truth in what he said to make her even more furious. "Get out! Get out before I have you thrown out," she said shrilly.

"Oh, I'm leaving. After meeting you, I find you even more common than I expected. And since the child has your blood in her veins, I can see I've made a mistake. You won't be hearing from me again."

He was gone, leaving Mara trembling with anger. Typically, she took it out on Jocko. "What right do you have interfering in my business?" she demanded.

Infuriatingly, he grinned at her and gave her a mocking salute. "Lovely, old girl. Just lovely. That's more like our old Mara."

He sauntered off, looking very pleased with himself.

But the anger didn't last. During the next few days, Mara sank back into apathy, eating when it seemed the only way to stop Clinker's fussing, refusing to see anyone, even Jocko, now. For hours at a time she sat by the window, staring out. She had set herself the task of remembering everything, every minute, of her life with Jaime, afraid that eventually his image would fade from her mind. And if that happened, then he would truly be dead, wouldn't he?

Clinker did her best. She sat with Mara by the hour, relaying circus news that once would have been amusing and entertaining. She read to her—novels, newspapers, magazines. But Mara was too apathetic to listen, and only wanted to be alone.

It was a month after the funeral, and Mara was sitting with Clinker in the salon. Clinker was doing needlepoint, a hobby she'd recently embraced. She had been talking nonstop for a long time, Mara only half listening, when suddenly her words began to register.

"—and then she did this absolutely smashing series of flanges, and the audience began counting, like they always do with you—"

"*Who* did a series of flanges, Clinker?"

"Why, Rosie Rushmore. She was a big star with Lasky Circus. Anyway, you know how Mr. Sam is always looking for a way to get his own back with old man Lasky? Well, he heard Rosie had left Lasky in a huff—something to do with her contract, which had run out. So he talked her into doing the evening performance last night. She was a big hit, so now he's decided to offer her a contract."

She giggled and rolled her eyes. "She's a real vamp. I just hope he keeps his head this afternoon at two when she signs the contract—" She stopped, popped her hand over her mouth. "Oh, Lord—me and my big mouth!"

Mara searched her memory. Rosie Rushmore . . . a Lasky Circus poster she'd once seen in a barbershop window came to her. Jaime had read off the shout line—"A second Princess Mara!"—and then he'd laughed at her indignation. She hadn't been mollified, even after he'd pointed out that imitation was the best flattery.

"Let me get this straight, Clinker," she said. "Mr. Sam is going to offer this Rosie Rushmore a contract? But why? The show doesn't need two female solo—" She stopped as realization came to her. "Why, that oily bastard! I suppose he offered her my private car, too?"

Clinker looked away. "You know you can't stay here indefinitely," she mumbled. "Even the wives of the artistes, if they take up a berth on the train, have to pull their own weight."

Mara's nostrils flared. "Well, we'll see about this," she said.

She stormed into her stateroom to look over her wardrobe. Everything looked so garish, so bright. In all of her extensive wardrobe there was nothing black, only one dark blue middy dress with a pleated skirt, a sailor collar, and a coral-colored bow scarf. She shrugged finally and laid it out on the bed.

For the first time in weeks, she really looked at herself in her dressing table mirror. Her skin had a waxy look, and her hair, which hadn't been washed for a week, lay in limp red strands around her face. She went to the door and beckoned to Clinker.

"Ask Lobo to fetch me a lemon from the cookhouse. I need it for a hair rinse—oh, and have him fetch the car. I don't want to get my shoes dusty walking across the lot."

Clinker hurried away to find Lobo, and Mara got clean undies from her bureau, found hose and a pair of navy blue pumps. An hour later, her hair towel-dried and piled on top of her head, freshly bathed and wearing light makeup, she put on a dress for the first time in several weeks. Her hair, although clean and shiny now, displeased her.

"There's a picture of Ruth Etting in last month's *Vogue*," Clinker, who had been hovering around, said. "I cut it out because her hairstyle seemed so right for you. Of course, long hair is part of your act, but this could be a good compromise. Short on the sides so it looks up-to-date, but still long in the back." She paused briefly, then added, "Rosie has a very short bob. Personally I don't like the way it's cut, on a slant, but she does look—well, very smart."

Mara gritted her teeth. "Smart, does she? I'll show her smart." She sat down in front of her dressing table mirror. "Trim it, but leave the back long."

Expertly, Clinker curled the hair at the side of Mara's face over her fingers, trimmed it neatly. When she was finished, she stood back, smiling. "You look about sixteen with that hair fluffed around your face."

And Mara, studying herself in the mirror, had to agree. Unexpectedly the crushing weight of grief, of loss, was back, almost overwhelming her. What did it really matter how she looked when Jaime wasn't there to see her?

On the other hand, how dare Mr. Sam hire another female soloist—and one who did the flanges, too? Didn't he have any loyalty at all? Well, she'd fix that little copycat. Vamp Mr. Sam and steal her act, would she? And she'd fix Mr. Sam, too.

She finished dressing, then stood looking at herself in the mirror. Just this morning she'd been thinking she looked like a ghost, but right now her face was flushed, her eyes bright.

"I need some new clothes," she said.

"Indeed you do. We can go shopping in Cincinnati next week. But first you have to take care of Rosie Roundheels."

The two women exchanged conspiratory smiles. Mara whirled

around, making the pleats below the dropped waist of the dress
flare out.

"How do I look?" she said.

"Swell," Clinker breathed. "Just like a princess."

Mara realized that she'd taken too much time getting ready
when she heard voices inside Mr. Sam's private domain, the
Silver Wagon. One voice was Mr. Sam's deep rumble, the other
a light, breathless female voice. She paused, but only to fix a
smile on her face. Was she too late? Had Rosie Rushmore already signed the contract?

Nothing of her inward doubts showed on her face as she swept
through the door. The woman sitting in a chair near Mr. Sam's
desk was younger than she'd expected, and prettier—but her chin
was too pointed, her lips too thin, her eyes too narrow. A weasel's face to match her weasel ways, Mara thought scornfully.
And she was done up like a clown in that too tight brown satin
chemise with a fringed skirt that showed too much of her bony
legs. . . .

After one swift look, she ignored the girl as if she weren't
there. Her arms outstretched, her smile wide, she advanced upon
Mr. Sam. The look of astonishment—and maybe guilt—on his
face as he jumped to his feet was gratifying. She meant to pay
him back for his disloyalty, but this wasn't the time. Still smiling, she reached up and planted a kiss on his cheek.

"Dear Mr. Sam," she crooned. "Did you think I was never
coming back? You've been such a peach. A good loyal friend,
that's what you are. I'll need a little practice to get my muscles
back in shape, but I'm sure I can make the first matinee of the
Cincinnati run. Is that soon enough?"

Mr. Sam cleared his throat nervously. He looked at her with
wary eyes, as if he was afraid she might explode. "I didn't
expect—of course, I'm delighted you're coming back to work.
Well, well—this is a surprise. It calls for a celebration—"

"That's all been arranged. I sent Clinker to the cookhouse to
ask Cookie to serve a late dinner tonight in my private car after
the evening show. Your favorite goulash and noodles, and Lobo
is rounding up some champagne, the real stuff, right off the
boat. I hope you won't disappoint me—"

"No, no. I'll be there, Mara."

Mara beamed at him. She gave him another kiss on the cheek,
and swept out of the Blue Wagon. She hadn't spoken one word
to the girl—and except for that initial glance, hadn't acknowl-

edged her presence. Which didn't mean she hadn't noticed the storm clouds gathering on Rosie Roundheels's face.

"And let's see how you get out of that, old dear," she said aloud.

But reaction had set in by the time she'd returned to the pull-man. She dropped into a chair and listlessly pulled off the bow under her chin. Clinker, who was back from the cookhouse, looked at her anxiously.

"How did it go?" she asked.

"First time I've ever seen Mr. Sam at a loss for words." But her smile faded quickly. "I'm having second thoughts, Clinker. What if I've lost my touch? Maybe I should just walk away from the whole thing."

"And do what?" Clinker asked. "You don't know anything else."

"I've got money in the bank."

"And how long would that last? Do you have enough to raise Vicky and give her a good education?"

Mara sighed. "No, probably not enough for that. Jaime—" She choked on the word, because it was the first time she'd said his name aloud since his death. "Jaime was always telling me to invest wisely, but I didn't think there was any hurry. I was wrong, wasn't I, Clinker?"

She began to cry, and Clinker put her arms around her. "Let it all out," she said. "It won't get better until you let it all out."

Mara cried for a while longer, and then she wiped away the tears and went into the lavatory to wash her face and put on fresh lipstick. It was time, she knew, to turn her back on grief, to come to terms with how it was going to be from now on. She doubted that she would ever be happy again—how could she be?—but she had responsibilities, a life to live, things to do before it was time to join Jaime in the *gadjo* heaven he had believed in so firmly, and about which she had her doubts.

CHAPTER 22

*D*URING THE THREE YEARS AFTER JAIME'S DEATH, MARA concentrated on two things—her career and her child. Her life was hectic, incredibly so sometimes, but she always managed to sandwich in time for Vicky. From noon until after the evening performance, she was involved with business, with promoting herself and the circus, with workouts, and, something she never slighted, her performances. Mornings, she devoted to Vicky, trying conscientiously to be both mother and father to her tiny daughter.

Not even to herself would she admit that part of her determination was to make up to Vicky for those weeks when she'd avoided her, when the sight of her daughter, who looked so much like Jaime, had been almost more than she could bear. Even now she sometimes felt the same grief, sharp and painful, when she heard Vicky's laugh or saw her smile, and then she had to force herself not to turn away.

Vicky, who had been an enchanting infant, was a beautiful toddler. Her auburn hair and startling blue eyes caught the fancy of everybody, and if Mara hadn't put her foot down, she would have been hopelessly spoiled. Luckily she had her father's sunny nature instead of Mara's volatile disposition. Everybody was her friend, whether Slim Jim Cody, the giant who was billed (untruthfully) as the tallest man in the world, or Doc McCall, who let her play with all the menagerie babies, or Donny Lyono, the surliest roughie on the lot.

Sometimes, as Mara watched Vickie make her way through the backyard, bestowing her smiles on everybody as if she had a thousand best friends, she felt an ache that bordered on envy. How different her own childhood had been—and how trusting Vicky was, how sure that everybody was her friend. Was that bad or good? Was it safe to go through life trusting other people? And how odd that only with her, who was so conscientious a mother, did Vicky always seem a little restrained.

But Vicky showed no reserve toward Jocko. He was her devoted slave. They spent long hours together while he, so impatient and critical with others, played games with her or read her stories she couldn't possibly understand. Even so, she listened patiently, as if sensing how important these times with her were to the tiny man.

True to a resolution she'd made herself when she'd turned down Earl St. Clair's offer, Mara was becoming very rich. Every week Clinker read her the financial reports that were forwarded to her by a New York stockbroker. Although she couldn't read the figures, Mara had a head for money and knew that she was prospering beyond her wildest childhood dreams. Mr. Sam, too, was showing signs of prosperity. His serviceable Ford sedan became a gleaming Hudson limo, and it was well known that he had remodeled and enlarged his mansion south of Orlando, turning it into a showplace.

As Mara's fame grew, the offers from other circuses increased, but she wasn't tempted to sign up with anyone else. She felt comfortable with Mr. Sam, although they had never really become personal friends. Still, they understood each other—and if she left him and signed on with the Big One, then she would be competing daily with the world's greatest circus acts. Her performances would be judged by their critical eyes— and in her heart, she knew that technically she couldn't compare with an artiste like Lillian Leitzel.

Here, at Bradford Circus, she was a queen, a legend in the making, Jocko called her. Like him, she enjoyed being a big frog in a small pond. Or was that term still true? Since its expansion in 1927, Bradford Circus had prospered and was fast becoming a formidable rival even to the larger circuses.

And of course, she did have a vested interest in the circus now. Mr. Sam had offered her stock in the show when he needed capital for expansion, but she'd opted to buy the circus's winter quarters land near Orlando instead. Owning land satisfied some need in her, and the rent the circus paid brought in a tidy sum every winter.

A year after Jaime's death, Mara took a lover, a young newspaper journalist who had come to interview her. He was handsome, funny, and he made her laugh. Although he satisfied her sexual needs, she felt emotionally empty after she'd been with him, and she finally broke it off. Clinker, who was growing more straitlaced every year, didn't try to hide her disapproval, and Jocko avoided Mara completely during her affair, not even coming to see Vicky until she'd sent the man packing.

During the winter seasons she accepted a few stage bookings, mostly in New York. They took her away from Vicky for long periods of time, but the pay for these short-term runs was so lucrative that she couldn't resist.

For one thing, her own personal expenses were very high, starting with clothes. One of her extravagances was to descend upon an exclusive dress shop and buy everything in sight. Every time she did, she thought about the day she'd been thrust out of her *kumpania*, naked as the day she was born.

Clinker and the other women in the circus got the benefit of these compulsive shopping binges. When her closets got too stuffed, she cleared out the old, giving it away. And if she got some secret satisfaction from seeing her gowns and shoes and hats on other women, just as she'd once worn her relatives' and Berty's discards, she kept it to herself.

Her excess earnings, she turned over to Mr. Sam's broker for investment. Once Jocko made a remark about her ending up owning the circus someday, and she hadn't laughed.

"How are those stock market investments Mr. Sam's broker is making for you doing?" he asked one evening. "What kind of an accounting does he give you?"

Silently she got out the last statements, both from her broker and Mr. Sam's accountant, that Clinker had been reading to her, and handed them to him. "Judge for yourself," she said.

It took him a while, but when he had finished poring over the statements, there was a thoughtful look on his clever face. "You're close to being a millionaire—at least on paper," he said.

"And I intend to get even richer. Isn't it about time you stopped throwing your money away on floozies and gambling and started thinking about your future?"

"My future—somehow that word doesn't seem to apply to me. But you're right. I can't work forever. I'm lucky to get through my routine these days. Another few years and it's the boneyard for this old nag."

Mara looked at him closely, alerted by the depression in his voice. The lines on his face made him look older than his age. Were those pain lines?

"You can always—" She stopped, but not in time.

"Join the ten-in-one like the other freaks? The circus is my life, but I'd give it up rather than have people gawking at me twenty times a day, asking me personal questions about my sex life because, after all, I'm not quite human."

His eyes were haunted, as if he saw something dark and dangerous up ahead, and Mara changed the subject, not wanting to see his pain.

A few days later he came to see her, looking very pleased with himself. "Well, I just took my first flier on the market. I sunk my savings in futures and made more money in one day than I did all last year."

Mara watched him with amusement as he strutted and bragged his way around her dressing tent, expounding on his cleverness, and lecturing her on the secrets of the stock market. All of a sudden, she noted, he was the expert and she was the novice. Wasn't it always that way with men? And Jocko, despite his size, was all man.

In June of '28, on Vicky's third birthday, Mara had a party for her. She invited Vicky's special friends among the circus children and included several of her daughter's favorite adults— Mr. Sam, Jocko, Clinker, Doc McCall, and of course, Lobo, who was also Vicky's willing slave.

The party was a success, although Mara thought the presents far too extravagant for a three-year-old. She couldn't help thinking about her own third birthday, which had passed unnoticed even by herself, as had all her birthdays until she'd turned fifteen.

What had happened to them, to her grandfather, her aunts and uncles, the cousins she'd grown up with? Did they ever think about her? Once, when she was staying in a hotel in New York, she had come face-to-face with a dark-skinned man who had paused in midstride to stare at her with heavy-lidded Rom eyes, and she was sure she heard him mutter the Rom word for *witch*. Had he merely taken a dislike to her on sight—or had he recognized her as a Rom despite her fur-trimmed coat, her cloche hat, and her stylish alligator purse?

Mara shuddered, suddenly very cold. Inevitably, as always when she thought of her childhood, her eyes moved to the jewelry chest where she kept her mother's tarot cards. Maybe it was time to burn them. After all, she was a *gadjo* now, not a superstitious, ignorant Rom. . . .

She unlocked the chest and took out the cards. They felt very cold, although it was warm in the salon. A shiver rippled through her; her grasp loosened, and the cards fell to the rug. She bent quickly to pick them up, not wanting Vicky, who was playing with her dolls on the sofa, to ask questions.

The cards had fallen facedown except for two: the Tower, which heralded disaster—and the Wheel of Fortune.

How strange—the first time she'd met Leo, he had recited the words to an old Rom song about the Wheel of Fortune to her. Had it been prophetic, a harbinger of what was to come?

As if she sensed her mother's distress, Vicky looked up from her dolls, and Mara bundled up the cards, thrust them back in the chest, and turned the key in the lock.

Tomorrow, she promised herself. Tomorrow she'd destroy them, once and for all. . . .

The 1929 season was one of the best the circus had ever had. Even Mr. Sam, who could find a dark cloud in every silver lining, had to admit that they had never drawn such crowds. "The whole damned country's on a merry-go-round ride," was his comment.

It had been a mild autumn, and Mr. Sam, always looking for added revenue, had booked several last-minute engagements in Ohio—to Mara's annoyance since she had accepted several winter club dates and had been planning a month in Florida with Vicky before she went off again.

One thing that tempered her irritation was the state of her finances. The stock market was rocketing out of sight, and her broker was predicting that it would be a bull market well into the thirties.

"This isn't the time for the weak and the timid," Jocko told Mara, his eyes taking on a feverish shine. "This is the chance of a lifetime, and I'm riding it all the way."

Mara agreed with his optimism. She, too, intended to ride it all the way. After he left her dressing tent, where they'd been having lunch, she put on her hat and walked over to the Blue Wagon to call her broker. But the circuits to New York were busy, and she returned to the tent to take an afternoon nap.

Refreshed by her nap, Mara was putting on makeup for the evening performance when she heard a noise at the door flaps. She put down her camel-hair powder brush and looked around. Mr. Sam was standing there, his face so ashen that her first thought was of Vicky.

She jumped to her feet, knocking over the dressing table stool.

"Vicky—is something wrong with Vicky?" she said, and in her mind's eye she saw the flames on the court card, the Tower.

Mr. Sam shook his head, and she allowed herself a sigh of relief. Because he'd given her such a scare, her voice was sharp as she added, "So what is it? An accident?"

He stared at her with red-rimmed eyes. "Accident? No, not an accident."

"Look, why don't you sit down? Are you sick or something?"

"Sick? Yes, I'm sick." His voice cracked, and for a moment she thought he was going to cry. "I just lost everything, my whole nut—and so did you."

Bewildered, she stared at him. "What are you saying?"

He put his hands over his face, as if he couldn't bear to look at her. "The stock market," he said thickly. "The bottom just fell out. All I have left is my circus stock and this season's receipts. Thank God I didn't gamble with that money."

She turned his words over in her mind, trying to make sense out of them. "How could it be gone? It was spread out over so many things—you called it diversification, and you told me yourself that there was no risk—"

"Don't you understand? I was wrong. Everybody was wrong. The stock market plunged and it's all gone. We're wiped out because our broker—may he burn in hell!—put it all on margin. We don't have a cent—in fact, we owe the brokerage money."

He went on explaining, as if talking about it gave him some relief, talking about ten percent margins and other things that meant nothing to her. But maybe it should have, she thought. Maybe she should have learned all she could about the stock market before she invested a penny. . . .

She sat down on the dressing table stool again, because her knees suddenly refused to hold her up. "Are you sure nothing's left?" she said, interrupting him.

"The winter quarters land—that's in your name. It's probably safe, but—" He stopped, blinking his eyes.

"But what?"

"I doubt you could raise more than a few thousand on it."

"But I paid you a hundred thousand dollars for the land," she protested.

"That was business. Nothing personal, you understand." He rubbed his face with the heels of his hands. "There's the winter rent you get, of course, which'll cover the taxes and keep up the roads and other facilities, so it won't be a drain on you, but there just isn't any market for that kind of wasteland. Too much sand and too dry for farming or orchards. I—well, you didn't ask the value of it, so I didn't exactly lie. I figured I'd buy it back from you later on and give you a reasonable profit.''

She almost laughed. Fancy that—a Rom being taken by a *gadjo*. But no, that wasn't right. She was no longer a Rom. She'd changed sides. Why did she keep forgetting that?

Mr. Sam looked away, as if ashamed to meet her eyes. ''I'll make it up to you, Mara. It's all my fault. I infected you with my own greed.''

As I did Jocko, she thought sickly.

''Jocko—does he know yet?'' she asked.

''If he's been listening to the news on the radio, he does. This'll wipe him out, too, because he's been playing the margin for all it's worth. He must owe his broker a fortune. You know what a gambler he is.''

''I know.''

He sighed deeply. ''I didn't want you to hear about it from anyone else. Sorry I had to tell you just before the evening performance. You can cancel out if you like.''

She shook her head. No, she would perform, if only to have something to keep her from falling to pieces. Besides, it was a matter of pride that she'd never missed a performance except when she was pregnant with Vicky, and later, after Jaime was killed.

''If it's any consolation, next year's bookings are already coming in, and 1930 looks to be another good year for the circus. I don't know how long that will last. This whole business could blow over or it could be the beginning of hard times. We can only hope for the best.''

She didn't answer. Yes, she could recuperate, and so could Mr. Sam, but what about Jocko? He didn't have enough time to start over again. . . .

Jocko sat in the middle of his bed, his legs stretched out in front of him. The bed was an antique, a child's sleigh bed, and he'd always been proud of its rooooo lines. He was in full makeup, wearing his tails, his top hat, and the monocle that had become his trademark. Usually he put on his makeup in Clown Alley, but today, because the pain in his back was so bad, he'd had no heart for the usual high jinks of his compadres and had dressed in his roomy compartment instead.

In his lap was the leather-bound scrapbook where he kept his press clippings and other mementos. Beside him, propped up against his leg, was a bottle of Jack Daniels. It had been full when he'd climbed up onto the bed half an hour ago; now it was only half-full.

He opened the scrapbook. Three items shared honors on the first page—a canceled steamboat ticket from England to New York, a hotel bill from his early weeks in New York, his first booking slip with a now defunct circus. The following pages held other souvenirs, including his first pay chit, the menu of a gourmet restaurant where he'd celebrated his first featured act, and a hotel bill for the night he'd lost his virginity to a dark-eyed show girl.

There were press clippings, the important ones, a chronological record of his career, and there were other mementos—a pressed flower, brown with age, a woman's handkerchief embroidered with the initial M, a piece of paper on which was painfully executed a dozen attempts to write the name *Mara*, a pearl button from a woman's blouse. The last item was a tiny bootee, pink.

Even though no one else was in the compartment, he felt uneasy. How often had he laughed, made pointed jokes about just such sentimentality in other people? But the important thing was not that people would probably laugh at this show of vanity, but that the scrapbook might cause embarrassment to others should it fall into the wrong hands.

With a stab of regret, he removed the sheet of memo pad paper with its damning practice scrawls, tore it into tiny pieces, and dropped them beside the bed. He tilted the bottle to his lips, took a long draw, for once deploring his capacity for alcohol. What it took to put other men under the table just brought him a gentle glow, a physical phenomenon in which he'd always taken a certain pride—until now.

He had just finished putting on his makeup when the news about the stock market crash had come over the radio. In fact, the radio was still on, and the thin edge of hysteria in the announcer's voice was beginning to get on his nerves. He finished off the bourbon, careful not to smudge his makeup, then took careful aim and heaved it at the radio, tumbling it to the floor. The silence was gratifying, and yet it made him even more aware of his aloneness.

He closed the scrapbook and laid it aside. His nose tickled and he sneezed, something that incited another laugh, because it was a milestone of sorts—his last sneeze on earth.

He rooted under his pillow and brought out the gun. It was beautifully crafted, an Italian-made pistol with a mother-of-pearl handle and an ash stock. A special gun, fit for a lord. Which made it quite appropriate for the occasion.

A memory nudged his mind. Someone had once tacked up a crudely drawn cartoon on his dressing mirror in Clown Alley. It showed a tiny man, up to his shoulders in the middle of a donicker in the act of reaching up to pull the handle to flush the toilet. There was no mistaking the identity of the man, with his top hat, his blissful painted-on smile, and his monocle.

The caption underneath, while not really funny, had stuck in his mind, and he'd never forgotten it.

Under his painted-on smile, Jocko's lips twitched with amusement. In the end, all you really had left was your sense of humor—and wasn't that a laugh!

He could have said, "Laugh, Clown, laugh," or maybe "Good night, Sweet Prince." Instead, he quoted the cartoon caption. "Good-bye, cruel world," he said, and putting the muzzle of the gun against the roof of his mouth, he pulled the trigger.

After Mr. Sam left, Mara finished dressing. Usually Clinker was here to help her with her hair and makeup, and she wondered vaguely where she could be. From outside the tent she heard voices, running feet, but no one came in. Her thoughts moved sluggishly. What would this disaster mean to her daughter? She had been so arrogant, turning down the St. Clair millions for Vicky, so sure she could provide for the future. Was it possible that Earl St. Clair had been wiped out by the crash, too?

She put on her costume. The spangles and sequins caught the light of the dressing table lamp and seemed to mock her with their sparkle. Wiped out—God, all that work, all that effort, and for what? To be told that you were back where you'd started nine years ago. . . .

She had just left the tent and was heading for the backyard when Lobo came loping up. His rough face, so much larger than other men's, looked strange, and she wondered if he had been investing his money in the market, too. Clinker, she knew for sure, followed the market avidly—how many other circus people had been wiped out today because they'd caught the get-rich-quick fever from Mr. Sam?

"You've heard the news?" she asked Lobo. He blinked once, his signal for yes. "Were you heavily invested, too?"

He gaped at her, looking bewildered, then shook his head. He made a gesture—palm down toward his knees, his sign for Jocko.

"Something's happened to Jocko? What is it?" she asked sharply.

He put his finger into his mouth, made a gesture that sent a shock wave coursing down her body.

"Jocko's—dead?"

He blinked twice, and then, amazingly, because he and Jocko had never gotten along, his eyes filled with tears.

"Was it suicide?" she asked, because she had to know.

He nodded, and the world did a slow swing around Mara. She heard the musical cue that signaled the end of the equestrian act, which preceded her in the line-up, and automatically she started walking toward the big top. Lobo fell in behind her, and she knew, if she turned around, she would see her own misery mirrored on his broad, rough face.

She wanted to cry, but she couldn't. Her loss, her pity, and yes, even her anger were too deep. *He shouldn't have done it,* she thought. *I didn't know he was a coward.*

Others, perhaps everybody in the backyard, had heard. She saw it in their faces, although no one spoke. The acts, most of whom had already performed and ordinarily would have been in their dressing tents, were still there. Silent, grim-faced, they parted for her. She didn't stop, not even when she passed the clowns, huddled together as if trying to keep warm. Afterward she could cry and scream and rage at fate, at whatever it was that eternally demanded a price for every bit of happiness. For now, she had a performance to give.

Inside the Big Top, Konrad Barker was announcing her act in his booming voice, extolling the pleasure in store for the audience. At the rolling of the trap drums, Lobo lifted her to his broad shoulder, and her lips curved into a wide smile as the white spotlight caught them. She waved and kept on smiling as Lobo, moving slower than usual, jogged across the tanbark toward the white rope that would bear her aloft.

She tossed off her velvet cape, and there was a roar of approval, followed by an expectant hush. Then she was climbing, stopping every few feet to throw out kisses, kindling the expectation of the crowd. But it was all mechanical, without her usual pleasure at commanding, for these twelve minutes twice a day, the total attention of the audience.

When she reached the rings, she threw herself into her routine, dipping and swinging and hanging precariously from the slender circles of metal, going through the motions, aware that she wasn't giving her best performance but also knowing that few in the stands would realize it.

Then it was time for the flanges.

Usually she played with the audience, flirting and smiling and making a false start or two, but today she flung herself toward the rope on its metal swivel, moving recklessly, the sheer physical effort, the feel of rope against her wrist, somehow comforting.

This is for you, Jocko, she thought as she maneuvered her body upward, then over, making a complete roll.

Normally, unless it was for the opening performance of a long run, she would have stopped at thirty-five, but her anger and grief demanded something more today, and she kept on going. The audience, who seemed to sense that this would be something special, chanted out ". . . forty-eight . . . forty-nine . . . fifty . . ." but she didn't stop, ignoring the growing ache in her wrist and shoulder.

Below, when she swung to the top of the turn, she saw, as through a haze, the white blur of hundreds of upturned faces. Among them was Lobo, his filled with concern. She thought she heard Mr. Sam's voice, calling her name, telling her that was enough, but nothing could stop her now. She was going for the record, doing it for Jocko. His death had to be recognized, his life had to be honored.

In a few days the circus would move on, leaving behind a diminutive body in a grave somewhere. He would be forgotten. In a short time it would be as if he had never existed. And that she couldn't tolerate.

But if this was the night she broke the flange record that Lillian Leitzel had set in 1924, her feat would be associated with Jocko's death. This much, to make sure he was remembered beyond a season or two, she could do for him.

One hundred forty . . . one hundred forty-one . . .

She saw images, phantoms of old memories. Jocko, the first time she'd met him, swaggering down the road that led to the cookhouse, saying things that had been beyond her limited grasp of English to understand. Jocko, curled up on her lap, his face buried in her breast. Jocko telling her small daughter a long, involved story about a princess with flame-red hair . . .

Two hundred . . . two hundred one . . .

The pain in her wrist was almost unbearable. Although she was good at this maneuver, she hadn't developed the thick chest and strong shoulder muscles that such a prolonged strain demanded. But she willed her weakness away, achieved a state in which the pain, while still there, seemed to be happening to someone else.

She heard the crowd's roar, felt the concern of the circus people who had crowded in from the backyard. It didn't matter. Everything in her strained toward the next turn and the next, because she was not willing to acknowledge that she might fail, that her body might not be as strong as her will.

Two hundred thirty-eight . . . two hundred thirty-nine . . .

She had reached Lillian Leitzel's record. One more turn would surpass it. The pain was worse now, breaking through her defenses, but she wasn't content with a tie. She had to break the record. Drawing upon some reserve of inner strength, she lifted her tired body one more time and flung it upward, then down.

There was a roar from the crowd, but even above it, she heard Konrad Barker's triumphant bellow, announcing that she had done it, that Bradford Circus's own Princess Mara had broken Lillian Leitzel's record for the flange, that they were privileged to be here when it happened. His words joggled her from her detachment, and looking down, she saw a stream of blood dripping from her wrist, staining her arm, and splashing carmine drops on her white costume.

Clinker will have a fit, she thought, and then, as if time had slowed to a stop, her numb hands opened, and the rope was slipping, slipping from her grasp. She heard a rush of sound, a long sigh of horror from the stands as she fell, the tanbark below rushing up to meet her.

She saw Lobo lumbering forward, but she knew with certainty that he would be too late to break her fall. Only by a second or two, but still—too late.

So this is how it ends, she thought just before she struck the ground.

CHAPTER 23

*F*IRST, MARA WAS AWARE OF PAIN. IT PERMEATED HER BODY, persistent and bone-deep. A rational part of her mind told her that it could be worse, that to feel nothing at all would be worse, but her brain refused to believe it and tried to retreat back into unconsciousness.

Then, intruding upon the pain, came sound. Voices, subdued, the words they spoke indecipherable. A soft, liquid noise, like a faucet dripping in a distant room. Someone moaning.

She tried to open her eyes, but a heavy weight seemed to press against her eyelids. Was she blind? Panic surged through her and she tried to speak, but again she was thwarted by her own inertia.

"Mara . . ." The voice was male, unfamiliar. "Can you hear me, Mara? You're in the hospital, and I'm Dr. Tope. You've been hurt, but everything's being done to make you more comfortable. I'm going to give you something for the pain, but first I want you to know that you're not in a life-threatening condition. Do you understand?"

The words sank through layers of consciousness. She knew something was expected of her, but what? A nod? But how could she nod when she had no control over her body?

"Move your fingers if you understand," the voice said, and she focused all her attention on this simple gesture. She must have responded satisfactorily, because the voice said, "That's a good girl. You'll sleep now, and all your questions will be answered when you awaken."

She wanted to tell him that she wasn't a girl but a grown woman, but it was too much effort. She thought she felt the prick of a needle, but she couldn't be sure. The pain began to

246

dull, and her thoughts clouded, finally dimming to nothingness again.

It must have been hours later that she awoke, because some internal clock in her mind told her she'd been asleep for a long time. The pain had returned, sharp and immediate, but it was a little less frightening now. There had been a man, a doctor, and he'd told her something important. Hadn't he said that she'd been hurt but that her injuries weren't life-threatening? Did that mean that in time she would be as good as new?

She opened her eyes. A woman, dressed in white and wearing the frilled cap of a nurse, was standing at the foot of the bed, making marks on a clipboard.

"Nurse . . ." Mara mumbled.

The woman looked up, smiled. "How do you feel, Mara?"

"Terrible . . . How bad . . . is it?"

The woman's eyes slid away. "Dr. Tope will be here shortly. He'll answer your questions. For now—are you thirsty?"

Mara discovered her mouth was very dry. She murmured, "Yes," and the woman brought her a glass of water and put a straw to her lips. It was so difficult to swallow that fear blossomed again. Was she paralyzed? She tried to move, but nothing happened.

"There—you'll feel better now," the nurse said. "The doctor will prescribe something for your pain."

A few minutes later, a small, thin-faced man came into the room. He met her stare with a long one of his own.

"Well, I see you're back with us. You're a famous young lady, I understand. The press has been bombarding us with questions about you. And your friends—there's quite a collection of them in the waiting room, hoping to see you. However, it's a bit too soon for visitors. Perhaps in a day or so—"

"How badly am I hurt?" she interrupted.

"You're in no danger. But you do have some healing to do. I suggest we wait until you feel a bit—"

"I want to know now," she said, her voice rising.

He made a helpless gesture. "Very well. Your left arm and leg are broken, as well as your collarbone. The bone in your left cheek was shattered—uh, cracked in several places—and you have a slight concussion. There are some abrasions, that sort of thing. I understand that your fall was partially broken by one of the circus attendants—"

"Lobo," she said thickly. "He's my rope handler."

"Well, he managed to divert your fall slightly or it would have been much worse.'' He must have sensed her concern because he added, ''He wasn't hurt except for a couple of bruises.

She closed her eyes briefly in relief, then asked, ''How long will I be out of the show?''

''It's much too early to think about that,'' he said quickly. ''I'm going to have Nurse Cummins give you a sedative now. If you're hungry, you can have some broth and a glass of milk.''

She wanted to tell him that it was the truth she wanted, but she knew it would be useless. So she closed her eyes, and later, after she'd taken a couple of yellow pills, she sank back into sleep.

The hospital allowed her to have a visitor that afternoon just after she awoke. Not so surprisingly, it was Mr. Sam. He stood by the bed, the lines grooved in his face even more pronounced than usual, and any hope she'd had that her injuries were minor was lost when she read the worry, the pity, in his eyes.

''Well, Mara, you broke the record. I doubt if even Leitzel can beat that one,'' he said.

Mara felt a small shock. She had forgotten about that—and about Jocko. A wave of grief threatened to overwhelm her. To thwart it, she asked quickly, ''How many?''

''Two hundred and forty.''

She closed her eyes. A tear trembled on her eyelashes, ran down the side of her face. Mr. Sam brushed it away, and it was such an unusual gesture from a man who seldom touched other people that she opened her eyes again.

''How's Vicky?'' she said.

''Thriving. We thought it best to keep the publicity from touching her, so Clinker took her to a hotel.''

Mara nodded her agreement. ''I don't want her to see me all bandaged up and in these casts. Did they tell you that my arm and leg are broken?''

''So I heard. Now, don't you worry about anything. Just get well, you hear?''

''Jocko—has he been—''

''All taken care of. I cabled his family in England, and they asked that his body be shipped there so he could be buried in the family plot.''

''How strange. Just like Jaime. After they were dead, then they were acceptable to their families again,'' she said bitterly.

''Don't fret about it, girl. Jocko was sick—he knew he didn't have long to live anyway. I think he was afraid of the pain.''

"Sick?"

"Yeah. The cancer was getting worse—"

"What are you saying? That he had cancer?"

"Of the spine. Incurable. It was pretty bad there at the last."

"But he never said anything to me."

"You know how proud he was, how he hated to admit weakness. I only found out by accident." He leaned forward suddenly and took her hand. "Look, you've had a terrible shock. Don't add guilt to it. He would have done it anyway. This business about the stock market—it just hurried things along. He must have bought the gun with suicide in mind."

She didn't totally believe him, and yet—all the signs had been there. She remembered how thin, how gaunt, Jocko had looked for the past few months. Had he been planning this, waiting until the pain got too much to bear?

"Don't worry about your hospital bills," Mr. Sam was saying now. "The circus will pick them up. I'm sorry that I—" But he couldn't seem to get the rest of the words out.

"I'm a grown woman," she said wearily. "I invested my money in the stock market because I was greedy. I'm not blaming you."

"Then don't blame yourself because Jocko took a plunge in the market, too. He would have gambled it away anyway."

She knew he was right. So why did she still feel as if she'd murdered her best friend? She closed her eyes, pretending to be asleep, and Mr. Sam went away.

Clinker came that evening, a welcome visitor. She held Mara's hand, and although she sounded brisk and matter-of-fact as she rushed into speech, her eyes were red and puffy, and Mara knew her friend had been crying.

"I was here earlier, but Mr. Sam wanted to talk to you, and they'd only let one visitor in. The oldest Martini girl is watching Vicky so I could come see you. A dozen women volunteered to stay with her, but of course, they won't be available after the circus moves on. Everybody sends their love and best wishes. You'd have a roomful of visitors right now, only the doctor says just one person a visiting hour."

She looked around the room at the abundance of flowers and stack of cards. "I'll be here every day, reporting on Vicky."

"And I'll be back to work before you know it," Mara said. "I might not be able to do the flanges for a while, but I can work up some kind of act on the rings."

Clinker's nod was listless; she began telling Mara about Vicky's conquest of the hotel staff where they were staying.

After Clinker was gone, the nurse came in with two more arrangements of flowers. "Your room has already reached the limit," she said cheerfully. "But I thought you'd like to see these before I take them to the wards."

She gave Mara a stack of cards. "You've had a lot of visitors, but Dr. Tope is adamant. Only relatives and your closest friends, one per visiting period. He did hold a meeting for the press, because they were cluttering up the waiting room. He was very discreet about your injuries, of course. Have you read any of your cards yet?"

"I'll look at them later," Mara said. "Do you know when the bandage on my face will come off?"

The nurse didn't seem to hear her question. She bustled around, putting fresh water in the flower vases, fluffing Mara's pillows, straightening her top sheet. When she went on to say that she thought she'd leave the violets after all, because they were so lovely, Mara knew she was avoiding the question.

The doctor told her the truth the next day.

"Your injuries are extensive. You fell on your left side, shattering the bones in your leg and arm. Since both are compound fractures, there's the problem of infection. You'll need hospitalization for quite a while, I'm afraid. As for your face—you won't look the same. However, they're doing great things with plastic surgery these days. Not my field, of course, but perhaps that's a possibility."

He paused, as if expecting some reaction, but when she was silent, he went on to say, "Let's look at the bright side. You're a strong, superbly healthy young woman. With the aid of a cane, you'll undoubtedly walk again. In time—and with good therapy—it's possible you'll be almost as good as new. So you won't be a cripple. But I have to tell you—there's no hope that you will be able to resume your career. I'm being blunt because I think you're the kind of person who would rather have the truth. Am I right?"

Mara didn't have hysterics, nor did she cry, but she also didn't answer his question. She lay as if dead, neither moving nor speaking, retreating into some refuge deep inside her own mind. Her despair was so devastating that she wanted to die and was resentful that Lobo had broken her fall.

In the middle of that long, long night, when the hospital was silent, her room dark, it came to Mara that she was already dead and that this was hell.

To never again hear the hush that fell in the stands when she appeared at the big top's back door, riding Lobo's broad shoulders like a queen, her legs nonchalantly crossed, her smile wide. To never again soar through the air or hear the sweet applause or bask in the love, the admiration, that flowed from the crowd, engulfing her in warmth. To never again be feted and entertained by the great or be interviewed by the press. To go back to being a nobody—yes, this *had* to be hell.

Most devastating of all was the knowledge that she had failed Vicky, had condemned Jaime's Princess Sunshine to a childhood, perhaps a lifetime, of poverty. How could she possibly face her daughter, knowing what was in store for her?

But what if the doctor was wrong, had made a mistake about the extent of her injuries, about her face? She had beat out other odds in her life. Surely she could beat out these, too. . . . Three days later, when they took off her facial bandages, she finally had to accept the truth. The face that stared out at her from the mirror the nurse reluctantly provided, even discounting the bruises and the raw abrasions that eventually would heal, was that of a stranger. A scar, too deep to ever completely heal, ran diagonally from her forehead to her chin. Oh, her face wasn't monstrous, repulsive, but it wasn't Mara either. It was altered, asymmetrical—and it was no longer beautiful and enchanting, would never be any of those things again.

The doctor talked about plastic surgery again, and reminded her of what they had done to Fanny Hurst's nose, which had been in all the gossip columns. He spoke about coming to grips with reality, about getting on with her life. She listened and didn't argue, but she knew his words for what they were— platitudes to calm the patient.

When she was alone again, she thought about a lot of things— her depleted savings, about greed and willfulness and arrogance. She thought of a future in which she would never again command a respectable, much less a high, salary. She saw herself as one of those poor souls who, unable to stay away from the circus they loved, took jobs as seamstresses or wardrobe women or ticket takers, an embarrassment to other performers, who didn't like to be reminded that they, too, were vulnerable and lived just one step away from the same fate.

Then there was Vicky. As an illiterate without any experience at earning a living except as a dancer or an aerialist, what kind of future could she possibly give her daughter? There would be no security, no fine education, none of the advantages that were Vicky's birthright.

Mara didn't sleep that night, not even with the pill the doctor prescribed for her, and in the morning, she rang for the nurse and asked her to contact Earl St. Clair, who lived in Boston, to tell him to please come to see her as quickly as possible about his granddaughter.

Jaime's father came two days later. He looked the same as the first time she'd seen him—tall and handsome and elegantly thin, a man whose white hair was the only sign that he was in his late fifties.

He stood by the bed, and what he was thinking was impossible to tell. "I'm sorry about your accident," he said, so dispassionately that the words meant nothing. "I hope you are on the road to recovery?"

"I'll be starting therapy in another week or so," she said, just as politely. "But I'll never fly again."

"Fly? Oh, you mean do aerialist work," he said.

There was a tinge of distaste in his voice that stirred her old anger. "Yes. Something as important to me as your law practice is to you, Mr. St. Clair," she said.

"I'm sure you're right. What is it you want to see me about?"

"It's Vicky. Do you still want her?"

There was a subtle change in his face, so subtle that only her Rom training caught it. Something—triumph, satisfaction?—tightened the muscles of his eyelids, and she knew then how much this meant to him. She wondered why she should be surprised. Men like Earl St. Clair didn't change their minds. They waited patiently, supremely confident that time was on their side.

"Of course," he said smoothly. "She's a St. Clair—the last of my particular branch of the family. Naturally we want the best for her."

"Like you, I want the best for my—for Jaime's daughter. It wouldn't be fair to keep Vicky when I can't provide for her adequately."

"You have no savings?"

"I was totally invested in the stock market, Mr. St. Clair. There's nothing left. I won't be able to return to the circus—and I'm not trained for anything else. Which is the only reason I'm considering—this."

"Just considering? You haven't already made up your mind?" There was a hint of mockery in his voice now.

"I have not. First I want some concessions on your part. I have to be sure that Vicky will receive the very best education."

"Of course. I enrolled her in the Cabot School the week she was born. It was my wife's school, and it's one of the finest in the country. Since it is located in Westchester County, and is both a boarding and a day school, she'll naturally live at home."

"And Vicky will be your heir?"

"I have no other."

"What about your personal feelings? She's a child who is used to a lot of love."

"She'll be raised as an American princess. Privileged but with obligations suited to her position. Every effort will be made to insure her a happy childhood."

She looked at him, suddenly afraid. Was she doing the right thing? What about love? He hadn't promised that *he* would love his granddaughter. But Jaime's mother—surely she would devote her life to her only grandchild. After all, just how much love did she herself have to give when her own heart was dead?

Earl St. Clair seemed to sense her uncertainty, her wavering. "You asked me to come here," he reminded her. "You must have been convinced that this was the best thing for Victoria. I promise you that she'll be given every opportunity to become a happy, well-adjusted woman. Can you offer her anything like that?"

The answer, or course, was no. "Then it's settled," she said heavily.

"No, not exactly." His flat Boston voice was crisp, decisive. "I want a few concessions on your part, too. I won't have the child torn between two loyalties. I don't want my wife to go through any more—heartache. It would kill her if, at some future date, you changed your mind and took her grandchild away. I expect you to sign a release, giving up all claim to Victoria. In return—" his nostrils flared briefly as if he'd caught a whiff of something unpleasant "—I'm willing to set up a trust fund in your name so you can live comfortably for the rest of your life. I don't want you on my conscience, you see. I also don't want you turning up to disrupt Victoria's life every time you have an impulse to see your child."

Mara closed her eyes to shut out his well-groomed face. Never see Vicky again? But that wasn't possible. She had assumed that she could visit Vicky often, send her gifts, write to her. And how about Vicky herself? What would she think about a mother who had abandoned her? It would be better if she had died in that fall. . . .

An idea took root. Dead—never to have to face the pity, the slow erosion of her past glory. To remain a legend, as she was now—yes, that would solve so many things, put a decent end to the past. . . .

She opened her eyes. "I have a better idea. What if everybody believed that I had died of my injuries?"

The man stared at her. "Are you suggesting—"

"Suppose I was being transferred to a private hospital in Boston to be closer to my in-laws. And suppose I didn't survive the trip. I would be buried in—oh, some out-of-the-way place along the route. You could arrange that. Jaime used to say that his father was an expert at arranging things the way he wanted."

She took a savage satisfaction in his involuntary flinch. But when he spoke, his voice was as cool as ever. "What about your friends?"

"I would be dead to them, too," she said wearily. "They could grieve for a while and then forget me."

He took his time. She could almost see the wheels turning in his mind. When he finally nodded, she knew she had won. Or had she lost? Of one thing she was sure. The legend of Princess Mara would live on for a while—if she was dead. A woman at the height of fame and success is killed in a fall on the same night that she is wiped out by the stock market crash. But first she breaks the record for doing a daring stunt, doing it in honor of her best friend, who had just committed suicide.

She could almost see the headlines.

After Earl St. Clair left, she told Clinker what she planned to do. Predictably her friend had hysterics, so much so that the nurse came and gave her a glass of water. When Clinker had calmed down enough to speak rationally again, she tried to change Mara's mind.

"It's insane! You can't do it, Mara. It just won't work."

"It will work, but I need your help."

"I won't do it. I refuse to get involved in such a terrible lie."

"If you're really my friend, you'll help me," Mara said relentlessly.

"But how can you fake your own death?" Clinker wailed. "You'll be recognized, and then—"

"Mr. St. Clair is arranging all the details. As for being recognized—I don't look like Princess Mara anymore."

Clinker averted her eyes. "You don't look bad," she said gruffly.

"I know I'm not repulsive. I thought I might be, you know. Everybody was acting so strange—"

"Dr. Tope told us there would be a severe change in your appearance, that we weren't to say anything about it to you until you were better. That's one reason why you weren't allowed many visitors. I—Mr. Sam and I thought that—well, that you were badly disfigured. But you really do look fine, you know, just not—not like you used to."

"I hate this face I'm wearing, Clinker." Bitterness colored Mara's voice as she thought of the black future ahead. "But I'll learn to live with it. I have no choice."

"You'll always be beautiful to me," Clinker said, tears filling her eyes.

"Then help me. Vicky will have a much better life with Jaime's parents. They'll come to love her. How can they help it?"

Clinker sighed. "You're right. She'd win the devil himself over."

"You see why I have to do it this way, don't you? I can't live with pity, with people lowering their voices around me, acting as if I'm an embarrassment. This way, I can start a new life—"

"Am I included in that life?"

Mara swallowed hard. A rush of gratitude thickened her voice as she said, "Of course. There'll be enough money for both of us. We can get a little cottage somewhere—where would you like to live? Florida? California? The Midwest?"

"I've always fancied California," Clinker said.

"Then it's settled. We'll make out. Later, I can get a job doing something—"

"I'll work, too." Clinker paused, thinking. "What about Lobo? He'd be lost without you. He's been hanging around the waiting room, looking so sad. He blames himself because he didn't catch you when you fell."

Mara felt a trickle of shame that she hadn't thought of Lobo. "Why not? He can be—oh, my brother. We can all be related, a brother and two sisters."

A giggle bubbled up in Clinker's throat. "What a combination—a giant, a princess, and a—"

"A good friend," Mara said softly.

Clinker's eyes filled with tears again. "I'll take care of you, Mara. Honest I will."

"Then we'd better start making some plans. Why don't you get Lobo in here—and if the nurse gives you any trouble, tell her you'll have another fit of hysterics if you don't get your way. And once we get settled somewhere, we'll start a new life. I already know the first thing I want to do."

"What's that?"

"I want to learn how to read and write."

BOOK TWO

Vicky's Story

CHAPTER 24

WHENEVER VICKY WANTED TO BE ALONE, SOMETIMES TO think out a problem or to read without interruptions or simply because she needed space around her, she saddled Misty, her favorite among her grandfather's stable of horses, and rode across the rolling hills of the St. Clair estate to the family cemetery. Today she had a particularly good reason for wanting to be alone—and for visiting her father's grave.

The cemetery, located in the northwest corner of the estate, was a serene place. Although no one in the family except Vicky came here these days, its ornamental shrubs and privet hedges, the maple trees that shaded the marble gravestones, were as meticulously cared for as the estate's formal Italian gardens. Even the lush grass that covered the graves was kept short, as regimented, Vicky often thought, as everything or everyone who came under Earl St. Clair's control—including herself. Although she would soon be eighteen, she despaired of ever being free of his domination.

While the mare grazed on the sweet grass near the ornate iron fence that surrounded the cemetery, Vicky sat cross-legged beside her father's grave. It was here she'd come with her childhood woes, her adolescent frustrations, and now her teenage dreams, ever since she could remember. How ironic that the only place she was free to speak her mind was among the dead, because nothing she said here would be reported back to her grandfather by toadying servants, later to be rehashed, explained, endlessly accounted for.

In one way, because reality never got in the way when she fantasized that her father, if alive, would advise and comfort her, and most of all, listen to her, it helped that she had no

recollection of him. She didn't even know what he looked like—
which was something she'd come here today to rectify.

Of course, her grandfather had no idea that she'd found the
photograph album. He didn't even know it still existed, because
he'd given orders that all his son's pictures be destroyed long
ago.

"Not that your grandfather hated Jaime, you understand,"
Grandmother Ada had once told her. "It's just that he was so
disappointed when Jaime gave up law school to marry your
mother."

Grandmother Ada was small-boned and fragile, and despite
her white hair and the multitude of wrinkles in her tissue-thin
skin, it was obvious that she had once been a very beautiful
woman. Ever since Vicky could remember, she had been an
invalid, confined to her room except on those rare occasions, at
Christmas and Thanksgiving, when her grandfather insisted she
be carried downstairs to dine with them in the formal dining
room. Those dinners were more like wakes than holiday celebrations, with Grandfather dominating the conversations and,
so often, admonishing Vicky about her many failings. No wonder Grandmother Ada stayed in bed most of the time.

Vicky thought about the conversation she'd had with her
grandmother that morning, remembering her determination to
get some answers about her parents.

"Why does Granddaddy get so furious when I ask questions
about my parents?" she had asked. "I don't even know my own
mother's name."

Grandmother Ada took a dainty sip from her teacup. "Her
name was Mara," she said calmly.

For a moment, surprise held Vicky speechless. "What was
her maiden name?" she managed finally.

"If she had a last name, I never heard it. We never met,
although I did see a photograph of her."

Vicky waited for her to go on; when her grandmother was
silent, she asked, "Do I look like her?"

"You both are redheads, but—no, you look just like your
father. You have his eyes—he had the bluest eyes, Victoria."

Her hand moved restlessly, plucking at the lace on her bed
jacket. Vicky knew she shouldn't pester her with questions, and
yet—her curiosity about her parents had been unsatisfied for so
many years.

Why the mystery? she wanted to ask. *What kind of woman
was my mother that my father was disowned for marrying her?*

*Why wasn't she buried beside him—and why does his grave have
the plainest stone in the family cemetery?*

Instead, she asked, "How did they meet? I already know she
was some kind of actress. I overheard you and Granddaddy
talking once, and he called her a—a cheap entertainer."

"You mustn't listen to other people's conversations, Victoria.
It's terribly gauche." But her grandmother's voice was absent,
as if her thoughts were elsewhere. She glanced toward the
door, twisting her lips as she did when she was undecided about
something. "I suppose there's no harm in it now that you're old
enough to be discreet. But you must promise not to repeat this
conversation to your grandfather. He'd be so furious."

"I promise," Vicky said, her mouth dry.

"Well, you mother *was* an entertainer, but she wasn't an actress. She was a circus performer, and quite famous, I understand."

Vicky was stunned. All her fantasies about her mother being
an actress in the movies, a café singer, or even a dancer, were
wrong. She'd been willing to accept that. But a *circus* performer? Circuses were—well, they were tawdry and cheap. . . .

"Oh, dear! I shouldn't have told you." Her grandmother's
fluty voice quavered with dismay. "Now you're going to ask me
a lot of questions I can't answer, and if Earl finds out, he'll be
so angry—"

"He won't find out. Please tell me more, Grandmother Ada."

"No, no. I've already said enough. You'll have to leave now,
dear. I'm very tired—"

"Then tell me about my father. Granddaddy never mentions
his name."

Her grandmother sighed. "I know. He blames himself—and
me—for not being more firm with Jaime, and maybe he's right.
I did spoil the boy. But then, he was so easy to spoil. In his own
way, your grandfather did love him, but he has such an unfor-
giving nature. Victoria, you must never cross your grandfather.
He can be so hard and inflexible. I disappointed him, and he
never forgave me. He wanted more sons, but after I had Jaime,
the doctors told us I'd never have any more babies. Earl knew
he'd made a mistake, marrying me. He needed a strong woman
who could give him a large family, but instead he got a sickly
wife." She gave a curious little laugh. "It almost seems like
poetic justice."

Vicky hid her impatience. Grandmother Ada was given to
long, rambling reminiscences about her years at Cabot, the same

day school Vicky now attended, about her coming-out parties
and her debut, about her wedding and four-month-long honeymoon in Europe. But she never spoke of her son—and Vicky
was determined that today she would finally get some answers
to the questions she'd lived with most of her life. After all, she
was almost eighteen, and would be having her own debut in the
fall. It was about time she knew the truth, no matter how unpleasant, about her parents.

She cast around for a relatively innocuous question. "Was
my—was Jaime a sickly baby?" she asked.

"Jaime? Whatever gave you such an odd idea? He was as
healthy as a baby can be. Of course, I couldn't take care of him
myself, but he never gave any of his nurses trouble. They all
adored him. He was so beautiful—always laughing, and so good-
natured. When he was older, Earl criticized Jaime and called
him a womanizer, but it wasn't true. It wasn't Jaime's fault that
all the girls chased him."

"And yet it was my mother he married," Vicky said. "They
were married, weren't they?"

"Why, of course! Earl and I didn't go to the wedding because—well, we disapproved. Your mother was—I'm afraid she
wasn't the kind of wife we wanted for Jaime. No one knew
where she came from, you see, and there were all kinds of tales
about her. She was already notorious by the time Jaime met
her." She sighed deeply and gave her untidy head a fretful shake.
"They'd only been married two years when Jaime was—when
he passed away. Then, two years later, your mother was killed
in a fall and—"

"What kind of fall?"

"Why, from a trapeze—or was it Roman rings? That's when
you came to live with us. I've often wished I'd defied your grandfather and gone to their wedding."

Vicky digested this, then asked, "Grandmama, do you have
any pictures of them?"

Her grandmother looked frightened. "Oh, no. Your grandfather would be furious if—he wants you raised as if we were
your parents. The past is the past. Best to put it behind you."

"But don't you see—if you and Granddaddy didn't make such
a mystery of it, I wouldn't be so curious."

Her grandmother gave her a sharp look. "Strange, you saying
that. I said those very words to Earl. But of course, he wouldn't
listen. He never listens to me, you know. It's as if I'm not really
here."

Vicky was silent. It was so hard to believe that these two people, always so formal with each other, had once been intimate enough to conceive a child. Had they ever loved each other? If so, what had eroded away that love? She felt a familiar ache, as if there were a hollowness in her chest—or maybe inside her heart. Somewhere in her past, at the perimeter of her memory, was—someone, a smile, a husky voice, warm arms, a time when the whole world was golden and safe. Was this the memory of her mother?

"Grandmama—you surely didn't destroy all my father's photographs," she said, her voice coaxing. "He was your only child."

But her grandmother wasn't listening now. There was a look on her face that came so often these days, a fixed smile, wandering eyes, a slackness around her mouth. That it had something to do with the brown liquid in the teacup her grandmother had been sipping steadily while they talked, Vicky was aware.

She often wondered where her grandmother got such an endless supply of sherry. For one thing, because of the war, there was a shortage of all kinds of liquor. One of the servants must be buying it for her—most likely her nurse, Mrs. Wright. But how did Grandmother Ada pay for it? She had no money of her own. Of course, she did have her jewelry. . . .

Vicky's eyes moved to the mahogany jewel chest, which sat on its own graceful table near the door. Since her grandmother's eyes were closed now, she rose quietly and went over to it.

Opening the drawers, one by one, she examined the display of jewelry. Her suspicions were confirmed when she realized some of the pieces—a garnet-and-diamond necklace, a sapphire ring, and the emerald bracelet that had belonged to her great-grandmother—were gone.

So that was how her grandmother bribed her nurse to supply her with sherry. Should she put a stop to it by going to Mrs. Wright and threatening to tell her grandfather? Of course, it would be an empty threat. She would never tell her grandfather that his wife was selling off her jewelry to buy liquor. It would only make Grandmama Ada's life even more miserable. . . .

Her grandmother moved restlessly on the massive bed that dwarfed her wasted body. Not wanting to be caught looking through her jewel chest, Vicky shut the drawer she'd been examining. As she was lowering the lid, her eyes fell on a tiny brass key. She picked it up, wondering what it unlocked. Certainly not the jewel chest, which had no keyhole.

Curious now, she examined the key more closely. It was old-fashioned, tarnished by age, obviously an antique. And the house was full of antiques, including the furniture in her grandmother's room. In fact, there were keyholes in most of the chests and bureaus, even in the small Queen Anne writing desk that sat between two windows.

She chose the Queen Anne desk as the most likely place to start. The drawer that was set in the curved front of the desk was locked, and when she examined the brass keyhole, she saw that it was badly scratched, as if the drawer had been locked and unlocked many times by an unsteady hand. She glanced toward the bed, saw that her grandmother was still dozing. Noiselessly she inserted the key, turned it, and pulled open the drawer.

Inside was a single item—a small, leather-bound photo album. Vicky didn't hesitate. She snatched up the album, tucked it under her arm, locked the drawer, and returned the key to the jewelry chest. Only then did she look around at her grandmother. Was Grandmama Ada really asleep? Her eyes were closed and she was lying very still—but she wasn't snoring, that soft little sighing sound that accompanied her frequent naps.

Salving her conscience with the thought that she would return the album as soon as she'd had a look inside, Vicky hurried away to her own room. But she didn't open the album immediately. Instead, she changed into riding clothes, the jodhpurs, tight-fitting jacket, and helmet that her grandfather, always a stickler for convention, insisted she wear even when she went riding alone around the estate.

With the album hidden away in the saddlebag that usually held a snack for herself and an apple for her mare, she had ridden toward the cemetery.

But now that she was here, sitting beside her father's grave with the leather-bound album resting on her knees, she found herself reluctant to open it. What if her father didn't live up to her expectations, her fantasies of him?

Darcy Woodrow, her best friend at school, thought it romantic that she had no memory of her parents. But Vicky knew that being an orphan wasn't romantic. It had been lonely, having no deep roots to keep her anchored in a safe harbor while she grew up. Sometimes she felt like a ghost, wandering through her grandfather's huge gray stone house with its gloomy corners and its unpredictable drafts.

Although it was imposing to look at, she knew from servants' talk that it was monumentally inconvenient, almost impossible to keep in the condition her grandfather demanded. And woe to the servant who fell down, even a little, on his job. She herself had had more nannies, all fired for little or no reason, than she could remember. Which was why she'd learned not to get too attached to any of them.

She often envied Darcy, who had such a normal life, and who lived in a modern house, with light wood furniture, vivid colors, and bright impressionist paintings that bore no resemblance to the dark oils that dominated the walls of her own home. Those portraits might be priceless, as her grandfather claimed, but she found the faces of her long-dead ancestors very depressing.

Sometimes she felt as if she were suffocating, a prisoner in her grandfather's house, constantly supervised, questioned about every move she made away from home. When, on very rare occasions, he did allow her to go to a school entertainment night, he was always waiting up for her when Johnson, his chauffeur, brought her home. What had the play been about? Had there been boys there? If so, had any of them spoken to her? What had they said?

It was open knowledge among her schoolmates that Vicky St. Clair's life away from school was as cloistered as a nun's. The day students could talk about their weekend dates, and the girls who lived in the dorms could brag about slipping out to meet a boy from nearby Sansun Academy behind the ivy-covered wall that separated the two schools, but not Vicky, because everybody would know she was lying.

When they spoke dreamily of kisses exchanged in the dark, she was silent. She envied them, and yet—none of the boys they talked about appealed to her. They seemed so young, maybe because she'd had so little experience with boys. Even so, she longed to have her first date, her first kiss, to receive a gift or a love letter from a boy.

When the Sansun boys were invited to Cabot School for the monthly dances, she had all the dance partners she could handle, but not one of them had ever invited her to meet him in town— or behind the notorious wall.

Vicky knew that the other girls called her the Princess behind her back, which bewildered her. Most of their parents were rich. After all, there were no scholarship students at Cabot School.

That she had made one good friend at school seemed something of a miracle. How could you make friends when you couldn't visit their homes—or invite them to yours? The other girls might whisper behind Darcy's back and say she was "fast," but she was fun to be with. She was also the daughter of her grandfather's stockbroker, which was why he grudgingly allowed Vicky to visit her on occasion. In fact, he had even allowed her to stay there overnight one memorable weekend. . . .

Vicky smiled, remembering the fun it had been, making cocoa in the Woodrows' big kitchen late at night, talking until almost morning, confiding her secrets—well, some of them—to Darcy. Did she dare tell her friend about the album—provided she found a picture of her father inside?

She ran her hand over the cover. Gingerly, as if the buttery soft leather might crack and break, she finally opened it.

The face of a young man, a color-tinted studio photograph, smiled up at her. Involuntarily she gasped. It was her own smile, her own face she saw—the same startling blue eyes, the same straight nose and wide, full-lipped mouth. Only the color of their hair was different. Where hers was auburn, her father's had been burnished gold. It was thick, curly: he wore it longer than the current military-short style, giving him an old-fashioned look.

For a long time she studied the photograph, questions crowding her mind. He was incredibly handsome, something she hadn't known before, even though her grandmother had said women chased him. And her mother—what had she been like? Had she been beautiful—or had a cheap prettiness captured Jaime St. Clair's heart?

Vicky turned the page and found herself smiling at the picture of a baby, dressed in lace-trimmed swaddling clothes. As she went through the pages slowly, stopping to study each photograph, she found it increasingly hard not to cry. All the pictures were of her father, progressing from baby to small boy to teenager to young man, ending finally with a snapshot of him as a college graduate in a cap and gown, smiling confidently into the camera.

The date on the back of the snapshot was 1924. So it must have been taken near the time he'd met her mother. No wonder she'd fallen in love with him. He was a girl's dream come true— or had her mother been a girl? If she'd already been famous, then perhaps she had been an older woman who had used her wiles to seduce an impressionable—and very rich—college boy. . . .

Vicky closed the album, feeling depressed. The photographs had raised more questions that they had answered. Dare she keep one of them? Would her grandmother miss it?

Vicky went through the album again, lingering over several of the snapshots—Jaime as a boy, sitting on a fat pony, his hair tousled and his smile sunny; Jaime, older now, on a horse, a dappled gray stallion, looking very much at ease; Jaime seated in the driver's seat of a rakish sports car; Jaime in evening clothes, a twinkle in his eye as if he were laughing at some private joke.

She felt a greedy desire to keep all of them, but in the end, she chose her father's graduation picture because it showed him as he'd been when he'd fathered her.

Wondering how two people from such different backgrounds could have met, much less married, she closed the album. As she got to her feet, a rectangular piece of cardboard, yellowed with age, fell on the grass at her feet. She picked it up and saw it was the photograph of a woman.

The postcard was in color—gaudy and poorly printed. The woman was shown full figure, sitting on a swing—no, a trapeze. Her head was held high, her smile radiant—and her hair was the color of flames. Her costume, all white net and sparkles, was daringly brief, and she looked like a fairy, getting ready to launch herself into the air.

Even before Vicky read the caption underneath—*Princess Mara*—she knew it was her mother. She waited for a surge of emotion—regret, sadness, even grief—but she felt nothing. This woman seemed to have nothing to do with her. Had it been her mother's arms that had held her as a child, her voice that had soothed away her baby fears? It was hard to believe. There was nothing even remotely maternal about the woman on the postcard. Yes, she had been beautiful, but it was an exotic beauty, completely alien to the world Vicky knew.

And how had the postcard, obviously the kind made for publicity purposes, come into her grandmother's possession? It was signed in ink, but only the word *Mara*, printed in large, childish letters. No "Love to my mother-in-law," or even "Best wishes, Ada." Had her father sent it to his mother? Maybe Grandmama Ada had found it in Jaime's room after he'd been banished. It was another mystery, one she would probably never solve. . . .

That evening, after her grandmother was asleep, Vicky stole into her room and returned the album to its hiding place. She kept her father's graduation photograph, and she also kept the postcard of her mother.

CHAPTER 25

*T*HE NEXT DAY, WHEN VICKY WAS EATING LUNCH WITH
Darcy under one of the huge oak trees that bordered the
campus, she showed her friend the two photographs.

"These were my parents," she said.

Darcy wore her honey-blond hair in a fashionable pompadour
that showed off her vivacious face and upturned nose; she was
much shorter that Vicky, with a well-rounded figure that wasn't
at its best in the severely tailored school uniform. Her amber-
colored eyes widened as she studied first the photograph, then
the postcard.

"So that's what they looked like," she said finally. "It gives
me goose bumps, just thinking about it. Both of them dying so
tragically, I mean."

Vicky stared at her in bewilderment. "How could you possibly know how they died when I just found out myself?"

Darcy popped both hands over her mouth. "Oh, rats. Look,
don't you dare tell your grandfather I spilled the beans. My
father would butcher me."

"Tell me what you know and I won't," Vicky said.

"Well . . . it isn't really much. Just what everybody knows
about Princess Mara. That she was this famous aerialist, a Gypsy
princess, who fell in love with your father, and how, after his
family disowned him for marrying her, he was shot by one of
her former lovers, and then a couple of years later, she was
killed, too, falling off a trapeze. I knew you were their daughter,
that it was a big secret—"

Her words echoed in Vicky's ears. —*he was shot by one of
her former lovers*— Was that true? Had one of her mother's
lovers killed her father? Was that why her grandparents never
spoke of Princess Mara, why she, her daughter, hadn't even

268

known her name until yesterday? And had her mother been a Gypsy? But that would mean that she was part Gypsy, too. . . .

Feeling a little sick, she took a deep breath, forcing air into her starved lungs. "Why didn't you tell me, Darcy?" she asked, her voice thin.

"I couldn't. I promised my dad. I don't think anyone else knows about—you know, who your mother was. At least, I've never heard any talk around school."

Vicky digested this for a moment. She wasn't so sure. Why else did they call her the Princess behind her back?

"What do you mean by 'what everybody knows about Princess Mara?' " she asked finally. "I didn't know. I never heard her name before yesterday."

Darcy shook her head. "Your grandfather keeps you locked in an ivory tower—or is that an ivy tower? I'll bet you've never read a novel in your life that wasn't a classic. *Yesterday's Shadows* was a big bestseller last year, and it was based on your mother's life. Everybody was reading it. Of course, it was fiction, but they say it was based on fact. About her being a Gypsy and having noble blood and being banished from her family because of a love affair with a commoner, I mean. There was an article about her in the *Tattletale*—because of the novel being so popular. Of course, you don't read scandal sheets either, do you?"

"No—and I hope you aren't going to repeat this conversation to anyone. I wouldn't want my private business aired around school."

Darcy stared at her. "You aren't *ashamed* of it, are you? Listen, if Princess Mara was my mother, I'd brag about it. Frankly, I think you're nuts."

Vicky forced a smile. "Nuts? Who sneaks out at night to go riding around in cars with boys? And who's going to get caught one of these days?"

Darcy giggled. "You don't know what you're missing. Think of the fun you could have if you'd do a little sneaking around, too."

"And how would I manage that? Climb the wall around the estate? The top is littered with broken glass, you know. Or maybe I could scale the gates. They're only twenty feet tall."

"I know what you mean. You're like the princess in that old fairy tale. 'Rapunzel, Rapunzel, let down your long, golden hair. . . .' "

"It's not quite that bad," Vicky protested.

"Bad enough, though. Well, you're almost eighteen. Your grandfather can't keep you locked up forever. It's a wonder he lets you out to go to school."

"It's a tradition. My grandmother Ada went to Cabot. So did her mother and aunts. I was registered here the week I was born—or so my grandmother told me once."

"Lord. Frankly, I think this grisly old place is overrated. 'Our girls are all ladies, don't you know?' " Darcy said in a good imitation of their dean's nasal drawl. "And it could be worse. You could've had a governess."

"And then I never would've met you," Vicky said.

" 'That is cor-rect, Miss St. Clair—but do watch your syntax.' " Darcy giggled when Vicky laughed. "And I have to admit I'm not overloaded with friends. My reputation for liking to have a good time scares off the Goody Two-Shoes around here. We make a good team, don't we? Both of us outsiders—sort of. Of course, it's different with you. You're a St. Clair. Everybody looks up to you and tries to copy the way you talk and all. If only you'd let go and have some fun. Of course, we'd have to figure a way to get you out of the dungeon first."

To Vicky's relief, the tower bell rang, announcing the end of lunch hour. As she deposited her milk carton and sandwich wrapping in a trash can, then headed toward her English IV class, she wondered uneasily if she'd made a mistake, showing Darcy those photographs. But then, if you couldn't trust your best friend, who could you trust?

It was a week later that she overheard the conversation that would change her life.

Ever since her seventeenth birthday, she'd been aware that her grandfather's attitude toward her had changed. Oh, he was as strict as ever, but now he included her when he had guests for dinner, whereas before, she'd eaten off a tray in her room those nights. Then, after the guests were gone, he would review the evening with her, pointing out all of her faux pas and exhorting her to behave like a proper St. Clair. She did her best, even though she knew that no matter how well she talked or behaved, she would never, ever please him.

Lately, too, he'd been bringing the name of one of his junior law partners into their conversations. Since he never did anything without a reason, she knew that sooner or later, she would find out why.

She knew who Gary Wisdom was, of course, because he was

a frequent dinner guest. The truth was, she didn't like him. Although he had a draft deferment because of something he called "my unfortunate rugby injury," he spoke cuttingly about draft dodgers and war shirkers. Which seemed hypocritical to Vicky for a man who was well aware that he was in no danger of going off to the Pacific or Europe to fight the war.

Slightly built, with a long, narrow nose, pale eyes slightly too close together, he reminded her of one of her grandfather's prize borzois—pale, languid, and just a little effete.

She also found him boring and dull, but she was always polite, since Grandfather Earl obviously approved of his junior partner, whom he called "an up-and-coming young lawyer who was going to make his mark in corporate law."

Vicky wandered restlessly around her room, stopping to stare absently at the large display of trophies she'd won at horse shows, then to study a collection of antique dolls in a glass-fronted cabinet. They had belonged to her great-grandmother, and she'd been forbidden to touch them until she was old enough to "be responsible." By then, of course, she'd lost all interest in playing with dolls.

The problem of Gary Wisdom, she decided, was like so many things in her life—dependent upon her grandfather's whim. The next time Gary came for dinner, she would turn up as ordered, dressed appropriately in one of the long evening skirts and white silk blouses that were as much a uniform as her school clothes, with her hair neat, no makeup on her face, not even the lipstick she applied after Johnson, the family chauffeur, dropped her off at school, and removed just before Johnson drove her back home that afternoon.

She would spend the whole long evening listening silently while her grandfather and Gary droned on about the law business and, inevitably, the war, which was fast winding down in the Pacific, until finally she could excuse herself and escape to her room.

But why was she thinking of Gary Wisdom when she had something much more exciting to think about right now—the blind date Darcy wanted to arrange for her?

"I've been dating this really keen guy, and he has a friend who wants to meet you. They've invited us out to dinner Friday night, and then to a movie afterwards. How about it, Vicky?"

"You know that's impossible. Who is your new boyfriend, anyway? Does he go to Sansun Academy?"

"Heavens no. He's been out of school for ages. And I met

him—well, through a friend. The thing is, it'll spoil everything if you don't go. Daddy is really sore because I charged some stuff on Mom's charge account last month. So I'm under restriction. No dates, not even a movie, for a month. But if you stay overnight and say you want to go to a movie, Daddy'll even let me borrow his car without grousing about gas rationing. They know how straitlaced you are, and besides, Daddy is always trying to suck up to your grandfather so he can sell him some more bonds or something. It's all such a bore, but they've got their back up this time and—you will do it, won't you?''

Vicky had told her again that it was impossible, but she'd been tempted, for just a few moments, to say yes. After all, she was old enough to go out to dinner and to the movies with a man. It might even be fun, and she'd be helping out a friend, too. . . .

Vicky realized where her thoughts were heading, and she gave herself a mental shake. No, it was impossible. If her grandfather found out, there was no telling what he'd do. He fired servants for breaking a crystal glass or being a few minutes late when he rang for his morning coffee. For such an infraction as lying to him, he would probably confine her to her room for the rest of the year.

There was another reason for turning down Darcy's offer. A blind date sounded—well, as if you couldn't get a date on your own. . . . A breeze sprang up, ruffling the sheer curtains at the windows, reminding her it was getting late. She changed for dinner, then decided there was still time to visit the new puppies her grandfather's grand champion borzoi bitch had dropped a few days earlier.

She was passing her grandmother's bedroom when she heard her grandfather's raised voice. When she heard her own name, she paused to listen.

"You of all people should understand why I can't allow Victoria to go away to college," her grandfather was saying. "Bad blood is bad blood, even when it's diluted with good, solid St. Clair stock. She's too much like her mother to take chances."

Her grandmother tried to say something, but his voice overrode hers. "The wise thing is to marry her off young, see that she's in the hands of someone who will not only take good care of her, but will keep her on a tight rein. And Gary Wisdom is the man I've chosen."

"But Vicky doesn't like him. She told me that he reminded her of a horse—or was it a dog? Anyway, she'd be miserable, married to him."

"Nonsense. She doesn't know what she wants. When the time comes, she'll come around—and she'll give me some fine grandsons. Gary has already agreed to have his name changed to St. Clair."

"You never learn, do you, Earl?" Grandmother Ada's voice was unexpectedly strong. "You made the same mistake with Jaime, trying to run his life. Never a word of praise, just constant criticism and—"

"My mistake, as you call it, was giving him too loose a rein. Well, I didn't make that mistake with Victoria. She'll do what I say or I'll disown her."

"Just like you did Jaime? It didn't work with him—he went right ahead and married that circus woman anyway, and what did it get you? You lost your only son because of your wicked, wicked pride."

There was a ominous silence. When he spoke again, Earl St. Clair's voice was edged with ice. "He made his own bed. I had nothing to do with it. And Victoria's got too much of both of them—and you—in her. She needs a strong hand or she'll turn into a hedonist like her mother or a weakling like Jaime or a drunk like you. So keep your nose out of this, you hear?"

Vicky put her hands over her ears, refusing to hear more. She hurried back to her room, wishing she were dead. She flung herself facedown on the bed, burying her flushed face in her pillow. How could her grandfather talk about her—and Grandmama—tnat way, say such ugly things about them? She had tried to believe that his coldness, his criticisms, were because he found it hard to show affection, because he wanted the best for her. But now she could no longer fool herself. He was incapable of love. All he wanted was to have his own way. One thing for sure—nothing or no one could ever make her marry a man she detested. This was the forties—he had to be crazy to think that he could marry her off to whomever he pleased. Just the thought of Gary Wisdom, with his clammy hands and his hot eyes, made her stomach roll. Standing up to her grandfather would be hard, but she had no other choice. In fact, she was ashamed that she hadn't done it long before this. He had called her weak—but she wasn't! And to prove it—yes, she knew just how to prove that she wasn't a jellyfish. . . .

Was this how her father had felt when he'd defied his father—scared and yet excited, too? The thought of her father having the courage to live his own life made her feel closer to him, much more than she'd ever felt to her grandfather. . . .

She took a deep breath, let it out slowly. Resolutely, not giving herself time for second thoughts, she picked up the brass French phone beside her bed, and when the operator came on, asked for Darcy's number.

A minute later, her friend's breezy voice came on the line. "Darcy speaking."

"This is Vicky. I've changed my mind. I'd love to go to the movies with you and your friends."

CHAPTER 26

AT FIRST, THE NOVELTY OF DEFYING HER GRANDFATHER—and the intrigue of convincing Darcy's parents that they would absolutely die if they didn't see *The Phantom of the Opera*—was enough to negate Vicky's uneasiness. Her first real doubt came when Darcy insisted that her cashmere sweater set and green plaid skirt would never do.

"You look so—so schoolgirlish in that outfit. Oh, I know that sweater set cost a fortune, but we're not going out with schoolboys, you know." She giggled suddenly; there was a glitter in her eyes that increased Vicky's doubts. "Wait until you see Matt! I'm really nuts about him."

Despite her reservations, Vicky agreed to wear one of Darcy's dresses, an ice-blue silk sheath with a draped front. Since she was several inches taller than Darcy, the skirt was too short, and she felt very uncomfortable with the amount of skin that showed through the keyhole neckline. Darcy, who was wearing a tight-fitting tunic with a flounce and exaggerated shoulder pads, assured her she looked keen, so she hid her doubts and returned the compliment.

It only took half an hour to drive from the exclusive Boston suburb where the Woodrows lived to the street where Darcy parked her father's Cadillac sedan, but it could have been on a different planet. The street was lined with third-rate movie houses, wholesale stores, and nightclubs that announced the presence of girls, girls, girls. Throbbing music, loud and raucous, poured out into the street from the café where, Darcy told her now, they were to meet their dates.

"I assumed we'd be meeting your friends at the movie house," Vicky said in dismay.

"Oh, Vicky. You are so naive. We aren't going to the movies. That was just to throw the bloodhounds off our trail. Come on, don't be so stuffy. You're going to love Matt's friend. He's really neat."

Hiding her doubts, Vicky followed her friend into the noisy café. It was dark and smoky, and the odor of stale beer was so strong that she found herself holding her breath. As Darcy led the way past a long bar, heading for a booth in the rear, Vicky's first impression was that all the patrons were men, many of them in uniform, who turned to stare at them. When her eyes adjusted to the change of light, she realized that there were a few women present, most of them sitting in pairs in the booths.

Without asking Vicky what she wanted, Darcy ordered two beers from a plump waitress. Vicky pretended to take an occasional sip, wishing it were a Coke. Darcy chatted nervously, her eyes fixed on the door. A few minutes later, when her friend's face took on a sultry smile, Vicky looked up to see two men coming toward them.

"The tall one's mine," Darcy whispered.

One look at her blind date and Vicky no longer had the slightest doubt that she'd made a mistake. Not only was he not the clean-cut type Darcy had described, but he was years older. Even Darcy grimaced and told her, sotto voce, that she was sorry, Matt had brought a substitute. "Well, looks aren't everything," she added, shrugging.

Matt, too, was a revelation. He was handsome in a dark, flashy way, but his eyes, as he looked Vicky over, were much too bold. After the third blue joke he told, Vicky wished more than ever that she were home in bed.

Dinner, to her dismay, consisted of slabs of gray-looking roast beef, served on white bread with a mound of watery mashed potatoes, the whole mess smothered in hot gravy. The food was greasy, much too salty, and even the few bites Vicky took left a dark brown taste in her mouth.

By now she knew the whole adventure would be a total disaster. Her date—Owen Something—had as little to say as she, but he never took his eyes off her. After the first few minutes, she was careful to keep her eyes fixed either on her plate or on Darcy's face.

Darcy, who never stopped talking, had that feverish look in her eyes again, and when Vicky realized that Matt was fondling her friend under the cover of the table, she finally gave up all pretense of eating and sat numbly, as far away from the rough-looking man beside her as the booth permitted, praying for the evening to end.

"So what do we do next?" Matt said when they had finished eating. "How about the Shadow Box?" He grinned at Vicky, his eyes busy surveying her keyhole neckline. "Darcy ever tell you how we met? I work at the Shadow Box, kind of like a bouncer, see. Darcy here had some kind of row with the guy she was with, and I stepped in, tossed him out, and we've been cozy ever since."

Darcy giggled. Vicky had always thought of her friend's giggle as infectious; now it grated on her nerves. "I've got a better idea," Darcy said. "Why don't we take in the carnival at the fairgrounds? It should be fun."

The two men exchanged glances; Owen shrugged, and Matt said, "Okay. Why not?"

Since no one had asked Vicky's opinion, she was silent. At least at a carnival she wouldn't have to dance with Owen, and there would be lots of other people around, too. But as soon as she got the chance, she was going to make an excuse—a headache, stomachache, a broken leg—and make Darcy take her home.

The midway of the Great Southern Show was going full blast when they got there. The noise was deafening, and not just the ear-piercing screams of the passengers on the Sky Rider roller coaster. With regularity, a high-pitched whistle of compressed air accompanied a ride called the Tipple-Top as its metal baskets went swirling up and down and around. There were staccato blasts of noise from the motorcycles inside the Wall of Death hippodrome, mingled with the gentler sounds of the merry-go-round, and the brash voices of pitchmen, touting their wares.

And then there were the odors—stale popcorn and hot grease and the sugary, too-sweet odor of saltwater taffy—none of them setting well with Vicky's already queasy stomach. Although still grimly trying to be a good sport, it seemed to her that she'd wandered into a nightmare.

"Hey, there's the Tunnel of Love," Matt said, squeezing Darcy's arm. "How about it, sport? Let's you and me take a spin through the tunnel."

"Yeah. I'm for it," Owen said. He gave Vicky a sidelong glance. "It could be fun."

Vicky stiffened at the thought of sitting close to him in the dark. "I'd rather not. Rides make me sick," she said, although she'd never been on one. "Actually, I don't feel so well. I think it was that beef sandwich. It had a strange taste."

"Oh, Vicky, you aren't going to get sick, are you?" Darcy wailed. "You're going to spoil everything."

"Maybe a drink of water would help," Vicky said, thinking fast. "I saw a fountain back that way. Why don't you come with me?"

"No, I'll stay here. And don't take too long." Darcy's voice was sulky.

Vicky didn't argue with her. With a feeling of relief, she hurried off. Somehow she had to get through the next hour or so—maybe she should pretend to feel faint as well as nauseous. It wouldn't be a lie. She did feel awful. Some of it was due to Owen Something, but mainly it was disillusionment. She had thought she knew Darcy, but a girl who let a man fondle her under her skirt was not someone she wanted as a friend. As to what they were doing during the ride here, with Darcy practically sitting in Matt's lap in the front seat, even though he was driving—well, she didn't want to even think about that.

A few minutes later, she located a women's rest room and was glad to find it empty. It was a dark, unpleasant place, obviously unsanitary, but at the moment, it seemed like a refuge. She turned on the faucet at a rusty sink and let cold water run over her wrists. In the blurred mirror above the sink, she caught a glimpse of her own face and realized she looked as sick as she felt.

Well, it was time she took a stand. When she went back, she would insist that Darcy drive her home—and the devil with her sulks. Darcy wasn't really her friend. She was spoiled rotten, used to using people—why hadn't she seen this before?

Her lips set in a determined line, Vicky washed her face in cool water, dried it with a rough paper towel, tidied up her hair, and immediately felt better. She took her time returning to the Tunnel of Love; when she saw the three of them waiting for her, her step slowed even more.

As she came up behind them, Matt was saying, "Jesus, Darcy, I thought you said she was a live one!"

"I thought she was. She's never acted like this before." Darcy's tone was defensive.

"Well, I have to admit she's a looker," Matt conceded.

"It ain't her looks I'm interested in," Owen growled. In the garish lights of the Tunnel of Love ride, his face had a coarse, unfinished look. "Hell, what I want is action. What's wrong with her, anyway? She acts like I'm poison."

"Maybe she don't like your ugly mug," Matt said.

Owen growled something Vicky didn't catch, and Matt laughed. "I'll bet I could warm her up," he said.

"Don't forget—you're my date!" Darcy's voice was shrill.

"Hey, baby, I was just kidding. You know I go for you. Didn't I tell you she was something special, Owen?" He hugged Darcy, his hand cupping her hip. "Say, I've got a great idea. Why don't you be a good sport and show my buddy some action? Looks like he's not going to get anywhere with your iceberg friend."

Darcy giggled. "You're terrible," she said, but the hot, excited look was back in her eyes.

Vicky felt a lurching sickness in the pit of her stomach. She turned and ran, wanting to escape not only the three of them, but the realization that her friend, whom she had defended so often to other girls, was all the things they said she was—and worse.

The carnival was closing down for the night. Vicky, still trying to decide what to do, was hiding out in an arcade, pretending an interest in a game of Fascination. The flashing lights, the irritating spiel of the man in attendance as he tried to lure more customers into his game, the noisy rattle of the machinery, made her head throb with pain.

Her main fear was that she would bump into Darcy and the two men again. When she'd run away from them, part of it was disgust, but it was also because she was afraid of her own flaring temper.

Anger was an emotion she never allowed herself. All the years of being punished for such minor crimes as raising her voice or running in the house or not immediately obeying her grandfather's orders had molded her into what she now was—controlled, wary, the opposite of impulsive. The other Vicky, who could explode into a white-hot rage, frightened her to death.

She had read enough psychology books to realize that her

rages had something to do with repression, with never being allowed to show her inner feelings, so she was always very careful to walk away from any situation that might trigger it off.

When she'd felt all the signs of temper—nausea, heat suffusing her head, and a choking sensation in her throat—she'd known she had to get away before she did something stupid, like slapping Darcy's cheap, lying face.

Even after the choking sensation went away, leaving her feeling drained and lethargic, she had stayed out of sight, pretending an interest in the arcade games, but now the crowds were thinning out, and she knew the arcade would soon be closing. Wanting to avoid the front of the arcade, which was open to the midway, she slipped out through a back door and found herself in a narrow passageway that ran between the row of concession stands and a long, narrow tent that housed one of the sideshows.

It was quieter here, the midway sounds muffled. Although it was unlighted, there was enough reflection from the midway to see by, and she moved carefully, picking her way around a pile of empty crates and a row of trash cans, hoping the passageway would come out on the parking lot. Maybe she could get a ride into the city from some family—or even borrow enough money for a phone call.

The nausea was back, which wasn't a surprise since she always felt sick after one of her rare tempers. She was wearing heels, which Darcy had practically forced upon her, and she wanted desperately to sit down and rest, but she didn't dare because it was so late.

She was thirsty, too, but even if she was willing to risk the midway, she had no money, not a penny, for a soft drink. How stupid to come out on a blind date without money! But then, she never carried money with her. When she shopped, it was always at stores where her grandfather had charge accounts. Johnson drove her to and from the stores as well as to school and to her riding academy, so she had no need for money, not even for tips.

She had assumed that everything would be provided by her date, and now she was stranded in this horrid place without a cent in her purse.

Did Darcy realize her predicament? What was her friend doing right now? Was she in some motel room with both those loathsome men? As for Darcy getting into trouble for what had happened tonight, her friend had probably concocted some lie to absolve herself from blame. Anyone who had gotten away with murder as long as Darcy had could explain away anything. And her parents would probably believe every word of it.

Well, she'd worry about that later. Right now she had to get home. She had no intention of returning to Darcy's house—let the little sneak explain *that*!—because from now on, Darcy didn't exist for her.

If only she had a dime, she'd call her grandfather and confess everything. He'd put her on restriction and she'd have to listen to endless lectures, but at least she'd be safe at home. . . .

She reached the end of the row of booths. She hesitated, not knowing which way to go. A couple, quarreling loudly, passed, and she shrank back, realizing they were both drunk. Maybe if she could find a guard or someone in authority, she could borrow a dime for a phone call. Surely Darcy and the two men were gone now. The midway should be safe enough. . . .

As she stepped out of the shadows, someone grabbed her shoulder. She gave a scream and tried to twist away, but a large hand clamped down over her mouth, and she fell backward, against a hard body. The odor of whiskey, of sweat, and something else unpleasant she couldn't identify made her gag as she tried to squirm out of the man's grasp.

In her struggle to escape, she kicked backward. Her heel cracked against his shin; he ripped off a vicious curse, and she recognized Owen's voice.

"Okay, you little tease," he said, his hot breath fanning her ear. "You've had your fun. Now it's my turn."

CHAPTER 27

IT WAS THE MOST TERRIFYING THING THAT HAD EVER HAP-pened to Vicky. Like every woman, she'd had her nightmares of being raped. She had dreamt of death, too, a violent one. But now reality put all those nightmares in the shade as the man dragged her backward, away from the light and into the darkness, his thick arm pressed against her windpipe, choking off her breath.

The first shock gone and desperate for air, she began to fight. Briefly she broke away, long enough to gasp out a cry for help. Then his arms were crushing her face against his leather jacket and blocking off her air again.

"Okay, we're going to have a little party. Don't give me any trouble or I'll work you over so your own mother won't know you."

His words revitalized her desperation. She began to fight again, using her feet, her elbows, twisting her body to break his smothering grasp. His fist crashed against the side of her head, knocking her to the ground, and something hard and brittle crackled under her body as he fell on top of her, crushing all the air out of her lungs. She took a shuddering breath, but when she tried to scream, he hit her again, this time on the chin.

The pain was so excruciating that she went limp. She felt a rush of cold air against her throat and realized he was pawing at her neckline, trying to rip the front of her dress open. She wanted desperately to fight back, but her strength had deserted her and she couldn't move. He threw her skirt up over her head, exposing her thighs, and she heard the whisper of a zipper and knew he had opened his fly.

Then—a miracle. Suddenly he was reeling backward, losing his balance and falling to the ground with a loud thump. In the sallow light she saw a figure looming over Owen, and she realized someone had come to her rescue.

"I'll kill you, you son of a bitch!"

It was Owen's hoarse voice. He was lifting himself, regaining his feet. The man, his head and shoulders silhouetted against the lights of the midway, was smaller than Owen, but there was something in his stance, an easy balance that marked him as dangerous.

Owen obviously thought so, too. Rubbing his mouth, he backed away. A moment later, he was shambling off into the darkness.

"You okay, lady?" the man asked.

"I—I think so. Thank God you happened along," was all she could think to say.

"I didn't happen along. That's my Skillo booth over there. I heard you yell and came to see what was going on. How'd you get in such a fix, anyway?"

"It was a blind date," Vicky said. Since the man hadn't moved, she struggled to her feet, unaided. "He got—uh, fresh, so I went to the rest room and never came back. But he found me anyway and—" She stopped, unable to go on.

"Yeah." He studied her closely, and she wished he weren't standing against the light, so she could see his face. "You need a doctor?" the man said with obvious reluctance.

"No, he didn't—I don't need a doctor. But I'd like to clean up a little before I go home. I'm not sure where the rest rooms are from here."

"They lock them up nights—you know, to keep the bums out. My rig's over in the backyard." He pointed toward the end of the midway. "If you want, you can clean up there. No one'll bother you."

The thought of washing her face was appealing, but still Vicky hesitated. Did she dare trust this man? What if she'd exchanged one rapist for another?

"Course, it's up to you," the man said, and the indifference in his voice decided her.

"Thank you," she said.

"You can fix yourself some coffee if you want, but be careful with the stove. It's butane and kinda tricky." He paused as if thinking something through. "I have to close down now, but I guess I can leave long enough to point out my rig."

"I'd appreciate that."

"Yeah, well, we better get moving. I don't want to leave the booth too long with the boards down."

His voice held impatience, and she was silent as she followed him down along the extension of the midway. A few minutes later, they came to parking lot filled with vehicles. The man pointed out a small, tear-shaped trailer, attached to a truck.

"Door's not locked. Just pull the string to turn on the light. There's a washbasin and water in the tank. Be careful you turn the spigot off all the way so it don't drip. There ain't no clean towels, so you'll have to use the one on the nail."

He turned and walked away, not waiting for her answer, and she wondered if he was sorry he'd been so quick to come to her rescue. For some reason, that was reassuring.

She found the door unlocked, as he'd stated, but it was a while before she located the string, hanging from the ceiling. She gave it a yank, and light came on from a naked bulb that hung from a wire that disappeared through an opening in the window. The trailer, she saw, was not only very cramped, but littered with everything from automobile parts to a stack of old western pulp magazines.

She wrinkled her nose, trying to identify the unpleasant odor. Fruit gone bad, machine oil, and other things she'd just as soon not identify, she decided. A folding metal daybed, the thin mattress covered with a wrinkled blanket and no sheets, sat open against one wall. From the clothes and other objects that were strewn around, it was obvious her rescuer seldom bothered to put anything away.

She got water from a small metal tank, and was very careful to turn the spigot off tightly. She washed quickly, drying herself with a slightly sour towel she found hanging on a nail. When she saw a safety pin lying on the floorboards, she used it to pin together the rip in her dress. She examined her reflection in an unframed mirror hanging on the wall above the washstand and discovered a large bruise, already turning black, on the side of her face; another one discolored her chin. Maybe—yes, maybe she could tell her grandfather she'd been in an accident.

She pushed a stack of clothes off the daybed and sat down. Her legs felt weak, and her face ached where Owen had struck her. She desperately wanted a cup of tea—but she had no idea how to make it. Suddenly she was shaking all over, the enormity of what could have happened if she hadn't been rescued finally sinking in. Maybe, if she just closed her eyes for a minute, she would feel better able to cope.

A hand shook her awake. She sat up with a cry of panic, her heart pounding in her chest. It was the man who had rescued her, and she got her first good look at him. Even after the other surprises of the evening, this one managed to catch her off guard. For one thing, he was younger than she'd expected. His eyes were deep-set, amber in the harsh light, and his hair, dark blond, covered his head in a mass of tight curls. His skin was tanned, and his teeth were very white, his mouth wide and well shaped. A giggle escaped her throat. How chagrined Darcy would be if she could see the "looker" who had rescued her.

The man frowned at her. "You ain't getting hysterical on me, are you?"

"I'm okay," she said, her amusement gone as quickly as it had come. "I guess it's reaction. I was pretty scared."

"You oughta be more careful who you take up with." He studied her closely. "How old are you, anyway?"

"Nineteen," Vicky said, and then wondered why she'd lied.

"You look older," he said, and she wanted to laugh.

"Thank you," she said.

"How about some coffee? There's still some left in the pot. I'll heat it up."

Not waiting for an answer, he went to light the burner under a smoke-blackened coffeepot. While it heated, he took two mugs from a cupboard, pushed a pile of socks off a table made of unfinished planks, and set out the mugs.

"Hope you don't use cream. Can't keep it from going sour."

Vicky started to tell him she never drank coffee, that she'd rather have tea, then changed her mind. He took off his jacket, and she saw he was wearing a navy-blue undershirt that had seen better days. A small blue anchor had been tattooed on his lower arm. She'd never seen a tattoo before, and she stared at it with fascinated eyes.

He caught her stare and told her, "Got that done in Pearl City. Some of the guys bet me I wouldn't, and I was all tanked up, so I went for it. Damned stupid thing to do."

"You were in the navy?"

"Yeah—on a mine sweeper. We got hit off Guam. I spent a couple months in Tripler—that's the big army hospital in Honolulu—and when they let me out, it was good-bye, Charlie, here's your discharge and thank you. Can't say I was sorry. I figured I'd done my share. Then I got this job—it's just temporary, until I get the money together for this act I want to buy."

"What kind of act?" she asked, not from any real interest but because talking kept her mind occupied.

"Trained dogs. Mixed breeds mostly. This guy I know wants to sell out. I learned how to work animals from my old man. He'd still be with Ringlings except he couldn't lay off the juice."

"He must have been good," she said politely. "Is that where you'll be working when your act is ready?"

"You pulling my leg? You don't *start* with Ringlings. Most acts don't end up with them, either."

He stopped to study her, and something moved behind the opaqueness of his eyes. "You wouldn't be in the market for a job, would you? I need an assistant to help out with the act."

"No, thank you. I'm not looking for a job."

He shrugged. "Just asking. I couldn't afford to pay you much at first, anyway. Room, board, and a little walking-around money is all."

He tested the side of the coffeepot with a wetted finger, and when it gave a pop, he filled the mugs and handed one to her.

Vicky took a cautious sip; it tasted like hot mud. Somehow she managed to choke down half of it without spluttering.

"So how you gonna get home? The buses stop running out this way after two. It's past that now," he said.

She tried out a smile on him. "If you'll lend me a dime, I can call my—a friend to pick me up."

"You don't even have a dime? That guy rob you, too?"

"No. I—I forgot to bring any money with me."

He shook his head. "You sure are one dumb broad. I thought all girls took mad money on their dates these days."

"Mad money?"

"Yeah—in case you get dumped."

"It never occurred to me that I might get dumped. I was double-dating with a girlfriend, the one who arranged the blind date. But she turned out not to be my friend, after all."

"It happens that way sometimes. Look, seeing as it's so late, why don't I drive you home—unless you live way out in the boonies. In that case, I'll drive you to a phone booth."

"It's only about—oh, a fifteen-minute drive from here," she said, shrinking the time by a good twenty minutes.

"You'll have to give me directions. I ain't familiar with Boston." He was already putting on his jacket. "I have to get some smokes, anyway. I ran out and I'm about to have a nicotine fit. You don't have any, do you?"

"Sorry. I don't smoke."

"It figures. Well, let's get going. It'll take me a couple minutes to unhitch the trailer. Gotta think about gas mileage, with rationing and all."

He pulled the string in the middle of the room, turning off the light. Somehow she wasn't surprised that not only did he disappear out the door, leaving her to grope her way across the trailer, but that he didn't wait to help her down the steps.

It figures, she thought, and found that she still could smile.

The tall wrought-iron gates that guarded the estate were standing open, something so unusual that Vicky's apprehension shifted to full gear. Her grandfather retired at eleven—and it was almost three now. Had Darcy called her grandfather to tell him they'd become separated at the carnival? Had the gate been left open for her?

She directed the man—she still hadn't learned his name—to pull up at the side of the driveway. "I'd better walk the rest of

the way," she said. "Maybe I can slip in without being seen.
That way I won't have to explain about my torn dress."

"Suit yourself." He leaned across her to open the door of the
truck.

She didn't get out immediately. "Thank you for everything."

"No sweat. Just be careful about blind dates in the future."

Vicky looked up the drive toward the house. Lights blazed in
two of the downstairs windows. Was her grandfather sitting there
in his den, like a spider waiting to jump on a juicy fly?

"You work here?"

The question startled her—until she realized it was a natural
one. "Yes," she said.

"You help out in the kitchen?"

"I'm an upstairs maid," she said, hiding a smile.

"Funny. I had you figured for a teacher, maybe a secretary."

"I don't know how to type, and you need a college degree to
teach," she said.

"You sure you don't want to take me up on that job offer? It's
better'n scrubbing out some rich dame's donicker. You get to
see a lot of new places, meet a lot of people."

"I'm afraid not—but thank you."

"Well, if you change your mind, look me up. Just ask for Jim
Riley. The show'll be here a couple more days before we move
on to Philly."

Vicky sensed his impatience to get back to his rig, so she
thanked him again and slid out of the truck. He already had the
door closed by the time she turned to wave good-bye. He geared
up the truck, and a moment later, he was gone, leaving a cloud
of exhaust fumes behind.

Vicky started up the driveway, her feet lagging. Jim Riley was
like a creature from another world, and yet, in his own offhand
way, he had been kind. He also hadn't made a pass at her. Which
could mean he was more sensitive than he looked, or, which
was more likely, that he simply hadn't been interested.

In any case, she was safely back home—and there was still
her grandfather to face. What kind of restriction would he put
her on? And how long would it be before he stopped lecturing her, going over and over her latest failing?

The double front door, very old and carved from slabs of
chestnut, was unlocked, and when she went inside, her grandfather was standing at the foot of the stairs, waiting for her.
Stony-faced, he took in her appearance, missing nothing, from

her ruffled hair and the bruises on her face to the pinned-together rip at her neckline.

"Trash—like your mother."

The words were cold, spoken without apparent emotion, but Vicky wasn't fooled. Her grandfather was in a fury—and nothing she said was going to help. Even so, she had to try.

"I—I had a quarrel with Darcy. I decided I'd better come home," she said quickly, saying the words she'd been rehearsing. "I was trying to get a taxi when a car sideswiped me and knocked me down. I'm not hurt, but my dress was torn and—"

"Liar." And again his lips barely moved.

"It's true, Grandpapa. We both lost our tempers and said some things that were—"

"Save your breath. Your friend called and told me what happened. I can't say I'm surprised. Bad blood will out—that's what I should have remembered."

"I don't know what Darcy told you, but—"

"She told me that you went to a movie—against my express wishes. You encouraged this—this man when he tried to pick you up. Your friend tried to talk sense into your head, but you took off with him. She called me as soon as she could, almost in hysterics because she was so worried about you."

"It's all a lie. She was just covering up for herself. She was the one who arranged the—" She stopped then because, in her grandfather's eyes, the truth would be as bad as Darcy's lies.

"I knew you'd come back eventually, your tail between your legs," he said, as if he hadn't heard her. "How did you get those bruises? Did the man get rough with you? What I'm really curious about is how you managed to sneak out all those nights without getting caught. Oh, yes, Darcy told me all about it once I threatened to change brokers. She knows what side her bread's buttered on."

"She was lying. Couldn't you tell that she was lying?" Vicky said.

Again, he didn't seem to hear her. "I could turn you out with only that—that hussy dress you're wearing on your back, but I've decided to be generous. You have ten minutes to pack what you can carry with you. Everything else will be turned over to a charity."

Her stunned silence seemed to annoy him, because he gave an impatient shrug. "Johnson will drive you wherever you want to go—within reason." His mouth twisted suddenly. "I'm sure you won't starve. Your kind can always earn a living walking the streets. Just don't expect any help from me. From now on, I don't have a granddaughter. And don't try to get in contact with your grandmother. She feels the same way I do."

The burning sensation, deep inside Vicky's skull, was back; she felt a deep pressure against her windpipe, as if someone were choking her. A scintillating light, jagged and white, shimmered at the perimeter of her sight. An urge, so violent that it shocked her, gripped her. If she'd had a weapon, she might have used it on him. Since her only weapon was her voice, she used words, overriding his attempt to interrupt.

"Yes, I'll leave. You reject me? Well, I reject you! Just remember this when you're all alone in this old mausoleum someday and no one in the whole world gives a damn if you live or die!"

She didn't wait to see his reaction. She ran past him, up the staircase. Although she wanted to leave everything she owned behind her, she knew that would be stupid. She would need clothes, other personal belongings.

It took her less than the ten minutes he'd allotted her to cram her two large suitcases full of clothes. Despite her burning desire to be gone, she made herself choose practical items—skirts, blouses, sweaters, underwear, a pair of pumps, walking shoes. At the last minute she stuffed in jodhpurs, a riding jacket, and boots, with some idea of getting a job at a riding academy.

When she was finished, she stripped off Darcy's dress, left it lying in the middle of the floor, and changed into slacks and a sweater, throwing an all-weather coat around her shoulders just before she picked up the luggage.

When she went downstairs, her grandfather was still standing in the middle of the hall. His face had a grayish cast, as if he had been dipped in ashes. After that first involuntary look, she ignored him and hurried across the black-and-white tiles of the entrance hall to the door and down the broad marble front steps.

Johnson, his dark face expressionless, was waiting in the Rolls. When he saw her, he hopped out and opened the rear door for her. He put the suitcases in the trunk, slammed down the lid, and got behind the wheel.

"Where to, Miss Victoria?" he said.

Vicky didn't answer immediately. She was penniless—her grandfather had seen to that. And without relatives or a real friend to take her in—she really only had one choice. "Take me to the Westchester Fairgrounds," she said.

Her last glimpse of her grandfather's house was through eyes filmed with tears. The downstairs lights shimmered like halos around the windows, and she thought she saw her grandfather's figure, silhouetted against the open door, but she couldn't be sure because the tears began coming down in earnest now. It had just occurred to her that she was leaving for good—and she hadn't said good-bye to her grandmother.

CHAPTER 28

*I*T HAD NEVER OCCURRED TO VICKY BEFORE THAT THERE could be such a difference in darkness. In the bedroom where she'd slept most of her life, darkness was total, silent, with the faint fragrance of linen sheets and her own delicate cologne surrounding her like a protective cocoon. But here, lying on an air mattress on the floor of Jim Riley's trailer, the darkness was none of these things. For one thing, it wasn't complete. A faint glow came through the small round windows, set on opposite walls of the trailer, and every few minutes or so, a light swept over the ceiling as a car passed on the pike that bordered the fairgrounds.

The odors, too, were intrusive. She'd noticed a sourness, like rotted fruit, earlier; now she was aware of dankness, of mildew and dust.

And there was constant sound. Sometimes it was voices, people passing the trailer, laughing and talking or quarreling. Other times, it was the hooting of an animal she couldn't identify. Once there was the deep rumbling of a truck, passing through the parking lot, and toward morning, the clatter of what she decided must be trash cans. Closer at hand, she could hear Jim Riley's breathing—regular, deep, obviously untroubled by his unexpected guest.

She should have been reassured by his indifference, but for some reason it only added to her discomfort. When he'd come to the door at her knock, he'd been wearing a ratty old seer-sucker robe with USN printed on the front—and, she was immediately aware, nothing else.

"Changed your mind, I see," was all he'd said. "You'll have to sleep on the floor. I'll blow up the air mattress for you." He went to put on the coffeepot.

The coffee was even viler than it had been earlier, but she finished it off, watching silently as he blew up a canvas-covered air mattress with a tire pump. He pushed aside a pile of dirty laundry and slid the mattress into the space.

"Better get some sleep," he said, and tossed her a blanket. With complete lack of self-consciousness, he stripped off his robe. She caught a glimpse of a well-developed male body before he slid under his own blanket. "Put the light off, willya?" he said, and turned his back.

It was a long moment before she followed his instructions. In the dark, she stripped to her panties and bra rather than hunt for her pajamas in her suitcases, folded her clothes over the back of a chair, and groped her way to the mattress. Its canvas cover felt clammy, and she wrapped herself in the blanket before she settled into its too-spongy softness.

It was a long time before she slept. Over and over, the events of the day played themselves out in her mind. She felt lost, miserably lonely, now that she no longer had her anger to sustain her. She knew she should feel grateful to Jim Riley for taking her in without asking a lot of questions, and yet—he might have shown a *little* interest. Of course, if he had, she probably would have bawled her eyes out. So what did she want from the man?

She slept finally, and it was the smell of coffee that awakened her. She opened her eyes to see Jim shaving himself at the wash-stand. To her relief, he was already dressed in corduroy trousers and a khaki shirt. Since he seemed oblivious to her, she studied him openly, wondering how old he was. He couldn't be more than twenty-two, so why did he seem so mature, without any hint of boyishness? Was it because he'd been in the navy?

He was also handsome—or was he really? On close inspection, his features were a little too blunt, his jaw a little too wide, his nose too large, and yet—she was very much aware of him as a man. A queer sensation, like a charge of electricity, moved through her, and she was aware suddenly of a restriction in her breathing. Was this how other girls felt when they got a crush on someone? Was it possible she could be attracted to a man so uncouth that he picked his teeth with his thumbnail—as he was doing now?

And what right did she have to feel superior, she who was dependent upon the man's charity? Vicky winced at the word. No, *not* charity. She would be earning her keep. And why should she care what her grandfather, always so fastidious, would say if he saw her now, sleeping on the filthy floor of a man she'd just met? He would assume the worst, of course, but he would be wrong. She had her pride—and it would sustain her while she learned how to get along in this strange new world. No matter what happened, she would never become any of the things he had called her. . . .

"You'd better hop to it," Jim said, and she realized he was watching her in the mirror. "I told Tuck—he's the old guy that's selling me his dog act—I'd be coming around this morning to start learning the act and to look over his rig. That's part of the deal. I'm going to hang on to my own rig, too. You know anything about driving a truck?"

Vicky sat up, keeping the blanket tucked around her. Was he going to stand here, watching her, while she dressed? "I took driving lessons in school. I've never driven a truck, but I'm sure I can learn."

"Well, we'll check you out on that later. Tuck's got this place in Florida he wants to retire to. He's willing to show me the ropes, but he's itching to head south as soon as possible. I guess he's having trouble with his lungs."

Since he didn't seem to expect an answer, Vicky nodded, wishing he would turn his back so she could retrieve her clothes.

"I made fresh coffee," Jim said. "There's some rolls in that paper sack over there. A little stale, but you can dunk them in the coffee."

He turned away and began tucking his blanket over the daybed mattress. By the time he'd turned around again, Vicky had snatched her clothes off the chair and had pulled them on.

Jim looked her over, frowning. "Those duds are pretty fancy. Don't you have any work clothes with you?" When she shook her head, he shrugged. "Well, you can buy some Levis later."

She waited for him to pour her some coffee. When he didn't, she found a mug that looked reasonably clean and poured it herself. This time, while it was still too strong, it did taste like coffee.

"How many dogs are there?" she asked, more to have something to say than from genuine interest.

"Ten that perform, five younger dogs still in training."

"Why did you chose this kind of act?"

"Like I said, my father was a dog trainer. He had monkeys once, but they were too dirty. Can't house-train them—those suckers shit all over the floor. The damned rig smelled like a toilet most of the time. They're touchy, too. Always getting sick and dying on you. Dogs are easier to handle—and they're a lot cheaper to replace."

"You must like dogs," Vicky ventured.

"I hate the bastards. My old man used to feed his dogs when he didn't feed me. But it's what I know. And a good dog act can always get on somewhere—and not just in a two-bit mudshow like this."

He tossed her the paper sack. "Better eat fast. Old Tuck ain't one for waiting around."

The roll was hard and tasted of stale paper, but she got it down since she was hungry and it was obvious she wasn't going to be offered anything else. A few minutes later, she discovered that "old Tuck" was not only irascible and contrary, but that he didn't have much use for women.

"Never had no woman in my act," he grumbled. "You sure you know what you're doing, Jim?"

"She'll add some class to the act," Jim said. "How about we get started?"

Still grumbling, the older man began setting up props. "Let Vicky do it," Jim said. "That'll be part of her job. Show her how you want them spaced."

For the next hour, Vicky learned how to set up the props and watched as Tuck ran through his act, showing Jim the signals and the routine. To her inexperienced eyes, the dogs, which ran from a huge German shepherd to a tiny terrier, seemed surprisingly well mannered. In fact, she much preferred their company to Tuck's.

As she groomed the dogs, following his directions, she tried to ignore the crick in her back from her night on the floor. The dogs, at least, seemed to appreciate her efforts. One of them, a tiny terrier named Whiskey, whined when she was finished and tried to insinuate himself onto her lap. She gave him a hug—and earned a lecture from the old man about spoiling working dogs. But when they were leaving, he told her grudgingly that she might be able to handle the job—eventually.

When they reached Jim's trailer, he left her at the door. "I've got some business to attend to before the midway opens," he said. "There's some canned soup if you get hungry. How about cleaning up this rig? But don't use up all the water. The tank's pretty low."

He was gone before she could ask him where to put her clothes.

In the full light of day, the trailer looked even dingier than ever. As she got herself more coffee and ate another of the stale rolls, she couldn't help thinking of the chilled fruit, the rasher of bacon and poached egg, the flaky biscuits, her grandfather's cook prepared for her every morning.

She unpacked her clothes, putting her sweaters and underwear on a shelf and squeezing the rest of her things into an already-stuffed closet. Jim had told her to clean up the trailer. The problem was—where were his cleaning supplies?

She looked through the built-in cupboards, found a selection of wrenches and hammers and other tools, but no broom, no dustpan, or scrub brush. The door opened behind her, and she turned, expecting to see Jim, but it was a woman who came in.

"Who the hell are you?" the woman demanded. She was young, pretty in a plump, overblown way. She was wearing what looked to be men's work pants, drawn tightly around her waist with a belt, and her sweater was so tight that it strained against her breasts.

"I'm Vicky—Jim's new assistant."

"Yeah? I've heard it called a lot of things, but never that. Where'd he find you?"

It occurred to Vicky that she didn't have to answer the woman's questions. "Jim should be back soon," she said, her voice clipped.

"Like that, is it? Listen, you tell Jim that Annie came by, you hear?" She flounced off, leaving behind the strong odor of "Evening in Paris."

Vicky returned to her cleaning. After she'd picked up all the soiled clothes, she didn't know what to do with them. Did Jim expect her to do his laundry, too? If so, where? She finally left them in a pile and used a whisk broom she found to sweep the floor. It took the rest of the afternoon to do the dishes, scour the tiny sink and table, and wash the floor, using a bar of Fels Naptha soap and a rag she found stuffed in the bottom of the closet.

When she was finished, she looked around doubtfully. Her labor, which had cost her two fingernails and palms reddened from the harsh soap, had improved the odor—but the linoleum was so scarred and stained, it didn't look much different than it had before.

Well, she'd ask Jim for money to get some decent cleaning tools—and if he wanted her to do his laundry, he'd have to show her how. If he questioned that, she'd just tell him that upstairs maids didn't do laundry. Thank heaven she hadn't told him she was a cook's helper.

Jim didn't return that afternoon. When it got dark outside, she opened a can of tomato soup, then ended up eating it cold because she was intimidated by the stove. Afterward she read a year-old western pulp magazine, finally gave that up, and turned on a small radio that had seen better days.

It was very late when Jim came home. By then, Vicky was in bed, trying to sleep. Whistling under his breath, he came up the steps, missed the top one, and when she heard him cursing, she pretended to be asleep. She found out he wasn't alone when she caught a whiff of "Evening in Paris."

"Your new girlfriend fell asleep on you," the woman said.

"How about running along, Annie?" Jim's voice was bored. "I gotta get some rest."

"So now you've got that fancy piece of tail, I'm not good enough for you. Well, that's okay with me. I've got other fish to fry." She went out, slamming the door behind her.

There was a rustling sound, and Vicky realized Jim was undressing. Since she already knew he slept in the nude, she couldn't resist opening her eyes a crack. His back was turned to her and he was bending over the daybed, spreading out the blanket. The overhead light fell across his back, revealing a thick, ropy scar that cut a crimson slash from his upper ribs to his buttocks. Another scar etched a similar line from his left thigh to the calf of his leg.

She felt a wave of pity, pity she knew he wouldn't appreciate. When he started to turn, she closed her eyes quickly, and after the light was out, she lay there, thinking of her problems.

For the time being, she was stuck here. But when she had saved a little money, she would find something more compatible to do. She just wasn't suited for this life, didn't like it, never would. But if she thought of it simply as a learning process, she could endure it for a while. After all, she didn't have much choice, did she?

During the next three days, Vicky often thought of her resolution, and knew she'd been right. Carnival life was a different world from the one she'd left, and one she couldn't wait to leave. The people, the few Jim bothered to introduce her to when they went to the cookhouse to eat, were wary, not particularly friendly, and she came to the conclusion that they didn't trust anyone they sensed was not their own kind. She didn't like cookhouse food either. Mostly it was too greasy, overcooked, and too heavily spiced. She also didn't like being stuck in the trailer every night with nothing to do—complaints she kept to herself.

The only bright spot was the dogs. Here, at least, she was accepted. In fact, they obeyed her much better than they did Jim.

"They figure you for the leader of the pack," Tuck, who had mellowed toward her, told her during a training session. "Ain't no accounting for it. You'd think it'd be Jim they'd take to, him being a male and all, but no, them dogs got their own ideas, and they've put the label of leader on you. He's got any sense, he'll let you do the act and him assist."

That seemed to amuse him, because he repeated it again, this time to Jim.

"You're never gonna get them dogs to mind you like they do the little lady. I seen it happen before with one of them Gypsy fellers. Mean as a rattler he was, but the animals just naturally took to him. Animals, they got their instincts. Figured the guy'd protect them, I suspect. Same with the little lady. You always had a way with dogs, gal?"

"I never really thought about it," Vicky said. "My grandfather has borzois, and they always seemed more my dogs than his."

"Borzois, you say?" Tuck rubbed his chin, his rheumy eyes reflective. "That's them Roosky dogs, ain't it? Pretty fancy breed. Your grandpa got money, has he?"

Too late, Vicky saw the trap she'd fallen into. "Actually, he didn't own them," she said hastily. "He showed dogs for other people. Borzois—Russian wolfhounds were his speciality."

The man grunted. "Well, give me a mongrel every time. Blue bloods are delicate—got no stamina nor brains."

Vicky started to point out that the best traits of a breed could be bred in when the ancestry was controlled, but something her grandfather had said to her stopped her.

"Bad blood will out," he had said, and he'd been talking about her, not his borzois.

"What's the matter, gal? You look like you seen a ghost."

Vicky made an effort to smile. "I guess I'm a little tired."

"Well, you've been working hard. Might have made a mistake, saying Jimbo here didn't need you in his act."

Jim was grooming one of the dogs, a part-collie with a heavy coat of hair. He didn't bother to look up.

Later, when they returned to the trailer, he told her, "I'm hungry—and I'm tired of eating cookhouse garbage. How about I go get some round steak and potatoes and you cook us a decent meal?"

Vicky looked at him in dismay. Not only didn't she have any idea how to cook, she had no desire to learn. "I don't know how," she admitted finally.

"You don't know how to cook? Where the hell was you raised—in a hotel?"

"I—my grandmother didn't want anyone underfoot when she was cooking," she improvised.

"Or maybe you think you're too good to cook for me, is that it?"

She stared at him in astonishment. His face was very red, and the muscles in his jaw were bunched as if he were gritting his teeth. Understanding came to her; his anger had nothing to do with cooking, but with what Tuck had said about the dog act.

"I don't want to take over your act, Jim," she said.

He gave her a long, hard look, turned on his heels, and started for the door. "I'll get a hamburger at one of the grab joints," he said over his shoulder. "And get everything tied down good, you hear? We're pulling out right after breakdown. It's a long haul to Philly."

He was gone before she could answer. She heated a can of tomato soup, having learned the mechanics of the crotchety stove, ate it with some stale oyster crackers she found in the cupboard, washed the dishes, and then began tucking breakable things behind the racks in the shelves and in the cupboards, securing the latches on the doors. She finished the soup for supper, and went to bed early.

At some point during the night, she awoke to find the trailer moving, and knew that they were on their way to Philadelphia.

CHAPTER 29

*T*HE NEXT MORNING, WHEN VICKY AWOKE, JIM WAS ASLEEP on the daybed. She dressed quickly, then opened the door to see what looked to be the same untidy row of trailers and vans and trucks they'd left behind in Boston, although she knew it wasn't. *So much for seeing new places,* she thought, and went to put on coffee and set out mugs.

When Jim stirred, yawned noisily, and then threw off his blanket, she averted her eyes quickly. When he had finished dressing and had returned from a visit to what he called the donicker, she set a mug of coffee and doughnuts in front of him at the plank table. He ate silently, but she knew he was watching her as she drank her own coffee and nibbled on a doughnut.

"Look, Vicky, about yesterday—I shouldn't've jumped on you like that," he said abruptly.

Vicky hid her surprise. "That's all right. I'm not trying to—to muscle in. I just want to do a good job—and fit in here."

"That won't be easy. Most carnies has seen nothing but hard times all their lives. But they got a lotta pride, and they don't like it if they think someone's high-hatting them. And yeah, I finally figured out you wasn't no upstairs maid."

She started to protest that she never high-hatted anyone, but he stopped her. "I figure your grandfather is really loaded to live in that place I took you to. I don't know why he kicked you out, but if you'd had some better place to go to that night, you never woulda come to me, asking for a job. So that puts you right down here with the rest of us. If you want to fit in, just mind your own business—and don't go around acting like you think you're better'n us."

He paused to give her a sidelong glance. "And you can start by learning how to cook. I'm getting ulcers from eating in grab

297

joints, and cookhouse food ain't much better. I'm no great shakes as a cook, but I can show you how to fry eggs and put together a decent pot of slumgullion.''

Although Vicky doubted she could ever master anything remotely complicated, she wanted to keep the peace, so she agreed to give it a try.

During the next days, Jim initiated Vicky into the complicated world of the carnival. She learned to call a tent a top, to not be indignant when someone referred to her as a broad, which wasn't an insult in carnival parlance, and to get huffy when called a jane, which was. Jim taught her how to cook—to a degree. Luckily his own tastes ran to eggs and fried meat and potatoes, and while she never became comfortable with the cranky stove, she mastered it enough to fix simple meals.

One of Jim's friends, a florid-faced woman who took tickets at the Wheel of Death, showed her how to use the washhouses provided by most of the fairgrounds. Vicky lost the rest of her fingernails on the washboards, got chapped hands, but she managed to keep Jim and herself supplied with clean clothes. She also insisted he purchase some inexpensive sheets and pillowcases, and some cleaning supplies.

She should have felt a sense of accomplishment, but it was mainly resentment that she felt. Only by reminding herself constantly that this was temporary, that as soon as the dog act was ready, she would begin to earn pay and build up an escape fund, did she get through the days without complaining. One solace was the dogs; they gave her what she needed most, acceptance and affection, and in return, she showered them with attention, even though she sensed Jim's disapproval.

When Jim suggested that she help him at the Skillo booth, she wanted to protest that she hadn't been hired for that. But she bit back her words and listened while he described her duties.

''You can help me set up and tear down the booth, stock the slum—that's the prizes—shelves, and wait on customers. And sometimes I'll use you as a stick.''

''Stick?''

''Yeah—you know, you act like a customer and I let you win. The marks stop to take a good look at your ass when you're bent over the counter, tossing rings, and when they see you winning, they figure that if a dame can win, so can they.''

''But—that's dishonest,'' she protested.

"Dishonest? Shit, it's them or us." He hesitated, then added, "It won't be forever. Sol Singer—he's the guy that owns the Skillo privilege—is looking around for someone to take over when I quit, but I figure to keep on working as long as possible. The extra bucks'll come in handy."

Vicky quickly learned the Skillo game routine, although she never lost her distaste for it. With morning rehearsals for the dog act, evenings spent at the Skillo booth, with cooking and cleaning and the never-ending laundry sandwiched in between, she fell into bed exhausted every night and rose in the mornings still tired. Jim, having taught her what needed to be done, turned all the household chores and care of the dogs to her, and only when she finally rebelled and told him that he'd have to help did he take over the daily dog grooming.

Often, after the Skillo booth closed, he disappeared for the night without explanation. Late in the morning hours, he would come in reeking of whiskey and perfume, and she knew he'd been with one of his women. That he had a wide variety to choose from, she couldn't help noticing. They hung around the booth, giggling and flirting, and it was all too obvious he took advantage of what was offered.

That everybody in the carnival assumed she was sleeping with him irked her. Once someone complimented him, not so quietly, on his summer wife, and when she asked Tuck later what that meant, he grinned, showing tobacco-stained teeth.

"Has Jimbo asked you to take a turn on the merry-go-round with him yet?" he asked.

"I don't understand—"

"That's to warn other fellers to keep hands off 'cause you're his summer wife. When a broad wants to break up with her old man, she tells him, 'I'm getting back on the carousel,' and he knows it's all over." He gave his honking laugh. "Saves all the expense and bother of a divorce, see?"

One thing that pleased her was the progress of the act. Tuck told her she was a natural with animals, and Jim, to her surprise, allowed her to handle some of the simpler tricks on her own. While he never asked her advice outright, he listened to her suggestions and sometimes followed them, even though he didn't bother to acknowledge her help afterwards.

The smallest of the adult dogs, the wirehaired terrier named Whiskey, was her favorite. He had adopted her as his master, paying only minimal attention to Tuck and Jim. His devotion was so flattering to her bruised ego that she found herself wishing she could smuggle him under her blanket at night to help chase away the loneliness that haunted her every time she thought of her grandmother. They hadn't been close, but Grandmama Ada had been kind in her own vague way. What had her grandfather told her to explain the disappearance of her granddaughter? One thing she was sure of. It would do no good to try to contact her, either by phone or mail. Neither would she ever get past the servants, who had undoubtedly had their orders to thwart any effort she made to contact Grandmama Ada.

They were playing a mid-Ohio fair when Tuck finally told Jim the act was ready for the carnival's stage show, a musical review with a duke's mixture of acts. Jim took Vicky into Dayton to a theatrical costume shop, where he chose a safari outfit for himself. When he tried it on, he strutted around in front of a three-way mirror, obviously pleased with his appearance.

It was the first time he'd shown any personal vanity, and Vicky had to smile, liking the change. Her own costume was the feminine version of Jim's, featured the same knee-length shorts, bush jacket, and pith helmet. It wasn't very becoming. The too-generously cut garments overwhelmed her slender figure, and she was well aware that khaki was not her best color. When she found herself wondering if he'd chosen these particular costumes on purpose, she shook off her suspicions. Jim Riley might be moody, hard to please, and impossible to understand, but he wasn't Machiavellian.

Their debut, in front of Mr. Montrell, the show's manager, came a few days later. During the tryout, they ran over a few minutes, and one of the dogs, a part-afghan hound with a touchy disposition, started a fight with another male, but Mr. Montrell seemed satisfied.

"It's still a little rough, but that's to be expected for a new act," was his comment. "We'll fit you in next week at one of the matinees."

To Vicky's surprise, Jim was elated. She had expected their less than perfect performance to trigger off one of his silent moods. Instead, he was smiling as they left the grandstand.

Vicky puzzled over his reaction. To her, the performance had been a disappointment. When she'd competed in horse shows, she'd always gone for the top trophy, knowing that second-best would never measure up to Earl St. Clair's expectations. Only first prize earned the reward she craved—her grandfather's praise.

Well, Jim might be satisfied with a passing mark, but not she.

Her pride demanded that their act be the best it could be, even if the show they appeared with was fourth-rate.

The following week, whenever she could fit it in, she worked with the dogs on her own. Jim shrugged off her efforts, obviously content with the act the way it was.

A week later, they gave their first performance. The matinee audience was rowdy and inattentive, even during the chorus revue, which featured a dozen half-nude dancers doing a tap number. The comedy skit that followed evoked few laughs, and Vicky found that she was very nervous, worried about the reception they would get.

There was little fanfare when their turn finally came. Mr. Montrell, dressed in a cowboy outfit, complete with an outsize Stetson hat, announced them; to Vicky's ears, he sounded as bored as the audience.

"Ladies and gentlemen and kiddies—I give you Jimbo's Mutts on Parade." And then they were on. The extra practicing paid off, and the dogs, from the big collie, Buster, to Whiskey, the tiniest of the lot, pranced through their tricks as if they had been born to it, obviously enjoying being the center of attention. Vicky wished she could do the same, but she felt uncomfortable in the spotlight with the eyes of the crowd upon her. Even so, she thought she was doing better than Jim, who seemed miscast in the role of animal trainer.

It came to her that he was too masculine, too much of a contrast to the dogs, that he would have done better to dress in ordinary clothes rather than something connected to most people's minds with big game hunting.

The thought slipped away from her as she got caught up in the act. The crowd was attentive now, responding to the antics of Whiskey, who was playing the scamp, tormenting the bigger dogs—and getting chased in the process, each time taking refuge in Vicky's arms, where he immediately regained his aplomb and barked his defiance. The act flowed so smoothly that it seemed over with too quickly. The audience obviously felt the same, because they applauded so vigorously that Mr. Montrell finally called for an encore.

Vicky had expected the dogs to perform well. What she didn't expect was the rush of pleasure she felt when the applause came rolling in. The encore was a controlled riot they'd practiced, with all the dogs turning in circles, the smallest two leaping into their trainers' arms at the finale. The only flaw was that both the dogs decided to jump into Vicky's arms, leaving Jim to take his bows alone.

Afterward, Mr. Montrell told them he was pleased with the act, that he would think about finding them a better place on the program. Jim didn't say much as they rounded up the dogs and headed back for the trailer, but she read his relief and satisfaction on his face.

They celebrated at a small bar near the fairgrounds that night. Tuck and a man named Clarence, whom Jim had known since childhood, celebrated with them. Although their carny jargon was sometimes obscure to Vicky, she listened with interest to the exchange of reminiscences. It was soon apparent to her that Jim had been badly mistreated as a youngster. Although he laughed when Clarence teased him about being the sorriest-looking kid he'd ever seen, always hitting him up for a meal or a place to hide out when his old man was on a rampage, she sensed his discomfort.

"I guess you're looking forward to retirement, Mr. Tucker," she said, hoping to change the subject. "When are you leaving for Florida?"

Tuck, who had downed several beers, got watery-eyed. "Tomorrow. And I'm not looking forward to it as much as I figgered. If I could afford to feed them dogs on my Social Security, I'd keep them for sure," he mourned.

"Come on, old man, don't give us that crap," Clarence said. "You're glad to get shed of them animals."

They began to quarrel good-naturedly, and under cover of their raised voices, Jim touched Vicky's hand. "Let's cut out of here," he said.

They walked back to the fairgrounds through the soft June night. The air had turned a little cool, but Vicky felt warm inside her light sweater. Jim took her elbow when they came to the busy highway, and after they'd crossed, she discovered they were holding hands. Although she was tall for a woman, she felt diminutive beside Jim, and at ease with him for the first time.

When they reached the trailer, to her surprise, Jim helped her up the three steps. He pulled the string, turning on the jerry-rigged light fixture, but he didn't move to put coffee on, as she expected. He kept looking at her, his gaze so intense that she was caught off guard.

"What is it?" she said.

He blinked, as if her words startled him. "There's some things

we should talk about, starting with your pay,'' he said finally.
"How about, instead of me paying you wages, I give you twenty-five percent of the profits after bills? It won't be much now—Montrell is real close with his money—but I don't figure on staying with this mudshow forever. I got myself an agent, and he's putting some feelers out. As soon as we can connect with something better, we'll move on. How does that grab you?'

Vicky took her time answering him. It was all so vague—twenty-five percent sounded generous, but this was after expenses. And why hadn't he been more specific, told her what Mr. Montrell was paying him? Was this a deliberate omission or just an oversight? On the other hand, Jim had taken her in, given her a place to stay, a job. She owed him something for that.

"Thank you," she said, but the words came out a little flat.

Jim's eyes narrowed as he stared at her. "Always so polite and ladylike. Only I've got a hunch you're just like any other broad behind those manners."

"I have no idea what you're talking about—"

"I'm talking about—this."

She wasn't prepared when he put his arms around her. Too surprised to struggle, she lost her chance to pull away. He kissed her, and at first, it was curiosity more than his hold on her that kept her there. Then, when the kiss went on, she suddenly was charged with a full-blown excitement and there was a heaviness, a pressure in her abdomen that bewildered her. Was this—desire? It wasn't particularly pleasant, and yet—she felt no urgency to move away. Was this why so many women succumbed to men they didn't even like?

Her mind, despite her inertia, was still under control—until Jim slid his hands under her sweater to fondle her breasts. His touch wasn't gentle; the palms of his hands were rough, rasping against her tender skin, but this only seemed to add to the excitement. She wanted more, wanted him to fondle her in other places, wanted him to satisfy the burning that had started up between her thighs. Awkwardly she pressed closer, and the feel of his hard, aroused body set up such a storm of pleasure that she lost all desire to resist.

Without protest, she let him undress her, then watched silently while he stripped off his own clothes. His arousal, so blatant and overwhelmingly masculine, sent a chill—or was it a thrill?—through her, but she let him lead her to the daybed. She lay back against the pillow, and when he rolled on top of her and kissed her again, she returned the kiss, opening her mouth to his tongue. It felt like a lance, probing the softness of her mouth, a promise of what was to come, and under a new surge of excitement, her skin grew hot and moist.

Feverishly Jim thrust his hand between her thighs, spreading them apart, and then lowered himself between. He lunged against her and she felt a hard pressure, followed by a shock of pain—and then everything fell apart.

The excitement, the passion, disappeared, leaving her disappointed and cold. She tried to get away, but it was too late. He was already inside her, frantically pumping away. She felt little pain now, but the embarrassment of being spread-eagle before him, like some ancient sacrifice, was humiliating. In the harsh light, his flushed face, his glazed and feverish eyes, were repulsive, and she wanted only for it to be over and done with.

When he collapsed upon her, she tried to wriggle out from under him, but he didn't move, and she finally stopped trying to escape. At least it was over—was he asleep?

She stared at his closed eyes, the relaxed muscles of his mouth, and for that moment, she loathed him. But then he sighed, murmured her name, and buried his face in her hair. She remembered how the scars in the small of his back had felt under her hand, and her anger left her as suddenly as it had come. She didn't love him, certainly didn't desire him, but he had been good to her—in his own way. Surely she could be generous. And besides, she had already lost her virginity. Did it really matter all that much now?

"You okay?" Jim asked, and there was enough concern in his voice that the rest of her resentment ebbed away.

"I'm fine," she said.

"You never did this before, did you?"

"No."

"That's what I figured." He eased away from her, reaching up to pull the light cord. "We'd better get some shut-eye. Hard day tomorrow."

She expected him to kiss her, but he rolled away, taking up more than his share of the narrow daybed. A few seconds later, he was asleep.

Vicky lay there, crowded between him and the wall, listening to his breathing. Did he expect her to return to the air mattress? Or was she now entitled to share his bed? She thought over what had happened, and she didn't know whether to laugh or cry. The truth was, she felt—frustrated. Yes, that was the word. And more than a little sore—which was to be expected the first time. Most of all she felt disappointed. She had expected so much and had gotten so little. Was this all there was to sex?

What about those old Victorian novels she'd found hidden away in her grandfather's library, behind a row of law books? They described sexual encounters that drove a woman mad with passion. Had they all been pure fiction? Was Jim a bad lover— or was she the one at fault? Was it possible that she was frigid? It was certainly true that Jim had waited a long time before he'd taken her to bed. Was he disappointed, too? He was used to women like Annie and the girls who hung around the Skillo game, with their hot eyes and eager smiles. Maybe he wished he'd never started this with her.

And just what had she expected from him? That he would be grateful for having deflowered a virgin? He probably preferred women like Annie, who knew how to please a man. It was obvious that to Jim, she was just another female, his latest summer wife.

One thing for sure, there was no question of love. She wasn't even sure if she *liked* Jim. If she was a convenience to him, that's what he was to her. Someone she could eventually turn her back on and leave without guilt as soon as she had acquired enough money to hold her over for a while.

So why did she feel like crying her eyes out?

CHAPTER 30

*J*IM WAS SITTING ON THE STOOL HE KEPT BEHIND THE *SKILLO* booth counter, watching Vicky as she moved down the midway toward him. Even after all these weeks, he hadn't lost his fascination with her long, elegant legs and the way she walked, as if she were floating.

And her beauty—it came to him as a small shock, each time

he saw her, how beautiful she was. Not cute or pretty or a looker. No, she was out-and-out beautiful, with that auburn hair, so thick and silky to touch, with those cool blue eyes and that full mouth, with the way the parts of her body went together so perfectly. . . .

The thing was, he'd never gone for that classy type before. So why *her*, out of all the women who had moved in and out of his life?

A man, accompanied by two kids, came up to the counter, but only to ask directions. After Jim pointed out the way to the saltwater taffy booth, he settled back, picking up his thoughts again.

Women—there had been women in his life since he was a snot-nosed kid of thirteen, who hardly knew what to do with the equipment nature had given him. He'd had his pick, starting with the hot-eyed circus wife who'd lured him into her bed with the promise of a new portable radio. She had paid off, too, and would have bought him a watch except that he'd wised up to the fact that a woman married to a jealous lion trainer meant trouble, big trouble.

At first, most of them had been older. A dancer from the hooch show, the wife of an equestrian who had hot pants, the tattooed lady in the ten-in-one who was an education in herself, all offering him what was so easy to take. Sex with no strings and no price tag.

Then, as he grew older, the women became younger—girls who hung around the midway, looking for excitement, the daughters of other carnies. While in boot training, he'd had a hot affair with the wife of a chief petty officer that had almost finished his military career before it started.

Since his return to civilian life, there'd been a whole string of one- or two-night stands with women he couldn't remember a few days later. He took them to bed, then got up and walked away without a backward look. Once, he'd taken on a summer wife, but that hadn't lasted long. He'd quickly become bored with her constant chatter, and was glad when she walked out on him.

He'd thought that this was what he wanted, that he needed variety—until Vicky had come into his life. And it was fear that had kept him from taking her to bed the first night he'd met her. Not physical fear, but the suspicion that *this* one could become a problem, that he might not want to walk away once he'd had sex with her.

So he'd left her alone on her air mattress while he slept a few feet away. Knowing his own needs, he'd made sure that they were well taken care of by other women. But it hadn't worked. She was like a disease that wouldn't go away. The truth was, he'd been hooked all along.

And now, even though she'd moved into his bed, it was pure misery. Oh, sure, he took her whenever he felt the urge, and he even tried to make it good for her. Which was a new switch, since he'd never worried before how the woman felt. But then, he hadn't known the frustration of wanting a woman who felt nothing for him, who submitted but never responded.

He could kid himself all he wanted, but he knew when a woman was really hot for him. Okay, Vicky never refused him, but she didn't really *feel* anything. Sometimes, when he first started kissing her, her skin would grow hot and her eyes would darken, but then, in the middle of it, she would withdraw into herself, and he would lose her. Not that it stopped him. He always took his own pleasure, but her coldness drove him mad, drove him to demands that he was ashamed of later. God, when he thought of all the women who had clawed and scratched at him, screamed when they came with him inside them—why had he fallen for someone who was as cold as an ice cube?

Night after night, as Vicky lay in his arms, her body unresistant but her mind somewhere else, while he labored to arouse her, his anger and frustration grew stronger, and he was afraid of it, afraid of the demon that lived inside him, afraid of his own jealousy

Whenever some guy looked at Vicky, when she talked to the marks that came up to the booth, his guts tightened and he wanted to lash out, destroy their fucking faces with his fists. And they weren't the only ones. The men who worked the midway looked, too. He'd seen their hot stares when Vicky walked by. Not that she encouraged them. No, she ignored the attention she got. But how could she miss it? And what if, someday, she was attracted to some other guy?

Funny how that coldness of hers reminded him of his mother. His father's dislike, even his brutality, never really got to him, but his mother's total indifference to him, her son, had driven him crazy.

Briefly he was back in that filthy van, sharing his floor mat with a couple of snuffling monkeys, the odor of sour milk and overripe bananas and animal excreta in his nostrils, his stomach growling with hunger because there was nothing to eat in the van except those fucking half-rotten bananas. . . .

"Sorry to be late," Vicky said, startling him. She was wearing a cotton blouse, embroidered with tiny flowers, and a full skirt. Her hair, which tumbled carelessly to her shoulders, had a burnished look in the sun, and he wanted to bury his face in that softness and inhale the fragrance that was always there. Despite the water restrictions, she kept herself immaculate and sweet-smelling, which set her apart from the other women of this blasted mudshow. And sometimes it was her fastidiousness that drove him crazy. It reminded him that she was too good for this life, too good for him, that eventually she would realize it and walk away. And then where would he be? He'd be alone, just as he'd been alone all his life, even when he was going at it hot and heavy with some broad. . . .

But he intended to keep her as long as he could. Which was why he cried poor all the time and never gave her a dime of her own. It was why he pretended to be disgusted with cookhouse food to keep her away from the other carnies, why he had her help out in the booth so he could keep his eye on her while he worked. Hell, he'd even given up his late night poker games with the guys.

"No sweat," he said aloud. "Why don't you start with the slum?"

Vicky put her purse away under the shelf. She never grumbled about the jobs he gave her, although she must be wondering why he hadn't stocked the racks himself with business so slow and him just sitting there on his ass. Why did it bug him so much that she never complained? Guilt? Hell, what did he have to feel guilty about? He'd taken her in when she was broke and needed a place to stay. He'd given her a job, treated her well, hadn't he? Had he ever once raised his hand to her? His mother would have thought she was in hog heaven with a man who didn't beat her all the time.

A customer came up, and Jim went into his spiel, half needling and half coaxing the man into trying a few balls. The words spun out automatically, perfected by practice, just like the sexy smiles for the younger women, the frank-and-earnest stuff that worked with the older ones. With the men, especially those his own age, he made it a challenge, a let's-see-if-you-can-take-me-buddy dare. With this guy, an older man, he used a smart-aleck approach that said, hey-pop-you're-over-the-hill. . . .

Looking sour, the mark tried a few balls, didn't even earn one of the slum prizes, tried another, won a Kewpie doll worth about seven cents, and finally walked away, not looking back. Vicky, who had finished stocking the lower racks of the display, put the empty boxes away under the counter. She stood looking up the concourse, watching a bunch of soldiers from a nearby army base who were hanging around the Ferris wheel. She seldom had small talk, which he appreciated, not liking women's chatter, but today, for some reason, her silence annoyed him.

"You sulking or something?" he asked aggressively.

"No. Are you?"

"Don't get smart with me," he growled.

"Then don't ask stupid questions," she retorted, and turned her back.

Without thinking, he reached out, grabbed her shoulder, and swung her around to face him. But his hand fell away when a customer, a young boy, appeared at the counter and piped, "Gimme three balls, mister."

By the time the boy left, three dimes later, Jim's temper was gone, and impulsively he said, "How about going off the lot for a couple beers and some hamburgers tonight after we close?"

She looked at him in surprise, but her nod was agreeable. "Thank you. That would be nice," she said politely.

He shook his head. "You never forget your manners, do you?"

A gleam of humor came into her eyes. "You'd understand if you ever met my grandfather."

"Strict, huh?"

"Very."

"He ever hit you?"

"Of course not. He wasn't—that wasn't his way. But he used his tongue. That may be worse."

Jim puzzled over that for a moment. "How do you figure that? My old man used to curse my mom and me like crazy. That never hurt. But when he laid onto me with his belt—yeah, that hurt."

Something shifted in her eyes. "I'm sorry. It must have been terrible."

He shrugged. "It wasn't no picnic. He liked to drink, and when he did, he got crazy. You know what I mean?"

"I think so."

"Which is why I try to stay away from the sauce. I don't wanna end up like my old man, six foot under at forty-five."

"The drinking killed him?"

"You could say that. He walked into the side of a truck while he was drunk. That's what killed him, but yeah, you could say booze did him in."

"Was this before you went into the navy?"

"Naw. I was stationed at Pearl when I got the word. My old lady was already dead. Had a tumor, wouldn't go to the doctor. Time she did, it was too late. How about you? How come you lived with your grandfather?"

"My parents died when I was really young. I don't remember them."

He eyed her curiously. A mystery here—but none of his business. Besides, the conversation was getting too personal. He was glad that two young couples came up just then.

It was a week later that the demon returned. Jim called it that because it seemed as if the rage came out of nowhere and had nothing to do with him, the real Jim Riley.

It happened after their act. As usual, Vicky got the most applause, and while he told himself that it was to be expected, someone who looked like Vicky, it did rankle. After all, Jimbo's Mutts on Parade was *his* act. He'd sweated blood, getting the money together to buy the dogs and rig from Tuck, learning the tricks and the patter that accompanied them. All Vicky had to do was work the dogs. So it made him sorer'n hell, seeing her take over that way. Even so, he pushed his irritation to the back of his brain. And maybe that was his mistake.

They were leaving the backyard with the dogs on their leashes when one of the clowns stopped Vicky and presented her with a bouquet of artificial flowers, pretended to swoon with his hand patting his chest. When Jim lost him temper and took a swing at the guy, he ducked easily, gave Jim the finger, and then disappeared behind the other clowns. Everybody laughed, and Jim stalked off without waiting for Vicky.

Even then it might have been all right if she'd kept her mouth shut. But when she came in, after putting the dogs away in the van for the night, she said in that clipped way that always riled him, "It was a joke, Jim. He's a show-off. He does that to all the women."

"Shut up," he said. He took another swig from the bottle of beer in his hand. It was warm, since they didn't have ice, and the beer tasted too malty, a little metallic. "Just shut up. You remind me of my old lady—always flapping your mouth."

She whirled to face him, her eyes stormy. "I don't have to

shut up. If you don't stop yelling at me, I'm going to walk out on you—''

That's when he hit her.

Vicky usually came awake quickly, ready to face the morning. Today she felt a reluctance to wake up, and tried to slip back into sleep. But the light against her eyes was too bright, and when she rolled to her side, away from it, pain shot through her cheek. Remembrance came in a rush, and she winced, not so much from the pain as from the memory of Jim's furious face, his hot eyes. He had struck her fully on the face before she could dodge, and for a moment she had been too stunned to move. Then, when she raised her hands to ward off further blows, she had seen something—horror?—in his eyes. He shook his head violently as if to clear it, and he'd reached out and tried to put his arms around her. When she flinched away, his eyes had turned sick and ashamed.

"God, Vicky—I'm sorry as hell. I don't know why I did that."

She didn't answer. So this was what it had come to—Jim was abusing her. What did she do now? Her first instinct was to run out the door, but she needed her clothes, needed money—and she didn't have a penny. He'd seen to that—on purpose, to keep her under his thumb. Why hadn't she realized this before?

"I acted like a jackass," Jim said, his voice hoarse. "I'm sorry as hell."

There was no doubting his sincerity, his remorse. His eyes were bloodshot, as if he were on the verge of crying, and a muscle in his cheek twitched spasmodically.

"You won't leave me, will you?" he said.

Leave him? And go where, do what? "No—but if you ever hit me again, I will," she said, meaning every word of it.

She accepted his embrace, and later, let him make love to her, but as he groaned with pleasure, something inside her remained very cold. He must have sensed it, because afterward, when his needs had been satisfied, he held her for a long time instead of rolling over and going to sleep as he usually did.

For the first time, he opened up to her. He talked about his father, who had beaten him regularly; about his mother, who hadn't given a damn what his father did as long as he let her alone. He described the filthy converted moving van they lived in, the overripe garbage and the animal excreta.

He talked about growing up knowing he had less value to his parents than one of their monkeys. And as he talked, the coldness inside Vicky thawed, and now she was the one holding Jim in her arms, promising him that she would never leave him, even though she knew it wasn't true.

It was a week later, while she was taking a nap between shows, that Jim returned to the trailer to tell her, his eyes bright with excitement, that the agent he was registered with had just contacted him about an offer for a circus job for the remainder of the season.

"Bradford Circus ain't Ringlings-B&B, but it's a good, solid show," he said. "They need an animal act to replace one that folded on them—and this is our chance to make it into the big time."

CHAPTER 31

MARA SAT WITH HER ELBOWS PROPPED ON THE VELVET-covered table in the center of the tent, absorbed in the spread of tarot cards before her. Usually she concentrated on the clients, on reading their expressions, their body movements, the small signs that gave away their thoughts, their deepest worries. But sometimes, like now, the cards spoke to her. When this happened, she listened, deciding just how much truth to reveal to the client.

In this case, the cards spoke of ill health, of tragedy, of betrayal. The client, a past-middle-aged-woman, sat tense and silent, as if she already knew what was coming. Or maybe, Mara thought, she knew the meaning of some of the cards. That happened sometimes, especially with the Devil and the Tower cards, and then she was careful to explain that it was the combination with other cards that told the full tale, that there was another factor, her own skill as an interpreter.

"I see a warning," she said finally. "Not a certainty, since the future is never fixed."

"What's the warning?" the woman said. She was wearing a cotton dress that had been washed so often that the colors had faded to an indeterminate gray. She wore no makeup, no jewelry, not even a watch, and the straw purse she carried had seen years of wear. Yet she was willing to pay to have her fortune told by Madam Rosa.

"Someone very close to you is not to be trusted," Mara said, making up her mind. This one would get the truth—some of it. "This person is young, related to you."

The woman twisted her straw purse between her hands. "That has to be Charley—my son."

Mara hid her satisfaction. A son—yes, that figured. "You love him very much—and he loves you. But his judgment is very poor. Do not sign any papers, or turn over anything valuable to him. He is very persuasive, but you must not give in."

"It's the farm," the woman said, sighing. It always surprised Mara how often, when it would be to their benefit to keep quiet, the customers came right out with facts. Which made her job easier, of course.

"Yes, it *is* a farm that's in danger," she said promptly. "You must not sell it or take out a mortgage on it. Your son has lied to you. The money he says he needs so urgently for an operation is really for—I believe his problem is gambling."

The woman blinked, unconsciously nodding her head, and Mara went on, "Yes, it is gambling. So protect yourself. Give your love, your moral support, but don't risk your farm. Later, when he needs a place to stay, you can offer him a home. And he will ask. It's in the cards."

She swept the cards together in a dramatic gesture. There were other things, but she wouldn't tell the woman. What good would a warning do against ill health? It might even bring it on faster.

The woman rose. "Thank you, Madam Rosa," she said. "I reckon I knew this all along, but I just couldn't see things straight." She fumbled in her straw purse. "How much do I owe you?"

"You can see my associate, Sister Clinker, on the way out. No, wait—this reading is free. When I laid out my own cards this morning, they told me that I should give free advice today. And I always listen to the cards."

"I don't need charity. I can pay."

"Not charity," Rosa said blandly, even while she wondered

why she was being so generous. "The cards tell me that the money you save will be put to good use."

The woman beamed at her. "I'll drop it in the collection box next Sunday."

And the wonder is that you really will, Mara thought.

After the woman left, Clinker came to the tent. "And how you going to give Mr. Sam twenty percent of nothing?" she demanded.

"He can add it to the privilege fee he charges me. Which should be free. After all, I gave him free rent on winter quarters all through the depression."

Clinker's lips tightened briefly. Her face had grown a few wrinkles through the years, but she still had more energy—and strong opinions—than women half her age. "The depression—it sure is queer that it took a war to bring this country out of the depression."

"You don't credit President Roosevelt for any of it?"

"Of course. But even he can't compare with a war," Clinker retorted. She straightened the chair the woman had used, then smothered the sandalwood incense punk that perfumed the air inside the tent. "The midway's almost empty. Time to close for lunch."

"No, not yet. Someone important's coming—I feel it in my bones." She laughed at the face Clinker made. "After all this time, you still don't believe in my bones, do you?"

"I think *you* believe in them. But you do fake a lot of what you say."

"Of course. I have to sometimes. The cards get tired just like anything else. So I get the client talking, and I study their faces, their gestures, and then I give them good, solid advice."

"And what about the times when you get that funny look in your eyes, like you just did with that woman, and your accent gets so thick, you could cut it with a knife?"

"Why, that's when the cards are using me as a conduit, speaking through me."

Clinker snorted. "Well, I'm a good Christian and I don't believe in all that Gypsy mumbo-jumbo. But I have to admit you're good at reading people's faces. Maybe your advice is worth what you charge, and maybe it isn't. And you can tend the door. I'm going to fetch us some lunch."

She flounced out, heading for the cookhouse. Mara smiled, knowing her friend's bark was worse than her bite. She also knew that for all her grumbling, Clinker loved dressing up in long skirts and bright blouses, clinking with gold jewelry, playing the mysterious and otherworldy Gypsy. Most of all, she loved being back with the circus again.

And so do I, Mara thought.

Suddenly restless, she rose and moved around the tent, not really seeing what was so familiar to her now. She had chosen red velvet to cover the table, the chairs, and the long library table that held the props of her profession—a crystal ball, black candles, a Bible, her mother's tarot cards, which she used only rarely these days.

The tent, red-and-white-striped outside to match its closest neighbor, the Big Top, was lined with black cloth, shot here and there with silver stars. The only light was the soft glow of a glass-paneled lamp that hung from the tent post above the table. Mara always wore brightly colored caftans with marching turbans that were specially made for her by a theatrical costumer in Tampa. Not only were they exotic, but the turbans hid her distinctive red hair. Other than that, she made no attempt to disguise herself with makeup. Because of the scar that had reconstructed her face, she knew there was little danger of being unmasked at this late date.

It was in the midthirties that her forced retirement had begun to pall. At first, she'd been so busy getting settled in the bungalow that had been her very first permanent home. Of course, it had turned out not to be permanent, but that had been off in the future when she'd bought the house on a tree-lined street in Santa Rosa.

It had been fun, refurbishing the roomy cottage, choosing, with Clinker's help, the homey furniture and carpets and curtains, the wallpaper and paint and paneling. Staying so busy had helped keep her mind off Vicky, and gradually some of the doubts, the guilt, had faded. But not entirely. Even now there were times when the yearning to see her daughter became almost unbearable.

Luckily, during those first few years after the accident, she had been caught up in the excitement of educating herself. It had taken her a year to learn to read really well, but once she could, she devoured books voraciously, all kinds of books, gobbling them down like a starved person turned loose in a bakery. She'd been in a delirium of discovery, intoxicated by all the knowledge at her fingertips, and she'd filled her life with books, enrichments like museums and art galleries, and taking classes in everything from current affairs to gourmet cooking. Sometimes Clinker had enrolled in classes with her, but with less and less real interest as time went by.

Oh, her friend had faked it admirably, and it had been a while before Mara caught on that Clinker was only indulging her, keeping her company, hiding her own homesickness and dissatisfaction with their exile.

It had been different with Lobo. The big mute had settled into his new life like a wet dog curled up before a roaring fire. He was popular around their neighborhood because he was willing to help a widow paint a fence, or repair the leaking faucet of some struggling divorced mother, cheerfully tolerating the kids who swarmed around him wherever he went, enthralled by the ugly giant with kind eyes who could speak only by gestures.

He gradually grew old before their eyes, fading away so slowly that Mara hardly noticed. One day, it seemed, he was strong and robust as ever and the next, he looked old and worn. Clinker noticed it first, that he slept later and later, moved more slowly, ate less, lost weight. When they took him to a doctor, it was only to be told that his heart, overtaxed by his size, was wearing out, that it was just a matter of time.

He died the sixth year of their exile, and it was a comfort to both of them to know that he faced his own death with a smile, as if glad to go. They buried him in a sunny cemetery on a hill overlooking Santa Rosa, and since they didn't know his last name, they invented one for him.

The gravestone read *Lobo Friend*, and it seemed a fitting name for the gentle giant.

It was soon after Lobo's death that Mara realized Clinker was unhappy. After a lot of soul-searching, it came to her that she, too, was bored, that an idle life without purpose wasn't for her. It was only then that she was willing to admit that it was time for another change.

Mara went to see Mr. Sam the winter of '35, making the trip to Tampa by train and then hiring a car to take her the rest of the way. When she'd decided to fake her death, she'd let him in on it, knowing that his help would be essential to the deception. He had agreed readily, probably, she suspected, in part because it would be an easy way out of their contract. She wondered, as the hired car sped along the highway, heading for Orlando, if he would recognize her, even though she'd called to tell him she was coming.

The town of Orlando had spread out in the direction of her

land, but was still far enough away that there hadn't yet been any complaints about noises or animal odors from its rural neighbors. The acreage, so sandy and dry, was not suitable for citrus farming; only tough, drought-resistant palmetto and scrub grew there. But the topology of the low hills that surrounded the site protected it from the worst of the winter winds off the gulf, always so surprisingly cold to tourists not familiar with Florida climate.

When the rented car turned off the highway, into the winter quarters, Mara looked around with proprietary eyes, noting the signs of hard times. With the whole country in the throes of the depression, she hadn't expected prosperity, of course—so why did she feel so guilty that she'd had it easy the past few years? Was it because of that trust fund Earl St. Clair had set up for her?

Mr. Sam, looking a little grayer, jumped to his feet when she came into the Blue Wagon, his gaunt face showing a rare pleasure. Her old vanity stirred, and she was glad that the past six years had been kind to her. The scars had been tempered by expensive plastic surgery, and her eyes, always one of her best features, were as green as ever. Other than covering her hair with one of the turbanlike hats that were currently in style, she hadn't bothered with a disguise, knowing the subtle rearrangement of her features would take care of that. Some of the old-timers might see the resemblance, but the last thing they'd be expecting was to see Princess Mara resurrected.

"How are you, Mr. Sam?" she said.

"Can't complain," he said, and pulled out a chair for her. "You look as pretty as ever," he said.

"Thank you. I know it isn't true, but I like hearing it." She looked around the familiar office, at the battered yellow oak desk, the mission chairs, the aging oak file cabinets. "Nothing's changed here. How's business?"

"Bad. It's hard times for the circus, just like everything else. People don't have the cash for ducats. They crowd the midway to gawk, but they don't go into the Big Top or the sideshows. Sometimes they buy frozen custard cones for the kids or pitch a few balls, but that's about all. We're just managing to keep our head above water, Mara. I don't know how long we can go on, and that's the truth. If we hadn't taken chickens and hams and vegetables in trade last summer, we would've lived on rice and beans. Can't even afford half pay this winter. Most of the winter crew is working for food and a bunk; the rest is on welfare, waiting for the season to start again."

"Would it help if I waive rent this year?"

Mr. Sam's eyes sharpened. "You'd do that, girl?"

"Consider yourself my guest—next year, too, if things don't improve. What do you say to that?"

"I'd say—what do you get out of it?"

"You're a suspicious man, Mr. Sam."

"I been around the barn a few times. And you always valued the almighty dollar as much as anyone. So what is it you want? My right arm?"

Mara smiled at him, genuinely amused. "That's what I like about you, Mr. Sam. You always get right to the point. I do have a favor to ask you. I know you've never allowed a fortune-teller on the midway, but it happens I'm very good with the tarot cards."

He looked at her skeptically. "You wouldn't pull the leg of an old friend, would you?"

"Of course not. I *am* a Gypsy, you know." At his snort, she went on, unoffended. "I learned to tell cards when I was a kid. Clinker and I need something to keep us busy. I'll furnish everything, all props and my own top. And we won't even take up berths in a sleeper, because I'm looking around for a truck and trailer. All I want is a decent location near the Big Top. You get a good cut and free rent for the winter."

"You know I don't like fortune-telling on the midway. That whole business smacks of the devil."

"The devil has nothing to do with it. It'll be clean—no grifting, strictly on the up and up."

"You sure you can handle it?" he said doubtfully. "It takes a special talent, telling fortunes and satisfying the customers."

"I can handle it." Mara reached in her bag and took out the new deck of tarot cards she'd bought before she left California. "And to prove it, I'll tell your fortune—for free. How about shuffling the deck?"

Mr. Sam shuffled the cards a few times, then handed them back. Mara cut them three times. She laid out the top card, a King of Pentacles, then placed another, the Knight of Pentacles, across it to form a cross.

"This is father and son—you and Michael. Everything you have, you will pass along to him—your experience, your counsel, your worldly goods."

"Tell me something new," he growled.

Unperturbed by his skepticism, she laid out the rest of the cards, then studied them in silence for a while. When she reached forward suddenly to tap the Ten of Swords, Mr. Sam gave a nervous start. Mara smiled inwardly. He might not believe in tarot cards, but right now he was sitting on the edge of his chair.

"This card means change, possibly trouble, in connection with your son. It is inevitable, but whether it is for the better or not depends on how you handle it. There will be quarrels—you won't let loose of the reins easily. And that's as it should be. Michael must prove himself first—but don't be too hardheaded or you will lose the thing you want most."

"You could say that about any father and son," Mr. Sam grumbled.

"But these are *your* cards," she said reasonably.

"What else do they say?"

"You've finally resolved a problem that has aggravated you for years. There will be no reoccurrence. It has something to do with—" She tapped another card. "With this woman, the Empress."

"How did you know that?" he said quickly.

"I didn't. But the cards did."

"Well, they're right. Belle and me were divorced last summer. We shoulda done it years ago, but she didn't want to give up her meal ticket, I guess. Then she met a retired lawyer who was rich enough to make it worth her while. I dug in my heels, and she was so afraid he'd get away that I got out cheap."

He rubbed his long chin, his eyes reflective. "Belle's still got Michael in one of those fancy snob factories in the East, trying to make a gentleman out of him." He gave a sly smile. "But he's already caught circus fever. Soon as he finishes college, I figure I'll start grooming him to take over for me someday. Can't live forever, you know."

"You'll live a long time—and be a thorn in everybody's side while doing it," she retorted.

He eyed her thoughtfully. "The cards tell you that?" he said, so seriously that she knew then that he was hooked.

"No, the cards didn't say that, but everybody knows you're too ornery to die young."

"You could be right. Well, I guess we got us a deal. How about a contract? I think we'd better make it legal."

It took him a while to alter one of his standard contracts. When he handed it to her, along with his fountain pen, she took her time reading it. From the chagrin on Mr. Sam's face, she knew he'd thought she was still illiterate—and had acted accordingly.

"I don't like a couple of these clauses you wrote in," she said. "Fifteen percent is fair. Thirty is robbery."

"Oh, did I write thirty? I meant twenty-five."

"Fifteen," she said firmly. "I'm paying for my own top and transportation, remember."

"Twenty and I'll throw in the services of a roughie for any hard work you need."

"Oh, I took that for granted—"

As she bargained with Mr. Sam, Mara discovered she was enjoying herself. She had missed these sessions—along with other things.

It was later, after the contract had been signed in duplicate, that Mr. Sam said expansively, "Well, welcome back, Mara."

"Not Mara," she said. "From now on, I'm Rosa Smith. Don't forget it."

And he hadn't. She was Madam Rosa to everybody from Mr. Sam to the newest First of May guy. Only Clinker, in the privacy of their trailer, still called her Mara.

As she told Clinker while they were packing for their move to Florida, "We're doing the right thing, Clinker. I'd be really happy if it wasn't for—" She broke off.

Clinker said it for her. "If it wasn't for Vicky. I know how you still pine for that girl. Have you ever thought about going to Boston and demanding to see her? She must be—oh, nine by now—"

"Ten in June. I've thought about contacting her. God knows, I've been tempted. But she thinks I'm dead. If she found out I was still alive, that I'd deserted her, she wouldn't want to see me."

Clinker started to say something, thought better of it, and silently returned to her packing.

CHAPTER 32

VICKY HAD KNOWN THAT THE GREAT SOUTHERN SHOW WAS on the lower rungs of the traveling show world, but she'd assumed that any other carnival or circus, no matter if it was a Sunday school operation, as Jim claimed, would be more of the same. So her first impression of Bradford Circus was a welcome surprise.

"No grift, no three-card monte or shell games, and no turning the duke—you know, short-changing the customers," Jim told her when she commented on the prosperous appearance of the circus. "Most of the big shows are clean these days. It don't pay to burn a town, 'cause then you can't book there again."

Ever since they'd checked in with the circus owner, a dour-looking man named Mr. Sam, there had been a new swagger in Jim's walk. Noting his high spirits, Vicky couldn't help wondering what this step up in the circus world meant to him. Was it some long-held dream? Or simply that he'd be making more money and have better working conditions, such as two instead of three shows a day?

She found herself wishing that he would let down his hair again the way he had the night he'd struck her. Since then, she had gone out of her way to please him. Not out of fear. No, it was just that he needed her, no matter how well he hid it. And she liked being needed.

She checked over the new costumes they'd been issued in wardrobe to wear in the spec. Following the theme of the show, Nations of the World, the costumes were Spanish, complete with a black lace mantilla for her and a toreador's cape for Jim. There were a few wrinkles in the cape, and she got out a battered flat iron, heated it on the stove, and began pressing out the wrinkles on the edge of the table, which she'd padded with an old towel.

321

Their debut, at the matinee performance that afternoon, had gone well. None of the dogs had been temperamental, and Jim had looked very handsome under the lights. Of course, they had been one of the side acts, performing to the blue seats while the center ring was given over to a tumbling act.

"You listening to me or daydreaming again?" Jim said. He was sitting on the daybed, drinking a mug of coffee.

"Sorry. I thought the act went well today, even if Mr. Sam only nodded when we came off. But maybe we should try something new, Jim."

"It's okay the way it is," Jim said.

"But it's a little old-fashioned, don't you think?"

Jim slammed his mug down, jarring the table. "I don't want you messing around with the act, you hear?" he said, and too late, she saw the tight look around his mouth and remembered that, so often, his periods of high spirits were quickly followed by his dark moods.

Her silence seemed to irritate Jim further. "You hear me? Don't mess with my act," he growled.

At his peremptory tone, resentment overcame her caution. "I hear you—but I just don't happen to agree. Of course, it *is* your act, so—"

There was no warning. Jim was off the daybed in one fluid movement; his fist crashed against her face before she could duck. There was a moment of pain, and then she found herself lying on the floor, staring up into his enraged face.

"I told you not to mouth off at me," he shouted. "You do it again and I'm going to knock the hell out of you, you hear?"

He stormed out of the trailer, letting the door slam behind him. The smell of scorching cloth aroused Vicky. She got up from the floor and sat the iron upright, fighting confusion and disappointment. He had promised—and he'd broken that promise the first time he'd lost his temper. It was time she faced the truth. Jim hadn't changed. He would never change. And she was right back where she'd started from--living with another bully, this time with one who was capable of doing more physical damage to her than tossing her out in the street.

An hour later, Jim returned to the trailer, looking sheepish and apologetic.

"It was just that you took me by surprise. I was really pissed off or I never woulda hit you. After all, I worked like a horse, getting the money together to buy out old man Tucker. It really got to me when you bad-mouthed the act. But I shouldn't've hit you. You know how crazy I am about you. It's just that blasted temper of mine—I swear it won't happen again. Just—just hang in there with me, Vicky.''

There were tears in his eyes, and suddenly Vicky was seeing the boy who had been beaten every day of his life until he was big enough to fight back. So she told herself that *this* time he really meant it, and forgave him. Later, when he went off to have some repairs done on the truck, she finished her house-keeping chores, checked on the dogs, and then, because she was feeling claustrophobic, she decided to take a walk before she dressed for the evening performance.

Before she left the trailer, she covered the bruise on her cheek with makeup, but she was well aware that it didn't hide the swelling. When she reached the midway, she almost turned back, but decided to go on because she was curious to see what the circus had to offer in the way of rides and game booths and other concessions.

The red-and-white tops looked very gay under a flawless July sky, and her spirits rose as she paused to watch a small boy laughing up at an orange balloon. It occurred to her that if she had some happy childhood memories of a circus or a carnival, she might have warmer feelings about them now.

She had just passed the Big Top when she spotted a miniature tent, so similar to its neighbor with its red-and-white striped canvas that it looked as if the larger tent had given birth to a pup. The thought amused her, especially when she read the banner that announced the services of a Madam Rosa, Gypsy Fortune Teller Extraordinaire, and she was smiling when a woman, dressed in a voluminous caftan, stepped out of the tent, right into her path.

"Excuse me," Vicky said politely, stepping aside.

But the woman didn't move. She was several inches shorter than Vicky, very petite even in the billowing caftan. The turban that completely covered her hair was multicolored silk, shot through with silver and gold threads, and her fingers and neck glittered with gold rings and chains. Her skin was pale beige, the color of ivory, and even in the strong sunlight, only a few fine lines showed at the corners of her eyes and mouth. A forked scar ran from her forehead, across her nose, and ended at her jawline, but oddly, it didn't detract from her attractiveness. In fact, it added a touch of mystery to what must once have been a face of great beauty.

Vicky realized she was staring, that the woman was staring back. Although there was no expression on her face, Vicky sensed her shock. "Who are you?" the woman demanded, and Vicky caught a faint accent in her husky voice.

"I'm with Jim Riley's dog act—"

"No, no. What's your *name*?"

"Vicky—Victoria St. Clair."

This time there was no mistaking the woman's reaction. She reeled as if she'd been struck, and automatically Vicky grabbed her arm to keep her from falling.

"Are you ill—uh, ma'am?" she asked.

"Madam Rosa—and I'm a little dizzy. Can you help me inside the tent?"

She leaned on Vicky heavily as they moved through the tent's open door flaps. "Over there—the chair," the woman said, and Vicky saw with relief that color was seeping back into her face. Another woman appeared from the rear of the tent. When she saw Madam Rosa, she made a tutting sound and rushed over to help her to the chair. She gave Vicky a glance, then stopped, her mouth falling open.

"Who are you?" she asked, exactly as Madam Rosa had.

"Vicky St. Clair," Vicky said, frowning at her.

"You look just like—"

"Would you fix us some tea, Clinker?" Madam Rosa interrupted. She took a deep breath, then smiled at Vicky. "You've been very kind. I insist you stay for tea."

"Thank you," Vicky said, then wondered why she'd accepted the invitation. Her grandfather had detested Gypsies, called them the dregs of the human race. She knew now that her own mother had been one—which was something she tried never to think about. Well, Madam Rosa was obviously a cut above most of the people she'd met since she left home, even if she was a Gypsy. . . .

The woman waved her toward another red velvet chair, and Vicky seated herself, looking around the tent. The canvas was lined with black velvet, which effectively blotted out most of the outside light. A large electric fan, sitting on the floor, circulated the air. From the rugs, scattered like jewels across the canvas floor, and what looked to be an antique lamp overhead, the fortune-telling business must be very good.

"Do you tell fortunes with a crystal ball?" she asked Madam Rosa when the silence seemed to stretch out too long.

"Sometimes. But I prefer tarot cards."

Again, Vicky noticed the huskiness in her voice. Her accent was unusual—a touch of British combined with a southern drawl and something else she couldn't identify.

"Are you really a Gypsy?" she asked impulsively.

"A Rom. We call ourselves Roms—short for Romany."

Vicky nodded, hoping she hadn't insulted the woman by calling her a Gypsy.

"I'd like to tell your fortune—no charge," Madam Rosa said. Her regard was so intent that Vicky wondered uncomfortably if the woman had noticed the swelling on her cheek.

"I'm afraid I don't believe in the occult," Vicky told her.

"You don't have to believe. Consider it a game."

Madam Rosa rose and went to a long library table, picked up a small wooden box that showed the dark brown patina of age. She took out a deck of cards that looked as old as the box.

"These are tarot cards. They belonged to my mother," she said. "You can see the markings are almost worn off. I use another deck for my clients."

Vicky wondered why she was being honored as she watched Madam Rosa shuffle the fragile old cards, her eyes closed, her mouth moving. Vicky caught a few words, but they meant nothing to her. Since she had had special tutoring in several languages and spoke conversational French, German, and Spanish, she was sure the words were not European. Were they Romany?

Madam Rosa opened her eyes. "When you shuffle the cards, you must concentrate on your heart's desire," she said. "Do not let negative thoughts creep in, and maybe I can tell you if your dreams are realistic."

Vicky took the cards and shuffled them slowly, trying to channel her thoughts. What exactly did she want out of life? Money enough so she would be independent, but not so much that she would be burdened. Peace. Someone who cared for her in a loving way. Children on whom she could lavish the love missing from her own childhood . . .

The woman took the cards from her hand and began laying them out on the table. Her lips moved again as she studied each card she put down. Slowly she lifted her face to look at Vicky. Her eyes, a brilliant green, held some deep emotion. Was it sadness?

"So little joy," she said heavily. "How is it possible that you have had so little joy in your life?"

Vicky felt uncomfortable suddenly. It was all nonsense, of course, but still—why did this woman's words disturb her so much? "Actually, I've had a very happy life," she said—then wondered why she had lied.

Madam Rosa tapped a card. "This says differently. The cards never lie. Sometimes the fortune-teller lies, but the cards—never."

Vicky blinked at the intensity in the fortune-teller's voice. Was it part of her act? But why was she bothering with a nonpaying customer?

"You're right," she said impulsively. "I was raised by my grandparents—my home life wasn't all that happy. My grandfather was very—very strict. I never managed to please him."

"And your grandmother?"

"She's been an invalid ever since I can remember. She seldom paid much attention to me."

"Why did you leave home?"

"I had a quarrel with my grandfather. I went to work in a carnival—for the man who owns the dog act."

The woman leaned forward slightly. "And you are happy with this man?"

Vicky hesitated, wondering where all this was leading. "We get along," she said finally.

"Your parents are dead?"

"My father was killed when I was a baby. My mother died when I was four. I don't remember either of them."

"You know nothing about them?"

"Very little. My grandfather disapproved of his son's marriage. My mother—well, I guess there was good reason for his disapproval. He refused to talk about either of them."

The fortune-teller was silent. She laid down another card, then another, completing an oddly shaped cross. She studied them for a while before she spoke.

"There is trouble ahead—some of it your own doing. You have much to learn about life, about people, and above all, about yourself. But happiness can be achieved—by determination, hard work, courage. Your cards show that you have a strong will. Use it wisely or it could become false pride."

A prickling sensation moved along Vicky's upper arms. She didn't believe a word of this—but the woman obviously did. As for the reading—it could fit almost anyone. Most people could fulfill their dreams with hard work, determination, and—what was the other? Courage?

"Thank you," she said, finally remembering her manners. "That was very interesting."

The woman stared at her. "You don't believe. Well, that's to be expected. The cards speak the truth—in time, you'll come to see this."

Vicky doubted that very much, but since it would be rude to say so, she gave a noncommittal nod.

The tall, thin woman Madam Rosa had called Clinker came back with their tea, and Vicky soon discovered that she was a fountain overflowing with advice. She warned Vicky to ease into circus life slowly, to be patient, and eventually she would be accepted. Since Vicky had no intention of staying around long enough for that to happen, she listened politely to the advice but made no comment.

When they had finished their tea, Clinker carried off the cups and disappeared again, leaving Vicky alone with the fortune-teller. They soon discovered some common interests—books and love of animals—and, to Vicky's surprise, Madam Rosa spoke French very well. By the time she got up to leave, they were on a first-name basis. Rosa seemed genuinely sorry to see her go. She invited Vicky to come back soon and offered to lend her a new novel by Anaïs Nin that she'd just finished. Vicky accepted both offers with pleasure, and as she walked back to the trailer to get dressed for the evening performance, she discovered that the depression that had dogged her earlier was gone.

After Vicky was gone, Clinker came out of the back of the tent, where they kept a cot and facilities for making tea. Mara, who was fighting tears, was glad that her friend didn't seem to notice as she went to stand at the tent entrance, staring after Vicky.

"She's just like her father," Clinker said finally.

Mara shook her head. "She *looks* like him, but I'm afraid she inherited her dark spirit from my side of the family," she said, sighing. "Did you notice that she has Jaime's smile, Clinker?"

"I noticed. What is she doing here, anyway? And that thing she said about there being reason for Earl St. Clair's disapproval of her mother—what was that all about?"

"Earl St. Clair got his revenge, I suspect. God knows what he's told her about me. As for how she turned up here—coincidences do happen, you know."

"Maybe she caught circus fever from you, and that's what drew her back.'

Despite her depression, Mara had to smile. "I doubt it. Circus fever may be in your blood, but not in mine. With me, it was vanity. Anything that put me in the limelight would have done just as well. Becoming a circus performer was just a means to an end."

"So why did you come running back to the circus?" Clinker said skeptically.

"Maybe I got tired of you moping around the house."

Clinker laughed, then returned to the subject of Vicky. "If we saw Vicky's resemblance to Jaime so quickly, what about the old-timers who knew him—and knew her as a child? And then there's her name—Mr. Sam is bound to put two and two together eventually."

"He'll keep his mouth shut—and so will the old-timers. They have about me."

The two women exchanged glances. No one in the circus had ever shown, by word or look, that they had guessed her secret— but Mara knew some of them had. The fact that Clinker, well-known to the old timers, was her companion was enough to raise a few speculations.

"I notice that Mr. Sam sends any writer who wants a story about Princess Mara to see you these days," Clinker commented.

"I'm the official keeper of the flame."

"So what if she"—Clinker gestured toward the midway— "catches on?"

"That will never happen," Mara said firmly.

The two women were silent, each busy with her own thoughts. "Did you see the swelling on her face?" Mara asked abruptly.

"I did. Someone's worked her over, probably the guy who owns the dog act. He's a handsome brute, all right, but there's something about him—"

"You've met him?"

"Cappy introduced us in the privilege tent last night. You know how he takes newcomers under his wing."

"Vicky wasn't with the man?"

"He said something about her nursing one of the dogs that was sick. Cappy told me privately that the guy is jealous of her."

"With reason?"

"Who knows. She's a beauty. I always knew she would be." Unexpectedly Clinker's eyes filled with tears. "It gave me a shock, seeing her like that. Why didn't you tell her who you are, Mara?"

"How could I? I made a terrible mistake, turning her over to Earl St. Clair to raise. If she found out the truth, that her grandfather arranged that trust fund for me, she'll think I did it for the money. Better if she keeps on thinking I'm dead."

Clinker gave her a cross look. "You did the best you could, Mara. I don't want you tearing yourself apart over this."

"You're right," Mara said, sighing. "Well, she's a grown woman now. It's too late to be her mother. But maybe I can be her friend. I think she needs one."

And Clinker nodded, looking as troubled as Mara felt.

CHAPTER 33

MR. SAM SELDOM CONCERNED HIMSELF WITH PERSONNEL matters these days, although he still handled the Big Top acts. With artistes, he'd learned it was best to trust his own judgment. Some acts could come on flashy in tryouts—and fade like hell before an audience. Others were nervous, unimpressive, when they were auditioning, but when they got in front of an audience, they came alive, shining all over the place.

He had an instinct for both kinds. A smell, he called it privately. And the new dog act, Riley and Company, had the aura of a winner.

Not that their routine was unusual. The same old stuff, really, but there was a—what his son Michael would probably call a rapport between the dogs and the girl in the act that was impressive. Oh, the guy, Jim Riley, was okay. But just as Dag Heller, his talent scout, had said after he'd caught their act in some two-bit mudshow, it was the girl who made the act.

Of course, an animal act always went over well with the kids. Dogs especially got to the little rug rats. And the men liked the girl, who had real class. The women liked the man, too, who was good-looking and had been raised around shows, which was a plus.

Which was why he was so nonplussed when, five days after

they joined the show, Konrad Barker came to him with a complaint.

He'd been having a cup of coffee with his son, Michael, going over some cost-accounting figures, and munching on one of the filled doughnuts Cookie had sent over from the cook tent, when the equestrian director came stalking in.

"We could have a domestic problem with the new dog act," he said. Like Cookie Gordon, Oly Johnson, and old Doc McCall, Konrad Barker went back a long way with the circus. He kept the Big Top running like well-oiled machinery and was the best equestrian director in the business, an opinion Mr. Sam was careful to keep to himself. Not that any other circus was apt to take on an old-timer like Konrad, who had the disposition of a Russian bear with a sore tooth. Still—he was always careful to listen to Konrad's advice, which usually was good.

"So? You know management don't interfere with domestic problems," he growled. Behind Konrad's head he was aware that Michael was grinning, obviously enjoying his encounter with the irascible equestrian director.

"Who said you should interfere? But you pay me to keep the artistes out of trouble, and I say we've got a hothead here. Jealousy is Riley's problem. He's already tried to lay one on that jerk-off, Jeckel, for whistling at the woman. Luckily someone hustled him away before Riley could deck him, or we'd have big trouble."

"So? Maybe Riley'd had a bad day," Mr. Sam said, bored with the conversation.

"Okay, don't say I didn't warn you. The woman turned up with bruises the next day. Which is their business. Some women like that kind of treatment. But if he's going to take a swing at anyone who looks at his woman, it's our business."

Mr. Sam knew he was right. "The woman—I've forgotten her name—"

"Vicky."

"Is this Vicky inviting the whistles?"

"All I know is she's been getting a lot of attention from some of our young bucks. It figures; she's built like a brick outhouse. She doesn't have much to say, what little I've seen of her during rehearsals and in the backyard. Could be shy. Could be scared of her old man. Who knows? But I think someone should talk to the guy, lay it on the line."

"I agree. You have my permission to do the honors."

"The hell I will. That's management's job."

Konrad stalked off, his wiry body stiff with indignation. Mr. Sam should have been amused because he'd routed the old fart, but he wasn't. Konrad had a nose for trouble—and it was almost as good as his own. He caught Michael's grin, and that made up his mind.

"Since you're personnel boss, this is your department. Talk to this fellow Riley and straighten him out. What we don't need is a hothead mucking things up. We've got enough troubles."

Michael lost his smile, and Mr. Sam regarded him with satisfaction. Michael was dark-haired and brown-eyed, like his mother, but Mr. Sam liked to think that his son had inherited his own solid good sense. Although he was proud of Michael, thought he was the best thing that had ever happened to him, he wasn't going to throw him the reins in a hurry. It took years to develop good judgment. As far as he was concerned, Michael was just like any other employee who was working his way up the management ladder. By the time he turned over the circus to him, the boy was going to be ready for it—and taking on unpleasant jobs was part of the game.

"You sure this is the right thing to do? It might make things worse," Michael said doubtfully.

"Nipping trouble in the bud is always best. If it wasn't for the girl, I'd kick them out. They're still on probation."

Michael frowned at him. "The *girl* got to you?"

"Not the way you're thinking, you knothead. It was—well, she's got something going with those dogs—and with the audience. Soon as J.C. gets back to work and you stop doubling up on jobs, you should take a look at the act and see if you don't agree."

Michael nodded. "Will do—and I'll have a talk with this Jim Riley. I hope he doesn't take it the wrong way. I hear he's a veteran, which could make it touchy."

"Yeah." Mr. Sam was careful to look disinterested. He knew how it had rankled Michael when he'd been turned down for military service, knew how it smarted to be the right age, ready, willing, and all fired up to do your duty and then be told by a recruiting officer that because you'd had rheumatic fever when you were seven years old, you weren't fit to serve your country. And if, deep in his own heart, he'd felt a giddy relief when he heard the news, he was smart enough to keep it to himself. . . .

Mr. Sam put on his panama hat and picked up the cane that was not an affectation, like most people thought, but something of a necessity since that last flare-up of arthritis. "I'll be over at Rosa's top having lunch," he said gruffly.

Michael grinned at him. "Give her a kiss from me," he said slyly. "Just make sure you tell her who sent it."

"One of these days that mouth of yours is going to get you in trouble," Mr. Sam said.

He stomped off, pretending anger, but secretly he was pleased. There was nothing going on between him and Mara, never had been, never would be, but something in him, male pride perhaps, liked being teased about their relationship. The same something always made him spruce up a bit before he went to see Mara.

"That son of mine is a smart-ass," he was telling her a few minutes later. They were sitting at the table where she gave her readings, eating corned beef sandwiches and drinking root beer. With the tent flaps closed, the sounds of the midway—the talker at the ten-in-one next door, the rattle of the hanky-panky apparatus, the grab joint talkers exhorting their wares—were muted, blurred by the drone of the electric fan.

"He's a fine, decent boy," Mara said sternly. "Don't be so hard on him."

Mr. Sam started to tell her to mind her own business, but he stopped just in time. Because Mara was right. Michael *was* a fine, decent man. Stubborn as a Missouri mule, but he was a hard worker, and he lived and breathed circus. Funny that last, when Belle had done her best to turn the boy against circus life. . . .

"Someday he'll be running the show, but not yet," he said. "Hell, I'm still in my prime."

Mara smiled and popped a ripe olive in her mouth; Mr. Sam cast around for a less-depressing subject than age. "From the bookkeeper's reports, the fortune-telling business is booming. Wish I could say that about other operations. These shortages are killing us. The grab stands run out of hot dogs halfway through the evening—and Cookie is always screaming about rationing. We had beans three times already this week. I'll be glad when things get back to normal."

"Those coal-mining strikes don't help. This being mining country, I got five or six miners' wives yesterday, worried sick because their men are on strike."

"With that Missouri hardhead taking over the White House, there's bound to be trouble," Mr. Sam, who was a staunch Republican, said sourly. "He'd lock horns with the devil to get his own way."

"Oh? Seems to me you told me once that you were born in Missouri, and you sounded pretty proud of it," Mara said, looking innocent.

He muttered something under his breath, eyeing her. She was wearing one of her fancy robe outfits, embellished by a rope of pearls at her neck. That they were real, he was well aware. Luckily they were so large and uniform in size that no one else would guess that the Bradford show's Gypsy fortune-teller often wore a fortune in pearls.

"So what else is new?" Mara asked.

"Konrad has the vapors again," he said. "The guy that has the new dog act took a swing at that idiot Jeckel for flirting with his woman. Konrad smells trouble."

Mara was a few moments answering him; her face had a drawn, tight look. "I met the girl yesterday afternoon."

"What do you think of her?"

"Good-looking. Younger than she looks. Bright. Very naive in some ways, mature in others."

Mr. Sam stared at her. What was going on inside that clever head? She sounded—soft. Which wasn't like Mara. Did the girl remind her of her own daughter? They'd be about the same age. He seldom asked Mara—or anyone else—personal questions, but this one he'd like to ask.

"I hear she's got bruises," he commented.

Mara moved restlessly. "I saw them."

"She must really go for the guy to take his abuse."

"Or maybe she doesn't. Maybe she thinks she doesn't have a choice."

"You lost me there—"

"She's all alone in the world. She may be staying with him because she doesn't have any money."

"Hell, that never stopped you. You never took anything off anyone without fighting back."

"We're two different people. I came equipped with enough stiff-necked pride to take on Hitler's army."

"Well, this girl doesn't have much gumption or she'd walk out on the guy. Can't say I admire that type of woman."

"I'm not sure I do either. God knows, I can't help her. Sometimes we have to let our kids make their own mistakes."

It took Mr. Sam a few seconds to catch the meaning of her

words. "My god—that's *your* Vicky! How the hell did she end up here?"

"I don't know the whole story. She thinks I'm dead, of course. Which is the way I want to keep it." Her face twisted with pain, and her eyes glistened with tears. "I'm aching to tell her who I am, Sam. But that bastard St. Clair raised her to think her mother was a whore—or maybe worse."

"So why don't you set her straight?"

"Don't you start! I've already gone through this with Clinker. I'm not going to do anything. It's all in the past, and there's where it should stay. And I wouldn't have told you except I knew you'd figure it out eventually."

Looking into her eyes, reading the pain there, Mr. Sam held his peace. Maybe she was right. Nothing good ever came from digging up old mistakes. But he made a private resolution to keep a close eye on the girl. In fact, he just might call in a marker. Nancy Parker's trailer was parked next to Riley's two rigs. Maybe he'd put a bug in Nancy's ear and ask her to get acquainted with the girl and find out what the hell was going on with her and Jim Riley.

Other than Rosa and Clinker, Vicky hadn't become acquainted with any of the circus people in the week they'd been with the show, not only because Jim had warned her to keep her distance, but also because she had no common ground with the few she had met. Not only did they speak their own language, but they were at home in this world—and she wasn't. She didn't like the dirt, the hard edges of a life that involved constant change. The lack of water was more than irritating; it was offensive. She was tired of having to pile on makeup so the spotlights wouldn't wash out her coloring, of the profanity that everybody used, of all the tawdry things that made up the circus world.

Most of all she was tired of trying to please Jim, of washing his underwear, cooking his meals and picking up after him, sleeping with him. She knew she should find a way to leave him, and yet—she did feel a certain responsibility toward him. In his way, he loved her. He was a man whom most women were attracted to. So why was it she could hardly stand to have him touch her?

She brooded over this, trying to understand her own confused feelings, as she sat beside the trailer, drying her hair in the sun. Cleanliness was another sore point. All her life she had used hot water lavishly, taking two showers a day and washing her hair every morning. She'd slept between sheets that were changed every other day, never put on an item of clothing that wasn't freshly laundered. Now Jim expected her to get along with a daily trickle of water because, he said, it was too much trouble, keeping the tank full.

She jumped as a voice hailed her. It was the woman who lived in the next trailer, the wife of an acrobat.

"Looks like we'll get well here in Ironton," the woman said. She was young, probably in her midtwenties, not really pretty but attractive and cheerful-looking. She was also very pregnant.

"Mr. Sam actually had a smile on his face this morning at the gripe meeting," she went on. "The show musta got its nut back this week."

Vicky smiled at her. "I'm keeping my fingers crossed," she said.

"I've been wanting to ask you if there's anything I can do to help you get settled in. I know how hard it is at first when you come to a new show. If you need a friend, just ask."

Vicky was touched by her offer. She did need a friend—desperately. "Thank you. You're very kind," she said, feeling a little shy.

"How about coming in for a glass of ice tea? You look hot, sitting there in the sun."

Vicky hesitated. Did having a glass of ice tea with a neighbor come under the heading of "messing around with other people"?

"My name is Vicky," she said, making up her mind. "I could really use something cold."

That was the start of her friendship with Nancy Parker. They talked about impersonal things—the baby Nancy was expecting, the scarcity of nylons and sugar, the gouging prices the shops in the vicinity of the fairgrounds charged circus people.

Nancy showed her a bootee she was crocheting, and when Vicky expressed interest in learning how to crochet, Nancy demonstrated a few elementary stitches. Vicky, who was starved for woman talk, was soon laughing at Nancy's sallies. She was glad that her new friend, like most circus people, asked no personal questions, even though she suspected Nancy was fishing for information when she remarked so artlessly that she and Jim Riley sure were a good-looking pair.

When Vicky got up to leave, Nancy insisted she take a ball of yarn and a hook with her for practice. Jim came home later and found Vicky curled up on the daybed, trying to master the stitches Nancy had shown her.

Her heart sank when she saw that he'd been drinking. "You take care of the dogs yet?" he said as a greeting.

"They're ready for the matinee," she said cautiously.

"So how come I saw Pixie scratching like hell when I came past the van?"

"I gave them baths and sprayed out the van. Maybe she picked up a flea from the ground."

" 'Maybe she picked up a flea from the ground,' " he mimicked in an unlikely Boston accent. "And maybe you're just plain lazy. I hired you to take care of the dogs, and that's what I expect. So put away that—what the hell is that you're working on, anyway?"

Vicky held up the bit of pink yarn. "It's a baby bootee—"

She got no further. Jim was upon her, jerking her to her feet, shaking her until her head bobbed uncontrollably. His face was engorged with blood, and his eyes had a glazed look. "Who you been messing around with?" he shouted. "You little whore—who knocked you up?"

She tried to answer him, but his hands were around her throat, choking off her breath. He flung her down on the daybed and started taking off his belt, holding her down with his knee.

"The bootees are for Nancy Parker's baby—she lives in the blue trailer," she said quickly. "I'm not pregnant—how could I be when you use condoms?"

The rage drained from his face slowly. Or maybe the word was reluctantly. Why did she have the feeling that he was disappointed because he didn't have any reason for his suspicions? When he sat down hard on the daybed and buried his face in his hands, she felt only a cold relief that she'd escaped another beating.

Too much, something sane and self-protective inside her said.

She got up, careful not to touch him. Her voice even and without emotion, she told him, "If you ever do that again, I'll leave you and go back to Boston even if I have to hitchhike."

Jim's hands fell away from his face, and she knew that he was ashamed of his violence. She listened silently as he told her he was sorry, that he'd just had a run-in with Mr. Sam's son, who had really pissed him off, that he didn't know what got into him sometimes, but it would never happen again.

She knew that Jim was no longer dangerous—but what about next time? What about tomorrow or the day after, when he lost his temper again? What about his jealousy, the rage that came out of nowhere, turning to violence?

She pretended to be asleep when he came to bed that night, and after a tentative touch, he let her alone. He fell asleep almost immediately, but Vicky lay awake most of the night, making plans.

Money, not nerve or opportunity, was the problem. Jim handled all the money, had even taken over grocery shopping, never giving her a dime. His claim that the dogs were eating up all their wages didn't hold water. The act was earning at least twice as much as it had at the carnival—and Jim always had enough to buy liquor. By keeping her broke, by making sure she had no friends to turn to, he had made it almost impossible for her to leave. And always, like a carrot before a mule, was his promise—a cut of the profits somewhere off there in the future.

Well, she didn't intend to be trapped here. She had already stayed too long with Jim. Maybe she could get a job at one of the concessions. She could be a cashier or take tickets or sell caramel popcorn, anything to earn some money. She could sleep in the women's sleeper, eat in the cookhouse, until she got a stake together. And when she did, then she would leave this miserable circus and never look back.

The next morning she waited until Jim went to get a haircut before she left the trailer. She had chosen her clothes carefully— a tartan skirt with a white silk blouse, calf-length boots, and a plain gold chain at her neck. Knowing she looked good gave her confidence, and since it was very unlikely anyone here would realize that the plaid skirt had been hand-loomed in Scotland, that the blouse was silk, and the chain pure gold, she didn't look overdressed.

When she reached the Silver Wagon, she hesitated, looking in through the screen door. Mr. Sam, the owner, was there, talking to two other men. Not wanting to intrude, she was turning away when a woman, sitting behind a desk just inside the door, looked up and spotted her.

"You want something, honey?"

"Can you tell me where I can find the personnel boss?"

"You looking for a job?"

"Yes, I am."

"You want to talk to Michael Bradford, but he isn't here right now. You can wait—or come back tomorrow."

She returned to her typing.

Uncertain what to do, Vicky stood there for a minute. She had just decided to come back the next day when Mr. Sam came to the door.

"If you're looking for Michael, he said something about going to the menagerie to talk to Doc McCall. You can try there."

Vicky was puzzled by the odd note in his voice. If it hadn't seemed inappropriate, she would have guessed he was amused. She thanked him and moved off, aware that he was still standing at the door watching her.

Since she hadn't been to the menagerie tent yet, Vicky looked with interest at the line of elephants tethered outside. A horse whinnied nearby, and she turned her attention to a small temporary corral, admiring the sleek Arabians and the sturdy Percherons with their broad, level backs. An Arabian stallion, sleek and lean, caught her eye, reminding her of her own favorite mare. What had happened to Misty? Now that she wasn't there to champion her, had her grandfather put her to sleep as he'd threatened to do when her foal-bearing years ended?

The thought of Misty, so proud and lovely, lying dead, was so painful that involuntarily she flinched.

"You scared of horses?" a male voice asked.

Vicky turned to look at the man. He was of average height, well built and lean, probably in his late twenties; his shirt sleeves were rolled up, revealing tanned, well-muscled arms. He wasn't handsome, not in a classical way, but there was no doubt he was a very attractive man, and from his easy, self-confident smile, she suspected he knew it.

"I was raised with horses," she said coolly.

His eyes roamed over her, taking in her plaid skirt, her boots. "Funny, I could have sworn I saw you flinch when Lo'Boy snorted just now."

"I'm looking for the personnel boss—I think his name is Michael?"

"You've found him. How can I help you?"

"I'm looking for work."

His eyebrows rose. "As a lark? Or maybe to win a bet with some of your school chums?"

"So I can eat," she retorted, resenting his amused tone as well as his words. "I have experience—I worked at the Great Southern Show. I can handle a ticket seller's or cashier's job."

He studied her, his eyes quizzical. "Now, why would a good-looking girl like you want to work for peanuts when you could be a model or a showgirl?"

"I prefer to keep my clothes on when I work. Do you have anything or not?"

Despite herself, her voice had a cutting edge, and she expected him to retaliate in kind. To her surprise, he gave her a genuine smile. "Sorry—that was uncalled for. Blame it on overwork. And I just might have something for you. The taffy booth cashier is quitting. Do you think you can handle it?"

In her relief, Vicky had to swallow hard before she said, "I'm sure I can."

"You say you worked for Great Southern? That's something of a gilly show, isn't it?"

"I needed a job badly. I met a man who'd just bought a dog act. He offered me a job as his assistant. Then he transferred to your show, and I came with him. But it isn't working out so—" She broke off when she saw the expression on his face change to a frown.

"You're Jim Riley's woman?" He shook his head before she could answer. "Sorry, lady. No deal. I'm not about to get involved in your domestic affairs."

She flushed, but she kept her voice even as she said, "I just work for Jim Riley. I need a change."

"That's your problem." For some reason, he sounded angry. "You'll have to work it out on your own."

He turned and walked away, not looking back.

CHAPTER 34

MICHAEL BRADFORD'S LOVE AFFAIR WITH THE CIRCUS HAD started the day his father took him, a chunky five-year-old, to Jacksonville for Bradford Circus's first performance of the season. Until then, he'd had no idea that the tall, gaunt-faced man who sometimes visited his mother owned a circus.

He knew what a circus was, of course. Clowns and elephants

and ladies in sparkling clothes who did scary things on high wires and swings. One of his friends had been to the Barnum & Bailey Circus in Sarasota and had brought back some brightly colored postcards, one of a funny-looking man with a red nose and another of a ferocious tiger with enormous teeth. When he'd asked his mother if they could go to the circus, too, she'd yelled at him and sent him to his room.

But she hadn't been able to stop the man she called Sam from taking Michael to see his circus. At first he'd been afraid, because the man had threatened to take his mother's house away if she gave him any more trouble about seeing the boy. But later, in the car, he told Michael to call him Pop and then talked about lion trainers—"Don't call them lion tamers, son, because no wild animal can ever really be tamed!"—and explained the difference between high school and rosinback horses.

And then Michael had seen the red-and-white striped tents, silhouetted against the sky, smelled the popcorn and the sugar candy, watched the clowns and the elephants, and the men, dressed in tights, doing somersaults in the air, heard the band blaring out one lively tune after another, rode the merry-go-round and fished for prizes in the fish pond, and suddenly he knew that this was what he wanted when he was grown, to be part of this glittering, exciting world.

Since then, he'd learned that the circus had its warts, that the glitter was often tarnished, but he'd never lost his first fierce determination to belong to it.

As soon as he was old enough, he'd defied his mother and signed on during school vacation as a roughie, doing any job assigned to him. He'd washed dishes in the cookhouse, helped the sails men mend canvas, washed down elephants and cleaned out stalls, and done a dozen other menial jobs. He hadn't liked some of them, but he'd never complained.

When he was sixteen, for one wonderful summer, he'd donned a hobo costume and been a Joey. The older clowns hadn't made it easy for him just because he was the owner's son, but he'd stuck it out. When they'd finally admitted him into their brotherhood, he'd been far prouder than when, a few years later, he graduated from Princeton with an M.B.A. degree.

After graduation, he'd told his father that he wanted to learn everything he could about running a circus. He hadn't played it coy. He'd come right out with his ultimate goal.

"When I'm ready, Pop," he said, looking his father straight in the eye, "I want you to turn the show over to me to manage.

No crap-outs at the last moment. Is it a deal? If not, I'll take my training somewhere else.''

Mr. Sam had agreed. Reluctantly, taking his time about it, but he'd finally agreed, realizing that if he didn't, he would lose his only son, with his fancy business degree, to another show.

Since then, Michael had worked eighteen hours a day, sometimes longer, learning the circus business. It had been his choice, taken after careful consideration, as was his habit. Rosa, his father's good friend, had told him once that he was a true Capricorn who thought out every decision he made, but once he did decide, he never looked back.

So why the hell did he feel so damned guilty for turning down that redheaded girl's request for a job?

He hadn't had a choice, once he'd discovered who she was. The circus was a narrow, tight world. There were rules, unwritten but binding, that existed in order to keep things running smoothly. And not interfering or taking sides in domestic affairs was one of the strongest. Of course, Riley and the girl weren't legally married, but that made no difference. If they lived together, in the eyes of the circus they were considered a married couple. And the old gag that a carny should be polite to another man's summer wife, because next season she could be his, didn't change that. If he'd given her a job, then he would've been interfering in a family quarrel and the whole circus would have lost respect for him.

And why had the old man sent the woman to see him? Mr. Sam had hired the dog act, so he must have known who she was. Was this another of the old man's asinine tests? When was he going to start trusting his own son's judgment, for God's sake?

Knowing all this, why had he hesitated to tell the girl that it was a no-go on the job? Was it the way she was dressed, in that hand-woven Scottish tartan skirt and white silk shirt, so like the girls he'd dated at Princeton? Of course, few of them could measure up to her when it came to looks. Was that why he'd almost given her the job?

Okay, admit it, Michael. She got to you. . . .

That crystalline beauty, warmed by all that auburn hair, not to mention the elegant lines of her body, had done something drastic to his breathing. He'd wanted to run his fingers through that hair, wanted to kiss her—was he going into early senility? The circus was full of good-looking women, most of the unattached ones eager to jump into his bed. But he'd never taken advantage of their inviting looks, not because he hadn't been tempted, but from sheer self-preservation.

The truth was that while he was a normal man with the usual sex drives, he was as careful about women as he was about everything else. At this point of his life, they just didn't enter into his plans. Later, when he had his future under control, then he would think about a wife, preferably a nonprofessional, someone to give him kids and a home life to come back to when the season was over each fall.

Meanwhile, he had his flings with women from time to time, but none of them worked for the circus. That kind of involvement only meant trouble, especially with the old man breathing down his neck all the time, just looking for mistakes. Which brought him back to the question of why Mr. Sam had sent the girl to him. Had it been a test to see if he could keep his hands off another man's summer wife?

When he returned to the Blue Wagon, he realized that Mr. Sam was itching to find out what had happened. For punishment, he gave his father a lazy grin, poured himself a mug of coffee, and set about teasing Mamie, his father's secretary. She was wearing a ballerina-length skirt with matching ballerina slippers, her hair teased into a high pompadour that made her look like a French poodle, and it was obvious, from the way she bridled and tossed her head, that she loved his attention. Since she was also married to the show's canvas boss, and was straight as a die, it was safe to indulge her.

Mr. Sam finally got impatient with their patter. "You talk to that gal who was looking for a job?"

"Who? Oh, you mean the redhead. I sent her packing. She looked like trouble to me. We've already got enough problems with sexpots, what with guys hanging around the Blue Wagon, flirting with your secretary."

Mamie giggled. "How you do go on, Mr. Michael," she cooed.

With satisfaction, Michael took in the chagrin on his father's face. Since Mr. Sam had held back his knowledge of who the girl was, there was nothing more he could say. Michael smiled to himself, but his satisfaction soon faded. What was it about the whole situation that made him feel in the wrong?

That night he made it his business to be standing at the back door during the evening performance, ostentatiously making a crowd count. From his vantage point, he watched the dog act and knew that his father had been right. The redhead was good, not only with the dogs but with the audience. When she smiled, you could almost feel the temperature rise in the stands. Which was strange, because she was such an iceberg away from the ring. Where had she learned her showmanship? Was she a natural? Too bad she was tied up with that Neanderthal, Riley. . . .

He realized where his thoughts were heading, and was disgusted with himself. After all, he wasn't some callow college kid with the hots. He was a reasonably mature man who had always been in control of himself, and he intended to keep it that way. . . .

As the circus followed the circuit route through central Pennsylvania, Vicky felt as if she existed in limbo. A tentative peace existed between her and Jim, but she felt edgy, apprehensive. If Jim had quarreled with her, she would have found some way to leave him, but he seemed eager to placate her and keep the peace. Since he made no fuss when she returned to the air mattress, saying it was too hot to sleep with him, she let things ride, hoping for the best.

And then, unexpectedly, she found a new interest that made her problems with Jim seem less important.

Having caught that one brief glimpse of the horses, it was inevitable that she would return to the menagerie. She was leaning against the corral gate, watching a young colt frolicking in the sun, when a short, slightly built man, dressed in a dapper riding habit, approached her. He introduced himself as Marcus Bearnaise, his accent so thick that it was hard to understand him. When she replied in her careful French, his eyes lit up and he began talking so rapidly that she finally asked him to speak in English.

"These people"—he waved his arms extravagantly—"they are so uncouth. Only because I am building up a stake do I work here, so far from civilization. When I return to France I will open a riding academy and teach people how to ride properly."

He looked Vicky over, his eyes frankly admiring. "Maybe you would like to take lessons from me? I am very good teacher."

"I've been riding since I was four," Vicky said. "These horses—all of them are yours?"

"Oh, no. Only the Arabians are mine. My wife and I do an equestrian act. We are very good. And you are the redhead who is with the new dog act. I hear you are very good, too. Your partner, not so good. Is true?"

"Not really," she said, feeling uncomfortable. "It's just that I have more patience with the dogs. I'd like to change a few things, but—well, it's Jim's act."

"Is bad situation, eh? So why do you stay with him?"

Vicky hesitated. Was this ordinary curiosity—or did he have a reason for the question? "We have a verbal contract," she finally said.

"Such contracts are good only when both parties are happy. They are easily broken. An illness that keeps you from performing . . ." He shrugged.

The turn of the conversation was making Vicky uneasy, so she asked him a question about one of his Arabians, a sleek beauty with flashing eyes who seemed a little too spirited for a show horse.

"That one—he has the devil in his shanks. His name is Lo'Boy—is very strange name, no? Very hard to handle, but ah, he *is* a beauty."

The horse, as if he knew they were talking about him, sidled up to the fence. He fixed his eyes on Vicky, whinnying. "Does he think I have some sugar for him?" she said, amused by his antics.

"He is curious about you. Maybe it is your red hair."

"Horses can't see colors—or so I've heard."

"Maybe not. Who can really tell? But he is interested in you."

She held out her hand, and the man snapped out a warning. "Watch out! He will bite you—"

But the horse was nuzzling Vicky, pushing his velvety nose into the palm of her hand. She let him nibble for a few moments, then rubbed the bone behind his ear. His nostrils flared and he rolled his eyes, pawing the ground, as if asking a question.

"You have charmed the devil, I see. I do believe he invites you to ride him."

"Could I? I would love to—"

"No, no. Do not be deceived. It would be too dangerous. Even I cannot always control him."

Vicky started to tell him that she'd ridden spirited horses all her life, but she had second thoughts. As she watched Marcus put one of the horses he was training through its paces, she wondered if he would have let her ride the stallion had she told about the cups she'd won in some of the toughest competitions in the country. Well, there was no reason why she couldn't go back to see the horse, maybe take him an apple, was there?

From then on, whenever she got the chance to get away for

an hour or so, Vicky went to visit the Arabian. The stable boys, most of them younger than Vicky, became accustomed to her and left her alone. She was always careful to give herself a good wash at the menagerie water faucet before she returned to the trailer, even though Jim never questioned her absences. In fact, he seldom spoke to her these days. He seemed sunk in apathy when he was there at all, and often he was gone for the whole night, coming in early in the morning without explanation. Suspecting that he was involved with another woman, she hoped that this would last until she was ready to leave.

One thing that was making things easier was his continued lack of sexual interest. Sometimes she would catch him staring at her, his eyes brooding, but since she'd left his bed, he hadn't made any advances. If he had, she would have refused him. And if he'd persisted, she had already made up her mind to pack her things and leave, no matter the consequences. As long as he left her alone, she would stick it out and hope for the best.

She continued to have coffee with Nancy, enjoying these visits very much. Often there were other women there, and she made an effort to be friendly, pleasant. The conversation was about the weather, which always loomed large in importance to the circus, or sometimes they gave Vicky advice about where to shop, because of her First of May status. Other things they gossiped about were the birth of babies, couples who had split up, acts that had joined the circus, and others who had left.

Vicky enjoyed these conversations, but she was so aware how temporary her life here was that it was hard to relate to women whose whole lives revolved around the circus. She also couldn't help noticing how narrow their interests were.

That in the world that existed outside the circus lot former occupants of Nazi detention camps were telling tales of pure horror, that a civil war raged in China, that the Phillipines had been given their independence, meant nothing to them. That rationing, including sugar and gasoline, was finally over, with inflation cutting into the value of their wages, did matter. And why, Vicky thought, was she surprised at this partisanship? When had her grandfather, during his monologues at the dinner table, ever commented on the problems of the poor and disfranchised?

The late summer days grew progressively hotter as they moved through Pennsylvania. Sometimes Vicky felt as if she were living in a boiler that was getting ready to explode, but she kept the trailer immaculate, provided Jim with good, plain food on demand, groomed the dogs every day.

They had just finished a four-day engagement in Harrisburg, with record crowds that had Mr. Sam beaming, when Vicky finally gave in to temptation and rode the stallion, Lo'boy.

It was a "still" day, which all the circus welcomed because of their unusually hectic schedule. Vicky went to the corral early that morning, slipping out of the trailer before Jim was awake. Since no one was about, she climbed over the corral fence and warily approached the Arabian.

Lo'Boy rolled his eyes at her, his ears twitching, but he came up and nuzzled her arm when she called his name. She gave him the sugar lump he was expecting, and then looked around. No one was in sight, which wasn't surprising. Most of the stable hands and beast boys, having hit the local bars the night before, would be sleeping it off, taking advantage of the open day.

Vicky looked with longing at Lo'Boy's shining chestnut back. Did she dare ride him? He whinnied softly, as if daring her, and she slipped up onto his bare back, moving so quickly that he only had time to lay back his ears before she was holding tightly onto his mane.

When he tossed his head and looked at her over his shoulder, his eyes showing white crescents, she expected him to bolt, but he surprised her. As sedately as her little mare, he pranced along the fence, sometimes getting so close that she knew it was deliberate.

"You old fraud," she told him affectionately. "Okay, I know you could do some damage to my leg if you got any closer to that fence. But if you do, you'll never get another apple or sugar lump out of me. N'est ce pas?"

The stallion shook his head, tossing his mane in the air, then settled down to a steady trot as if saying, "Who, me? Why I'm just a pussycat."

"So let's see what you can do," she said, and dug her heels into his ribs.

The next few minutes, as they circled the corral, Lo'Boy was as responsive to her guidance as one of her grandfather's champion show horses. Marcus had told her that he'd bought the horse from another circus. It was obvious that Lo'Boy had been well trained. Did his spookiness with Marcus stem from a history of abuse from a male rider?

Curiosity made her venture further. Dropping her head scarf

on the ground, she brought the horse about with the pressure of her knees, and when they were opposite the scarf, she bent sideways to snatch it up. Lo'Boy leaned with her, making it easier to reach the scarf, and she laughed aloud with excitement.

After a few more minutes, she slid off the Arabian and led him toward the stable tent. So the stallion had been playing games with Marcus. All he really needed was to be taught who was boss.

It was that way with people, too. Give them an inch, they took a mile. Show the slightest weakness and they walked all over you—or worked you like a horse and found excuses not to pay you a just wage. From now on, it was going to be different. "I want my pay," she was going to tell Jim. . . .

She was grooming the stallion when Marcus came into the stall. "Couldn't resist trying him out, eh?" he said.

She gave him a guilty look. "I know I should've asked your permission first—"

He waved off her apologies. "You're better than I expected—and I expected a lot. But next time, use a saddle and reins, and make sure someone's there to pick you up in case he tosses you. He was in a good humor today."

"The next time?"

"How would you like to work with me? Katrine is five months pregnant. In a month she must quit to wait for baby. I will need a replacement until she can return." His eyes were shrewd as he studied her reaction. "Of course, I cannot pay you until you start with act, but the training, it will be free."

Vicky's first impulse was to accept, but immediately obstacles came to her. Since she was planning to leave the circus as soon as she collected her money from Jim, it wouldn't be fair to Marcus to go to the trouble of training her. Oh, she would love working with horses again—but not here. She loathed the circus—and besides, if she did start training, how could she possibly keep it from Jim?

He'd been so strange the past three days, sitting for hours with a can of warm beer in his hand, listening to country music on the radio, saying nothing, not moving. If she told him she intended to train for Marcus's equestrian act, he'd surely kick her out immediately, and then she'd never get the money he owed her. And how could she manage for a month without any pay coming in?

No, better to stick to her plans—but keep this option open as long as possible, just in case. . . .

"I'll think about it," she told Marcus. "There're a few problems I'll have to work out."

"You think about it. We will talk of it again in a few days."

CHAPTER 35

*O*NE OF THE DUTIES THAT MARA HAD TAKEN ON WAS COUNseling the circus people. Not that anyone called it that. They came for tarot card readings, and invariably they poured out their problems in the process. Sometimes she gave them advice. Other times, when she knew it would be useless, she simply listened, then made sure the tarot reading was optimistic. She never felt guilty about this. After all, in the course of her life, she had made every mistake in the book. Who was more qualified to counsel troubled souls?

Today it was the sixteen-year-old daughter of the Woroski family. She'd been slipping out to meet one of the roughies, a college kid earning summer money by working for the circus, and now he'd skipped out, leaving her pregnant and desperate and in a near-suicidal mood.

Mara advised the girl to tell her father the whole story, pointing out that he wasn't going to toss her out, no matter how angry he got, because the pony drill she did was the highlight of her family's equestrian act. Money, if not fatherly love, would keep Stephen Woroski from going too far. A slap or two, perhaps. But he wouldn't banish her—and she should keep this advantage in mind when she confessed her condition.

The girl stopped crying to listen, and when she left, she looked almost cheerful.

"Rosa, the gypsy mother hen, strikes again," Clinker said. "Doesn't it bother you, using that hokey-pokey to interfere in other people's lives?"

"It wasn't my advice. It was the cards speaking," Mara said virtuously.

Clinker made a rude sound. "Personally I think she should marry the Martini boy. He's always been crazy about her. Maybe she'll appreciate him now that she's been made a fool of by Joe College."

Mara stared at her. "That's what you used to call Jaime," she said.

"Yeah—but he didn't disappear after he got you in bed."

"Maybe I'm better in bed than that poor girl is."

Clinker's smile was absent. "You still miss him, don't you?"

"Oh, yes. People tell you that time heals all things, but it hasn't helped much with me."

She started to list other platitudes that weren't necessarily true when a half-forgotten memory suddenly surfaced, silencing her.

That afternoon when she'd still been nursing Vicky—Jaime had come into the salon from work, and because it was raining outside, his hair had glistened with beads of moisture. *Silver on gold,* she'd thought.

With the curtains drawn, and the sound of rain striking the metal roof of the pullman car, they seemed to be in their own private world. Jaime took off his wet clothes and put on his robe, then sat there, drying his hair with a towel and watching her as she nursed their baby.

She caught the expression in his eyes, and in the way that happened between them sometimes, understood what he was thinking. When the baby was asleep, back in her crib, she bared her breasts again and, without saying a word, offered them to Jaime.

He buried his face in their softness and suckled her, and as she felt the contractions start up deep inside her, she wondered dreamily what images were going through his mind. Was he a baby again, taking nourishment from his mother's breast? No, Jaime's mother had never nursed him, he'd told her once, because she'd been so ill after he was born. So was he pretending he was Vicky, his own baby, suckling her mother's thin, blue milk? It didn't matter. She was satisfying some need of his, and she was content.

Later, he made love to her but with a difference. Before their lovemaking had always been tempestuous, fierce and wild, but this time he touched her with reverence, and while she was moved by his tenderness, it was her old lover she wanted. So she'd teased him, taunted him, and in the end, he made love to

her with the frenzy that always aroused her own sexuality to a
feverish peak. . . .

The memory faded, and Mara sighed deeply. God, she did
miss him. How long did she have to wait until she was finished
with this life and was with him again? And what if his religion
was wrong? What if he was truly gone and this feeling she had
so often that he was still with her, watching over her, was only
a specter of her own mind?

She discovered her cheeks were wet, and she brushed the tears
away impatiently, conscious of Clinker's watching eyes. "I'm
hungry," she said brusquely. "It's my turn to fix lunch—which
means you get canned soup and toasted cheese sandwiches."

She went to open a can of soup, to put it on to heat while she
grilled cheese sandwiches. When the food was ready, she set up
the breakfast bar with silverware and napkins, put out the food.
They were almost finished when someone knocked at the door.
"Now, who could that be?" Clinker fretted as she went to answer it.

It was Vicky; she was wearing men's Levis and a man's blue
work shirt, knotted at her waist. To Mara's amusement, she still
managed to look as elegant as a high-spirited Thoroughbred.
"May I speak to Rosa?" she said.

Silently Clinker ushered her inside and then disappeared into
the tiny bedroom, closing the folding door behind her. From
where, Mara knew, she would be straining her ears to hear every
word they spoke.

"I don't want to bother you," Vicky said, "but—do you have
time to give me a reading?"

Mara hid her surprise. She knew who believed and who didn't,
and her daughter was a disbeliever. So why had she really come
here? "Why don't you sit down and tell me what's on your
mind?" she asked.

Vicky dropped into the chair opposite Mara. "It's—well, the
truth is, I need a job. I approached Michael Bradford about
working on the midway, but he turned me down. I thought—
would it be okay to approach one of the concessionaires directly? Some of them are independent, aren't they?"

"Where personnel is concerned, Michael has final say. That's
to keep grifters off the lot."

Color rose to Vicky's pale cheeks, and Mara realized it was
anger that made her eyes so bright. "Michael Bradford is de-
testable," she said fiercely. "He was rude and—and impossible!"

Mara hid a smile. "Most people think Michael is very polite," she said.

"Well, he treated me like I was dirt. It was all I could do not to tell him off."

"Just as well you didn't since he's Mr. Sam's son," Mara said dryly. "Are you hungry? Would you like a sandwich and a glass of iced tea?"

"I'm not hungry—but I would like the tea. It's so hot outside."

As Mara poured her a glass of tea, Vicky looked around the trailer, her eyes lingering on the shelves of books that reflected Mara's eclectic tastes. "Your trailer is very nice," she said, and unexpectedly, Mara was caught up in a wave of déjà vu. Jaime had used those same words the first time he'd seen the salon in her railroad car.

"It's furnished, on a very much smaller scale, like the pullman car of an artiste who used to be with the circus," she said deliberately.

"Oh? Who was that?"

"Her name was Princess Mara."

She saw Vicky's eyes darken, saw her fingers tightened around the glass in her hand. "You—you knew Princess Mara?"

"Oh, yes. We were very good friends."

"Did you know her husband, too?"

"Jaime? Of course."

Vicky took a long drink of tea, as if her mouth was dry. "She was with this circus? Somehow I had the impression she was with Ringling Bros—"

"Never. She was the star here—until her tragic death," Mara said, and despite herself, her voice was unsteady. "I knew her daughter, too. I changed that baby's nappies, fed her and rocked her, and sang her to sleep. Her father called her Princess Sunshine, and she's grown to be every bit as beautiful as she was as a child."

Vicky stared at her. It seemed to take her an inordinately long time to absorb the meaning of Mara's words. "You know who I am?"

"From the moment we bumped into each other on the midway. You're the image of your father, you know. Which is strange, because he was so masculine, and there's nothing the least bit boyish about you."

Vicky was silent for a moment. "I didn't know what he looked like until a few weeks ago, when I found an old album in my grandmother's desk.''

''An old album?''

''Photographs of my father since he was a baby.''

''I don't suppose you brought it with you, did you?'' Mara asked carefully.

''I only kept my father's college graduation picture. And a postcard with my mother's picture on it.''

Mara sighed, trying not to show her disappointment. What she wouldn't give for a baby picture of Jaime. ''Earl St. Clair shouldn't have done that, cut you off from your past,'' she said aloud.

''He's a cruel man. I didn't realize that until recently. Whenever he criticized me or punished me, he said it was for my own good, but he liked it, liked having an excuse to put me on restriction. No matter what I did or how well I did it, I could never please him. I expect it was his way of getting back at my parents.''

''And that's why you ran off with the first man who came along?''

''It wasn't like that, Rosa. I went to a carnival with a blind date. He was horrid. Jim rescued me, and offered me a job, which I turned down, but he did drive me back home. It was very late by the time we got there, but my grandfather was waiting up for me. He accused me of—of terrible things, and then he gave me ten minutes to pack and get out. I accepted Jim's job offer. I didn't have anywhere else to go, you see. But I think now I made a mistake. He frightens me sometimes—do you know what I mean?''

Mara felt a chill. Oh, yes, she knew what Vicky meant, all right. Was it true that things ran in cycles? It had been a jealous lover who had cost her the person she loved most in all the world. Was the pattern repeating itself here?

''You're afraid that he will harm you physically? Hasn't that already happened?''

''Yes. And I am afraid he'll do it again. I just don't understand him—it's as if I don't really exist as a person, that I'm just a symbol for something he desperately wants and can't have.''

Mara was silent. Was that what she had been to Leo—a symbol of something or someone that he'd lost? How strange that this girl, so inexperienced about people, had hit upon the truth—if she really had. Probably this man, Riley, was simply a drunk—and drunks had unpredictable tempers. . . .

"Some men think their women expect to be abused, you know," she said. "Have you invited that kind of treatment?"

Vicky's eyes flashed. "No. I told him that if he ever hit me again, I'd leave. He hasn't touched me since."

Mara nodded, relieved. "My best advice to you is to get out of that situation as fast as you can."

"I agree. Which is why I'm looking for a job. I was thinking about contacting the concessionaires on my own. But if Michael Bradford has final say, I guess that's out."

"You don't have any money?"

"Jim has never paid me any wages. He has a dozen excuses, but I'm sure now that he just wants to keep me under his thumb. And yet—he must know it won't work forever." She met Mara's steady gaze, and another flush colored her pale face. "I didn't come here to ask for money. Since you've told me what I wanted to find out, I think I'd better leave."

She rose, looking very young, very regal. "Thank you for the tea," she said, and then she was gone.

Clinker came out of the bedroom. "Well, she's a cool one," she said. "She never asked one question about her mother, and only one about her father. It's strange how two people who were raised by the same man could be so different. Jaime was so warm and outgoing."

"Maybe she's the same—underneath that shell," Mara said.

"Maybe. Or maybe she is more like her grandfather than you'd like to think." She gave Mara's stiff face an appraising look. "Let her go, Mara. She isn't a four-year-old child now. She has to make her own decisions, fight her own battles." When Mara didn't answer, she began clearing the card table. "We'd better get set up for business."

Mara sighed. "You're right. With times the way they are, the circus needs my twenty percent."

"But not enough for you to make that twenty-five percent?" Clinker said wickedly.

"Hell, no!" Mara said before she realized Clinker was teasing her. She stalked into the bedroom, but she already felt better. Clinker could always do that to her. A good friend was priceless—could she be that kind of friend to her daughter, even though they seemed to have so little in common?

She applied fresh makeup, including the lightly tinted cream she used to cover her scar. It didn't hide it completely, but it blended her skin tones. Once, she had grieved over the loss of what she had once had in such abundance, but no longer. Now she was used to the scar, had grown comfortable with it. Sometimes she even thought it added character to her face.

And why had she told her daughter that she'd known Princess Mara and Jaime? That she knew Vicky was their daughter? Why hadn't Vicky asked her more questions about her parents? There had been something there, a wariness in those cool blue eyes that deflected confidences. Was Vicky ashamed of being the daughter of a circus performer? Or had she refrained from asking any questions for fear she would find out her mother was a Gypsy?

Prejudices, no matter how other things changed, never really died out, and prejudice against Gypsies, some of them well founded, were as strong as ever. Why did it bother her more now than it had when she'd first left the tribe? Was it the knowledge that along with the Jews, the Nazis had murdered whole tribes of Roms in their concentration camps?

She finished dressing, then went to her jewel chest to select several gold chains to wear. Strange that she still loved the glitter of gold as much as ever. They said that food was the final greed of the aged, but she wondered if it wasn't love of personal adornment. How many old women had she seen with jewelry covering their wrinkled throats and fingers? And when they came in for their readings, those women, they always asked about money first, then health and family, and finally, way down the line, about a man.

Well, *she* wasn't old. She was still a handsome woman—wasn't that the word the reporter who'd done the article about her for *The Brunswick Herald* had used to describe her?

"You still have your juices, Mara," she told her image in the mirror. "Maybe you should do something about it."

"You talking to yourself again?" Clinker called.

"Why not? That way I'm sure of getting an intelligent answer."

Clinker made one of her tutting sounds. Mara discovered she was smiling again, her mood changed. Once she'd told Clinker that she kept her around for laughs, and there was enough truth in that for her to feel a little guilty now. Clinker was sure to disapprove if she took a lover again. Which wasn't going to stop her. Old Doc McCall's new assistant—he was fun to talk to, intelligent and warm. Fifteen years younger than she, but what did that matter? She didn't want to marry him, for God's sake. She'd seen him without his shirt, working over a horse, and he had a great body. She'd always been partial to men with good bodies—and he'd been giving her the eye ever since he'd reported in last month.

Clinker called her, reminding her of the time, and she tucked a stray strand of hair under her turban, got her big carryall, and went to join her friend.

Tomorrow, she promised herself. *I'll see if I can't start things perking with that young vet tomorrow.*

CHAPTER 36

*I*T WAS VERY DARK IN THE BAR, WHICH WAS HOW JIM PRE-ferred it. Since the saloon was close to the railroad tracks, most of the patrons there were railroad men, wearing their gray-and-white seersucker caps and overalls. In the yeasty darkness, he felt anonymous and, even when someone glanced in his direction, invisible.

He had come here to get drunk. Since it was a still day, he had nothing else to do, no reason to stay sober. Let Vicky take care of the goddamned dogs. It was her job, wasn't it? Let her clean up the urine stink and scrub down the van. He'd given her orders before he left, and while she hadn't argued with him or asked what the hell he was going to do while she scrubbed out the van, he'd caught that look, the one that said he was less than nothing, that as soon as she could, she was taking off.

And then what would he do?

He had lost her. He saw it in her eyes when she looked at him—which she did only when she couldn't avoid it. He read it in her slight shrinking away when he came too close in the cramped trailer, the tightening of her lips when he snapped the radio on to country music or a baseball game. He hated her. He loved her. He hated and loved her.

He'd been happy—well, as happy as anyone could be these days—before she came into his life. He'd worked hard to buy the dog act, just as he'd worked hard all his life. He'd never had it soft the way she had, living in that big house that looked like a hotel with her servants and horse cups and private school.

She thought her grandfather was rough on her? What a joke! She'd never gone hungry or been beaten with a belt until she thought she'd die, never been cursed until her ears stung.

So okay, she'd lost her folks young. He'd had both of his, and neither had given one hot damn for him. Any day he would have traded both of them for a good meal instead of the moldy hot dogs and orange Crush he'd been raised on—when he got lucky.

The day he'd finally lit into his old man and kicked his ass good had been the best day of his life. It still made him laugh, remembering the scared look on the prick's face. As for his ma—she'd always taken the old man's part. The two of them had fought like a couple of wild dogs, but it was them against everybody else, including him.

Things had been a lot better after he'd walked out, of course. He'd worked hard, earned pretty decent pay, gone without a lot until he had enough to buy the act. And then *she'd* come along and ruined everything. Even the fucking dogs took to her better than they did him. No wonder he drank. She made him drink. Always so hoity-toity. He saw the way she turned up her nose when he got close. Once she'd even told him that he needed a bath. Scrubbing herself all the time as if she'd been contaminated just being in the same trailer with him.

But God, he did want her. It was a torment, lying there every night, watching her give herself a sponge bath, wanting to grab her and throw her on the daybed. The flowery scent of her skin, the softness of her body, the feeling, like nothing else in the world, when he sank into her. Then the sweet release, like dying and going to heaven. Oh, yes, he wanted her. And he'd take her, too, whether she wanted it or not, except he knew what would happen.

So far and no further, that's how it would be. He would get all excited, reach that point just before he exploded, and then— nothing. The power would fade, his dick would shrivel, and then she would know that he was that pitiful thing, a man who could get it up but who lost it before he finished the act.

And what if she laughed? What if she called him what he was—a loser? He should have seen the writing on the wall that first time. Oh, she'd been excited enough at first. When he'd touched her down there, she'd been moist, hot, ready. Then he'd taken her and she'd stiffened up, froze on him, and for a brief second he'd been sure that it was all over for him, too, that he'd lost it. It hadn't happened that time, but it had begun there. Now—hell, he was afraid to try again now.

Maybe—what was it that blonde in Biloxi had said to him once? That he came on too strong, that women weren't like men, that the pump had to be primed? He'd thought she was smarting off, but maybe she was right—about some women. But what about all those dames who'd scratched and screamed like hell when they came? Vicky never came. She just lay there, letting him do all the work.

And that's why he couldn't perform these days. It was driving him crazy. *She* was driving him crazy. It had been so simple before he hired her. When he saw a broad he wanted, he came on to her. If she wanted it, okay, they got together and did it. And no one had ever complained before. Not that she complained. Oh, no, she just locked those lips together and looked at him. And it was like ice, digging into his guts, that look. It said that he was an ignorant jerk, that she was too good for him. It said that as soon as she could, she would leave him.

So he hated her. And he loved her—if love was this black obsession, this need to be with her, this grinding jealousy every time she was out of his sight. And the rage—he lived with it all the time now. Used to be, for long periods, he could push it out of his mind, this black cloud, edged with red, that had got him into hot water so many times. . . .

Jim finished his beer and went back to the trailer. Vicky was there, taking a sponge bath, using a galvanized pail for a tub. He went past her without speaking, got himself another beer, threw himself on the daybed, and pretended to fall asleep.

He watched her through half-closed eyes as she rinsed herself, the water glistening on her smooth shoulders and her tight little buttocks, and he wanted to put his hands on her, touch her, take her. She dried herself with a towel, then hung it up to dry. The gesture, the neat way she arranged the towel over the back of a chair as if to remind him that he seldom hung up anything, seemed like a slap in the face.

He got up, carefully quiet, and was upon her before she could turn. She swung her head around, her eyes startled, and it was the distaste on her face that was the final straw. He threw her facedown on the daybed and fell on top of her, and lust surged through him, a welcome return. Suddenly he was sure that this time he could do it—if he didn't think too much first. Her struggle to escape excited him at the same time it infuriated him. She was trying to deprive him of what he needed so badly and cheat him of his satisfaction. He hit her with his fist, then pushed her face into the pillow, held it there until she stopped struggling and went limp. Without bothering to take off his shirt, he stripped off his Levis, shoes, socks, and jockey shorts, then forced her thighs apart and fell between them.

His lust, hot and urgent, lasted until he penetrated her, and then it all went away. He collapsed on top of her, sobbing under his breath.

Because, if he was no longer a man, then what was he?

Vicky took a deep, gasping breath and began to struggle again. The rage boiled up inside him again; he grabbed her by the hair, flipping her over and lifting her half off the daybed. His fist crashed into her mouth, splitting her upper lip. The blood on her face gave him a savage satisfaction, and he raised his fist to hit her again. But this time, he pulled the blow before it landed. Like his lust, the desire to hurt had vanished, gone along with everything but the black sinkhole of depression.

He told himself that what he needed was a drink, and he flung himself off the daybed. He didn't look at her as he got the bottle he kept under the washstand, uncorked it, and raised it to his lips.

The sharp burnt-wood taste of whiskey flooded his throat, soothing him. This was one thing he could always depend on. It didn't condemn him, didn't look at him with scorn because of his faults, the things he lacked. It was his friend, his only friend, and he sat down at the table with his friend in front of him to get drunk.

Once, Vicky moved as if she meant to get up, but he raised his fist and made a threatening gesture. Her chin was covered with blood, and her eyes had a dazed look, as if she was half-out, but he felt no pity. She was to blame for his failure—and he meant to punish her. In a little while, when he was good and ready, he was going to fix her good. This time he'd make sure she never left him, because when he got finished, no other man would have her. But first—he needed some help from his friend. He couldn't do it unless he was all tanked up. . . .

He took out the pocketknife he always carried, snapped open the blade, and laid it in front of him on the table. Vicky's eyes widened as she looked at the knife. To make sure she got the point, he told her what he was going to do as soon as he'd finished off the bottle. If she screamed, he reminded her, no one would come to her aid. This was a domestic quarrel—and circus people don't interfere in other people's domestic business. Hadn't she learned that much by now? Of course, she was pretty stupid about some things. All that education, all those languages and stuff she'd learned, and for what? All of it useless in real life. Well, she'd be a lot smarter when he got through with her. When he was ready, he was going to fix it so she'd never look the same again. She'd go through life with people looking away when she passed, like they did Barky the Dog-Faced Boy.

And then she would have to stay with him, because who else would want her?

The room grew dark as the sun set outside, but he didn't bother to pull the light cord. He drained the bottle, tried to get up, but suddenly something heavy, an invisible weight, was holding him in the chair, and his eyes were closing, refusing to open. He slipped forward, his face buried in his arms. Well, he'd rest a minute, and then he'd get up and do what he had to do. . . .

After Vicky had left Rosa and Clinker, she'd taken her time returning to Jim's trailer. Because of the dogs, they had parked near the menagerie, not only for privacy, but to keep down complaints that the dogs' barking kept other people awake. It was still hot, even though the sun was almost to the horizon, and she stopped once to wipe her face with the edge of her sleeve.

Already she was regretting that she hadn't asked Rosa more about her parents—or maybe it was best this way. How could it change anything to know how they'd met or how long they'd been married before her father's death or if he had really been killed by her mother's ex-lover? So she'd held back, and she'd read disappointment and possibly disapproval in the Gypsy woman's eyes.

Vicky circled a row of empty holding cages that were parked near the menagerie tent. When she was in sight of the trailer, she stopped, reluctant to go on. For a while she stood in the lengthening shadows, wishing she had some other place to go.

Jim was becoming so strange—sometimes, when he stared at her, she was sure she saw madness in his eyes. A shiver ran through her, but she went on, hoping that he was still off somewhere with his buddies, drinking away the still day.

When she went inside the trailer, she was relieved to find it empty. She put on water to heat for coffee, knowing Jim would ask for it the minute he walked in the door. But he still wasn't home by the time it had finished perking, so she decided this was a good opportunity to take a bath without an audience. She poured water into the pail she used for bathing, undressed, and began her sponge bath.

Jim came in just as she was rinsing the soap off her body. After one quick glance, he ignored her, got a beer, and threw himself on the daybed. For some reason, it seemed to annoy Jim that she bathed every day. She only wished he did, too.

She had just finished drying herself and was reaching for her robe when Jim came off the sofa without warning and grabbed her.

The next few minutes were humiliating, painful, a nightmare. When she struggled, he hit her. Only half-conscious from the blow that rocked her head back violently, she was vaguely aware that he was raping her—no, he stopped almost before he began and flung himself off the bed. She opened her stinging eyes, and watched as he got a bottle of whiskey from under the washstand and began drinking from it. After a few minutes he took out his pocketknife and began to talk, his tone monotonous and even, making threats that froze the blood in her veins. She lay there, not daring to move, not even to cover herself, knowing that not only was she in danger of a beating, but that he meant to maim her. Then, just when she had resigned herself to the worst, Jim passed out. The anticlimax was too much for her, and she began to laugh, couldn't seem to stop. Knowing it was hysteria, she crammed her fist in her mouth, and it was the pain from her split lip that finally stopped her. She tried to think what to do next. For now, she was safe, but how long would Jim be out? She had to leave—but she wanted to take what was hers with her. Already he was moaning, muttering disconnected words.

"Ma . . . hurts . . . . hurts . . ."

Was he dreaming—or was he reliving some memory, dredged up from the past? Whatever it was, she didn't dare be here when he came to. Those threats may have been his way of controlling her—or they could have been real. Either way, she was leaving for good this time.

She started to sit up, and pain shot through her lip. She touched it gingerly, then looked down at the blood on her hand. She must look a mess—how bad was it this time? She slid off the sofa and began to dress, throwing on the first things that came to hand. She was stuffing clothing into one of her suitcases when Jim groaned and tried to raise his head. She stopped breathing, staring at him. He opened his eyes, but he seemed to be having trouble focusing them. "Want . . . drink," he said thickly.

Vicky swallowed hard. "You finished off the bottle—but I know where there's another one," she lied.

Jim tried to get to his feet, but couldn't manage it. "Feet," he said fretfully. "Something's wrong . . . feet."

"I saw a beast boy hide a bottle in one of the holding cages." She edged toward the door. "I'll go get it for you."

He heaved himself to his feet, and waggled his finger at her. "You trying trick me. . . I'm coming . . . with you. Gimme hand here."

Vicky took a couple of steps closer. When he made no move to hit her, she slid under his arm, supporting his weight as he sagged against her. The odor of whiskey made her nostrils flare, but she didn't make the mistake of showing her revulsion. She wanted to remind him that he was naked from the waist down, but she was afraid of setting off his temper again. Together they staggered toward the door, then down the steps and across the road toward the row of holding cages.

The menagerie tent was dark except for a naked light bulb that hung over the entrance. At the other end of the road, the trailers and vans and converted buses of the circus people were mostly dark, although she saw a light here and there. Most of the people were taking advantage of the still day to shop in town or take in a movie or go to a bar. There was no one in sight as she steered Jim to the first of the holding cages, up the metal steps, and through the open gate.

She lowered him to a pile of clean straw, then stood back, edging toward the door, expecting him to demand the bottle. Instead, he sank back with a groan, mumbled something about taking a little nap. He was already snoring when she left the cage, locking it behind her.

She hesitated, eyeing the key in the Yale lock. When he came to, he'd realize she'd tricked him, so she didn't want him to get out until she was off the lot. He'd be safe in the cage—one of the menagerie men would let him out in the morning. She took the key with her when she left.

Back in the trailer, she finished packing, but it was becoming increasingly hard to think. Her lip throbbed so painfully that she knew she had to do something about it. She went to the mirror and examined her reflection. The whole side of her face was swollen, already turning blue, and her lip was twice its usual size, still oozing blood where it was cut.

She cleaned up the cut, put a bandage over it to stem any
further bleeding, and then, realizing that no matter what happened, she'd need money, she picked up the jacket Jim had
discarded and went through the pockets quickly, but found nothing there except some change. She put the change in her pocket,
then searched Jim's jeans, found his wallet in his back pocket.

But except for a few dollars, the wallet was empty.

She sat down hard on the daybed, nursing her stinging lip
with her hand. She had taken it for granted that he kept his
money on him. None of the circus people used banks. Not only
were they suspicious of them, but they lived from payday to
payday.

Was Jim an exception? It was so unlikely, especially since
she'd never seen him with a bankbook, that she began searching
the trailer. If he had the money hidden, it would be some unlikely place—and she didn't have much time. Also, she had
cleaned every inch of the trailer many times. If there was a
hiding place, it was too cleverly hidden for her to find in a few
minutes.

She finally gave it up. Pretty soon people would be returning
from town—and someone, a guard or one of the beast boys who
bunked in the menagerie tent, would probably find Jim. Before
that happened, she intended to be on her way, money or no
money.

She was walking down the road, lugging her heavy suitcases
and heading toward the backyard area, which she had to pass to
reach the highway, when dizziness almost overcame her again.
She sat down on a suitcase, put her head between her knees, but
it didn't help much. Aware that she was in no condition to hitch
a ride into town, she tried to think what to do. The only thing
that occurred to her was to go to Rosa for help. The Gypsy
woman might not approve of her, but Rosa had been her mother's friend. Surely she would lend her a few dollars for bus fare
so she could get away before Jim came to.

When she felt steady enough, she rose, took a firm grip on
the suitcases, and went on, stopping to rest again when she came
in sight of Rosa's trailer. It was parked under a tree, where it
got the shade during the day. She wondered why it was that Rosa
rated a favored spot among the trailers and rigs owned by management personnel and star artistes who preferred to travel in
their own trailers rather than on the circus train.

One thing for sure. Rosa wasn't living from hand to mouth
like most circus people. Her trailer was an expensive model,

and the jewelry she wore was genuine. Vicky had been an audience too many times while her grandmother droned on about her jewelry, describing the history of each piece in her jewel chest, pointing out how to tell a flawed jewel or pearl from a perfect one. She hadn't paid a lot of attention to those lectures, their value being the attention of her grandmother, but she knew enough to recognize genuine pearls from fake.

It took the remainder of her waning strength to stumble the last few yards to Rosa's trailer. A haze obscured everything except what was directly in front of her. When she reached the trailer, she stopped to catch her breath—and to muster her courage.

A light showed at the window, for which she was grateful. At least she wouldn't be wakening Rosa out of a sound sleep. She knocked on the door, then waited. Waves of dizziness came and went, making it hard for her to stay on her feet. There was a squeaking sound as the door opened, and Clinker, wearing a cotton nightgown, looked out at her through the screen door, her eyes wary. Vicky tried to say something, but all that came out was a croaking sound.

Clinker's face grew dim. Vicky's feet slid out from under her and she slipped forward onto the ground like a rag doll that had just lost all its stuffing. She was aware of Clinker's voice asking questions, of being helped to her feet and led inside. She fell rather than sat on the down-filled cushions of the sofa, and her head lolled backward. The trailer whirled around her, a profusion of colors and shapes that made no sense. A laugh struggled up through her throat and escaped.

"Oh, Lord, just what we need—a drunk woman," Clinker grumbled. But she slipped off Vicky's shoes and lifted her feet onto the sofa, got her settled against a pillow.

"What's wrong with her?" Rosa's anxious voice said.

"Someone's worked her over—probably that asshole she lives with," Clinker said. "At first I thought she was drunk, but there's no liquor on her breath."

"You'd better get Doc McCall," Rosa said. A cool hand touched Vicky's forehead. "She's got a fever—and look at her face! I'll kill him! So help me, I'll kill the bastard!"

"Be careful. She's conscious—she's just got her eyes closed. I'll go fetch the doc, but you be careful what you say."

Things got very confused again. Vicky thought Clinker left the trailer, but she couldn't be sure, because when she opened her eyes, there still seemed to be two women in the room. Someone placed a wet cloth on her forehead. A hand brushed her hair back from her face.

She drifted into sleep, and her last thought was how strange it was that although the woman was speaking a strange language, she knew Rosa was telling her to rest and not to worry, that she was safe now.

The circus awakened early, even though it was the morning after a still day. In the men's sleeping tents, the cook boys crawled out of their bunks, yawning and scratching, and staggered off to the men's donicker, then to the cook tent to start coffee for other early risers, to set the tables in the short end of the cook tent with cutlery and china, to lay out coffee mugs, paper napkins, and plates near the steam table on the long side of the tent.

Cookie and his assistants arrived soon afterward to roll out biscuit dough and mix pancake batter, make oatmeal and Cream of Wheat, scramble eggs, fry rashers of bacon and slices of ham for the work crews—roughies and canvas men, elephant men and stable help, who in turn would feed and groom the menagerie animals.

As it happened, it was one of the cat men who found Jim. He had gone to clean out the holding cages that would transport the big cats from the menagerie tent to the Big Top for the matinee performance. When he reached the end cage, he found a half-naked man sprawled out on his back in the straw.

He began to grin when he recognized Jim Riley, who had decked him a couple of days earlier in a bar brawl. Okay, it hadn't been a smart move, calling Riley a bowwow because he had a dog act, but then, he'd been pretty tanked up. He sure hadn't deserved being worked over by that hotheaded son of a bitch. . . .

He was still standing there grinning when Jim awoke, groaning and clutching his head. He stared around with bleary eyes, and he looked so comical, with his bare shanks showing below his shirt, that the cat man began to laugh. Jim cursed him, and the more he did, the more the man hooted. The noise brought others. They broke up, too. Who could help it? The guy looked so ridiculous, standing there in the holding cage with everything hanging out.

The cat man was so busy laughing that he didn't notice when Jim Riley stopped cursing and just stood there, glaring at his tormentors. None of them recognized the madness in his eyes. They did try to find the key, which was missing from the lock.

But it wasn't until the menagerie boss turned up to find out what the racket was all about and ordered someone to break the fucking lock that they let him out.

By then it was too late. Jim had finally gone over the edge, into madness.

CHAPTER 37

VICKY'S FIRST AWARENESS WAS OF COMFORT, OF BEING ENveloped in soft warmth. The second was that this was impossible. She had left all that behind her when Grandpapa had thrown her out of his house. So she must still be asleep—only, how was it possible that such a pleasant dream could be so real? She moved her head, felt a throbbing pain in her upper lip, and she knew then she wasn't dreaming, after all.

Reluctantly she opened her eyes and discovered she was lying in a narrow bed, on a soft mattress, covered by a snowy white sheet. That's when she remembered Jim, the beating, his threats, how she'd locked him in a holding cage so she'd have time to pack her things and leave.

She pulled the sheet up over her face, trying to shut out the memory. She had escaped, but that didn't end it. Jim must be free by now. Surely someone had let him out of the cage. Was he sleeping off his drunk or was he out there with his hate, looking for her?

By now she should be on the highway, hitchhiking a ride away from Madison, away from Wisconsin. How long had she slept? And where was Rosa?

A sound made her start. She flung the sheet off her face, already poised for flight. But it was Rosa, pushing aside a folding door. She was holding a coffee mug, and as Vicky met her eyes, a memory stirred—a soft hand on her forehead, a soft voice, whispering words of comfort she couldn't remember. Had it been a dream?

Rosa set the mug of coffee down on the tiny table next to the bed. "How do you feel?" she asked.

"My lip hurts, but I'm fine otherwise," Vicky said, sitting up, only then realizing that someone must have undressed her, because all she was wearing was a thin batiste gown. She touched her lip with an experimental finger, winced when she felt the bandage there.

"Don't worry. It will heal," Rosa said briskly. She pointed to a narrow door. "The donickers's there. When you've had your coffee, we'll talk."

She was gone before Vicky had time to ask any questions. Vicky visited the donicker, a chemical type unfamiliar to her, then dressed quickly. Her purse was sitting on top of her suitcases, which filled most of the remaining space in the tiny bedroom. She got her comb, ran it through her hair, but she didn't bother with lipstick. It would look ridiculous with the bandage, anyway.

When she pushed aside the folding door, carrying the still-full coffee mug, she found Rosa and Clinker waiting for her, sitting side by side on the small down-filled sofa. Neither of them smiled as she dropped into a chair opposite them. Feeling unwanted, Vicky sipped the coffee, even though it was cold now. Her stomach rumbled, reminding her that she hadn't eaten for almost twenty-four hours, and when Clinker offered to fix her some toast, she accepted gratefully.

After Clinker had disappeared into the tiny pullman kitchen, Rosa said, "I have something to tell you." Although she was dressed and made-up for the day, she looked a little pale, and her eyes were pink, as if she hadn't slept well the night before. "But first I want to know what happened between you and Jim Riley."

Since Vicky didn't want to think about it, much less talk about it, it was a few moments before she said, "After I left here, I went back to the trailer. I was taking a bath when Jim came home. He grabbed me, threw me on the daybed. I thought he wanted to make love, but he struck me instead. He had been drinking heavily, and he was saying crazy things about cutting my face so no other man would want me. When he passed out, I got dressed and started to pack, but he woke up and wanted more whiskey. I told him there was some hidden in one of the holding cages across the road. When he went into the cage, he passed out, and I locked him in. Then I finished packing and came here."

"So that's how he got in the cage," Rosa said, nodding.

Vicky rose to her feet. "I'd better go before he finds out I'm here—"

"Sit down. He's no danger to you now," Rosa said. She fingered the strand of pearls at her throat, her eyes on Vicky's face. "Do you love the man, Vicky? Is that why you stayed with him?"

Vicky shuddered. "Love him? I hate him. I felt sorry for him at first, but now I just want to get away as quickly as possible."

"That won't be necessary. Jim Riley won't ever hurt you again." She paused briefly, as if bracing herself for her next words. "He's dead—he killed himself last night."

Vicky's whole body jerked. There was a buzzing inside her head, as if a bee had wandered into her brain. "Killed himself? But I never saw a gun in his trailer."

"He used a pocketknife."

"Oh, God—was it my fault? Did I drive him to it?" She was asking herself the question, but Rosa answered.

"He was crazy, Vicky. Before he killed himself—" her voice faltered briefly "—he killed the dogs."

The dizziness was back, but now it had a companion— nausea. It clawed at the back of Vicky's throat, threatening to overwhelm her. But strangely, the nausea also steadied her, because she fought against it, won out against the dizziness. When she was conscious of her surroundings again, she realized that Rosa was crouching beside her, holding her hand. She smelled of sandalwood, of something else that was spicy and familiar. Chrysanthemums, Vicky thought.

"I know this is a shock," Rosa said. "But it happened. There isn't anything you can do to change it. If you had stayed, he might have killed you, too. There was a note, addressed to Mr. Sam. He said he was tired of living, that he was taking the dogs with him. He didn't mention you in the note. So don't feel guilty. It had nothing to do with you."

"Nothing to do with me?" Vicky said incredulously. "Maybe if I had loved him—but I didn't. The only things I've ever really loved were my horses and my grandfather's borzois, and that wretched little mongrel that was always upstaging the other dogs in the act. My grandfather had it all wrong. He said I'd inherited my mother's hot blood, but my blood is as cold as ice. I hated it when Jim touched me—and it drove him crazy. That's why he took his own life."

She began to cry, and the thing that shamed her was that she wasn't crying for Jim. She was crying for Whiskey, a mongrel dog who had come from an animal shelter and who hadn't even been a registered thoroughbred.

After a while Rosa put two pills in her hand, handed her a glass of water, and told her to swallow them. She found herself back in Rosa's soft bed, and when oblivion hovered at the edges of her consciousness, she welcomed it as if it were her only friend.

When she awoke, the sun was high in the sky, and the trailer was very quiet. She lay there for a while, thinking of the future. She regretted the tragedy with all her heart, and if she could have gone back and done things differently, she would have. But she couldn't feel grief for Jim, only relief that she was still alive, still relatively unscathed. For the dogs, those innocent victims of Jim's madness, she felt a deep, wrenching sorrow. But they were dead and she was alive—and her problems hadn't gone away. She still was broke, and she still needed a job.

She said as much later, after she'd dressed and joined Rosa and Clinker, who were just finishing their lunch.

"I had a job offer from Marcus Bearnaise last week," she told them. "His wife is pregnant and he'll need an assistant in his act shortly. He's willing to train me—and it's something I can do. I've been showing horses since I was six. My wages won't start for a month, so I need a job to tide me over. I'm going to talk to Michael Bradford again. He can't have any objection now. After all, Jim is—is gone. If he gives me a job, he won't be interfering in a domestic matter."

Rosa glanced at Clinker, then looked away. "You want to stay with the circus?" she said. "I had the impression that you hate this life."

"I do hate it. But riding is something I can do."

"You won't get anywhere with Mr. Michael," Clinker spoke up. "He's as stubborn as his old man. And circus folks are superstitious—once they get it in their heads you're a Jonah, they'll cut you dead. I advise you to move on, find a job somewhere else."

Rosa gave her friend a long, cold look, but she addressed her next remark to Vicky. "Michael's trailer is parked at the end of this row, the silver one with blue shutters. He should be there—

he usually takes a nap in the afternoon. You may as well tackle him now.''

Michael seldom took a nap during the day, although everybody thought he did. What he really did was read, listen to his favorite jazz records, give his brain—and his voice—a rest. Today was no exception. He was reading Theodore Deiser's new novel, *The Bulwark*, while his record player belted out New Orleans jazz, but he was finding it hard going. There had been the investigation into Jim Riley's suicide, which had been a headache because dealing with local authorities, always so willing to believe the worst of ''carnies,'' usually was a headache.

Luckily, that business today had been cut-and-dried. Riley had left a note, saying he was tired of living, saying he'd killed the dogs because he hated their smell, their yapping, even the way they wagged their fucking tails. He hadn't mentioned the girl, Vicky, and since she was gone, no one else had either. The circus, as usual, had closed ranks against their common enemy, the silver badges, not because they cared what happened to the girl, but because the quicker trouble was covered over, the quicker forgotten.

Even though there was no indication of foul play, the local police chief had taken a hard-nosed stance, asking questions that had nothing to do with Riley's death. Knowing that he had the power to kick ass, he'd postured and blustered and made it hard on everyone. Madison, Wisconsin, was a good circus town, one that they wanted to play again, and so a few bills had found their way into the police chief's pocket and he'd finally closed his investigation. But not before he'd had the last word.

''You people better straighten up and fly right,'' he said. ''Next time you come this way, I don't want no trouble, you hear?''

Then there'd been the burial arrangements for Riley. The show would be moving out in the morning, and someone would have to stay behind to see that the man got a decent burial. Ordinarily the wishes of relatives would be honored, but Jim had put ''no relatives'' on his application form, so he would be buried in a local cemetery among strangers, his rigs sold to pay burial expenses.

The old man had been madder than hell, of course. He'd ranted about bad publicity, and even about bad luck. And then he'd dumped it into his, Michael's, lap.

''You handle it,'' he'd snarled. ''It'll be good practice for you.'' Before Michael could respond, he'd crammed his panama hat over his ears and left the Silver Wagon, leaving Michael to deal with the authorities, the disposal of the dogs, and funeral arrangements for Riley.

It seemed strange to Michael that no one had expressed even the most conventional regret. On his way to his trailer, when he stopped by the stake-and-chain wagon, where the workingmen hung out in their off time, one of Jim Riley's drinking cronies had ventured an opinion about what had set him off.

''It's that girl. He was crazy about her, but she didn't give a damn about him. When she up and left, it musta set him off. He shouldn't've killed them dogs, though. They was valuable animals. Someone else could've handled the act.''

The other men, squatting on the ground, drinking coffee and smoking, had nodded, and Michael had been left with the suspicion that none of them had been particularly surprised that Jim Riley had gone over the edge. Gussy Cootz, the circus blacksmith, said he'd seen it coming, that Jimbo'd had a funny look in his eyes lately, which hadn't meant anything to him then, but did now.

Luckily, circus memory was short. By the end of the season, Jim Riley would be all but forgotten. There'd be no entry about him in the route book Mr. Sam kept so meticulously for posterity, because entries he made were very selective.

Good houses were recorded as sellouts or straw shows, rotten ones—''playing to Mr. Patch''—as breaking even, while the real disasters, like their venture into Pennsylvania Dutch country two years ago, were listed as ''a little disappointing.'' And tragedies that might reflect against the show weren't recorded at all. Posterity was going to get a very distorted view of circus history someday—which wasn't so surprising for a profession that was built on fantasy.

So no one would remember Riley for long. He hadn't been popular or the kind of bigger-than-life figure who spawns legend or retellable anecdotes. He would disappear like a stone tossed into a pond. The circus might be like a small town in many ways, but not when it came to having a long memory.

Michael put the whole thing out of his mind as he fixed himself the one drink he allowed himself every afternoon—a shot of Kentucky whiskey in the same amount of water with a single ice cube from his minute refrigerator. It was one of his few indulgences, and he used it as a way of relaxing before the evening routine started.

Very early in the morning, the first section of the train would be moving out, and he would be leaving even earlier so he'd be in Ashton, Wisconsin, their next stop, before it arrived. One of his duties was hiring the temps, the extra laborers needed at every stop. With so many men just back from Europe and more recently from the Pacific, looking for work, there was little problem finding enough bodies. The problem was quality, hiring men who gave full measure for minimal wages.

He had returned to his book, when he heard a rap at the door. He said a word not meant for polite company, and laid his book aside. Everybody knew better than to disturb him while he was "napping." So it must be something important—and he'd had it with crises for the day.

He took his time going to the door. His whole body stiffened when he saw the girl standing there. Her face was badly bruised and she was wearing a bandage on her upper lip. He was surprised—and dismayed—at the quick thrill of anger that went through him.

"May I talk to you, please?" she said.

He opened the door and let her in. "What is it?" he said warily.

"I—I suppose you know what happened?"

"Concerning what?"

"Jim's suicide. They say he killed the dogs, too."

"You heard right. What happened to your face? Did Riley hit you?"

She nodded, blinking her eyes. "I packed my things and left—"

"But not before you locked him into an empty holding cage. The whole circus was there, laughing at him."

Briefly, anger flared in her eyes. "That bothers you—but not that I did it because I was in fear of my life?"

He had the grace to feel embarrassed, but he wasn't about to admit it. "Well, you don't have to worry about him now, do you?"

"You blame me because he committed suicide, I suppose. Well, I'm sorry about that. But surely you can see that he was crazy. Otherwise, he wouldn't have—" her voice thickened suddenly "—killed the dogs."

"Yes, I think he was crazy. Why didn't you leave him the first time he abused you?"

"I did try," she said stiffly. "I asked you for a job, but you turned me down. I had no money, no place to go, no friends to take me in while I looked for work. It's easy for you to say that I should have left, but then, you've never walked in my shoes, have you?''

He was silent, for the reason that she was right. But she could be more sorry, more—what the hell did he want from her? More display of guilt, even if she didn't feel it? ''What do you want to see me about?''

''I still need a job—''

''Someone put you up last night,'' he interrupted. ''Why don't you hit him up for a loan?''

She stared at him; a twitch started up in her cheek and he braced himself, expecting her to explode. Instead, she said, ''Is that job still open?''

''No.'' He hesitated, then dug into his pocket for his wallet. ''Here.'' He held out several bills. ''This is enough for bus fare back to Boston. You must have friends there.''

She stared at the money, then at him; a deep flush spread over her throat and face. She slapped the money from his hand, so quickly that he didn't have time to step back. The money fluttered to the floor around his feet.

''No, thank you,'' she said in her crisp Boston voice. She turned on her heel and fled, slamming the door behind her, and he stood there, knowing he'd been right to turn her down for a job, but also wishing he'd handled the whole situation differently.

Vicky returned to Rosa's trailer to get her suitcases. On the way, she replayed her encounter with Michael Bradford in her mind. One look into those cold, judging eyes and it should have been obvious that she'd be wasting her time asking him for a job. That remark he'd made her about getting money from her ''friend''—it hadn't even occurred to him that it might be a woman who had held out a helping hand. Well, the hell with him. She didn't need his job.

If Marcus Bearnaise's offer was still open, she would accept it, eat as little as possible to make the few dollars she'd taken from Jim's wallet last until she started drawing wages. As for transportation during hauls, she would sleep in Lo'Boy's stall on the train. No one would bother her there because of the stallion's reputation for wildness. She'd made it this far—and while she might be a little battered, she wasn't going to give up. One thing for sure—she would use the circus to get what she wanted, but she'd never forget—or forgive—the way she'd been treated—never!

CHAPTER 38

SEVERAL TIMES DURING EACH SEASON, MR. SAM MADE IT A point to call a grievance meeting. Tensions built up during the long, hot summers, and it was best to air any controversy that might fester, eventually erupting into real trouble. Usually the meetings were held in the ring tent on the second morning of a three-day run. Everybody, from the lowliest roughie to top management, was welcome to have their say, air their complaints, get their gripes off their chest. Most of the time the complaints were easily resolved, but sometimes a donnybrook would start up that took all of Mr. Sam's small store of patience to handle.

Today, along with a complaint (unjustified) about cookhouse food, a mix-up in berth assignments in the married couples' sleeper, and a feud that had erupted between sisters-in-law in the Alhambra risley troupe, two concessionaires, who wanted the same privilege spot on the midway, had gotten into it hot and heavy. After an exchange of insults, one had threatened to knock the hell out of the other—and things had gone downhill from there.

Mr. Sam had lost his temper and threatened to break both their contracts, a confrontation Michael had watched with mixed emotions. His father had finally settled things, although not to either man's satisfaction, but losing his temper hadn't helped any—a view Michael kept to himself.

As he walked back to the Silver Wagon with his father, Michael brought up his own grievance. "I hear Marcus is going ahead with his plans to train the redhead for his act. I wonder how she got to him."

"Marcus says she's a damned good horsewoman."

"She's trouble, Pop."

"Marcus is a perfectionist when it comes to his act. If she wasn't good, he wouldn't take her on."

The tolerance in his father's voice irritated Michael. "Or maybe he would. He has an eye for the ladies, and this one seems to know how to get under a man's skin."

"You include yourself in that, boy?"

"Hell, no." Something Mr. Sam had said suddenly got through to him. "You talked to Marcus about this?"

"He might have mentioned he was thinking about training the girl to fill in for Katrine."

"When was this?"

"Oh, could've been last week."

"And you didn't tell me?"

"Don't get your back up. I don't tell you everything I hear. Besides, it slipped my mind."

"Nothing slips that steel trap you call a mind. And I'm pissed off because I want her off the lot."

Mr. Sam frowned at him. "She wasn't to blame for what Riley did. He didn't even mention her in his suicide note. You ask me, boy, you're getting pretty high-handed these days."

"It's my job to stop trouble before it starts. And a woman like that can do more damage than a bull elephant in *musth*."

"Why don't you give her a chance? She's staying with Rosa, who will keep an eye on her, and if she can't hack it with Bearnaise, okay. But give the little lady a chance."

He stalked away, leaving Michael steaming. Give the little lady a chance—someone must have said that about Mata Hari at least once, and look what had happened.

Ted Bietecker, the canvas boss, hailed him with a complaint about two roughies who had blown the show, and he pushed the problem of Vicky to the back of his mind. It was an hour later, when he stopped by Jim Riley's rigs to see if they had been cleaned up as ordered, that he found the dog lying in the tall grass behind the trailer. It was the "scamp" dog of the act, a small terrier named Whiskey, although badly hurt, he was still alive.

Despite her assurances to Rosa and Clinker that she had a job with Marcus Bearnaise, Vicky was well aware that he might have changed his mind. As Clinker had pointed out, circus people, especially artistes who had dangerous acts, were superstitious, and no matter who was to blame for Jim's suicide, it was obvious that Vicky hadn't brought him good luck.

When she arrived at the corral the next morning, having spent the night on a cot in Rosa's trailer, Marcus was already there. "I heard you left the lot," he said.

"I'm still here. Is your offer still open?"

"Why would I change my mind?" he said, and went on to demonstrate the various talents and peccadilloes of his Arabians. Although no one came near them, Vicky was aware of curious—and maybe disapproving—glances in their direction.

Midway through the morning, Marcus's wife, a young, dark-haired woman in the middle stages of pregnancy, brought them a thermos of coffee. "So you're Vicky," she said in a thick German accent, looking Vicky—and her bruises—over.

"I saw your act last week," Vicky told her. "I'm afraid I'll be a poor substitute for you."

"Marcus thinks you'll do fine—did he tell you his idea for a new routine?"

"I have not yet told her, Katrine." Marcus drank from the metal cup his wife had handed him, then touched his upper lip with an immaculate handkerchief. "The idea came to me when I saw you riding Lo'Boy. You looked so—what is the word? Snooty? Suppose, I ask myself, this very elegant lady, wearing a fancy riding habit and a dashing little derby, trots out into the arena and does a few tricks, nose in air, and oh, so refined. Then this hobo fellow, wearing a wool cap and raggedy clothes, wanders into the ring, sees the beautiful lady, and is instantly smitten. He tries to get her attention by applauding loudly, but the lady snubs him. He persists, finally getting onto a horse and doing these very difficult tricks to impress her. Gradually she warms to him, and finally they end up on the same horse, doing tricks together. What do you think, *mon ami*?"

Vicky stared at him. Was *that* how he saw her, snooty and nose in the air? "I think it's a wonderful idea," she said diplomatically.

For the rest of the morning, they rehearsed basic procedures. Marcus was a perfectionist, but so was Vicky. Even if she had resented his impatient orders, the horses would have made it worthwhile. When Vicky finally returned to Rosa's trailer, she was hot and tired, but also feeling relaxed and comparatively content. Clinker was doing some mending, and Rosa, looking very exotic in an embroidered caftan and matching turban, had been reading a book; she laid it aside to smile at Vicky.

"How did it go?" she asked.

"Very well, I think."

"Come sit down," Rosa said, patting the cushion beside her. "Tell me about the rehearsal."

For the next few minutes, Vicky described the new routine Marcus was putting together. Rose listened silently, her eyes never leaving Vicky's face.

"Does Michael Bradford know you're taking Katrine's place in the act?" Clinker asked.

"If he doesn't, I'm sure he will soon. Enough people saw us practicing." She hesitated, then asked Rosa, "Will this cause trouble for Marcus?"

"Marcus is a star," Rosa said. "He would be offended if anyone, including Michael, tried to tell him who to use in his act. I guess you've noticed that he's something of an autocrat?"

"I noticed, I noticed," Vicky said ruefully, and Rosa laughed. But not Clinker.

"So where do you plan to bunk until you're on the payroll?" she asked.

"She's going to sleep here on the cot," Rosa said before Vicky could speak.

Clinker's lips tightened, and Vicky wished she were in the position to say that she had another place to stay. Since it wasn't true, she remained silent. Rosa rose, sighing. "Time to open up shop again. You coming, Clinker?"

"I want to finish mending this blouse," Clinker said, her tone testy. "I'll be along in a few minutes."

After Rosa left, the two women were silent. A fly buzzed at the window, a drowsy sound. The backyard was located near a highway, and the wind brought the odor of exhaust fumes through the door Rosa had left open. Vicky searched her mind for something to say, finally decided that silence was safer.

"You hadn't ought to take advantage of Rosa's good nature," Clinker said abruptly.

"I won't. As soon as I start drawing wages—"

"Here." Clinker reached in her pocket and thrust a handful of bills at her. "This is enough to get you out of here."

Vicky stared at the crumbled bills. "I don't want your money. I'll move into the women's sleeper as soon as I'm on the payroll. Besides—" she took a long breath, fighting not to show her deep hurt "—it's really none of your business."

"You're wrong. I've been Rosa's friend for a long time, and I'm not going to stand still for you hurting her. In fact, I'm going to talk to Mr. Michael about this. He's just looking for an excuse to get rid of you.''

She didn't wait for Vicky's answer. She started for the door, but before she reached it, she stopped, turned. "And don't you get any ideas about snitching Rosa's jewelry.''

After Clinker was gone, Vicky sat there, determined not to cry. This was the second person who'd tried to pay her to leave—why did Clinker dislike her so? It was almost as if she was afraid of her. Had she meant it when she'd said she would get Michael to evict her from the circus? Maybe, before that happened, she should talk to him and convince him she wasn't a trouble-maker—or whatever he thought she was. . . .

Michael's least favorite sideshow was the one that circus people called the ten-in-one, and outsiders called the freak show. It wasn't the anomalies he disliked. In the main, they were decent and hardworking, their only difference from ordinary people being the fact that they were curiosities whom others were willing to spend money to gawk at. It was the customers who disgusted him, which was why he usually avoided the ten-in-one top. But he'd heard rumors that there was trouble between Barky, the dog-faced boy, and Mr. Universe, the circus's current giant, and it was time to investigate.

Usually the giants were the most gentle of men. As if nature, in giving them great height and strength, had decreed that this was enough, they seldom were the cause of any trouble. Unfortunately Mr. Universe was that rarity among giants, a belligerent and arrogant man who considered himself superior to the other anomalies. He jockeyed for the most favored position just opposite the entrance, and took extra time during the show to tout the postcards that brought in additional money to the anomalies. Lately he'd been badgering Barky, who was timid, unaggressive, and not quite bright, making his life miserable.

Barky, his misformed face glum, was still on his platform, laboriously counting the change he'd made that afternoon selling postcards. Because he'd had no schooling (''Who'd wanta sit in a classroom with me, boss?'' he'd said to Michael once), he was having a hard time of it.

"Hi, boss,'' he lisped when he saw Michael. His upper lip was so badly cleft that when he smiled, he seemed to be all gums and teeth. "I hear the Big Top had a real good house yesterday. You think we're gonna make our nut here?''

"If the weather holds out, we will," Michael said. "What's this I hear about Mr. U. giving you a hard time?"

The smile slipped off Barky's face. "Aw, we get along okay."

Michael studied him doubtfully. Was he afraid of the giant? Or was this a circus man's natural instinct against causing trouble? "You don't have to take his shit, you know."

"He's just antsy 'cause he's been getting them dizzy spells again, boss. Some towner asked him if it was true that giants die young, and it's been on his mind."

Michael nodded, knowing he'd get no complaints from Barky. The anomalies might fight among themselves, but like the clowns, they were a tight-knit group who closed ranks when there was any outside interference. Well, he'd have a talk with Mr. Universe. He wouldn't warn him off Barky, but he would lie a little and say it wasn't true about giants dying young, that he'd know several who'd lived to a ripe old age. . . .

He had just left the tent when he almost bumped into Vicky. She was wearing a man's work shirt, tucked into snug-fitting Levis, with a wide belt around her narrow waist. Although she smiled at him, it was a tight smile, as if she was forcing herself to be pleasant.

"So you're still here," he said.

"Madam Rosa is putting me up until I start drawing pay," she said. "I began training with Marcus Bearnaise this morning. That's what I want to see you about—in private."

Michael realized that they had an audience, a trio of roughies who were repairing the ten-in-one's bally platform. "You can walk along with me to my trailer," he said tightly.

She followed him as he stalked away. They were stopped twice, both times by someone with a complaint, and each time she waited far enough away to be out of hearing range, a politeness that irritated rather than appeased Michael.

The trailer, which had been closed up for several hours, had a musty smell. He opened the windows before he pointed to a camp chair and told her to sit down.

"How did you get to know Rosa?" he asked.

"I met her while I was with Jim. That's where I spent the last two nights."

"Rosa is always taking in strays. Someday it's going to get her into a lot of trouble," he said sourly.

"She's been good to me, and I appreciate it. As soon as I can pay the fee, I'll move into the women's sleeper." She paused briefly, then added, "I won't cause any trouble. I promise I can get along with circus people—"

"But you don't like them much, do you? You think they're crude and uncouth. Well, you're right—and you're also wrong. Most of them are decent people who just happen to function best here, where they can get some respect. Some are true artistes who are only happy when they're performing in front of an audience. Others are misfits, outcasts from society—like the anomalies. Where else could someone like Barky earn a living? And some are hiding—from the law, from old sins, from themselves. The point is that no one cares as long as they pull their own weight. And they're leery of you because they have an instinct about people who look down on them. That's what will keep them from accepting you, not that business with Jim Riley."

"I don't look down on them," she protested. "And I can't understand what I've done to make you so anxious to get rid of me!"

Her eyes held hurt, but Michael wouldn't allow himself to soften. Oh, she was beautiful, all right. People bandied that word around so much that it had almost lost its meaning, but in Vicky's case, the word was justified. But she had no warmth, even when she was trying to enlist his sympathy.

In fact, it was time to order her off the lot, even if it meant trouble with Marcus and the old man. He opened his mouth to speak, but a whimpering sound, followed by a sharp little bark, stopped him—or maybe it was the shock on Vicky's face that stopped him.

"That's Whiskey!" she exclaimed. "You said he was dead!"

She didn't wait for an answer. She pushed past Michael and headed for the curtain that partitioned off his sleeping area. Michael followed her and watched as she bent over the terrier, who was curled up in a box beside Michael's cot. As she touched him, the dog whimpered again and tried to lick her hand.

She started to pick him up, but Michael stopped her. "Can't you see he's hurt?" he demanded.

She gave him a defiant look. "He's mine. Mr. Tucker gave him to me. Why didn't you tell me last night that he was here?"

"Because he wasn't here then. I found him near Riley's trailer this morning. Doc McCall had a look at him, says he'll be all right—provided he isn't moved."

She sat back on her haunches. "I'll leave him here for now, but when he's better, I'm coming to get him."

"That suits me. You can come see him whenever you like," he added, surprising himself.

"Does that mean—?"

"It means I'm giving you a chance—and a berth in the single women's sleeper. But the first time you cause any trouble, out you go. Say good-bye to your dog—I'll wait for you outside."

He pushed his way through the curtain and went to pour himself another drink. Funny how the woman kept throwing him off balance. He just couldn't seem to pin a label on her. Through the curtain, he heard the murmur of her voice. What was she saying to the mutt? That everything was going to be all right, now that Mommy was here? Her affection for the animal seemed genuine enough. Or did she realize the terrier's monetary value as a trained show dog? Was that why she was so fierce about collecting what was hers?

It was obvious that she'd gotten under Mr. Sam's skin. Since she was only a third his age, if that, this was something he intended to put a stop to. She had driven one man to suicide. He wasn't about to stand by and watch her take the old man for a ride, too.

For now, there wasn't much he could do about getting rid of her. But if she stepped out of line, if she gave him the least excuse, then out she went. He had to protect his own, didn't he?

CHAPTER 39

MICHAEL WAS SURPRISED TO SEE HOW MANY PEOPLE HAD come to watch the tryout for Marcus Bearnaise's new routine. This late in the season, since there was no longer much jockeying around for better positions on the big top's line-up, there should have been little interest. And yet the ring tent, when Michael arrived, was studded with small groups of people, not all of them artistes, who had obviously come to see how Marcus's new assistant would work out.

Despite himself, Michael felt a little sorry for her. This was the toughest audience Vicky would ever face—and they were already predisposed against her. Did Marcus know what he was doing? To Michael, it seemed doubtful that the cocky little Frenchman understood that Vicky hadn't endeared herself to most of the people here today.

On the other hand, the old man was obviously on her side— or was he? Right now he looked like a man who had just swallowed a gnat. Rosa, who was standing beside him, wore an enigmatic smile, while it was easy to read her friend Clinker's disapproving expression.

There was a stir near the entrance as Marcus, wearing a hobo costume that he'd obviously borrowed from one of the joeys, led the handsomest of his Arabians into the ring tent. He was smiling, obviously highly gratified by the attention.

Following close behind was Vicky, leading another Arabian. She was dressed in traditional riding clothes, her hair tucked under one of those stiff little derbies Michael had always thought so unattractive. What Vicky thought when she saw the crowd was impossible to guess. Even when she greeted Rosa, she seemed detached, as if she weren't really there. Strange that she had won the partisanship of a woman who was such a good judge of character as Rosa.

He watched as Vicky mounted the horse in a graceful movement that showed her perfect posture to advantage. She obviously was a skilled equestrienne, but show business demanded more than that. It took showmanship, timing, an acute awareness of what people expected for their money. No amateur, however well trained, could perform in a professional manner without special training. Since he'd deliberately stayed away from the corral where Marcus had been working with Vicky for the past three weeks, he had no idea what to expect.

To his surprise, Nancy Parker, who had done an acrobat act with her husband before she got pregnant, came forward to greet Vicky. Vicky's response was a smile so warm that he felt a small shock. So she could thaw out—was this the face Rosa and the old man saw? And why, since his own taste ran to warm, responsive women, was his own response to that smile so visceral?

He watched, unconsciously frowning, as Rosa, moving in that graceful glide that negated her limp, joined Vicky and Nancy

Parker. Rosa smiled up at Vicky. "Are you nervous?" Michael heard her say.

"Scared to death," Vicky confessed.

"Well, don't be. Everybody here wants the act to be good. The better the show, the better for the circus." Rosa hesitated, then added, "Everybody is nervous at a tryout. I remember the first time Princess Mara tried out. She was scared, just like you. But she came through like a trouper."

A look passed between the two women that Michael couldn't interpret. He could have sworn that Rosa had joined the circus years after the famous aerialist's death. It was obvious his memory was faulty. After all, he'd only visited the circus a few times before his mother sent him away to boarding school. He searched his memory, came up with an image right out of a fairy tale, someone all flaming red hair and deep green eyes, all sugar-spun candy and excitement. That had been Princess Mara, of course—strange he couldn't remember Rosa from those days.

"Okay," Mr. Sam called out impatiently. "Let's get this on the road. You ready, Marcus?"

Marcus, who was something of a dandy, looked out of place in rough clothing that could have come right off the back of a street bum. He nodded to Mr. Sam, then faded backward, away from the ring.

Vicky smiled and bowed, a little stiffly, Michael thought, and then began putting the Arabian through some fancy footwork. Michael knew what she was doing was much more difficult than it looked to the uneducated eye, but it wasn't show material, and he wondered what the hell was going on. Even when the pace quickened and Vicky began to do sideslips around the ring, she never lost that cool detachment. In fact, it bordered on haughtiness now.

And then Marcus appeared at the edge of the arena, weaving slightly and talking to himself. He pulled a bottle from his rear pocket, raised it to his lips. But before he could drink, he spotted Vicky, who was performing a fork-split, and his eyes widened dramatically, the bottle falling from his hand. He slapped both hands over his heart as if he'd been stabbed.

By Cupid's arrow? Michael thought, amused in spite of himself as he recognized a variation of an old high wire act in which a clown, seemingly drunk, wanders out onto the high wire and goes through a series of near catastrophes, ending up in a flurry of intricate moves. But this act had something new—the haughty personality of the girl involved.

First Marcus tried to mount the horse Vicky was riding on, was tumbled into an ignoble heap when it slid away under him. After a few more unsuccessful tries, he bumbled into the second horse, which he managed to mount only after several attempts. Meanwhile, Vicky was performing what Michael recognized as a surprisingly complicated routine, all the time seemingly unaware of the intruder who was trying so desperately to capture her attention.

After a few hair-raising maneuvers, her own horse bolted, and then it was Marcus to the rescue. When she gave him a kiss of gratitude, he went crazy and performed the complicated tricks he was famous for, and now it was Vicky's hands that were clasped over her heart.

It was corny, melodramatic, masterful, and the audience who had come with doubts responded with a satisfying round of applause when Vicky and Marcus, now on the same horse, rode off into the sunset, presumably to do even more exciting things. They came back for a bow, and as Vicky slid to the ground, smiling at the audience, Michael recognized something rare, even with top artistes.

Presence, he thought. *The little redhead has got stage presence. . . .*

He left the tent, deep in thought. So he had been wrong. She was a natural performer, and Mr. Sam's interest in her was professional, not sexual. And what about his own interest? He wasn't proud of his physical reaction when she'd smiled at the crowd.

Well, so be it. He wasn't going to do anything about it. In fact, he meant to stay out of her way—and hope that Katrine returned to the act as quickly as possible.

Vicky's first performance in the Big Top with Marcus was almost anticlimactic. Although the response from the audience was more than gratifying, she felt a little letdown. It took a while for her to dissect the feeling and figure out that she was disappointed because Marcus, while using her effectively in the act and capitalizing on her appearance, was also careful not to give her anything special to do that might draw attention away from his own performance. He was the star of the act, and he wasn't about to let her steal even a modicum of his applause. He had even shortened her solo at the beginning, coming onstage just as she had finished making her first round.

She talked it over with Rosa, as she so often did these days.

She had just finished having lunch with Rosa and Clinker, during which Rosa had talked about the circus, about the intricacies of relationships, the alliances and feuds between the artistes, the personalities and foibles of everyone from Mr. Sam to the lowest roughie.

Vicky knew what Rosa was trying to do, and she was grateful, even though she found it hard to muster interest.

"So how are you getting along with Marcus?" Rosa finally said, as if sensing her wandering attention.

"We get along fine—as long as I do everything his way," Vicky said. "I suggested a change today and he had a tantrum. Later Katrine took me aside and asked me sweetly not to argue with him because he was an artiste and very sensitive. You'd think he was a little tin god."

"To Katrine, he is. He's also something of a womanizer. You will be careful, won't you? You wouldn't want to cause any trouble between those two, would you?"

She had asked it as a question, and Vicky felt a wave of irritation. "No. I don't want to cause anyone trouble. What makes people here think the worst of me? Why do they see me as some kind of menace?"

Clinker shook her head. "It's your attitude, girl. You aren't very friendly, you know."

"It isn't my nature to—to gush over people. I guess I take after my father's side of the family," Vicky said, more hurt than she cared to admit.

"If so, it jumped one generation," Clinker retorted. "Your father made friends wherever he went."

"So maybe I inherited my bad traits from my mother," Vicky said bitterly. "I hear she was very vain."

"Oh, yes, she was," Rosa said, sighing. "Vain about her beauty, about her talent, her fame. And then—it was all gone in just a few seconds."

"Did you like her?"

"Like her? I'm not sure. But I did admire her. Too much, I think."

Clinker set her cup down with a clatter. "Mara was a wonderful person," she said, giving Rosa a hard look. "Oh, she liked to have her own way. I'll grant you that. But she was kind, a wonderful friend. And your father was crazy about her. You should have seen them together. Jaime was—the newspapers called him a golden boy, whatever that's supposed to mean. And Princess Mara was queen of this circus."

She fixed her eyes on Vicky, and her expression softened. "You were his Princess Sunshine. He used to put you up on his shoulder and race around with you shrieking and carrying on. Of course, you don't remember any of that. You were just two when he—when it happened."

She fell silent, and Vicky glanced at Rosa, expecting some comment. But Rosa was studying the tea leaves in the bottom of her cup as if she found something fascinating there. "Oh, yes, he did love both his princesses," Rosa said finally. "And how your mother did love him."

Vicky discovered a lump in her throat. "Tell me about my mother," she said impulsively.

During the next few minutes, as if the words had been bottled up, waiting to be released, Rosa described a girl, a Rom, who, at an age three years younger than Vicky, had been disowned and thrown, stark naked and beaten, into a ditch by her family, who had fought her way, step to step, to fame and fortune. She told Vicky how her parents had met, the word "Harvard" sounding strange in her faintly accented voice, told how Jaime St. Clair had given up his birthright for a girl who couldn't write her own name, and how they had loved each other, been happy together. She skipped over Jaime's death, but she did describe Mara's years of widowhood, how she'd reached the pinnacle of fame before fate snatched it all away in one split second.

When she was finished, Vicky's eyes were full of tears, tears for her parents, who had died so young—and also for herself because she'd been cheated out of so much.

"Are you ashamed of your Romany blood?" Rosa asked abruptly.

"It doesn't seem to have anything to do with me," Vicky said, a little surprised by the question. "After all, I'm only one-fourth gypsy, you know."

If her answer disappointed Rosa, it didn't show. She began making brisk noises about getting back to the midway, a signal, Vicky knew, that it was time for her to leave.

As Vicky walked slowly toward the women's sleeper, she thought over the past hour. The woman she vaguely remembered from her childhood—had that been her mother or her English nanny or perhaps Rosa herself? Well, she was glad she'd had that conversation with Rosa. In the future, she would do her best to be more friendly, even though she didn't expect to be with the circus more than a few more weeks. Not that she hoped to make any new friends. But it would be more pleasant if she

could feel as comfortable with these circus people as she did
with horses—or with Whiskey, her dog.

CHAPTER ·40

*D*URING THE NEXT FEW WEEKS, AS *OCTOBER* DREW TO A
close and the end of the season drew near, Vicky found a
new, if guarded, acceptance among the other circus personnel.
Not that they were overly friendly. But they exchanged greetings
when their paths crossed hers, even stopped to pass along circus
news, and when she went into the cook tent to eat, for the first
time she felt comfortable, joining the other artistes in the short
side of the tent.

She had been assigned a berth in one of the sleeping cars,
which she shared with a motley group of single artistes, and
although she was more of a spectator than a real participant of
the lively exchange of conversation during the hauls between
engagements, she no longer felt an outsider. Rosa's friendship,
too, she soon discovered, was enough to get her accepted by a
large proportion of the circus. Only Michael, who pointedly
ignored her, made her feel unwelcome.

Although she resented his attitude, she did have to admit that
she could find no fault where Whiskey was concerned. Because
pets weren't allowed in the women's sleeping car, she'd been
forced to leave him with Michael. Since he'd told her in an
offhand way that he would be busy from ten to twelve every
morning, so he expected her to do the honors and give the dog
his midmorning walk then, she got to see Whiskey every day.

Her friendship with Nancy, who was gloriously pregnant now,
continued. Like Rosa, Nancy's whole world revolved around
the circus, and the stories she told about her childhood with her
parents' acrobatic troupe were both fascinating and, to Vicky,
mystifying.

"You don't feel as if you were cheated, not having a normal home?" she asked one day. They were working on the baby's layette, and the morning sun, streaming in through the windows of the trailer, revealed Nancy's slightly puffy face and swollen ankles.

Nancy looked surprised. "Cheated? Why would I? I've never wanted anything else."

"What would you do if—" Vicky stopped, but Nancy understood.

"If I couldn't work the mats anymore? Why, I'd ask Mr. Sam for another job. I wouldn't like it, you understand, but I wouldn't want to live outside. I'd rather take ducats or even pearl-dive for Cookie and get dishwater hands." She giggled suddenly. "As long as I keep my figure, I can always get a job in the hooch show."

"You have to be joking!" Vicky said, shocked.

"Yeah, I'm kidding. I'd hate to earn my living wiggling my backside, even if Johnny would let me. But it's honest work. Mr. Sam doesn't allow any touchy-touchy stuff."

Vicky shivered. "I'd hate it."

"Well, it's part of the circus. Of course, if I ever caught Johnny flirting with one of the dancers, I'd cut off his balls with a butcher knife."

Vicky laughed at the picture of Nancy, who was so petite despite her pregnancy, tackling her muscular husband with a butcher knife. As Nancy went on to relate a bit of gossip about a run-in Mr. Sam'd had with a sticky-fingered concessionaire, she reflected how lucky it was that she'd made a friend her own age in this unlikely world.

A month after Vicky joined Marcus's act, Nancy delivered a seven-pound son, whom she named Alexander. He was an active, bouncy baby, who fascinated Vicky, maybe because she'd never been around a baby before. Although she was squeamish about changing diapers, and handed him back quickly to his mother when he became wet, she loved to hold him whenever she got the chance.

She was baby-sitting while Nancy was off doing some shopping when a strange thought came to her. Most women dreamed of having children of their own, but she never had. While she'd been sleeping with Jim, the possibility that she might get pregnant hadn't worried her, yet when he was drinking heavily, he'd sometimes failed to take precautions. Even so, she'd never missed even one period. Was she barren? Or was she so frozen inside that she simply didn't provide a warm, welcoming place for a baby to take root?

And wasn't she lucky not to be bearing Jim's child right now? She tried to think of him, of what had happened, as little as possible. That part of her life was over, and she'd learned a lesson from it—and from her grandfather. She'd never again let a man have such power over her.

And no, she no longer felt guilty that Jim had died by his own hand. Why should she? She didn't feel anything at all. As for why she sometimes woke up crying in the middle of the night, that had nothing to do with Jim. Women did cry over nothing at all sometimes, didn't they?

Rosa was just finishing with a customer, an acne-pocked teen-age boy, obviously there at the urging of his buddies, who were outside right now, snickering and acting silly, the way teenagers did these days. She was giving him safe advice, that he should be careful about choosing his friends because some of them were out to get him into trouble, when Michael stuck his head through the tent flap. He mouthed the words, "I want to talk to you," and then ducked out again. She got rid of her customer, who left looking a little sheepish, and Michael came in, grinning.

She smiled back with affection. She'd always been partial to Mr. Sam's kid, ever since, barely out of diapers, he'd followed his father around winter quarters like a solemn little owl. She'd never met his mother, but she'd heard that she was a cold fish. Luckily, Michael showed none of his mother's coldness—except to Vicky.

"How's business?" Michael asked, which she knew was a social rather than a business question.

"Slow. This hot spell is keeping them home."

"Yeah, it's a worry—along with the shortages and other things. Tires for the trucks are really getting to be a problem—and parts are practically nonexistent. I'll be glad when the factories get geared up again for civilian products. Luckily, everybody seems starved for entertainment. If I can just convince the old man to modernize the show, we could have a great season next year."

"How modernize it?" Mara asked, frowning.

"People are tired of the same old routines. They're seeing all sorts of exciting things in the movies—they expect more flash for their money. Tradition is fine, but there's no reason not to use a few stage devices in the acts. Even that old fogy Joe Lasky is going that way. I hear he's hired himself a stage production manager. What we need is something to draw them in, then knock them dead.''

"Well, if you can move Mr. Sam, you're a miracle man. Of course—'' she gave him a sidelong glance ''—he did go for Marcus Bearnaise's new routine.''

"Nothing new there. It's just a variation of the old tramp high-wire gag.''

"Maybe it's Vicky that makes it seem so fresh. She really does have class, don't you think?''

The question, although it sounded innocent, didn't deceive Michael. Rosa was partial to the girl—he wished he could figure out why.

"She's a good equestrienne,'' he conceded. Then he ruined it by adding, "Why do you stick up for her so much?''

"Let's turn that around. Why do you dislike her?''

Michael regarded her with gloomy eyes. There was no clear answer to her question. Why did he dislike Vicky—or was that the right word? *Cautious* was a better one. *Wary* even more accurate.

"How can you explain why you like this person, dislike that one?'' he said. "The first time I saw her, I knew she meant trouble. I felt it in my bones.''

"I'm the one who's supposed to have sensitive bones,'' Rosa said. "You're supposed to be the hard-nosed businessman. Why don't you give her a chance? Everybody's talking about this antagonism between you two.''

Michael shrugged, dismissing the subject. "I came to tell you your new canvas's come. The tent men can put it together tomorrow after they set up the big top in Peru—''

They talked about the new top, and then Rosa offered to tell Michael's cards, something she did regularly, with him refusing most of the time since he didn't believe in such things. Today, to his surprise, he found himself agreeing to a reading.

He expected Rosa to hand him the fancy tarot deck she used for her customers, but instead, she dug out a small wooden box from the voluminous purse he'd never seen her without, extracted a tattered tarot deck, handed them to him to shuffle.

Hiding his amusement, he did what she asked and gave them back with the not so funny quip that now he knew what to get her for Christmas—a new deck of cards. Rosa didn't smile at his joke. Her expression very grave, she laid out the cards, stopping to touch each card and consider it carefully. When she finally raised her eyes to look at him, the expression on her face made him want to squirm.

She tapped a card, a man standing at a table upon which four objects were displayed. "This is your card—the Magician."

"What, not the Emperor?" he joked.

"The Magician represents new projects, a man who has the willingness to accept the changes offered by life," she said, as if he hadn't spoken. "In reverse, it shows a man who sacrifices love and warmth for ambition. This will lead to unhappiness, even though money and fame are attained."

"Then I'm glad the card isn't reversed," he said, not altogether joking.

Again, she ignored his remark. She pointed to two cards near the end of the spread. "Strength—this card shows the strength of love," she said. "See the maiden with the flowers in her hair? That eight lying on its side above her head is the sign of infinity. This could be your fate—a good woman who will support you all your life. And the Lovers card next to it predicts the fulfillment of love. We Gypsies give this card the meaning of a desire to keep love virginal and fresh. It's also a warning that you can't have your cake and eat it, too."

"*That's* an old Gypsy saying?" Michael said. Rosa, the matchmaker—who would have thought it? And just who did she have in mind for him? Surely not her protégé, Vicky. What a disaster that union would be. Talk about the Magician card in reverse. . . .

Rosa tapped a highly colored card, an upside-down man with a long beard. "The Hermit card, reversed. I see family trouble—close to home."

"What's unusual about that?" he said, laughing. "I'm always fighting with the old man."

"And this card, the Sun in reverse—it clouds the future. Trouble—yes, there will be trouble in the circus."

"What kind?" he asked, interested despite himself. He'd long suspected that the wisdom Rosa's cards dispatched was a reflection of her own shrewd observations and knowledge of human nature, and also her own private sources of information. If she has chosen this way to pass along something he should know, so be it.

"Not fire. Not a blowdown. Trouble with outsiders, I would guess. But it will work out. Nothing too serious or lasting. More aggravation than anything else." She hesitated, then added, "I

understand the Lasky Brothers show is playing Peru this weekend."

Michael lost his amusement. "How did that happen? Their
itinerary calls for Indianapolis."

"A cloudburst last week washed out the lot they'd contracted
for. So they're making a wildcat stop in Peru, hoping to cover
their nut."

"Where did you hear this?"

"One of their advance men is an old friend. He dropped by
to say hello and, I suspect, to give me a friendly warning. He
doesn't care much for Joe Lasky. He called him a hard-ass."

"You should be working for military intelligence, Rosa. The
war would've been over three years earlier."

"I do have my sources," Rosa said, looking smug.

"I wonder what Lasky hopes to gain. He must know we have
the contract for the old county fairgrounds, which is high and
dry and in a central location. The only other lot big enough to
accommodate a circus is a mudhole in the river bottoms. So we
have a big advantage."

The next morning, when the advance trucks and the first section of the train arrived at the fairgrounds, Michael found out
how wrong he'd been. The Lasky show was not only there, it
was already set up for business, having arrived the day before.
The contract Joe Lasky produced had been signed by His Hon-
or, the mayor of Peru, and it predated by two weeks their
own, which had been signed by the town's city manager. It did
no good to complain to the mayor.

"Some kind of mix-up," he told them blandly. "So sorry . . ."

In the end, it was the Bradford Circus that set up in the riv-
erside lot, after padding the muddy spots with thick layers of
expensive straw. The Indian summer weather remained torrid,
and the spare crowd that came were out of sorts, unresponsive
to the show in the Big Top, the sideshows, and even the usually
popular midway games and rides.

It wasn't just the customers. The circus people reacted predictably, and there was muttering about getting those bastards,
of paying them back.

"Trouble in town last night," Mr. Sam told Michael when he
reported in the next morning. As usual, he was already there
working on his books when Michael came into the Blue Wagon.
"Some of our boys mixed it up with those Lasky hooligans. I

don't know who started it, but that hothead Murphy is in the
hospital with a knife wound in his shoulder. He claims he was
minding his own business, taking a leak in the alley behind a
saloon, when three of the Lasky guys jumped him. My guess is
that he started it—the dumb mick.''

Michael swore. ''How bad is it?''

''He'll be back to work in a few days. Lucky he's got a thick
skin.'' He gave a sour grin. ''He managed to put two of them
in the hospital, too. Hope he doesn't decide to finish them off
before he gets out.''

Michael swore again.

''This is bad business, Michael. Leaves a sour taste in the
locals' mouths. It could burn this town for us. We'll have one
helluva time getting another permit here. We can't afford much
more of this kind of trouble.''

Michael nodded agreement. ''Maybe we should have a pow-
wow with Lasky and try to clear the air.''

''The only thing that would clear the air is a shootout between
me and that prick. He's been after my hide ever since I stole
your mother right from under his ugly nose. I wonder why I
went to so much trouble. The challenge, I guess.''

Michael was silent. He knew his mother's faults—possessive,
hard to please, self-centered—but she *was* his mother, after all.

His father gave him a sidelong look. ''Sorry, boy. Shouldn't've
said that. My fault as much as your mother's, the trouble between us. Guess I should keep remembering that she gave me
one helluva good son.''

Michael hid his surprise and merely grinned, but he thought
about those words often in the following days. Was the old man
mellowing? Did that mean he had changed in other ways? He
would find out during the winter, when he approached him about
changes he was convinced they must make if they hoped to keep
afloat in the changing postwar world.

It should have pleased Michael that he seldom saw Vicky as
they moved through Indiana and then into Illinois. Oddly, he
felt disappointed—and for no reason he could pin down. It
seemed obvious that if he wanted to avoid her, she also wanted
to avoid him, and that she was doing a good job of it. He knew
she was still walking her dog every morning, and from the weight
Whiskey was putting on, she was also bringing him treats. He
thought of leaving a note, reminding her that fat dogs were
unhealthy dogs, but restrained himself. Whiskey did, after all,
belong to her. Once, when he stopped by his trailer to change

into town clothes for an interview with the entertainment columnist of a local newspaper, she was there—but she slipped away with only a nod for greeting. He was surprised—and alarmed—by his own disappointment. And why did he think about her so often? Was he in danger of making an ass out of himself, just as so many other men undoubtedly had—including that poor obsessed fool, Jim Riley? Well, there was no way he was going to fall into *that* trap. Hell, she wasn't even his type.

Chicago was in the midst of another unseasonable heat wave when they arrived for a week's engagement, one of the last of the 1945 season. Although the sun had been up only a few hours, the air was already sultry, overladen with moisture from an early morning shower.

Michael, who was overseeing the unloading of the flatcars, filling in for John Paley, the trainmaster, who was down with a bad cold, edged his forefinger inside the rim of his cap to wipe away the sweat. Like the rest of the circus, he had hoped for a favorable weather report, but it was the same old prediction—just enough rain during the night to raise the humidity, accompanied by another sweltering late fall day.

Unless the heat wave broke, this engagement would be a bust. If this was the trouble Rosa's cards had predicted, it was a humdinger. . . .

One of the canvasmen, a middle-aged man who was a chronic grumbler, came up with a complaint, this time about the noise in his sleeping car. With his new position of assistant manager, Michael had his finger into anything and everything. Since he acted as liaison between Mr. Sam and his employees, someone was always bending his ear with gripes. Mainly it was small problems, but some were potentially bad—such as the shortage of sawdust. A muddy midway was an uninviting one—and they didn't need that problem at this point in the circuit.

He settled the sawdust problem, after several phone calls and the calling in of a favor from one of the local distributors, then decided to reward himself with a cup of coffee in the cook tent. He had just gotten settled with his coffee when he was accosted by Konrad Barker. The elderly equestrian director looked even more out of temper than usual as he plopped down opposite Michael.

"Marcus is screaming to high heavens. That redheaded girl didn't show up for rehearsals this morning. She wasn't in her berth in the women's sleeper last night, either. You think something happened to her?''

Michael maintained a cool smile. "Maybe she took off with some towner."

"Naw, I don't think so. Her duds are still in the sleeper. Would she leave her clothes behind?''

"You're asking me? You know her better than me."

"Well, she's a quiet one, and those are the ones who can surprise you. Maybe you're right and she met some towner with a bankroll. It's happened before. Marcus will just have to improvise."

"He can do a single. Cut it to six minutes and lengthen the ballet with some extra web work," Michael advised. He hesitated, then added, "Anyone ask Rosa about the girl? She's pretty tight with her."

"Yeah. Marcus talked to her. She got all upset. Said she hadn't seen Vicky for a couple days."

One of the work crew bosses came up with a voucher for Michael to sign, and when he turned back, the equestrian direction had left. Michael returned to work, but he couldn't get Vicky out of his mind. Had she gone off with someone and missed the train—or had she been in an accident? Surely she wouldn't leave without her clothes and the pay that was due her tomorrow. Well, he'd speak to the old man about it. Maybe he knew what the hell had happened to the woman.

CHAPTER 41

ALTHOUGH THE EVENING PERFORMANCE HAD BEEN WELL received, Vicky wasn't satisfied. Again, Marcus had stumbled out into the arena early, drastically shortening her opening routine. It wasn't that she was hungry for applause, but it just wasn't fair that he would cut into her solo time. Her routine was every bit as difficult as his, and she resented the high-handed way he'd been treating her lately, as if he were jealous of the attention she got from the audience.

Her mood went from bad to worse when she returned to the dressing tent she shared with a dozen other women. Two of the ballet women, who had just discovered they were being romanced by the same man, got into a fight and rolled on the floor, scratching and biting and eventually knocking over a dressing table and scattering powder throughout the tent.

Totally disgusted, Vicky changed quickly, took her costume to the wardrobe tent, and then went strolling aimlessly down the midway, reluctant to return to the train. She was passing a souvenir stand that was already packing up for the move to Chicago when a familiar voice hailed her.

"Hey, Vicky—wanna go into town with a bunch of us for a little dancing and a beer? We've got three hours before the second section pulls out for Chicago."

It was one of the Wesky twins, brothers who did a spectacular double trap act. Tom was a redhead with the compact body of an acrobat, who blithely went in and out of girlfriends, as mercurial as the wind.

"Sounds like fun," she said, surprising herself.

Later, when so many of them piled into Tom's car that the overflow was forced to utilize another sedan, she knew she'd made a mistake. She wasn't really in the mood for dancing—and she didn't even like beer.

The roadhouse they stopped at was undeniably seedy. Most of the tables were packed, the cigarette smoke hanging in layers near the ceiling, and the blare of a country band was overwhelming. Since it was impossible to talk in a normal voice, they ended up shouting at one another, which didn't help Vicky's already jangling nerves. But she tried to be a good sport, to laugh when it was expected, to drink a little of the beer Tom bought for her. Since the dance floor was so crowded, she refused his invitation to dance, pleading fatigue, and he took it good-naturedly and went off to ask another girl.

When he didn't return, she wasn't offended. After all, it wasn't a real date—and he had come here to dance. After a while, when the noise got to be too much, she slipped away to the ladies' room.

There was a small lounge, shabby and not very clean. She dropped into a wicker chair and closed her smarting eyes. She may have dozed; when a group of chattering and giggling women, most of whom looked to be even younger than she, invaded the lounge, she realized she'd been there much too long. She ran a comb through her hair, repaired her lipstick, and went outside, only to find that a strange group was occupying the table where she'd been sitting.

She realized immediately what must have happened. Tom had been off somewhere with his dancing partner, and with two cars, each group had assumed she was with the other. Or maybe they hadn't even noticed she was missing. Whatever the reason, she was stranded here—and she had no idea where "here" was.

She checked her purse, found a dollar and some change in her wallet, certainly not enough for taxi fare back to the fairgrounds. She bit her lip, staring around. The place, which had seemed run-down but friendly enough when she was with her own group, now took on a sinister air. Which, she told herself firmly, was stupid. All she had to do was call a cab, and when she got back to the fairgrounds, she could borrow enough to pay her fare.

But it wasn't that easy. When she called the number the bartender gave her, the dispatcher, a woman, asked her destination, and when she said the city fairgrounds, the dispatcher told her she would have to pay her fare in advance.

"We been stiffed too many times by you carnies," she said.

Vicky hung up, knowing it would do no good to point out that she was with a circus, not a carnival. She looked around, hoping to see someone she knew, but they were all strangers. A couple of men, sitting at the end of the bar, had been openly listening to her phone conversation. One leered at her.

"Hey, lady, you wanna ride? We'll take you out to the fairgrounds, and it won't cost you one red cent." He winked at the bartender. "Clyde here will vouch for us, won't you, Clyde?"

The bartender grunted and went to draw a beer for a customer. Vicky tried to ignore the men, which didn't go over very well. "Say, don't be snooty. We know how you carny dames are. You sell it out there, why not here?"

She didn't answer; she looked around, found an empty table, and settled herself with her back to the bar. The waitress came up, and she ordered a Coke. When it came, she sipped it slowly, trying to think what to do next and fighting her rising panic. Already the first section of the train would have moved out—the phone in the Silver Wagon, which Mr. Sam controlled, would be disconnected by now, so it would do no good to phone.

Behind her, the music blared, and her head throbbed in time

with the beat. She glanced around and discovered she was the focus of several pairs of male eyes. Did they think she was a hooker, plying her trade?

The waitress came up again and she explained her problem. The woman, who was plump and no longer young, shrugged. "You'll have to talk to the boss. I'll send him over."

She flounced off, taking the empty glass with her, and a few minutes later, a heavyset man came over to the table. "I hear you got troubles. Your friends dumped you, huh? Can't understand that, a looker like you. But what the hell—I get a lot of business from you carnies. Maybe I'll stake you to cab fare. But you'll have to wait until we're closed. Got too much to do now to worry about anything else." His eyes flicked over her. "How about I send over a drink? You look like you could use it."

Vicky started to say, "No, thank you," but she didn't get the chance. There was a loud crash near the bar, where two men were squaring off at each other. They began exchanging blows, and when another man tried to intervene, both of them turned on him, and suddenly the room exploded with fighting men, and women's screams.

The club manager cursed and hurried away. A beer bottle whizzed past Vicky's head and crashed against the wall behind her. She took cover under the table, feeling not only afraid but also very much aware of how ridiculous she must look.

When she heard a police whistle, she breathed a sigh of relief, only to realize a few minutes later, when she was herded along with the rest of the people into a van, that her relief had been premature. Somewhere on the way to the police station, she discovered her purse was missing, but when she complained to the policeman in charge, he told her to shut up and sit down.

The station house where the van was unloaded swarmed with Saturday night brawlers, prostitutes, harried policemen with arguing or sullen people in tow, and she was hustled into a small holding cell with several other women. One by one they were let out to be questioned by policemen sitting behind battered desks. Vicky's interviewer was shuffling through a stack of papers when she sat down on the splintery chair beside the desk.

"Name?" he said, his voice bored.

"What's the charge, officer? I didn't do—"

"Disorderly conduct, inciting a riot, assault and battery," he interrupted. "Now, you going to make this easy on both of us or do you want to go back into the holding cell until morning?"

"But I didn't do anything. I was minding my own business when the fight broke out. I didn't know anyone there—"

"So let's add soliciting to the charges," he said.

"Now, wait a minute. I'm not a—a—" But she couldn't get out the word.

"So what were you doing alone in the crummiest dive in the North Division? Come on, lady, your name and address."

She started to give her name, but stopped. What if there was some kind of permanent record? No, she didn't want that. Since she didn't have any identification with her, she could give any name.

"Vicky Brown," she said.

"Address?"

"I'm with the Bradford Circus," she said.

This time he looked her over, his eyes speculative. "Yeah? What do you do?"

"I'm an equestrienne," she said. "I was with several others from the circus. We stopped to have a beer. I went to the ladies' room, and when I came out, they had gone. We came in two cars, so I suspect they each thought I was in the other car—"

"Yeah, yeah. I gotta hand it to you, lady. That's pretty good. So where's your ID?"

"I lost my purse when the place was raided."

"Personally, I figure you were soliciting. Which is what I'm putting down."

"But I'm telling the truth!" she protested.

"So tell it to the judge in the morning. He just might believe you."

He got up and motioned for her to follow him. She bit down on her lip to keep from screaming. Some of this was bad luck, being in the wrong place at the wrong time, but some her own fault, too. She never should have gone with Tom Wesky. Was it possible that she'd been stranded on purpose? Was it some kind of practical joke?

At the end of a long hall, the policeman threw open a door and motioned for her to go inside. Although the room wasn't really a cell, its single window was barred. She turned to make one more appeal to the policeman, but he was already closing the door. The sound of the lock, clicking into place, made her shudder, but it was the sight of the large, muscular woman, sitting on a bunk and watching her like a stalking cat, that turned her blood to water.

* * *

Rosa got Vicky's telegram the next afternoon. She was frantic with worry, had been since she realized Vicky was missing, and yet it was a minute before she could bring herself to rip open and read the Western Union envelope one of the roughies had brought to her trailer.

She had expected bad news, tragic news even, but not this. Vicky had been picked up at a roadhouse, charged with soliciting, something so unlikely that it was almost laughable. The telegram was an appeal for help.

"Arrested for soliciting during fight in roadhouse. Need bail money." It was signed Vicky.

She started to call Clinker, who was visiting a friend in the next trailer, but an idea came to her, stopping her. Vicky was obviously safe enough, locked up at the police station. So maybe she could use this business to good purpose. What had Vicky's cards said? That there would be trouble that ended in triumph? Of course, she was taking a chance. It could backfire and make things worse. On the other hand, life was a crap shoot at the best of times, wasn't it?

She went into her bedroom, got an Ace bandage from a drawer. Sitting on the edge of the bed, she wrapped it around her ankle, taking care to make it look neat and professionally done. Only then did she call Clinker and ask her to fetch Michael as fast as she could.

Michael was in a temper. Although he valued Rosa's friendship highly, he resented the errand he'd been forced to do for her. Why had Rosa insisted that he be the one to bail Vicky out of jail? Oh, she'd given a lot of reasons, and some of them had made sense at the time, but now that he'd had time to think it over, he just couldn't buy her assertions that as assistant manager, he could best represent the circus and bail Vicky out.

"I'd go myself in a minute," Rosa said, looking very pale with her bandaged foot resting on a hassock. "But I got so upset when the telegram came that I fell and sprained my ankle."

"What about Clinker? I'm busy as hell, Rosa—"

"I'm calling in a marker, Michael. You owe me one for that time you got in trouble with that showgirl and I covered for you with Mr. Sam."

"Hell, that was five years ago, Rosa!"

"Then it's about time you paid your debt. Anything at all, you said, if I remember correctly."

In the end, he agreed to make the trip back to Kokomo, but

he wasn't happy about it. Soliciting, for God's sakes! That cold fish? Of course, common wisdom said that hookers were cold sexually. So maybe she picked up a few extra bucks that way, although—hell, he didn't believe it! Vicky might be a lot of things, but he'd bet his last dime that she wasn't a hooker.

He found himself grinning. He hated to admit it, but there was something satisfying about this business. St. Michael to the rescue—and he was going to enjoy watching her face when he walked into that police station. . . .

As it happened, Rosa's belief that he could just waltz in and set things right was overly optimistic. The judge, a dried-up man with a sour expression, obviously disapproved of circus people—or maybe people in general. Not only did he make Michael pay Vicky's full fine on the spot, but he made him directly responsible for her future conduct. It didn't seem to occur to him that both of them would be out of his jurisdiction in a matter of minutes.

During the whole proceedings, while the judge lectured Vicky about her lack of judgment for going to a notorious roadhouse, she stood with her eyes downcast, her face very pale. Whatever had happened to the solicitation charge, it wasn't mentioned. The fine was for disturbing the peace, and Vicky looked so humiliated that Michael was ashamed of his former inclination to gloat. Vicky was suffering—and he didn't like it. Not one bit.

She didn't speak until they were in his car, driving away from the municipal parking lot, and only then when he asked her if she felt okay. Her answer, that she felt fine, thank you, was so obviously a lie that he didn't probe. In the sullen light of an overcast day, her skin had a grayish look, and there were dark circles under her eyes.

They were passing a motel when he impulsively turned in and parked. "You need some rest. You can't go back to the show looking like a ghost," he said gruffly.

He considered it an indication of her state of mind that she didn't argue with him.

After he'd registered, he slid back under the steering wheel. "Rosa sent you a change of clothes," he said. "Why don't you take a shower, then crawl into bed and get some rest? I've got some things to do—you'll have the cabin to yourself. I don't suppose you slept much last night?"

Vicky shuddered, couldn't seem to stop shaking. "It was a nightmare," she said, her voice choked. "The woman I was locked up with—she was a pervert. She tried to—"

She began to cry, and he put his arm around her, turned her face in to his shoulder. Something very strange was happening to him, something he was wary of. He had always known that he wanted her. God, how could he not know that? But he hadn't realized until now that part of his antagonism was self-defense. Right now he wanted to tilt windmills for her, wanted to protect her and make things right. Most of all, he wanted to get his hands on whoever had left her stranded in that lousy roadhouse.

"Who was it?" he said. "Who took you to that place?"

She straightened, wiped her face on her sleeve. "It wasn't anyone's fault. There was a whole gang of us. I went to the ladies' room, sat down to rest my ears from the noise, and must have dozed off. When I went back, they were gone. There were two cars—I'm sure each one assumed I was in the other car. Then there was a fight and the police came, took everybody to the station house. I lost my purse somewhere, and that's why they held me. I'm lucky they let me send that telegram."

"So that's what happened. Well, you'll feel better when you've had a shower and a nap."

The motel was luxurious, one of a well-known chain. When Michael switched on a light, the room sprang to life, looking welcoming and even cozy. "Make yourself comfortable," he said. He set down the small overnight case Rosa had given him. "I don't know what she packed, but I expect it's appropriate. I'll be back in a couple of hours. You going to be okay now?"

Listlessly she nodded. "It's going to be so difficult, getting new identification," she said fretfully. "I wonder what happened to my purse. I don't remember seeing it after the fight."

"Did you have much money in it?"

"No, just a couple of dollars. I was trying to talk the nightclub manager into vouching for me so I could get a cab back to the fairgrounds when the fight started."

"Well, it's all over now. Try not to think about it," he said. "Why don't I bring back some food? Are hamburgers and fries okay?"

"Don't bother bringing me anything. I'm not hungry." Her voice was stiff as she added, "I'll pay back the fine as soon as I get paid."

"I'm not worried," he said. He started for the door, and as he passed a mirror that hung above a bleached oak chest, he caught a glimpse of her image. She was crying again. He started on, only to change his mind and turn back. When he put his arms around her, she leaned against him briefly, then pulled away to give him a wobbly smile.

"I need a bath," she said. "I don't think I'll ever get rid of the smell of that place." She hesitated, then added, "I really am grateful. I don't know why it's always so hard for me to say thank you."

"Maybe you didn't hear it often enough when you were a kid." He pointed to the bathroom. "Take a long soak. Meanwhile, I'll see if I can find something better than hamburgers."

"I love hamburgers," she said. "I was just being bitchy."

A few minutes later, Michael found a phone booth and started calling around, finally locating Mr. Sam in the dining room of his favorite Chicago hotel, where he was having a late lunch with another circus owner. Not to his surprise, Mr. Sam grumbled about his absence. Since Michael had decided to keep the whole incident to himself, he laid it off to having met "an old friend" and getting tied up longer than he expected. Mr. Sam grunted, then told him to get his butt back as soon as possible or he was going to dock him a week's pay.

Michael called the fairgrounds, was gratified to find that the phone in the Silver Wagon had been connected. He left a message for Rosa, saying all was well. Later, he stopped at a variety store, bought a lipstick, a comb, and a small leather handbag with a matching woman's wallet.

Since he'd only been gone for thirty minutes, he stopped for a drink at a neighborhood bar, then looked around until he found a Chinese restaurant that had takeout. Not knowing Vicky's taste, he bought a variety of dishes, enough for several people, and went back to the motel.

When he let himself in with his key, the radio was playing softly, and the clean, medicinal odor of Ivory soap hung in the air. Vicky was asleep on the bed, the sheet pulled up to her chin. She had washed her hair, and it had dried to an auburn tangle around her face.

She awoke as he was setting the cartons of food down on a nearby table. She looked at him so shyly that he had to smile. What had happened to that cool, measuring expression that always made him want to either kick her or kiss her? Was it a defense? Was this the real Vicky, vulnerable and uncertain? If so, he was in real trouble, because he wanted this one even more than he had the other one.

"You've been very nice," she said. "I—I want to thank you for not asking a lot of questions."

"Well, there is no way I'm ever going to believe you were soliciting," he said brusquely.

Strangely, this seemed to annoy her. "Why not? Don't you think I could attract any customers?"

"That isn't what I meant. I can see you doing a lot of things, but not that. You're too—uh, fastidious. And before you start throwing things, that's a compliment."

She stared at him for a long moment as if weighing his words. She smiled, and his breath caught sharply.

God, lady, don't you have any sense at all? Don't you realize that we're alone here in this motel room, and from that pile of clothes on the floor, you're naked under that sheet, and I'm a man. God knows, I'm a man . . . and I've never felt more like one than right now.

He saw the expression on her face change, and only then realized he said something, God knew what, aloud. He groaned, turned away from the surprise—or was it fear?—in her eyes. He had almost reached the door when he felt her hand on his arm, holding him back.

"I know you're a man," she said softly. "I've been very much aware of it for a long time."

"What does that mean?" he said hoarsely.

"I was protecting myself. Being careful."

"What you're feeling right now is gratitude. You know that, don't you?" he said, not because he wanted to but because it was only fair to point out the truth.

"It's not gratitude. I know Rosa sent you, that you probably resented it. But I want—hold me, Michael. Just hold me for a little while and maybe I can get that place out of my mind."

He put his arms around her and pulled her up close. She needed comfort; anyone who offered sympathy would have sufficed right now. He knew that, and for a little while this was enough. And then it wasn't enough. He pressed his hand against the small of her back, and his aching, needing body stirred, giving him away. He thought she would pull back then, but she settled up against him with a sigh, mutely giving him permission to go on.

He knew he was taking advantage of her, of the fright she'd had, but that didn't stop him. Nothing short of an earthquake could have stopped him. Her body, so supple and yet so firm, fit his perfectly. Heat rose to his head, and his body tingled, hardened even more. He knew he was lost when she raised her arms and slid them around his neck.

"I want you, Vicky," he said against her ear. "Oh, God, I do want you, Vicky."

Vicky heard his words, but she didn't answer. Something was going on inside her body that filled her with wonder—and disbelief. She'd felt desire before, had gone through the usual adolescent blossoming and sometimes had been moved by Jim's kisses, but this was different. This made her knees buckle, turned her body incredibly weak. It frightened her, too, even while it lured her, and in the end, overwhelmed her. She liked the pressure of Michael's erection against her thigh, liked it even more when she moved slightly so the hardness pressed against the soft flesh between her thighs.

Michael groaned like a man in pain. He kissed her, and her lips opened to him, allowing him to plunder her mouth. The male odor of his body was an aphrodisiac, promising mysterious delights to come. His hand tightened on her back, forcing her even closer, and her thighs yielded, opened to the pressure as if she'd lost all power to resist. Not that she wanted to. She wanted more, wanted all he could give. She was so absorbed in her own reaction that she hardly noticed when he steered her toward the bed and lowered her onto the mattress.

His hand trembled as he touched her lips, tracing their outline with his fingertip. "I've dreamt about your mouth," he said. "I thought I was going crazy, having erotic dreams about you."

He pulled away the sheet she'd wrapped around her, and his breath whistled in his throat as he stared down at her naked body. He touched her breast with his fingertips and then began a slow exploration of her body, touching her breasts, the hollow of her stomach, the soft mound of her pubic hair.

When he went further, when he used his tongue to arouse her, she trembled violently, frantic that he would stop, that somehow she would be cheated as Jim had always cheated her, taking her so far and then no further.

Michael seemed almost to be reading her mind, because he murmured reassuring words against her hot flesh, promising her that it would be as good for her as it was for him.

Wanting to please him, she fumbled for his belt, but he pushed her hands aside. "I don't think I can hold back if you touch me," he said, his voice strained.

She watched him hungrily as he undressed. His body was lean, well shaped; his chest was smooth, with little hair, but he was all man, a man in the throes of sexual excitement, and the sight of his arousal filled her with a hot sweetness.

He kissed her, and her skin tingled and grew even hotter. She hadn't known how sensitive the small hollow behind her ear, the flesh beneath her breasts, the crease behind her knee, were until he kissed her, stroked her there.

And there were other erotic places. She gasped, then relaxed, when he fondled her buttocks, then traced a pattern with his fingertips between her thighs. When he took even more liberties, the feeling was so delicious, the little bursts of pleasure so irresistible, that she moved frantically, straining toward fulfillment.

But again he murmured against her hot flesh, telling her to relax, to let it happen, to trust him.

When he took her, he moved with skill, with long, slow strokes that told her that he would satisfy her first. The surge, when it came, was sharp, overwhelming, and she lost all touch with reality as she was caught up in pure, erotic pleasure. The rush ebbed, then soared again, something so astonishing that she forgot to breathe.

Above her, Michael cried out, saying her name, and she knew he had reached his own erotic pinnacle. She felt a sudden tenderness for him, a pride that she could bring such pleasure to this hard, tough man. She also knew that this wasn't a one-time thing with her, that she wanted more from him. Why hadn't she realized this earlier? Had she been afraid to let down her defenses for fear he didn't feel the same way? He'd made his contempt for her so clear—why was she assuming that this part had changed?

Michael collapsed upon her. He rolled to his side, then to his back, taking her with him until now she lay on top of him. He stroked her hair back from her face, touched the tip of her nose with his finger as if putting his mark on her.

"This won't do, you know," he said. "Too many things could happen. We've both got too much pride and too much temper. I think we should get married so we have to stay around and work out our differences. What do you say to an elopement? Say, today if we can get a license?"

Rosa was drinking her afternoon tea, her bandaged foot propped up on a stool, when she heard the news. It was Clinker who brought it—which was no surprise. Clinker always was first to know when anything, good or bad, happened around the circus.

And this was good news, so good that she closed her eyes against the rush of thankfulness. She had been given the thing she wanted most, to see her daughter safe, the daughter she'd failed so terribly. God had been good to her, even though she hadn't really deserved it.

"So you pulled it off," Clinker said, and there was a grudging admiration in her voice. "How did you know?"

Rosa opened her eyes. "It was in the cards."

Clinker snorted. "Don't give me that malarkey. You made a couple of shrewd guesses. But I have to admit they fooled me. I would have sworn those two hated each other's guts."

"Oh, ye of little faith! If you're so sure it's all nonsense, why are you always after me to tell your cards?"

"Never mind that. You deliberately sent Michael after Vicky because you hoped this would happen. Well, they're married, but I'm not sure you did them a favor. Mr. Sam is clumping around, madder than hell because they didn't ask his permission."

"That won't last. He wants grandchildren. And he admires Vicky. I think he's a little afraid of her, but that isn't bad. They'll get along just fine."

"You're sure of that, are you? Happy endings and all that. Well, it can be dangerous, poking your nose into other people's lives."

Mara's smugness fled. "You're right. And this is the last time I interfere. It's hands off from now on. Let them solve their own problems." She hesitated, thinking. "It won't be easy for either of them. Vicky hates the circus—and it's Michael's whole world. Maybe Michael will be enough for her. Maybe she'll have a family and be so busy, she won't mind this life."

"Or maybe she'll turn Bradford Circus into some kind of Junior League," Clinker retorted.

"Not with Mr. Sam around, she won't."

"Or Michael. He can handle her," Clinker said, nodding.

"Well, it's going to be interesting, the immovable object meeting the irresistible force."

"Meaning?"

"Never mind. I'm betting on Vicky."

Clinker's eyes gleamed. "How much?"

"Say—a fiver?"

"Make that a tenner and you've got a bet," Clinker said.

BOOK THREE

Michelle's Story

CHAPTER 42

ALL NIGHT LONG, THE SINGING OF STEEL WHEELS AGAINST
steel rails and the swaying of the pullman car had soothed
Michelle's sleep. It was the silence that awakened her. She
opened her eyes, and even before she was fully awake, she was
already smiling.

It was still very early. She could just make out the gray rec-
tangle of the window at the foot of her berth. She snuggled down
into her comforter, thinking of the day—no, the days, weeks,
months!—that lay ahead. Because *this* time Daddy had won, and
this summer, just like her brother, Danny, she would travel with
the circus until school started up again in the fall.

There was another reason for rejoicing, too. Danny, who had
just celebrated his sixteenth birthday, seldom included her in his
plans these days. She understood this, but she resented it, too.
After all, she was fourteen now, and even when she'd been
younger, she'd never tattled on him. Not only because he
would've been furious with her, but also because, if she had,
Papa would have given him a good thrashing. And she didn't
want that.

She knew, for instance, that Danny had been responsible for
the fire that burned down the horse barn in winter quarters. He
and one of the grooms had been smoking in the loft when the
hay caught on fire. The groom had run away, never to be seen
again, but Danny had stayed to fight the fire. He'd saved the
horses, and everybody, including Papa and Grandpa Sam, had
treated him like a hero. Only she, who had heard Danny and
his friend talking up in the loft earlier and smelled the smoke,
knew the truth.

Since the horses had been saved, she'd held her tongue when
the absent groom got blamed for the fire. After all, he *was*

guilty. He just wasn't exclusively guilty. Later, she'd told Danny what she knew, and instead of being grateful, he'd threatened her. Her feelings had been so hurt that she'd cried, and then he'd been sorry and said, "Okay, I owe you one, Carrots."

Michelle smiled into the grayness of dawn. Today, Danny was going to pay up. Whatever he was planning when they reached Atlanta, she was going to be in on it. Not that he was very happy about that.

"I know you've got a bet on with Bobby Dugan," she'd told him last night just before they'd boarded the second section of the circus train. And because she didn't much like Bobby, who worked in the cook tent and who had a funny way of eyeing her, she didn't try to hide her disapproval. "If you don't include me—well, I might tell Papa."

"That's blackmail," Danny said. Unlike Michelle, who had inherited their mother's red hair and blue eyes, Danny was dark-haired and brown-eyed like their father, whom he already topped by two inches. As usual, his smile was lazy, good-natured, but Michelle watched him warily, knowing how mercurial his temper could be.

"Maybe so, but it's no worse than burning down a barn," she retorted. "I heard you talking to Bobby this afternoon during the blessing." The blessing, by Father O'Rourke, was a tradition on the day the circus train left Orlando for its summer tour. "You've got something planned, and I want to be in on it."

"You little sneak," Danny said. "One of these days those big ears of yours are going to get you in trouble."

"You owe me one for not telling Papa about the fire," she pointed out. "And all I'm asking is to go along."

"You'd just get in the way."

"No, I won't," she said eagerly, sensing that he was weakening.

"Well—okay, but I won't be responsible for you. If anything happens, you're on your own."

"I can take care of myself."

"Just don't say I didn't warn you, rat-fink," he said darkly.

Michelle grinned at him. The insult didn't bother her, now that she'd gotten her own way. Although she knew he would die before admitting it, Danny had a soft spot for her. In return, she adored her big brother. True, he teased her unmercifully sometimes, but he often covered up for her, and a couple of times he'd even taken the blame for things she'd done, like when she'd let her cat sleep in the house one rainy night and he had pissed all over Mama's Persian rug.

The thought of her mother eroded some of her good spirits. Why did Mama always seem so—well, disappointed in her? No matter what she did or how hard she tried, she just couldn't please her. Her final report card had been all A's except for one B+, but all Mama had said was that she'd have to work harder on her French next year.

That quarrel between Papa and Mama she'd overheard last week, for instance—it had been about her, and Papa had taken her part. She hadn't been able to sleep, and she'd come downstairs to get a glass of milk, hoping that would help. She was passing the living room, what Mama called the drawing room, when she heard them talking.

The house, so big and empty when her father was gone, always seemed so much smaller when he was home. Which was strange, because he wasn't all that large. His voice, although he never spoke loudly, seemed to fill the empty corners and erase the echoes.

Mama was different when he was home, too. She seemed younger, happier, and even prettier—if that was possible. Her face glowed and she laughed a lot, and she had no eyes for anyone but Papa.

Michelle often wondered why Mama didn't go with him on the circuit. The family pullman car was so roomy and comfortable. They even had their own galley for when the cookhouse was closed down during hauls. So why didn't Mama stay with Papa all summer instead of just joining him for short visits?

That was one of the things they were quarreling about when she paused outside the door. Maybe she should have gone on, but she'd been too curious—Papa was always saying that she had more curiosity than an elephant child.

She heard her own name, which was why she crouched down beside the half-open door to listen. After all, they were talking about her, weren't they? Didn't she have a right to know what they said? Through the crack in the door, she heard the snapping of the fire, and she had a vision of the two of them, sitting side by side on the big ivory-colored sofa, drinking pink wine.

But tonight there was none of the soft murmuring and laughing that always made her feel so left out. Her father's voice was edged with anger as he said, "You expect too much from Michelle, Vicky. All those lessons—French and Spanish and music. She's a very—very earthy child, and you aren't going to make a Boston debutante out of her, no matter how hard you try.''

"She's a tomboy—and I blame you for that. And besides, what's wrong with trying to make a lady out of her?'' Mama's voice, usually so controlled, was pitched so high, it hurt Michelle's ears.

"You turned your back on that kind of life once. Why do you want it for Michelle?''

"I didn't turn my back. I had no choice. But Michelle is a St. Clair, too,'' Mama said. "You keep forgetting that. I want her to be ready if she ever has the opportunity to move in those circles.''

"In other words, you're grooming her to be a rich man's wife,'' he said. "I suppose you feel you lost your chance when you married me?''

There was a long silence, and when Mama finally spoke, her voice had softened. "You know I've never regretted marrying you, Michael.''

"But you wish I had chosen a more dignified profession, something respectable and socially correct,'' he said, and Michelle winced at the bitterness in his voice.

"You have an M.B.A. from Princeton,'' Mama said. "You could do anything you want. The circus is a headache—you worry constantly about how to keep it going, and your father's on your back all the time. When are you going to stop beating yourself to death? It isn't worth it—''

"But it is. The circus is more than just a way to earn a living. We've been married seventeen years, and yet you still won't accept how I feel about the circus. It would be different if I'd ever lied to you, Vicky. But I told you, the day we got married, that I would never change, that the circus was in my blood. I know how you feel about it, and I haven't asked you to share that life, no more than you want to. I've kept my part of the bargain—''

"You sound like a banker, talking about a loan,'' she said coldly.

"But isn't that exactly what you want me to be? A banker?'' he said.

Michelle, listening in the hall, put her hands over her mouth to keep from laughing. Papa, with his little jokes and his warm eyes and great smile, a cold-eyed banker? She'd seen the bankers in their dark suits, who came to talk to Papa and Grandpa Sam sometimes. Papa could never be one of them—didn't Mama see that?

"There's nothing wrong with being a banker," her mother said. "My great-grandfather was one—"

"But not your father. I wonder sometimes if you have any of him in you at all. You certainly don't have any of your mother in you."

Again, there was a long silence. When her mother spoke, her voice sounded so queer that Michelle was tempted to peek around the door and look at her. "Why do you say that?"

"Come on, Vicky. I know who your mother was."

"How long have you known?"

"Pop told me right after we eloped."

Mama said a word that made Michelle jump. "He had no right—he's never approved of me. And you—why haven't you said something about it before?"

"It was your own business."

"So why do you bring it up now?"

"Because it's time you remembered that it isn't just St. Clair blood Michelle inherited. She's fourteen. This fall she'll be going off to that fancy school in Boston you went to. She deserves this summer with the circus."

Mama must have started to speak, because Papa added, "Wait. Let me finish. I've given in on the boarding school because I'm tired of arguing about it. But I will have my way about this. You're welcome to come, too, you know."

"No, thank you. And you aren't being fair. I haven't interfered with Danny, have I? I let him go off with you every summer because, God knows, I don't have much choice. But it's different with Michelle. Can't you see that? I want her to be a lady, to have a different kind of life. And rubbing shoulders with riffraff is not my idea of what's best for her."

"I'm not going to argue about that. We've been through it too many times already. Michelle is old enough to spend the whole summer with the circus. Those flying visits, sandwiched in when you can tear yourself away from your clubs and charity committees and your riding competitions, aren't enough. If you're worried about her, then come along, too. It's your choice. Since you brought up the subject of fairness, consider this—Michelle loves the circus. Is it fair to deprive her of what's her birthright just because of your own prejudices?"

"I suppose this is your way of telling me that nothing I can say is going to change your mind?"

Papa didn't answer that, not directly. His voice took on a coaxing tone as he said, "Vicky, I miss you during the summer."

"I get lonely, too," she said.

"Then come with us this summer. Get involved. Take on a job—how about helping me with the publicity? You'd be great at that. Or if you like, you can refurbish the pullman. The circus will spring for it. If you don't want to eat in the cook tent, we'll have food sent over—or I'll assign you a cook, if you like. Just be there for me."

This time the silence was so long that Michelle gave in to temptation and eased her head around the door opening. Her mother, wearing one of her long hostess gowns, was curled up on one of the sofas that flanked the fireplace. Papa, looking very handsome in a dark maroon robe, was leaning against the marble mantelpiece, watching her.

Michelle studied her father's half smile and then turned her attention to her mother. Mama's face was very pink, and there was a softness in her eyes that made Michelle's heart jump with hope. Then Mama pressed her lips together in a gesture Michelle knew too well, and she was sure that once again, her mother would have her own way. She'd talk Papa out of letting her go, and then she'd be stuck at home all summer, taking riding and music lessons, being tutored in French and literature, but never math, which was her love. And Danny would have all the fun—

"Very well. You can take Michelle," her mother said. "But next fall, she goes to school in Boston."

"And you? Are you coming, too?"

Mama plucked at the front of her hostess gown, avoiding his eyes. "I can't. I'd just be in the way. You need all your attention for your business."

"Our business, Vicky."

"It's never been mine. I've always been an outsider to the circus."

"I don't agree, but—have it your way. Just think of this—you can expose Michelle to that upper-crust life all you want, but she'll return to the circus, Vicky, just like I did. It's in her blood."

"No one is born with circus fever. Of course, she loves being with you. In your eyes, she can do no wrong. Sometimes I wonder if you'd even bother to come home if it wasn't for Michelle. She'll come back looking like a ragamuffin, of course.

Last year when I let her visit you that week, she came home so brown that she looked like a—" She broke off.

"Like a Gypsy? Is that what you meant to say?"

"Like a ragamuffin."

"So why don't you come along and make sure she doesn't go out into the sun without a hat?" Papa said.

"That wasn't my only objection. She was noisy and overexcited and—"

"She was happy. She loved every moment of it. She's made friends with—"

"With a bunch of misfits." Mama's voice was tight with distaste.

"With Rosa and Clinker. With Young Doc. With the Valucchi children. All very respectable people, even by your standards. She had so many guardians that she was safer there than here in Orlando. Rosa would have taken a gun to anyone who even looked at her cross-eyed."

"Oh, yes, Rosa—I suppose she filled Michelle's head full of Gypsy lore. No wonder she's been so—so intractable lately. Do you really think Rosa is the kind of influence an imaginative child like Michelle needs?"

"Rosa loves Michelle—and she'd loved you if you ever gave her a chance. You seldom bother with her, not even during the winter months, when she's just a few miles away."

"I don't want to talk about Rosa. I want to settle this business about Michelle. She goes with you this summer, but in the fall, she starts school at Cabot. Is it agreed?"

"I don't seem to have a choice, do I? But I should warn you that when she's old enough to make up her own mind, she'll choose the circus. I say that from experience. All those years my own mother exposed me to the so-called better life, and yet I never wanted anything else. It will be the same with Michelle—"

Michelle didn't wait to hear any more. She'd heard this particular quarrel before. Quietly she crept away, forgetting what she'd come downstairs for, and eased her way up the hall stairs, avoiding the boards that might creak under her weight.

She'd remembered the milk as she was crawling back into bed, but she'd fallen asleep anyway, and had dreamed that she was in the spec, riding Connie, her favorite of all the elephants, and wearing a costume covered with rhinestones and sequins.

And now, just a week later, here she was, with the whole summer stretched out before her. As for the price she must pay, being banished to cold Boston for the winter, that was a long way off. Maybe, by next fall, her mother would have changed her mind. After all, there were plenty of private schools near Orlando. Surely Papa could talk Mama into choosing one of those.

Suddenly aware of the time, Michelle slid out of her berth, shivering as her bare feet touched the cold floor. Hugging her chest with her arms, she went to the window to look out. Through the morning mist she saw a row of huge gray shadows, moving majestically past the train, and her heart thrilled with excitement. The elephants—how she loved them, especially Connie, who had been her friend as long as she could remember!

A soft glow cut through the mist, and she realized it would soon be dawn. She pulled down the window shade and turned on the overhead light before she pulled off her nightgown. Hurrying now, she opened the storage drawer under the berth and got out underwear, jeans and sneakers, and a sweatshirt, and for the early morning chill, an oversized windbreaker she'd coaxed out of Danny.

She started to put on her underwear, but her own naked image in the mirror above the built-in washbasin stopped her. Just last month, Papa had reminded Mama that she was no longer a child even if she looked like one. Which meant he hadn't really looked at her closely lately. Her body, ivory-pale in the overhead light, was no longer thin and straight and shapeless like a child's.

Gingerly she touched one budding breast. Sometimes they tingled so that she could hardly stand it. She was different in other ways, too. She had strange feelings, strange thoughts about—well, things like wondering what it felt like to be kissed by a boy.

It was all very annoying—and she didn't have time to worry about it now. Danny had warned her that if she wasn't ready when he tapped on the door, he was going on without her. But she would be ready when he came. In fact, she meant to watch his door just in case he "forgot" that he'd promised to take her with him.

Hurrying now, she dressed. At the last moment, she tucked her telltale hair up inside one of Danny's old caps. No use advertising that she was up and about this early, when the whole circus acted like they were her keepers.

A disquieting thought came to her. Danny's warning, that she might be sorry if she insisted on coming along, had sounded sincere. Maybe she should—no, she wasn't going to be scared off! She was tired of always being a good little girl who had to keep clean and mind her manners. "Mama's little angel," Danny had called her more than once.

She gave her image in the mirror a secretive little smile. There was a lot Mama didn't know. Papa pretty much let her run loose the times he managed to persuade Mama to let her come for a visit. What would she say if she knew that Rosa, who told fortunes for a living, was her very best friend at the circus? Although she was even older than Mama, who was almost forty, Rosa seemed younger somehow, and she was more fun than any of the girls Michelle went to school with, most of whom were so silly about boys and the Beatles and other rock stars.

Rosa could talk about anything. She knew so many stories, too. Sometimes they were about circus people, about things that had happened, old scandals and what she called "lessons from life." She knew all about Gypsies, who were not at all like Mama thought. Of course, they did things they shouldn't, like stealing and cheating people out of their money, but only because they were forced to. And they weren't dregs of society, like Mama said. They had their own religion and they lived by very strict rules and customs that were older than time.

But if you weren't one yourself, you had to watch out for them. They didn't see anything wrong with cheating *gadjos*, which was anyone who wasn't a Rom—and they could tell you the biggest lies and look you right in the eye while doing it.

"Ask a dozen Roms the same question and you'll get a dozen different answers," Rosa had told her once. "Ask one Rom the same question a dozen times and you'll still get a dozen different answers."

There were other friends she never talked about at home, like Barky the Dog-faced Boy. Only, he was a grown man, almost as old as Papa. At first, she'd been afraid of him because he was so ugly, but then he'd picked her up that time she'd taken a bad fall off a rope web in the ring tent. His eyes had been so soft and warm and concerned that she'd never been afraid of him since. But Mama wouldn't approve of that friendship any more than she'd approve of her swiping raisin bread from the cookhouse to take to Connie whenever she got the chance.

Connie was the oldest elephant in the circus, and her very special friend. Once when Danny and one of his buddies had been teasing her, she'd hid behind Connie, and the old elephant had lifted her trunk and trumpeted so loud that the boys had run off.

Young Doc was her friend, too. He wasn't really young, of course, any more than Barky was a boy. He and Rosa were good friends, and he looked out for Michelle when she visited the menagerie. Danny wasn't allowed to go there anymore, which really made him mad.

"Not until you learn some responsibility," Papa had told him after he'd caught Danny teasing the cubs of Poppy, the Bengal bitch.

There was Cookie, too, who always saved her a big piece of chocolate cake when he baked. She wasn't supposed to eat chocolate, but oh, she did love it. And besides, what Mama didn't know didn't hurt her. That's what Cookie always said when he slipped her the cake, wrapped in aluminum foil. He always winked when he said it, too. Only, he didn't call Mama that, of course, or even Mrs. Bradford, like the other circus people did. He called her Queen Vee.

He called her, Michelle, Princess Carrot, but this spring he'd changed that to Princess Michelle—and then he'd winked at Black Joe, his assistant.

There were other friends whom Mama probably wouldn't approve of. The Valucchi family, for instance. They didn't speak English, but that was okay, because they did speak French. Peter Valucchi was her own age, and he'd taught her tumbling and other acrobatics, something she kept to herself. Only, the last time she'd gone to winter quarters with Papa, Peter had acted—funny. He'd invited her to go into the practice barn to watch him do a new trick, but then he'd crowded up against her, and tried to kiss her.

She'd hit him with a rake, and he'd called her a stuck-up bitch. But she'd taught him a lesson he wasn't likely to forget in a hurry. The shock on his face when she'd poked him in the ribs with that rake—yeah, there were a lot of things her mother didn't know about her. . . .

A sound in the passageway outside her door alerted her. She eased the door open, and when she saw Danny, tiptoeing past, she opened it all the way and glared out at him.

He gave her a sheepish smile. "I was just getting ready to knock," he said.

"I'll just bet you were."

"Well, I was. And you'd better shake a leg if you want to come along."

Michelle didn't bother to answer. Silently she followed him down the passageway, past the other compartments, all of which were empty since Papa slept in the stateroom at the other end of the car, and Grandpa Sam was staying at a hotel in Atlanta. In a couple of weeks Mama would be joining them for a few days, and then the fun would stop—at least until she went away again.

But this was today, and she was off on an adventure. Her heart swelled with excitement suddenly. It was good to be alive—and wasn't she the luckiest girl she knew, having a grandfather and father who owned their own circus?

CHAPTER 43

ALTHOUGH SHE WOULDN'T HAVE ADMITTED IT TO A SOUL, not even Clinker, there were times when Mara wondered if it wasn't time to retire. After all, she would be sixty in two more years. It wasn't that she had tired of the circus—how could you tire of something as essential to your well-being as breathing?— but just that she didn't have the energy, the get-up-and-go, as Mr. Sam called it, nor the patience with others she used to have.

For the past hour, she'd been pretending to listen to one of Mr. Sam's droning reminiscenses, while actually her thoughts were far away. In a few minutes she would have to leave her comfortable (and brand spanking new) Winnebago motor home for the midway. Clinker was already there, setting up the props, preparing the first of several pots of Earl Grey tea that would see them through the long afternoon and evening.

Since this was Atlanta, the circus's first stop every spring for the past twenty years, a good percentage of her customers would be repeaters. Although they paid to get their cards read, she knew that the majority of them wouldn't follow the advice they got. Maybe, she thought, feeling depressed, they simply needed someone to give them her undivided attention for a few minutes. And who would have thought, back when she was Bradford Circus's star attraction, that she would end up in the same circus, telling fortunes to the wives of farmers and shoe clerks?

She must have sighed, because Mr. Sam broke off a rambling account about a ducat scam he'd once thwarted to peer at her over the rim of his glasses. He had aged since retirement; there was a slackness around his jawline, a puffiness in his eyelids. Was he drinking too much these days? Sometimes he seemed a little befuddled, which certainly wasn't like Mr. Sam. He had also become even more testy, taking offense easily. Would that happen to her once she retired?

"You haven't heard a word I said," Mr. Sam grumbled. "You're in some kind of fog today."

"Sorry, Sam. I was thinking about Michelle. I thought for sure she'd be here early this morning to have breakfast with Clinker and me. This is usually her first stop of the day. Clinker made up waffle batter, just for her."

"Haven't seen her—or our grandson," Mr. Sam said. "Guess they got more interesting things to do than visit with old folks like me."

"Old? You're a long way from being old, Sam."

He grinned at her, showing a set of impossibly perfect teeth. "Get along with you. I know what I look like. Should, seeing as I have to look at this mug every morning when I shave. Don't know why I bother. Who cares if a retired old fogy like me has a few whiskers."

"You didn't retire. You just turned the hard work over to Michael. Count your blessings."

He glowered at her. "Blessings, is it? Sometimes I feel like I'm talking to air, trying to give that boy advice. And the workmen these days—used to be they were real men. Oh, sometimes they drank too much and got into fights, but they gave an honest day's work for a day's pay, and you could tell what sex they were. Now the young ones look like a bunch of females, hair down their necks. If it was me, I'd fire the lot of them. Not that I ever interfere. No, I don't give advice unless it's asked for."

"I'm sure Michael is grateful for your advice," she murmured, managing not to laugh.

"Maybe so and maybe not. When we found out that Lasky bunch had booked the same dates we had here in Atlanta, he just shrugged, said something about free enterprise. Free enterprise, my ass! That Lasky upstart figures that now I'm retired, he can move in on our territory. You know, girl, it ain't much fun, getting old, is it?''

Although it was in the form of a question, Mara didn't answer. Forgetting that just a few minutes earlier, she'd been thinking much the same, she was offended by the question. After all, she was a generation younger than Mr. Sam—why had he included her in *his* category? She certainly didn't feel old—why should she? She still had a lover to keep her bones warm. Let Clinker pull her long nose and give out those sighs of hers. There was nothing like a man to keep you young.

"You still seeing Young Doc?" Mr. Sam said, as if he'd caught her thought.

"We're old friends," she said noncommittally.

"It doesn't bother you that he's married?"

"So? We're just friends—and besides," she answered incautiously, "he and his wife have been separated for years."

She hadn't seen Young Doc for two months. He'd been in California, brushing up on new animal surgical techniques at the University of California at Davis. When she joined him in his motor home tonight, he would have champagne on ice waiting, and afterward—well, it would be an exciting evening.

No, she didn't love him. She was still in love with Jaime, always would be. But that didn't mean she didn't enjoy the companionship, and yes, the sex she had with Young Doc. She was human, had human needs—and Young Doc was as good a lover now as he'd been seventeen years ago when they'd first become lovers. The fact that he was married to a woman who wouldn't give him a divorce made it better. No pressure about a marriage she didn't want . . .

Mr. Sam took out the big railroad watch he'd carried ever since she'd known him. "I don't want to keep you," he said. "Maybe I'll drop around tomorrow again—Michael don't much care for me hanging around the Blue Wagon. Maybe it's time I reminded him again that the circus still belongs to me."

Mara bit down hard on her lip. She wanted to tell him to stop being a cantankerous old fool, but she knew better. Opposition only exacerbated Mr. Sam's stubbornness. It was a good thing Michael had the kind of patience his father had never had. . . .

"Did you see much of Vicky this winter?" Mr. Sam asked.

"She's been busy—and so have I."

"So you say. It's a shame the way she neglects her old friends."

"When Michael is home for the winter, they like to be together," she said defensively.

Mr. Sam grunted. "Well, the boy's always been a fool where she's concerned. Can't understand that woman. She should be making the circuit with Michael. She's just like my old lady. Turned her back on the circus."

"It reminds her of—of an unpleasant time in her life."

"Hell, Mara, it's been seventeen years! I never thought Michael would put up with her nonsense this long. And now she's trying to turn his own kids against him."

"Not against him. She just doesn't want the circus for them."

"Well, make excuses for her if you want. No one else sees it that way. They call her the Queen Vee." He gave a snorting laugh. "Queen *Vee*—get it?"

"I get it. And I have to go. You want to walk over to the midway with me?"

She pretended not to see how long it took Mr. Sam to struggle to his feet. She went into the bedroom to get a scarf that matched her long, full skirt. She arranged it over one shoulder, then tucked the ends in under the hammered copper belt at her waist. Not bad for fifty-eight, she thought as she surveyed herself in the mirror.

Mr. Sam was waiting for her, leaning on his cane, when she went outside. She was checking the door to make sure it was locked when one of the management trainees came running up.

"Mr. Sam, I think you'd better come. I can't find Mr. Michael—and there's been trouble over at the Lasky lot. It has something to do with his kids."

Although Danny had ignored Michelle ever since they'd left their pullman car, she was content to trail along behind him, absorbed in the bustle around them as they headed for the gilly wagon, the shuttle bus that provided transportation between the railroad spur and the circus lot.

About them, the workmen were still unloading the flatcars. Underfoot was the gravel the advance crew had put down to cover any ruts in the ground that might hang up wheels. All debris, whether bottles, wires, or just plain trash, had been removed to save the feet of the working elephants. Planks and ramps had been installed at the end of the seventy-foot flatcars, and the menagerie had already been unloaded. As she hurried in Danny's wake, Michelle kept an eye out for Connie, her elephant friend. She'd stuffed a loaf of bread she'd swiped from the pantry at home inside her suitcase, and right now it was buttoned inside her windbreaker, her gift to Connie.

As they passed an empty stock car, she wrinkled her nose. Not that the animal odors really bothered her. In fact, she preferred them to the acrid odor of too strong coffee that wafted from the privilege car.

They reached the gilly bus and swung aboard. Although the driver, a veteran of the circus, recognized Danny, his greeting nod was reserved. But he smiled at Michelle, told her in a thick Arkansas accent that she got prettier every year.

When the gilly bus dropped them off in the middle of the circus lot, ten minutes later, it was awash with activity. There was an order about setting up that never varied. First to go up was the cook tent, where coffee and doughnuts were served to all comers, then the Big Top, followed by a small city of tents to house everything from the menagerie and sideshows to Rosa's fortune-telling operation. This early in the season, Michelle noted, everything looked bright and fresh, sparkling clean.

Amidst the hectic bustle, the lot swarmed with agents, bringing supplies to fill the needs of the circus—machine and fuel oil, stock feed, fruits for the apes, meat for the big cats, who devoured twenty pounds or more each per day, eggs and beans and steaks for the cook tent, hot dogs and hamburgers and ice cream for the grab joints.

The day before, such items as hay, straw, coal, and coke had already been delivered. As Papa had once told her, the circus was big business—and like any other business, it must run like clockwork.

She sniffed happily as they approached the cook tent. She expected Danny, who seldom missed a meal, to turn in, but he hurried past, glancing down at the watch that had been his sixteenth birthday present from Grandpa Sam.

Glumly Michelle subdued her hunger by nibbling on a hunk torn from the loaf of bread in her windbreaker, wishing she had one of Cookie's fat doughnuts instead. She had to hurry to keep up with Danny's long stride, and she wondered if he was trying to lose her. When he stopped near the horse tent, she wasn't surprised to see Bobby Dugan coming toward them.

"Hey, I thought you'd chickened out." He gave Michelle a sly grin. "What are you doing here, little sister?"

"She's coming along," Danny said shortly.

"You think that's a good idea? She might get—well, hang you up."

"Let me worry about that," Danny said, scowling at him. "Where's the car you borrowed?"

"Out in the lot. Say, it's later than we planned. You sure you want to go through with it?"

"I'm here, aren't I? If you want to forfeit the bet, okay."

"Don't you just wish. I thought—"

"You thought wrong. Come on, both of you."

Michelle trailed behind again, careful to avoid looking at Bobby. She didn't like him, the way he never seemed to really look directly at people. What's more, she had a hunch Danny didn't much like him, either.

The car was an ancient Ford. Its rusting body was spotted with patches of gray paint, and its wheels looked as if they would cave in any minute.

"Did you get the—you know, the stuff?" Danny asked Bobby, who was already behind the steering wheel. At Bobby's nod, he climbed into the front seat, leaving the backseat to Michelle.

"Hey, Michelle, there's room up here for three," Bobby said.

Before she could answer, Danny said, "Knock it off, Bobby. Let's go."

For the next forty-five minutes, while they rattled down the highway, then through a series of suburbs, there was little conversation. Michelle was too stubborn to ask questions, but she was already wishing she hadn't insisted on coming along, especially when she saw a sign advertising their approach to the Lasky Circus. Why was Bobby taking them there, into enemy territory? Did the bet have something to do with Lasky Circus, maybe that Danny could sneak into the Big Top without paying?

The lot was adjacent to a big shopping center. There were even a few permanent buildings, including a stable. Michelle, despite her fierce partisanship, had to admit that in terms of the number of attractions, the Lasky Circus compared very favorably to her own family's circus.

They parked in the visitors' lot. Bobby got a heavy brown bag from the trunk and handed it to Danny, who took it without comment. Again, Michelle held back a little as her brother and his friend bypassed the midway and headed for the back of the lot. Her uneasiness grew as they approached a cluster of buildings. When they reached the first building, the boys ducked behind it. As Michelle followed, she caught a glimpse of a sign, tacked up over a door, and realized it was being used as a menagerie.

Several men, dressed in work clothes, passed, arguing good-naturedly, and the three of them flattened themselves in a tall stand of weeds. From the conversation of the men, they were heading to the cook tent, and her stomach rumbled, reminding her again that she hadn't yet eaten her own breakfast.

"Stay here—and don't move," Danny whispered. Bent low, he scurried toward a door, still carrying the brown paper sack. A moment later, he had disappeared inside the menagerie.

Beside her, Bobby had settled down into a crouching position; she didn't like the gloating look in his eyes. He expected Danny to get in trouble, she knew instinctively, but she would die before she asked him what her brother was up to.

A few minutes later, she discovered her foot had gone to sleep. She shifted her position, only then noticing that Bobby had moved closer. He reached out to put his hand on her knee, and she gave him a shove that made him lose his balance. He ripped out a curse as he sat down hard on his rear.

"You try anything like that again and I'm going to tell Danny," she whispered hotly.

"You just do that, and I'll claim you were coming on to me. And if he starts anything—" He made a quick gesture, and suddenly there was a knife in his hand.

"What the hell's going on here?"

Michelle twisted around so abruptly that Danny's cap flew off her head. The speaker was young, probably no more than a year or so older than Danny; he was fair-haired and tall, looking like a movie cowboy in Levis and a Stetson hat. He was also the best-looking boy she'd ever seen.

"You bothering the kid, fellow?" he drawled. He even sounded like a movie cowboy, she decided.

"Mind your own business, bud. She's my sister—"

"He's lying," Michelle said indignantly.

"I figured that. Okay, you—take off. And if I see you around, I'll have you tossed off the lot."

Bobby's face drew up in an ugly frown; he didn't move. "He's got a knife," Michelle said quickly.

"I saw it. But I'm not a girl, and he's going to leave quietly before he gets in real trouble."

Bobby gave an insolent shrug; he moved away, taking his time, even swaggering a little.

"How did you know he wouldn't come at you with his knife?" Michelle asked.

"I didn't. I like to live dangerously." He grinned at her, and she had to swallow hard. He really was incredibly handsome. "You going to be all right?" he added.

She nodded, suddenly shy. "I'm okay. Thank you for—you know, running him off."

"That's okay." He looked her over, taking in her jeans and the outsize windbreaker. "You must be one of the Gleason girls my brother just hired. I heard one of them was a redhead—and pretty as they come."

"Your brother?"

"Steve Lasky—the guy that hired you. He's the circus manager. I'm David Lasky." He didn't seem to notice her start. "What do they call your color of hair?"

"Red," she said shortly.

"I'll bet they call you Carrots." He grinned at her frown. "How old are you, Carrots?"

"My name is Michelle—and how old do you think I am?"

"Well, at first I thought you were just a kid, but now I can see you're much older than that—say, sixteen?"

She smiled at him. "You're a good guesser," she said, which wasn't really a lie. "How old are you?"

"Seventeen. I'll be a senior at Sansun Academy this fall. That's in—"

"Boston. I know. This fall I'm going to Cabot."

He gave her a slow smile. "So we'll be neighbors, huh? Maybe those Cabot dances won't be so grim next year."

A warmth invaded her cheeks. She cast around for something adult to say, only to remember that Danny would be coming back any minute now. And how were they going to get home without Bobby's car?

"I have to go," she said, hoping he'd take the hint and leave. "Thank you again for—you know, chasing away that man."

"No thanks necessary." He moved a little closer. "However, if you really want to show your gratitude—"

"How?" she said a little nervously.

"A kiss. Just a little one—here." He tapped his cheek.

Michelle stared at him, uncertain if he was serious. He gave her a smile that made her skin tingle, and she thought—why not? A kiss on the cheek didn't mean anything. She leaned forward, meaning to kiss his cheek, but at the last moment he turned his head and the kiss landed squarely on his mouth. It was just a brushing of lips, but it sent a shock along her nerve endings. She jumped back, feeling confused.

"That was very nice—but much too short," he said, grinning.

Before she could answer him, two men erupted through the menagerie door. One was a tall, muscular man with dark hair and angry eyes. He was holding Danny by the collar. Danny tried to twist out of his grasp, lost his balance, and landed in a heap on the ground. He didn't try to get up. Michelle could almost smell his fear. When the man stepped closer, as if to grab him by the collar again, all her protectiveness rose. She grabbed a stick and hurried toward them.

"Let him alone, you bully," she stormed. "You touch him again and I'll hit you with this stick."

"Put that down before you poke out your eye," the man growled. "If you're in on this, you're in big trouble."

"Hey, cool it, Steve." It was David Lasky, and she realized, her heart sinking, that the dark-haired man was his brother. "She couldn't be in on anything. I've been talking to her for the past ten minutes. What the hell's going on, anyway?"

"I caught this piece of crud slapping pink paint on the elephants." His voice was full of anger. "He'd already covered six of them and was working on Belle when I stopped him."

Michelle gasped in dismay. So that's what the bet had been! How *could* he? She gave her brother a reproachful stare, and he ducked his head, looking sheepish.

"I didn't hurt them" he muttered. "It was just a joke. The paint'll come off."

"But it will get in the creases in their hide and take a ton of turpentine to get it out," Michelle said, forgetting their audience in her anger. "You know how sensitive their noses are, Danny, and besides, the turpentine will sting."

"So you *are* with this jerk," Steve Lasky said.

"Let her alone. She didn't know about the—she just came along for the ride," Danny said.

"Is this guy your boyfriend?" David asked Michelle.

"He's my brother."

"I think they're part of the Gleason family," David told his brother.

"I've never seen either of them before. Just who the hell are you, anyway?"

"I'm Michelle and this is Danny," she said, then hurried on to say, "He didn't mean any harm. It was just a prank."

"Prank, hell." Steve Lasky's expression was so ferocious that she shrank back.

"Can't you see you're scaring the kid?" his brother said.

"She has good reason to be scared. Let's see what you're hiding inside your jacket. At this stage, a bomb wouldn't surprise me."

Knowing she had no choice, Michelle unbuttoned her windbreaker, and took out the loaf of bread. Steve Lasky stared at it, at the place where a hunk had been torn out, and for a moment she thought he was going to smile. If so, he changed his mind.

"What is it? Bait to keep the elephants quiet while your brother decorated them?" he demanded.

Michelle bristled. "The bread was for Connie, one of our elephants. Only I didn't get a chance to give it to her before—" She broke off, realizing her mistake.

"Connie—I've heard of her. A real old-timer with the Bradford operation." He frowned at her. "You must be Michael Bradford's kids. Somehow, I'm not surprised."

"Why don't you let them go, Steve?" David said. "I'm sure he's learned his lesson, and Michelle didn't have anything to do with it."

"Michelle, is it? She's too young for you. She couldn't be more than thirteen."

"Mind your own business, big brother," David said.

"Danny won't do it again," Michelle spoke up quickly. "I promise he won't."

Steve stared down at Danny's sullen face. "Not here, he won't. I'm probably making a mistake, but I'm going to turn you over to your old man. I hope he lays it onto your backside with his belt—and stay away from here in the future, you two. Next time, I won't be so easy on you."

Michelle almost told him that she wouldn't come near his crummy circus for any reason, but wisely she only tossed her head and scowled at him. His lips twitched, and she resented the way he examined her with insulting thoroughness.

"I see what you mean," he told his brother. "Give her a few years and she'll be a menace to every red-blooded man in sight."

"You've got that wrong, big brother. She doesn't need a few more years. I think I'll marry her when she finishes growing up."

Michelle couldn't help smiling at him. He was joking, of course—both of them were. How strange that his compliment pleased her, while his brother's made her want to hit him with the stick in her hand. It came to her that her brother, who usually was quick to speak up and justify himself, had been surprisingly quiet. Maybe, she thought soberly, he was trying to decide what to tell Papa.

Although Michelle was still angry with her brother, she felt sorry for Danny when their father, his face tight, collected them in the Lasky Circus's Blue Wagon with a chilly "Thank you" to Steve Lasky, then drove them back to the fairgrounds. He didn't say a word in the car—and neither did Michelle or Danny, who for once had the good sense to hold his tongue.

When they reached their pullman, he marched them into the salon. Michelle knew they were really in for it when she met the coldness in his eyes.

Danny spoke up first. "Michelle didn't have anything to do with—you know, what happened," he said.

Papa studied him as if he were an interesting bug. "She knew you were up to something, or why did she go to the Lasky lot with you? She's old enough to make up her own mind, and she has to take some of the blame."

His voice, which has started off calmly, roughened. "Why did you do such a stupid thing? It'll be all over the circuit, that Michael Bradford can't control his wild kids. Where were your brains—and your conscience, tormenting those elephants? I might expect it from you, Danny, after some of the stunts you've pulled, but I thought you had more sense, Michelle."

"It was all my idea," Danny said. "I just didn't think—"

"No, you didn't think. You never do. But you, Michelle—I talked your mother into letting you come along this summer, told her you were responsible and mature. Well, she obviously knows you better than I did. For two cents, I'd send you back to Florida on the next train."

Michelle blinked hard, determined not to cry. "Please, Papa—don't send me back," she pleaded.

He studied her contrite face for a long moment. "Very well. I'll probably regret this, but I'll give you a choice. You can go back to Florida—or you're confined to the train for the next two weeks. It's up to you."

"I'll stay on the train," Michelle said meekly.

"You'll spend your time studying those books your mother sent along. I'll lay out some lessons for you."

"Yes, Papa," she said.

"As for you, Danny, you're going to be working so hard this summer that you won't have any energy left for practical jokes. For a starter, I'm turning you over to Cookie. He can always use an extra pot scrubber. Let's see if hard labor will take the starch out of you. Also, you don't get any pay until you've paid Steve Lasky the cost of having those elephants cleaned up. And don't go whining to your grandfather, asking for money, or I'll think of something worse.''

After he was gone, Danny regarded Michelle with gloomy eyes. "I should've known he'd go easy on you," he said.

Michelle glared at him. "Easy? I might as well be in jail. And it's all your fault.''

"Hey, didn't I tell him you weren't to blame? Besides, you did blackmail me into taking you along.''

There was enough truth in that to silence Michelle, but after Danny disappeared into his own room, she thought over what had happened and knew her father was right to punish her. Maybe it was time she started thinking for herself—and grew up.

After all, she'd just had her first kiss from a boy, hadn't she? And come to think of it, her first proposal, too.

As Steve Lasky walked back to the menagerie with David, he listened to his younger brother with jaundiced ears. David had been talking nonstop about the Bradford girl, whom he called Carrots. According to him he'd saved her from an attack by a vagrant, and in appreciation she had given him a kiss. It wasn't that he didn't believe that something along those lines had occurred. It was just that David tended to embroider his own achievements.

As for the girl—yes, he agreed with David that she had been special. Even in jeans and that outsize windbreaker, she had looked like a porcelain doll. Not that he was stupid enough to voice this opinion to David.

It had dismayed him when, at his grandfather's death, he'd discovered that Joe Lasky had dumped the responsibility of his younger brother into his lap. The management of the circus, he could handle. Since his parents' death in a freak car accident when he was David's age, he'd been training for this job, spending every summer under this grandfather's thumb. Since the old man's death a year ago, he'd made all the decisions, kept everything going at a healthy profit, despite the decline in circus attendance around the country. It was the guardianship of his younger brother that bugged him, gave him the most trouble.

The trust his grandfather had set up for David laid it all out. David would come into the trust when he was twenty-one—

unless he, Steve, decided against it. He could postpone turning it over until David was twenty-five—or he could terminate it at any time and turn the money back into the general funds of the circus. It was totally up to him.

David bitterly resented this, of course. And so did he. It was a responsibility he didn't want. Still—he had to take it seriously, and it did have one advantage. David wanted the trust fund so badly that it did keep him in line—most of the time.

"—listening to me or not?" David's voice intruded upon his thoughts.

"You were talking about the little redhead. Who, I might point out, couldn't possibly be over thirteen, if that."

"Fourteen is my guess." David grinned at him. "A delicious little morsel, right?"

"If you say so," Steve said, hurrying his step.

"I do say so. She's going to enroll at Cabot this fall. You can bet I'll be attending their dances, fruit punch or not."

Steve gave him a hard look. "Stay away from her, David."

"Why, older brother, you sound downright protective of Carrots. Now, why is that? Don't tell me she got to you!"

Steve started to blast him, then changed his mind. David was baiting him—and he wasn't about to play that game. But he *was* going to keep an eye on David this winter. The one thing he didn't need was a renewal of that asinine feud with the Bradford family that had died with his grandfather. He also didn't want the little redhead involved with David, who had quite a reputation, even at seventeen, with girls.

And what a pity the dates were all wrong. If Michelle Bradford were a few years older than fourteen or he a few years younger than twenty-eight, he just might—hell, what was he thinking! This whole business had thrown him off balance today. And right now, he had more important things to think about, such as seeing that the pink paint was removed from those poor elephants' hides. . . .

CHAPTER 44

*O*NE OF THE BEST THINGS ABOUT BEING WITH THE CIRCUS, in Michelle's opinion, was eating her meals in the cook tent. At home, her mother's taste in food ran to vegetables, steamed and served without sauces, salads without dressing, broiled fish and chicken without butter. As Danny had once said, "Man, I wish Mama would get off her health kick."

But eating in the cook tent was different. There were such things as chili, spaghetti, slumgullion and country fried steak with cream gravy, thick slices of ham fried to a golden brown. And the desserts—oh, those chocolate cakes!

Another reason she loved to eat in the cook tent was because there was always so much going on. Sometimes one of the younger married couples would have a yelling fight, or the clowns, who never ate in makeup, would stir everything up with one of their elaborate practical jokes. Or maybe an artiste would come in with a new summer wife, setting everybody to buzzing.

Every meal was different. She was welcome to sit anywhere she wanted, so she spread herself around. One of her favorite tables, when she got there early enough, was with the anomalies, who always welcomed her kindly. It was just recently that she'd understood why. So many people, including circus folk, didn't like eating with the freaks. It didn't bother her at all to watch Barky put tiny bites of food into the cavity formed by his ruined mouth, and she wasn't offended when Little Edna, the fattest woman in the world, finished off a whole cake in one setting. It wasn't, Little Edna told her, sighing, that she was all that greedy, but if she started losing weight, how would she earn a living?

Rosa and Clinker seldom ate in the cook tent, but when they did, Michelle sat with them. Rosa was always so interested in Michelle's life that she told her all her secrets, her dreams. In fact, they shared a secret that no one else in the whole world knew except Clinker.

The secret had something to do with Michelle's grandmother—actually, it had *everything* to do with her. Mama's mother had not only been an artiste, an aerialist, but she'd been very famous. Her name had been Princess Mara, and she'd been real royalty. Only, it was Gypsy Royalty, so in most people's eyes, it didn't really count. Princess Mara's father had been head of his tribe, and he'd been very cruel. When Mara had refused to marry an old man he'd picked out for her, he'd disowned her—which was why she only had one name.

Rosa had been Princess Mara's best friend. Whenever authors wanted to write about her, they came to Rosa. Clinker disapproved of this, said it took up too much of her time, but then, Clinker disapproved of a lot of things. Sometimes, when Rosa was in a mellow mood, she told Michelle stories about how Princess Mara had met her husband, Michelle's grandfather, and how she'd gone through so much hardship before she became famous. Tucked away in Michelle's compartment on the train was a book Rosa had given her that told all about Princess Mara's life.

"I don't want you to forget her," Rosa said when she gave her the book. "Someone has to remember her the way she was. This book doesn't tell all the story—but it's as close as any they've written."

The book had been a bestseller and was still in print. Michelle had read it several times, and every time she did, she dreamt that she was Princess Mara, that she was soaring high, high, high above the arena, doing the flange turn, the blood running down her arm.

Today she was eating breakfast with some of the workmen in the long side of the tent. Earlier, she'd asked Cookie for a loaf of raisin bread for Connie, but he wouldn't give her any, saying she should stay away from the elephant tent today. All he would tell her was that there'd been trouble there last night.

So she'd carried her breakfast to the workmen's table, and kept her hears open while she ate. Sure enough, one of the canvasmen started talking about an accident outside the menagerie where the elephants were tethered. A towner, a teenager, had been teasing the elephants, poking them with a nail on a long stick. He got too close to Connie, and she knocked him down with her trunk, then sat on him so he couldn't get up. He was in the hospital in very bad condition now.

Michelle didn't learn any more because someone remembered she was there and shushed the canvasman. When she asked him where Connie was now, he told her gruffly that she'd better talk to her old man about it. Only, when she went to the Blue Wagon, Papa wasn't there. All his secretary would say was that he was off the lot.

Michelle headed for the menagerie next. As she walked along the row where the elephants were tethered, she stopped to rub an inquisitive trunk here, to speak to an old friend there. All the elephants knew her, of course, and although she wasn't supposed to go too near them, she paid no attention to the warning. She had a way with animals, or so Young Doc said, and if that meant they were her friends, it was true enough.

She reached the end of the line of bulls, but the last space, where Connie was always tethered, was empty.

Her mouth went dry as a terrible suspicion struck her. Had Connie been destroyed, the way they sometimes did with rogue elephants? She looked around frantically, but the only person in sight was one of the elephant trainers, a man called Cotton. When he pretended not to notice her, even after she called his name, her apprehension crystallized into fear.

"What happened to Connie?" she demanded, planting herself directly in front of him.

"You ain't heard?"

"Heard what?"

"Oh, shit. Well, you hafta find out sometime. There was trouble last night. This kid had been tormenting the bulls, sticking them with a nail, and when he got too near Connie, she knocked him down and then sat on him. Time we hauled her off, the kid was in real bad shape. We got him to the hospital right away, but I just heard he didn't make it."

He pulled off his cap and scratched his head. "I'm real sorry, Michelle. There wasn't nothing your pa could do. The sheriff come here early this morning with a truck to haul her away, and he had a warrant. Mr. Michael had to turn her over. It's rotten, I know, but the law's the law."

"What's going to happen to her, Cotton?" she asked, on the verge of tears.

"Well, there'll be a hearing. Connie's valuable property. They hafta go through the legal stuff, but it don't look good for the old bull."

Michelle shivered, suddenly very cold. "Where did they take her?" she asked.

Cotton shrugged. "I don't know. The hearing is set for tomorrow, but I figure it's just for show. The towners don't understand that animals ain't humans, that they live by their instincts, see?"

"But Connie never did anything like this before," Michelle protested.

"Yeah—only, you can't talk sense to towners."

He spit on the ground to show his contempt and then went back to work.

Michelle started back to the Blue Wagon, in the hope that Papa had returned by now. She met Danny on the access road. He was shoveling gravel into a pothole, looking glum. True to his word, Papa had kept her brother busy for the past month, mostly doing manual labor. When he saw Michelle, he propped the shovel up against his wheelbarrow.

"I see you heard about the old bull. She's the one you're always feeding, isn't she?"

Too choked up to speak, Michelle nodded.

Danny gave her an awkward pat on the shoulder. "I'm sorry, Carrots. Papa tried to cool things with the sheriff, but he's a real red-neck, bound and determined to set an example. That's how the silver badges get re-elected, I guess. It's always safe to come down hard on circus people."

"Do you know where the sheriff took Connie?"

"To the county animal shelter, I heard. Look, don't feel so bad, I know you're soft on that bull, but she *is* awful old, even for an elephant."

"But she must be so afraid—and lonely. She's used to having the other bulls around her—and what if they hurt her, taking her out of that truck?"

"Well, there's nothing you can do about it. Why don't you let Papa handle things?"

Resentment washed over Michelle. He didn't really care. All Danny ever cared about was his own comfort and pleasure. Without a word, she turned and hurried away, knowing what she had to do. Danny called after her, but she didn't turn around.

On her way to the city bus stop just outside the fairgrounds, she stopped at the cook tent and swiped one of the loaves of bread that were cooling on a wire rack. With the bread tucked under her arm, she hurried to the bus stop. A bus came along in a few minutes, and after she'd boarded it and dropped her fare in the box, she asked the bus driver if she'd need a transfer for the line that went closest to the animal shelter.

The driver told her that she was already on the right bus, and a while later he called, "Animal Shelter," and then gave her directions before she got off the bus.

A few minutes later, Michelle was standing in front of a large red brick building that looked as if it had once been a foundry. The COUNTY ANIMAL SHELTER sign above the entrance told her that it was the right building, but another one, tacked on the door, said the facility was closed for the day. Not ready to accept this, she tried the doorknob, but it didn't turn. When she pounded on the door, no one came.

She was turning away when a familiar sound, the trumpeting of an elephant, stopped her. Connie . . . So she *had* come to the right place. But how to get inside? Surely there was a rear entrance—or was it necessary to find a way *inside*? No ordinary cage would hold a full-grown elephant. How could they even get Connie through the door?

She started around the corner of the building with the idea of looking for another entrance. The building was relatively narrow, and where it ended, a high wall began. A sound confirmed her suspicion that Connie was being held outside. There was no mistaking that rhythmical thump, thump, thump. Connie was showing her displeasure at being confined in a strange place.

Michelle looked around for a ladder. She didn't find one, but there was a collection of garbage cans and empty crates sitting on the curb. She rolled two of the garbage cans against the wall, chose the sturdiest-looking of the wooden crates to balance on top of them. Too agitated to worry about splinters, she climbed on top of the crate, and raised her head above the top of the wall.

She found herself looking down into an L-shaped courtyard. Half of it was cemented over, the other half hard-packed earth. Connie was staked out near the center, each of her thick legs chained to steel spikes that had been driven deep into the ground. From a long, low building in the rear of the courtyard, she heard other animals—barks, whines, the yowling of cats.

She climbed up on the wall, dropped the loaf of bread she was holding to the ground, then let herself over the edge. Briefly she dangled there, getting up the courage to let go. A moment later, she hit the ground so hard that the breath was knocked out of her lungs, but other than scraped knees and hands, she was unhurt.

Connie spotted her and threw back her trunk to trumpet a welcome. She was making so much noise that Michelle knew the building must be deserted or someone would have come running. She was resentful that they'd left Connie here alone, until it occurred to her that there was no one to stop her from taking Connie away—provided she could figure out how to release the elephant from her chains.

Connie gave another trumpet, and Michelle picked up the bread and hurried toward her, making soothing sounds, as if hushing a child.

"I brought you a treat," she told Connie. "But you have to stop making such a racket."

Connie lowered her trunk and nuzzled Michelle's face, snorting softly. As Michelle tore off hunks of the bread and fed her, the elephant rocked slowly back and forth, a sure sign that she was upset. Michelle's heart twisted with pity—and fear. She was here, true, but now what did she do?

She jumped nervously when she heard the tinkling of shattering glass, followed by a triumphant roar of men's voices. In the kennels, a rising storm of barks, yelps, howls, broke out. Michelle looked around wildly for someplace to hide, but the courtyard was devoid of anything but another huge pile of empty crates.

The big elephant moved restlessly, her small eyes showing fear. When she threw up her trunk again, trumpeting her distress, Michelle saw her as outsiders would, a huge and dangerous rogue, capable of killing a human simply by sitting on him, and she forgot her personal fear in her concern for her friend.

"No—be quiet, Connie," she said anxiously. "You'll only make things worse—"

A door in the brick building crashed open, and a man burst into the courtyard. He was brandishing a piece of iron pipe, and the raw hate in his eyes paralyzed Michelle.

"There's the killer," he shouted. "Let's get him!"

Other men poured into the courtyard. As they rushed toward Connie, Michelle knew she had to stop them. Without further thought, she flung herself in front of the elephant, spread out her arms as if that could stop the horde. The first man to reach her was cursing; he knocked her to one side and she fell to her knees, the pain making her cry out.

"Get away from that killer, you little fool," the man snarled. "You're lucky to still be alive."

He grabbed her by the arm and hauled her to her feet. She tried to tell him that he was making a mistake, that Connie was gentle and kind, that she'd often fallen asleep between the elephant's feet when she was a kid.

But the man didn't listen to her. None of them listened to her. They were too filled with their hate, their blood lust—and maybe with their fear. One man, older than the others, finally pulled her to one side.

"Here now, this is no place for a girl," he said, not unkindly. "Harry, you take her outside. We don't want no witnesses to what we gotta do."

"But Connie isn't dangerous," Michelle pleaded. "It was an accident—"

"It wasn't no accident, girl. That beast is a killer, and the circus oughta be sued, letting it out where it can kill people. Here, Harry, take her outside and make sure she don't come back."

The burly man he called Harry grabbed Michelle by the arm and dragged her toward the brick building. She tried to fight him, but he was too strong, and eventually she found herself outside the building, the door locked behind her. Although she knew it was useless, she pounded on the door until her hands were bruised and bleeding, then collapsed on the walk.

She began to wail, her voice keening out her grief. In all her life, she had never felt so helpless before. Surrounded by people who loved her, she had always been able to influence others, to be listened to. But not this time.

She felt such a savage hatred for the men that when a hand touched her shoulder, she lashed out with her fists, only to connect empty air.

"I'm not going to hurt you—it's Michelle, isn't it?"

Michelle blinked away her tears, and focused her eyes on a familiar face—Steve Lasky's face. "What are *you* doing here?" she blurted.

"To see what I can do to stop that mob before they get out of hand. One of my men heard a bunch of hotheads talking in a bar about lynching the old bull. Your father wasn't on the lot when I called, but I left a message for him to come right away. My man is trying to round up some of my own workers, but no one's showed up yet, and it looks like I'll have to tackle them on my own. Maybe I can defuse things until help comes."

"Why would you care? Connie isn't *your* elephant," she said belligerently.

His mouth tightened, but his voice was even when he said, "Circus people have to stick together."

Michelle stared at him doubtfully. There were so many of them and only one of him. She started to warn him, but her fear for Connie was stronger than concern for a man she hardly knew, a Lasky at that. "I tried to stop them," she said. "But they put me out. You have to stop them—"

"I'll do my best. But you stay out here, where you'll be safe. A mob is capable of anything."

"The door is locked, but they got in through a window. I heard the glass break," she said urgently. "You can stop them, can't you?"

He stared at her a moment as if he wanted to say something, then turned and ran toward the corner of the building. Michelle hugged her chest with her arms, feeling rebellious. She couldn't just sit here and do nothing. She would go crazy if she didn't know what was happening—and maybe she could help. Surely they wouldn't hurt Connie if there were two witnesses.

Filled with an urgency that bordered on panic, she jumped to her feet and rushed toward the corner where Steve had disappeared. She found the broken window a few seconds later. Careless of the jagged edges of the broken glass, she climbed through, hurried across an office and down a long hall, heading for the rear of the building.

Even above the uproar of the kennels, she could hear Connie's frantic trumpeting. She burst out into the courtyard, and when she saw what was happening, she began to scream. The men had piled the empty crates around and under Connie, and had already set it on fire. The flames licked at the old elephant's belly, and her trunk was waving frantically, her eyes rolling in her head. The piercing squeals that escaped Connie's throat sounded just like a woman screaming. . . .

Michelle ran toward the fire, mindless with rage and grief, and when one of the men tried to stop her, she thrust him aside with a strength she hadn't known she possessed. She came to a stop when she saw Steve Lasky, realizing only then why the men had fallen silent.

He was standing beside the burning crates, and his face was so pale that it was a moment before she recognized him. He was holding a small gun; it was pointed at the men. Even as she watched, several of the men started toward him.

Michelle screamed a warning, and he turned his head to look at her. He said something—it could have been, "I'm sorry"—and then he shifted the gun and pointed it toward the fire.

Michelle's overloaded mind played a trick on her. It rejected the next sound. Then she saw Connie crumple to her knees and roll to her side like the floundering of a great gray whale. There was another shot, and she knew that Connie was dead, that nothing she could do, not her screams nor her promises to God, could save her old friend.

A searing grief enveloped her. She found herself screaming again, this time words, the kind that would have earned her a mouthful of soap if her mother had heard them.

The men gave way as she rushed toward the blaze, some part of her still denying the truth, still convinced that if she just did *something*—rubbed the sensitive spot above Connie's eye socket, scratched behind her fan-shaped ear—a miracle would happen and Connie would rise to her feet again.

Steve Lasky's swift action saved her from the flames. She fought him wildly, using her feet and her nails and even her teeth, but it was no use. Her struggles were in vain, and her only satisfaction was the scratches she managed to leave on his face.

"I'm sorry, Michelle," he said when she finally gave up. There was no anger, only a deep weariness, in his voice. "I had to do it—she would have suffered so much if I hadn't killed her."

"Murderer! Murderer! I hate you!" she shouted.

Steve's grasp loosened and he let her go. Then other arms were holding her—her father's arms. She heard voices, shouts, the sound of a fist hitting flesh, and she knew that help had finally come—too late. She began to sob, shuddering sobs that shook her whole body. If only Steve had waited a few more seconds—but he hadn't, and she'd never forgive him, not if she lived for a hundred years.

The fighting only lasted a few minutes. There were curses, a lot of threats, exchanges of angry words, but it was just the face-saving bluster of men who were ashamed of the violence they'd unleashed. Eventually they melted away, leaving Steve and his men to put out the flames.

Michelle refused to leave. The stench of burning flesh was in her nostrils; permanently etched in her brain was the image of Connie's charred body.

She had seen violence before, but never such hatred, such driving, mindless cruelty. Never again would she smile when Clinker talked about a quarrel between two circus men that had ended in a fistfight. Violence, any kind of violence, was ugly and hateful and terrifying. She would never, even after the memory faded, be quite the same. And the one she blamed was not the lynch mob, who already were faceless and anonymous, but Steve Lasky.

In her father's arms she wept quietly, sure that her heart was broken, that it would never mend.

Steve tried to talk to her before he left. She was sitting on a crate, staring down at her dusty sneakers, waiting for her father to take her home, when Steve crouched down beside her.

"I'm sorry, Michelle," he said softly. "It was one of the hardest things I've ever done in my life."

"You could have waited—you had a gun! You could have held them off, made them kick out the fire. I'll never forgive you, never!"

He stared into her stormy eyes. The hair on one side of his head was singed, and his face was so gray that the scratches on his cheek stood out in stark detail. One of them was still bleeding, but she felt no guilt. The scratches would heal, but Connie, her gentle old friend, was dead, shot by this man.

"I know you're still in shock," Steve Lasky said. "But I hope that eventually you'll understand. I couldn't let her suffer. And the threat of the gun wouldn't have stopped them from attacking me, yet I couldn't shoot another man, not even to save her. Someday you're going to be one hell of a woman. You're loving and loyal, and you've got more courage than all that mob put together. But I hope that somewhere along the way, you also develop understanding."

Papa came up then and lifted Michelle to her feet. There were smudges of soot on his face, and his eyes were red-rimmed, as if he'd been crying. He held out his hand to Steve Lasky. "Thank you, Lasky. It seems I owe you another one."

Michelle stared at him in disbelief. He was thanking the man who had killed Connie. With a sob, she turned her back on both of them and began to run, wanting only to escape the knowledge that she was alone in her grief, that no one else shared her pain, her disillusionment.

CHAPTER 45

As soon as Michelle came into the room she shared with two other Cabot juniors, she knew that Joan, the one she liked the least, had been complaining about her again. Although her relationship with her roommates was not particularly close, still she had shared the chocolates Rosa sent her from time to time, had listened to their woes, lent them clothes, and helped them with their math. So she'd thought they had accepted her—which was more than her classmates during her freshman and sophomore years at Cabot had done.

Part of it had been her own fault. Her freshman year, she'd been so homesick that she'd kept to herself at first, and when she did finally open up, she'd talked too much about the circus, unaware that it was an alien and very grubby world to these girls from protected and privileged New England backgrounds.

For the first time in her life, people returned her goodwill and friendliness with coolness, even snubs. Here she was the outsider, a First of May guy. *And I hate it,* she thought fiercely. *I can't wait until I return to the circus for good. . . .*

She searched her memory now, but could think of nothing she'd done that might have offended Joan. In fact, she'd bent over backward this past year to get along with her. Next year, as a senior, she would have a private room, and she was looking forward to it, having discovered how precious privacy could be.

"What's happening?" she said now, forcing a casualness she didn't feel.

"You expecting something to happen—at Cabot? How droll," Joan said in her flat New England drawl. The drawl wasn't affected. She came from one of the first families of Boston, and several generations of her female ancestors had attended Cabot

School, once Mrs. Cabot's School for Refined Young Ladies. What's more, she never let anyone forget it.

"Just asking a civil question and hoping for a civil answer," Michelle said, suddenly tired of always being the one to back off.

"My, we *are* touchy today, aren't we?" Joan said.

"We were talking about the Valentine dance next Friday." Lanie, Michelle's other roommate, was plump and pretty—and also a born peacemaker. "Seems we're all expected to turn up. No excuses unless we break a leg or get the plague. We have to set an example for the daring little plebes." Lanie hesitated, then added, "You *are* going, aren't you?"

Michelle hadn't intended to. She considered the dances a waste of time. Now, because she sensed Joan was a little too interested in her answer, she smiled pleasantly and said, "Oh, I expect I will."

"I suppose you'll be hogging all the boys, as usual," Joan said disagreeably.

So that was it. Joan was jealous. If only her roommate knew how little it mattered whether or not she had many—or any—dance partners. "I'm not interested in anything heavy," she said with an idea toward appeasement. "Which makes me safe. The guys know I won't read anything into it if they ask me to dance."

Joan glowered at her. "So how come you danced with Allie Forester three times last week at his frat's party?"

Allie Forester. Surely it wasn't Allie the Creep Joan had set her cap for—or maybe it was. Joan liked her men rich, rich, rich, and Allie was certainly that. She might even have fallen for that uncool line of his.

"He danced with a lot of girls," she pointed out. "Including you. He told me he had a thing for you, but you wouldn't give him a tumble."

It wasn't true. What Allie had really said was he thought her roommate was a drag—but what the hell. A sulky Joan was pretty hard to take. She flung herself into a chair, pretending not to see the surprise in Joan's eyes—and the flush that spread over her long, narrow face. Joan wasn't pretty, but she had—well, a certain élan. *Like Mama,* Michelle thought, with a pang. *Joan and Mama would get along just fine. . . .*

She caught a glimpse of herself in the mirror above the dressing table they all shared. Earthy, Papa had once called her. And she was certainly that—along with a lot of other things. What had happened to the girl who had come here three years ago?

The change had been so gradual that she had hardly noticed it. Just when had her mouth taken on that sexy look? And her skin that—call it a glow. Her eyes were still too large for her triangular face, but now they looked—well, one of the boys she'd danced with at the frat party had told her she had bedroom eyes. And her hair, that impossible mop of red hair, had darkened drastically. No one had called her Carrots in years. . . .

The thing was, she wasn't sure she liked the new Michelle. Being the center of male attention made her uncomfortable. Which didn't make sense when every girl she knew wanted just that. No wonder they'd never really taken to her. She was too different. She just didn't belong. Sometimes she felt years older than her schoolmates, even the seniors, and certainly older than those infants at Sansun Academy. Other times, she felt as if she hadn't yet grown up. For one thing, she was still a virgin, and what's more, she intended to stay that way. Not for her those messy wet kisses and fumblings in the dark. . . .

"I sure hope David Lasky comes to the dance," Lanie said dreamily. "But he probably won't. The one time he did come, he only stayed a hour or so before he cut out."

"David Lasky?" Michelle fought hard to keep her voice cool. "Should I know him?"

"Oh, that's right. You didn't go to the Thanksgiving dance, did you? All the girls were coming on to him. He's a senior at the Academy, new this year. Great smile, great build, and all this curly blond hair. I danced with him once, but there were no vibes on his part. He didn't come to the Christmas party. I guess he thought it was a drag, chaperons and fruit punch and that dreary band."

"Oh, Lanie, you always play it safe." Joan's drawl held spite. "You never get interested in anyone you can *get*. It's always a teacher or someone who's hung up with another girl. Sometimes I think you're afraid of sex!"

Lanie raised her eyebrows. "Sex at one of *our* school dances?"

"Don't be dense. You make the contact there and then later—well, over the wall and into the arms of love." Joan rolled her eyes, and Lanie giggled.

The conversation turned into familiar channels—the school's absurdly outdated dress code and then a rumor that the two schools would combine and turn coed. Although Michelle was careful to laugh at the right places, it was David Lasky she was thinking about. Could there be two David Laskys, both with

great smiles and curly blond hair? If this was the same boy she'd
met the day Danny had painted the Lasky Circus elephants pink,
why was he just a senior? When she realized he hadn't enrolled
at Sansun Academy three years ago, she'd assumed he'd gone to
another school. He should have finished school that year. Was
it possible he'd been ill?

One thing for sure. She had only been half-serious when she'd
said she would attend the dance. Now wild horses couldn't keep
her away.

Usually Michelle dressed to blend in with the crowd, this after
her freshman rebellion period, when she'd dressed only to shock.
Today, as she dressed for the dance, she chose a knee-length
blue silk bubble dress that her mother had given her for her
seventeenth birthday. As a rule, she wouldn't be caught dead in
anything Vicky chose for her, but today, this one seemed just
right—if a little on the Barbie doll side.

Her reasons were twofold. On the off chance that David Lasky
would attend the dance, she wanted to—what? Show him that
she had grown up? Also, Joan's snide remark that she hogged
all the boys had burrowed in like a burr, and this was her way
of thumbing her nose at her roommate.

She didn't need Lanie's compliments and Joan's narrow-eyed
appraisal to realize how she looked. She'd get a lot of attention,
and it wouldn't mean a thing, because she wasn't interested in
boys—not in general.

Unlike the other girls at Cabot, she had never had a crush on
a boy or even on a rock star. She didn't go into fits over pock-
marked screamers or lank-haired men with gyrating hips. That
whole scene bored her, although she was careful to keep this to
herself. She only had one ambition, and that was to get through
the next year and a half so she could go to work for Papa. They'd
already talked about it, and he was starting her out as a bookkeeper, working in the Red Wagon.

It had taken her a while to get over Connie's death, and although the violence, the horror, still haunted her dreams, she'd
come to terms with it. Hindsight and the passage of time had
made her realize that Steve Lasky had done the brave, the right,
thing, risking his own neck in order to save her old friend from
a terrible death by fire. And yet—she still felt an antipathy toward him, unfair though she knew it to be.

Luckily, that terrible day hadn't affected her devotion to the circus. As Rosa had pointed out more than once, brutal things happened everywhere, not just around a circus.

Although she spent her Christmas vacations with Mama in Florida, she followed the circuit with Papa during the summer, refusing to let the knowledge that she was hurting Mama bother her too much. Someday she intended to help Papa run the circus, so she tried to learn all she could about its logistics and its day-to-day operation.

She still hadn't told Mama she wasn't going to college. Mama expected her to enroll at Sarah Lawrence, the college she herself had once planned to attend. What her mother didn't understand was that college would be a waste of time. After all, *someone* from the present generation should be ready to take over someday. Danny obviously wasn't interested.

Unconsciously she sighed. Danny—he had been in and out of several schools the past couple of years, always starting out with so much promise and always ending up in disgrace. Sometimes it was drinking or girl trouble, but mostly it was gambling that got him in big trouble.

"I've got an incurable case of gambler's fever," he'd told her at Christmas.

"What's gambler's fever?"

"A rare disease that isn't in the medical books and which has no cure. It strikes when the cards are hot—and also when they're not." And then he'd smiled, looking not at all ashamed of himself.

Danny had never made any bones about his disinterest in the family business. Someday Papa—and Grandpa Sam—would give up on him, and when that happened, Michelle meant to be ready. So she didn't dare waste four years learning unneeded skills.

She loved Danny—who didn't?—but he was weak. Under his management the circus would fall apart. And that mustn't happen. The livelihood of too many people depended upon Bradford Circus. It was one of the few family-owned ones still around. As long as it remained healthy, it was a haven for artistes and circus people who couldn't make it in the big circuses, the ones run strictly by profit-and loss sheets.

In preparation, she had signed up for all the math and advanced accounting courses she could find at a school that specialized in subjects to enhance the social graces. It was one of the last schools of its kind in the country—and as far as Michelle was concerned, it was as obsolete as the dodo bird.

Michelle finished brushing out her hair. If only it weren't so damned curly. This year, curly was out and straight was in—she did envy Joan her long, poker-straight hair. Her roommate didn't even have to iron it like some of the other girls did.

"Are you ready, girls?" the house mother's fluty voice floated in from the hall. "You should be there early—you have reception line duty, you know."

Lanie groaned. "Reception line! Honestly—that went out with the ark. What a drag!" She whirled in front of the mirror, her pink miniskirt billowing out above her plump knees. "How do I look?" she said.

"Great—just like a little pink valentine," Joan said.

"You look gorgeous, Lanie. And I love your dress, too, Joan," Michelle said, hoping to defuse Joan's spite. "Where did you get it?"

"Mums bought it for me in New York," Joan said, preening herself. "It's one of a kind."

Meaning it's a designer's original, Michelle thought. "Your mother has perfect taste," she murmured, and didn't point out, as she rightfully could have, that the op art fabric, however stylish, made Joan's angular figure look like a barber pole.

The ballroom—actually, the school auditorium—was festooned with pink paper garlands and pink heart-shaped balloons. Joan surveyed it with bored eyes. "I don't believe it. Couldn't the decoration committee come up with *something* more original than pink hearts?" she said, not bothering to lower her voice.

"I think it looks nice," Lanie protested. "Sort of festive—you know?"

"God—you do have strange taste. Well, I just hope it's worth the bother," Joan grumbled, and for once, Michelle had to agree with her.

Later, as she was sipping a cup of punch—pink, of course—that her latest dance partner had brought her, listening while he tried out his best line on her, she felt a tingling along her spine. Knowing someone was watching her, she turned her head slowly. She met the eyes of a tall, fair-haired man, standing by the door, and the blood rushed to her head, making her dizzy.

For a moment longer, their eyes met, and then David Lasky was looking away, his face a mask of indifference.

"Hey, you okay?" her dance partner asked.

"It's too hot in here," she said. "I think I'll go outside for some fresh air."

"I'll go with you," he said, brightening.

"No—no, you go dance with someone. I'd rather be alone," she said, wanting only to escape. It was obvious David hadn't recognized her, and she felt disappointed—and madder than hell.

She felt a welcome coolness against her flushed cheeks when she got her wrap and then slipped out one of the doors that led to the patio behind the gym building. She wasn't alone—but most of the others there were couples, absorbed in each other. She found a bench well away from the gym, tucked her legs under her, glad to be alone while she dealt with her thoughts.

She started violently when a hand touched her arm. Even in the semidarkness, she knew it was David Lasky. "So you did enroll at Cabot," he said.

"I thought you didn't recognize me," she said.

"Oh, I recognized you, all right. I was just playing it cool in case you didn't remember me."

"Imagine that," she said. "Nice line."

She felt giddy, as if there had been alcohol in that punch after all, when he sat down beside her, so close that his leg brushed hers. "I'm not handing you a line. I never forgot you—or that kiss. Was it your first?"

"What do you think?" she temporized.

"I think it was."

"It wasn't *your* first."

He grinned at her. "Of course not. I was sixteen and a male."

"If ever I heard a sexist remark, that's it."

"Uh-huh. I told you that when you grew up, I was going to marry you. And here you are, all grown-up."

"Is that a proposal?" she said, laughing.

"A premature one. But something happened to me when I saw you a few minutes ago. I don't know yet just what it is or where it will lead, but it knocked me for a loop. Was it that way with you?"

And Michelle, mesmerized by the seriousness in his voice, by the warm pressure of his thigh against hers, by three years of dreams, found herself nodding.

"Good. I'm glad that settled. So what's been happening to you these past years?"

"I've been growing up," she said. "How about you?"

He shrugged. "The family decided I needed some practical experience. They sent me off to Europe to learn the circus business from an old friend of my granddad's. I felt I was just marking time. Maybe I've been waiting for you to grow up."

"You didn't try all that hard to find me," she said.

"How could I, off in Europe? But believe me, I never forgot you."

Two girls passed; from their sidelong glances, the gossips would be buzzing tomorrow. David took her arm and pulled her to her feet. "We can't talk here. How about meeting me tomorrow in town? You do have town privileges, don't you?"

Michelle didn't even hesitate. "Yes. Where and when?"

"Have lunch with me—eleven-thirty at Sears Tavern." He smiled down at her. "I think it's time we found out just what's going on between us, don't you?"

And Michelle, caught up in a wave of excitement, nodded again.

The yeasty odor of beer, of hamburgers grilling over charcoal, struck Michelle's nostrils as she pushed open the door of Sears Tavern. She had never been here before—it was off limits to Cabot students because it served alcohol—but she'd heard of it, of course. She wondered uneasily if anyone from school had spotted her going in, then forgot it when she saw David, waving to her from a booth in the rear of the tavern.

He rose, smiling, as she approached, and when she started to slip into the seat opposite him, he motioned for her to join him on his side of the booth.

A waiter came up, and David ordered hamburgers, fries, and selected an imported beer to drink, and she couldn't help being impressed by his poise. He had learned more in Europe than how to run a circus, she thought.

"I hope that smile's for me," David asked.

"Actually, I was smiling at a private joke."

"You've pierced my heart." He picked up her hand and placed it in the middle of his chest. "Feel how it's jumping all around?"

"Indigestion," she said.

He groaned. "I didn't sleep much last night," he said. "I kept thinking about you."

Michelle withdrew her hand, a little disappointed by the glibness in his voice. "I missed the ten-thirty bus. I'm sorry I was late," she said, not adding that she'd missed it in order to avoid the company of her roommates, who had come into town to shop.

"You should be. I was beginning to think you weren't coming. Is there any other guy I have to worry about?"

He took her hand again and Michelle felt befuddled, acutely aware of the pressure of his hand. ''No one special,'' she said.

''They must all be blind.'' His eyes caught the light as he smiled at her. How odd, she thought in confusion. All this time, she'd remembered them as brown, but they were blue—an even lighter blue than her own.

The waiter brought their order. To her surprise—wasn't love supposed to ruin your appetite?—she was ravenous. She munched on her fries, listening to his banter, and the excitement, the tension, grew, making it hard to respond in the same light tone. If he didn't touch her soon, she'd die—and if he did, she would die anyway. Once, when his hand brushed hers, she felt a jolt along her arm. She told herself it was static electricity, but she couldn't make herself believe it.

She had only been half listening to David, so she was startled when he suddenly dropped his half-eaten hamburger on his plate. ''Let's get out of here,'' he said, his voice rough.

''But—where would we go?''

''A friend of mine has an apartment in town. We can talk there without anyone interrupting us,'' he said.

Michelle was sexually inexperienced, but not so naive that she didn't know what he was proposing. She wanted to go with him, to be alone with him, to let him make love to her, but what if he thought she was easy and cheap?

''I'm sorry.'' He sounded so contrite that she almost patted his hand. ''I'm rushing you. Forgive me, will you?''

She stared at him numbly. She should be relieved, but instead, she was only aware of disappointment. ''I don't know why you're apologizing,'' she said, doing her best to sound casual. ''We can't sit here all afternoon, and it's too cold to just walk around.''

''Are you sure?'' he said.

''I'm sure.''

''We'll just talk, get to know each other better. We have so much to catch up on, you know.''

And talk they did—as they drove through the small town of Coopersville. Michelle was amazed how comfortable and at ease she felt with David, how many things they seemed to have in common, including the same taste in movies and music. They finally stopped in front of a shabby apartment building, and after he'd ushered her into an apartment that had obviously been rented furnished, he fixed coffee and dug out a coffee cake from a tiny refrigerator.

The living room was furnished in glossy, pseudo-Swedish furniture, but the shabby sofa was comfortable, and the February wind, rattling the windowpanes, made the drab room seem almost cozy once David lit a fire in the fireplace. The logs were artificial, but Michelle fancied she could smell wood burning.

"I would offer you a drink," David said lazily, "but I don't suppose you indulge?"

"Sometimes I have a sherry when I'm visiting my friend Rosa. But my mother is positively paranoid about alcohol. Maybe that's why my brother drinks too much."

"Your brother?"

"Danny. He's older than me by three years."

"Of course—the elephant painter."

"I suppose the Bradfords are quite a subject of conversation with your family. I've heard stories about the dastardly Laskys all my life."

"We're sort of like Romeo and Juliet, right?"

"How so?"

"Well, we met when you were only fourteen." He grinned at her flush. "Our families have this ongoing feud, and the way I feel right now, I'm going to do my best to become your lover."

He leaned toward her and took both her hands in his. "You are so beautiful, Michelle."

She gave him a troubled look. Again, the compliment had come so easily to his lips. Was it a line, one he fed all his women?

"I'm not beautiful, David. I'm a carrot top, and my skin is much too pale when I don't have a tan. And I don't need compliments to make me feel good. I'm comfortable with the way I look."

"Silly Michelle. Wonderful, silly Michelle. Don't you know what that mouth does to me? And your hair—I want to tangle my fingers in that hair and never let go."

He kissed her then, a slow, undemanding kiss, and because it was undemanding, she relaxed against him. The kiss deepened, and something inside her, something wild and untamed and too new to be controlled, responded. She found herself clinging to him, letting his tongue intrude. Only, it wasn't an intrusion. It was welcome, wanted, desired. When he touched her throat with his fingertips, she threw back her head, giving him easier access.

Gently he pushed her backward until they were both stretched out full-length on the sofa. His body, strong, hard, and undeniably aroused, pressed against her, sending erotic messages up and down her body. She knew she should stop him, but even more she wanted him to keep touching her, kissing her, wanted him to do more to her aching, burning body. . . .

His hand slipped inside her blouse, arousing and mesmerizing her at the same time. She hadn't known how sensitive her breasts were until he touched her, stroked her, there. He nuzzled her, and when she felt his tongue against her breasts, she realized how adroitly he'd unbuttoned her blouse and pushed aside her bra.

Entranced by the fire that his touch had stoked, she didn't resist, even when he suckled her breast with his open mouth. She told herself that anytime she wanted to, she could stop him—but not yet. Not until she had to.

His hands moved downward, over her hip and under her skirt, and again she didn't protest as he parted her thighs, opening them to his touch.

He was breathing so hard now that she was alarmed for him. When she looked at him, she saw that his eyes were glazed, his face flushed, and she felt a sense of wonder that just touching her could affect him so strongly, She also felt a reluctant to disappoint him, deny him what he wanted so badly. *A little longer,* she thought, *and then I'll stop him.* . . .

He was doing something outrageous to her now, tangling his fingers in the downy mound that was as red as the hair on her head. "Oh, God," he moaned. "I can't stop. You're driving me crazy."

Some part of Michelle knew that he was too experienced to lose control that easily, but suddenly it didn't matter. He was stroking her where no man had ever touched her before, probing her soft flesh with his fingers, and a pressure was building, building. Suddenly it blossomed into pure sensation, a white-hot rush of pleasure that went on and on and never seemed to stop.

She gasped, clutched at him wildly, unable to grasp what was happening, and then the sensation ebbed, leaving her limp and drained and weak. She expected him to go on, to take her now, but instead, he pulled away.

"I didn't mean to go that far. Will you forgive me?" he said.

She looked at him in bewilderment. Forgive him for giving her such a gift? Forgive him for awakening her to all the possibilities of being a sexual being?

"You can't, can you? I told you we would just talk and then

I lost my head and—I hope you don't think I planned this, Michelle.''

He looked so unhappy that she put her arms around him. And because she knew he was still unsatisfied, that he must be in pain—hadn't she heard that it was very painful for a man to go so far and not be satisfied?—she put her hand on the bulge in his trousers, pressed it gently.

He caught his breath and then he was kissing her, fervent, frantic kisses that stirred her passion again. As he undressed her, he kissed the flesh he exposed, and although she welcomed each kiss, she wished he would hurry and finish what they'd started.

While he undressed, she watched with fascinated eyes. She wasn't new to nudity—after all, she'd been surrounded most of her life by people who took it for granted—but never before had she really appreciated the beauty of the male body. His muscles were smooth and taut, close to the bone, his chest covered with fine, silky hair, and she stared openly at his erection. Here, too, he was symmetrical, beautifully formed, and she wanted to be possessed by him, to have it inside her. She raised her arms in invitation, and he sank down on the sofa beside her and buried his face in the hollow between her breasts.

"I want this to be good for you," he muttered against her skin. He caressed her, stroked and fondled her, and again the realization that only someone experienced in sex would know exactly how to arouse a woman. But what did it matter? She was thankful that he knew so well how to use his fingertips, his mouth, his tongue, to make her flesh throb, to send her out of her mind. He could have been one of the fumblers who jumped on top of a girl and took her virginity without finesse. Instead, he entered her carefully, and only the strain on his face, the rigid line across his upper lip, said how much he was holding back.

"Relax, Michelle," he whispered, his breath stirring the tiny hairs at the side of her face. "Trust me. . . ."

And she did. When she felt the rush of passion, she moved against him frantically, and when the soaring, the bursting loose, the ultimate pleasure, came, she fancied she could feel the vibrations even in her bones, and she knew that the first time had only been a prelude to this, the real thing.

She was floating down from the pinnacle when David gave a strangled cry and she felt a warm gushing inside. He collapsed upon her, breathing hard. "Oh, God—you are something special, Carrots."

She didn't answer. In the afterglow of love, she tightened her arms around him, not wanting him to withdraw from the warm sheath of her body. Because then she would start thinking about consequences, thinking about what she had just lost.

A tear ran down her cheek, and he touched his finger to it, tasted it. "Very salty," he said soberly. "Did I hurt you?"

"No, no. I thought it would hurt, but—"

"That's because there was no hymen."

"But—I was a virgin."

"I know. Sometimes it happens that way. Riding a horse will do it. Have you done much of that?"

"Since I was old enough to hold on."

"It was right for you, wasn't it? I could feel it happening, and God, it drove me out of my mind!"

"I didn't know it would be like that. I thought—well, that the first time would be messy and something you just got through as quickly as possible."

He laughed, then sobered quickly. "Do you know what we've got going for us, Michelle? It doesn't happen like this for everyone. And the funny thing is that I knew it would be this way back when we first met. Did you feel it, too?"

Michelle nodded—but a little absently. Something was happening that she hadn't known was possible. Where he had filled her, he was filling her again, and she knew that he was aroused, ready to make love a second time.

"Are you sorry you gave me your virginity?" he said softly, and she was glad that he didn't call it her cherry, making it sound cheap and vulgar.

"A little—but I'm glad it was you."

He reached above her head and pulled a faded afghan over them. "I don't want to move," he said, "but I also don't want you to get cold."

She pressed up closer to him. "As if I could—considering what's happening down there."

He laughed softly, and then he was nuzzling her breasts with his lips. They made love again, and this time he showed her ways to please him, and although some of the things were strange, she did them willingly, wanting to bind him to her, make her necessary to him.

"You're wonderful," David groaned. "Wonderful and generous and exciting."

"You're wonderful, too," she said, breathless because he was

caressing her buttocks in a way she hadn't known until now—
how could she?—was so erotic.

He slid inside her, and she rejoiced in the way his whole body
trembled, in the way he gasped, as if he couldn't find his breath.
The fire inside her flared, and everything stopped except the
urgency, the swift rise to fulfillment.

Afterward, they lay in each other's arms for a long time before
they dressed. As if their lovemaking had aroused other hungers,
they ate every crumb of the coffee cake and finished off the pot
of coffee. As they laughed and talked and teased each other,
Michelle discovered that she was totally happy. Later, she knew,
there would be regrets to cope with, but for now she only wanted
to savor every moment of being in love with David.

During the next few weeks, Michelle discovered she possessed a real talent for subterfuge. She invented excuses to go
into town every Saturday—and to go alone. As a senior, David
had no such problem. He had his own car, a rakish new Ford
Mustang, an abundance of freedom, and, she eventually discovered, the apartment was always at his disposal because he paid
the rent.

"You must have a big allowance," she said when he confessed one afternoon that there was no friend.

"It's just adequate. I think Steve would like to cut me off with
even less, but that wouldn't look good, would it? He has control
of my trust fund until I'm twenty-one—or even twenty-five, if
he wants to get nasty. My grandfather really messed me up on
that trust—hell, Steve is only eleven years older than me. Well,
once I get possession, I can thumb my nose at him."

Michelle digested this information for a moment. "Are you
going to work for your brother after you graduate this June, or
go to college?" she asked.

"Both. School in the winter, work in the summer. He made
that very clear when I came back from Europe."

"I'll be working for Papa next summer," she said, trying to
sound casual. "Maybe we'll run into each other somewhere.
We do seem to hit the same towns a lot."

"Not so often since the old man died. He was the one who
wanted to continue the vendetta. Besides, I think it's about time
the feud stopped, don't you?"

"I do. I always thought it was pretty silly, anyway."

David grinned and pulled her close. "So we don't get to play
Romeo and Juliet, after all. And let's not talk about the future.

We have today, tomorrow, and the rest of the winter and spring. Let's make the most of it, shall we?''

Michelle let him kiss her, kissed him back. They made love, but for the first time, a tiny part of herself held back. Today, tomorrow, and the rest of winter and spring, he'd said—but what about after that, what about the rest of their lives?

CHAPTER 46

*O*NE OF THE PLEASURES THAT *ROSA* ALLOWED HERSELF WAS a rest between the matinee rush and the evening performance. Sometimes she didn't even bother to go to her motor home in the backyard, preferring to simply stretch out for a nap on the camp cot behind the curtain in the rear of the tent.

Clinker, who had her own routine, used this time to visit friends, catching up on the latest news. These days, the circus was buzzing with rumors of financial trouble. And with good reason, was Rosa's opinion. The circus was still solvent, but profits were down, forcing a tightening of the belt when it came to new equipment, new costumes, and pay raises that kept up with inflation.

The sad thing was that despite its reputation as one of the most respected circuses in the country, Bradford Circus was falling behind the times. And the main reason for that was sitting across the table from her now, drinking a glass of Clinker's famous tiger milk, and keeping her from her afternoon nap.

She looked at Mr. Sam with mingled affection and exasperation. One of these days, Michael was going to elope to another circus, and all because of Mr. Sam, who balked at every innovation his son proposed.

Mr. Sam had been droning on for the past half hour. She hadn't been listening, but it didn't matter because she knew he'd forgotten he had an audience. Right now, he was reminiscing about his early circus days.

"—and then, just when the war was winding down, the French flu hit again. So many of us down, we had to cancel the rest of the tour. Large gatherings were banned by the government, so we couldn't have gone on anyway. There in Medford, where we were stranded, we fixed up the Big Top for a hospital, separated the cots with sheets hanging over ropes. We took in some of the towners, too, because their hospitals were full. Some of our women had nursing experience, and one of the local doctors and Doc Smithers—he was our vet then—did all they could. Then, wouldn't you know it, this rumor started that we'd brought in the flu, and there was trouble with the towners—"

Mara stifled a yawn. She'd heard this tale so many times before. Well, old men did ramble on, and Mr. Sam was—how old was he, anyway? He had that lean, close-to-the-bone look that could fool you. Still had his own hair—would Michael keep his, too? It wouldn't matter to him, but it probably would to Vicky.

She sighed, and because it always made her a little sad to think about her daughter, she broke in on Mr. Sam's soliloquy. "How old were you when all this happened, Sam?"

Mr. Sam blinked, as if the interruption confused him. "Oh, I musta been—well, I was born in '90, so I guess I was in my midtwenties. Would've been in the war except for my feet. Flatter'n a Percheron's backside, my arches. I went to enlist, and they wouldn't take me. Saddest day of my life—we knew what we were fighting for in that war, which is more than you can say about what's going on over there in Vietnam. Lots of our men were in the Great War. Jesse Olson came back with his leg gone up to the knee, and some of them, Jack Tuff and—what was that fellow's name? The one who did the double flip-flop off the black rosinback?—he and Jack never made it home."

Mara studied him, adjusting her ideas. "So you were only fifteen years older than me when I joined the circus? Funny—I thought you were at least forty."

He smiled as if she'd complimented him. "Always did look older than I was. That was a big help when I took over after the old man died. It was the flu took him away, the first time it came around. Left me with the circus to run. Lucky I was up to it."

"So is Michael," she said slyly.

"Yeah, I guess so." But his voice was unenthusiastic. "We don't see things the same way, but I let him run things and don't interfere."

"You really believe that, Mr. Sam?" she said.

He gave her an indignant look. "Hell, I don't bother him. Oh, I come along on the circuit 'cause I don't have nothing else to do, but I keep my nose out of the business. I give him some advice from time to time, but he doesn't have to follow it."

"And of course, you never remind him who really owns the show?"

"Well, I got a right to state my opinion when I don't like some of his crackpot ideas. Those new songs the band's been playing—sound like ten cats fighting all at once. Trash music, if you ask me. People like the old songs, the standards—"

"Time moves on, Sam. You mean you didn't make some changes after you took over?"

"Well, sure. But that was different. My old man was rooted in the past. If we hadn't changed, we would have gone under—" He stopped, glowering at her. "Okay, you made your point. You always were a smart-ass. I haven't forgotten how you talked me into selling the Florida property to you."

"You overcharged me—and you can't complain. You've had cheap winter quarters all these years," she reminded him.

His frown deepened, but he didn't challenge her statement. She had increased the rent through the years, but only enough to cover rising taxes and insurance—and she'd turned down offers for the land that could have made her rich. Of course, she was already that—not that anyone, even Clinker, knew about her investments in real estate, her conservative portfolio of stocks and bonds.

"I got a letter from Michelle yesterday," she said, wanting to change the subject. "Hard to believe she's a junior, isn't it?"

He grunted. "Hard to believe that mother of hers sent her off to Boston to get educated when she should be living at home." He gave Rosa an appraising look. "Funny how much the girl reminds me of you. Has your disposition. Now, the boy—" He broke off.

"Danny reminds you of Jaime, even though he has Michael's coloring," she said calmly. "You can say it. It doesn't hurt like it used to. Yes, he has Jaime's charm and ease with people, but Jaime wasn't a gambler."

Mr. Sam bristled as he always did at any criticism of his grandson. "He'll settle down. That boy's pure gold." He paused, his eyes reminiscent. "You never knew I had two sons, did you?"

"Two sons? No, I didn't."

"Well, Michael had an older brother. Only lived to be seven, and then the meningitis took him off." His jaw moved from side to side as if the words left a bad taste in his mouth. "It sure knocked his ma and me for a loop when Sammy, Jr., died. He used to follow me around like he was my shadow." His pale eyes watered and he shook his head as if rejecting the tears.

"I never knew about him."

"Well, it's not easy, even now, talking about the boy. Seemed like the whole world caved in when he died. I couldn't take it in at first—it was a while before I got over it."

"Michael must have been a comfort to you," she said.

"Michael—" He looked blank for a moment. "Oh, sure. Belle was carrying him when Junior died. I guess it did help."

But it didn't, she thought. *You're still mourning your firstborn, and you think you've found him again in Danny.*

Despite her pity, she felt like shaking the old man. Didn't he realize that the grandchild he should be proud of was Michelle? Jaime would have adored both his grandchildren, but he would have seen them through objective eyes. Which was more than Mr. Sam did. And wasn't that true of her, too? Didn't she see Michelle as the daughter she had always wanted—loving and affectionate and, yes, admiring?

She sighed at her own folly, and got up to replenish the thick, creamy concoction in Mr. Sam's glass, wishing she could discuss her worries about Michelle with him. In her pocket, Michelle's letter crackled, reminding her of her alarm when she'd first read that letter yesterday.

"You'll never believe who's a senior at Sansun Academy, Rosa," the letter had started out. "It's David Lasky! In fact, he's my—well, you'd call him my boyfriend. Nowadays, we call him my old man. Rosa, I know I can tell you because you're so broad-minded, but don't tell Clinker! She'd have a fit. David and I are lovers, have been since February. Sometimes I have to pinch myself to believe it. You've never seen him, have you? He is—well, he's wonderful! His hair is the color of saltwater taffy. It's almost as curly as mine, and he wears it as long as his school's code will allow.

"He's older than the other seniors because he spent two years in Europe, learning the circus business. Actually, he's a man, not a boy, and we're very serious about each other, but you mustn't tell anyone. David's older brother still has hard feelings toward the Bradfords, and until David is twenty-one, he has to do pretty much what his brother says. After that, it won't matter because he'll come into a trust fund his grandfather set up for him, and he can do anything he wants.

"I have to admit I'm disappointed that he doesn't have much interest in the circus business. You know how I feel about that. But this was before I fell in love with David. Rosa, I can't think of anything else these days! Sometimes I think I'll go crazy, waiting until we can be together all the time instead of having to sneak around and meet in the apartment he rented in Coopersville—"

Mara realized that Mr. Sam was still rambling on, talking about the son he'd lost. She took a sip of her tea, wishing she were alone so she could read Michelle's letter again. Why did it bother her so much? It was inevitable that Michelle, with her fire and her intense nature, would go all out when she eventually lost her heart to a boy.

It wasn't just my temper she inherited, she thought, and suddenly she was fifteen again, in a dilapidated barn in the Cincinnati river bottoms with the odor of sweet hay in her nostrils, her body on fire for a man. She'd always known that Michelle, when she matured, would have her passionate nature. Did her uneasiness stem from the fact that it was David Lasky, Joe Lasky's grandson, whom Michelle had fallen in love with?

No, it wasn't that. The feud had ended with Joe Lasky's death. It was something else—some rumor, some gossip she'd heard about Lasky's youngest son.

Well, she'd ask Clinker about it. She would know, if anyone did. Of course, she'd have to be subtle. Clinker, who knew her so well, would pounce on any suggestion that she had a personal interest in David Lasky. And if she was right, if David wasn't the kind of man she wanted for Michelle? Well, then she just might do something about it, like contacting his brother, Steve Lasky. . . .

Steve Lasky seldom took a day off during the summer, even when there was a rare still day, but when the phone call came from Rosa, the legendary Gypsy fortune-teller with the Bradford Circus, he made arrangements for his assistant to take over for the day and drove into Baltimore for a meeting with Rosa.

His curiosity stirred by her cryptic statement that it involved a matter of vital—and mutual—concern, he wondered if she'd had a donnybrook with Michael Bradford and was planning to elope to another circus.

This suspicion was put to rest almost immediately after they met in an elegant little French restaurant in downtown Baltimore. Rosa, to his surprise, was not the blowsy, aging woman he'd half expected. She was elegantly dressed in a coffee-colored silk dressmaker's suit, with a matching turban, looking years younger than he knew her to be. He would have sworn, despite their size, that the pearls she wore were genuine. If so, they had set her—or someone else—back a small fortune.

"You're undoubtedly wondering why I asked for his meeting," she said once they had ordered. "I chose this place, away from the fairgrounds, because I didn't want any false rumors to start that I'm planning to leave Bradford Circus."

"I see," he said, hiding his disappointment. "So what is the mutual concern you mentioned?"

She took her time answering. In fact, he thought she seemed a little embarrassed as she fumbled with her napkin, folding it carefully over her knees. "You've met Michael Bradford's daughter, I understand," she said finally. "What did you think of her?"

Steve's face relaxed into a smile. "She's very special. One of the gutsiest kids I've ever met."

"She's no longer a kid, Steve. She's seventeen and very grown-up—in some ways. In other ways, she is still an innocent. In fact, that's why I asked you to meet me. It involves Michelle— and your brother."

Steve frowned at her. "David? What has he got to do with Michelle?" he said sharply.

In answer, she handed him a letter, then sat there silently while he read it. He looked up finally. "Hell," he said explosively.

"Exactly. Michelle is very dear to me. I just can't stand by and watch her get hurt. I know your brother's reputation—he's a womanizer, along with other . . . weaknesses. He'll break Michelle's heart. What are you going to do about it, Steve?"

"I'm going to stop it," he said grimly.

"You can do that?"

"Oh, yes. I control David's trust fund."

"And you share my—my dismay?"

"I have a very special affection for Michelle, Rosa. I've never forgotten what happened when her elephant was killed. Maybe I owe her something."

"Then I leave it in your hands." There was relief in Rosa's voice. She gave him a smile that made him wonder what she'd looked like as a young woman. "Michelle is like my own daugh-

ter. I want only the best for her. She's devoted to the circus, you
know. When she marries, I hope it will be to someone who feels
the same way. Do you understand what I'm saying?''

He stared into her expressive eyes. "I think I do," he said
slowly.

The waiter came with their order, and for the rest of the meal,
they talked about other things. By the time they were finished,
Steve felt as if he'd known Rosa—and admired her—all his
life. He also knew something else. Rosa had not only come to
ask him to break up his brother's affair with Michelle, which she
could have done by phone, she was also here to take a good
look at a possible husband for her young friend.

He didn't know whether to be amused—or touched. He drove
back to the fair grounds in a very thoughtful mood.

When David rented the furnished apartment in Coopersville,
it had been his way of thumbing his nose not only at the antiquated rules of Sansun Academy, but at his brother. Of course,
it had served more than one purpose. During the year, he'd
entertained several girls there—but that was before he'd met
Michelle again.

Although he grumbled to Michelle about being older than the
other seniors, secretly he enjoyed the respect he got. The rumors
of his sexual adventures were highly exaggerated, but he never
bothered to correct them. He was, after all, something of an
expert, having learned the art of seduction when most guys his
age were still getting their sex with a *Playboy* centerfold in one
hand. If his brother hadn't held the threat of taking away his
trust fund over his head, he wouldn't even be at Sansun. He
hated the school, hated the stupid discipline and having to follow
rules. It had been his antipathy for rules that had landed him in
The Trouble.

He always thought of it like that, in capital letters. It wasn't
as if he'd committed a real crime. Hell, he'd only been seventeen
when he and Sheila got together for the first time. It had been
her doing as much as his. That summer, she'd managed to turn
up everywhere he went, flaunting herself, tantalizing him with
her lush figure and those pouty lips. How could he possibly have
passed her up? He'd been as horny as any other seventeen-year-
old, maybe more so.

But he had held back at first because she was one of the
Martizan girls. The Martizans were high fliers, old circus, and
very touchy about their daughters. He'd known about the old

man's reputation for being hard-nosed, and how tough Sheila's brothers were, but when she'd snuck into his compartment during an overnight haul, he'd lost his head, and in a few minutes, they were going at it hot and heavy. He'd thought he was one cool stud when it came to sex, but she'd taught him things he hadn't known.

And then, he'd gotten her pregnant. Or so she said.

It had ended up one helluva mess. There was no way he was going to marry her, like she wanted, and yet—there *were* Sheila's father and brothers, all of whom had a reputation for taking care of people who offended them.

So he'd gone to Steve, and that self-righteous bastard had put the screws in him. He'd help him out, get David out of their reach by sending him to a friend in Europe whose family owned a circus, and when things were cool, he could come back and finish school. But if he didn't toe the line, he could forget about ever collecting his trust fund. He could starve, for all Steve cared.

The odd thing was that David had enjoyed his sojourn in Europe. Sure, he'd worked his ass off at all kinds of junk jobs, but he had seen things that broadened his outlook, stretched his consciousness. And the girls—God, there wasn't anything like European girls. Tall, blond Swedes and short, dark-skinned Italians. And the Germans—so matter-of-fact about sex and yet so inventive in bed.

Not that it had been easy, leading an active sex life. Hans Schmidt, who managed the circus for his family, was always coming down on him, checking up on him. He suspected that Steve had told his friend to not only work him hard but to keep him on a close rein. Well, he'd still had his fun, but one thing had come clear to him—he wanted nothing to do with the family business except to collect his share of the profits.

When Steve finally told him he was free to come home, to enroll at Sansun Academy, he hadn't argued. School was a breeze next to pounding spikes into the ground. The Trouble had blown over. That bitch Sheila had finally confessed that she wasn't sure who had fathered her brat, that she'd used her pregnancy to try to get herself a husband (at seventeen!), and so he'd gotten off the hook. And now he just had to sweat out another year until he turned twenty-one. Once Steve had turned his trust over, he could spit in his brother's eyes—and put the circus behind him for good.

Which was still his plan, even though Michelle had changed things.

David leaned against the window frame, staring down at the shabby street below his apartment. Michelle—God, she had gotten into his blood! He hadn't dreamt he could fall so hard for a girl. They had come and gone, the Sheilas and the Maries and the Gretas, quickly seduced and just as quickly forgotten.

He hadn't counted on someone like Michelle coming along. She was an original, all that fire and generosity, just for him. He never tired of making love to her. In fact, he never tired of being with her, period. When he didn't see her for a while, he ached for her, and he was scared to death something would happen and he'd lose her.

And wouldn't Steve laugh if he knew his younger brother, whom he'd once called "a crazy young stud with the morals of an alley cat," had been struck down by a half-pint girl with hair the color of carrots? Talk about irony.

And if Michelle, with her sometimes disconcerting honesty and lack of guile, ever found out that he'd lied about his exile to Europe, how would that go down? She believed every word he told her now—but how fast would that change if she found him out?

There were so many things to consider—in a few weeks, he would graduate. Steve expected him to work for him this summer, then go off to Princeton in the fall. Michelle would be working for her father, and after that, she still had another year at Cabot. There just didn't seem to be any way they could get married soon.

Well, he'd think of something.

The phone rang behind him. He swung around and stared at it, frowning. Only one person, Michelle, knew this number, and she was off on some field trip today. The only reason he'd had the phone installed was so she could reach him here evenings. . . .

The phone rang again, and this time he picked it up. "You okay, Michelle?" he said.

There was a long pause. "Hello, David," his brother's voice said.

David grimaced, but he pumped cheerfulness into his voice. "This is a surprise, elder brother. How did you get this number?"

"Never mind that. Why the hell did you rent an apartment? You know it's against Sansun rules."

"Hey, this place belongs to a friend of mine—"

"Don't lie to me. You pay the rent. And you're in big trouble. Don't you have any sense at all?"

Anger made David incautious. "Listen, Steve, I'm twenty years old. I can get along without your advice."

"You're shit. That's what you are. You rented that apartment so you could take Michelle Bradford there. She's—how old? Sixteen?"

"Seventeen," he said sullenly. So Steve knew about Michelle, too. . . .

"I knew you were a jerk, but not so low that you'd hit on a girl that young, one that special."

"What do you know about her? You only saw her once."

"Twice. Long enough to know that she's too good for you. You fool! The feud may be over, but what if Michael Bradford finds out you've been sleeping with his seventeen-year-old daughter?"

"How can he find out?"

"I did."

"So you did. Which raises an interesting question. I know Michelle hasn't told a soul, and I sure haven't."

"Never mind that. I've put up with as much as I'm going to take from you. You end it with that girl, and right away, or you can forget the trust fund—permanently. Is that clear?"

Bitterness welled up inside David, but he managed to keep it out of his voice. "You've got things all wrong. I'm serious about Michelle. I want to marry her."

"And how do you plan to support her?"

"Hey, I can get a job. And you should be happy. You've been wanting to merge with her old man's circus, right? If it was all in the family, that should make it easier to convince old man Bradford it's a good deal."

"You always have an angle, don't you? Well, I'm not going to let you ruin that girl's life. She's infatuated with you, but that's all it is. So make it a clean break."

"Why are you so concerned about Michelle? If it wasn't ludicrous, I'd—hell, that *is* the answer. Mr. Perfect is lusting after a seventeen-year-old girl!"

"You have a filthy mind, David. Yes, I *am* concerned about Michelle. But I'm more concerned about the circus. I'm not going to let you start up that feud again, which is what would happen if Michael Bradford finds out you've been fooling around with his daughter. So break it off, like right now, or—"

"The hell I will. I love Michelle—this isn't some one-night stand with me. I'm marrying her, and I might not wait until she's eighteen. How do you like that?"

"If you do, forget your trust fund. I'll turn the money back to the circus account. I have that option, you know. I'll give you three days to think how it would be to work hard for a living—and to remember your expensive tastes."

The phone clicked in David's ear.

It took David the full three days grace period to make his decision. He loved Michelle, yes, but he was also a realist. Oh, if he were the hero type, he'd tell Steve to go to hell, get a job, and marry Michelle. But this was real life, and he knew his weaknesses. Working for slave wages, living on the edge of poverty—it just wasn't for him. He'd go bonkers, and in the end, he'd blame Michelle. No, he was doing her a favor, dumping her.

As for his brother—all his life he'd played second fiddle to Mr. Perfect. For now, he had to do things Steve's way, but someday—yeah, someday it would be his turn, and then he'd pay that bastard back. . . .

CHAPTER 47

*F*OR HER FIRST TWO AND A HALF YEARS AT CABOT, MICHELLE had marked time, waiting for graduation, when she would rejoin the circus, the only world she'd ever wanted. After she and David became lovers, all that changed. The months between February and June were a time of magic, of excitement and heightened awareness. Colors seemed brighter, her senses sharper, her emotions a crazy mix of joy and, inexplicably, a not unpleasant melancholy.

Her mood swings were dramatic. She laughed a lot, cried just as easily, touched by things as small as an old woman sitting alone on a park bench, holding a tiny kitten. Children at play delighted her. Love songs thrilled her, sent her blood pounding in her throat, and when she went to a rock concert with David, it was all she could do not to dance in the aisles like some adolescent teenybopper.

She was wildly, almost maniacally, happy. Part of it was David's lovemaking. Intellectually she realized that she was one of those rare women who are almost as quickly aroused as a man, that undoubtedly she could respond sexually to other attractive men. But not, she was sure, the way she responded to David's lovemaking. Other girls, when they were letting down their hair and being honest, admitted that while they loved foreplay, loved being the center of a man's attention, they could take or leave the act itself. But she loved the act as much, she suspected, as David did. Which made the relationship very special indeed, especially since some of her euphoria also stemmed from her feeling of belonging, of finding someone who came from the same background and talked her own language.

She refused to allow anything negative to intrude upon her happiness. That David was careless with money, sometimes borrowing from her, she brushed aside, especially since he was so ashamed when he had to admit that he didn't have the money to take her to a concert or even to put gas in his car. As for forgetting to pay it back—well, he had a lot on his mind.

His brother was to blame, of course, for giving him such a niggardly allowance. She did ask him how he could afford to own such an expensive car, but he'd explained that by saying he'd saved up for it while working in Europe.

They made plans. When David graduated, he would go to work for his brother, impress him with his maturity, and then, when Steve had turned over his trust fund money, they would be married—and the devil with both of their families. Eventually her parents and his brother would come around. Families always did, didn't they?

Michelle tried not to think of June, which was approaching at such a rapid rate, because it meant that she and David would be separated for the summer. On the other hand, she wanted the time to pass quickly, because it hurried the day when they would be together forever.

Forever. God, that had a good ring. . . .

The night before David's graduation, they spent in each other's arms. He couldn't seem to get enough of her. She had enlisted the help of Lanie—luckily, Joan had already departed for home—who thought it a great lark, covering for her so she could stay out all night. David's lovemaking had never been sweeter, more fervent, and she was sure that, like her, he was thinking about the long summer of separation ahead.

Very early the next morning, when David drove her back to the campus, he kissed her for a long time, looking so forlorn that she couldn't help crying. After she got out of the car, he sat there for a long moment, staring at her, before he finally started up his car and drove away.

When she reached her room, she was so exhausted that she fell onto her bed without taking off her clothes. She only intended to close her eyes for a few minutes, but she fell asleep as soon as her head hit the pillow.

Lanie shook her awake. "Come on, sleepyhead. You've got to get out of those wrinkled clothes before someone starts asking questions." Her eyes were bright with curiosity. "How did it go? Was it—you know, everything you expected?"

Michelle smiled to herself. Lanie thought this was her first time with David. What would her roommate think if she knew she'd had sex—no, she hated that expression!—that she and David had been lovers for months?

"You did get those pills, didn't you?" Lanie added.

Again, Michelle wanted to smile. She'd been on the pill since February. "Indeed I did," she said lightly. "And David is a wonderful lover."

Lanie sighed. "What I wouldn't give if he looked in my direction. I think I'd forget you and me were good friends!"

Michelle looked at her with real affection. Why hadn't she seen that Lanie really was her good friend earlier? Had she missed other opportunities to make friends because she'd been so wrapped up in resentment?

"Are you going to David's graduation?" Lanie asked.

"No. He got a call from his brother ordering him to join the circus in Newark tomorrow, so he won't be at the ceremonies today."

Michelle had been surprised when David told her about his brother's phone call. It seemed so unreasonable, even for a man who never hesitated to disrupt other people's plans.

"Well, that gives you more time for packing," Lanie was saying. "We have to be out of our rooms for sure by Tuesday. Half the school's already gone."

She sounded so wistful that Michelle put aside her own concerns. Of course—Lanie's parents were dead, so school was probably the closest thing to a home she had. How strange that she'd never wondered before if Lanie was lonely. "Where will you go this summer?" she asked.

"Oh, the usual. Guess I'll sign up for a counselor's job in the Berkshires again. I'm going to spend a couple of weeks on Martha's Vineyard with my guardian and his new wife. This is the first time he's invited me. I guess he figured that a single man couldn't put up a teenager without it causing talk."

"How would you like to spend the summer with a circus?" Michelle asked impulsively.

Lanie gave her a startled look. "You mean—?"

"You can live with Papa and me in our private car. There's plenty of room. I'm sure he can find a job for you if you want to earn money. How about it? You'll love Papa. He's really super. And wait until you meet Danny, my brother—but don't fall in love with him. He isn't someone you can depend upon."

Lanie jumped up and hugged her. "I accept, I accept! I've always thought you were the luckiest girl alive, your grandfather actually owning a circus!"

Michelle frowned at her. "You did? Funny, I got the impression that everybody at Cabot looked down on circus people. That's why I never talk about it."

"You crazy kid! Everybody thinks it's terribly romantic, you coming from such an exotic background. If someone said anything to—you know, hurt your feelings, it was only because they were jealous. I hope you set them straight."

"I retreated into a shell," Michelle confessed. "I guess I was overwhelmed that first year. As a rule, I'm—well, I do have quite a temper."

Lanie giggled. "You? You're a pussycat."

There was a rap on the door, and the floor monitor stuck her head in, waving an envelope.

"Mail call—special delivery for you, Michelle."

Michelle took the letter, recognized David's bold handwriting, and retreated to her bed to read it. Her first love letter— how like David to realize how lonely she'd be feeling today.

She tore the envelope open, smiling in anticipation, and then, as she read the first lines of the letter, the world collapsed around her like Rosa's deck of tarot cards.

"My dearest Carrots," David had written. "I know it's rotten of me not to tell you this in person, but I just had to spend one more night with you before—well, before you find out about Steve.

"He knows about us, and he's crazy mad. He refuses to listen to reason. If I want my trust fund—and remember he has complete control over it and can dissolve it at any minute—I must give you up. That's the only thing that will satisfy him. I know how this sounds. You're thinking how weak I am. I prefer to call it being realistic. Those years I spent in Europe, doing manual labor, taught me one thing about myself. I'm just not cut out for a life of poverty—or even near poverty. I'm too used to—well, not wealth, but a very comfortable life. If I turned my back on my inheritance to marry you, eventually both of us would be miserable. You won't believe this now, but I'm doing it for you as much as me.

"Please forgive me. I do love you, Carrots."

He'd signed it David, but he should have signed it Judas.

Michelle sat there, the letter crumpled in her hand. With wild eyes, she looked around the familiar room, at the Filmore Auditorium poster that Lanie was so proud of, at the faded patch on the wall where Joan's favorite montage had hung, at the hand-embroidered quilt Rosa and Clinker had sent her when she was a freshman, and she wanted to destroy something, wanted to slash the poster and the treasured quilt to shreds, wanted to smash the wall mirror to smithereens.

She did none of these things, of course. Neither did she faint, although the room had a tilted look. Sensibly, she put her head down between her knees until the dizziness went away. But she couldn't dismiss so easily the rage, hot and brutal, that wracked her. It wasn't directed at David. He was weak. His excuses couldn't hide that. But it was his brother she blamed. He had played on David's weakness, and she hated him for that. She wanted revenge, hungered for it—only, there was nothing she could do that could possibly hurt him the way he'd hurt her.

She smoothed out the letter and read it again.

Finally she began to cry.

CHAPTER 48

A S FAR AS MICHAEL WAS CONCERNED, IT HAD BEEN ONE helluva morning. First there'd been a mechanical breakdown of one of the light wagon generators, and then a complaint from a local city councilman about an irregularity in the water permit. He'd put his best electrician to work on the generator and had exerted all his diplomacy on the councilman, finally soothing his ruffled feathers by presenting him with a handful of free passes, which was what it had all been about, of course. When the councilman was gone, he left the Blue Wagon in his secretary's capable hands and took the gilly wagon back to the train.

Looking forward to a quick shower, a change of clothes, and maybe a short nap before the afternoon matinee, he hurried up onto the pullman car's platform. Like his father, he'd missed few performances since he'd become manager. His presence there at the back door, clipboard in hand, was the glue that held the show together as much as the prompts from the music director, and the perfect timing of Sam Marks, the equestrian director who had replaced Konrad Barker when he'd finally retired.

To his surprise, since he'd turned off the air conditioning earlier, a blast of cool air greeted him when he opened the door. He stopped in the entrance, looking around, and when he saw the matched set of suitcases sitting by the sofa, he began to smile, knowing that Vicky was paying him a surprise visit.

Despite his instinctive pleasure, he felt a little wary, too. Their last meeting had been anything but pleasant. She had been furious because, for yet another time, he'd refused to even discuss leaving the circus, and she'd shown her displeasure by developing a convenient headache. So why had she turned up here without any warning? Was something wrong?

471

His breath caught as Vicky appeared in the stateroom door. Her hair, smooth and glossy and the color of fall oak leaves, swung free, the way she seldom wore it these days. She had changed into a summer robe, and her figure, almost as perfect as the day he'd married her, showed to advantage through gossamer material. God, how she could still take his breath away!

There were times, when she was flaying him with her tongue, that he wished she'd get a little fat or grow a few gray hairs. Maybe then, was his reasoning, she wouldn't expect perfection in others. But she wouldn't be Vicky either, and it was Vicky he loved to distraction. . . .

"This is a surprise," he said, trying for casualness.

"I know," she said, smiling.

He went to give her a husbandly kiss on the cheek. He wanted to do more, to kiss her violently, but he was sure that would be a mistake.

"I missed you," she said. "It's been six weeks."

"And two days, and—uh, three hours," he said, and despite himself, his voice came out a little hoarse.

"How would you like some company for the rest of the circuit?" she said.

"Are you—are you all right, Vicky?"

She stepped away from him. "Of course I'm all right. Does something have to be wrong just because I want to be with you? If you don't want me to stay—"

"Of course I want you to stay. Every year I try to talk you into coming with me for the summer."

"Not lately," she said, her voice low. "I don't think we even discussed it this spring."

He stared at her, trying to see behind her words. Was she accusing him of being indifferent? Of neglecting her? The truth was, he had simply gotten tired of asking her and having her refuse. Okay, some of it was resentment. Being separated eight or more months every year was not his idea of a perfect marriage.

"I guess that's my answer," she said, and he knew he'd been quiet too long. "I suppose you've found other interests?"

He frowned at her. What the hell was going on here? Was she jealous? She must know he didn't play around with other women. Yes, there had been that brief episode with the woman journalist who'd interviewed him last season. It had been exciting as hell—until the morning after, when he'd realized that the chase was more exciting than the catch, that the only woman he really wanted was Vicky.

Had Vicky found out? Was this why she was here?

"Why don't you tell me what's really on your mind?" he said gently.

"I got lonely," she said. Unexpectedly her eyes were wet. "I thought—well, Michelle will be working for you full-time after she graduates. And Danny is already here. I thought we should be a family again. And besides—I'm tired of being a summer widow."

Instinct told Michael that this wasn't the whole story. It was also obvious that she didn't intend to confide in him. Whatever it was, it didn't even matter. What did was that she was here, that there would be no more summer loneliness. Maybe they could turn back the clock to the way it used to be. It wasn't just sex he missed, although that had always been good between them. It was the intimacy, the closeness of those first years.

Not that he blamed the slow decline of their marriage on Vicky. God knew he wasn't innocent. He could have gone into another business, given her the stable life she'd always craved. But he'd wanted things his own way, and he hadn't given an inch.

And now it looked as if he'd won, after all. . . .

He reached out and took her hand, smiling into her eyes. Although he was already aroused, he didn't make the mistake of rushing her. He kissed her cheek, then her eyebrow, then her mouth.

"I've missed you, Vicky," he said against her ear. "I'm glad you're here. I hope you never leave."

She snuggled closer. Already her heartbeat rate had quickened—and so had her breathing. How strange that she was such a passionate woman when outwardly she was so cool. The Ice Queen, one of the riggers had called her once, not knowing Michael was listening. Ice and fire was more like it—was that why he had never lost his need for her?

He pulled her closer, buried his face in her hair. It smelled like carnations, the perfume she favored. It was obvious that she wanted him to make love to her, and God knew he was more than willing. After six weeks of abstinence, he was horny as a teenager.

"What do you say we both go to Michelle's graduation next month?" he said, wanting to please her.

She pulled away a little to look at him. "Can you get away?

That's the weekend the show's booked for that long run in Cleveland, isn't it?''

"The old man can take over for a few days. It'll make him feel useful.''

She smiled at him. "In an emergency, maybe Danny could step in.''

"Right," he said, hiding his doubts. "We can leave a couple of days early, stop somewhere along the way for some time alone together, then surprise Michelle by both turning up at her graduation. How does that sound?''

"Like heaven," she said, and kissed him. "And let's discuss it later.''

"Oh? You got something more interesting to talk about?''

She slid her hand inside his belt. "Not talk. Action is what I crave,'' she said.

It seemed to Michelle, as she stood on the lush green lawn in front of the school chapel, that she was viewing the world through a long-distance telescope. The other graduates, looking like flowers in their pastel dresses, each surrounded by parents and guests, the teachers in their somber clothes that looked like uniforms but weren't, didn't seem quite real.

She'd had this feeling of detachment so often this past year, as if she were living on a different plane. In some ways the detachment was comforting because it protected her from pain. She went through the motions, talking and laughing and making all the right moves, protected by a wall nothing could penetrate, not even this most recent hurt.

It wasn't that she had expected her father to come to her graduation. For him to leave in the middle of an important booking like Cleveland would have meant all kinds of difficulties for the circus. But it had never occurred to her that her mother wouldn't be here on this important day. All through the program, she'd searched the audience with her eyes, not giving up until she'd examined every row.

And wasn't it interesting that while it hurt, it was a gentle ache, not the same as it would have been a year earlier? Oh, yes, she had changed. She was no longer a stupidly naive girl. She'd grown wiser, less gullible. The odd thing was that her classmates believed that she'd come out of her shell, when actually she had merely retreated behind a thicker one. Couldn't they see that she no longer cared what they thought about her? Maybe that was the secret of her recent popularity. That she really didn't give a damn.

Her student advisor had put it succinctly. "You've become a mature person, Michelle." This after Michelle had just been elected senior class president. How strange to be complimented for becoming cynical, indifferent to other's people's opinion, for retreating behind a protective shell. . . .

"Michelle, that pink dress is absolutely fabulous on you. Whoever said a redhead shouldn't wear pink?" It was Lanie, looking like a buttercup in a pale yellow dress. "Guess what?" she rushed on. "I'm going to work for my guardian this summer. Can't you just see me, typing out contracts and filing away important papers?"

"You'd better learn the alphabet first," Michelle teased.

A middle-aged man, looking a little uncomfortable in a too heavy three-piece suit, and a rather dowdy younger woman came up. The woman put her arm around Lanie and gave her a hug. Michelle went through the amenities of being introduced to Lanie's guardian and wife with only half her attention. She still hoped to see her mother coming toward her through the crowd.

Lanie was babbling on about her summer plans when Mr. Bevens, the assistant dean, touched Michelle's arm to get her attention. His face was grave, off-color, and even before he spoke, she knew that something was wrong.

What she couldn't possibly guess was just how wrong that something was.

After the funeral, that sad, dark-hued double funeral of her parents, attended by the whole circus, including the anomalies, Mara and Clinker rode back to the lot with Michelle in one of the long black limos provided by the funeral parlor. Danny, who had looked like Little Boy Lost all through the services, was riding with Mr. Sam in the limo behind them.

Clinker, her handkerchief pressed against her red-rimmed eyes, snuffled now and then, but for once, she had nothing to say. Michelle was silent, too. She sat staring straight ahead, as if she had been struck blind, and Mara, fighting her own shock and almost unendurable grief, couldn't think of any way to comfort her.

What could she say? That sometimes death was a blessing? Both of them, Michael and Vicky, had been in perfect health. How could death be a blessing to people who had a long life to look forward to? Nor could she say that they had gone so quickly that it was doubtful they'd known what was happening. No one knew if they had died when the runaway truck struck them head on or if they had suffered agonies of pain before death released them. Even to mention it would only evoke images of a fiery highway accident on a lonely Pennsylvania road. . . .

Nor could she say that time would heal all wounds. She, who still nursed wounds from Jaime's death, wouldn't have been very convincing.

Oh, Jaime, the beautiful daughter we made together is gone. I made so many mistakes, failed her so many times. When you see her, tell her I loved her. Make her welcome with your love. . . .

The thought of Jaime calmed her, as it always did, and suddenly, as if he had whispered the right words in her ear, she knew what to say.

"Your mother came to see me a week ago," she said, breaking the long silence. Clinker turned her head to look at her, and Michelle's eyes lost some of their blindness. "She asked me to read her cards."

"And did you?" Michelle's voice was wooden, the words a little slurred.

"I tried, but the cards were silent. When the person reading them loves—is deeply involved with the subject, they sometimes withhold sad news."

"If they had taken a different route—or if they'd flown or gone by train—they'd still be alive. And why were they together anyway? They haven't taken a trip together in years."

"They were on a second honeymoon. I don't know if it matters to you, Michelle, but they were very close, very happy, this last month. Your mother was going to make the circuit this year so the family would be together again. After they went to your graduation, they were going to bring you back with them."

"And if Papa had stayed with the circus, Mother would have flown to my graduation and they'd both be alive today," Michelle said bitterly. "What good are your cards if they can't warn you in advance of danger?"

"They were very happy this past month. Surely that's important. To die when you're happy—how much better than to die when you're not."

Michelle began to cry, her whole body shaking with sobs. Mara gathered her up in her arms, ignoring Clinker's frown and sharp "Now see what you've done!"

Michelle cried for a while, then stopped. Mara wiped her face with a tissue, held it while she blew her nose. Later, when they were back in the pullman, she gave Michelle a sleeping pill, then sat beside her, holding her hand, until she fell asleep.

Clinker was waiting, slumped in a chair, when Mara returned to the salon. "She's asleep. I have to go to Mr. Sam now. He'll need me," Mara told her.

Clinker nodded agreement. "They'll all need you now, Mara," she said, her voice heavy.

Mr. Sam was sitting in the roomy compartment he used when he traveled with the show. His gaunt face reminded Mara of the painting of a dying Italian warrior she had once seen on a museum tour.

"Can I do anything for you?" she asked, knowing it was a meaningless question. He had just lost his only son—what could anyone possibly do for him?

Surprisingly, he answered her question. "I could use some coffee. Seems like I'm just too tired to get it myself."

Glad to have something to do, Mara made coffee in the galley, then carried two mugs to Mr. Sam's compartment. She put one mug into his hand and sat down opposite him. He nursed the mug between his hands as if they were very cold.

"Well, Mara, here we are," he said. "Two old folks who have just lost their only kids. I never once told Michael I loved him, Mara. Oh, I guess he knew how I felt, but I wish I'd told him."

"I loved him, too. He was the son I never had."

"Your Vicky and me were never close, but I admired her. She had lots of class—and most of the time, she made Michael happy." Mr. Sam's face twisted suddenly. "Oh, God—it's so rotten, outliving your own kid. How are we going to get along without them? Ask your cards that, Mara."

"We have two wonderful grandchildren. We should count our blessings."

He took a sip of coffee, swallowed it. "Danny and Michelle. Yes, we have to think of them. We're all they have now."

"You'll be busy. The circus needs a strong hand at the helm."

"I'm too tired. Too old. Someone else will have to take over."

"Michelle—you could train her."

"Michelle? She's too young." He ruminated for a while. "Danny will have to take over. I'm just not up to it, Rosa."

Mara, aware of his stubbornness, his prejudices, didn't argue with him, although she could have pointed out that Michelle, with her fine, orderly mind, her passion and dedication to the circus, was the logical one to train as manager. It was the wrong decision, but time would have to prove that to Mr. Sam. Meanwhile, she would keep her eye on Danny, who was lovable, sunny-natured—and also lazy, a born gambler and womanizer.

Maybe she'd get out the tarot deck tonight and see what they had to say. Or maybe she wouldn't. If the circus was about to run into hard times, did she really want to know about it?

CHAPTER 49

THERE WAS ALWAYS A CERTAIN AMOUNT OF GRUMBLING around the workmen's tables in the long end of the cookhouse. A circus person who didn't bitch was considered an oddball. But there was a new intensity about the gripes during the season of '68, a year after Danny took over as manager.

One thing was the weather. Always capricious in the Midwest, it had been unusually so this year, creating all manner of difficulties, from a blown-down top in Dayton to a spring hailstorm in Terre Haute to a rumble with towners during a three-day run in Akron that resulted in injuries on both sides.

But most of the grumbling had to do, not with the weather, but with circus management. There were growls that Danny Bradford was too young, too lazy—and too oversexed. That he was never there when he was needed. When emergencies arose, he was always off the lot, and other people, mainly his sister, was forced to make decisions for him. What the circus needed, was the general consensus, was a strong hand at the helm. Mr. Sam, for all his age and antiquated ideas, could have handled things, but he was under the weather and spent most of his time in his pullman these days.

Mara, more worried than she was willing to admit to Clinker, had even started to eat breakfast in the cookhouse, just to find out what the thinking was among the rank and file. There was talk about Danny's expensive wardrobe, his flashy new foreign car, about his gambling and his women and the wild parties he threw in hotels along the circuit. To Mara, the stories cut deep, because she saw in Danny the live-for-today ways of her own people.

She held off talking to him. They were good friends, had been since he was old enough to spend his summers with the circus, but she was realistic enough to know that she had no real influence on him.

So she hoped for the best, kept trying to convince herself that it was only a matter of time until he grew up and began accepting responsibility. It wasn't until the bank auditors came for their midseason audit that she realized just how bad things were.

Mr. Sam came to see Mara that afternoon. His face was even grayer than usual, and she saw something in his eyes that she'd never seen there before—defeat. "What's wrong, Sam?" she asked quickly.

"Someone's been tampering with the books."

"Someone? Who?" Mara asked, even though she already knew what the answer must be.

A nervous tic started up in Mr. Sam's cheek. He rubbed the palm of his hand over his face as if checking to see if it was still there. "The bank auditors are still trying to pin it down."

"What'll happen when they find out who it is?"

He blinked his heavy-lidded eyes; the despair on his face made her wince. "They'll prosecute. They have the right. Goddammit! I told Michael not to take out that loan!"

"The circus needed new canvas and equipment—"

"We could've made it without them. Hell, we were doing great before he went off on that fool second honeymoon with—" He broke off, not finishing the sentence.

"You need a cup of coffee," she said, holding tightly on to her temper.

"What I need is a good stiff drink," he said gruffly.

Mara didn't remind him that the doctors had forbidden him alcohol. She went the cabinet where she kept her liquor, poured him a shot of scotch, put it into his hand. His hand shook so he could hardly get it to his mouth. She had no doubts that Danny was the one who had embezzled the money. Had her grandson realized the seriousness of what he was doing? Probably not. She'd encountered his inability to call a spade a spade before. If it were his own money he had squandered, she could understand. But to risk the whole circus, the livelihood of people he'd known all his life—that was inexcusable.

"If the money was paid back, would the bank back off?" she said.

Mr. Sam shrugged listlessly. "Probably. They're only interested in getting their money back. But who's going to lend money to a circus on the brink of bankruptcy?"

"How much?"

"Close to a million. How the hell could he spend a million dollars in just one year?"

So it was out in the open. It *was* Danny—and Mr. Sam was well aware of it.

"Gambling," she said. "It goes fast when you gamble. Remember Jocko died broke—and he had earned top salary most of his adult life."

"But he gambled with his own money. He didn't steal it." He swallowed the rest of his scotch, coughed, wiped his mouth. "God, my own grandson, a thief."

"And mine," Mara said softly.

"Where did I go wrong, Mara? Did I spoil the boy too much? Did I look the other way too often?"

"Loving someone and not seeing their faults is human. You can't blame yourself for being human. I looked the other way, too." She paused, then asked, "What are you going to do next, Sam?"

Mr. Sam fingered the loose flesh under his chin. His eyes had a sunken look that made him look very old. "Try to negotiate another loan if I can. When this gets out, the big boys will be standing in line, trying to take over what's left of the circus. But they won't offer a penny to bail it out. I got a merger offer a few months ago from that Lasky fellow—you know, Joe Lasky's son."

"What did you tell him?"

"Turned him down. Hell, he wants full management powers. You know what would have happened. Wherever there was a duplication of jobs, his guys would've been in, and ours out. So I turned him down. After I finished talking to the bank people, I called Lasky, asked if he still wanted to make a deal. But he said he'd just ordered a whole lot of new equipment and had too much of his capital tied up in that."

"How much would it take to clear things with the bank?"

"Close to a million—I just told you that."

"Why don't you ask me for a loan?"

"You? I'm talking big money, Mara. Even if you could raise that much, why would you take such a risk?"

"Danny's my grandson, too," she reminded him. "I don't want to see him rotting away in prison for embezzlement."

"Are you saying—can you raise that much money?"

"I can get it," she said shortly.

"What kind of deal do you want?"

"It would be a loan. To be paid back in the usual terms. But there's a condition."

"What condition? My left hand?" he said, sounding more like his usual irascible self.

"Danny can stay on in a job that doesn't involve handling money, but I want Michelle brought in as manager."

Mr. Sam glared at her from under his heavy brows. "Michelle? Why, she's just a kid. Besides, she—"

"Don't say it, Sam."

"Look, I know there's a lot of this woman's lib stuff going around, and maybe they should get the same pay for the same job as a man. But the circus is different. The bosses won't take their orders from a woman, even if she is Michael's kid."

"Michelle has already made a lot of the decisions around here this past year. It isn't unique. Women have managed circuses before, you know."

"Widows who had worked with their old man for years before they took over—mature women who knew the score. But Michelle's only nineteen. Men three times her age aren't going to take orders from a nineteen-year-old girl."

"These men have known Michelle all her life. She's one of them. If you stand behind her, back her up all the way and teach her what you know without undermining her authority, it will work. And that's my deal. I'll bail you out, but Michelle will take over as manager. And she's not to know about this. She has to believe you borrowed the money from—say, an old friend. I want her to believe you're the one who wants her in as manager."

"I'm not much good at lying," he growled.

"It wouldn't be a lie if you could see your hand before your nose," she retorted.

Mr. Sam's answer to that was a grunt. "So you're bailing me out for the second time," he said heavily. "You saved my hide back there during the depression when you waived rent for winter quarters those six years. Funny—I didn't much like you at first. Thought you were pushy, out for all you could get, a real tough bimbo.''

"You were right. I was. Still am. And that's why I'm going to have my lawyer draw up the loan papers, all nice and legal. I don't want to end up living on Social Security and dog food someday." Her eyes softened as she looked at him. "And I don't want that to happen to you, either."

He sighed heavily. "It won't. I'm not going to live that long. Doctors give me six months, maybe a year. My ticker's running down like a rusty old clock. Congestive heart failure, they call it. Which is why this business with Danny hit me so hard. I won't be here to see it through to the end. But I feel better, knowing you're going to be around, watching out for our grand-kids."

Mara was silent for a long time, fighting shock and an unexpectedly deep grief. "Do they know?" she asked finally.

"Naw. It'd only worry them."

Mara nodded agreement. Michelle would have enough to worry about in the coming months, and besides, it was best to keep some bad news to yourself.

CHAPTER 50

SINCE MICHELLE HAD TAKEN OVER MANAGEMENT OF THE circus, she was always careful not to let down her guard in front of other people, but today she was tempted to burst out crying and wring her hands like a heroine in an old melodrama.

Too much, she thought. *It's just too much.*

The first thing on the agenda of the weekly staff meeting, always held in the Silver Wagon for privacy, was a report by Alan Waters, the ticket boss. He had worked for Mr. Sam for twenty-five years, and the gloom on his middle-aged face reflected the news that receipts for their three-day Springfield run were at an alarming low. This she had known, since she always did a head count of the Big Top audience during each performance, and she knew attendance had fallen off drastically. But the concession stands, the rides, even the always well attended hooch show, had also been down, much below what she had hoped for.

"The take's way off, thirty percent below the last time we played Springfield," Alan growled. "And you can blame it on the Lasky operation. They took the cream right off the top, booking in here a week before we opened. No working stiff's gonna take his family to two circuses a week apart. Someone oughta put a bomb in that guy's car."

"Or maybe someone should have checked out the schedule better," Clarence Beebe, the canvas boss, said.

Since the whole staff had had a say in the scheduling that spring, including Clarence, Michelle's voice was testy as she said, "It wouldn't have helped. Lasky booked this date after the season started."

"Even so, we managed to make our nut," Cody, the advertising boss, said.

"We have to do better than break even," Michelle said. "We're facing that balloon payment on the bank loan next month, remember?"

"Why don't you ask for another extension?" Clarence asked.

"I may have to—but it's only postponing the problem," Michelle said. "Our cash flow is too tight—we don't have enough slack."

"Yeah—and we need new light wagon equipment," Terry said. "Next time, it could break down in the middle of a show. The customers don't remember later that they got their money back, only that they just saw half the show."

"We got other things to worry about, too." It was the equestrian director. He pulled at his long nose, looking gloomy. "The Lawson troupe won't be coming back next year. They got an offer from the Robinson show."

That's when Michelle had thought that it was just too much. Even so, she hid her dismay.

"It was inevitable, I guess. We can't match what the big shows pay," she said, trying to sound unconcerned. The Lawson troupe, a couple and their two oldest sons, who did a spectacular pole act, were one of the show's best drawing cards and got star treatment, but they had three younger children still in school in Florida. She couldn't blame them for looking out for themselves, but she wondered if they would have stayed if her grandfather or father were still manager.

After the others had aired their problems and left the Silver Wagon, Michelle slumped down at her desk, resting her head on folded arms. *Too much*, she thought again.

There was the sound of the screen door opening, and she straightened immediately, wiping the worry from her face before she turned. She was relieved when she saw it was Rosa. Despite her depression, she forced a smile. Although Rosa had to be in her midsixties, she had slipped from being attractive to handsome without a ripple. Her eyes were the same brilliant green Michelle remembered from her childhood, and her skin, although it had a fragile look these days, was still flawless. The few wrinkles she had didn't show under her subtle makeup.

Rosa didn't smile back. "Something's wrong," she said immediately.

"A dozen things are wrong—including the big balloon payment coming due on the bank loan I negotiated this spring so we could get the show on the road," Michelle said.

"You'll meet it. The rest of the stops on the circuit are good circus towns. We'll get well by the end of the year."

"True—unless the weather goes sour or Steve Lasky does another of his wildcat bookings. I don't know how he does it—but I'm sure it's deliberate. And I thought that stupid feud was over."

Rosa looked thoughtful. "Maybe he's trying to push the show into that merger."

Michelle's smile vanished. "Merger? What merger?"

"Mr. Sam didn't tell you about that?"

"No. What's it all about?"

"Steve Lasky made Mr. Sam an offer a year ago, his second in the past three years. It does make sense. Both shows play the Midwest and East, and the Lasky show's weaknesses are our show's strengths—and vice versa."

Michelle shook her head so vigorously that the barrette she wore in her hair flew off. "I'd never merge with that bastard."

"Surely you don't still blame him for Connie's death?" Rosa paused to study Michelle's tight face. "No, it's something else—did he have anything to do with you and David breaking up?"

"He had everything to do with it—and I don't want to talk about it, Rosa."

Rosa nodded—which was one of the things that made her so special, Michelle reflected, already ashamed of her outburst. "I came over to ask about Mr. Sam. Have you heard from him lately?'' Rosa said.

"I called Florida this morning, talked to his housekeeper. She says he refused to get out of bed yesterday. He told her he was going to take root and turn into a vegetable.''

"Well, that's Mr. Sam. Stubborn as a horsefly, opinionated as a mule—and I hope he can make the circuit with us next year.''

"I do, too. So many times, I want to ask his advice. I'd be calling him all the time, but the doctor says we're not to worry him.'' She paused, her eyes reflective. "We've never been really close, you know. I always thought he favored Danny over me. I didn't realize he—well, approved of me until he made me manager.''

Michelle gave Rosa a rueful smile. "Not that he did me a favor. I wasn't ready, Rosa. I'm still not ready. Running a circus is so much more than logistics. I can handle that, but it's dealing with other people, all the nuances of this business, that I need to learn. The staff has helped, but they can only do so much.''

"You're doing just fine," Rosa said soothingly. "You started out with a big handicap, the circus in poor financial condition— and then Mr. Sam's heart attack. But we're still hanging on. Your father would have been proud of you, Michelle.''

Michelle's eyes filled with tears. To hide them from Rosa's sharp eyes, she got up and went over to the water jug to get a glass of water.

"If you're heading toward the midway, I'll walk over with you,'' Rosa offered. "I want to go by the cookhouse. Clinker's been under the weather again. Wants some lime water. That's her cure for everything, you know.''

"She hasn't been at all well this year, has she?'' Michelle said, glad the subject had changed.

"No. And I'm worried about her,'' Rosa said. "I finally got her to agree to go see a doctor next week. And this winter, I'm going to make her take a long rest. I can be just as stubborn as she.''

Michelle agreed that yes, indeed, Rosa could be every bit as stubborn as her friend, Clinker—or Mr. Sam. As she locked up the Silver Wagon, she felt much more optimistic. Sometimes, all it took was a good friend who was willing to listen.

Mr. Sam and Clinker died that winter.

Mr. Sam passed away in his sleep in the big house in Orlando that he'd built for his wife. He was buried in a cemetery near Sarasota next to his parents' graves. Mara was deeply grieved, but there was the consolation that it had been an easy death, that he'd led a long, full life.

It was different with Clinker. In her heart, Mara had known that her friend was very ill, but because Clinker wouldn't talk about it, saying only that she felt tired and needed rest, she had pushed her fears to the back of her mind.

Even so, it shouldn't have been such a surprise when the doctor took her aside after one of Clinker's respiratory attacks and told her that if her friend had any family, they should be notified. The thought of life without her friend filled her with grief—and self-pity. Once Clinker was gone, there was no one in the world who had known her as Princess Mara. As Rosa Smith, she was as respected as anyone else in the circus world and had many friends. She was loved by her grandchildren—by Michelle, and to a lesser degree, by Danny. But they were from another generation, another time. In the realest sense of the word, she would be alone. And she was no longer used to being alone.

So she slipped into the hospital chapel and made a few promises to the *gadjo* God and also, playing it safe, to a few Rom deities who were just as dim in her mind, and then she summoned up a smile and went back to Clinker's hospital room.

Clinker's responding smile held a tinge of irony, and Mara knew her friend was well aware how little time she had left. "What did that fool doctor say to you?" Clinker asked, blunt as ever.

"That you're the worst patient they've ever had at Tampa Memorial."

Clinker didn't return the insult with one of her own, as she once would have. "Don't send for my sisters. I hardly know them anymore—and they don't have the money to come here from Missouri."

"Don't worry about that—"

"I want your promise. My friends, the ones that matter, are all here in Florida."

Mara nodded, and Clinker's face relaxed. She had always been thin; now she was so gaunt that her cheekbones stood out under her skin. A memory came to Mara, of Clinker the first time she'd met her. She had never been beautiful, but she had glowed with youth, with health, with hope. The hope had died when she'd been jilted by—what had his name been? It had been so very long ago. . . .

Clinker's hand clutched her arm. "How long did he give me?" she asked.

"A couple of decades—maybe three if you give up your motorcycle," Mara said.

But Clinker didn't smile at the joke. "How long?" she said insistently.

"A year—maybe, two."

Clinker settled back with a sigh. "He's wrong. A week at the most." She blinked hard, as if the light hurt her eyes. "I'm slipping away, Mara. I can feel it—it's like sand running out of one of those hit 'em bags. And it's almost run out."

Mara started to say that was nonsense, but Clinker was already going on. "There's something I've been wanting to tell you. It's been bothering me for years."

"Come on—you've never been able to keep anything from me. I probably already know—"

"It was Lobo and me. Back in California, we used to wait until you were asleep and then—well, he would come to my room."

"You and Lobo—?"

"Were sleeping together, yes."

Mara tried to sort out her reaction. She was chagrined that she hadn't suspected, but also very hurt. "Why did you hide it? Did you think I wouldn't understand about loneliness?"

"Loneliness, hell." Clinker gave a small, secret smile. "Lobo was a great lover. He never disappointed me. And he was so damned grateful—it used to make me cry, how grateful he was."

"Why did you keep it a secret, Clinker?"

"Because it was private. I didn't want to share it. Besides—" Clinker plucked at her sheet with thin fingers "—I was ashamed."

"Ashamed? Because Lobo was a mute?"

"Hell, no. Because I'd already made such a to-do about being respectable. I just couldn't admit that I was human, like everybody else, I guess. Lobo understood. He worshiped you, you know. He didn't want to do anything that might make you think less of him." She sighed fretfully. "I didn't talk much to him— I was afraid you'd hear, and besides, he couldn't talk back. He loved me, you know, in a different way than he loved you. After we made love, he used to stroke my hair, and I always felt so safe, lying there in the dark with him."

She began to cry, and Mara held her hand. "I'm glad you told me," she said, although she wasn't sure that was true.

"It didn't seem right, holding out on you when you always tell me everything."

"What makes you think I tell you everything?" Mara said. "I have my secrets, too."

Clinker stopped crying; the old curiosity shone in her wet eyes as she stared up at Mara. "What secrets?" she demanded.

Mara laughed, and after a moment, Clinker laughed, too. She fell asleep a few minutes later, and when Mara bent to kiss her, her cheek felt very cold, as if she were already drifting away from life.

The next morning, very early, Clinker passed away in her sleep.

Mara took her body back to California. She buried her old friend in the cemetery on a Santa Rosa hillside, next to Lobo's grave.

CHAPTER 51

ONE CHORE MICHELLE DISLIKED WAS OCCASIONALLY HAVING to delve into Mr. Sam's old files. Those dusty papers, especially the route books Mr. Sam had kept so religiously for the past forty-five years, reminded her all too vividly of the things she didn't know about running a circus.

Ordinarily she wouldn't have been hunting through the rusty cabinets Mr. Sam had called the archives, but today her secretary, Aggie Coles, was off with a cold, and there was a canceled check she needed.

It was the first time they'd played Louisville in almost three years. This morning a dealer had turned up, bill in hand, claiming that he hadn't been paid for a truckload of hay he'd delivered three years ago, and threatening to put a lien on the circus.

Michelle knew it was up to her to prove that the bill had been paid. After a short search, she'd found the invoice, stamped *paid,* among her father's meticulously kept records, but she needed the canceled check, too. So here she was, digging through old folders, even though she had a dozen other things to do.

She finally found the canceled check and was closing the file drawer when her eyes fell on another folder. *Lasky Circus,* it read. Curious, she pulled it out and flipped it open. It held a motley collection of old show bills, correspondence between her grandfather and the Lasky Circus, and, in a small notebook, a record of every grievance against the Laskys that Mr. Sam had accrued over the years.

She shuffled through the contents of the folder, stopping to read one particularly acrimonious letter from Joe Lasky to her grandfather. Such a waste, she thought. All that trouble—and over a woman whom Mr. Sam must have wished a thousand times he hadn't married.

According to gossip, Grandma Bradford had been a tartar who had made Mr. Sam's life hell. If Joe Lasky had only known it, Mr. Sam had done him a favor—or would her grandmother have been different with a different husband? Had she regretted her choice and thrown it up to Mr. Sam every chance she got? They'd stayed together for years before the divorce, so they must have started out loving each other. Or had it been pride that kept them together, the unwillingness to admit their mistake?

As for the feud—it had survived far longer than it should have. Maybe it had built upon itself, one grievance giving birth to the next. It was even possible that they'd both enjoyed it, that it had added spice to their lives. Certainly Mr. Sam had never been more animated than when he was denouncing his rival.

Michelle was about to close the folder when she spotted a note, written in her father's handwriting. She pulled it out and read it, and her eyebrows came together in a frown. It was a rough draft of a letter, addressed to Steve Lasky. It thanked him for his offer of a merger, and then her father had gone on to say that he was thinking it over and was inclined to say yes—provided he could talk his father into it and the terms were agreeable. It asked for a meeting—and then, as if there had been an interruption, it broke off in midsentence.

Michelle rubbed her forehead, trying to think. What had happened? Why hadn't her father finished drafting the letter? She looked at the date again. A month before his death—was that significant? Well, she would never know the answer. But it did show one thing, that her father had entertained the idea of a merger with their old enemy.

She put the letter back in the folder, suddenly depressed. In the long run, what did it matter? He obviously hadn't sent the letter, or the circus would be Bradford and Lasky by now. . . .

As for her, she was glad it hadn't gone through. The thought of having to deal with Steve Lasky as an equal partner chilled her blood. And yet—if it had been a fait accompli when her father was killed, she wouldn't be in the position now of having to go it alone.

Well, maybe things would be better next year. It just had to be.

It was the season of 1970, and a malaise hung over the circus. It affected everybody, from the equestrian elite to the lowest roughie. When Michelle came into the cookhouse or privilege tent, she could see the evidence of it in eyes that didn't quite meet hers, in too hearty greetings, in smiles that were only on the surface, in the things that weren't said.

She wouldn't have minded so much, this consensus of worry, if their attitude toward her had changed. But they still felt protective toward her, Michael's little girl, and she often suspected that lesser disasters were deliberately kept from her in order not to worry her.

That they didn't blame her made it worse instead of better. It made her feel guilty, and she began getting what the doctor she consulted called anxiety attacks, where she couldn't seem to catch her breath, and her heart beat too rapidly. It became increasingly hard to make a decision, mainly because she was so afraid of making a mistake. Sometimes it was simply that she didn't have enough detail about a problem to come up with an answer. The staff, whether because they'd lost faith in her judgment or because they wanted to save her from more stress, went their own way more and more.

Her inability to grab hold and take complete charge was humiliating, and she often wished that Danny were still manager, despite his sticky fingers. Since Mr. Sam had replaced him, he had been working with the advance crew, and he seemed perfectly content to stay there. When, after her grandfather's death, she'd asked him to take on the assistant manager's job, he'd declined with thanks, saying he was happy where he was.

"This job was made for me," he said, his smile as cocky as ever. "For one thing, the circus picks up the tab for my hotel rooms, and if I—uh, indulge a little occasionally, I still have a place to sleep nights.''

Luckily, the season, which had started out slowly, had changed for the better, and they often played to straw houses. The weather was balmy, unusually so for a midwestern summer, just the kind circus people pray for. The bank had granted the circus a six-month extension on their loan, and with cash on hand to pay day-to-day bills and meet the payroll, things were looking up. The circus might be shabby, with its faded canvas, its less than sparkling costumes, but they were still operating in the black, with every indication that they could meet the next payment on their bank loan, something she tried to take heart from.

And then disaster struck, in the form of a gray-haired man in a charcoal-gray business suit.

His name was Henry Alden, and he was a fussy-looking man with a precise way of speaking, a nervous habit of squeezing the end of his nose. He appeared without warning during the lunch hour while Michelle was alone in the Blue Wagon, carrying a black leather satchel and, of all things, an umbrella. He was such a stereotype of a bank auditor that Michelle knew what he was even before he introduced himself.

Despite her apprehension, she offered him a cup of coffee, which he refused, then a glass of cold water, which he accepted. After he set down his empty glass, he wiped his face with a handkerchief, even though it was cool inside the long trailer van. That's when he told her that the bank had sent him to close down the circus unless their bank loan was paid immediately—in full.

"I'm sorry, miss. A new board has taken over. While they're sympathetic to your problems, they also have a responsibility to their stockholders. And your loan is six months in arrears.''

"But we've paid the interest on time every month since it fell due,'' she protested.

"If it were up to me, I'd let it ride another six months,'' he told her, looking very human suddenly. "I'm a circus buff, you see. Belong to the Circus Fans of America. Unfortunately, I'm just the messenger.''

"But business has been excellent. We should be able to pay the principal off by the end of the season.''

"I'm sorry. We've had an offer from another circus for your holdings—provided there's a foreclosure.''

"Steve Lasky,'' she said, her nostrils flaring with anger. "He's behind this, isn't he?''

He took off his glasses, polished them vigorously. "I'm not at liberty to say."

"Never mind. You don't have to."

For the next hour, Michelle put aside her anger, and set about flattering and coaxing and using the circus's financial records to prove that the circus was running in the black. She even appealed to his confessed love of the circus, and when he left, an hour later, Mr. Alden was in possession of a check that almost wiped out the circus's cash reserves—but she had a month's extension on the loan.

For a long time, Michelle sat behind the old desk that had belonged to her great-grandfather, her face buried in her arms, and her thoughts were grim and crackling with anger.

How could she possibly come up with the money in one month? Even if every performance for the rest of the month was a straw house, and every ride, every sideshow on the midway, was packed to capacity, there still wouldn't be enough to pay off the full bank loan in a month.

But surely there must be *some* way to meet that payment. This was one of the oldest and most respected shows in the country. The name alone must be worth something, enough for some bank or independent party to take a chance.

The answer came to her then. It had been there all along, lurking in the back of her mind. She got up and went to the file cabinet that held the archives, and got out the folder marked "Lasky Circus." She found the rough draft of the letter her father had written and never mailed. For a long time she stood there, studying it, knowing what she had to do and dreading it so much, she felt sick to the stomach.

But there was more at stake than her pride and her antipathy toward Steve Lasky. The livelihood of several hundred people depended upon her. For them, she must put aside her own feelings, and go to Steve Lasky to ask for a loan, or, as a last resort, a merger.

But oh God, how she dreaded it!

The Lasky Circus was playing a four-day run in Indianapolis. Michelle arrived at the municipal airport in the middle of the morning, but she didn't leave for the fairgrounds immediately. Instead, she rented a hotel room, took a shower and washed her hair, then changed into the clothes she'd brought along.

She had chosen them with care. "Use the ammunition the Lord gave you," Rosa had told her when she'd gone to her for advice. "Steve Lasky is just as susceptible as any man. Maybe more so—in your case. It's possible he feels guilty for breaking up your affair with his brother."

So Michelle had chosen one of the draped skirts that were currently so popular, a white silk blouse that revealed while it seemed to conceal, a braided leather belt to emphasize her slender waist, and plain pumps that showed off her long legs. All underplayed but, she hoped, effective. She let her hair hang loose, having learned that what she'd once detested was truly her crowning glory, and she made up her face with care.

When she was finished, she was satisfied that while she looked her best, it wasn't apparent that she'd taken any special pains.

But her confidence took a nosedive an hour later, when she met Steve's hard stare. Those dark brown eyes didn't miss a thing—including, she was sure, both her suppressed anger and her nervousness.

"Well, this is a surprise, Miss Bradford," he said. There was no special inflection in his voice, certainly only politeness, so why did she feel so threatened?

She gave him her best smile. "Surprise? But I sent you a wire, saying I'd be here today to discuss a business matter." This was a lie; she had decided to tackle him without advance warning.

"I'm afraid it didn't arrive." He pulled out a chair for her. A middle-aged woman, who had been typing at a desk nearby, came up with a paper for Steve to sign, and Michelle took advantage of the interruption to look around the motor van that served as the show's Blue Wagon. She couldn't help comparing its opulence with the shabbiness of her own Blue Wagon. Not only was the van spacious, but the furniture was modern, obviously expensive, and the business equipment was the best available.

No sentimentality here, she thought, thinking of the battered oak desk that had served four generations of Bradfords. The woman left the van, saying something about a lunch break, and Steve returned his attention to Michelle.

"So you're here on business. I'm disappointed. I thought it might be a social call," he said.

"Why would I come so far for a social call?" she said.

"So far? Oh, that's right. You're playing St. Louis, aren't you?"

"You keep up with our itinerary?"

"As you do ours," he said smoothly. "Can I offer you a drink?"

Michelle wanted to accept. Not only did she need the forti-
fication of alcohol, but her mouth was so dry, it was hard to
talk. But it was one thing to propose a merger with the enemy,
another to drink with him.

"No, thank you," she said politely.

His eyebrows rose. "Come now. You're thirsty. I saw you
glance at the water jug when you came in."

"Very well. Water will be fine," she said. Realizing that she
was forgetting her promise to Rosa to hide her dislike, she forced
a smile.

Steve got her a glass of distilled water from the jug, then
settled back in his chair. "What's this all about, Michelle?" he
said, and now he was all business.

Michelle reached into her handbag and produced her father's
letter. "I found this while going through my father's files. It
seems that he was thinking seriously about accepting your offer
of a merger. If he hadn't been killed—" She shrugged. "It really
surprised me, and yet—it does make sense."

Steve glanced at the letter, then back at her. "So what you're
saying is that you are ready to consider a merger?"

"I'd like to hear your offer," she said coolly.

"Oh, would you? But maybe I've changed my mind."

Michelle's fingers tightened around her purse clasp. Was he
playing with her? Well, she was going to call his bluff. She
forced a cool smile. "Then I'm wasting my time, aren't I?"
She got up, smoothed down her skirt as if preparing to leave.

He looked amused. "Do sit down. And let's stop playing
games. You have a large overdue bank loan, and the bank is
eager to call it in. I believe there's been some interest from
another show to buy up your assets."

She fought a swift rise of temper. When she was sure she
could speak calmly, she said, "Whatever makes you think that?
We've had record crowds—"

"Things are different from when I made your father—and
grandfather—that offer. Why merge when it's possible I can pick
up your equipment and animals for the price of your bank loan?"

"It isn't equipment they pay to see," she snapped. "We have
a reputation for always putting out a great show. Our artistes are
not only tops, they're loyal. I doubt very much if any of them
would work for an outfit that has pulled so many dirty tricks
through the years."

"You might be surprised. It's odd how quickly loyalty flies
out the window when a good contract is offered."

Michelle knew he was right. Some acts would accept a contract with the devil if the money was right. But he was also wrong. Others would not. They would go to other shows instead. But then there were those old-timers who, if the circus went under, couldn't find a job in any circus because they were too old. . . .

"However, I still might be interested," Steve went on. "Under certain conditions, a merger could be attractive."

Michelle wet her lips with her tongue. "Certain conditions?"

"That it be more than a business merger. None of this business of your people versus my people. If the merger is presented as a natural progression, with no hint of a takeover or a buyout, there would only be the normal problems of combining two operations inside a family business."

Michelle shook her head. "You've lost me. How is that possible?"

"Marriage would make it a family business."

Michelle's mind played a trick on her. For a split second, she thought he was talking about David and her. Then, as she took in his steady regard, she realized what he really meant.

"You want me to marry *you*! You have to be crazy!" she exclaimed.

"It's logical. I'm not engaged, and neither are you. In fact, you don't have a relationship of any kind going."

"You've been spying on me!"

"Just keeping tabs on my competitor," he said blandly. "A marriage between us would solve a lot of problems. I've been wanting to expand, but the competition between our circuses makes that impractical. But if we were married—well, just think of the positive side. A big wedding, lots of publicity because the story would be a natural, two circus dynasties uniting. It would solve everything—"

"It wouldn't solve anything. I wouldn't marry you if you were—"

"Please! No clichés. Just imagine the possibilities. 'Bradford and Lasky, back together again.' You have to admit it has a nice ring."

"I can't believe any of this. I'm good enough for you now, but you had a fit when David and I wanted to get married. What's changed? If you thought you had to protect David from me—"

"Why do you assume that it was David I wanted to protect?" Although his voice was still easy, his eyes were deadly serious. "When I found out what was going on, I kept thinking about a very special girl who was willing to tackle me to save her brother from punishment—and the guts to confront a lynch mob to rescue her elephant friend. How could I let David ruin that girl's life? And he would have. Eventually he would have started looking around for other women to stroke his ego. I love my brother, but I know him, too. Usually he doesn't do any harm. The kind of girls he favors are able to take care of themselves. But it was different with you. I knew you would be badly hurt if you married him. Maybe he was really in love with you, but he would have ruined your life anyway. Where women are concerned, he's a weakling. And you deserve better than that."

"What you're saying is that I deserve *you*? You broke up David and me just because you were concerned about me? That's crazy. You hadn't seen me since I was fourteen!"

"Seven years ago, I saw the woman you would become, and I wanted that woman."

"I don't believe any of this," she cried. "This is some kind of game you're playing."

"It's no game. Why do you find it so hard to believe?"

"Hardheaded businessmen like you don't fall in love that easily," she said scornfully.

"I'm not sure 'fall in love' are the right words. Admired you, yes. Wanted to marry you, yes. I've wanted to since you were fourteen."

"That's sick! You were in your twenties—"

"Actually, I was closer to thirty," he said.

She brushed aside the correction with an angry gesture. "The offers for a merger you made Mr. Sam and my father—is that what they were all about? This—this obsession of yours?"

"Oh, no. I'm a hardheaded businessman—as you pointed out. The merger would have been in both our best interests. I realized several years ago that we can't go on dividing the take, competing with each other in the same markets. But if we combine, we can survive, even in a world that has so many other entertainment options."

How cold and logical he sounded—and yet, he'd said he'd wanted to marry her for seven years. Was he talking about lust? That was hard to believe—hell, she didn't believe it!

"Why all this nonsense about marriage? If you want a merger, I'm willing—provided the terms are right."

"Sorry. Marriage is part of the deal. And I'm talking about a real marriage. Children, the whole works." There was no humor in his eyes now. "I put marriage on hold seven years ago to give you time to grow up. Well, you're all grown-up now."

Michelle was silent, trying to make sense of his words. Unexpectedly his face relaxed into a smile. "Are you still sore at me for shooting your elephant, Michelle?" he said softly.

"No," she said honestly. "I understand now why you did it. You saved Connie from a horrible death, and I thank you for that."

He nodded. "Eventually you'll realize breaking up your engagement to David was the right thing to do, too."

Her softness vanished. "You had no right—"

"Maybe not. But you'll be happy with me. Maybe not right away, but eventually. I'll be good to you, Michelle, good *for* you. We'll work together and bring our circuses to their full potential. I have plans—but we'll talk about that later. I want the wedding as soon as possible. I've waited a long time for you."

"But you never came to see me," she protested. "You didn't try to—to—"

"Court you? You had this fixation against me. Oh, yes, I know the things you've said about me. Very interesting. And humbling."

She frowned at him. "So you do have a spy planted in our show."

He didn't seem to hear her. "We're playing St. Paul next week, and since you'll be in Minneapolis, why don't we take a day off and have one hell of a wedding? Think of the publicity possibilities."

"Trust you to think of that," she muttered.

"Would you expect me *not* to think of it?"

She knew he was right. Mr. Sam would have thought of it. Her father would have thought of it. Why didn't she admit that it was a practical solution to her problems? But the thought of being intimate with a man she hardly knew, a man she disliked, was so distasteful that a shudder rippled over her. Could she actually go through with it even to save the circus?

"I won't rush you into bed, Michelle," Steve said, his tone wry. "I'll give you time to get used to the idea before I claim my—what do you call it? Marital rights? I'm willing to court you, but I won't wait forever. Do you understand? I don't want any claims later that you thought I was asking for a marriage in name only."

It was a long time before she nodded. He had her in a box,

and too much was at stake that involved the welfare of people she cared for, people who had been her friends all her life. It did make some kind of cold, pragmatic sense. Many marriages were based on just such reasoning. So she would honor their deal and marry him, but she wasn't about to give him children. No matter what he wanted, as far as she was concerned, this wasn't part of the bargain.

CHAPTER 52

MICHELLE WAS AWARE THAT ROSA, HER FACE FLUSHED WITH excitement, was talking to her. Dully she wondered why Rosa, usually so perceptive, didn't sense her misery. She knew that she looked, as Rosa said, like a fairy princess in her white lace dress, her wreath of tiny white roses, the strand of milky pearls that Steve had given her as a wedding present, but couldn't her friend see that inside she was cold as ice?

Now that her wedding day was here, it didn't help to remind herself that she had no choice, that she had to save the circus, no matter what it cost her. All she could think of was the finality of what she was doing, the reality of living with, sleeping with, being the wife of, a ruthless, uncaring man whom she didn't love, didn't even respect.

"Well? Is it a secret or not?" Rosa asked as she straightened the lace at Michelle's throat.

"Secret?"

"Where Steve is taking you for your honeymoon—you haven't heard a word I've said, have you?" Rosa said, shaking her head. She was looking particularly handsome in a lapis-blue silk gown. It had been a shock when she'd suddenly discarded the turbans that were her trademark. Michelle had never known what color her hair was, but she'd always assumed she was dark. She still didn't know; since it was now an iron-gray that emphasized her friend's still brilliant green eyes.

"I give up," Rosa threw up her hands, laughing. She sobered quickly. "I have something to tell you. I've held off because I didn't want to add to your worries."

Michelle felt a thrill of alarm. "You aren't sick, are you?"

"Lord, no. I never get sick. But I *am* tired. I want to retire. So I won't be coming back to the circus next spring. I've been looking around, and I've found you a replacement. She's a Hungarian, very good. Not as good as me, of course, but—"

She went on talking about her replacement, but Michelle was too shocked to listen. *But I need you,* she wanted to say. *I'm desperately unhappy, and I need you to be here, to listen to me, give me advice. . . .*

She clenched her teeth to keep the words from escaping. She owed Rosa so much—how could she ask her to stay on when it was obvious that she'd just been waiting for things to straighten out? No wonder she had seemed so relieved when she'd heard about the merger. . . .

Michelle put her arms around Rosa. She was several inches taller than the older woman, but she was aware of this only when they were standing together. For such a tiny person, it was strange how Rosa could project such a strong presence. Would she herself ever be half the woman her old friend was?

"I love you, Rosa," she said, her voice unsteady. "I'll miss you."

"This was the wrong time to tell you," Rosa said, looking contrite. "I should have waited until you came back from your honeymoon."

"There won't be a honeymoon. We've decided to postpone it until the season's over," Michelle said.

"That does seem sensible, only—well, there's never a better time for a honeymoon than just after the wedding."

"How would you know?" Michelle teased. "No man ever talked you into walking down the aisle."

But Rosa wasn't smiling. "One did," she said, her tone reflective.

"You've been married?"

"Oh, yes. He died—a long time ago—"

A rap on the door interrupted her; a moment later, Steve came in. "How are things going, Michelle?" he said, his eyes taking in her lace gown, the roses in her hair, lingering on the pearl necklace he'd given her.

"You shouldn't be here," Rosa scolded. "It's bad luck for the groom to see the bride before the wedding."

"Then I'd better leave. We're going to need all the luck we can get," Steve said.

His eyes sought out Michelle as if he was waiting for something. She wanted to smile, but she could only stare back, knowing how stiff and unresponsive she must look.

"You've been crying," he said abruptly.

"Blame it on me, Steve," Rosa said. "I picked the wrong time to tell Michelle that I'll be leaving the show at the end of the season." She studied Steve's face, and what she saw there obviously pleased her. "You're both going to be very happy."

"Did the cards tell you that?" Michelle said tightly.

"Of course. First a few problems, but then—"

"Then the deluge," Steve said dryly.

They smiled at each other, and Michelle felt a stab of jealousy. Why had Rosa taken to Steve so fast despite all the things he'd done to sabotage the circus? It was almost as if they were allies—or conspirators. Rosa was fiercely partisan—did she see Steve as some kind of rescuer, a knight on a white horse, come to marry the princess and save the circus?

After Steve left, Rosa, who never fussed, fussed over Michelle's hair and straightened a tiny rose in her wreath that didn't need straightening. She left finally to check on Cookie and his helpers, who were preparing the wedding dinner in the cookhouse.

Michelle wasn't sorry to see her go. She needed a few minutes alone to catch her breath. All morning the circus lot had been buzzing, alive with an air of festivity. Everybody seemed to be involved in some way with the wedding preparations. Michelle didn't blame them for their excitement, but she felt a little lonely, too. They loved her, she knew that, but they also couldn't help being aware that it was Steve who had saved their jobs, their future. How much of the excitement and high spirits was due to relief?

A few minutes later, Michelle's bridesmaids came for her, a bevy of women in a variety of summer dresses. Rather than show favoritism, she'd asked anyone who wanted to be her bridesmaid to draw lots, and the winners were such a duke's mixture in their finery that she couldn't help smiling. Whether it was Greta Muelhauser, who had the pivot position in an all-woman tumbling act and who topped six feet by two inches, or Missy Elaine, billed (erroneously) as the smallest woman in the world, or Glad Gordon, a curvy member of the aerial ballet, it was obvious they were enjoying their roles as bridesmaids.

It came to Michelle that they all hungered for the same things that towner women did. This wedding was theirs, too, a symbol that dreams of romance came true, even for circus women. Well, she wouldn't let them down. She might be filled with despair, but she would smile and try to look radiant, like a bride should. She had done the right thing, no matter what her motive. In time, Steve would get tired of a wife who didn't love him. When that happened, they would quietly part and go their own ways.

One thing she had to be thankful for: David, who had been living in Europe since Steve had turned his trust fund over to him, had sent his regrets. She wouldn't have wanted him here today, a guest at her wedding to his brother. It was hard enough, faking the happy bride image for her friends. Having David here would have made it impossible. It wasn't that she still loved him. But his presence would have evoked too many memories, memories that should remain buried.

The Big Top, where the wedding was to be held, had been transformed into a bower. Rosa must have bought out all the florists in St. Paul *and* Minneapolis, Michelle decided. Flower garlands decorated the bandstand, the support poles, the temporary altar in the center ring. Everybody was dressed in his or her best, and it was obvious that there had been some tippling during the day.

What had Rosa said? That no woman ever forgot her wedding day? Well, she wouldn't forget hers, but not because she was marrying the man she loved. She'd remember it for the outpouring of love from these people, the responsibility for whom she'd inherited along with the circus and Mr. Sam's estate in Orlando. And in the months ahead, this was what she had to keep remembering, not the vows she was exchanging with Steve, not the kiss he gave her at the end, not even the look in his eyes that she didn't even try to interpret.

Michelle spent her wedding night alone. Steve, honoring his promise to give her time, had left her at the door of her stateroom with a brief kiss, saying he'd crash on the sofa in the salon. "I'll be leaving early in the morning for Youngstown," he said. "So I'll say good-bye now. This next month, I'll be in and out, of course, but why don't we put everything personal on hold until the season's over and we're back in Florida? Then we'll talk."

Despite her fatigue, Michelle didn't sleep well. She was overstimulated from too much talking, too much excitement, too much champagne. She knew Steve was restless, too, because she heard him moving around in the salon. The clink of glass against glass told her that he'd helped himself to a drink, and the light that showed under the stateroom door didn't go out until almost dawn.

She told herself that he'd made the rules, that blackmailers deserved everything they got, but there was a nagging feeling that it would be so easy just to get up and join him, let him make love to her. No matter about his practical motives for instigating this marriage, he did want her. And after all, it wasn't as if she were a virgin with a virgin's fears and romantic fantasies.

She fell asleep finally, and in the morning when she awakened, Steve was gone. The note he left was kind, affectionate; it was also very impersonal.

The next month was hectic. The process of combining the two circuses would take place in winter quarters before the 1973 season began, but in the meantime, there were the usual crises, the rapid breakdowns and put-ups entailed in a series of one-night stands, the inevitable letting down that was endemic at the end of the season. Steve came and went, making personnel evaluations but doing it so inconspicuously that Michelle was sure no one was unduly alarmed.

Michelle, the target of endless teasing, often had to grit her teeth not to explode at some particularly heavy-handed remark. She was sick of having to keep a happy smile on her face, sick of pretending she wasn't relieved that Steve was away most of the time, tending to his own circus.

She also couldn't help noticing that during his brief visits, the management staff and bosses went to him with their questions, their problems. She tried not to feel hurt, but what it all boiled down to was the fact that Steve had the sureness, the authority, the experience, that she didn't have. And he was also a man— and thirteen years older than she.

Then the final advertising bill was posted, placed upside down to denote the circus's last appearance of the year. The season was over, and the personnel drew their final pay envelopes. Next year, thanks to Steve, there would be spring call notices in the *Billboard*, calling them back to work. Which was something they all knew—and something she must keep remembering.

During a general meeting in the ring tent, Steve had promised that there would be work for those who wanted to stay with the new combined circus. Some would by necessity have to take a lesser job. As he pointed out, there were only so many management and boss openings. On the other hand, there was a very strong possibility that the circus would launch a second string in '74. It had worked well for Ringlings-B&B and other circuses, and if he decided to go that way, there would be more foreman, management, and skilled workmen's openings.

Michelle, standing at Steve's side, couldn't help resenting how quickly authority had moved into his hands. She had expected it, of course, but it still rankled that even the most loyal of her people addressed their remarks to Steve when he asked for questions at the end of the meeting.

Traditionally Steve's circus wintered on leased property south of Orlando, but after examining the facilities at the Bradford lot, Steve told Michelle that he'd decided to move the whole operation there, that he had already appropriated her Silver Wagon for his office.

They were in the Blue Wagon, the aging boxcar that she'd taken over as her own headquarters during the winter. Since this was obviously the "discussion" he'd promised earlier, her nerves were on edge, her temper close to the surface.

"Oh? Nice of you to tell me," she said.

"Sorry. I've been in complete charge so long that—well, I see I'll have to change my ways."

"I *am* an equal partner," she pointed out.

"Right." He hesitated, then added, "Look, Michelle, we got off on the wrong foot, and I'm sorry about that. I'm a blunt man, and I've had to be—" He fumbled for a word.

"Ruthless?" she said.

His face tightened. "Is that how you see me? If I were really ruthless, I would have culled out half your work force by now."

"Oh, I doubt that. I *am*, as I'm getting tired of pointing out, an equal partner."

He was silent for a long moment, watching her. He sighed finally, and said, "No, you aren't, Michelle. You signed away that right. I have the final say."

Shock hit Michelle with almost physical force; for a moment she felt dizzy. "What are you saying?"

"Surely you read the merger agreement."

"Of course I did. And my lawyer looked it over and explained some of the legal gobbledygook. He didn't say anything about you being the final authority."

"It was there, in the contract. Yes, it was in legalese—which is why I advised you to have your lawyer read it over and explain it to you. I wasn't trying to cheat you. I thought you understood the ramification of that clause. There can only be one final authority, Michelle. Businesses run by committees, especially one that has to have fast decisions, can end up in chaos. There isn't time for committee meetings when you're constantly on the move.''

Michelle wanted to protest against his cool, logical words, but she was all too aware that she'd been in a state of chaos herself at the time she'd agreed to marry him. Had she signed away her birthright, failed her own people, through her stupidity?

"Look, this is obviously a shock, although it's hard to believe your lawyer didn't discuss it with you," Steve said.

"He didn't say anything about my giving up my authority," she said hotly. The air seemed too close, the room too hot. "I don't know how you got to him, but you must have been planning this all along, you bastard!"

His face darkened. "I was honest with you. If your own lawyer didn't protect your interests, I'm sorry. But you did sign that contract, and this is how it's going to be. Don't worry. I'm sure we'll see things the same way most of the time. But when we don't, the final decision is mine. After all,'' he pointed out with sickening logic, "I have been in charge of the Lasky show for several years. Your experience is much more limited.''

"I was thrust into the manager's job without any training, but if my—if there hadn't been a problem with the reserve fund, we would have made it through. Well, the hell with you. You want authority, you've got it, but not over me. I'm leaving—''

"No, you aren't. You're staying, and you're going to cooperate and maintain a supportive image or so help me, I'll replace every one of your people.''

Michelle fought to control her too rapid breathing. Usually, as soon as she felt an anxiety attack coming on, she breathed into a brown paper bag to increase the carbon dioxide in her lungs, but she'd waited too long this time.

"What is it?'' Steve said sharply.

"I'm going to be sick,'' she managed. She turned and hurried into the supply room, where she kept a supply of paper bags. It took several minutes, but eventually her breathing returned to normal. When she came back into the office, Steve was still there, waiting for her.

"You okay?'' he said, his face pale.

"Something I ate," she said stiffly. "I think you'd better leave. I don't feel at all well."

"Okay—but this isn't the end of our discussion. We have to talk, Michelle."

The next day, Michelle was so busy with a load of end-of-the-season paperwork that she didn't have time to worry where Steve was. Only when he appeared late that afternoon did she wonder if he'd been deliberately avoiding her.

"I'm taking you out for dinner," he said. "I think we both need a break."

She wanted to refuse, but common sense told her that she would just be postponing the inevitable. "I have to go home to change," she said.

"I'll pick you up at seven-thirty." He hesitated, then added, "One thing we need to discuss is where we'll live. If you have some particular fondness for Mr. Sam's old place, we can live there. My house is smaller and not so fancy, but it's much closer to winter quarters. I'll leave it up to you."

Knowing this concession was a sop to counteract the usurping of her authority, she didn't answer. She returned to her ledgers, and when she looked up again, he was gone.

Michelle wasn't sure why she took such pains getting dressed that evening. It wasn't that she wanted to impress Steve—even if that were possible. He hadn't gone out of his way to compliment her about anything since the wedding. Most of the time he was all business. She knew this was part of his promise to let things ride until the season was over. Still—he might have mentioned the good job she'd done, organizing the move back to Florida.

So maybe it was pique that made her choose her sexiest dress, spend a little more time than usual over her makeup and hair. Feeling a little self-conscious, she opened the door when Steve rang the bell at exactly seven-thirty, and his reaction—the slight widening of his eyes, his hesitation before entering—was very gratifying.

Even so, all he said was, "Ready to go, Michelle?"

Hiding her irritation, she slipped into her wrap. "Where are we going?" she asked.

"La Bourgogne—in Orlando. Great French food, plenty of room between the tables, very art deco."

As they drove toward the restaurant, their conversation was easy, comfortable. She had already seen his charm at work on other people, but even so, when it was directed to her, it was surprisingly effective. It came to her that this was the first time they had ever been at ease with each other.

There were other surprises which didn't fit the image she had of Steve—such as his sense of humor. The third time she found herself laughing at one of his anecdotes, this one about a particularly sultry artiste who was systematically working her way through the bachelors of the Big Top show, she told herself that she had to be careful. It was obvious that he was bending over backward to be pleasant—but why? Was this the night he intended to exercise his conjugal rights? He had said he wanted a family—if this was his intent, he was in for a disappointment because she'd started on the pill a week before the wedding.

The restaurant, small and elegant, and Steve told her, named after a similar place in Paris, sat on one of Orlando's many lakes. The lights on the deck reflected across the water as they walked along the lake toward the restaurant. Michelle paused to watch a large swan, followed closely by a line of cygnets, float past.

"Idyllic scene, isn't it?" Steve said, "Hard to believe that death could be lurking there, out of sight."

She gave him a puzzled look. "Death?"

"Like as in the midst of life we are in death."

"What *are* you talking about?"

"Alligators. Every once in a while one wanders into this lake and then—zap, the tender little cygnets disappear, one by one."

She shuddered. "What a morbid thing to say!"

"I'm a realist—most of the time. The few times I've stepped out of character, I've brought a lot of grief down upon my head. And that's one thing we have to talk about. But not now. Let's postpone all serious conversation until after we've wined and dined."

The meal, as Steve had promised, was superb. The Bradford Circus's latest Cookie was Chicano, and although Michelle loved Mexican food, she'd eaten enough chili, tacos, and refried beans the past few years to appreciate the fine French cooking. She also couldn't help being impressed by Steve's impeccable French as he'd ordered *magret de canard* and artichokes stuffed with parsley.

"Did you take French at college?"

"I majored in languages," he said. "I had this urge to join the diplomatic corps. It wasn't a complete waste, because the languages have been useful. The last time I counted, eight different languages are being spoken by our artistes—including Texan."

Michelle laughed. "It's seven with us—including Basque. Since the Basque risley act are the only ones who speak it, it's something of a problem. Luckily, all of the tumblers also speak Spanish."

"No one, but no one, can speak Basque unless they were born to it," Steve said, laughing.

Michelle stared at him, fascinated by the change on his austere face when he laughed. It occurred to her that he was a very attractive man with his thick brown hair, his deep-set eyes, and strong features. Not like David, who was the stuff women's dreams were made of, but in his own way—yes, Steve *was* attractive, especially when he smiled. No wonder the circus women, young and old, preened for him.

"Why the diplomatic corps?" she asked. "Surely you must have known that someday you'd be running the circus."

"The usual teen rebellion—which didn't last past graduation. But I still have dreams of putting down roots in one place. If I can swing an idea I have, maybe I can have it both ways."

"What idea?"

He didn't answer immediately. He finished his wine, set the glass down. "Have you ever been to Europe?" he asked then.

"Unfortunately, no," she said. "Does your idea have something to do with Europe?"

"In a way. There are state or city circuses in most European countries—and elsewhere. Berlin has one. China and Russia, too. The circus has a permanent home, and the customers come to them. The artistes and management and other employees live ordinary lives except that their jobs are with a circus."

"That's your idea—a state-funded circus? But our government doesn't sponsor opera or ballet or even a national theater. Why would they fund a circus?"

"I wouldn't want government funding, even if it were available. But a privately owned theme park, a permanent site for the circus—that's what gets me excited. And this area of Florida, where there's a concentration of entertainment facilities, including Disney World, would be ideal. The tourists already flock here for recreation—why not include a day at the circus?"

"What exactly are you talking about?"

"A recreation park, built around the circus theme. A look backward, into the past, with the pomp and ceremony of the Barnum days perhaps. Buildings that look like tents with red-striped roofs, a menagerie, a petting zoo, plenty of rides for the kids, and a good dinner club for the adults. A hotel—well, that's a really far-off dream. A mixture of the old blended with the new. What do you think of my dream, Michelle?"

Michelle thought a moment, wondering at the intensity in his voice. "I love your dream," she said. "I hope you make it come true someday."

He smiled at her; for a moment, she thought she read satisfaction in his eyes. "Oh, I intend to. But it will take enormous capital—and a good site to build on. You know how land has skyrocketed lately, especially around Tampa and Orlando. There's very little suitable land left. Of course—" he paused briefly "—there's your winter quarters lot. It's perfect for what I need. An easy distance from airports and railroads, within half an hour's distance from Orlando via a major highway."

Michelle's body stiffened with outrage as realization came to her. "You've already talked to Rosa about it, haven't you? And she refused to sell because of the circus using the land as their winter quarters. So *this* is why you wanted that merger so badly! Your reasons never did ring true. You think because of the merger, she'll be willing to sell."

He didn't deny it. In fact, he seemed eager to tell her about it. "It's perfect for a theme park. The land is well drained, at the junction of two major highways, and it has its own natural water sources, which is a big plus in Florida. Rosa is willing to sell and finance it herself at a very decent rate of interest—an interest-alone agreement until the park starts to show a profit. She's even willing to invest some of her own money in it—"

The hurt was so deep that Michelle wanted to lash out at him, hurt him. "So that's it. I had the feeling you two knew each other. The word *conspirators* even came to mind. Did she buy a husband for me, Steve?"

"It wasn't that way, Michelle. When I went to see her, I told her how I felt about you, that I wanted to marry you, take care of you. She wanted it, too. She loves you as if you were her own daughter. Which is something I can understand, since you're very lovable. Prickly as an armadillo, but lovable." He tried out a smile, but she only stared back, stony-faced. "I can see this was the wrong time to tell you this, but I thought you were—"

"Gullible? Stupid and naive? Well, you just blew it, buster. The food, the charm, the great conversation—we were supposed to end up in bed, weren't we? And then what? I would be so impressed with your expertise that I would turn into a simpering little bride? And in gratitude, Rosa would sign over the lot to you?''

She paused, something else suddenly coming clear to her. "She used the bank auditor's visit to make sure I'd go to you for help. She gave me this song and dance about having spent all her money to help a friend. Did she instigate this whole damned thing?''

"You have it all wrong. She was concerned about you, about the circus. She could have given you the money to cover the bank note, but then what? The circus needs a complete rehauling, enormously expensive new equipment, new canvas all around. And you, at this stage of the game, just aren't equipped yet to pull it off.'' His voice hardened. "You should be grateful someone cares about you that much.''

"Oh, yes. I'm grateful, all right. That I found out about this—this scheme in time. How can you look at yourself in the mirror, Steve? Don't you feel any shame?''

"Why should I? I told you I'm a realist. I want a real marriage—that was no lie. And I want to share it with you. Also the truth.'' The waiter came up with their bill, and Steve dropped a few bills on the tray, then said, "Let's get out of here. Why don't we go to my motor home and finish this conversation there?''

They were silent as they drove back to winter quarters, where Steve's motor home was parked. Michelle's anger had already begun to fray at the edges. After all, Rosa had done what she had to save the circus. She had been devious, yes. But then, Rosa had always been devious, and it hadn't bothered her before.

As for Steve—she had gone into their marriage with her eyes wide open. She already knew that he was a practical man who put business above everything else. Why feel so angry and betrayed because her suspicions had been confirmed? Even if she'd known the whole story earlier, wouldn't she have married him anyway for the sake of saving the circus?

When they reached Steve's motor home, he unlocked the door, then stood aside so she could enter. She was already familiar with his rig, but she looked around now, wondering if he had planned to seduce her here or wait until he took her home. If this was still his plan, he was in for a big surprise. She'd made a bargain and she wouldn't renege, but it would be in her own time, on her own terms. . . .

She refused his offer of a drink, and he got himself a beer from the galley, then joined her on a red leather sofa.

"I know we have a lot of problems to thrash out, but I want to try to make a go of our marriage," he said then.

"Oh? Why not be honest? The only reason you married me was to manipulate Rosa, to play on her concern for me. So call our marriage what it really is—a business deal. I don't blame Rosa. She came from another culture, where arranged marriages are the norm. She's too smart to believe that you really give a damn about me, that you'd been waiting seven years for me to grow up."

Steve's face hardened. He set down the beer can and then he was moving toward her so fast that she didn't have time to recoil before he had his arms around her. She had thought she was strong for a woman, that he wasn't particularly muscular, but it took her only a few moments to realize her mistake. Even so, she was determined not to give in. Why should she when there was no longer a reason to consummate their marriage? She fought him silently, and only when he had finally subdued her by the simple matter of pinning her to the sofa with his full weight was she forced to stop struggling.

She stared up at his face and a wave of pure fear silenced her. What if he hurt her? From the white line across his upper lip, he was furious enough—or was that anger she saw on his face? He bent closer, and when she realized he meant to kiss her, she concentrated on keeping her lips pressed tightly together.

His kiss was surprisingly gentle, so gentle that involuntarily she relaxed, and his wily tongue slipped past her lips, probed deeply into her mouth. Her breathing accelerated, partly with panic, and she started to struggle again, tried to tell him to let her up, that she was having an anxiety attack. Desperately she gasped for air, and he must have taken it for an invitation, because he kissed her again, taking her remaining breath away. She tried to roll away, but he was holding her too tightly, and a darkness gathered at the edges of her sight.

Part of her remained aware. She knew, for instance, that he was undressing her, then himself. She gulped in great breaths of air, which only made it worse, then held her breath. He was touching her now, and through the mist she saw the hunger, the tension, on his face. Her breathing was slowly returning to normal, but she could take no comfort in that, because she still found it hard to breathe. This time her own traitorous body was the problem.

Steve was fondling her breasts, touching her intimately, seeking out the erotic places of her body, and she didn't want him to stop, not until he'd satisfied the need he'd aroused in her. Suddenly it didn't matter who he was, only that he had started something that she wanted to go on.

His lovemaking was surprisingly generous. He wooed her with his lips, his hands, his virile body, not rushing toward his own satisfaction. His body was lean, like David's, but there the resemblance ended. Dark brown hair covered his muscular chest, and his nipples were the color of mahogany. His skin had a subtle scent, like a sandalwood fan someone had once given her, and when he touched the moist valley between her thighs, his hands trembled and there were two white lines beside his mouth as if he were in pain.

The man she'd known, all business and logic, had disappeared, replaced by this man, who stroked her, fondled her, finally sending her into a mindless spiral to paradise, even though it was obvious that his own needs were even more urgent.

When she came back to earth, she felt depleted, satiated, but she also felt a warmth toward Steve, who was still unsatisfied, that took her by surprise. She knelt before him and pushed against his chest with both hands until he was stretched out on the sofa. Her hair veiled her face as she bent over his groin and took him in her mouth. He groaned and thrashed around, helpless under the pressure of her lips.

I could kill him now—and he couldn't stop me, she thought— then wondered why his helplessness evoked only tenderness. She slid upward until she was straddling him, and slowly eased her body down until he filled her. Gently she rocked above him, wanting to make it good for him, wanting to give him his own ride to paradise. But then the urgency, the wildness, was back, and now she was the one who groaned with pleasure as she reached the pinnacle of pleasure again.

Beneath her, Steve's body jerked violently and there was a rush of warmth inside her. "Oh, God, Michelle, I've waited so long for this," he groaned.

Tenderness washed over her. Part of it stemmed from the release of tension, the sensory relief he'd just given her, but not all. The bliss on his face was undeniable, and for the first time, she was ready to believe that he was in love with her.

He reached up, pressed his forefinger against her lips and then to his. "Sweet," he said. "Your kisses are so sweet, Michelle."

She laughed, feeling as if she were seventeen again. No, not

seventeen. At seventeen, she had been in love with David, and
his lovemaking had changed her from a child to a woman. But
what she'd just experienced had been even more earth-shattering.
Which was all very strange, because David had been a better
lover than his brother.

Or maybe her memory was faulty.

Certainly David and she hadn't fitted together as if they were
two parts of a whole. He had been too large for her, sometimes
causing her pain, while Steve—he was just right. Did such pragmatic things matter all that much? Before today she wouldn't
have believed so, and yet—right at the moment, even though
she was satiated from their lovemaking, she was acutely aware
of his naked body, pressing against her side.

She glanced down at him, at his limp, relaxed body, and an
impish impulse seized her. She reached over and patted the now-
depleted instrument of her satisfaction.

"Poor thing," she cooed. "Did it finally get its little feet
wet?"

Steve exploded; he threw back his head and roared, and she
smiled at him, pleased by his reaction.

"I can't believe you said that," he said, wiping his eyes. "My
little fourteen-year-old has grown up."

She giggled, she who never giggled. "You're sick—you know
that? Lusting for a fourteen-year-old girl."

"But I didn't lust for you back then. Well, maybe there was
a little lust mixed in with my admiration. And does this mean
that you're willing to give our marriage a chance?"

She was a long time answering. Did the fact that they were
great together in bed—no, in this case, on the sofa—mean all
that much? There were so many things against their having a
good marriage. But why was she hesitating? She'd been willing
to live with Steve when she thought she was indifferent to him
sexually. Why not consider this a bonus, something extra she
hadn't expected?

"I'm willing to give it a try," she said. "But one thing I want
you to understand. I'm not going to be your little yes woman
who agrees with everything you say. When I think I'm right, I'll
tell you so."

He grinned at her. "I wouldn't have it any other way. Pax?"

"Pax," she said, against all her better judgment.

CHAPTER 53

*T*O OUTSIDERS, THE CIRCUS SEEMS TO LAY DORMANT DURING the winter months, waiting for spring. In reality, there is constant activity. Animals have to be fed, groomed, trained, and sometimes bred; equipment repaired, painted. A payroll has to be met for those workers who remain at winter quarters at half pay, their meals provided by a reduced cookhouse crew. Scheduling for the next season begins almost as soon as the old tour is over. Once booking dates are confirmed, contracts for supplies must be let out months in advance, involving complicated paperwork. Canvas has to be repaired or replaced, rides put into tip-top condition, and new costumes designed, made up, ready for final fittings when the artistes report in the spring.

And then there is the never-ending paperwork, the government tax forms, record compiling, invoices. Books have to be balanced, accounts put in order, along with a multitude of other tag ends left over from the old season.

This year, most of these latter tasks were Michelle's responsibility. Although she resented being relegated to the role of paper shuffler, there was a certain logic to it. She had been trained for it—and she was still a novice at handling personnel, mapping out route sheets, making decisions that involved detailed scheduling. She had depended upon her staff for this the past year, and as she'd found out, they hadn't always used good judgment.

Despite this, she couldn't help feeling like a fifth wheel when, as personnel began to report in, a month earlier this year because of the merger, she sat in on Steve's weekly gripe sessions. He listened patiently to complaints and recitals of problems, and she had to admit that his decisions were always logical, tactful, including, when possible, the ideas of the complainers, who went away satisfied they'd had a fair hearing even when they didn't get their own way.

Still, it rankled that she had been stripped of the power to grant a salary advance or settle a dispute or admonish someone who had stepped out of line, without first asking Steve's permission. Her only comfort were those old friends who hadn't been won over, who dropped by the Blue Wagon often to talk about old times. She encouraged rather than discouraged these visits, even though they cut into her work time.

Increasingly, during the late winter months, the only time she and Steve really seemed on the same wavelengths was in bed. After she had sold her grandfather's house, she had moved in with Steve. She often regretted it, especially since the money from the sale had gone into the general circus funds. She and Steve ate their meals together in the cookhouse, but she had little to say to him and soon began making excuses to eat at a different time.

Steve treated her with courtesy, but there was a wariness between them that got in the way of real intimacy. She was harboring too much distrust and resentment, and she was content to simply live from day to day, accepting their surprisingly good sex life as something apart from the rest of their relationship.

If Steve felt her lack of warmth, it obviously didn't bother him. Sometimes, as they shared a meal, she would look up to find him watching her, his eyes so somber that she would feel an odd pang of regret that their marriage was failing.

Meanwhile, the newly combined circuses were undergoing a transformation. The theme of the year was Legends of America, and to Michelle's surprise, Steve turned over the problem of costuming the show to her. Although she suspected this was another sop to placate her for the usurping of her authority, she threw herself into it, determined to go a good job. She did extensive research, solicited advice from the wardrobe women, from professional costumers, and from those artistes who wintered in the area, and came up with an innovative, yet practical, collection.

When Steve viewed the sketches, fabrics, and prop samples, he said, "Good job, Michelle." Since he didn't make any suggestions for changes, she knew he was satisfied, which was gratifying, but she couldn't help feeling disappointed, too. Her father would have complimented her extravagantly, but Steve acted as if she'd only done what he had expected of her.

Soon after the management personnel reported in, Steve called a meeting in the Silver Wagon, where he had established his own office. He told the staff that he had ordered a new red, white, and blue big top, an inventive design with bale ring, four center poles, and twelve-foot side walls that permitted more seating than the old one. Other new tents, including ones to house the ten-in-one and the kid's petting zoo, had also been ordered and would match the red-white-and-blue theme of the show.

The midway, too, was undergoing changes. By renovating the best from both circuses, and adding new rides and concession booths only as needed, expenses would be minimized. Not to Michelle's surprise, the prospect of new canvas and equipment won over the management staff, but when Steve unveiled his new transportation plan, Michelle had finally had enough. She spoke up, voicing the reservations reflected on other faces.

"The railroad is traditional for both our circuses," she protested. "We know what to expect, and the kinks have been worked out over the years. Using a fleet of trucks is not only expensive, because we have to invest in our own equipment, worry about gas shortages, and carry additional mechanics, but it leaves us open to all sorts of local and state regulations—"

"Those things are already being worked out," Steve interrupted impatiently. "It's about time we stopped putting up with the railroads' indifference to our special needs. If we travel exclusively by motor, we have complete control—barring acts of nature. Then there is the improved scheduling. We can go into recreational areas that aren't serviced by railroad, ones we've had to pass up before. And there're other advantages—no need for cumbersome transfers of equipment and animals from the railroad spurs to the lots, which means less laborers, and no gilly wagons are needed to move personnel back and forth to the train."

And also no private pullman car for the owner and his new wife, Michelle thought. "It would take dozens of trucks and semis to haul all the equipment and animals and personnel," she said. "The seating equipment alone would fill several trucks."

"The trucks are being customized to eliminate wasted space—"

"What about the animals? How many semis does it take to haul sixteen elephants?"

"I'm cutting down on the animals," he said calmly. "We won't need draft horses or work elephants. As for the exotic animals, the novelty is gone. They simply don't draw the crowds they once did.''

She felt as if he'd struck her. ''A circus isn't a circus without elephants!''

''There'll be elephants. Just not as many.'' He hesitated, looking at her. ''If you like, we'll use the ones from your show and sell ours.''

She wanted to scream at him, tell him what he could do with his ''plan,'' but he was already going on, discussing the fleet of trucks he'd contracted for. ''It's a matter of good design. The right combinations provide the most efficient use. Several semis will pull two twenty-seven-foot trailers each, and the donicker trailer has nine booths, with plenty of room at the end to store shop repair equipment.''

''A nine-seater, huh?'' Maxie Costa said, and the other men chuckled.

''Right. The chemical donickers fit even the most stringent code, and we won't be dependent upon the antiquated plumbing in some of the fairgrounds. All the semis and trucks have extra storage boxes behind the cab, and one truck–fifth wheeler will serve a double purpose—the truck as the gilly wagon around the lot, and the trailer as an extra sleeper.''

''How about the clowns?''

''They'll have to share one of the dressing vans with other artistes, which eliminates the necessity of setting up dressing tops.''

''They're going to scream about losing Clown Alley,'' Michelle warned.

''They'll adjust,'' he said shortly.

She would have lost the battle with her temper then, but her show's new veterinarian, just out of school and worried about his job, asked a question about the animals, and she used the diversion to slip away.

She started in on Steve as soon as he came in the door that night. ''Thanks for consulting me before you obligated the circus for a fleet of new trucks,'' she stormed.

Steve moved past her and went into the kitchen. She followed him, stood waiting for an answer. He plugged in the coffeepot, set out mugs and spoons. Like the rest of the house, the kitchen was strictly utilitarian, reflecting what had been, for so many years, a purely masculine household. She hadn't bothered to make any changes because she'd been too busy—and maybe because, in her heart, she'd known all along that her stay here was apt to be temporary.

"Well?" she said finally. "Don't you have something to say?"

He turned to look at her. There was a coolness in his eyes that put her on the defensive. "The order for the trucks was placed a year ago, before the merger. It takes that long for customizing. Besides, I knew that by the time your buddies and you had hashed it over, you'd end up objecting if I went out and ordered a five-inch patch for the old top."

"That remark is totally out of line," she snapped.

He made a weary gesture. "Sorry. I'm dead beat, Michelle. Can't we talk about this tomorrow?"

"I want to talk about it now. Is this how it's going to be, you doing what you want and then telling me about it later?"

"It's not like that. Maybe I should have talked it over with you, but transportation is my territory. Did I interfere with the costuming? No, because that was *your* territory."

"So that's why you dumped it in my lap instead of letting wardrobe handle it as usual. So you could use it as an excuse to stop consulting me about what you do!"

"I asked you to handle it because our combating wardrobe mistresses can't agree about anything. I kept Mary on because she's an old friend of yours, but it isn't working out. One of them will have to take a demotion—"

"And of course, it will be Mary."

"She should have retired years ago, Michelle. In fact, there's a lot of deadwood that should be culled out."

"And of course, there're no old-timers in *your* show that should retire."

"No, there are not. You can't allow sentiment to affect your decisions in this business."

His words, reflecting all she'd feared, took her voice away. By the time she recovered, he had taken his coffee into the living room, leaving her standing there, fuming.

Later, when Steve turned to her in bed, she told him coldly that since he was so tired, maybe it was best they both get some sleep. He didn't argue; he turned to his side and went to sleep with insulting haste, but Michelle lay awake for a long time, nursing her resentment. She finally came to a decision. If all she meant to him was a convenient body when he wanted sex, then she just wouldn't be available in the future. Because she had her pride. It was about all she did have these days.

The next night she refused him again, this time pleading a

headache. Although he nodded his understanding, there was a hard glint in his eyes when he told her he hoped she'd feel better soon. The third night, she didn't bother with an excuse. She simply told him she wasn't in the mood, so sorry.

The next day, Steve moved his clothes and other belongings into another bedroom. He didn't approach her again.

There was a celebration after the last stragglers had reported in for the 1973 season. It had been Michelle's idea, the first she'd proposed since their estrangement, so she was a little surprised when Steve agreed. He even gave her credit when he made a brief welcoming speech at the beginning of the gala dinner the cooks had prepared. She felt a warm glow as the circus people cheered lustily—until she looked up and found Steve watching her, his expression unreadable.

As she glanced around at the noisy party, she couldn't help thinking how different the merging of the two circuses had been from what she'd expected. Although there was still wariness between them, there was no open hostility. Only the two bandmasters managed to get into a quarrel before dinner. Steve had solved the problem of two bandmasters by assigning the evening performance to one, the matinee to the other. It hadn't set well with either, but then, she reflected, everybody knew that bandmasters were temperamental.

To her surprise, the displaced equestrian director, from her own show, had taken his relegation to second-in-command in stride. "Felix Howden's got a lot more mileage on me," he said, winking. "I figure I'll wait him out. Meanwhile, this gives me more time to develop some ideas I have. The program needs to be jazzed up. Faster timing, more flash, better patter in the introductions. Old Felix is out of step with the seventies. When he retires, I'll be right there, in line for the top spot again."

Since he'd only been with Bradford Circus four seasons, she'd been touched by his loyalty—until he went on to say that it was the chance to work with her husband that had made him decide to stay on in second place rather than take another offer he'd had.

Michelle looked up at the banner, spread across the wall of the cookhouse. *Bradford and Lasky Circus*. At least Steve had put the Bradford name first. Strange that things had returned full circle. "Bradford and Lasky Circuses, Back Together Again!" was what the 1973 season's advertising posters would read.

The circus had received a lot of good publicity from the wedding. As Steve had predicted, the ending of the feud, the merger of both the circuses and the Bradford and Lasky heirs, was a natural for entertainment journalists trying to find something new to write about. How ironic that both mergers had been for business reasons. . . .

Michelle must have sighed, because she looked up to meet Steve's eyes. There was an intentness there, as if he were trying to decipher her sigh. They hadn't slept together since he'd moved into another bedroom, and while she was convinced she'd done the right thing, the physical aspect was annoying. She was horny as hell these days, a condition that humiliated her. Not that it was Steve she wanted, per se, she told herself. She was just naturally passionate.

"You looked as if you were a hundred miles away," Steve said.

"I was."

"What were you thinking? I know it wasn't about me."

"Why on earth would you say that?"

"You were smiling."

"I was thinking of Rosa," she lied. "She's doing private readings, and she has a new lover, a retired banker who's been spending a lot of money on her. All that talk about being tired was just that, talk."

"Maybe not. Maybe she was tired of being the circus guru," he said.

Michelle gave him a cold look. "I wonder what would happen to your deal with Rosa if she knew about that contract clause that gives you control of my circus?"

"She already knows," he said calmly. "Which brings up a question. Why haven't you been over there in Sarasota, crying on her shoulder about your miserable marriage?"

"Because Rosa still believes in fairy tales," she reported. "If it pleases her to believe our marriage is pure bliss instead of pure hell, why disillusion her?"

"Careful. People are watching. We don't want them to think we're quarreling," he said.

"But we aren't," she said sweetly. "I wouldn't waste my time quarreling with a bastard who lies and cheats and walks all over people to get what he wants."

The muscles in Steve's jaw tightened. "Don't call me that again," he said softly. "Enough is enough."

"And just how do you intend to stop me?"

"Oh, I have my ways. For instance, it's over time for your friend Benny Hyde to retire, don't you think? The other clowns are carrying him these days."

She realized he was baiting her, but she couldn't help responding. "Just you try. I'll put him on my personal staff. *That* little clause gives me the right to hire my own staff."

"And will you put Jigger Higgins and Mary and all your other cronies on your personal staff?" he said, his eyes gleaming.

"You bastard!" she hissed.

He was silent for a long moment. "I warned you," he said.

He turned away, and Michelle took a long drink of wine to ease her suddenly dry throat. There had been a real threat in the flatness of his voice—not that she was afraid of him. After all, what could he do to her that he hadn't already done?

Two mornings later, she found out. When she went to the Blue Wagon after breakfast, she discovered that the old railroad car had been stripped of everything—office equipment, her desk, her file cabinets, her personal belongings. In one corner, several floorboards had been removed, leaving a gaping hole. Seething with rage, she stormed across the strip of lawn that separated her office from the Silver Wagon.

Steve looked up as she threw open the screen door. Before she could speak, he said, "We had to move your office to the old cottage. Dry rot in the floorboards. The carpenter boss is putting it on his list—should get to it by sometime in May."

"The cottage doesn't have any heat, not since the space heater was removed. It's drafty as hell, and the paint's peeling off the walls," she said, trying to speak calmly, because Steve's secretary wasn't even trying to pretend that she wasn't listening. "Besides, it's a good half mile from here, more than that from the backyard. No one wants to walk that far for—" She stopped, staring at his thin smile.

"I thought you'd welcome the peace and quiet. You have so many interruptions, what with your old buddies dropping by to commiserate with you, that it must be hard to get anything done."

She took a deep breath, determined to keep her cool. "There's no reason why I can't share your office."

"It's already too crowded in here. You'll just have to put up with a little inconvenience for a while."

He turned back to the papers on his desk. She wanted to kick his chair out from under him, but she restrained herself. She had known that he was ruthless, but she hadn't realized before that he could be petty.

"You think you've won this round, but it isn't over yet," she said. She turned on her heel and started for the door.

She'd almost reached it when his voice stopped her. "Of course, if you promise to drop the name calling and the under-handed campaign you've been conducting against me, I might talk the carpenter crew into tackling those repairs next."

"And you can go straight to hell, you—you elephant killer," she said.

She was out the door before he could react. Aware that he had come to the door and was watching her, she forced herself to walk to her car even though she wanted to run. As she drove the half mile to the near derelict cottage that had been her grand-father's hideaway, she made a vow. She would make do there if it killed her.

Two weeks later, Michelle looked around the cottage with satisfaction. She had installed a new space heater, charging it to the circus, had hired several local painters to scrape and paint the cottage inside and out, had moved in a few pieces of her mother's furniture from storage to make things comfortable.

Although she didn't want to admit it, she had managed to do a record amount of work, even with the painters there, working out of one of the bedrooms. Not that her old friends had ne-glected her. It was just that there was much less casual dropping in for a cup of coffee and a chat. She had also removed all her belongings from Steve's house and transferred them here.

Since she'd moved out of Steve's house, she'd seen very little of him. Which was a relief. She found it difficult to even speak to him these days, much less eat with him. Not that he'd asked her to join him . . .

Unexpectedly her eyes filled with tears. She shook her head, repudiated them, and when she heard someone coming up the walk, she turned away from the door, wiping her face on her sleeve.

"Hi, Carrots," a familiar voice said.

For a long moment she couldn't move. Then, when she turned and saw David, smiling at her from the door, she couldn't speak.

"Sorry—I guess it *is* a shock, me walking in on you like this," he said, and she remembered that David, unlike his brother, always found it easy to apologize.

"How are you, David?" she said, not knowing what else to say.

"If that's a social question, I'm fine. If you want the truth, I feel like hell. I knew seeing you would be rough, but I didn't know it would tie my guts into a knot. God, I've missed you, Michelle. It's been a hellish three years."

"I find that hard to believe—"

"There's never been a day that I haven't thought of you and regretted what I did. I don't have any excuses, only that I was too damned stupid to realize what I was giving up. I should have told Steve to take the blasted trust and donate it to the SPCA."

"I'm afraid I put *you* out of my mind rather quickly—especially after I met Steve again," she said coolly.

He took a step closer, studying her face. "Are you happy, Michelle?"

"Very happy," she lied.

"Then why have you been crying?"

"I cry very easily. Someone drops their hat and I cry. I get a hangnail and I cry. It's my safety valve."

"And what happened this time to make you cry?"

"I can't remember—and how did you know I was here?"

"Steve's clerk told me. She looked as if she could tell me a lot more if I'd just ask the right question. Is something wrong between you and Steve?"

"Of course not. Didn't you know? It's a marriage made in heaven."

"And not a convenient consolidation?"

"Why on earth would you say that?"

"Because I can't believe that a warmhearted, passionate woman like you would fall for an iceberg like Steve. It just doesn't add up. Of course, he's always been interested in you—which is the real reason he broke us up. I could kick myself for not catching on sooner." His lips twisted into a smile. "I don't know why I'm surprised. I fell for you the first time I saw you. Remember? I told you I was going to marry you when you grew up."

Michelle felt a trickle of pain. So many things had started that day. How disappointed Steve must be that *he'd* wasted so many years waiting for her to grow up, only to find that he'd married a shrew. . . .

"I still love you, Michelle," David said softly. "I guess I always will. If Steve hadn't interfered, we would be married now, maybe have a couple of kids."

Michelle took in his smile; there was no denying that he was still the handsomest man she'd ever seen. So why did his words leave her so cold?

"And of course, you couldn't have stood up to him, could you? It would have meant that you'd have to work for a living," she said.

There was a flicker of resentment in his eyes, but his voice was very earnest as he said, "You have good reason to be bitter. But you have to understand that I was in a bind. It would've been years before I could earn a decent living. That fancy prep school diploma from Sansun didn't mean anything without a college degree to go with it. I would've been lucky to get a job as a supermarket clerk. And you deserved better, Michelle. I couldn't ask you to marry a man who couldn't give you anything but poverty."

"Thousands of women do—every day. You sure it wasn't because *you* didn't want to live without all those things?"

"I admit I like luxuries," he said. "And I didn't intend for our separation to be permanent. I planned to come back for you once I had my trust fund."

"Oh? Funny. I don't remember reading anything about that in the one letter you sent me."

"I wrote a dozen letters—and then tore them up. I felt it wasn't fair to ask you to wait for me. I guess I was stupid. I should have spelled it out. I was devastated when I found out you and Steve were married. That's when I realized he'd planned it all along. He reminds me of one of those trap-door spiders, lying in wait and pouncing when the time is ripe. He doesn't love you, Michelle. He doesn't have it in him to love anyone."

She looked into his eyes and knew that he believed what he was saying, which was a different thing from its being true. Suddenly she was weary of the conversation, weary of David's attempts to play on her emotions. *I've grown up finally,* she thought. *But David hasn't.*

"I think you'd better go, David," she said.

He rose, but not to leave. Carefully, as if afraid of her reaction, he put his arms around her shoulders. She knew she should pull away, but his arms were comforting and familiar, if no longer exciting. When she let him kiss her, his lips were firm, the kiss very skilled, and she reflected that he had always been a good lover. Something—a reflex from the past or maybe just her long abstinence—stirred, and she allowed the kiss to go on.

She didn't realize they weren't alone until she heard a curse. By the time she'd pulled away, Steve was already halfway across the room. His face was ashen, and his eyes—she flinched at the fury in his eyes.

"Get out," he told David. "Get out before I beat the shit out of you!"

"You're too late. This time you lose, big brother!"

It happened so quickly that it was all over before Michelle could scream a warning. Steve struck David fully on the jaw and sent him reeling backward. He crashed against the wall and slid down to the floor.

All Michelle's natural instincts for the underdog came to the fore. "You bastard," she screamed at Steve. "*You* don't want me, but you can't stand the thought that David does. Well, this is the end. Tomorrow I'm filing for a divorce!"

CHAPTER 54

*S*TEVE HAD RUSHED OUT OF THE COTTAGE, LEAVING MIchelle and David alone, for the simple reason that he was afraid of what he might do if he stayed there any longer. The look of triumph on his brother's face, the knowledge that David had won after all, was too much to handle. Another minute and he would have thoroughly thrashed the brother who had been a thorn in his side all his life.

And Michelle—God, her words, that she was getting a divorce, still rang in his ears. Rosa had warned him the last time he'd called her to ask her advice.

"Remember that Michelle is fiercely loyal to the circus people. You're right—some of them should be retired. But remember they're her family, Steve, and act accordingly. Court her—right now she sees you as some kind of enemy. Tell her you love her, make her believe it. Is that so hard for you to do?"

And of course, it had been. He'd been so afraid of being rejected. After all, she'd banished him from her bed. Yes, he had been the one to move into another bedroom, but this was after he'd lain there awake three nights in a row, smelling her perfume, feeling the warmth from her body, wanting her so badly that it was pure agony, not grabbing her and making love to her. How much could a man stand, for God's sake?

And now—it was all over. David had won. Had he been waiting for this moment for a long time? Probably. The day Steve had turned over the trust fund to David, lulled by his seeming interest in the circus and his uncomplaining hard work, David had told him that now it was his turn, that someday he was going to pay him back for lording it over him all those years, for breaking up his affair with Michelle. He hadn't seen David since—not until he'd walked into the cottage and found Michelle in his brother's arms.

Steve had almost reached the Silver Wagon when he realized that he'd left his car at the cottage. He didn't go back for it, afraid of what he still might do to David. Instead, he went back to work. It didn't ease the pain, but at least it kept him from going crazy.

That evening, he went to pick up his car. The cottage was dark, and when he went inside and checked the closets, he found that one of Michelle's suitcases was gone.

He called Rosa from the cottage phone.

"Michelle's left me," he told her without preamble. "Have you heard from her?"

There was a long silence. "No. What happened?"

"Hell, I blew it, Rosa. I lost my temper and decked David—"

"David? He's back?"

"Oh, yes. And she's left with him."

"Are you sure?"

"She told me she was getting a divorce. I guess that's plain enough."

"Was she angry when she said it?"

"You could say that. She called me a few names first and then said she was getting a divorce."

"She won't. She loves you, Steve. And she does have my—one helluva temper. Let it alone. She'll come back. I promise you she'll come back."

"And if she doesn't?" His voice was bleak. "What do I do then? I love her, Rosa. I've never loved any other woman that way."

"Do you want me to tell your cards?" Rosa said, so seriously that for the first time that day, Steve found himself smiling.

"I don't think that would change anything, do you?" he said gently.

"Probably not. If she calls—what do I say to her?"

"You might tell her I love her—not that she'll give a damn," he said bitterly, and hung up.

After Michelle got rid of David, she packed a bag and left winter quarters.

She hadn't left with him, even though he'd begged her to after Steve had stormed out of the cottage. Although she no longer was angry with David, she didn't have the slightest desire to be with him. He was more attractive than ever, still had that basic sweetness that so effectively hid his many weaknesses, but he no longer mattered to her. In the end, it was her indifference that convinced him.

Michelle spent the next two nights in a motel in Tampa. She stayed in her room, sending out for food, then letting it sit untouched to grow cold. She didn't bother to unpack or even to shower. Most of the time she lay on the bed, staring up at the ceiling. When a maid came to clean the room, Michelle told her that she was recovering from the flu and sent her away.

At the end of the second day, she called Rosa.

"I've been expecting your call," Rosa said. "Steve is going crazy. He thinks—he's afraid something's happened to you."

"Why would he care, Rosa?" There was no sarcasm, only disbelief in the question.

"Because he loves you."

"Loved. You used the wrong tense."

"Loves—as in still does."

"Did he tell you that?"

"He did, but it wasn't necessary. After all, I'm an expert on love—remember?"

"Even experts can be wrong. I messed up royally, Rosa. I really did."

"Well, you're not alone. Steve should have opened up to you more instead of expecting you to read his mind. Am I right?"

"I don't know, Rosa. I'm too confused right now to think straight." She hesitated briefly. "Will you call and tell him I'm all right?"

"Are you sure that's true?"

"I just need some time to myself."

"And after that—what then?"

"That's what I need to think about."

She heard Rosa's sigh. "Go back to him, honey. Work on your marriage. You've got everything going for you."

After she'd hung up, Michelle sat for a long time, staring into space. *Because he loves you* . . . Was that merely wishful thinking on Rosa's part?

After a while she got up and snapped on the television set, not caring what was on, but needing the sound for company. But the flickering screen only irritated her, and she switched it off again.

She set herself a task. Day by day she relived the past few months, remembering so many things about her relationship with Steve that hadn't registered then but suddenly made sense.

What it all boiled down to was what she'd said to Rosa. She had messed up royally. She had acted like the fourteen-year-old girl she'd been when Steve first met her. Because everything hadn't gone her way, because she had failed her own people and felt guilty and ashamed, she had sulked, taken offense, allowing her resentment to erode their marriage.

She hadn't given Steve credit for anything, including his treatment of Danny. How strange that he had succeeded with her brother where Papa and Granddad Sam had failed. Steve had seen Danny through dispassionate eyes, had realized that he would be a natural to assist Scotty Douglas, the circus's advertising manager. His outgoing nature, his way with people, would be an asset in the job, Steve had pointed out, and from Scotty's satisfaction with the promotion plans for the season that Danny had helped work out, he was right.

Steve had been right about other things, too. No one had really suffered from the merger. Those who had retired, whether voluntarily or not, had been treated well, given a respectable pension from circus reserve funds. Those from her own circus who stayed on, Steve treated with the same courtesy he did his own people. In fact, she suspected most of them wished the merger had taken place two years earlier.

As for his treatment of her—he had acted with remarkable restraint. Although he must have been furious with her many times, he hadn't retaliated in kind. Even after she'd withdrawn the one thing that had been right in their marriage, he hadn't put any pressure on her. And yet she knew that he was a highly sexual person. How many men would have been so patient?

Did she love him? Was this what her misery was all about?

Had it crept up so gradually that she hadn't recognized it for what it was? Lust, she had called what she'd felt when they made love. But now she saw that she had wanted him because of what he was, not because of any chemistry between them.

Michelle slept for the first time in forty-eight hours, and when she awoke, she took a much-needed shower, washed and dried her hair, then put on fresh jeans and a sweatshirt that said, "Bradford and Lasky Circus, Back Together Again," and returned to winter quarters.

Steve wasn't in the Silver Wagon, but his secretary told Michelle that he'd gone to the old cottage to take a nap. From her avid curiosity, Michelle knew that their estrangement must be a matter of open gossip.

She found Steve in the living room of the cottage, staring at an afternoon sports program on TV. He hadn't heard her come in, so she stood watching him, trying to reconcile the many images she had of Steve with the man in front of her.

There was the Steve who had killed the elephant, who had broken up her affair with David, who had manipulated her into marriage and then brought her circus back from the edge of bankruptcy, who had made love to her so passionately.

Then there was the Steve before her. His shoulders had a slumped, defeated look, as if, thinking himself to be alone, he had let down his guard; his skin was off-color, his eyelids red-rimmed, and there were dark shadows under his eyes. Had she put them there with her sulks and her tantrums, with her desertion?

He looked up and saw her, and it hurt that there was only wariness in his eyes.

"So you've finally come back for the rest of your clothes," he said heavily.

"Yes, I'm back. But not for my clothes."

He didn't ask her to explain. He motioned to a pitcher on the coffee table. "Lemonade," he said. "Made from a mix, so it isn't all that great. You want a glass?"

She shook her head and dropped down in to the chair opposite him.

"What did you mean—you didn't come back for your clothes?" he asked belatedly.

Michelle discovered she didn't know what to say. That she wanted another chance? That maybe this time they could make it work? That she'd been a fool? All true—and yet it was impossible to state it so baldly. Steve wasn't helping with his silence. Had she made a mistake, coming here?

"I didn't leave with David," she said finally.

"Why not?"

"I don't want him. That's all over now."

She thought she saw something stir, come alive, deep in his eyes. "So you finally realized he wasn't right for you," he said. "Have you decided yet who is?"

"You. You're right for me."

He stared at her as if trying to digest her words. "You already know I love you, Michelle, but it can't be the way it was," he said finally. "I don't have to tell you that this is a hard life. I need to know that you'll back me all the way, the same way I'll back you when you need it. I can offer you a stable life, a home. Maybe, if the theme park materializes, even one that doesn't move on wheels. And I can offer you my love. I'll never let you down—I promise you that. We won't always agree—hell, we won't agree even half the time!—but I'll be there when you need me. Is that enough?"

Michelle listened to his words, listened to what was behind them. He was right—their marriage would be stormy. They would quarrel, disagree about many things, but they could make it work because they had so much going for them—the same goals, the same dedication to the circus. There was something else that would bind them to each other—and it was about time she did something about it.

She got up and went over to him. She didn't kiss him. She was making a statement, and it had to be very clear. Wordlessly she unbuckled his belt, then unbuttoned his jeans, exposing him to her eyes. He was already aroused, and when she stripped off her own jeans, then sank down on his lap, the glass in his hand fell to the floor, spilling lemonade on the rug. Neither of them noticed. The house could have been swallowed up by one of Florida's sinkholes and they wouldn't have noticed.

They made love. It was frenzied, violent, but because it was Steve who took her with near savagery, it was all right. It would always be all right. Not quiet and tame and idyllic, but still all right for both of them.

EPILOGUE

*T*HE LIMO BRAKED SUDDENLY, SENDING MARA SWAYING FOR-
ward against her seat strap, and she realized that she'd been
napping. In the front seat, the young driver muttered something
under his breath. It was quite an imaginative curse, and she hid
a smile when he gave the mirror a guilty glance. She could have
told him that she knew every curse in the book, some he'd probably never heard of, but she didn't.

Dignity, she thought. *In the end, the one thing we all try to
cling to is dignity.*

"Quite a crowd," the man commented when he realized she
was awake. "Looks like Circus U.S.A. is a real winner."

Mara didn't answer. She was too busy studying the festive
crowd that streamed toward the entrance of the theme park.
They must have given out balloons in the parking lot, because
every child seemed to have one, and it pleased her that they
were red, white, and blue, the trademark of the old Bradford
Circus. Did these people feel the magic, the excitement, of the
circus that was like nothing else in the world? Or was it just
another entertainment to them, a way to pass a few hours, something they forgot by the time they returned home?

She regretted now that she'd fallen asleep. Soon she would be
seeing Michelle, and she still hadn't made her decision. Was it
time to tell her granddaughter who she really was?

Michelle already knew that her grandmother had been Princess Mara. She'd told her that much when she was still a small
girl because she'd wanted Michelle to know about the blood that
flowed in her veins from the one of her grandmothers, blood
that was far more ancient than her other grandparents' New
England blue blood had been.

But if Michelle learned, at this late date, that her grand-

530

mother, the legend, was really Rosa, the old Gypsy fortune-
teller, would the truth ruin her pride in her heritage? Rosa, with
her scarred face and her lovers and her strange ways, bore no
resemblance to Princess Mara, who had died such a romantic
death and who would never age, never lose her beauty or her
glamour.

Would Michelle, despite her loving heart and her loyalty, be
dismayed to learn that her grandmother, the legend, was still
alive?

Mara sighed deeply, and with the sigh made up her mind. It
was too late. She had lived too long with the lie to tell the truth
now. In the end, the legend had taken on an entity of its own.
She owed the woman she'd once been the right to her legend. If
this be vanity, so be it. She'd never pretended to be modest—or
even very truthful, if it came to that. What Rom ever worried
about truth?

Just last month there'd been another book about Princess
Mara, which had been optioned for a movie. Loretta, the woman
who "did" for her, alternately bullying and pampering her, had
read it to her when she took her afternoon rests. The book was
full of inaccuracies, of course, glorifying the circus for the wrong
things, shorting its real value, as all such books did. That hadn't
lessened her enjoyment. The whole book had been a paean to
Mara's memory, making her seem larger than life.

Larger than life. A legend in her own time. Yes, she'd been
all of that. . . .

Mara permitted herself another smile. Now that the decision
had been made she meant to enjoy this outing—her last if you
could believe that old humbug, Dr. Robbins. Well, no denying
it. She was old. She didn't need the exaggerated respect she
received these days to realize that. But she had no regrets—well,
not many. She'd lived an exciting life, far more flamboyant and
richer than the dreams she'd had when she was very young. Not
that she'd ever doubted that she would do something exciting
with her life. She'd been so sure that she could control her own
destiny. And in many ways, she had.

How many people got the chance to feed the flame of their
own legend? Princess Mara was the essence of glamour, of romance. But not Rosa Smith. No, Rosa was another woman living a different, more obscure life. And yet—she couldn't
complain. Who hadn't wished, at one time or another, that they
could attend their own funeral, smell the funeral flowers, listen
to the eulogies, count the tears on the faces of the mourners?

And there had been compensations. She'd led a full life as Rosa Smith, who had been wiser, more caring, and yes, more humble than Mara. She'd played an important part in the lives of those she loved best. Not an overt part, but still, her influence had been felt. Not that she'd ever interfered, she thought virtuously.

The limo inched forward, toward the park. Shaped like a huge clown's face, the entrance promised entertainment, excitement. The drive beyond was lined with flowering shrubs, like any well-mannered park, but when they reached the first concession booths, she felt the old excitement stir.

She was glad they hadn't made the mistake of fancying it up too much. Everything was clean, orderly, but there was a touch of vulgarity about the profusion of balloons, blowing gaily in the wind, about the bright banners and the colorful flags. There was a fish-in-the-pond booth with its rows of slum, then a game of chance she recognized as a new version of the old Fascination game. Other booths sold cotton candy and popcorn, peanuts and hamburgers and the crusty filled buns that Floridians called Cuban sandwiches. She saw Michelle's hand in the advertised menu choices at one stand. Tacos and burritos and chili—Michelle had always been a nut about Mexican food. . . .

Then there were the rides, a whole galaxy of them, followed by more booths, old favorites like the ducking stand and the weight guesser, side by side with an arcade that featured the latest video games. Something for everybody—oh, yes, this was undiluted circus, changing with the times and yet always the same. Trust Steve to realize that kids wanted the latest technology along with balloons, that their parents wanted nostalgia, a chance to relive the best times of their past.

There were also innovations the old circus had never had. Iron benches under trees that must have been transplanted already full-grown, testifying that Steve had spared no expense to fulfill his dream. Michelle's dream, too, she amended. It had started with Steve, but Michelle had adopted it wholeheartedly.

They drove past the petting zoo, the ten-in-one, the building that discreetly advertised "dancing girls from all over the world." Some things never change, she thought indulgently, remembering her own days as a hooch dancer.

The grab joints had certainly changed. Now there were groupings of tables and chairs under red, white, and blue umbrellas, where the customers could sit while they ate. Mara wasn't sure she approved. Wasn't part of the fun of going to a circus walking along the midway with a hot dog in one hand, a bottle of pop in the other?

The limo stopped in front of a large building, shaped like a giant tent, whose banners were billowing in the Florida breezes. Michelle was there to greet her, looking trim and splendid in a red, white, and blue middy and slacks that showed off her long legs. She had told Mara that they were going to change themes every three years, the way the circus always had, and the first theme was patriotic. "America the Beautiful," she'd called it.

Mara smiled, noting how well Michelle looked. She was three months pregnant, although she hadn't told anyone except Steve yet. But the cards had tattled on her, and Mara had to resist the temptation to congratulate her as she kissed Michelle's cheek. No, let her granddaughter reveal the news in her own sweet time. She and Steve had waited so long, almost ten years—and besides, Michelle had always loved secrets. Now she had one all her own.

"Rosa, you're our guest of honor," Michelle said, hugging her. "I'm putting you in the owner's box. Steve and I have to be at the back door during the matinee, but as soon as the finale is over, I'll come for you. We're having a celebration, nothing elaborate because we don't want to tire you out, but I've invited some of your friends. I've already warned them I won't have them bothering you until after the show. Wait until you see the elephant march! Twenty bulls, the biggest we could find—and one darling little dwarf. We named him Lord Jocko after that clown friend of Princess Mara's."

Mara wanted to tell her that Jocko had been a midget, not a dwarf. But then—what did it matter? Jocko would have loved it, having an elephant named after him.

Michelle escorted Mara to the owner's box. It was very plush, set in the center of the star seats. Mara, always aware of an audience, forced her tired back to its most regal position as she seated herself. After Michelle left her, she gazed up at the arched roof. It could have been the canvas of a big top, and for a moment, she was sure she could smell the tanbark.

The lights dimmed and the spec began.

For the next two hours, she was bombarded with the sonorous voice of the equestrian director, with pomp and pageantry, with spectacular acts that rivaled anything she had seen in the past. It was a perfect blend of the old and the new. Something for everyone, she thought as she was caught up in the old magic again.

Then finally the show had almost ended. The acrobats and the tumblers and the equestrians on their rosinbacks, the elephants and lions and gay little prancing high school horses, had left the arena, and only one clown, a bozo with a bulbous nose and a painted-on smile, remained. He took a final pratfall, bounded to his feet and gave the audience a sweeping bow, and then he scampered toward the back door, followed by a roar of applause.

The lights came up, and the applause faded—slowly, slowly— in gradually diminishing waves as if the audience was reluctant to return to reality, to everyday life.

And this, Mara thought with sudden clarity, was the secret of the circus and why it would never die, that for a little while, a short interlude of time, it brought magic into lives that had so little magic.

There was a stirring, a rustling, like a deep sigh, and the auditorium slowly emptied. Mara sat on, her eyes closed, waiting for Michelle to come and escort her to the party. Images and memories, bits and pieces from the past, played themselves out in her brain. A vision of something yet to come made her smile. Michelle's baby would be a girl, and they would call her Rosa.

I wish they'd name her Mara, she thought, but the thought was already drifting away.

She opened her eyes and saw that the seats nearby had filled again, this time with familiar faces. There was Lobo, towering over the others, his big, dumb face wreathed in a smile; and Clinker, in the seat beside him, was waving to her. There was Mr. Sam and her old friend Jocko, resplendent in evening clothes and a top hat. Doc McCall and Young Doc were both there, too, and three of the Cookies—were they all coming to the party, too?

No, that couldn't be. There was some reason why that couldn't be, but at the moment she was just too tired to figure it out. . . .

She heard a voice then, a young, vibrant, familiar voice, and she smiled happily at Jaime, who was standing at the entrance of the box, smiling at her and holding out his hand.

"It's time to go, Mara," he said.

As light and graceful as a young girl, she rose from her seat and joined him, leaving her old, worn-out body behind. "I'm ready, Jaime," she said, taking his hand.

Michelle came a little later, hurrying because she'd been delayed by a last-minute emergency. She found Rosa slumped in her chair, her head resting against the back, and she knew she was dead, even before she touched the silent pulse in Rosa's throat. She cried, and yet the grief was touched with relief, because now Rosa, who had so much pride, would never suffer the indignities of extreme old age.

For a long moment she looked down at the face she'd loved so much. Rosa had died with a smile on her face—what had she been thinking about as life ebbed from her body? She had lived such a full life. So much tragedy and yet so much happiness. It all balanced out, didn't it? And secrets—so many secrets, including the one that Rosa had kept to the end, not knowing that Michelle had figured out her friend's true identity years ago.

Michelle smiled through her tears. She bent and kissed her grandmother's still warm cheek. "Good-bye, Princess Mara," she said, and went to get help.

RUTH WALKER

Where hopes and dreams reach for the skies...

Tai – daughter of a disgraced officer, follows
her own secret dream in a world of loneliness and
crushing hostility.

Bobby Jo – the Chaplain's lively daughter,
breaks loose, with devastating results for herself
and her family.

Shelley – the General's pampered child, fights
passionately for her independence, but shocks her
parents, and herself.

Crystal – determined to succeed where her
despised father failed, she ruthlessly plans to
acquire the status she has always craved.

They were the wives and the daughters of the men
who were married to the Air Force. Yet each of
them cherished her own dream of freedom . . .

FICTION/SAGA   0 7472 3098 6   £3.99

More Compulsive Fiction from Headline:

RUTH WALKER

**From exclusive spas to shady singles bars,
they're all members of**

It all began in a divorce lawyer's waiting room ...

There were five of them with appointments to see San
Francisco's most prestigious divorce lawyer. Five
women, five incredible stories and – minutes later –
five fascinatingly intertwined lives . . .

Chanel Devereau – all her life she'd longed to be
accepted by society, and for that she'd throw
aside anything, even her daughter, and her only
chance to love.

Ariel Di Russy – mysterious and otherworldly, even
her vast fortune could not shield her from the sinister
manipulations of her psychiatrist husband.

Morning Glory Brown – she grew up in the ghetto,
unloved and abused. Marriage was her escape – and
her biggest mistake.

Stephanie Cornwall – she was happy being a wife
and mother, until the day she walked in on a
terrible truth.

Janice Morehouse – her marriage to a Stanford
professor seemed made in heaven, but her new-found
independence revealed some disturbing cracks.

"Enjoyable . . . long, hot and light" *Publishers Weekly*

Also by Ruth Walker from Headline
AIRFORCE WIVES

FICTION/SAGA   0 7472 3260 1   £3.99

A selection of bestsellers from Headline

FICTION

ONE GOLDEN NIGHT	Elizabeth Villars	£4.99	☐
HELL HATH NO FURY	M R O'Donnell	£4.99	☐
CONQUEST	Elizabeth Walker	£4.99	☐
HANNAH	Christine Thomas	£4.99	☐
A WOMAN TO BE LOVED	James Mitchell	£4.99	☐
GRACE	Jan Butlin	£4.99	☐
THE STAKE	Richard Laymon	£4.99	☐
THE RED DEFECTOR	Martin L Gross	£4.99	☐
LIE TO ME	David Martin	£4.99	☐
THE HORN OF ROLAND	Ellis Peters	£3.99	☐

NON-FICTION

LITTLE GREGORY	Charles Penwarden	£4.99	☐
PACIFIC DESTINY	Robert Elegant	£5.99	☐

SCIENCE FICTION AND FANTASY

HERMETECH	Storm Constantine	£4.99	☐
TARRA KHASH: HROSSAK!	Brian Lumley	£3.99	☐
DEATH'S GREY LAND	Mike Shupp	£4.50	☐
The Destiny Makers 4			

All Headline books are available at your local bookshop or newsagent, or can be ordered direct from the publisher. Just tick the titles you want and fill in the form below. Prices and availability subject to change without notice.

Headline Book Publishing PLC, Cash Sales Department, PO Box 11, Falmouth, Cornwall, TR10 9EN, England.

Please enclose a cheque or postal order to the value of the cover price and allow the following for postage and packing:
UK: 80p for the first book and 20p for each additional book ordered up to a maximum charge of £2.00
BFPO: 80p for the first book and 20p for each additional book
OVERSEAS & EIRE: £1.50 for the first book, £1.00 for the second book and 30p for each subsequent book.

Name ....

Address ....

....

....